Lord of Shadows

Also by Cassandra Clare

THE MORTAL INSTRUMENTS

City of Bones

City of Ashes

City of Glass

City of Fallen Angels

City of Lost Souls

City of Heavenly Fire

THE INFERNAL DEVICES

Clockwork Angel

Clockwork Prince

Clockwork Princess

THE DARK ARTIFICES

Lady Midnight

Lord of Shadows

Queen of Air and Darkness

The Shadowhunter's Codex

With Joshua Lewis

The Bane Chronicles

With Sarah Rees Brennan
and Maureen Johnson

Tales from the Shadowhunter Academy

With Sarah Rees Brennan, Maureen Johnson,
and Robin Wasserman

Lord of Shadows

CASSANDRA CLARE

THE DARK ARTIFICES

BOOK TWO

Margaret K. McElderry Books

NEW YORK LONDON TORONTO SYDNEY NEW DELHI

MARGARET K. McELDERRY BOOKS
An imprint of Simon & Schuster Children's Publishing Division
1230 Avenue of the Americas, New York, New York 10020

For information about special discounts for bulk purchases, please contact
Simon & Schuster Special Sales at 1-866-506-1949 or business@simonandschuster.com.
The Simon & Schuster Speakers Bureau can bring authors to your live event.
For more information or to book an event, contact the Simon & Schuster Speakers Bureau
at 1-866-248-3049 or visit our website at www.simonspeakers.com.
Also available in a Margaret K. McElderry Books hardcover edition
Cover design by Russell Gordon
Interior design by Mike Rosamilia
The text for this book was set in Dolly.
Manufactured in the United States of America
First Margaret K. McElderry Books paperback edition November 2018
2 4 6 8 10 9 7 5 3 1
The Library of Congress has cataloged the hardcover edition as follows:
Names: Clare, Cassandra, author.
Title: Lord of Shadows / Cassandra Clare.
Description: First edition. | New York : Margaret K. McElderry Books, [2017] |
Series: The dark artifices ; book 2 | Summary: "Emma Carstairs has finally avenged her parents.
She thought she'd be at peace. But she is anything but calm. Torn between her desire for her parabatai
Julian and her desire to protect him from the brutal consequences of parabatai relationships, she has
begun dating his brother, Mark. But Mark has spent the past five years trapped in Faerie; can he ever
truly be a Shadowhunter again? And the faerie courts are not silent. The Unseelie King is tired of the
Cold Peace, and will no longer concede to the Shadowhunters' demands. Caught between the demands
of Faerie and the laws of the Clave, Emma, Julian, and Mark must find a way to come together to
defend everything they hold dear—before it's too late"— Provided by publisher.
Identifiers: LCCN 2017288805| ISBN 9781442468405 (hardcover) |
ISBN 9781442468412 (paperback) | ISBN 9781442468429 (eBook)
Subjects: CYAC: Supernatural—Fiction. | Demonology—Fiction. | Magic—Fiction. | Fantasy. |
Los Angeles (Calif.)—Fiction.
Classification: PZ7.C5265 Lo 2017 | DDC [Fic]—dc23
LC record available at https://lccn.loc.gov/2017288805

For Jim Hill

I said: Pain and sorrow.
He said: Stay with it. The wound is the
place where the Light enters you.
—Rumi

PART ONE

Dreamland

———◆———

Dream-Land
By Edgar Allan Poe

By a route obscure and lonely,
Haunted by ill angels only,
Where an Eidolon, named Night,
On a black throne reigns upright,
I have reached these lands but newly
From an ultimate dim Thule—
From a wild weird clime that lieth, sublime,
Out of Space—out of Time.

Bottomless vales and boundless floods,
And chasms, and caves, and Titan woods,
With forms that no man can discover
For the dews that drip all over;
Mountains toppling evermore
Into seas without a shore;
Seas that restlessly aspire,
Surging, unto skies of fire;
Lakes that endlessly outspread
Their lone waters—lone and dead,—
Their still waters—still and chilly
With the snows of the lolling lily.

By the lakes that thus outspread
Their lone waters, lone and dead,—
Their sad waters, sad and chilly
With the snows of the lolling lily,—
By the mountains—near the river
Murmuring lowly, murmuring ever,—
By the gray woods,—by the swamp
Where the toad and the newt encamp,—
By the dismal tarns and pools
Where dwell the Ghouls,—
By each spot the most unholy—
In each nook most melancholy,—

There the traveller meets aghast
Sheeted Memories of the Past—
Shrouded forms that start and sigh
As they pass the wanderer by—
White-robed forms of friends long given,
In agony, to the Earth—and Heaven.

For the heart whose woes are legion
'Tis a peaceful, soothing region—
For the spirit that walks in shadow
'Tis—oh, 'tis an Eldorado!
But the traveller, travelling through it,
May not—dare not openly view it;
Never its mysteries are exposed
To the weak human eye unclosed;
So wills its King, who hath forbid
The uplifting of the fringed lid;
And thus the sad Soul that here passes
Beholds it but through darkened glasses.

By a route obscure and lonely,
Haunted by ill angels only,
Where an Eidolon, named Night,
On a black throne reigns upright,
I have wandered home but newly
From this ultimate dim Thule.

1

Still Waters

Kit had only recently found out what a flail was, and now there was a rack of them hanging over his head, shiny and sharp and deadly.

He had never seen anything like the weapons room at the Los Angeles Institute before. The walls and floors were white-silver granite, and granite islands rose at intervals throughout the room, making the whole place look like the arms and armor exhibit at a museum. There were staves and maces, cleverly designed walking sticks, necklaces, boots and padded jackets that concealed slim, flat blades for stabbing and throwing. Morning stars covered in terrible spikes, and crossbows of all sizes and types.

The granite islands themselves were covered with stacks of gleaming instruments carved out of *adamas,* the quartz-like substance that Shadowhunters mined from the earth and that they alone knew how to turn into swords and blades and steles. Of more interest to Kit was the shelf that held daggers.

It wasn't that he had any particular desire to learn how to use a dagger—nothing beyond the general interest he figured most teenagers had in deadly weapons, but even then, he'd rather be issued a machine gun or a flamethrower. But the daggers were works of art, their hilts inlaid with gold and silver and precious gems—blue sapphires, cabochon rubies, glimmering patterns of thorns etched in platinum and black diamonds.

He could think of at least three people at the Shadow Market who'd buy them off him for good money, no questions asked.

Maybe four.

Kit stripped off the denim jacket he was wearing—he didn't know which of the Blackthorns it had belonged to originally; he'd woken up the morning after he'd come to the Institute to find a freshly laundered pile of clothes at the foot of his bed—and shrugged on a padded jacket. He caught a glimpse of himself in the mirror at the far end of the room. Ragged blond hair, the last of fading bruises on his pale skin. He unzipped the inside pocket of the jacket and began to stuff it with sheathed daggers, picking the ones with the fanciest hilts.

The door to the weapons room swung open. Kit dropped the dagger he was holding back onto the shelf and turned around hastily. He thought he'd slipped out of his bedroom without being noticed, but if there was one thing he'd come to realize during his short time at the Institute, it was that Julian Blackthorn noticed everything, and his siblings weren't far behind.

But it wasn't Julian. It was a young man Kit hadn't ever seen before, though something about him was familiar. He was tall, with tousled blond hair and a Shadowhunter's build—broad shoulders, muscular arms, the black lines of the runic Marks they protected themselves with peeking out from the collar and cuffs of his shirt.

His eyes were an unusual dark gold color. He wore a heavy silver ring on one finger, as many of the Shadowhunters did. He raised an eyebrow at Kit.

"Like weapons, do you?" he said.

"They're all right." Kit backed up a little toward one of the tables, hoping the daggers in his inside pocket didn't rattle.

The man went over to the shelf Kit had been rifling through and picked up the dagger he'd dropped. "You picked a good one here," he said. "See the inscription on the handle?"

Kit didn't.

"It was made by one of the descendants of Wayland the Smith, who made Durendal and Cortana." The man spun the dagger between his fingers before setting it back on its shelf. "Nothing as extraordinary as Cortana, but daggers like that will always return to your hand after you throw them. Convenient."

Kit cleared his throat. "It must be worth a lot," he said.

"I doubt the Blackthorns are looking to sell," said the man dryly. "I'm Jace, by the way. Jace Herondale."

He paused. He seemed to be waiting for a reaction, which Kit was determined not to give him. He knew the name Herondale, all right. It felt like it was the only word anyone had said to him in the past two weeks. But that didn't mean he wanted to give the man—Jace—the satisfaction he was clearly looking for.

Jace looked unmoved by Kit's silence. "And you're Christopher Herondale."

"How do you know that?" Kit said, keeping his voice flat and unenthusiastic. He hated the name Herondale. He hated the *word*.

"Family resemblance," said Jace. "We look alike. In fact, you look like drawings of a lot of Herondales I've seen." He paused. "Also, Emma sent me a cell phone picture of you."

Emma. Emma Carstairs had saved Kit's life. They hadn't spoken much since, though—in the wake of the death of Malcolm Fade, the High Warlock of Los Angeles, everything had been in chaos. He hadn't been anyone's first priority, and besides, he had a feeling she thought of him as a little kid. "Fine. I'm Kit Herondale. People keep telling me that, but it doesn't mean anything to me." Kit set his jaw. "I'm a Rook. Kit Rook."

"I know what your father told you. But you're a Herondale. And that does mean something."

"What? What does it mean?" Kit demanded.

Jace leaned back against the wall of the weapons room, just under a display of heavy claymores. Kit hoped one would fall on his head. "I know you're aware of Shadowhunters," he said. "A lot of people are, especially Downworlders and mundanes with the Sight. Which is what you thought you were, correct?"

"I never thought I was a *mundane*," said Kit. Didn't Shadowhunters understand how it sounded when they used that word?

Jace ignored him, though. "Shadowhunter society and history—those aren't things most people who aren't Nephilim know about. The Shadowhunter world is made up of families, each of which has a name that they cherish. Each family has a history we pass on to each successive generation. We bear the glories and the burdens of our names, the good and the bad our ancestors have done, through all our lives. We try to live up to our names, so that those who come after us will bear lighter burdens." He crossed his arms over his chest. His wrists were covered in Marks; there was one that looked like an open eye on the back of his left hand. Kit had noticed all Shadowhunters seemed to have that one. "Among Shadowhunters, your last name is deeply meaningful. The Herondales have been a family who have shaped the destinies of Shadowhunters for generations. There aren't many of us left—in fact, everyone thought I was the last. Only Jem and Tessa had faith *you* existed. They looked for you for a long time."

Jem and Tessa. Along with Emma, they had helped Kit escape the demons who had murdered his father. And they had told him a story: the story of a Herondale who had betrayed his friends and fled, starting a new life away from other Nephilim. A new life and a new family line.

"I heard about Tobias Herondale," he said. "So I'm the descendant of a big coward."

"People are flawed," said Jace. "Not every member of your family is going to be awesome. But when you see Tessa again, and you will, she can tell you about Will Herondale. And James Herondale. And me, of course," he added, modestly. "As far as Shadowhunters go, I'm a pretty big deal. Not to intimidate you."

"I don't feel intimidated," said Kit, wondering if this guy was for real. There was a gleam in Jace's eye as he spoke that indicated that he might not take what he was saying all that seriously, but it was hard to be sure. "I feel like I want to be left alone."

"I know it's a lot to digest," Jace said. He reached out to clap Kit on the back. "But Clary and I will be here for as long as you need us to—"

The clap on the back dislodged one of the daggers in Kit's pocket. It clattered to the ground between them, winking up from the granite floor like an accusing eye.

"Right," Jace said into the ensuing silence. "So you're stealing weapons."

Kit, who knew the pointlessness of an obvious denial, said nothing.

"Okay, look, I know your dad was a crook, but you're a Shadowhunter now and—wait, what else is in that jacket?" Jace demanded. He did something complicated with his left boot that kicked the dagger up into the air. He caught it neatly, the rubies in the hilt scattering light. "Take it off."

Silently, Kit shucked off his jacket and threw it down on the table. Jace flipped it over and opened the inside pocket. They both gazed silently at the gleam of blades and precious stones.

"So," Jace said. "You were planning on running away, I take it?"

"Why should I stay?" Kit exploded. He knew he shouldn't, but he couldn't help it—it was too much: the loss of his father, his hatred of the Institute, the smugness of the Nephilim, their demands that he accept a last name he didn't care about and didn't want to care about. "I don't belong here. You can tell me all this stuff about my name, but it doesn't mean anything to me. I'm Johnny Rook's son. I've been training my whole life to be like my dad, not to be like *you*. I don't need you. I don't need any of you. All I need is some start-up money, and I can set up my own booth at the Shadow Market."

Jace's gold eyes narrowed, and for the first time Kit saw, under the arrogant, joking facade, the gleam of a sharp intelligence. "And sell what? Your dad sold information. It took him years, and a lot of bad magic, to build up those connections. You want to sell your soul like that, so you can scratch out a living on the edges of Down-world? And what about what killed your dad? You saw him die, didn't you?"

"Demons—"

"Yeah, but somebody sent them. The Guardian might be dead, but that doesn't mean no one's looking for you. You're fifteen years old. You might think you want to die, but trust me—you don't."

Kit swallowed. He tried to picture himself standing behind the counter of a booth at the Shadow Market, the way he had for the past few days. But the truth was he'd always been safe at the Market because of his dad. Because people were afraid of Johnny Rook. What would happen to him there without his dad's protection?

"But I'm not a Shadowhunter," Kit said. He glanced around the room, at the millions of weapons, the piles of *adamas*, the gear and body armor and weapon belts. It was ridiculous. He wasn't a ninja. "I wouldn't even know how to start to be one."

"Give it another week," Jace said. "Another week here at the Institute. Give yourself a chance. Emma told me how you fought off those demons who killed your dad. Only a Shadowhunter could have done that."

Kit barely remembered battling the demons in his father's house, but he knew he'd done it. His body had taken over, and he'd fought, and he'd even, in a small, strange, hidden way, enjoyed it.

"This is what you are," said Jace. "You're a Shadowhunter. You're part angel. You have the blood of angels in your veins. You're a Herondale. Which, by the way, means that not only are you part of a stunningly good-looking family, but you're also part of a family that owns a *lot* of valuable property, including a London town house and a manor in Idris, which you're probably entitled to part of. You know, if you were interested."

Kit looked at the ring on Jace's left hand. It was silver, heavy, and looked old. And valuable. "I'm listening."

"All I am saying is give it a week. After all"—Jace grinned— "Herondales can't resist a challenge."

"A Teuthida demon?" Julian said into the phone, his eyebrows crinkling. "That's basically a squid, right?"

The reply was inaudible: Emma could recognize Ty's voice, but not the words.

"Yeah, we're at the pier," Julian went on. "We haven't seen anything yet, but we just arrived. Too bad they don't have designated parking spots for Shadowhunters here. . . ."

Her mind only half on Julian's voice, Emma glanced around. The sun had just gone down. She'd always loved the Santa Monica Pier, since she was a little girl and her parents had taken her there to play air hockey and ride the old-fashioned merry-go-round. She loved the junk food—burgers and milk shakes, fried clams and giant swirled lollipops—and Pacific Park, the run-down amusement park at the very end of the pier, overlooking the Pacific Ocean.

The mundanes had poured millions of dollars into revamping the pier into a tourist attraction over the years. Pacific Park was full of new, shiny rides; the old churro carts were gone, replaced by artisanal ice cream and lobster platters. But the boards under Emma's feet were still warped and weathered by years of sun and salt. The air still smelled like sugar and seaweed. The merry-go-round still spilled its mechanical music into the air. There were still coin-toss games where you could win a giant stuffed panda. And there were still dark spaces under the pier, where aimless mundanes gathered and sometimes, more sinister things.

That was the thing about being a Shadowhunter, Emma thought, glancing toward the massive Ferris wheel decorated with gleaming LED lights. A line of mundanes eager to get on stretched down the pier; past the railings, she could glimpse the dark blue sea tipped with white where the waves broke. Shadowhunters saw the beauty in the things mundanes created—the lights of the Ferris wheel reflecting off the ocean so brightly that it looked as if someone were setting off fireworks underwater: red, blue, green, purple, and gold—but they saw the darkness, too, the danger and the rot.

"What's wrong?" Julian asked. He'd slid his phone into the pocket of his gear jacket. The wind—there was always wind on the pier, the wind that blew ceaselessly off the ocean, smelling of salt and faraway places—lifted the soft waves of his brown hair, made them kiss his cheeks and temples.

Dark thoughts, Emma wanted to say. She couldn't, though. Once Julian had been the person she could tell everything. Now he was the one person she couldn't tell anything.

Instead she avoided his gaze. "Where are Mark and Cristina?"

"Over there." He pointed. "By the ring toss."

Emma followed his gaze to the brightly painted stand where people competed to see who could toss a plastic ring and land it around the neck of one of a dozen lined-up bottles. She tried not to feel superior that this was apparently something mundanes found difficult.

Julian's half brother, Mark, held three plastic rings in his hand. Cristina, her dark hair caught up in a neat bun, stood beside him, eating caramel corn and laughing. Mark threw the rings: all three at once. Each spiraled out in a different direction and landed around the neck of a bottle.

Julian sighed. "So much for being inconspicuous."

A mixture of cheers and noises of disbelief went up from the mundanes at the ring toss. Fortunately, there weren't many of them, and Mark was able to collect his prize—something in a plastic bag—and escape with a minimum of fuss.

He headed back toward them with Cristina at his side. The tips of his pointed ears peeked through the loops of his light hair, but he was glamoured so that mundanes wouldn't see them. Mark was half-faerie, and his Downworlder blood showed itself in the delicacy of his features, the tips of his ears, and the angularity of his eyes and cheekbones.

"So it's a squid demon?" Emma said, mostly just to have something to say to fill the silence between her and Julian. There were a lot of silences between her and Julian these days. It had only been two weeks since everything had changed, but she felt the difference profoundly, in her bones. She felt his distance, though he had never been anything but scrupulously polite and kind ever since she had told him about her and Mark.

"Apparently," Julian said. Mark and Cristina had come into earshot; Cristina was finishing her caramel corn and looking sadly into the bag as if hoping more would appear. Emma could relate. Mark, meanwhile, was gazing down at his prize. "It climbs up the side of the pier and snatches people—mostly kids, anyone leaning over the side taking a picture at night. It's been getting braver, though. Apparently someone spotted it inside the game area near the table hockey—is that a *goldfish*?"

Mark held up his plastic bag. Inside it, a small orange fish swam around in a circle. "This is the best patrol we've ever done," he said. "I have never been awarded a fish before."

Emma sighed inwardly. Mark had spent the past few years of

his life with the Wild Hunt, the most anarchic and feral of all faeries. They rode across the sky on all manner of enchanted beings—motorcycles, horses, deer, massive snarling dogs—and scavenged battlefields, taking valuables from the bodies of the dead and giving them in tribute to the Faerie Courts.

He was adjusting well to being back among his Shadowhunter family, but there were still times when ordinary life seemed to take him by surprise. He noticed now that everyone was looking at him with raised eyebrows. He looked alarmed and placed a tentative arm around Emma's shoulders, holding out the bag in the other hand.

"I have won for you a fish, my fair one," he said, and kissed her on the cheek.

It was a sweet kiss, gentle and soft, and Mark smelled like he always did: like cold outside air and green growing things. And it made absolute sense, Emma thought, for Mark to assume that everyone was startled because they were waiting for him to give her his prize. She was, after all, his girlfriend.

She exchanged a worried glance with Cristina, whose dark eyes had gotten very large. Julian looked as if he were about to throw up blood. It was only a brief look before he schooled his features back into indifference, but Emma drew away from Mark, smiling at him apologetically.

"I couldn't keep a fish alive," she said. "I kill plants just by looking at them."

"I suspect I would have the same problem," Mark said, eyeing the fish. "It is too bad—I was going to name it Magnus, because it has sparkly scales."

At that, Cristina giggled. Magnus Bane was the High Warlock of Brooklyn, and he had a penchant for glitter.

"I suppose I had better let him go free," Mark said. Before anyone could say anything, he made his way to the railing of the pier and emptied the bag, fish and all, into the sea.

"Does anyone want to tell him that goldfish are freshwater fish and can't survive in the ocean?" said Julian quietly.

"Not really," said Cristina.

"Did he just kill Magnus?" Emma asked, but before Julian could answer, Mark whirled around.

All humor had gone from his expression. "I just saw something scuttle up one of the pilings below the pier. Something very much not human."

Emma felt a faint shiver pass over her skin. The demons who made the ocean their habitation were rarely seen on land. Sometimes she had nightmares where the ocean turned itself inside out and vomited its contents onto the beach: spiny, tentacled, slimy, blackened things half-crushed by the weight of water.

Within seconds, each of the Shadowhunters had a weapon in hand—Emma was clutching her sword, Cortana, a golden blade given to her by her parents. Julian held a seraph blade, and Cristina her butterfly knife.

"Which way did it go?" Julian asked.

"Toward the end of the pier," said Mark; he alone had not reached for a weapon, but Emma knew how fast he was. His nickname in the Wild Hunt had been *elf-shot*, for he was swift and accurate with a bow and arrow or a thrown blade. "Toward the amusement park."

"I'll go that way," Emma said. "Try to drive it off the edge of the pier—Mark, Cristina, you go down under, catch it if it tries to crawl back into the water."

They barely had time to nod, and Emma was off and running. The wind tugged at her braided hair as she wove through the crowd toward the lighted park at the pier's end. Cortana felt warm and solid in her hand, and her feet flew over the sea-warped wooden slats. She felt free, her worries cast aside, everything in her mind and body focused on the task at hand.

She could hear footsteps beside her. She didn't need to look to know it was Jules. His footsteps had been beside hers for all the years she had been a fighting Shadowhunter. His blood had been spilled when hers was. He had saved her life and she had saved his. He was part of her warrior self.

"There," she heard him say, but she'd already seen it: a dark, humped shape clambering up the support structure of the Ferris wheel. The carriages continued to rotate around it, the passengers shrieking in delight, unaware.

Emma hit the line for the wheel and started shoving her way through it. She and Julian had put glamour runes on before they'd gotten to the pier, and they were invisible to mundane eyes. That didn't mean they couldn't make their presence felt, though. Mundanes in line swore and yelled as she stomped on feet and elbowed her way to the front.

A carriage was just swinging down, a couple—a girl eating purple cotton candy and her black-clad, lanky boyfriend—about to climb in. Glancing up, Emma saw a flicker as the Teuthida demon slithered around the top of the wheel support. Swearing, Emma pushed past the couple, nearly knocking them aside, and leaped into the carriage. It was octagonal, a bench running around the inside, with plenty of room to stand. She heard yells of surprise as the carriage rose, lifting her away from the scene of chaos she'd created below, the couple who'd been about to board the wheel yelling at the ticket taker, and the people in line behind them yelling at each other.

The carriage rocked under her feet as Julian landed beside her, setting it to swinging. He craned his head up. "Do you see it?"

Emma squinted. She *had* seen the demon, she was sure of that, but it seemed to have vanished. From this angle, the Ferris wheel was a mess of bright lights, spinning spokes, and white-painted iron bars. The two carriages below her and Julian were empty of people; the line must still be sorting itself out.

Good, Emma thought. The fewer people who got on the wheel, the better.

"Stop." She felt Julian's hand on her arm, turning her around. Her whole body tensed. "Runes," he said shortly, and she realized he was holding his stele in his free hand.

Their carriage was still rising. Emma could see the beach below, the dark water spilling up onto the sand, the hills of Palisades Park rising vertically above the highway, crowned with a fringe of trees and greenery.

The stars were dim but visible beyond the bright lights of the pier. Julian held her arm neither roughly nor gently, but with a sort of clinical distance. He turned it over, his stele describing quick motions over her wrist, inking runes of protection there, runes of speed and agility and enhanced hearing.

This was the closest Emma had been to Jules in two weeks. She felt dizzy from it, a little drunk. His head was bent, his eyes fixed on the task at hand, and she took the opportunity to absorb the sight of him.

The lights of the wheel had turned amber and yellow; they powdered his tanned skin with gold. His hair fell in loose, fine waves over his forehead. She knew the way the skin by the corners of his mouth was soft, and the way his shoulders felt under her hands, strong and hard and vibrant. His lashes were long and thick, so dark that they seemed to have been charcoaled; she half expected them to leave a dusting of black powder on the tops of his cheekbones when he blinked.

He was beautiful. He had always been beautiful, but she had noticed it too late. And now she stood with her hands at her sides and her body aching because she couldn't touch him. She could never touch him again.

He finished what he was doing and spun the stele around so the handle was toward her. She took it without a word as he pulled aside the collar of his shirt, under his gear jacket. The skin there was a shade paler than the tanned skin on his face and hands, scored over and over with the faint white Marks of runes that had been used up and faded away.

She had to move a step nearer to Mark him. The runes bloomed under the tip of the stele: agility, night vision. Her head reached just to the level of his chin. She was staring directly at his throat, and saw him swallow.

"Just tell me," he said. "Just tell me that he makes you happy. That Mark makes you happy."

She jerked her head up. She had finished the runes; he reached to take the stele from her motionless hand. For the first time in what felt like forever, he was looking directly at her, his eyes turned dark blue by the colors of the night sky and the sea, spreading out all around them as they neared the top of the wheel.

"I'm happy, Jules," she said. What was one lie among so many others? She had never been someone who lied easily, but she was finding her way. When the safety of people she loved depended on it, she'd found, she could lie. "This is—this is smarter, safer for both of us."

The line of his gentle mouth hardened. "That's not—"

She gasped. A writhing shape rose up behind him—it was the color of an oil slick, its fringed tentacles clinging to a spoke of the wheel. Its mouth was wide open, a perfect circle ringed with teeth.

"*Jules!*" she shouted, and flung herself from the carriage, catching onto one of the thin iron bars that ran between the spokes. Dangling by one hand, she slashed out with Cortana, catching the Teuthida as it reared back. It yowled, and ichor sprayed; Emma cried out as it splashed her neck, burning her skin.

A knife punched into the demon's round, ribbed body. Pulling herself up onto a spoke, Emma glanced down to see Julian poised on the edge of the carriage, another knife already in hand. He sighted down along his arm, let the second knife fly—

It clanged off the bottom of an empty carriage. The Teuthida, incredibly fast, had whipped its way out of sight. Emma could hear it scrabbling downward, along the tangle of metal bars that made up the inside of the wheel.

Emma sheathed Cortana and began to crawl along the length of her spoke, heading toward the bottom of the wheel. LED lights exploded around her in purple and gold.

There was ichor and blood on her hands, making the descent slippery. Incongruously, the view from the wheel was beautiful, the sea and the sand opening in front of her in all directions, as if she were dangling off the edge of the world.

She could taste blood in her mouth, and salt. Below her, she could see Julian, out of the carriage, clambering along a lower spoke. He glanced up at her and pointed; she followed the line of his hand and saw the Teuthida nearly at the wheel's center.

Its tentacles were whipping around its body, slamming at the heart of the wheel. Emma could feel the reverberations through her bones. She craned her neck to see what it was doing and went cold—the center of the ride was a massive bolt, holding the wheel onto its structural supports. The Teuthida was yanking at the bolt, trying to rip it free. If the demon succeeded in disengaging it, the whole structure would pull away from its moorings and roll off the pier, like a disconnected bicycle wheel.

Emma had no illusions that anyone on the wheel, or near it, would survive. The wheel would crumple in on itself, crushing anyone underneath. Demons thrived on destruction, on the energy of death. It would feast.

The Ferris wheel rocked. The Teuthida had its tentacles fastened firmly to the iron bolt at the wheel's heart and was twisting it. Emma redoubled her crawling speed, but she was too far above the wheel's middle. Julian was closer, but she knew the weapons he was carrying: two knives, which he'd already thrown, and seraph blades, which weren't long enough for him to reach the demon.

He looked up at her as he stretched his body out along the iron bar, wrapped his left arm around it to anchor himself, and held the other arm out, his hand outstretched.

She knew, immediately, without having to wonder, what he was thinking. She breathed in deep and let go of the spoke.

She fell, down toward Julian, stretching out her own hand to reach for his. They caught and clasped, and she heard him gasp as he took her weight. She swung forward and down, her left hand locked around his right, and with her other hand she whipped Cortana from its sheath. The weight of her fall carried her forward, swinging her toward the middle of the wheel.

The Teuthida demon raised its head as she sailed toward it, and for the first time, she saw its eyes—they were oval, glossed with a protective mirrorlike coating. They almost seemed to widen like human eyes as she whipped Cortana forward, driving it down through the top of the demon's head and into its brain.

Its tentacles flailed—a last, dying spasm as its body pulled free of the blade and skittered, rolling along one of the downward-slanted spokes of the wheel. It reached the end and tumbled off.

In the distance, Emma thought she heard a splash. But there was no time to wonder. Julian's hand had tightened on hers, and he was pulling her up. She slammed Cortana back into its sheath as he hauled her up, up, onto the spoke where he was lying so that she collapsed awkwardly, half on top of him.

He was still clasping her hand, breathing hard. His eyes met hers, just for a second. Around them, the wheel spun, lowering them back down toward the ground. Emma could see crowds of mundanes on the beach, the shimmer of water along the shoreline, even a dark head and a light one that could be Mark and Cristina. . . .

"Good teamwork," Julian said finally.

"I know," Emma said, and she did. That was the worst thing: that he was right, that they still worked so perfectly together as *parabatai*. As warrior partners. As a matched pair of soldiers who could never, ever be parted.

Mark and Cristina were waiting for them under the pier. Mark had kicked off his shoes and was partway into the ocean water. Cristina was folding away her butterfly knife. At her feet was a patch of slimy, drying sand.

"Did you see the squid thingie fall off the Ferris wheel?" Emma asked as she and Julian drew near.

Cristina nodded. "It fell into the shallows. It wasn't quite dead, so Mark dragged it up onto the beach and we finished it off." She kicked at the sand in front of her. "It was very disgusting, and Mark got slime on him."

"I've got ichor on me," Emma said, looking down at her stained gear. "That was one messy demon."

"You are still very beautiful," Mark said with a gallant smile.

Emma smiled back at him, as much as she could. She was unbelievably grateful to Mark, who was playing his part in all this without a word of complaint, though he must have found it strange. In Cristina's opinion, Mark was getting something out of the pretense, but Emma couldn't imagine what. It wasn't as if Mark liked lying—he'd spent so many years among faeries, who were incapable of untruths, that he found it unnatural.

Julian had stepped away from them and was on the phone again, speaking in a low voice. Mark splashed up out of the water and jammed his wet feet into his boots. Neither he nor Cristina was fully glamoured, and Emma noticed the stares of mundane passersby as he came toward her—because he was tall, and beautiful, and because he had eyes that shone brighter than the lights of the Ferris wheel. And because one of his eyes was blue, and the other one was gold.

And because there was something about him, something indefinably strange, a trace of the wildness of Faerie that never failed to make Emma think of untrammeled, wide-open spaces, of freedom and lawlessness. *I am a lost boy*, his eyes seemed to say. *Find me.*

Reaching Emma, he lifted his hand to push back a lock of her hair. A wave of feeling went through her—sadness and exhilaration, a longing for something, though she didn't know what.

"That was Diana," Julian said, and even without looking at him, Emma could picture his face as he spoke—gravity, thoughtfulness, a careful consideration of whatever the situation was. "Jace and Clary have arrived with a message from the Consul. They're holding a meeting at the Institute, and they want us there now."

2

BOUNDLESS FLOODS

The four of them went straight through the Institute to the library, without pausing to change their gear. Only when they'd burst into the room and Emma realized she, Mark, Cristina, and Julian had all tracked in sticky demon ichor did she pause to wonder if perhaps they should have stopped to shower.

The roof of the library had been damaged two weeks before and hastily repaired, the stained-glass skylight replaced with plain, warded glass, the intricately decorated ceiling now covered over with a layer of rune-carved rowan wood.

The wood of rowan trees was protective: It kept out dark magic. It also had an effect on faeries—Emma saw Mark wince and look up sideways as they entered the room. He'd told her proximity to too much rowan made him feel as if his skin were powdered with tiny sparks of fire. She wondered what effect it would have on a full-blood faerie.

"Glad to see you made it," said Diana. She was sitting at the head of one of the long library tables, her hair pulled back into a sleek bun. A thick gold chain necklace glittered against her dark skin. Her black-and-white dress was, as always, pristinely spotless and wrinkle free.

Beside her was Diego Rocio Rosales, notable to the Clave for being a highly trained Centurion and to the Blackthorns for having the nickname Perfect Diego. He *was* irritatingly perfect—ridiculously handsome, a spectacular fighter, smart, and unfailingly polite. He'd also broken Cristina's heart before she had left Mexico, which meant that normally Emma would be plotting his death, but she couldn't because he and Cristina had gotten back together two weeks ago.

He cast a smile at Cristina now, his even white teeth flashing. His Centurion pin glittered at his shoulder, the words *Primi Ordines* visible against the silver. He wasn't just a Centurion; he was one of the First Company, the very best of the graduating class from the Scholomance. Because, of course, he was perfect.

Across from Diana and Diego sat two figures who were very familiar to Emma: Jace Herondale and Clary Fairchild, the heads of the New York Institute, though when Emma had met them, they'd been teenagers the age she was now. Jace was all tousled gold handsomeness, looks he'd grown into gracefully over the years. Clary was red hair, stubborn green eyes, and a deceptively delicate face. She had a will like iron, as Emma had good cause to know.

Clary jumped to her feet now, her face lighting up, as Jace leaned back in his chair with a smile. "You're back!" she cried, rushing toward Emma. She wore jeans and a threadbare MADE IN BROOKLYN T-shirt that had probably once belonged to her best friend, Simon. It looked worn and soft, exactly like the sort of shirt Emma had often filched from Julian and refused to give back. "How did it go with the squid demon?"

Emma was prevented from answering by Clary's enveloping hug. "Great," said Mark. "Really great. They're so full of liquid, squids." He actually seemed pleased about it.

Clary let Emma go and frowned down at the ichor, seawater, and unidentifiable slime that had transferred themselves to her shirt. "I see what you mean."

"I'm just going to welcome you all from over here," said Jace, waving. "There's a disturbing smell of calamari wafting from your general direction."

There was a giggle, quickly stifled. Emma glanced up and saw legs dangling between the railings of the upstairs gallery. With amusement, she recognized Ty's long limbs and Livvy's patterned stockings. There were nooks up on the gallery level that were perfect for eavesdropping—she couldn't count how many of Andrew Blackthorn's meetings she and Julian had spied on as kids, drinking up the knowledge and sense of importance that being present at a Conclave meeting brought.

She glanced sideways at Julian, seeing him note Ty and Livvy's presence, knowing the moment he decided, as she had, not to say anything about it. His whole thought process was visible to her in the quirk of his smile—odd how transparent he was to her in his unguarded moments, and how little she could tell what he was thinking when he chose to hide it.

Cristina went over to Diego, bumping her hand gently against his shoulder. He kissed her wrist. Emma saw Mark glance at them, his expression unreadable. Mark had talked to her about many things in the past two weeks, but not Cristina. Not ever Cristina.

"So how many sea demons does that make it?" asked Diana. "In total?" She gestured for everyone to take seats around the table. They sat down, squelching slightly, Emma next to Mark but across from Julian. He answered Diana as calmly as if he *wasn't* dripping ichor onto the polished floor.

"A few smaller ones this past week," said Julian, "but that's normal when it storms. They wash up on the beach. We ran some patrols; the Ashdowns ran some farther south. I think we got them all."

"This was the first really big one," said Emma. "I mean, I've only seen a few that big before. They don't usually come up out of the ocean."

Jace and Clary exchanged a look.

"Is there something we should know about?" Emma said. "Are you collecting really big sea demons to decorate the Institute or something?"

Jace leaned forward, his elbows on the table. He had a calm, catlike face and unreadable amber eyes. Clary had once said that the first time she'd ever seen him, she'd thought he looked like a lion. Emma could see it: Lions seemed so calm and almost lazy until they exploded into action. "Maybe we should talk about why we're here," he said.

"I thought you were here about Kit," Julian said. "What with him being a Herondale and all."

There was a rustle from upstairs and a faint muttering. Ty had been sleeping in front of Kit's door for the past nights, an odd behavior no one had remarked on. Emma assumed Ty found Kit unusual and interesting in the manner that he sometimes found bees and lizards unusual and interesting.

"Partly," said Jace. "We just returned from a Council meeting in Idris. That's why it took us so long to get here, though I wanted to come as fast as possible when I heard about Kit." He sat back and threw an arm over the back of his chair. "You won't be surprised to know there was a great deal of discussion about the Malcolm situation."

"You mean the situation where the High Warlock of Los Angeles turned out to be a spree killer *and* a necromancer?" Julian said. There were layers of implication clear in his voice: The Clave hadn't suspected Malcolm, had approved of his appointment to the post of High Warlock, had done nothing to stop the murders he committed. It had been the Blackthorns who had done that.

There was another giggle from above. Diana coughed to hide a smile. "Sorry," she said to Jace and Clary. "I think we have mice."

"I didn't hear anything," Jace said.

"We're just surprised the Council meeting ended so quickly," Emma said. "We thought we might have to give testimony. About Malcolm, and everything that happened."

Emma and the Blackthorns had given testimony in front of the Council before. Years before, after the Dark War. It wasn't an experience Emma was excited to repeat, but it would have been a chance to tell their side of what had happened. To explain why they had worked in cooperation with faeries, in direct contradiction of the Laws of the Cold Peace. Why they had investigated the High Warlock of Los Angeles, Malcolm Fade, without telling the Clave they were doing it; what they had done when they had found him guilty of heinous crimes.

Why Emma had killed him.

"You already told Robert—the Inquisitor," said Clary. "He believed you. He testified on your behalf."

Julian raised an eyebrow. Robert Lightwood, the Inquisitor of the Clave, was not a warm and friendly sort of man. They'd told him what had happened because they'd been forced to, but he wasn't the kind of person you could imagine doing you favors.

"Robert's not so bad," Jace said. "Really. He's mellowed since becoming a grandfather. And the fact is, the Clave was actually less interested in you than they were in the Black Volume."

"Apparently nobody realized it was ever in the library here," said Clary. "The Cornwall Institute is famous for having a considerably large selection of books on dark magic—the original *Malleus Maleficarum*, the *Daemonatia*. Everyone thought it was there, properly locked up."

"The Blackthorns used to run the Cornwall Institute," said Julian. "Maybe my father brought it with him when he got the appointment to run the Institute here." He looked troubled. "Though I don't know why he would have wanted it."

"Maybe Arthur brought it," suggested Cristina. "He's always been fascinated with ancient books."

Emma shook her head. "Can't have. The book had to have been here when Sebastian attacked the Institute—before Arthur came."

"How much of the fact that they didn't want us there to testify had to do with them discussing whether I ought to be allowed to stay?" said Mark.

"Some," Clary said, meeting his gaze levelly. "But, Mark, we never would have let them make you return to the Hunt. *Everyone* would have risen up."

Diego nodded. "The Clave has deliberated, and they're fine with Mark remaining here with his family. The original order only forbid Shadowhunters from looking for him, but he came to you, so the order hasn't been contravened."

Mark nodded stiffly. He had never seemed to like Perfect Diego.

"And believe me," Clary added, "they were very happy to use that loophole. I think even the most faerie-hating of them feel for what Mark went through."

"But not for what Helen has gone through?" said Julian. "Any word on her return?"

"Nothing," said Jace. "I'm sorry. They wouldn't hear of it."

Mark's expression tensed. In that moment, Emma could see the warrior in him, the dark shadow of the battlefields the Wild Hunt stalked, the walker among the bodies of the dead.

"We'll keep at them," said Diana. "Having you back is a victory, Mark, and we'll press that victory. But right now—"

"What's happening right now?" Mark demanded. "Isn't the crisis over?"

"We're Shadowhunters," Jace said. "You'll find that the crisis is never over."

"Right now," Diana went on, "the Council just finished discussing the fact that large sea demons have been spotted all up and down the coast of California. In record numbers. There have been more seen in the past week than in the past decade. That Teuthida you fought wasn't an outlier."

"We think it's because Malcolm's body and the Black Volume are still out there in the ocean," said Clary. "And we think it may be because of the spells Malcolm cast during his life."

"But a warlock's spells disappear when they die," protested Emma. She thought of Kit. The wards Malcolm had placed around the Rooks' house had vanished when he died. Demons had attacked within hours. "We went up to his house after he died, to look for evidence of what he'd been doing. The whole thing had disintegrated into a slag heap."

Jace had disappeared under the table. He appeared a moment later, holding Church, the Institute's part-time cat. Church had his paws stuck straight out and a look of satisfaction on his face. "We thought the same thing," said Jace, settling the cat on his lap. "But apparently, according to Magnus, there are spells that can be constructed to be *activated* by a warlock's death."

Emma glared at Church. She knew the cat had once lived in the New York Institute, but it seemed rude to show preference so blatantly. The cat was lying on his back on Jace's lap, purring and ignoring her.

"Like an alarm," Julian said, "that goes off when you open a door?"

"Yes, but in this case, death is the open door," said Diana.

"So what's the solution?" asked Emma.

"We probably need his body to turn the spell off, so to speak," said Jace. "And a clue as to how he did it would be nice."

"The ruins of the convergence have been picked over pretty thoroughly," Clary said. "But we'll check out Malcolm's house tomorrow, just to be sure."

"It's rubble," Julian warned.

"Rubble that will have to be cleared away soon, before mundanes notice it," said Diana. "There's a glamour on it, but it's temporary.

That means the site will only be undisturbed for another few days."

"And there's no harm taking a last look," said Jace. "Especially as Magnus has given us some idea what to look *for*." He rubbed Church's ear but didn't elaborate.

"The Black Volume is a powerful necromantic object," said Perfect Diego. "It could be causing disturbances we cannot even imagine. Driving the deepest-dwelling of sea demons to crawl up onto our shores means mundanes are in danger—a few have already disappeared from the Pier."

"So," said Jace. "A team of Centurions is going to arrive here tomorrow—"

"Centurions?" Panic flashed in Julian's eyes, a look of fear and vulnerability that Emma guessed was visible only to her. It was gone almost instantly. "Why?"

Centurions. Elite Shadowhunters, they trained at the Scholomance, a school carved into the rock walls of the Carpathian Mountains, surrounded by an icy lake. They studied esoteric lore and were experts in faeries and the Cold Peace.

And also, apparently, sea demons.

"This is excellent news," said Perfect Diego. He *would* say that, Emma thought. Smugly, he touched the pin at his shoulder. "They will be able to find the body and the book."

"Hopefully," Clary said.

"But you're already here, Clary," said Julian, his voice deceptively mild. "You and Jace—if you brought in Simon and Isabelle and Alec and Magnus, I bet you could find the body right away."

He doesn't want strangers here, Emma thought. People who would pry into the Institute's business, demand to talk to Uncle Arthur. He had managed to preserve the Institute's secrets even through everything that had happened with Malcolm. And now they were threatened again by random Centurions.

"Clary and I are only stopping by," Jace said. "We can't stay and search, though we'd like to. We're on assignment from the Council."

"What kind of assignment?" Emma said. What mission could be more important than retrieving the Black Volume, clearing up the mess Malcolm had made once and for all?

But she could tell from the look that Jace and Clary exchanged that there was a world of more important things out there, ones she couldn't imagine. Emma couldn't help a small explosion of bitterness inside, the wish that she were just a bit older, that she could be equal to Jace and Clary, know their secrets and the Council's secrets.

"I'm so sorry," Clary said. "We can't say."

"So you're not even going to be here?" Emma demanded. "While all this is going on, and our Institute is invaded—"

"Emma," Jace said. "We know that you're used to being alone and untroubled here. To having only Arthur to answer to."

If only he knew. But that was impossible.

He went on, "But the purpose of an Institute is not just to centralize Clave activity, but to house Shadowhunters who must be accommodated in a city they don't live in. There are fifty rooms here that no one is using. So unless there's a pressing reason they can't come . . ."

The words hung in the air. Diego looked down at his hands. He didn't know the full truth about Arthur, but Emma guessed that he suspected.

"You can tell us," Clary said. "We'll keep it in the strictest confidence."

But it wasn't Emma's secret to tell. She held herself back from looking at Mark or Cristina, Diana or Julian, the only others at the table who knew the truth about who really ran the Institute. A truth that would need to be hidden from the Centurions, who would be duty-bound to report it to the Council.

"Uncle Arthur hasn't been well, as I assume you know," Julian said, gesturing toward the empty chair where the Institute's head would normally have sat. "I was concerned the Centurions might worsen his condition, but considering the importance of their mission, we'll make them as comfortable as possible."

"Since the Dark War, Arthur has been prone to flare-ups of headaches and pain in his old wounds," added Diana. "I'll run interference between him and the Centurions until he's feeling better."

"There's really nothing to worry about," said Diego. "They're Centurions—disciplined, orderly soldiers. They won't be throwing wild parties or making unreasonable demands." He put an arm around Cristina. "I'll be glad to have you meet some of my friends."

Cristina smiled back at him. Emma couldn't help but glance toward Mark to see if he was looking at Cristina and Diego the way he often did—a way that made her wonder how Julian could miss it. One day he would notice, and there would be awkward questions to answer.

But that day wouldn't be today, because sometime in the past few minutes Mark had slipped soundlessly out of the library. He was gone.

Mark associated different rooms in the Institute with different feelings, most of them new since his return. The rowaned library made him tense. The entryway, where he had faced down Sebastian Morgenstern so many years ago, made his skin prickle, his blood heat.

In his own room he felt lonely. In the twins' rooms, and Dru's or Tavvy's, he could lose himself in being their older brother. In Emma's room he felt safe. Cristina's room was barred to him. In Julian's room, he felt guilty. And in the training room, he felt like a Shadowhunter.

He had made unconsciously for the training room the moment he'd left the library. It was still too much for Mark, the way that

Shadowhunters hid their emotions. How could they bear a world where Helen was exiled? He could hardly bear it; he yearned for his sister every day. And yet they all would have looked at him in surprise if he had cried out in grief or fallen to his knees. Jules, he knew, didn't want the Centurions there—but his expression had hardly changed. Faeries could riddle and cheat and scheme, but they did not hide their honest pain.

It was enough to send him to the weapons rack, his hands feeling for whatever would let him lose himself in practice. Diana had owned a weapons shop in Idris once, and there was always an impeccable array of beautiful weapons laid out for them to train with: Greek *machaera*, with their single cutting edges. There were Viking *spatha*, two-handed claymores and *zweihänder*, and Japanese wooden *bokken*, used only for training.

He thought of the weapons of faerie. The sword he had carried in the Wild Hunt. The fey used nothing made of iron, for weapons and tools of iron made them sick. The sword he had borne in the Hunt had been made of horn, and it had been light in his hand. Light like the elf-bolts he had shot from his bow. Light like the wind under the feet of his horse, like the air around him when he rode.

He lifted a claymore from the rack and turned it experimentally in his hand. He could feel that it was made of steel—not quite iron, but an iron alloy—though he didn't have the reaction to iron that full-blooded faeries did.

It did feel heavy in his hand. But so much had been feeling heavy since he had returned home. The weight of expectation was heavy. The weight of how much he loved his family was heavy.

Even the weight of what he was involved in with Emma was heavy. He trusted Emma. He didn't question that she was doing the right thing; if she believed it, he believed in her.

But lies didn't come to him easily, and he hated lying to his family most of all.

"Mark?" It was Clary, followed by Jace. The meeting in the library must be over. They had both changed into gear; Clary's red hair was very bright, like a splash of blood against her dark clothes.

"I'm here," Mark said, placing the sword he'd been holding back in the rack. The full moon was high, and white light filtered through the windows. The moon traced a path like a road across the sea from where it kissed the horizon to the edge of the beach.

Jace hadn't said anything yet; he was watching Mark with hooded golden eyes, like a hawk's. Mark couldn't help but remember Clary and Jace as they had been when he'd met them just after the Hunt had taken him. He'd been hiding in the tunnels near the Seelie Court when they'd come walking toward him, and his heart had ached and broken to see them. Shadowhunters, striding through the dangers of Faerie, heads held high. They were not lost; they were not running. They were not afraid.

He had wondered if he would have that pride again, that lack of fear. Even as Jace had pressed a witchlight into his hand, even as he had said, *Show them what a Shadowhunter is made of, show them that you aren't afraid*, Mark had been sick with fear.

Not for himself. For his family. How would they fare in a world at war, without him to protect them?

Surprisingly well, had been the answer. They hadn't needed him after all. They'd had Jules.

Jace seated himself on a windowsill. He was bigger than he had been the first time Mark had met him, of course. Taller, broader shouldered, though still graceful. Rumor had it that even the Seelie Queen had been impressed by his looks and manner, and faerie gentry were rarely impressed by humans. Even Shadowhunters.

Though sometimes they were. Mark supposed his own existence was proof of that. His mother, the Lady Nerissa of the Seelie Court, had loved his Shadowhunter father.

"Julian doesn't want the Centurions here," said Jace. "Does he?"

Mark looked at them both with suspicion. "I wouldn't know."

"Mark won't tell us his brother's secrets, Jace," said Clary. "Would you tell Alec's?"

The window behind Jace rose high and clear, so clear Mark sometimes imagined he could fly out of it. "Maybe if it was for his own good," Jace said.

Clary made an inelegant doubtful noise. "Mark," she said. "We need your help. We have some questions about Faerie and the Courts—their actual physical layout—and there don't seem to be any answers—not from the Spiral Labyrinth, not from the Scholomance."

"And honestly," Jace said, "we don't want to look too much like we're investigating, because this mission is secret."

"Your mission is to Faerie?" Mark guessed.

They both nodded.

Mark was astonished. Shadowhunters had never been comfortable in the actual Lands of Faerie, and since the Cold Peace they'd avoided them like poison. "Why?" He turned quickly from the claymore. "Is this some kind of revenge mission? Because Iarlath and some of the others cooperated with Malcolm? Or—because of what happened to Emma?"

Emma still sometimes needed help with the last of her bandages. Every time Mark looked at the red lines crossing her skin, he felt guilt and sickness. They were like a web of bloody threads that kept him bound to the deception they were both perpetrating.

Clary's eyes were kind. "We're not planning to hurt anyone," she said. "There's no revenge going on here. This is strictly about information."

"You think I'm worried about Kieran," realized Mark. The name lodged in his throat like a piece of snapped-off bone. He had loved Kieran, and Kieran had betrayed him and gone back to the Hunt, and whenever Mark thought about him, it felt as if he were bleeding from someplace inside. "I am not," he said, "worried about Kieran."

"Then you wouldn't mind if we talked to him," said Jace.

"I wouldn't be worried about him," said Mark. "I might be worried about *you*."

Clary laughed softly. "Thank you, Mark."

"He's the son of the Unseelie Court's King," said Mark. "The King has fifty sons. All of them vie for the throne. The King is tired of them. He owed Gwyn a favor, so he gave him Kieran in repayment. Like the gift of a sword or a dog."

"As I understand it," said Jace, "Kieran came to you, and offered to help you, against the wishes of the fey. He put himself in grave danger to assist you."

Mark supposed he shouldn't be surprised that Jace knew that. Emma often confided in Clary. "He owed me. It was thanks to him that those I love were badly hurt."

"Still," said Jace, "there is some chance he might prove amenable to our questions. Especially if we could tell him they were endorsed by you."

Mark said nothing. Clary kissed Jace on the cheek and murmured something in his ear before she headed out of the room. Jace watched her go, his expression momentarily soft. Mark felt a sharp stab of envy. He wondered if he would ever be like that with someone: the way they seemed to match, Clary's kind playfulness and Jace's sarcasm and strength. He wondered if he had ever matched with Kieran. If he would have matched with Cristina, had things been different.

"What is it you mean to ask Kieran?" he said.

"Some questions about the Queen, and about the King," said Jace. Noting Mark's impatient movement, he said, "I'll tell you a little, and remember I should be telling you nothing. The Clave would have my head for this." He sighed. "Sebastian Morgenstern left a weapon with one of the Courts of Faerie," he said. "A weapon that could destroy us all, destroy all Nephilim."

"What does the weapon do?" Mark asked.

"I don't know. That's part of what we need to find out. But we know it's deadly."

Mark nodded. "I think Kieran will help you," he said. "And I can give you a list of names of those in Faerie to look for who might be friendly to your cause, because it will not be a popular one. I do not think you know how much they hate you. If they have a weapon, I hope you find it, because they will not hesitate to use it, and they will have no mercy on you."

Jace looked up through golden lashes that were very like Kit's. His gaze was watchful and still. "Mercy on *us*?" he said. "You're one of us."

"That seems to depend on who you ask," Mark said. "Do you have a pen and paper? I'll start with the names. . . ."

It had been too long since Uncle Arthur had left the attic room where he slept, ate, and did his work. Julian wrinkled his nose as he and Diana climbed the narrow stairs—the air was staler than usual, rancid with old food and sweat. The shadows were thick. Arthur was a shadow himself, hunched over his desk, a witchlight burning in a dish on the windowsill above. He didn't react to Julian and Diana's presence.

"Arthur," Diana said, "we need to speak with you."

Arthur turned slowly in his chair. Julian felt his gaze skate over Diana, and then over himself. "Miss Wrayburn," he said, finally. "What can I do for you?"

Diana had accompanied Julian on trips to the attic before, but rarely. Now that the truth of their situation was known by Mark and Emma, Julian had been able to acknowledge to Diana what they had always both known but never spoken about.

For years, since he was twelve years old, Julian had borne alone the knowledge that his uncle Arthur was mad, his mind shattered during his imprisonment in the Seelie Court. He had periods of lucidity, helped by the medicine Malcolm Fade had provided, but they never lasted long.

If the Clave knew the truth, they would have ripped Arthur away from his position as Institute head in moments. It was quite likely he would end up locked in the Basilias, forbidden from leaving or having visitors. In his absence, with no Blackthorn adult to run the Institute, the children would be split up, sent to the Academy in Idris, scattered around the world. Julian's determination to never let that happen had led to five years of secret keeping, five years of hiding Arthur from the world and the world from Arthur.

Sometimes he wondered if he was doing the right thing for his uncle. But did it matter? Either way, he would protect his brothers and sisters. He would sacrifice Arthur for them if he had to, and if the moral consequences woke him up in the middle of the night sometimes, panicked and gasping, then he'd live with that.

He remembered Kieran's sharp faerie eyes on him: *You have a ruthless heart.*

Maybe it was true. Right now Julian's heart felt dead in his chest, a swollen, beatless lump. Everything seemed to be happening at a slight distance—he even felt as if he were moving more slowly through the world, as if he were pushing his way through water.

Still, it was a relief to have Diana with him. Arthur often mistook Julian for his dead father or grandfather, but Diana was no part of his past, and he seemed to have no choice but to recognize her.

"The medication that Malcolm made for you," said Diana. "Did he ever speak to you about it? What was in it?"

Arthur shook his head slightly. "The boy doesn't know?"

Julian knew that meant him. "No," he said. "Malcolm never spoke of it to me."

Arthur frowned. "Are there dregs, leftovers, that could be analyzed?"

"I used every drop I could find two weeks ago." Julian had drugged his uncle with a powerful cocktail of Malcolm's medicine the last time Jace, Clary, and the Inquisitor had been at the Institute. He hadn't dared take the chance that Arthur would be anything but steady on his feet and as clearheaded as possible.

Julian was fairly sure Jace and Clary would cover up Arthur's condition if they knew it. But it was an unfair burden to ask them to bear, and besides—he didn't trust the Inquisitor, Robert Lightwood. He hadn't trusted him since the time five years ago when Robert had forced him to endure a brutal trial by Mortal Sword because he hadn't believed Julian wouldn't lie.

"You haven't kept any of it, Arthur?" Diana asked. "Hidden some away?"

Arthur shook his head again. In the dim witchlight, he looked old—much older than he was, his hair salted with gray, his eyes washed out like the ocean in the early morning. His body under his straggling gray robe was skinny, the point of his shoulder bone visible through the material. "I didn't know Malcolm would turn out to be what he was," he said. *A murderer, a killer, a traitor.* "Besides, I depended on the boy." He cleared his throat. "Julian."

"I didn't know about Malcolm either," Julian said. "The thing is, we're going to have guests. Centurions."

"Kentarchs," murmured Arthur, opening one of his desk drawers as if he meant to search for something inside. "That is what they were called in the Byzantine army. But a centurion was always the pillar of the army. He commanded a hundred men. A centurion could mete out punishment to a Roman citizen that the law usually protected them from. Centurions supersede the law."

Julian wasn't sure how much the original Roman centurions and the Centurions of the Scholomance had in common. But he suspected he got his uncle's point anyway. "Right, so that means we're going to have to be especially careful. With how you have to be around them. How you're going to have to act."

Arthur put his fingers to his temples. "I'm just so tired," he murmured. "Can we not . . . If we could ask Malcolm for a bit more medicine . . ."

"Malcolm's dead," Julian said. His uncle had been told, but it didn't seem to have quite sunk in. And it was exactly the sort of mistake he couldn't make around strangers.

"There are mundane drugs," said Diana, after a moment's hesitation.

"But the Clave," Julian said. "The punishment for seeking out mundane medical treatment is—"

"I know what it is," Diana said, surprisingly sharply. "But we're desperate."

"But we'd have no idea about what dosage or what pills. We have no idea how mundanes treat sicknesses like this."

"I am not *ill*." Arthur slammed the drawer of the desk shut. "The faeries shattered my mind. I *felt* it break. No mundane could understand or treat such a thing."

Diana exchanged a worried look with Julian. "Well, there are several paths we could go down. We'll leave you alone, Arthur, and discuss them. We know how important your work is."

"Yes," Julian's uncle murmured. "My work . . ." And he bent again over his papers, Diana and Julian instantly forgotten. As Julian followed Diana out of the room, he couldn't help but wonder what solace it was that his uncle found in old stories of gods and heroes, of an earlier time of the world, one where plugging your ears and refusing to listen to the sound of the music of sirens could keep you from madness.

At the foot of the stairs, Diana turned to Julian and spoke softly. "You'll have to go to the Shadow Market tonight."

"What?" Julian was thrown. The Shadow Market was off-limits to Nephilim unless they were on a mission, and always off-limits to underage Shadowhunters. "With you?"

Diana shook her head. "I can't go there."

Julian didn't ask. It was an unspoken fact between them that Diana had secrets and that Julian could not press her about them.

"But there'll be warlocks," she said. "Ones we don't know, ones who'll keep silent for a price. Ones who won't know your face. And faeries. This is a faerie-caused madness after all, not a natural state. Perhaps they would know how to reverse it." She was silent a moment, thinking. "Bring Kit with you," she said. "He knows the Shadow Market better than anyone else we could ask, and Downworlders there trust him."

"He's just a kid," Julian objected. "And he hasn't been out of the Institute since his father died." *Was killed, actually. Ripped to pieces in front of his eyes.* "It could be hard on him."

"He'll have to get used to things being hard on him," said Diana, her expression flinty. "He's a Shadowhunter now."

3

WHERE DWELL
THE GHOULS

Vicious traffic meant it took Julian and Kit an hour to get from Malibu to Old Pasadena. By the time they found parking, Julian had a pounding headache, not helped by the fact that Kit had barely said a word to him since they'd left the Institute.

Even so long after sunset, the sky in the west was touched with feather-strokes of crimson and black. The wind was blowing from the east, which meant that even in the middle of the city you could breathe in desert: sand and grit, cactus and coyotes, the burning scent of sage.

Kit leaped out of the car the minute Julian turned the engine off, as if he couldn't stand spending another minute next to him. When they'd passed the freeway exit that went to the Rooks' old house, Kit had asked if he could swing by to pick up some of his clothes. Julian had said no, it wasn't safe, especially at night. Kit had looked at him as if Julian had driven a knife into his back.

Julian was used to pleading and sulks and protestations that someone hated you. He had four younger siblings. But there was a special artistry to Kit's glaring. He really meant it.

Now, as Julian locked the car behind them, Kit made a snorting sound. "You look like a Shadowhunter."

Julian glanced down at himself. Jeans, boots, a vintage blazer that had been a gift from Emma. Since glamour runes weren't much use at the Market, he'd had to fall back on pulling down his sleeve to cover his Voyance rune and flipping up his collar to conceal the very edges of Marks that would otherwise have peeked out from his shirt.

"What?" he said. "You can't see any Marks."

"You don't need to," said Kit, in a bored voice. "You look like a cop. All of you always look like cops."

Julian's headache intensified. "And your suggestion?"

"Let me go in alone," Kit said. "They know me, they trust me. They'll answer my questions and sell me whatever I want." He held out a hand. "I'll need some money, of course."

Julian looked at him in disbelief. "You didn't really think that would work, did you?"

Kit shrugged and retracted his hand. "It could've worked."

Julian started walking toward the alley that led to the entrance to the Shadow Market. He'd only been there once, years ago, but he remembered it well. "So, let me guess. Your plan was to take some money from me, pretend you were going to the Shadow Market, and hop a bus out of town?"

"Actually, my plan was to take some money from you, pretend I was going to the Shadow Market, and hop on the Metrolink," said Kit. "They have trains that leave this city now. Major development, I know. You should try to keep track of these things."

Julian wondered briefly what Jace would do if he strangled Kit. He considered voicing the thought aloud, but they'd reached the end of the alley, where a slight shimmer in the air was visible. He grabbed Kit by the arm, propelling them both through it at the same time.

They emerged on the other side into the heart of the Market. Light flared all around them, blotting out the stars overhead. Even the moon seemed a pale shell.

Julian was still gripping Kit's arm, but Kit was making no move to run. He was looking around with a wistfulness that made him look young—sometimes it was hard for Julian to remember that Kit was the same age as Ty. His blue eyes—clear and sky-colored, without the green tinge that characterized the Blackthorns' eyes—moved around the Market, taking it in.

Rows of booths were lit with torches whose fires blazed gold, blue, and poison green. Trellises of flowers richer and sweeter-smelling than white oleander or jacaranda blossoms cascaded down the sides of stalls. Beautiful faerie girls and boys danced to the music of reeds and pipes. Everywhere were voices clamoring for them to *come buy, come buy*. Weapons were on display, and jewelry, and vials of potions and powders.

"This way," said Kit, pulling his arm out of Julian's grip.

Julian followed. He could feel eyes on them, wondered if it was because Kit had been right: He looked like a cop, or the super-natural version, anyway. He was a Shadowhunter, had always been a Shadowhunter. You couldn't shed your nature.

They had reached one of the Market's edges, where the light was dimmer, and it was possible to see the white lines painted on the asphalt under them that revealed this place's daytime job as a parking lot.

Kit moved toward the closest booth, where a faerie woman sat in front of a sign that advertised fortune-telling and love potions. She looked up with a beaming smile as he approached.

"Kit!" she exclaimed. She wore a scrap of a white dress that set off her pale blue skin, and her pointed ears poked through lavender hair. Thin chains of gold and silver dangled around her neck and dripped from her wrists. She glared at Julian. "What is he doing here?"

"The Nephilim is all right, Hyacinth," Kit said. "I'll vouch for him. He just wants to buy something."

"Doesn't everyone," she murmured. She cast Julian a sly look. "You're a pretty one," she said. "Your eyes are almost the same color as me."

Julian moved closer to the booth. It was at times like this he wished he was any good at flirting. He wasn't. He had never in his life felt a flicker of desire for any girl who wasn't Emma, so it was something he'd never learned to do.

"I'm seeking a potion to cure madness in a Shadowhunter," he said. "Or at least to stop the symptoms for a while."

"What kind of madness?"

"He was tormented in the Courts," Julian said bluntly. "His mind was broken by the hallucinations and potions they forced on him."

"A Shadowhunter with faerie-caused madness? Oh my," she said, and there was skepticism in her tone. Julian began to explain about Uncle Arthur, without using his name: his situation and his condition. The fact that his lucid periods came and went. The fact that sometimes his moods made him bleak and cruel. That he recognized his family only part of the time. He described the potion Malcolm had made for Arthur, back when they trusted Malcolm and thought he was their friend.

Not that he mentioned Malcolm by name.

The faerie woman shook her head when he was done. "You should ask a warlock," she said. "They will deal with Shadowhunters. I will not. I have no desire to run afoul of the Courts or the Clave."

"No one needs to know about it," said Julian. "I'll pay you well."

"Child." There was an edge of pity in her voice. "You think you can keep secrets from all of Downworld? You think the Market hasn't been buzzing with the news of the fall of the Guardian and the death of Johnny Rook? The fact that we now no longer have a

High Warlock? The disappearance of Anselm Nightshade—though he was a terrible man—" She shook her head. "You should never have come here," she said. "It's not safe for either of you."

Kit looked bewildered. "You mean him," he said, indicating Julian with a tilt of his head. "It's not safe for him."

"Not for you, either, baby boy," said a gravelly voice behind them.

They both turned. A short man stood in front of them. He was pale, with a flat, sickly cast to his skin. He wore a three-piece gray wool suit, which must have been boiling in the warm weather. His hair and beard were dark and neatly clipped.

"Barnabas," said Kit, blinking. Julian noticed Hyacinth shrinking slightly in her booth. A small crowd had gathered behind Barnabas.

The short man stepped forward. "Barnabas Hale," he said, holding out a hand. The moment his fingers closed around Julian's, Julian felt his muscles tighten. Only Ty's affinity for lizards and snakes, and the fact that Julian had had to carry them out of the Institute and dump them back in the grass more than once, kept him from pulling his hand away.

Barnabas's skin wasn't pale: It was a mesh of overlapping whitish scales. His eyes were yellow, and they looked with amusement on Julian, as if expecting him to jerk his hand away. The scales against Julian's skin were like smooth, cold pebbles; they weren't slimy, but they felt as if they ought to be. Julian held the grip for several long moments before lowering his arm.

"You're a warlock," he said.

"Never claimed anything different," said Barnabas. "And you're a Shadowhunter."

Julian sighed and pulled his sleeve back into place. "I suppose there wasn't much point in trying to disguise it."

"None at all," said Barnabas. "Most of us can recognize a Nephilim on sight, and besides, young Mr. Rook has been the talk of the town." He turned his slit-pupilled eyes on Kit. "Sorry to hear about your father."

Kit acknowledged this with a slight nod. "Barnabas owns the Shadow Market. At least, he owns the land the Market's on, and he collects the rent for the stalls."

"That's true," said Barnabas. "So you'll understand I'm serious when I ask you both to leave."

"We're not causing any trouble," said Julian. "We came here to do business."

"Nephilim don't 'do business' at Shadow Markets," said Barnabas.

"I think you'll find they do," said Julian. "A friend of mine bought some arrows here not that long ago. They turned out to be poisoned. Any ideas about that?"

Barnabas jabbed a squat finger at him. "That's what I mean," he said. "You can't turn it off, even if you want to, this thinking you get to ask the questions and make the rules."

"They do make the rules," said Kit.

"Kit," said Julian out of the side of his mouth. "Not helping."

"A friend of *mine* disappeared the other day," said Barnabas. "Malcolm Fade. Any ideas about *that?*"

There was a low buzz in the crowd behind him. Julian opened and closed his hands at his sides. If he'd been here alone, he wouldn't have been worried—he could have gotten himself out of the crowd easily enough, and back to the car. But with Kit to protect, it would be harder.

"See?" Barnabas demanded. "For every secret you think you know, we know another. I know what happened to Malcolm."

"Do you know what he did?" Julian asked, carefully controlling his voice. Malcolm had been a murderer, a mass murderer. He'd killed Downworlders as well as mundanes. Surely the Blackthorns couldn't be blamed for his death. "Do you know *why* it happened?"

"I see only another Downworlder, dead at the hands of Nephilim. And Anselm Nightshade, too, imprisoned for a bit of simple magic. What next?" He spat on the ground at his feet. "There might have been a time I tolerated Shadowhunters in the Market. Was willing to take their money. But that time is over." The warlock's gaze skittered to Kit. "Go," he said. "And take your Nephilim friend with you."

"He's not my friend," said Kit. "And I'm not like them, I'm like you—"

Barnabas was shaking his head. Hyacinth watched, her blue hands steepled under her chin, her eyes wide.

"A dark time is coming for Shadowhunters," said Barnabas. "A terrible time. Their power will be crushed, their might thrown down into the dirt, and their blood will run like water through the riverbeds of the world."

"That's enough," Julian said sharply. "Stop trying to frighten him."

"You will pay for the Cold Peace," said the warlock. "The darkness is coming, and you would be well advised, Christopher Herondale, to stay far away from Institutes and Shadowhunters. Hide as your father did, and his father before him. Only then can you be safe."

"How do you know who I am?" Kit demanded. "How do you know my real name?"

It was the first time Julian had heard him admit that Herondale *was* his real name.

"Everyone knows," said Barnabas. "It's all the Market has been buzzing about for days. Didn't you see everyone staring at you when you came in?"

So they hadn't been looking at Julian. Or at least not just at Julian. It wasn't much comfort, though, Jules thought, not when Kit had that expression on his face.

"I thought I could come back here," Kit said. "Take over my father's stall. Work in the Market."

A forked tongue flickered out between Barnabas's lips. "Born a Shadowhunter, always a Shadowhunter," he said. "You cannot wash the taint from your blood. I'm telling you for the last time, boy—leave the Market. And don't come back."

Kit backed up, looking around him—seeing, as if for the first time, the faces turned toward him, most blank and unfriendly, many avidly curious.

"Kit—" Julian began, reaching out a hand.

But Kit had bolted.

It took Julian only a few moments to catch up with Kit—the boy hadn't really been trying to run; he'd just been pushing blindly through the crowds, with no destination. He'd fetched up in front of a massive stall that seemed to be in the middle of being torn apart.

It was just a bare latticework of boards now. It looked as if someone had ripped it to pieces with their hands. Jagged bits of wood lay scattered around on the blacktop. A sign dangled crookedly from the top of the stall, printed with the words PART SUPERNATURAL? YOU'RE NOT ALONE. THE FOLLOWERS OF THE GUARDIAN WANT YOU TO SIGN UP FOR THE LOTTERY OF FAVOR! LET LUCK INTO YOUR LIFE!

"The Guardian," Kit said. "That was Malcolm Fade?"

Julian nodded.

"He was the one who got my father involved in all that stuff with the Followers and the Midnight Theater," said Kit, his tone almost thoughtful. "It's Malcolm's fault he died."

Julian didn't say anything. Johnny Rook hadn't been much of a prize, but he was Kit's father. You only got one father. And Kit wasn't wrong.

Kit moved then, slamming his fist as hard as he could into the sign. It clattered to the ground. In the moment before Kit pulled his hand back, wincing, Julian saw a flash of the Shadowhunter in him. If the warlock wasn't already dead, Julian believed sincerely that Kit would have killed Malcolm.

A small crowd had followed from Hyacinth's stall, staring. Julian put a hand on Kit's back, and Kit didn't move to shake him off.

"Let's go," Julian said.

Emma showered carefully—the downside of having your hair long when you were a Shadowhunter was never knowing after a fight if there was ichor in it. Once the back of her neck had been green for a week.

When she came out into her bedroom, wearing sweatpants and a tank top and rubbing her hair dry with a green towel, she found Mark curled up at the foot of her bed, reading a copy of *Alice's Adventures in Wonderland*.

He was wearing a pair of cotton pajama bottoms that Emma had bought for three dollars from a vendor on the side of the PCH. He was partial to them as being oddly close in their loose, light material to the sort of trousers he'd worn in Faerie. If it bothered him that they also had a pattern of green shamrocks embroidered with the words GET LUCKY on them, he didn't show it. He sat up when Emma came in, scrubbing his hands through his hair, and smiled at her.

Mark had a smile that could break your heart. It seemed to take up his whole face and brighten his eyes, firing the blue and gold from inside.

"A strange evening, forsooth," he said.

"Don't you forsooth me." She flopped down on the bed next to him. He wouldn't sleep on the bed, but he didn't seem to mind using the mattress as a sort of giant sofa. He set his book down and leaned back against the footboard. "You know my rules about forsoothing in my room. Also the use of the words 'howbeit,' 'wella-day,' and 'alack.'"

"What about 'zounds'?"

"The punishment for 'zounds' is severe," she told him. "You'll have to run naked into the ocean in front of the Centurions."

Mark looked puzzled. "And then?"

She sighed. "Sorry, I forgot. Most of us mind being naked in front of strangers. Take my word for it."

"Really? You've never swum naked in the ocean?"

"That's kind of a different question, but no, I never have." She leaned back beside him.

"We should one day," he said. "All of us."

"I can't imagine Perfect Diego ripping off all his clothes and leaping into the water in front of us. Maybe just in front of Cristina. Maybe."

Mark clambered off the bed and onto the pile of blankets she'd put on the floor for him. "I doubt it. I bet he swims with all his clothes on. Otherwise he'd have to take off his Centurion pin."

She laughed and he gave her an answering smile, though he looked tired. She sympathized. It wasn't the normal activities of Shadowhunting that were tiring her out. It was the pretense. Perhaps it made sense that she and Mark could only unwind at night around each other, since there was no one, then, to pretend for.

They were the only times she had relaxed since the day Jem had told her about the *parabatai* curse, how *parabatai* who fell in love would go insane and destroy themselves and everyone they loved.

She'd known immediately: She couldn't let that happen. Not to Julian. Not to his family, who she loved too. She couldn't have stopped herself loving Julian. It was impossible. So she had to make Julian not love her.

Julian had given her the key himself, only days before. Words, whispered against her skin in a rare moment of vulnerability: He was jealous of Mark. Jealous that Mark could talk to her, flirt with her, easily, while Julian always had to hide what he felt.

Mark was leaning against the footboard beside her now, his eyes half-closed. Crescents of color under his lids, his eyelashes a shade darker than his hair. She remembered asking him to come to her room. *I need you to pretend with me that we're dating. That we're falling in love.*

He'd held out his hand to her, and she'd seen the storm in his eyes. The fierceness that reminded her that Faerie was more than green grass and revels. That it was callous wild cruelty, tears and blood, lightning that slashed the night sky like a knife.

Why lie? he'd asked.

She'd thought for a moment he'd been asking her, *Why do you want to tell this lie?* But he hadn't been. He'd been asking, *Why lie when we can make it the truth, this thing between us?*

She'd stood before him, aching all the way down to the floor of her soul, in all the places where she'd ripped Julian away from her as if she'd torn off a limb.

They said that men joined the Wild Hunt sometimes when they had sustained a great loss, preferring to howl out their grief to the skies than to suffer in silence in their ordinary gray lives. She remembered soaring through the sky with Mark, his arms around her waist: She had let the wind take her screams of excitement, thrilling to the freedom of the sky where there was no pain, no worry, only forgetfulness.

And here was Mark, beautiful in that way that the night sky was beautiful, offering her that same freedom with an outstretched hand. *What if I could love Mark?* she thought. *What if I could make this lie true?*

Then it would be no lie. If she could love Mark, it would end all the danger. Julian would be safe.

She had nodded. Reached her hand out to Mark's.

She let herself remember that night in her room, the look in his eyes when he'd asked her, *Why lie?* She remembered his warm clasp, his fingers circling her wrist. How they had nearly stumbled in their haste to get nearer to each other, colliding almost awkwardly, as if they'd been dancing and had missed a step. She had clasped Mark by the shoulders and stretched up to kiss him.

He was wiry from the Hunt, not as muscled as Julian, the bones of his clavicle and shoulders sharp under her hands. But his skin was smooth where she pushed her hands down the neck of his shirt, stroking the top of his spine. And his mouth was warm on hers.

He tasted bittersweet and felt hot, as if he had a fever. She instinctively moved closer to him; she hadn't realized she was shivering, but she was. His mouth opened over hers; he explored her lips with his, sending slow waves of heat through her body. He kissed the corner of her mouth, brushed his lips against her jaw, her cheek.

He drew back. "Em," he said, looking puzzled. "You taste of salt."

She drew her right hand back from its clasp around his neck. Touched her face. It was wet. She'd been crying.

He frowned. "I don't understand. You want the world to believe we are a couple, and yet you are weeping as if I have hurt you. Have I hurt you? Julian will never forgive me."

The mention of Julian's name almost undid her. She sank down at the foot of her bed, gripping her knees. "Julian has so much to cope with," she said. "I can't have him worrying about me. About my relationship with Cameron."

Silently, she apologized to Cameron Ashdown, who really hadn't done anything wrong.

"It's not a good relationship," she said. "Not healthy. But every time it ends, I fall back into it again. I need to break that pattern. And I need Julian not to be anxious about it. There's already too much—the Clave will be investigating the fallout from Malcolm's death, our involvement with the Court—"

"Hush," he said, sitting down next to her. "I understand."

He reached up and pulled the blanket down from her bed.

Emma watched him in surprise as he wrapped it around the two of them, tucking it around both their shoulders.

She thought of the Wild Hunt then, the way he must have been with Kieran, huddling in shelters, wrapping themselves in their cloaks to block the cold.

He traced the line of her cheekbone with his fingers, but it was a friendly gesture. The heat that had been in their kiss was gone. And Emma was glad. It had seemed wrong to feel that, even the shadow of it, with anyone but Julian. "Those who are not faeries find comfort in lies," he said. "I cannot judge that. I will do this with you, Emma. I will not abandon you."

She leaned against his shoulder. Relief made her feel light.

"You must tell Cristina, though," he added. "She is your best friend; you cannot hide so much from her."

Emma nodded. She had always planned to tell Cristina. Cristina was the only one who knew about her feelings for Julian, and she would never for a moment believe that Emma had suddenly fallen in love with Mark instead. She would have to be told for practicality's sake, and Emma was glad.

"I can trust her completely," she said. "Now—tell me about the Wild Hunt."

He began to speak, weaving a story of a life lived in the clouds and in the deserted and lost places of the world. Hollow cities at the bottom of copper canyons. The shell of Oradour-sur-Glane, where he and Kieran had slept in a half-burned hayloft. Sand and the smell of the ocean in Cyprus, in an empty resort town where trees grew through the floors of abandoned grand hotels.

Slowly Emma drifted off to sleep, with Mark holding her and whispering stories. Somewhat to her surprise, he'd come back the next night—it would help make their relationship seem convincing, he'd said, but she'd seen in his eyes that he'd liked the company, just as she had.

And so they'd spent every night since then together, sprawled in the covers piled on the floor, trading stories; Emma spoke of the Dark War, of how she felt lost sometimes now that she was no longer searching for the person who'd killed her parents, and Mark talked about his brothers and sisters, about how he and Ty had argued and he worried he'd made his younger brother feel as if he wasn't there to be relied on, as if he might leave at any minute.

"Just tell him you might leave, but you'll always come back to him," Emma said. "Tell him you're sorry if you ever made him feel any different."

He only nodded. He never told her if he'd taken her advice, but she'd taken his and told Cristina everything. It had been a huge relief, and she'd cried in Cristina's arms for several hours. She'd even gotten Julian's permission to tell Cristina an abbreviated version of the situation with Arthur—enough to make it clear how badly Julian was needed here at the Institute, with his family. She'd asked Julian's permission to share that information; an extremely awkward conversation, but he'd almost seemed relieved that someone else would know.

She'd wanted to ask him if he'd tell the rest of the family the truth about Arthur soon. But she couldn't. Walls had gone up around Julian that seemed as impenetrable as the thorns around Sleeping Beauty's castle. She wondered if Mark had noticed, if any of the others had noticed, or if only she could see it.

She turned to look at Mark now. He was asleep on the floor, his cheek pillowed on his hand. She slid off the bed, settling among the blankets and pillows, and curled up next to him.

Mark slept better when he was with her—he'd said so, and she believed it. He'd been eating better too, putting on muscle fast, his scars fading, color back in his cheeks. She was glad. She might feel like she was dying inside every day, but that was her problem— she'd handle it. No one owed her help, and in a way she welcomed the pain. It meant Julian wasn't suffering alone, even if he believed he was.

And if she could help Mark at all, then that was *something*. She loved him, the way she should love Julian: Uncle Arthur would have called it *philia*, friendship love. And though she could never tell Julian about the way she and Mark were helping each other, it was at least something she felt she could do for him: make his brother happier.

Even if he'd never know.

A knock on the door yanked her out of her reverie. She started up; the room was dim, but she could make out bright red hair, Clary's curious face peering around the door's edge. "Emma? Are you awake? Are you on the *floor*?"

Emma peered down at Mark. He was definitely asleep, huddled in blankets, out of Clary's view. She held up two fingers to Clary, who nodded and shut the door; two minutes later Emma was out in the hallway, zipping up a hoodie.

"Is there somewhere we can talk?" Clary said. She was still so small, Emma thought, it was sometimes hard to remember that she was in her twenties. Her hair was caught back in braids, making her seem even younger.

"On the roof," Emma decided. "I'll show you."

She led Clary up the stairs, to the ladder and trapdoor, and then out to the dark expanse of roof. She hadn't been there herself since the night she'd come up with Mark. It seemed like years ago, though she knew it was only weeks.

The day's heat had left the black, shingled roof sticky and hot. But the night was a cool one—desert nights always were, the temperature dropping like a rock as soon as the sun set—and the breeze off the ocean ruffled Emma's damp hair.

She crossed the roof, with Clary following, to her favorite spot: a clear view of the ocean below, the highway folded into the hill below the Institute, mountains rising behind in shadowy peaks.

Emma sat down on the roof's edge, knees drawn up, letting the desert air caress her skin, her hair. The moonlight silvered her scars, especially the thick one along the inside of her right forearm. She had gotten it in Idris, when she'd woken up there screaming for her parents, and Julian, knowing what she needed, had put Cortana into her arms.

Clary settled herself lightly beside Emma, her head cocked as if she were listening to the breathing roar of the ocean, its soft push-pull. "Well, you've definitely got the New York Institute beat in terms of views. All I can see from the roof there is Brooklyn." She turned toward Emma. "Jem Carstairs and Tessa Gray send their regards."

"Are they the ones who told you about Kit?" Emma asked. Jem was a very distant, very old relative of Emma's—though he looked twenty-five, he was more like a hundred and twenty-five. Tessa was his wife, a powerful warlock in her own right. They had uncovered the existence of Kit and his father, just in time for Johnny Rook to be slaughtered by demons.

Clary nodded. "They're off on a mission—they wouldn't even tell me what they were looking for."

"I thought they were looking for the Black Volume?"

"Could be. I know they were headed for the Spiral Labyrinth first." Clary leaned back on her hands. "I know Jem wishes he was around for you. Someone you could talk to. I told him you could always talk to me, but you haven't called since the night after Malcolm died—"

"He didn't die. I *killed* him," Emma interrupted. She kept having to remind herself that she had killed Malcolm, shoved Cortana through his guts, because it seemed so unlikely. And it hurt, the way brushing up suddenly against barbed wire hurt: a surprising pain out of nowhere. Though he had deserved it, it hurt nonetheless.

"I shouldn't feel bad, right?" Emma said. "He was a terrible person. I had to do it."

"Yes, and yes," said Clary. "But that doesn't always fix things." She reached out and put her finger under Emma's chin, turning Emma's face toward her. "Look, if anyone's going to understand about this, I will. I killed Sebastian. My brother. I put a knife in him." For a moment Clary looked much younger than she was; for a moment, she looked Emma's age. "I still think about it, dream about it. There was good in him—not much, just a tiny bit, but it haunts me. That tiny potential I destroyed."

"He was a *monster*," Emma said, horrified. "A murderer, worse than Valentine, worse than anyone. You had to kill him. If you hadn't, he would have literally destroyed the world."

"I know." Clary lowered her hand. "There was never anything like a chance of redemption for Sebastian. But it doesn't stop the dreams, does it? In my dreams, I still sometimes see the brother I might have had, in some other world. The one with green eyes. And you might see the friend you thought you had in Malcolm. When people die, our dreams of what they could be die with them. Even if ours is the hand that ends them."

"I thought I would be happy," Emma said. "For all these years, all I've wanted was revenge. Revenge against whoever killed my parents. Now I know what happened to them, and I've killed Malcolm. But what I feel is . . . empty."

"I felt the same way, after the Dark War," Clary said. "I'd spent so much time running and fighting and desperate. And then things were ordinary. I didn't trust it. We get used to living one way, even if it's a bad way or a hard one. When that's gone, there's a hole to fill. It's in our nature to try to fill it with anxieties and fears. It can take time to fill it with good things instead."

For a moment, Emma saw through Clary's expression into the past, remembering the girl who'd chased her into a small room in the Gard, refused to leave her alone and grieving, who'd told her, *Heroes aren't always the ones who win. They're the ones who lose, sometimes. But they keep fighting, they keep coming back. They don't give up.*

That's what makes them heroes.

They were words that had carried Emma through some of the worst times of her life.

"Clary," she said. "Can I ask you something?"

"Sure. Anything."

"Nightshade," Emma said. "The vampire, you know—"

Clary looked surprised. "The head vampire of L.A.? The one you guys discovered was using dark magic?"

"It was true, right? He really was using illegal magic?"

Clary nodded. "Yes, of course. Everything in his restaurant was tested. He certainly was. He wouldn't be in prison now if he hadn't been!" She put a hand lightly atop Emma's. "I know the Clave sucks sometimes," she said. "But there are a lot of people in it who try to be fair. Anselm really was a bad guy."

Emma nodded, wordless. It wasn't Anselm she'd been doubting, after all.

It was Julian.

Clary's mouth curved into a smile. "All right, enough of the boring stuff," she said. "Tell me something fun. You haven't talked about your love life in ages. Are you still dating that Cameron Ashdown guy?"

Emma shook her head. "I'm—I'm dating Mark."

"*Mark?*" Clary looked as if Emma had handed her a two-headed lizard. "Mark Blackthorn?"

"No, a *different* Mark. Yes, Mark Blackthorn." A touch of defensiveness crept into Emma's voice. "Why not?"

"I just—I never would have pictured you together." Clary looked legitimately stunned.

"Well, who did you picture me with? Cameron?"

"No, not him." Clary pulled her legs up to her chest and rested her chin on her knees. "That's just the thing," she said. "I—I mean, who I pictured you with, it doesn't make any sense." She met Emma's confused look with a lowering of her eyes. "I guess it was nothing. If you're happy with Mark, I'm happy for you."

"Clary, what are you not telling me?"

There was a long silence. Clary looked out toward the dark water. Finally she spoke. "Jace asked me to marry him."

"*Oh!*" Emma had already begun opening her arms to hug the other girl when she caught sight of Clary's expression. She froze. "What's wrong?"

"I said no."

"You said *no?*" Emma dropped her arms. "But you're here— together—are you not still . . . ?"

Clary rose to her feet. She stood at the roof's edge, looking out toward the sea. "We're still together," she said. "I told Jace I needed more time to think about it. I'm sure he thinks I'm out of my mind, or—well, I don't know what he thinks."

"Do you?" Emma asked. "Need more time?"

"To decide if I want to marry Jace? No." Clary's voice was tense with an emotion Emma couldn't decipher. "No. I know the answer. Of course I want to. There's never going to be anyone else for me. That's just how it is."

Something in the matter-of-factness of her voice sent a slight shiver through Emma. *There's never going to be anyone else for me.* There was a recognition of kinship in that shiver, and a bit of fear, too. "Then why did you say it?"

"I used to have dreams," Clary said. She was staring out at the path the moon left across the dark water, like a slash of white bisecting a black canvas. "When I was your age. Dreams of things that were going to happen, dreams of angels and prophecies. After the Dark War was over, they stopped. I thought they wouldn't start again, but just these past six months, they have."

Emma felt a bit lost. "Dreams?"

"They're not as clear as they used to be. But there's a sense—a knowing something awful is coming. Like a wall of darkness and blood. A shadow that spreads out over the world and blots out everything." She swallowed. "There's more, though. Not so much an image of something happening, but a knowledge."

Emma stood up. She wanted to put a hand on Clary's shoulder, but something held her back. This wasn't Clary, the girl who'd comforted her when her parents had died. This was Clary who'd gone into the demon realm of Edom and killed Sebastian Morgenstern. Clary who'd faced down Raziel. "A knowledge of what?"

"That I'm going to die," Clary said. "Not a long time from now. Soon."

"Is this about your mission? Do you think something's going to happen to you?"

"No—no, nothing like that," Clary said. "It's hard to explain. It's a knowledge that it will happen, but not exactly when, or how."

"Everyone's afraid of dying," Emma said.

"Everyone isn't," said Clary, "and I'm not, but I am afraid of leaving Jace. I'm afraid of what it would do to him. And I think being married would make it worse. It alters things, being married. It's a promise to stay with someone else. But I couldn't promise to stay for very long—" She looked down. "I realize it sounds ridiculous. But I know what I know."

There was a long silence. The sound of the ocean rushed under the quiet between them, and the sound of the wind in the desert. "Have you told him?" Emma asked.

"I haven't told anyone but you." Clary turned and looked at Emma anxiously. "I'm asking you for a favor. A huge one." She took a deep breath. "If I do die, I want you to tell them—Jace and the others—that I knew. I knew I was going to die and I wasn't scared. And tell Jace this is why I said no."

"I—but why me?"

"There isn't anyone else I know I could tell this to without them freaking out or thinking I was having a breakdown and needed a therapist—well, in Simon's case, that's what he'd say." Clary's eyes were suspiciously bright as she said her *parabatai*'s name. "And I trust you, Emma."

"I'll do it," Emma said. "And of course you can trust me, I won't tell anyone, but—"

"I didn't mean I trusted you to keep it a secret," Clary said. "Though I do. In my dreams, I see you with Cortana in your hand." She stretched upward, nearly on her tiptoes, and kissed Emma on the forehead. It was almost a motherly gesture. "I trust you to always keep fighting, Emma. I trust you not to ever give up."

It wasn't until they got back into the car that Kit noticed that his knuckles were bleeding. He hadn't felt the pain when he punched the sign, but he felt it now.

Julian, about to start the car, hesitated. "I could heal you," he said. "With an *iratze*."

"A what now?"

"A healing rune," said Julian. "It's one of the gentlest. So it would make sense if it was your first."

A thousand snide remarks ran through Kit's head, but he was too tired to make them. "Don't poke me with any of your weird little magic wands," he said. "I just want to go"—he almost said *home*, but stopped himself—"back."

As they drove, Kit was silent, looking out the window. The freeway was nearly empty, and stretched ahead of them, gray and deserted. Signs for Crenshaw and Fairfax flashed by. This wasn't the beautiful Los Angeles of mountains and beaches, green lawns and mansions. This was the L.A. of cracked pavement and strug-gling trees and skies leaden with smog.

It had always been Kit's home, but he felt detached as he looked at it now. As if already the Shadowhunters were pulling him away from everything he knew, into their weird orbit. "So what happens to me?" he said suddenly, breaking the silence.

"What?" Julian frowned at the traffic in the rearview mirror. Kit could see his eyes, the blue-green of them. It was almost a shocking color, and all the Blackthorns seemed to have it—well, Mark had one—except for Ty.

"So Jace is my actual family," Kit said. "But I can't go live with him, because him and his hot girlfriend are going off on some sort of secret mission."

"Guess you Herondales have a type," Julian muttered.

"What?"

"Her name's Clary. But basically, yes. He can't take you in right now, so we'll do it. It's not a problem. Shadowhunters take in Shadowhunters. It's what we do."

"You really think that's such a good idea?" Kit said. "I mean, your house is pretty screwed up, what with your agoraphobic uncle and your weird brother."

Julian's hands tightened on the wheel, but the only thing he said was, "Ty isn't weird."

"I meant Mark," said Kit. There was an odd pause. "Ty *isn't* weird," Kit added. "He's just autistic."

The pause stretched out longer. Kit wondered if he'd offended Julian somehow. "It's not a big deal," he said finally. "Back when I went to mundane school, I knew some kids who were on the spec-trum. Ty has some things in common with them."

"What spectrum?" Julian said.

Kit looked at him in surprise. "You really don't know what I mean?"

Julian shook his head. "You may not have noticed this, but we don't involve ourselves much with mundane culture."

"It's not mundane culture. It's—" *Neurobiology. Science. Medicine.* "Don't you have X-rays? Antibiotics?"

"No," Julian said. "For minor stuff, like headaches, healing runes work. For major things, the Silent Brothers are our doctors. Mundane medicine is strictly forbidden. But if there's something you think I should know about Ty . . ."

Kit wanted to hate Julian sometimes. He really did. Julian seemed to love rules; he was unbending, annoyingly calm, and as emotionless as everyone had always said Shadowhunters were. Except he wasn't, really. The love that was audible in his voice when he said his brother's name put the lie to that.

Kit felt a sudden tightness through his body. Talking to Jace earlier had eased some of the anxiety he'd felt ever since his father had died. Jace had made everything seem like maybe it would be easy. That they were still in a world where you could give things chances and see how they worked out.

Now, staring at the gray freeway ahead of him, he wondered how he could possibly have thought he could live in a world where everything he knew was considered wrong knowledge to have, where every one of his values—such as they were, having grown up with a father who was nicknamed Rook the Crook—was turned upside down.

Where associating with the people his blood said he belonged to meant that the people he'd grown up with would hate him.

"Never mind," he said. "I didn't mean anything about Ty. Just meaningless mundane stuff."

"I'm sorry, Kit," Julian said. They'd made it to the coast highway now. The water stretched away in the distance, the moon high and round, casting a perfect white path down the center of the sea. "About what happened at the Market."

"They hate me now," Kit said. "Everyone I used to know."

"No," said Julian. "They're afraid of you. There's a difference."

Maybe there was, Kit thought. But right now, he wasn't sure if it mattered.

4

A WILD WEIRD CLIME

Cristina stood atop the hill where Malcolm Fade's house had once been, and gazed around at the ruins.

Malcolm Fade. She hadn't known him the way the Blackthorns had. He'd been their friend, or so they'd thought, for five years, living only a few miles away in his formidable glass-and-steel home in the dry Malibu hills. Cristina had visited it once before, with Diana, and had been charmed by Malcolm's easy manner and humor. She'd found herself wishing the High Warlock of Mexico City was like Malcolm—young-seeming and charming, rather than a grouchy old woman with bat ears who lived in the Parque Lincoln.

Then Malcolm had turned out to be a murderer, and it had all come apart. The lies revealed, their faith in him broken, even Tavvy's safety at risk until they'd managed to get him back and Emma had dispatched Malcolm with a sword to the gut.

Cristina could hear cars whizzing by on the highway below. They'd climbed up the side of the hill to get here, and she felt sweaty and itchy. Clary Fairchild was standing atop the rubble of Malcolm's house, wielding an odd-looking object that looked like a cross between a seraph blade and one of those machines mundanes used to find metal hidden under sand. Mark, Julian, and Emma were ranged around different parts of the collapsed house, picking through the metal and glass.

Jace had opted to spend the day with Kit in the training room at the Institute. Cristina admired that. She'd been raised to believe nothing was more important than family, and Kit and Jace were the only Shadowhunters of the Herondale bloodline alive in the world. Plus, the boy needed friends—he was an odd little thing, too young to be handsome but with big blue eyes that made you want to trust him even as he was picking your pocket. He had a gleam of mischief about him, a little like Jaime, her childhood best friend, had once had—the sort that could tip over easily into criminality.

"*¿En que piensas?*" asked Diego, coming up behind her. He wore jeans and work boots. Cristina wished it didn't annoy her that he insisted on pinning his Centurion badge even to the sleeve of a completely ordinary black T-shirt.

He was very handsome. Much handsomer than Mark, really, if you were being completely objective. His features were more regular, his jaw squarer, his chest and shoulders broader.

Cristina shoved aside a few chunks of painted plaster. She and Diego had been assigned the eastern segment of the house, which she was fairly sure had been Malcolm's bedroom and closet. She kept turning up shreds of clothes. "I was thinking of Jaime, actually."

"Oh." His dark eyes were sympathetic. "It's all right to miss him. I miss him too."

"Then you should talk to him." Cristina knew she sounded short. She couldn't help it. She wasn't sure why Diego was driving her crazy, and not in a good way. Maybe it was that she'd blamed him for betraying her for so long that it was hard to let go of that anger. Maybe it was that no longer blaming him meant more blame laid on Jaime, which seemed unfair, as Jaime wasn't around to defend himself.

"I don't know where he is," Diego said.

"At all? You don't know where he is in the world or how to contact him?" Somehow Cristina had missed this part. Probably because Diego hadn't mentioned it.

"He doesn't want to be bothered by me," said Diego. "All my fire-messages come back blocked. He hasn't talked to our father." Their mother was dead. "Or any of our cousins."

"How do you know he's even alive?" Cristina asked, and instantly regretted it. Diego's eyes flashed.

"He is my little brother, still," he said. "I would know if he was dead."

"Centurion!" It was Clary, gesturing from the top of the hill. Diego began to jog up the ruins toward her without looking back. Cristina was conscious that she'd upset him; guilt spilled through her and she kicked at a heavy chunk of plaster with a bolt of rebar stuck through it like a toothpick.

It rolled to the side. She blinked at the object revealed under it, then bent to pick it up. A glove—a man's glove, made of leather, soft as silk but a thousand times tougher. The leather was printed with the image of a golden crown snapped in half.

"Mark!" she called. "*¡Necesito que veas algo!*"

A moment later she realized she'd been so startled she'd actually called out in Spanish, but it didn't seem to matter. Mark had come leaping nimbly down the stones toward her. He stood just above her, the wind lifting his airy, pale-gold curls away from the slight points of his ears. He looked alarmed. "What is it?"

She handed him the glove. "Isn't that the emblem of one of the Faerie Courts?"

Mark turned it over in his hands. "The broken crown is the Unseelie King's symbol," he murmured. "He believes himself to be true King of both the Seelie and the Unseelie Courts, and until he rules both, the crown will remain snapped in half." He tilted his head to the side like a bird studying a cat from a safe distance.

"But these kind of gloves—Kieran had them when he arrived at the Hunt. They are fine workmanship. Few but the gentry would wear them. In fact, few but the King's sons would wear them."

"You don't think this is Kieran's?" Cristina said.

Mark shook his head. "His were . . . destroyed. In the Hunt. But it does mean that whoever visited Malcolm here, and left this glove, was either high in the Court, or the King himself."

Cristina frowned. "It's very odd that it's here."

Her hair had escaped from its braids and was blowing in long curls around her face. Mark reached up to tuck one back behind her ear. His fingers skimmed her cheek. His eyes were dreamy, distant. She shivered a little at the intimacy of the gesture.

"Mark," she said. "Don't."

He dropped his hand. He didn't look angry, the way a lot of boys tended to when asked not to touch a girl. He looked puzzled and a little sad. "Because of Diego?"

"And Emma," she said, her voice very low.

His puzzlement increased. "But you *know* that's—"

"Mark! Cristina!" It was Emma, calling to them from where she and Julian had joined Diego and Clary. Cristina was grateful not to have to answer Mark; she raced up the pile of rocks and glass, glad her Shadowhunter boots and gear protected her from stray sharp edges.

"Did you find something?" she asked as she approached the small group.

"Have you ever wanted a really up-close look at a gross tentacle?" Emma asked.

"No," said Cristina, drawing closer warily. Clary did appear to have something unpleasantly floppy speared on the end of her odd weapon. It wriggled a bit, showing pink suckers against green, mottled skin.

"No one ever seems to say yes to that question," said Emma sadly.

"Magnus introduced me to a warlock with tentacles like this once," Clary said. "His name was Marvin."

"I assume these aren't Marvin's remains," Julian said.

"I'm not sure they're anyone's remains," said Clary. "To command sea demons, you'd need either the Mortal Cup or something like this—a piece of a powerful demon you could enchant. I think we have some definite evidence that Malcolm's death is tied to the recent Teuthida attacks."

"Now what?" said Emma, side-eyeing the tentacle. She wasn't a huge fan of the ocean, or the monsters that lived in it, though she'd fight anything or anyone on dry land.

"Now we go back to the Institute," said Clary, "and decide what our next step is. Who wants to carry the tentacle?"

There were no volunteers.

"You've got to be kidding," Kit said. "There's no way I'm jumping off that."

"Just consider it." Jace leaned down from a rafter. "It's surprisingly easy."

"Give it a try," Emma called. She had come to the training room when they'd gotten back from Malcolm's, curious to see how it was going. She had found Ty and Livvy sitting on the floor, watching as Jace tried to convince Kit to throw a few knives (which he was willing to do) and then to learn jumping and falling (which he wasn't).

"My father warned me you people would try to kill me," Kit said.

Jace sighed. He was in training gear, balanced on one of the intricate network of rafters that intersected the interior of the training room's pitched roof. They ranged from thirty to twenty feet above the floor. Emma had taught herself to fall from those exact rafters over the years, sometimes breaking bones.

A Shadowhunter had to know how to climb—demons were fast and often multi-legged, scurrying up the sides of buildings like spiders. But learning how to fall was just as important.

"You can do it," Emma called now.

"Yeah? And what happens if I splatter myself all over the floor?" asked Kit.

"You get a big state funeral," Emma said. "We put your body in a boat and shove you over a waterfall like a Viking."

Kit glared at her. "That's from a movie."

She shrugged. "Maybe."

Jace, losing patience, launched himself from the highest rafter. He somersaulted gracefully in the air before landing in a soundless crouch. He straightened up and winked at Kit.

Emma hid a smile. She'd had a horrendous crush on Jace when she was twelve. Later that had turned into wanting to *be* Jace—the best there was: the best fighter, the best survivor, the best Shadowhunter.

She wasn't there yet, but she wasn't done trying, either.

Kit looked impressed despite himself, then scowled again. He looked very slight next to Jace. He was close to the same height as Ty, though less fit. The potential Shadowhunter strength was there, though, in the shape of his arms and shoulders. Emma had seen him fight, when in danger. She knew what he could do.

"You'll be able to do that," Jace said, pointing up at the rafter, and then at Kit. "As soon as you want to."

Emma could recognize the look in Kit's eye. *I might never want to.* "What's the Nephilim motto again?"

"'We are dust and shadows,'" said Ty, not looking up from his book.

"Some of us are very handsome dust," Jace added, as the door flew open and Clary stuck her head in.

"Come to the library," she announced. "The tentacle is starting to dissolve."

"You drive me wild with your sexy talk," said Jace, pulling on his gear jacket.

"*Adults,*" said Kit, with some disgust, and stalked out of the room. To Emma's amusement, Ty and Livvy were instantly on their feet, following him. She wondered what exactly had sparked their interest in Kit—was it just that he was their age? Jace, she imagined, would have put it down to the famous Herondale charisma, though from what she knew, the Herondales who had immediately predated him had been pretty low on the stuff.

The library was in a certain amount of chaos. The tentacle *was* starting to dissolve, into a sticky puddle of green-pink goo that reminded Emma horribly of melted jelly beans. As Diana pointed out, this meant that the time left to identify the demon was shortening quickly. Since Magnus wasn't picking up his phone and no one wanted to involve the Clave, this left good old-fashioned book research. Everyone was handed a pile of fat tomes on sea creatures, and they dispersed to various parts of the library to examine paintings, sketches, drawings, and the occasional clipped-in photo.

At some point during the passing hours, Jace decided that they required Chinese food. Apparently kung pao chicken and noodles in black bean sauce were a requirement every time the New York Institute team had to engage in research. He hauled Clary off to an empty office to conjure up a Portal—something no other Shadowhunter besides Clary could do—promising them all the best Chinese food Manhattan had to deliver.

"Got it!" Cristina announced, about twenty minutes after the door had closed behind Jace and Clary. She held up a massive copy of the *Carta Marina.*

The rest of them crowded around the main table as Diana confirmed that the tentacle belonged to the sea demon species Makara, which—according to the sketches between the maps in the *Carta Marina*—looked like a part-octopus, part-slug thing with an enormous bee head.

"The disturbing thing isn't that it's a sea demon," said Diana, frowning. "It's that Makara demon remains only survive on land for one to two days."

Jace pushed the library door open. He and Clary were loaded down with green-and-white take-out boxes marked JADE WOLF. "A little help here?"

The research team disbanded briefly to lay out food on the long library tables. There was lo mein, the promised kung pao chicken, mapo tofu, *zhajiangmian*, egg fried rice, and delicious sesame balls that tasted like hot candy.

Everyone had a paper plate, even Tavvy, who was arranging toy soldiers behind a bookcase. Diego and Cristina occupied a love seat, and Jace and Clary were on the floor, sharing noodles. The Blackthorn kids were squabbling over the chicken, except for Mark, who was trying to figure out how to use his chopsticks. Emma guessed they didn't have them in Faerie. Julian sat at the table across from Livvy and Ty, frowning at the nearly dissolved tentacle. Amazingly, it didn't seem to be putting him off his food.

"You are friendly with the great Magnus Bane, aren't you?" Diego said to Jace and Clary, after an affable few minutes of everyone chewing.

"The *great* Magnus Bane?" Jace choked on his fried rice. Church had taken up residence at his feet, alert for any evidence of dropped chicken.

"We're friendly with him, yes," Clary said, her mouth twitching at the corner. "Why?"

Jace was turning purple. Clary thumped him on the back. Church fell asleep, his feet waving in the air.

"I would like to interview him," Diego said. "I think he would make a good subject for a paper for the Spiral Labyrinth."

"He's pretty busy right now, what with Max and Rafael," said Clary. "I mean, you could ask . . ."

"Who's Rafael?" Livvy asked.

"Their second son," said Jace. "They just adopted a little boy in Argentina. A Shadowhunter who lost his parents in the Dark War."

"In Buenos Aires!" Emma exclaimed, turning to Julian. "When we saw Magnus at Malcolm's, he said Alec was in Buenos Aires, and that he was going to join him. That must have been what they were doing."

Julian just nodded, but didn't look up at her to acknowledge the shared memory. She shouldn't expect him to, Emma reminded herself. Julian wasn't going to be the way she remembered again for a long time, if ever.

She felt herself blush, though no one seemed to notice but Cristina, who shot her a look of concern. Diego had his arm around Cristina, but her hands were resting in her lap. She gave Emma a slight wave, more of a finger wiggle.

"Maybe we should get back to discussing the matter at hand," Diana said. "If Makara remains only last a day or two on land . . ."

"Then that demon was at Malcolm's house really recently," said Livvy. "Like, well after he died."

"Which is odd," Julian said, glancing at the book. "It's a deep-sea demon, pretty deadly and *very* big. You'd think someone would have noticed it. Plus, it can't possibly have wanted anything from a collapsed house."

"Who knows what desires a sea demon might possess?" said Mark.

"Assuming it wasn't after Malcolm's collection of elegant tentacle warmers," said Julian, "we have to imagine that it was most likely summoned. Makara demons just don't come up on land. They lurk on the ocean's bottom and sometimes pull ships down."

"Another warlock, then?" Jace suggested. "Someone Malcolm was working with?"

"Catarina doesn't believe Malcolm worked with anyone else," said Diana. "He was friendly with Magnus, but he was otherwise something of a loner—for obvious reasons, it now appears."

"If he *was* working with another warlock, he wouldn't be likely to advertise the fact, though," said Diego.

"It certainly appears Malcolm was determined to cause mischief from beyond the grave if anything happened to him," said Diana.

"Well, the tentacle wasn't the only thing we found," Cristina said. "Mark, show them the glove."

Emma had already seen it, on their way back from Malcolm's, but she leaned in along with everyone else as Mark drew it from his jacket pocket and laid it on the table.

"The sigil of the Unseelie King," said Mark. "A glove such as this is rare. Kieran wore such when he came to the Hunt. I could identify his brothers, sometimes, at revels, by their cloaks and gloves or gauntlets such as these."

"So it's odd Malcolm would have one," said Livvy. Emma didn't see Ty beside her; had he gone into the book stacks?

"No faerie prince would part with such a thing willingly," said Mark. "Save as a special mark of favor, or to bind a promise."

Diana frowned. "We know Malcolm was working with Iarlath."

"But he was not a prince. Not even gentry," said Mark. "This would indicate that Malcolm had sworn some kind of a bargain with the Unseelie Court itself."

"We know he went to the Unseelie King years ago," said Emma. "It was the Unseelie King who gave him the rhyme he was supposed to use to raise Annabel. 'First the flame and then the flood—'"

"'In the end, it's Blackthorn blood,'" Julian finished for her.

And it nearly had been. In order to raise Annabel, Malcolm had required the sacrifice and blood of a Blackthorn. He had kidnapped Tavvy and nearly killed him. Just the memory of it made Emma shiver.

"But this was not the sigil of the King that long ago," said Mark. "This dates from the beginning of the Cold Peace. Time works differently in Faerie, but—" He shook his head, as if to say *not that differently.* "I am afraid."

Jace and Clary exchanged a look. They were on their way to Faerie, weren't they, to look for a weapon? Emma leaned forward, meaning to ask them what they knew, but before she could get the words out, the Institute doorbell rang, echoing through the house.

They all looked at each other, surprised. But it was Tavvy who spoke first, looking up from the corner where he was playing. "Who's here?"

If there was one thing Kit was good at, it was slipping out of rooms unnoticed. He'd been doing it all his life, while his father held meetings in the living room with impatient warlocks or jumpy werewolves.

So it wasn't too much of a challenge to creep out of the library while everyone else was talking and eating Chinese food. Clary was doing an imitation of someone called the Inquisitor, and everyone was laughing. Kit wondered if it occurred to them that it was weird to endorse a governmental position that sounded like it was all about torture.

He'd been in the kitchen a few times before. It was one of the rooms he liked best in the house—homey, with its blue walls and farmhouse sink. The fridge wasn't badly stocked either. He guessed Shadowhunters were probably hungry pretty frequently, considering how often they worked out.

He wondered if he'd have to work out all the time too, if he became a Shadowhunter. He wondered if he'd end up with muscles and abs and all that stuff, like Julian and Jace. At the moment, he was more on the skinny side, like Mark. He lifted his T-shirt and gazed at his flat, undefined stomach for a moment. Definitely no abs.

He let the shirt fall and grabbed a Tupperware container of

cookies out of the fridge. Maybe he could frustrate the Shadow-hunters by refusing to work out and sitting around eating carbs. *I defy you, Shadowhunters*, he thought, thumbing the top off the container and popping a cookie in his mouth. *I mock you with my sugar cravings.*

He let the door of the fridge fall shut, and nearly yelled out loud. Reflexively, he swallowed his cookie and stared.

Ty Blackthorn stood in the middle of the kitchen, his head-phones dangling around his neck, his hands shoved into his pockets.

"Those are pretty good," he said, "but I like the butterscotch ones better."

Thoughts of cookie-related rebellion floated out of Kit's head. Despite sleeping in front of his room, Ty had hardly ever spoken to him before. The most he'd probably ever said at once was when he was holding Kit at knifepoint in the Rooks' house, and Kit didn't think that counted as social interaction.

Kit set the Tupperware down on the counter. He was once again conscious of the sense that Ty was studying him, maybe count-ing up his pluses and minuses or something like that. If Ty was someone else, Kit would have tried to catch his eye, but he knew Ty wouldn't look at him directly. It was kind of restful not to worry about it.

"You have blood on your hand," Ty said. "I noticed it earlier."

"Oh. Right." Kit glanced down at his split knuckles. "I hurt my hand at the Shadow Market."

"How?" Ty asked, leaning against the edge of the counter.

"I punched a board," Kit said. "I was angry."

Ty's eyebrows went up. He had interesting eyebrows, slightly pointed at the tops, like inverted Vs, and very black. "Did it make you feel better?"

"No," Kit admitted.

"I can fix it," Ty said, taking one of the Shadowhunters' magic pencils out of his jeans pocket. Steles, they were called. He held out his hand.

Kit supposed he could have refused to accept the offer, the way he had when Julian had suggested healing him in the car. But he didn't. He held his forearm out trustingly, wrist turned upward so the blue veins were exposed to the boy who'd held a knife to his throat not that long ago.

Ty's fingers were cool and careful as he took hold of Kit's arm to steady it. He had long fingers—all the Shadowhunters did, Kit had noticed. Maybe it had something to do with the need to handle a variety of weapons. Kit was caught up enough in wondering about it to only flinch slightly when the stele moved across his forearm, leaving a feeling of heat as if his skin had passed over a candle flame.

Ty's head was down. His black hair slanted across his face. He drew the stele back when he was finished, letting go of Kit.

"Look at your hand," he said.

Kit turned his hand over and watched as the tears over his knuckles sealed themselves together, the red patches turning back to smooth skin. He stared down at the black mark that spread across his forearm. He wondered when it would start fading. It weirded him out, stark evidence that it really was all true. He really was a Shadowhunter.

"That is pretty cool," he admitted. "Can you heal literally anything? Like what about diabetes and cancer?"

"Some diseases. Not always cancer. My mother died of that." Ty put his stele away. "What about your mother? Was she a Shadowhunter too?"

"I don't think so," Kit said. His father had sometimes told him his mother was a Vegas showgirl who'd taken off after Kit was born, but it had occurred to him in the past two weeks that his father might not have been entirely truthful about that. He certainly hadn't been about anything else. "She's dead," he added, not because he thought that was likely the case but because he realized he didn't want to talk about her.

"So we both have dead mothers," Ty said. "Do you think you'll want to stay here? And become a Shadowhunter?"

Kit started to answer—and stopped, as a sound like a low, sweet bell tolling echoed through the house. "What's that?"

Ty raised his head. Kit got a quick flash of the color of his eyes: true gray, that gray that was almost silver.

Before he could answer, the kitchen door swung open. It was Livvy, a soda can in her left hand. She looked unsurprised to see Kit and Ty; pushing between them, she jumped up onto the table, crossing her long legs.

"The Centurions are here," she said. "Everyone's running around like chickens with their heads cut off. Diana went to welcome them, Julian looks like he wants to kill someone. . . ."

"And you want to know if I'll go and spy on them with you," said Ty. "Right?"

She nodded. "I'd suggest somewhere that we won't be seen, because if Diana catches us, we'll be making up beds and folding towels for Centurions for the next two hours."

That seemed to decide things; Ty nodded and headed for the kitchen door. Livvy jumped off the table and followed him.

She paused with a hand on the doorframe, looking back over her shoulder at Kit. "You coming?"

He raised his eyebrows. "Are you sure you want me to?" It hadn't occurred to him to invite himself—the twins seemed like such a perfect unit, as if they needed no one but each other.

She grinned. He smiled hesitantly back; he was plenty used to girls, even pretty girls, but something about Livvy made him feel nervous.

"Sure," she said. "One warning—rude and catty comments

about the people we're spying on are required. Members of our family exempted, of course."

"If you make Livvy laugh, you get double points," Ty added, from the hallway.

"Well, in that case . . ." Kit started after them. What was it Jace had said, after all? Herondales couldn't resist a challenge.

Cristina looked with dismay at the group of twenty or so Centurions milling around the massive entryway of the Institute. She'd only had a short time to prepare herself for the idea of meeting Diego's Scholomance friends, and she certainly hadn't planned to do it wearing dusty gear, with her hair in braids.

Oh well. She straightened her back. Shadowhunter work was often dirty; surely they wouldn't be expecting her to look pristine. Though, she realized as she glanced around, they certainly did. Their uniforms were like regular gear, but with military-style jackets over them, bright with metal buttons and sashed crossways with a pattern of vine staffs. The back of each jacket bore the symbol of the Centurion's family name: a sandy-haired boy had a wolf on his back, a girl with deep brown skin had a circle of stars. The boys had short hair; the girls wore their hair braided or tied back. They looked clean, efficient, and a little alarming.

Diana was chatting with two Centurions by the door to the Sanctuary: a dark-skinned boy with a *Primi Ordines* insignia, and the boy with the wolf jacket. They turned to wave at Diego as he came down the stairs, followed by Cristina and the others.

"I can't believe they're here already," Emma muttered.

"Be gracious," said Diana in a low voice, sweeping up to them. Easy for her to say, thought Cristina. *She* wasn't covered in dust. She took hold of Emma by the wrist, seized Julian with her other hand, and marched them off to mingle with the Centurions, thrusting Julian toward a pretty Indian girl with a gold stud in her nose, and depositing Emma in front of a dark-haired girl and boy—very clearly twins—who regarded her with arched eyebrows.

The sight of them made Cristina think of Livvy and Ty, though, and she glanced around to see if they were peering down from the second floor as they often did. If they were, she couldn't see them; they'd probably gone off to hide, and she didn't blame them. Luggage was strewn all around the floor: Someone was going to have to show the Centurions to their rooms, welcome them, figure out how to feed them. . . .

"I didn't realize," Mark said.

"Didn't realize what?" Diego said; he had returned the greeting of the two boys who had been talking to Diana earlier. The boys started across the room toward them.

"How much like soldiers Centurions look," said Mark. "I suppose I was thinking of them as students."

"We *are* students," Diego said sharply. "Even after we graduate, we remain scholars." The other two Centurions arrived before Mark could say anything else; Diego clapped them both on the back and turned to introduce them. "Manuel, Rayan. This is Cristina and Mark."

"*Gracias*," said the boy with the sandy hair—it was a light brown, streaked and bleached by the sun. He had an easy, sideways grin. "*Un placer conocerte.*"

Cristina gave a little gasp. "You speak Spanish?"

"*Es mi lengua materna.*" Manuel laughed. "I was born in Madrid and grew up in the Institute there."

He *did* have what Cristina thought of as a Spanish accent— the softening of the c sound, the way *gracias* sounded like *grathiath* when he thanked her. It was charming.

Across the room, she saw Dru, holding Tavvy by the hand— they'd asked her to stay in the library and watch him, but she'd wanted to see the Centurions—come up to Emma and tug on her sleeve, whispering something in her ear.

Cristina smiled at Manuel. "I almost did my study year in Madrid."

"But the beaches are better here." He winked.

Out of the corner of her eye, Cristina saw Emma go up to Julian and awkwardly tap his shoulder. She said something to him that made him nod and follow her out of the room. Where were they going? She itched to follow them, not to stay here and make conversation with Diego's friends, even if they were nice.

"I wanted the challenge of speaking English all the time—" Cristina began, and saw Manuel's expression change—then Rayan took her sleeve and drew her out of the way as someone hurtled up to Diego and grabbed his arm. It was a white girl, pale and round-cheeked, with thick brown hair pulled back in a tight bun.

She crashed into Diego's chest, and he went a sort of watery color, as if all the blood had drained from his face. "Zara?"

"Surprise!" The girl kissed his cheek.

Cristina was starting to feel a little dizzy. Maybe she'd gotten too much sun out at Malcolm's. But really, it hadn't been *that* much sun.

"I didn't think you were coming," Diego said. He still seemed starkly shocked. Rayan and Manuel were starting to look uncomfortable. "You said—you said you'd be in Hungary—"

"Oh, that." Zara dismissed Hungary with a wave. "Turned out to be completely ridiculous. A bunch of Nephilim claiming their steles and seraph blades were malfunctioning; really it was just incompetence. So much more important to be here!" She looped her arm through Diego's and turned to Cristina and Mark, smiling brightly. She had her hand tucked into Diego's elbow, but the smile on her face turned stiff as Cristina and Mark stood in silence, staring, and Diego looked increasingly as if he were going to throw up.

"I'm Zara Dearborn," she said, finally, rolling her eyes. "I'm sure you've heard about me. I'm Diego's fiancée."

5

EARTH AND HEAVEN

Emma led Julian through the building, through hallways familiar to both of them even in the dark. They were silent. Emma's braids swung as she walked. Julian focused on them for a moment, thinking about the thousands of times he'd walked beside Emma on their way out of the Institute, carrying their weapons, laughing and chatting and planning about whatever it was they were going to face.

The way his heart always lightened as they stepped out of the Institute, ready to climb into the car, drive fast up the highway, wind in their hair, salt taste on their skin. The memory was like a weight against his chest now as they stepped into the flat, sandy area behind the Institute.

Jace and Clary were waiting for them. Both were wearing gear jackets and carrying duffel bags. They were speaking to each other intently, their heads bent together. Their shadows, cast into razor-edged precision by the late afternoon light, seemed to merge together into one.

Emma cleared her throat, and the two of them broke apart.

"We're sorry to go like this," Clary said, a little awkwardly. "We thought it would be better to avoid questions from the Centurions about our mission." She glanced around. "Where's Kit?"

"I think he's with Livvy and Ty," Emma said. "I sent Drusilla to get him."

"I'm here." Kit, a blond shadow with his hands in his pockets, shouldered open the Institute's back door. Light-footed, Julian thought. A natural characteristic of Shadowhunters. His father had been a thief and a liar. They were light-footed too.

"We have something for you, Christopher," Jace said, unusually somber. "Clary does, at least."

"Here." Clary stepped forward and dropped an object that flashed silver into Kit's open hands. "This is a Herondale family ring. This belonged to James Herondale before it was Jace's. James was close with several of the Blackthorns, when he was alive."

Kit's face was unreadable. He closed his fingers around the ring and nodded. Clary put her hand against his cheek. It was a motherly sort of gesture, and for a moment, Julian thought he saw vulnerability flash across Kit's features.

If the boy had a mother, Julian realized, none of them knew anything about her.

"Thanks," Kit said. He slid the ring onto his finger, looking surprised when it fit. Shadowhunter family rings always fit; it was part of their magic.

"If you're thinking about selling it," Jace said, "I wouldn't."

"Why not?" Kit raised his face; blue eyes looked into gold. The color of their eyes was different, but the framing was the same: the shape of their eyelids, the sharp cheekbones and watchful angles of their faces.

"I just wouldn't," said Jace, with heavy emphasis; Kit shrugged, nodded, and vanished back into the Institute.

"Were you trying to scare him?" Emma demanded, the moment the door shut behind him.

Jace just grinned sideways at her. "Thank Mark for his help," he said, pulling Emma into a hug and ruffling her hair. The next few moments were a flurry of hugs and good-byes, Clary promising to send them a fire-message when she could, Jace making sure they had Alec and Magnus's phone number in case they ran into trouble.

No one mentioned that technically, they had the Clave if they ran into trouble. But Clary and Jace had learned to be wary of the Clave when they were young, and it appeared that getting older hadn't dimmed their suspicions.

"Remember what I told you on the roof," Clary said to Emma in a low voice, hands on the younger girl's shoulders. "What you promised."

Emma nodded, looking uncharacteristically serious. Clary turned away from her, raising her stele, preparing to make a Portal into Faerie. Just as the shapes began to flow under her hands, the doorway starting to shimmer against the dry air, the Institute door banged open again.

This time it was Dru, her round face anxious. She was twisting one of her braids around her finger.

"Emma, you'd better come," she said. "Something's happened with Cristina."

He wasn't going to play their stupid spying game, Kit thought. No matter how much fun the twins seemed to be having, wedged into a corner of the second-floor gallery and looking down onto the main entryway, securely hidden from sight by the railings.

Mostly the game involved trying to figure out what people were saying to each other from their body language, or the way they gestured. Livvy was endlessly creative, able to imagine dramatic scenarios between people who were probably just chatting about the weather—she'd already decided the pretty South Asian girl with the stars on her jacket was in love with Julian, and that two of the other Centurions were secretly spies from the Clave.

Ty made rarer pronouncements, but Kit suspected they were

more likely to be right. He was good at observing small things, like what family symbol was on the back of someone's jacket, and what that meant about where they were from.

"What do you think of Perfect Diego?" Livvy asked Kit, when he returned from saying good-bye to Clary and Jace. She had her knees drawn up, her arms wrapped around her long legs. Her curling ponytail bounced on her shoulders.

"Smug bastard," said Kit. "His hair's too good. I don't trust people with hair that good."

"I think that girl with her hair in a bun is angry with him," said Ty, leaning closer to the railing. His delicate face was all points and angles. Kit followed his gaze downward and saw Diego, deep in conversation with a pale-skinned girl whose hands were flying around as she spoke.

"The ring." Livvy caught Kit's hand, turning it over. The Herondale ring glinted on his finger. He'd already taken note of the delicate carving of birds that winged their way around the band. "Did Jace give you that?"

He shook his head. "Clary. Said it used to belong to James Herondale."

"James . . ." She looked as if she were making an effort to remember something. She gave a squeak then and dropped his hand as a shadow loomed over them.

It was Emma. "All right, you little spies," she said. "Where's Cristina? I already looked in her room."

Livvy pointed upward. Kit frowned; he hadn't thought there was anything to the third floor but attic.

"Ah," Emma said. "Thanks." She shook out her hands at her sides. "When I get hold of Diego . . ."

There was a loud exclamation from below. All four of them craned forward to see the pale girl slap Diego sharply across the face.

"What . . . ?" Emma looked astonished, then furious again. She whirled and headed for the stairs.

Ty smiled, looking with his curls and light eyes for all the world like a painted cherub on a church wall.

"That girl *was* angry," he said, sounding delighted to have gotten it right.

Kit laughed.

The sky above the Institute blazed with color: hot pink, blood red, deep gold. The sun was going down, and the desert was bathed in the glow. The Institute itself shimmered, and the water shimmered too, far out where it waited for the sun's fall.

Cristina was exactly where Emma had guessed she would be: sitting as neatly as always, legs crossed, her gear jacket spread out on the shingles beneath her.

"He didn't come after me," she said, as Emma drew closer to her. Her black hair moved and lifted in the breeze, the pearls in her ears glimmering. The pendant around her neck shone too, the words on it picked out by the deep glow of the sun: *Blessed be the Angel my strength, who teaches my hands to war, and my fingers to fight.*

Emma collapsed onto the roof next to her friend, as close as she could get. She reached out and took Cristina's hand, squeezing it tightly. "Do you mean Diego?"

Cristina nodded. There were no marks of tears on her face; she seemed surprisingly composed, considering. "That girl came up and said she was his fiancée," Cristina said. "And I thought it must be some sort of mistake. Even when I turned and ran out of the room, I thought it must be a mistake and he would come after me and explain. But he didn't, which means he stayed because of her. Because she really is his fiancée and she matters to him more than I do."

"I don't know how he could do it," Emma said. "It's bizarre. He loves you so much—he came here because of you."

Cristina made a muffled noise. "You don't even like him!"

"I like him—well, liked him—sometimes," Emma said. "The perfect thing was kind of annoying. But the way he looked at you. You can't fake that."

"He has a fiancée, Emma. Not even just a girlfriend. A fiancée. Who knows how long he's even been engaged? *Engaged*. To get *married*."

"I'll crash the wedding," Emma suggested. "I'll jump out of the cake, but not in a sexy way. Like, with grenades."

Cristina snorted, then turned her face away. "I just feel so *stupid*," she said. "He lied to me and I forgave him, and then he lied to me again—what kind of idiot am I? Why on earth did I think he was trustworthy?"

"Because you wanted to," Emma said. "You've known him a long time, Tina, and that does make a difference. When someone's been part of your life for that long, cutting them out is like cutting the roots out from under a plant."

Cristina was silent for a long moment. "I know," she said. "I know you understand."

Emma tasted the acid burn of bitterness at the back of her throat and swallowed it back. She needed to be here for Cristina now, not dwell on her own worries. "When I was little," she said, "Jules and I used to come up here together at sunset practically every night and wait for the green flash."

"The what?"

"The green flash. When the sun goes down, just as it disappears, you'll see a flash of green light." They both looked out at the water. The sun was disappearing below the horizon, the sky streaked red and black. "If you make a wish on it, it'll come true."

"Will it?" Cristina spoke softly, her eyes on the horizon along with Emma's.

"I don't know," Emma said. "I've made a lot of wishes by now." The sun sank another few millimeters. Emma tried to think what she could wish for. Even when she'd been younger, she'd understood somehow that there were some things you couldn't wish for: world peace, your dead parents back. The universe couldn't turn itself inside out for you. Wishing only bought you small blessings: a sleep without nightmares, your best friend's safety for another day, birthday sunshine.

"Do you remember," Emma said, "before you saw Diego again, you said we should go to Mexico together? Spend a travel year there?"

Cristina nodded.

"It'd be a while before I could go," said Emma. "I don't turn eighteen until the winter. But when I do . . ."

Leaving Los Angeles. Spending the year with Cristina, learning and training and traveling.

Without Jules. Emma swallowed against the pain the thought caused. It was a pain she'd have to learn to live with.

"I'd like that," Cristina said. The sun was just a rim of gold now. "I'll wish for that. And maybe to forget Diego, too."

"But then you have to forget the good things as well as the bad ones. And I know there were good things." Emma wound her fingers through Cristina's. "He's not the right person for you. He isn't strong enough. He keeps letting you down and disappointing you. I know he loves you, but that's not enough."

"Apparently I'm not the only one he loves."

"Maybe he started dating her to try to forget you," Emma said. "And then he got you back, even though he didn't expect to, and he didn't know how to break it off with her."

"What an idiot," said Cristina. "I mean, if that were true, which it isn't."

Emma laughed. "Okay, yeah, I don't buy it either." She leaned forward. "Look, just let me beat him up for you. You'll feel so much better."

"Emma, no. Don't lay a hand on him. I mean it."

"I could beat him up with my feet," Emma suggested. "They're registered as lethal weapons." She wiggled them.

"You have to promise not to touch him." Cristina glared so severely that Emma raised her free hand in submission.

"All right, all right, I promise," she said. "I will not touch Perfect Diego."

"And you can't yell at Zara, either," Cristina said. "It's not her fault. I'm sure she has no idea I exist."

"Then I feel sorry for her," Emma said. "Because you're one of the greatest people I know."

Cristina started to smile. The sun was almost completely down now. A year with Cristina, Emma thought. A year away from everything, from everyone that reminded her of Jules. A year to forget. If she could bear it.

Cristina gave a little gasp. "Look, there it is!"

The sky flashed green. Emma closed her eyes and wished.

When Emma got back to her bedroom, she was surprised to find Mark and Julian already there, each of them standing on opposite sides of her bed, their arms crossed over their chests.

"How is she?" Mark said, as soon as the door closed behind Emma. "Cristina, I mean."

His gaze was anxious. Julian's was stonier; he looked blank and autocratic, which Emma knew meant he was angry. "Is she upset?"

"Of course she's upset," Emma said. "I think not so much because he's been her boyfriend for a few weeks again, but because they've known each other for so long. Their lives are completely entwined."

"Where is she now?" Mark said.

"Helping Diana and the others fix up the rooms for the Centurions," said Emma. "You wouldn't think carrying sheets and towels around would cheer anyone up, but she promises it will."

"In Faerie, I would challenge Rosales to a duel for this," said Mark. "He broke his promise, and a love-promise at that. He would meet me in combat if Cristina consented to let me be her champion."

"Well, no luck there," said Emma. "Cristina made me promise not to lay a hand on him, and I bet that goes for you two, too."

"So you're saying there's nothing we can do?" Mark scowled, a scowl that matched Julian's. There was something about the two of them, Emma thought, light and dark though they were; they seemed more like brothers in this moment than they had in a long time.

"We can go help set up the bedrooms so Cristina can go to sleep," said Emma. "Diego's locked in one of the offices with Zara, so it's not like she's going to run into him, but she could use the rest."

"We're going to get revenge on Diego by folding his towels?" Julian said.

"They're not technically his towels," Emma pointed out. "They're his friends' towels."

She headed for the door, the two boys following reluctantly. It was clear they would have preferred mortal combat on the greensward to making hospital corners for Centurions. Emma wasn't looking forward to it herself. Julian was a lot better at making beds and doing laundry than she was.

"I could watch Tavvy," she suggested. Mark had gone ahead of her down the corridor; she found herself walking beside Julian.

"He's asleep," he said. He didn't mention how he'd found time to put Tavvy to bed in between everything else that had happened. That was Julian. He found the time. "You know what strikes me as odd?"

"What?" Emma said.

"Diego must have known his cover would be blown," said Julian. "Even if he wasn't expecting Zara to come with the other Centurions tonight, they all know about her. One of them would have mentioned his fiancée or his engagement."

"Good point. Diego might be dishonest, but he's not an idiot."

"There are ways you could hurt him without touching him," Julian said. He said it very low, so that only Emma could hear him; and there was something dark in his voice, something that made her shiver. She turned to reply but saw Diana coming down the hall toward them, her expression very much that of someone who has caught people slacking off.

She dispatched them to different parts of the Institute: Julian to the attic to check on Arthur, Mark to the kitchen, and Emma to the library to help the twins clean up. Kit had disappeared.

"He hasn't run away," Ty informed her helpfully. "He just didn't want to make beds."

It was late by the time they finished cleaning up, figured out which bedroom to assign to which Centurion, and made arrangements for food to be delivered the next day. They also set up a patrol to circle the Institute in shifts during the night to watch for rogue sea demons.

Heading down the corridor to her room, Emma noticed that a light was shining out from under Julian's door. In fact, the door was cracked partway open; music drifted into the hallway.

Without conscious volition, she found herself in front of his room, her hand raised to knock on the door. In fact, she *had* knocked. She dropped her hand, half in shock, but he had already flung the door open.

She blinked at him. He was in old pajama bottoms, with a towel flung over his shoulder, a paintbrush in one hand. There was paint on his bare chest and some in his hair.

Though he wasn't touching her, she was aware of his body, the warmth of him. The black spiraling Marks winding down his torso, like vines wreathing a pillar. She had put some of them there herself, back in the days when touching him didn't make her hands shake.

"Did you want something?" he asked. "It's late, and Mark is probably waiting for you."

"Mark?" She'd almost forgotten Mark, for a moment.

"I saw him go into your room." Paint dripped from his brush, splattered on the floor. She could see past him into his room: She hadn't been inside it in what felt like forever. There was plastic sheeting on some of the floor, and she could see brighter spots on his wall where he'd clearly been retouching the mural that ran half-way around the room.

She remembered when he'd painted it, after they'd gotten back from Idris. After the Dark War. They'd been lying awake in bed, as they often did, as they had since they were small children. Emma had been talking about how she'd found a book of fairy tales in the library, the kind that mundanes had read hundreds of years ago: how they'd been bloody and full of murder and sadness. She'd spoken of the castle in Sleeping Beauty, surrounded by thorns, and how the story had said that hundreds of princes had tried to break through the barrier to rescue the princess, but they'd all been pierced to death by thorns, their bodies left to whiten to bones in the sun.

The next day Julian had painted his room: the castle and the wall of thorns, the glint of bone and the sad prince, his sword broken at his side. Emma had been impressed, even though they'd had to sleep in her room for a week while the paint dried.

She'd never asked him why the image or the story called to him. She'd always known that if he wanted to tell her, he would.

Emma cleared her throat. "You said I could hurt Diego, without laying a hand on him. What did you mean?"

He pushed his free hand through his hair. He looked disheveled— and so gorgeous it hurt. "It's probably better if I don't tell you."

"He hurt Cristina," Emma said. "And I don't even think he cares."

He reached up to rub the back of his neck. The muscles in his chest and stomach moved when he stretched, and she was aware of the texture of his skin, and wished desperately she could turn back time somehow and be again the person who wasn't shaken to pieces by seeing Julian—who she'd grown up with, and seen half-clothed a million times—with his shirt off. "I saw his face when Cristina ran out of the entry hall," he said. "I don't think you need to worry that he isn't in any pain." He put a hand on the doorknob. "No one can read someone else's mind or guess all their reasons," he said. "Not even you, Emma."

He shut the door in her face.

Mark was sprawled on the floor at the foot of Emma's bed. His feet were bare; he was half-rolled in a blanket.

He looked asleep, his eyes shadowy crescents against his pale skin, but he half-opened the blue one when she came in. "Is she really all right?"

"Cristina? Yes." Emma sat down on the floor beside him, leaning against the footboard. "It sucks, but she'll be okay."

"It would be hard, I think," he said, in his sleep-thickened voice, "to deserve her."

"You like her," she said. "Don't you?"

He rolled onto his side and looked at her with that searching faerie gaze that made her feel as if she stood alone in a field, watching the wind stir the grass. "Of course I like her."

Emma cursed the intensity of faerie language—*like* meant nothing to them: They lived in a world of love or hate, scorn or adoration. "Your heart feels something for her," she said.

Mark sat up. "She would not, I think—feel that way about me."

"Why not?" Emma said. "She certainly isn't stuck-up about faeries, you know that. She's fond of you—"

"She is kind, gentle, generous-hearted. Sensible, thoughtful, kind—"

"You said 'kind' already."

Mark glared. "She is nothing like me."

"You don't have to be like someone to love them," said Emma. "Look at you and me. We're pretty similar, and we don't feel that way about each other."

"Only because you're involved with someone else." Mark spoke matter-of-factly, but Emma looked at him in surprise. *He knows about Jules*, she thought, for a moment of panic, before she remembered her lie about Cameron.

"Too bad, isn't it," she said lightly, trying to keep her heart from hammering. "You and I, together, it would have been . . . such an easy thing."

"Passion is not easy. Nor is the lack of it." Mark leaned into her. His shoulder was warm against hers. She remembered their kiss, thought of her fingers in his soft hair. His body against hers, responsive and strong.

But even as she tried to grip tight to the image, it slid away between her fingers like dry sand. Like the sand on the beach the night Julian and she had lain there, the only night they'd had together.

"You look sad," said Mark. "I am sorry to have brought up the matter of love." He touched her cheek. "In another life, perhaps. You and I."

Emma let her head fall back against the footboard. "In another life."

6

There the Traveller

Since the kitchen was too small to hold the inhabitants of the Institute plus twenty-odd Centurions, breakfast was set up in the dining room. Portraits of Blackthorns past looked down on plates of eggs and bacon and racks of toast. Cristina moved unobtrusively among the crowd, trying not to be seen. She doubted she would have come down at all if it hadn't been for her desperate need for coffee.

She looked around for Emma and Mark, but neither of them were here yet. Emma wasn't an early riser, and Mark still tended toward the nocturnal. Julian was there, dishing up food, but he was wearing the pleasant, almost blank expression he always wore around strangers.

Odd, she thought, that she knew Julian well enough to realize that. They had a sort of bond, both of them loving Emma, but separated from each other by the knowledge Julian didn't realize she had. Julian trying to hide that he loved Emma, and Cristina trying to hide that she knew. She wished she could offer him sympathy, but he would only recoil in horror—

"Cristina."

She nearly dropped her coffee. It was Diego. He looked awful—his face drawn, bags under his eyes, his hair tangled. He wore ordinary gear and seemed to have misplaced his Centurion pin.

She held up her hand. *"Aléjate de mí, Diego."*

"Just listen to me—"

Someone moved between them. The Spanish boy with the sandy hair—Manuel. "You heard her," he said, in English. No one else was looking at them yet; they were all involved in their own conversations. "Leave her alone."

Cristina turned and walked out of the room.

She kept her back straight. She refused to hurry her steps—not for anyone. She was a Rosales. She didn't want the Centurions' pity.

She pushed through the front door and clattered down the stairs. She wished Emma was awake. They could go to the training room and kick and punch away their frustrations.

She strode on unseeing until she nearly collided with the twisted quickbeam tree that still grew in the shabby grass in front of the Institute. It had been put there by faeries—a whipping tree, used for punishment. It remained even when the punishment was over, when rain had washed Emma's blood from the grass and stones.

"Cristina, *please.*" She whirled. Diego was there, apparently having decided to ignore Manuel. He really did look awful. The shadows under his eyes looked as if they had been cut there.

He had carried her across this grass, she remembered, only two weeks ago, when she had been injured. He had held her tightly, whispering her name over and over. And all the time, he'd been engaged to someone else.

She leaned back against the trunk of the tree. "You really don't understand why I don't want to see you?"

"Of course I understand it," he said. "But it's not what you think."

"Really? You're *not* engaged? You're not supposed to marry Zara?"

"She is my fiancée," he said. "But—Cristina—it's more complicated than it looks."

"I really don't see how it could be."

"I wrote to her," he said. "After you and I got back together. I told her it was over."

"I don't think she got your letter," Cristina said.

Diego shoved his hands into his hair. "No, she did. She told me she read it, and that's why she came here. Honestly, I never thought she would. I thought it was over when I didn't hear from her. I thought—I really thought I was free."

"So you broke up with her last night?"

He hesitated, and in that moment of hesitation, any thought that Cristina had been harboring in the deepest recesses of her heart, any fleeting hope that this was all a mistake, vanished like mist burned away by the sun. "I didn't," he said. "I can't."

"But you just said you did, in your letter—"

"Things are different now," he said. "Cristina, you'll have to trust me."

"No," she said. "No, I won't. I already trusted you, despite the evidence of my own ears. I don't know if anything you said before was true. I don't know if the things you've said about Jaime are true. Where is he?"

Diego dropped his hands to his sides. He looked defeated. "There are things I cannot tell you. I wish you could believe me."

"What's going on?" Zara's high, clear voice cut across the dry air; she was walking toward them, her Centurion pin gleaming in the sun.

Diego glanced at her, a look of pain on his face. "I was talking to Cristina."

"I see that." Zara's mouth was set into a little smile, a look that never seemed to leave her face. She swept a glance over Cristina and put her hand on Diego's shoulder. "Come back inside," she said.

"We're figuring out what grids we're going to search today. You know this area well. Time to help out. Tick, tick." She tapped her watch.

Diego looked once at Cristina, then turned back to his fiancée. "All right."

With a last superior glance, Zara slipped her hand into Diego's and half-dragged him back toward the Institute. Cristina watched them go, the coffee she had drunk roiling in her stomach like acid.

To Emma's disappointment, the Centurions refused to allow any of the Blackthorns to accompany them on the search for Malcolm's body. "No, thanks," said Zara, who appeared to have appointed herself unofficial head of the Centurions. "We've trained for this, and dealing with less experienced Shadowhunters on this kind of mission is just distracting."

Emma glared at Diego, who was standing next to Zara. He looked away.

They were gone almost all day, returning in time for dinner, which the Blackthorns wound up making. It was spaghetti—lots of spaghetti. "I miss the vampire pizza," Emma muttered, glaring at an enormous bowl of red sauce.

Julian snorted. He was standing over a pot of boiling water; the steam rose and curled his hair into damp ringlets. "Maybe they'll at least tell us if they found anything."

"I doubt it," said Ty, who was preparing to set the table. It was an activity he'd enjoyed since he was little; he loved setting up each utensil in precise and even repeated order. Livvy was helping him; Kit had skulked off and was nowhere to be found. He seemed to resent the intrusion of the Centurions more than anyone else. Emma couldn't really blame him—he'd barely been adjusting to the Institute as it was, when in swept these people whose needs he was expected to cater to.

Ty was mostly right. Dinner was a large, lively affair; Zara had somehow managed to wedge herself in at the head of the table, ousting Diana, and gave them an abbreviated account of the day— sections of ocean had been searched, nothing significant found, though trace elements of dark magic indicated a point farther out in the ocean where sea demons clustered. "We'll approach it tomorrow," she said, elegantly forking up spaghetti.

"How are you searching?" Emma asked, her eagerness to know more about advanced Shadowhunting techniques outweighing her dislike of Zara. After all, as Cristina had said earlier, the situation wasn't really Zara's fault; it was Diego's. "Do you have special gear?"

"Unfortunately, that information is proprietary to the Scholomance," Zara said with a cool smile. "Even for someone who's supposed to be the *best* Shadowhunter of her generation."

Emma flushed and sat back in her chair. "What's that supposed to mean?"

"You know how people talk about you in Idris," said Zara. Her tone was careless, but her hazel eyes were dagger points. "Like you're the new Jace Herondale."

"But we still have the old Jace Herondale," said Ty, puzzled.

"It's a saying," Julian said, in a low voice. "It means, like, someone just as good."

Normally he would have said, *I'll draw it for you, Ty.* Visual representations of sometimes-confusing expressions, like "he laughed his head off" or "the best thing since sliced bread" resulted in hilarious drawings by Julian with explanatory notes about the real meaning of the expression underneath.

The fact that he didn't say it made Emma look at him a little more sharply. His hackles were up because of the Centurions, not that she blamed him. When Julian didn't trust someone, all his protective instincts kicked into gear: to hide Livvy's love of computers, Ty's unusual way of processing information, Dru's horror movies. Emma's rule breaking.

Julian raised his glass of water with a brilliantly artificial smile. "Shouldn't all Nephilim information be shared? We fight the same demons. If one branch of Nephilim has an advantage, isn't that unfair?"

"Not necessarily," said Samantha Larkspear, the female half of the twin Centurions Emma had met the day before. Her brother's name was Dane; they shared the same thin, whippety faces, pale skin, and straight dark hair. "Not everyone has the training to use every tool, and a weapon you don't know how to wield is wasted."

"Everyone can learn," said Mark.

"Then perhaps one day you will attend the Scholomance and be trained," said the Centurion from Mumbai. Her name was Divya Joshi.

"It's unlikely the Scholomance would accept someone with faerie blood," said Zara.

"The Clave is hidebound," said Diego. "That is true."

"I dislike the word 'hidebound,'" said Zara. "What they are is traditional. They seek to restore the separations between Downworlders and Shadowhunters that have always been in place. Mixing creates confusion."

"I mean, look at what's happened with Alec Lightwood and Magnus Bane," said Samantha, waving her fork. "Everyone knows that Magnus uses his influence with the Lightwoods to get the Inquisitor to let Downworlders off the hook. Even for things like murder."

"Magnus would never do that," Emma said. She'd stopped eating, though she'd been starving when they'd sat down.

"And the Inquisitor doesn't try Downworlders—only Shadowhunters," said Julian. "Robert Lightwood couldn't 'let Downworlders off the hook' if he wanted to."

"Whatever," said Jessica Beausejours, a Centurion with a faint French accent and rings on all her fingers. "The Downworlder-Shadowhunter Alliance will be shut down soon enough."

"No one's shutting it down," said Cristina. Her mouth was a tight line. "That's a rumor."

"Speaking of rumors," said Samantha, "I heard Bane tricked Alec Lightwood into falling in love with him using a spell." Her eyes glittered, as if she couldn't decide if she found the idea appealing or disgusting.

"That's not true," said Emma, her heart beating fast. "That is a *lie*."

Manuel raised an eyebrow at her. Dane laughed. "I wonder what will happen when it wears off, in that case," he said. "Bad news for Downworlders if the Inquisitor's not so friendly."

Ty looked bewildered. Emma could hardly blame him. None of Zara's circle seemed to care about facts. "Didn't you hear Julian?" he said. "The Inquisitor doesn't supervise cases where Downworlders have broken the Accords. He doesn't—"

Livvy put her hand on his wrist.

"We all support the Accords here," said Manuel, leaning back in his chair.

"The Accords were a fine idea," said Zara. "But every tool needs sharpening. The Accords require refining. Warlocks should be regulated, for instance. They are too powerful, and too independent. My father plans to suggest a registry of warlocks to the Council. Every warlock must give their information to the Clave and be tracked. If successful, it will be expanded to all Downworlders. We can't have them running around without us being able to keep tabs on them. Look what happened with Malcolm Fade."

"Zara, you sound ridiculous," said Jon Cartwright, one of the older Centurions—about twenty-two, Emma would have guessed. Jace and Clary's age. The only thing Emma could remember about him was that he had a girlfriend, Marisol. "Like an ancient Council member, afraid of change."

"Agreed," said Rayan. "We're students and fighters, not

lawmakers. Whatever your father may be doing, it's not relevant to the Scholomance."

Zara looked indignant. "It's just a registry—"

"Am I the only one who's read *X-Men* and realizes why this is a bad idea?" said Kit. Emma had no idea when he'd reappeared, but he had, and was idly twirling pasta on his fork.

Zara began to frown, then brightened. "You're Kit Herondale," she said. "The lost Herondale."

"I didn't realize I was lost," said Kit. "I never *felt* lost."

"It must be exciting, suddenly finding out you're a Herondale," Zara said. Emma restrained the urge to point out that if you didn't know much about Shadowhunters, finding out you were a Herondale was about as exciting as finding out you were a new species of snail. "I met Jace Herondale once."

She looked around expectantly.

"Wow," said Kit. He really *was* a Herondale, Emma thought. He'd managed to insert Jace-levels of indifference and sarcasm into one word.

"I bet you can't wait to get to the Academy," said Zara. "Since you're a Herondale, you'll certainly excel. I could put in a good word for you."

Kit was silent. Diana cleared her throat. "So what are your plans for tomorrow, Zara, Diego? Is there anything the Institute can do to assist you?"

"Now that you mention it," Zara said, "it would be incredibly useful . . ."

Everyone, even Kit, leaned forward with interest.

"If, while we were gone during the day, you did our laundry. Ocean water does ruin clothes quickly, don't you find?"

Night fell with the suddenness of shadows in the desert, but despite the sound of waves coming in through her window, Cristina couldn't sleep.

Thoughts of home tore at her. Her mother, her cousins. Better, past days with Diego and Jaime: She remembered a weekend she had spent with them once, tracking a demon in the dilapidated ghost town of Guerrero Viejo. The dreamlike landscape all around them: half-drowned houses, feathery weeds, buildings long discolored by water. She had lain on a rock with Jaime under uncountable stars, and they had told each other what they wanted most in the world: she, to end the Cold Peace; he, to bring honor back to his family.

Exasperated, she got out of bed and went downstairs, with only witchlight to illuminate her steps. The stairs were dark and quiet, and she found her way out the back door of the Institute with little noise.

Moonlight swept across the small dirt lot where the Institute's car was parked. Behind the lot was a garden, where white marble classical statues poked incongruously out of the desert sand.

Cristina missed her mother's rose garden with a sudden intensity. The scent of the flowers, sweeter than desert sage; her mother walking between the orderly rows. Cristina used to joke that her mother must have a warlock's help in keeping the flowers blooming even during the hottest summer.

She moved farther away from the house, toward the rows of hollyleaf cherry and alder trees. Drawing closer to them, she saw a shadow and froze, realizing she had brought no weapons with her. *Stupid,* she thought—the desert was full of dangers, not all of them supernatural. Mountain lions didn't distinguish between mundanes and Nephilim.

It wasn't a mountain lion. The shadow moved closer; she tensed, then relaxed. It was Mark.

The moonlight turned his hair silvery white. His feet were bare under the hems of his jeans. Astonishment crossed his face as he saw her; then he walked up to her without hesitation and put a hand on her cheek.

"Am I imagining you?" he said. "I was thinking about you, and now here you are."

It was such a Mark thing to say, a frank statement of his emotions. Because faeries couldn't lie, she thought, and he had grown up around them, and learned how to speak of love and loving with Kieran, who was proud and arrogant but always truthful. Faeries did not associate truth with weakness and vulnerability, as humans did.

It made Cristina feel braver. "I was thinking about you, too."

Mark feathered his thumb across her cheekbone. His palm was warm on her skin, cradling her head. "What about me?"

"The look on your face when Zara and her friends were talking about Downworlders during dinner. Your pain . . ."

He laughed without humor. "I should have expected it. Had I been an active Shadowhunter for the past five years, I would doubtless be more used to such talk."

"Because of the Cold Peace?"

He nodded. "When a decision like that is made by a government, it emboldens those who are already prejudiced to speak their deepest thoughts of hate. They assume they are simply brave enough to say what everyone really thinks."

"Mark—"

"In Zara's mind, I am hated," said Mark. His eyes were shadowed. "I am sure her father is part of that group that demands Helen remain prisoned on Wrangel Island."

"She will come back," Cristina said. "Now that you have come home, and fought so loyally for Shadowhunters, surely they will let her go."

Mark shook his head, but all he said was: "I am sorry about Diego."

She reached up and put her hand over his, his fingers light and cool as willow branches. She wanted to touch him more, abruptly, wanted to test the feel of his skin under his shirt, the texture of his jawline, where he had clearly never shaved and never needed to. "No," she said. "You're not, not really. Are you?"

"Cristina," Mark breathed, a little helplessly. "Can I . . . ?"

Cristina shook her head—if she actually let him ask, she'd never be able to say no. "We can't," she said. "Emma."

"You know that's not real," Mark said. "I love Emma, but not like that."

"But it's important, what she's doing." She drew away from Mark. "Julian has to believe it."

He looked at her in puzzlement and she remembered: Mark didn't know. Not about the curse, not that Julian loved Emma, or that Emma loved him.

"Everyone has to believe it. And besides," she added hastily, "there's Kieran. You only just ended things with him. And I just ended things with Diego."

He only looked more puzzled. She supposed faeries had never adopted the human ideas of giving each other space and having time to get over relationships.

And maybe they were stupid ideas. Maybe love was love and you should take it when you found it. Certainly her body was screaming at her mind to shut up: She wanted to put her arms around Mark, wanted to hold him as he held her, feel his chest against hers as his expanded with breath.

Something echoed out in the darkness. It sounded like the snap of an enormous branch, followed by a slow, dragging noise. Cristina whirled, reaching for her balisong. But it was inside, on her nightstand.

"Do you think it's the Centurions' night patrol?" she whispered to Mark.

He was looking out into the darkness too, narrow-eyed. "No. That was not a human noise." He took out two seraph blades and pressed one into her hand. "Nor was it an animal."

The weight of the blade in Cristina's hand was familiar and comforting. After a moment's pause to apply a Night Vision rune, she followed Mark into the desert shadows.

Kit opened his bedroom door a crack and peered through.

The hallway was deserted. No Ty sitting outside his door, reading or lying on the floor with headphones on. No lights seeping from underneath other doors. Just the dim glow of the rows of white lights that ran across the ceiling.

He half-expected alarms to go off as he crept through the silent house and opened the front door of the Institute, some kind of shrieking whistle or burst of lights. But there was nothing—just the sound of an ordinary heavy door creaking open and shut behind him.

He was outside, on the porch above the steps that led toward the trampled grass in front of the Institute, and then the road to the highway. The view over the cliff and down to the sea was bathed in moonlight, silver and black, a white path slashing across the water.

It was beautiful here, Kit thought, slinging his duffel bag over his shoulder. But not beautiful enough to stay. You couldn't trade a beach view for freedom.

He started down the stairs. His foot hit the first step and went out from under him as he was yanked backward. His duffel bag went flying. A hand was gripping his shoulder, hard; Kit wrenched himself sideways, nearly falling down the steps, and flung out his arm, colliding with something solid. He heard a muffled grunt— there was a barely visible figure, just a shadow among the shadows, looming over him, blocking the moon.

A second later they were both falling, Kit thudding to the porch on his back, the dark shadow collapsing on top of him. He felt sharp knees and elbows poke into him and a moment later a light flared: one of those stupid little stones they called witchlights.

"Kit," said a voice above him—Tiberius's voice. "Stop

thrashing." Ty shook his dark hair out of his face. He was kneeling over Kit—sitting on his solar plexus, pretty much, which made it hard to breathe—dressed all in black the way Shadowhunters did when they went out to fight. Only his hands and face were bare, very white in the darkness.

"Were you running away?" he said.

"I was going for a walk," said Kit.

"No, you're lying," said Ty, eyeing Kit's duffel bag. "You were running away."

Kit sighed and let his head fall back with a thump. "Why do you care what I do?"

"I'm a Shadowhunter. We help people."

"Now *you're* lying," said Kit, with conviction.

Ty smiled. It was a genuine, light-up-your-face-type smile, and it made Kit remember the first time he'd met Ty. Ty hadn't been sitting on him then, but he had been holding a dagger to Kit's throat.

Kit had looked at him and forgotten the knife and thought, *Beautiful.*

Beautiful like all the Shadowhunters were beautiful, like moonlight shearing off the edges of broken glass: lovely and deadly. Beautiful things, cruel things, cruel in that way that only people who absolutely believed in the rightness of their cause could be cruel.

"I need you," Ty said. "You might be surprised to hear that."

"I am," Kit agreed. He wondered if anyone was going to come running. He couldn't hear approaching feet, or voices.

"What happened to the night patrol?" he demanded.

"They're probably half a mile from here," said Ty. "They're trying to keep demons from getting near the Institute, not keep you from getting out. Now do you want to know what I need you for, or not?"

Almost against his will, Kit was curious. He propped himself up on his elbows and nodded. Ty was sitting on him as casually as if Kit was a sofa, but his fingers—long, quick fingers, deft with a knife, Kit recalled—hovered near his weapons belt. "You're a criminal," Ty said. "Your father was a con man and you wanted to be like him. Your duffel bag is probably full of things you stole from the Institute."

"It . . . ," Kit began, and trailed off as Ty reached over, yanked the zipper on the bag down, and eyed the cache of stolen daggers, boxes, scabbards, candlesticks, and anything else Kit had scavenged revealed in the moonlight. ". . . might be," Kit concluded. "What's that got to do with you, anyway? None of it's yours."

"I want to solve crimes," Ty said. "To be a detective. But nobody here cares about that sort of thing."

"Didn't you just all catch a murderer?"

"Malcolm sent a note," Ty said in a withering tone, as if he were disappointed that Malcolm had ruined crime-solving with his confession. "And then he *admitted* he did it."

"That does rather narrow down the list of suspects," Kit said. "Look, if you need me so you can arrest me for fun, I feel I should point out it's the sort of thing you can only do once."

"I don't want to arrest you. I want a partner. Someone who knows about crimes and people who commit them so they can help me."

A lightbulb went off in Kit's head. "You want a—wait, you've been sleeping outside my room because you want a sort of Watson for your Sherlock Holmes?"

Ty's eyes lit up. They still moved restlessly around Kit as if he were reading him, examining him, never quite meeting Kit's own, but that didn't dim their glow. "You know about them?"

Everyone in the whole world knows about them, Kit almost said, but instead only said, "I'm not going to be anybody's Watson. I don't want to solve crimes. I don't care about crimes. I don't care if they're being committed, or not committed—"

"Don't think of them as crimes. Think of them as mysteries. Besides, what else are you going to do? Run away? And go where?"

"I don't care—"

"You do, though," said Ty. "You want to live. Just like everyone else does. You don't want to be trapped, is all." He cocked his head to the side, his eyes a depthless almost-white in the witchlight glow. The moon had gone behind a cloud, and it was the only illumination.

"How'd you know I was going to run away tonight?"

"Because you were getting used to it here," said Ty. "You were getting used to us. But the Centurions, you don't like them. Livvy noticed it first. And after what Zara said today about you going to the Academy—you must feel like you're not going to have any choices about what you do, after this."

It was true, surprisingly so. Kit couldn't find the words to explain how he'd felt at the dinner table. As if becoming a Shadowhunter meant being shoved into a machine that would chew him up and spit out a Centurion.

"I look at them," he said, "and I think, 'I can't possibly be like them, and they can't stand anyone different.'"

"You don't have to go to the Academy," said Ty. "You can stay with us as long as you want."

Kit doubted Ty had the authority to make a promise like that, but he appreciated it regardless. "As long as I help you solve mysteries," he said. "How often do you have mysteries to solve, or do I have to wait until another warlock goes crazypants?"

Ty leaned against one of the pillars. His hands fluttered at his sides like night butterflies. "Actually, there's a mystery going on right now."

Kit was intrigued despite himself. "What is it?"

"I think they're not here for the reason they claim they are. I think they're up to something," Ty said. "And they're definitely lying to us."

"Who's lying?"

Ty's eyes sparkled. "The Centurions, of course."

* * *

The next day was blistering hot, one of those rare days when the air seemed to stand still and the proximity of the ocean offered no relief. When Emma arrived, late, for breakfast in the dining room, the rarely used ceiling fans were whirling full speed.

"Was it a sand demon?" Dane Larkspear was asking Cristina. "Akvan and Iblis demons are common in the desert."

"We know that," said Julian. "Mark already said it was a sea demon."

"It slithered off the moment we shone witchlight upon it," said Mark. "But it left behind a stink of seawater, and wet sand."

"I can't believe there aren't perimeter wards here," Zara said. "Why has no one ever seen to it? I ought to ask Mr. Blackthorn—"

"The perimeter wards failed to keep out Sebastian Morgenstern," said Diana. "They weren't used again after that. Perimeter wards rarely work."

She sounded as if she were struggling to keep her temper. Emma couldn't blame her.

Zara looked at her with a sort of superior pity. "Well, with all these sea demons crawling up out of the ocean—which they wouldn't be doing if Malcolm Fade's body wasn't in there somewhere, you know—I think they're called for. Don't you?"

There was a murmur of voices: most of the Centurions, except for Diego, Jon, and Rayan, seemed to be in agreement. As they made plans to set the wards up that morning, Emma tried to catch Julian's eye to share his annoyance, but he was looking away from her, toward Mark and Cristina. "What were you two doing outside last night, anyway?"

"We couldn't sleep," Mark said. "We bumped into each other."

Zara smiled. "Of course you did." She turned to whisper something into Samantha's ear. Both girls giggled.

Cristina blushed angrily. Emma saw Julian's hand tighten on his fork. He laid it down slowly next to his plate.

Emma bit her lip. If Mark and Cristina wanted to date, she'd give them her blessing. She'd stage some kind of breakup with Mark; their "relationship" had already done a lot of what it needed to do. Julian could barely look at her anymore, and that was what she'd wanted—wasn't it?

He didn't seem happy about the idea that she and Mark might be over, though. Not even a little bit. If he was even thinking about that. There had been a time when she could always tell what Julian had on his mind. Now, she could read only the surface of his thoughts: His deeper feelings were hidden.

Diego looked from Mark to Cristina and stood up, shoving back his chair. He walked out of the room. After a moment, Emma dropped her napkin onto her plate and followed.

He had stomped all the way to the back door and out into the parking lot before he noticed she was following him—a sure sign he was upset, given Diego's level of training. He turned to face her, his dark eyes glittering. "Emma," he said. "I understand you wish to scold me. You have for days. But this is not a good time."

"And what would be a good time? You want to pencil it into your day planner under Never Going to Happen?" She raised an eyebrow. "That's what I thought. Come on."

She stalked around the side of the Institute, Diego reluctantly following. They reached a spot where a small mound of dirt rose between cacti, familiar to Emma from long experience. "You stand there," she said, pointing. He gave her a disbelieving look. "So we won't be seen from the windows," she explained, and he grouchily did as she'd asked, crossing his arms across his muscular chest.

"Emma," he said. "You do not and cannot understand, and I cannot explain to you—"

"I bet you can't," she said. "Look, you know I haven't always been your biggest fan, but I thought a lot better of you than this."

A muscle twitched in his face. His jaw was rigid. "As I said. You cannot understand, and I cannot explain."

"It would be one thing," Emma said, "if you'd just been two-timing, which I still would think was despicable, but—Zara? You're the reason she's here. You *know* we aren't— You know Julian has to be careful."

"He should not worry too much," said Diego tonelessly. "Zara is only interested in what profits her. I do not think she has any interest in Arthur's secrets, only in getting attention from the Council for completing this mission successfully."

"Easy for you to assume."

"I have reasons for everything I do, Emma," he said. "Maybe Cristina does not know them now, but one day she will."

"Diego, *everyone* has reasons for everything they do. *Malcolm* had reasons for what he did."

Diego's mouth flattened into a thin line. "Do not compare me to Malcolm Fade."

"Because he was a warlock?" Emma's voice was low, dangerous. "Because you think like your fiancée does? About the Cold Peace? About warlocks, and faeries? About *Mark*?"

"Because he was a murderer." Diego spoke through his teeth. "Whatever else you think of me, Emma, I am not a senseless bigot. I do not believe Downworlders are lesser, to be registered or to be tortured—"

"But you admit Zara does," said Emma.

"I have never told her anything," he said.

"Maybe you can understand why I'm wondering how you could prefer her to Cristina," Emma said.

Diego tensed—and shouted. Emma had forgotten how fast he could move, despite his bulk: He leaped back, cursing and kicking out with his left foot. Muttering in pain, he kicked off his shoe. Columns of ants marched over his ankle, scurrying up his leg.

"Oh, dear," said Emma. "You must have stood on a red-ant hill. You know, accidentally."

Diego slapped the ants away, still cursing. He'd kicked away part of the top of the mound of dirt, and ants were pouring out of it.

Emma stepped back. "Don't worry," she said. "They're not poisonous."

"You tricked me into standing on an anthill?" He had shoved his foot back into his shoe, but Emma knew he'd have itchy bites for a few days unless he used an *iratze*.

"Cristina made me promise not to touch you, so I had to get creative," Emma said. "You shouldn't have lied to my best friend. *Desgraciado mentiroso*."

He stared at her.

Emma sighed. "I hope that meant what I think it meant. I'd hate to have just called you a rusty bucket or something."

"No," he said. To her surprise, he sounded wearily amused. "It meant what you thought it meant."

"Good." She stalked back toward the house. She was almost out of earshot when he called after her. She turned and saw him standing where she'd left him, apparently heedless of the ants or the hot sun beating down on his shoulders.

"Believe me, Emma," he said, loudly enough for her to hear him, "no one hates me more than I hate myself right now."

"Do you *really* think so?" she asked. Emma didn't shout, but she knew the words carried. He looked at her for a long moment, silently, before she walked away.

The day stayed hot until the late afternoon, when a storm rolled in over the ocean. The Centurions had left before noon, and Emma couldn't help but stare out the windows anxiously as the sun set behind a mass of black and gray clouds on the horizon, shot through with heat lightning.

"Do you think they'll be okay?" Dru asked, her hands worrying the hilt of her throwing knife. "Aren't they out in a boat? It looks like a bad storm."

"We don't know *what* they're doing," Emma said. She almost added that thanks to the Centurions' snobbish desire to conceal their activities from the Institute's Shadowhunters, it would be very difficult to rescue them if something dangerous *did* happen, but she saw the look on Dru's face and didn't. Dru had practically hero-worshipped Diego—despite everything, she was probably still fond of him.

Emma felt briefly guilty about the ants.

"They'll be fine," said Cristina reassuringly. "Centurions are very careful."

Livvy called Dru over to fence with her, and Dru trailed off toward where Ty, Kit, and Livvy stood together on a training mat. Somehow Kit had been convinced to don training gear. He looked like a mini Jace, Emma thought with amusement, with his blond curls and angular cheekbones.

Behind them, Diana was showing Mark a training stance. Emma blinked—Julian had been there, a moment ago. She was sure of it.

"He went to check on your uncle," Cristina said. "Something about him not liking storms."

"No, it's Tavvy who doesn't like . . ." Emma's voice trailed off. Tavvy was sitting in the corner of the training room, reading a book. She remembered all the times Julian had disappeared during storms, claiming Tavvy was frightened of them.

She slid Cortana into its sheath. "I'll be back."

Cristina watched her go with troubled eyes. No one else seemed to notice as she slipped out the training room door and down the hallway. The massive windows spaced along the corridor let in a peculiar gray light, hazed with pinpoints of silver.

She reached the door to the attic and ran up the stairs; though she didn't bother to conceal the sound of her footfalls, neither

Arthur nor Julian seemed to have noticed her when she entered the main attic room.

The windows were tightly closed and sealed with paper, all except one, over the desk at which Arthur sat. The paper had been torn away from it, showing clouds racing across the sky, colliding and untangling like thick rounds of gray and black yarn.

Trays of uneaten food were scattered on Arthur's several desks. The room smelled like rot and mildew. Emma swallowed, wondering if she'd made a mistake in coming.

Arthur was slumped in his desk chair, lank hair falling over his eyes. "I want them to go," he was saying. "I don't like having them here."

"I know." Julian spoke with a gentleness that surprised Emma. How could he not be angry? She was angry—angry about everything that had conspired to force Julian to grow up years too fast. That had deprived him of a childhood. How could he look at Arthur and not think of that? "I want them to go too, but there's nothing I can do to send them away. We have to be patient."

"I need my medicine," Arthur whispered. "Where is Malcolm?"

Emma winced at the look on Julian's face—and Arthur seemed suddenly to notice her. He raised his eyes, their gaze fixing on her—no, not on her. On her sword.

"Cortana," he said. "Made by Wayland the Smith, the legendary forger of Excalibur and Durendal. Said to choose its bearer. When Ogier raised it to slay the son of Charlemagne on the field, an angel came and broke the sword and said to him, 'Mercy is better than revenge.'"

Emma looked at Julian. It was shadowy in the attic, but she could see his hands clenched at his sides. Was he angry at her for following him?

"But Cortana has never been broken," she said.

"It's only a story," Julian said.

"There is truth in stories," said Arthur. "There is truth in one of your paintings, boy, or in a sunset or a couplet from Homer. Fiction is truth, even if it is not fact. If you believe only in facts and forget stories, your brain will live, but your heart will die."

"I understand, Uncle." Julian sounded tired. "I'll be back later. Please eat something. All right?"

Arthur lowered his face into his hands, shaking his head. Julian began to move across the room to the stairs; halfway there, he caught Emma's wrist, drawing her after him.

He exerted no real force, but she followed him anyway, shocked into compliance simply by the physical sensation of his hand on her wrist. He only touched her to apply runes these days—she missed those friendly touches she was used to from the years of their friendship: a hand brushing her arm, a tap on her shoulder. Their secret way of communicating: fingers drawings words and letters on each other's skin, silent and invisible to everyone else.

It seemed like forever. And now sparks were racing up her arm from that one point of contact, making her body feel hot, stinging, and confused. His fingers looped her wrist as they went out the front door.

When it closed behind them, he let go, turning to face her. The air felt heavy and dense, pressing against Emma's skin. Mist obscured the highway. She could see the heaving surfaces of gray waves slapping against the shore; from here, each looked as big as a humpbacked whale. She could see the moon, struggling to show itself between clouds.

Julian was breathing hard, as if he'd been running flat out for miles. The dampness of the air stuck his shirt to his chest as he leaned back against the wall of the Institute. "Why did you come to the attic?" he said.

"I'm sorry." She spoke stiffly. She hated being stiff around Jules. They'd rarely had a fight that didn't end in a casual apology

or joking. *I had this feeling, that you needed me, and I couldn't not come.*
"I understand if you're angry—"

"I'm not angry." Lightning sizzled out over the water, briefly whitening the sky. "That's the hell of it, I can't be angry, can I? Mark doesn't know a thing about you and me, he isn't trying to hurt me, none of it's his fault. And you, you did the right thing. I can't hate you for that." He pushed off from the wall, took a restless few paces. The energy of the pent-up storm seemed to crackle off his skin. "But I can't stand it. What do I do, Emma?" He raked his hands through his hair; the humidity was making it curl into ringlets that clung to his fingers. "We can't live like this."

"I know," she said. "I'll go away. It's only a few months. I'll be eighteen. We'll take our travel years away from each other. We'll forget."

"Will we?" His mouth twisted into an impossible smile.

"We have to." Emma had begun to shiver; it was cold, the clouds above them roiling like the smoke of a scorched sky.

"I should never have touched you," he said. He'd drawn closer to her, or maybe she'd moved closer to him, wanting to take his hands, the way she always had. "I never thought what we had could break so easily."

"It's not broken," she whispered. "We made a mistake—but being together wasn't the mistake."

"Most people get to make mistakes, Emma. It doesn't have to ruin their whole lives."

She closed her eyes, but she could still see him. Still feel him, inches away from her, the heat of his body, the scent of cloves that clung to his clothes and hair. It was making her insane, making her knees shake as if she'd just staggered off a roller coaster. "Our lives aren't ruined."

His arms went around her. She thought for a moment of resisting, but she was so tired—so tired of fighting what she wanted. She hadn't thought she'd ever get this, Jules in her arms again, all lean muscle and taut tension, strong painter's hands smoothing down her back, his fingers tracing letters, words, on her skin.

I A-M R-U-I-N-E-D.

She opened her eyes, appalled. His face was so close it was almost a blur of light and shadow. "Emma," he said, his arms leashing her, pulling her closer.

And then he was kissing her; they were kissing each other. He drew her against him; he fit her body to his, curves and hollows, muscles and softness. His mouth was open over hers, his tongue running gently along the seam of her lips.

Thunder exploded around them, lightning shattering against the mountains, blazing a path of dry heat across the inside of Emma's eyelids.

She opened her mouth under his, pressed up against him, her arms wrapping around his neck. He tasted like fire, like spice. He ran his hands down her sides, over her hips. Drew her more firmly against him. He was making a low sound in his throat, a sort of anguished wanting sound.

It felt like forever. It felt like no time at all. His hands molded the shape of her shoulder blades, the curve of her body beneath her rib cage, thumbs arching over the crests of her hips. He lifted her up and against him as if they could fit into each other's empty spaces, as words spilled from his mouth: frantic, hurried,

"Emma—I need you, always, always think about you, I was wishing you were with me in that goddamned attic and then I turned around and you were there, like you heard me, like you're always there when I need you. . . ."

Lightning forked again, illuminating the world: Emma could see her hands on Julian's shirt hem—what the hell was she thinking, was she planning for them both to strip down on the Institute's front porch? Reality reasserted itself; she pushed away, her heart slamming against her chest.

"Em?" He looked at her, dazed, his eyes sleepy and hot and wanting. It made her swallow hard. But his words echoed in her head: He'd wanted her, and she'd come as if she'd heard him call— she'd *felt* that wanting, known it, not been able to stop herself.

All these weeks of insisting to herself that the *parabatai* bond was weakening, and now he was telling her they'd just practically read each other's minds.

"Mark," she said, and it was just one word but it was *the* word, the most brutal reminder of their situation. The sleepy look left his eyes; he whitened, aghast. He raised a hand as if he meant to say something—explain, apologize—and the sky seemed to rip down the middle.

They both turned to stare as the clouds directly above them parted. A shadow grew in the air, darkening as it neared them: the figure of a man, massive and bound in armor, bareback on a red-eyed, foaming brindled horse—black and gray, like the storm clouds overhead.

Julian moved as if to thrust Emma behind him, but she wouldn't budge. She simply stared as the horse came to a neighing, pawing stop at the foot of the Institute steps. The man looked up at them.

His eyes, like Mark's, were two different colors, in his case blue and black. His face was terrifyingly familiar. It was Gwyn ap Nudd, the lord and leader of the Wild Hunt. And he did not look pleased.

7

SEAS WITHOUT A SHORE

Before Julian or Emma could speak, the front door of the Institute slammed open. Diana was there, with Mark just behind her, still in his training clothes. Diana, in a white suit, looked as beautiful and formidable as always.

Gwyn's towering brindled horse reared as Mark approached the top of the steps. Catching sight of Emma and Jules as they strode toward him, Mark looked more than a little surprised. Emma's cheeks felt as if they must be burning, though when she looked at Julian, he seemed unruffled, cool as always.

They joined Mark just as Diana swept to the top of the steps. The four Shadowhunters stared down at the Hunter—his horse's eyes were blood-red, and so was the armor that Gwyn wore: tough crimson leather, torn here and there by claw marks and the rips made by weapons.

"Because of the Cold Peace, I cannot bid you welcome," Diana said. "Why are you here, Gwyn Hunter?"

Gwyn's ancient gaze glided up and down Diana; there was no malice in it or arrogance, only the faerie appreciation for something beautiful. "Lovely lady," he said, "I do not think we have met."

Diana looked momentarily nonplussed. "Diana Wrayburn. I'm the tutor here."

"Those who teach are honored in the Land Under the Hill," said Gwyn. Under his arm he carried a massive helmet decorated with a stag's antlers. His hunting horn lay across the pommel of his saddle.

Emma boggled. Was Gwyn *hitting* on Diana? She didn't know faeries did that, exactly. She heard Mark make an exasperated noise.

"Gwyn," he said, "I give you fair greetings. My heart is gladdened to see you."

Emma couldn't help wondering if any of that was true. She knew Mark had complicated feelings for Gwyn. He'd spoken of them sometimes, during the nights in her room, head on his hand. She had a clearer picture of the Wild Hunt now than she'd ever had before, of its delights and horrors, of the strange path Mark had been forced to make for himself between the stars.

"I would that I could say the same," said Gwyn. "I bring dark news from the Unseelie Court. Kieran of your heart—"

"He is not of my heart any longer," interrupted Mark. It was a faerie expression, "of my heart," the closest they might come to saying "girlfriend" or "boyfriend."

"Kieran Hunter has been found guilty of the murder of Iarlath," said Gwyn. "He stood trial at the Court of the Unseelie, though it was a short affair."

Mark flushed, tensing all over. "And the sentence?"

"Death," said Gwyn. "He will die at the moon's rise, tomorrow night, if there is no intervention."

Mark didn't move. Emma wondered if she should do something— move closer to Mark, offer comfort, a gentling hand? But the expression on his face was unreadable—if it was grief, she didn't recognize it. If it was anger, then it was unlike any anger he had shown before.

"That is sad news," Mark said finally.

It was Julian who moved then, stepping to his brother's side. Julian put a hand on Mark's shoulder; Emma felt relief flood through her.

"Is that all?" Gwyn said. "Have you nothing else to say?"

Mark shook his head. He looked fragile, Emma thought worriedly. As if you could see through his skin to the bones underneath. "Kieran betrayed me," he said. "He is nothing to me now."

Gwyn looked at Mark in disbelief. "He loved you and he lost you and he tried to get you back," he said. "He wanted you to ride with the Hunt again. So did I. You were one of our best. Is that so terrible?"

"You saw what happened." Mark did sound angry now, and Emma herself could not help but remember: the twisted quickbeam tree she had leaned against while Iarlath whipped Julian and then her, and Kieran and Mark and Gwyn watched. The pain and the blood, the lashes like fire against her skin, though nothing had hurt as much as watching Julian be hurt. "Iarlath whipped my family, my friend. Because of Kieran. He whipped Emma and Julian."

"And now you have given up the Hunt for them," said Gwyn, his two-colored eyes flicking toward Emma, "and so, there is your vengeance, if you wanted it. But where is your compassion?"

"What do you want of my brother?" Julian demanded, his hand still on Mark's shoulder. "Do you want him to grieve visibly for your amusement? Is that why you came?"

"Mortals," Gwyn said. "You think you know so much, yet you know so little." His large hand tightened on his helmet. "I do not want you to grieve for Kieran. I want you to rescue him, Mark Hunter."

Thunder rumbled in the distance, but in front of the Institute, there was only silence, profound as a shout.

Even Diana seemed struck speechless. In the quiet, Emma could hear the sounds of Livvy and the others up in the training room, their voices and laughter.

Jules's expression was flat. Calculating. His hand on Mark's shoulder was a tight grip now. *I want you to rescue him, Mark Hunter.*

Anger swelled quickly inside Emma; unlike Jules, she didn't bite it back. "Mark is not of the Wild Hunt any longer," she said hotly. "Don't call him 'Hunter.' He isn't one."

"He is a Shadowhunter, isn't he?" asked Gwyn. Now that he had made his bizarre request, he seemed more relaxed. "Once a hunter, always a hunter of some sort."

"And now you wish me to hunt for Kieran?" Mark spoke in a strange, halting tone, as if he were having difficulty getting the words out past his anger. "Why me, Gwyn? Why not you? Why not any of you?"

"Did you not hear me?" said Gwyn. "He is held captive by his father. The Unseelie King himself, in the depths of the Court."

"And is Mark indestructible, then? You think he can take on the Unseelie Court where the Wild Hunt can't?" It was Diana; she had moved down a step, and her dark hair blew in the desert wind. "Yours is a famous name, Gwyn ap Nudd. You have ridden with the Wild Hunt for hundreds of mortal years. There are many stories about you. Yet never had I heard that the leader of the Wild Hunt had succumbed to madness."

"The Wild Hunt is not subject to the rule of the Courts," said Gwyn. "But we fear them. It would be madness *not* to. When they came to take Kieran, I, and all my Hunters, were forced to swear a life oath that we would not challenge the trial or its outcome. To attempt to rescue Kieran now would mean death for us."

"That's why you've come to me. Because I didn't swear. Because even if I did, I can lie. A lying thief, that's what you want," Mark said.

"What I wanted was one I could trust," said Gwyn. "One who has not sworn, one who would dare the Court."

"We want no trouble with you." It was Julian, keeping his voice level with an effort that Emma suspected only she could sense. "But you must see that Mark cannot do what you're asking. It is too dangerous."

"We of the Folk of the Air do not fear danger, nor death," said Gwyn.

"If you don't fear death," said Julian, "then let Kieran meet it."

Gwyn recoiled at the coldness in Julian's voice. "Kieran is not yet twenty."

"Neither is Mark," said Julian. "If you think we're afraid of you, you're right. We'd be fools not to be. I know who *you* are, Gwyn— I know you once made a man eat his own father's heart. I know you took the Hunt from Herne in a battle over Cadair Idris. I know things that would surprise you. But I am Mark's brother. And I will not let him risk himself in Faerie again."

"The Wild Hunt is a brotherhood as well," Gwyn said. "If you cannot bring yourself to help Kieran out of love, Mark, do it out of friendship."

"Enough," Diana snapped. "We respect you here, Gwyn the Hunter, but this discussion is at an end. Mark will not be taken from us."

Gwyn's voice was a bass rumble. "What if he chooses to go?"

They all looked at Mark. Even Julian turned, dropping his hand slowly from Mark's shoulder. Emma saw the fear in his eyes. She imagined it was echoed in her own. If Mark still loved Kieran—even a little bit—

"I do not choose it," said Mark. "I do not choose it, Gwyn."

Gwyn's face tightened. "You have no honor."

Light speared through gaps in the clouds overhead. The storm was moving toward the mountains. The gray illumination cast a film across Mark's eyes, rendering them unreadable. "I thought you were my friend," he said, and then he turned and stumbled back into the Institute, the door slamming shut behind him.

Gwyn began to dismount, but Diana raised her hand, palm out. "You know you cannot enter the Institute," she said.

Gwyn subsided. For a moment, as he gazed at Diana, his face looked lined and old, though Emma knew he was ageless. "Kieran is not yet twenty," he said again. "Only a boy."

Diana's face softened, but before she could speak, Gwyn's horse reared up. Something flew from Gwyn's hand and landed on the step below Diana's feet. Gwyn leaned forward, and his horse exploded into motion, its mane and tail blurring into a single white flame. The flame shot toward the sky and vanished, disappearing into the night's fretwork of clouds.

Julian shouldered the door of the Institute open. "Mark? Mark!"

The empty foyer swung around him as he turned. Fear for his brother was like pressure on his skin, tightening his veins, slowing his blood. It wasn't a fear he could put a name to—Gwyn was gone; Mark was safe. It had been a request, not a kidnapping.

"Jules?" Mark appeared from the closet beneath the staircase, clearly having just hung up his jacket. His blond hair was tousled, his expression puzzled. "Did he leave?"

"He's gone." It was Emma, who had come in behind Julian. Diana, a step after her, was closing the front door. Mark went straight across the room to Emma without a pause and put his arms around her.

The jealousy that flared through Julian took his breath away.

He thought he had gotten used to seeing Emma and Mark like this. They weren't a particularly demonstrative couple. They didn't kiss or cuddle in front of other people. Emma wouldn't, Julian thought. She wasn't like that. She was determined, and she was matter-of-fact, and she would do what needed to be done. But she wasn't cruel.

It was Mark who reached for her, usually—for the small, quiet things, the hand on the shoulder, the brushing away of a stray eye-lash, a quick embrace. There was an exquisite pain in watching that, more than there would have been in seeing them passionately embracing. After all, when you were dying of thirst, it was the sip of water you dreamed about, not the whole reservoir.

But now—the feel of holding Emma was so close, the taste of her still on his mouth, her rose-water scent on his clothes. He would play back the scene of their kiss over and over in his head, he knew, until it faded and fragmented and came apart like a photo-graph folded and unfolded too many times.

But it was too close now, like a just-delivered wound. And see-ing Emma in Mark's arms was a sharp splash of acid on raw skin, a brutal reminder: He couldn't afford to be sentimental, or to think of her as possibly his, even in an imaginary someday. To consider possibilities was to open yourself up to pain. Reality had to be his focus—reality and his responsibilities to his family. Otherwise he would go insane.

"Do you think he'll come back?" Emma drew back from Mark. Julian thought she cast him an anxious sideways glance, but he wasn't sure. And there was no point wondering. He crushed his curiosity down, brutally.

"Gwyn?" said Mark. "No. I refused him. He won't beg and he won't return."

"Are you sure?" Julian said.

Mark gave him a wry look. "Do not let Gwyn fool you," he said. "If I do not help him, he will find someone else to do it, or he will do it himself. Kieran will come to no harm."

Emma made a relieved noise. Julian said nothing—he was won-dering about Kieran himself. He remembered how the faerie boy had gotten Emma whipped bloody, and broken Mark's heart. He remembered also how Kieran had helped them defeat Malcolm. Without him they would have had no chance.

And he remembered what Kieran had said to him before the battle with Malcolm. *You are not gentle. You have a ruthless heart.*

If he could have saved Kieran by risking his own safety, he would have. But he would not risk his brother. If that made him ruthless, so be it. If Mark was right, Kieran would be fine anyway.

"Diana," said Emma. Their tutor was leaning against the closed front door, looking down at her palm. "What did Gwyn throw at you?"

Diana held out her hand; glimmering on her brown skin was a small golden acorn.

Mark looked surprised. "That is a fair gift," he said. "Should you crack open that acorn, Gwyn would be summoned to aid you."

"Why would he give Diana something like that?" asked Emma.

The ghost of a smile touched Mark's mouth as he began to mount the stairs. "He admired her," he said. "It is rare I have seen Gwyn admire a woman before. I had thought perhaps his heart was closed to that sort of thing."

"Gwyn has a *crush* on Diana?" Emma inquired, her dark eyes brightening. "I mean, not that you're not very attractive, Diana, it just seems sudden."

"Faeries are like that," said Julian. He almost felt for Diana—he had never seen her look so rattled. She was worrying at her lower lip with her teeth, and Julian remembered that Diana really wasn't very old—only twenty-eight or so. Not that much older than Jace and Clary.

"It doesn't mean anything," she said. "And besides, we have more important things to think about!"

She dropped the acorn into Mark's hand just as the front door flew open and the Centurions poured in. They looked wind-tossed and soaking wet, every one of them drenched. Diana, seeming relieved to no longer be talking about her love life, went off to find blankets and towels (drying runes notoriously worked well to dry your skin, but didn't do much for your clothes).

"Did you find anything?" Emma asked.

"I think we've located the likely spot where the body sank," said Manuel. "But the sea was too rough for us to dive for it. We'll have to try again tomorrow."

"*Manuel*," Zara said warningly, as if he'd revealed the secret passcode that would open the gates to Hell under their feet.

Manuel and Rayan rolled their eyes. "It's not like they don't know what we're looking for, Zara."

"The Scholomance's methods are secret." Zara thrust her damp jacket into Diego's arms and turned back to Emma and Julian. "Right," she said. "What's for dinner?"

"I can't tell any of them apart," said Kit. "It's the uniforms. It makes them all look the same to me. Like ants."

"Ants don't all look the same," said Ty.

They were sitting at the edge of the second-floor gallery overlooking the main Institute entryway below. Wet Centurions scurried to and fro; Kit saw Julian and Emma, along with Diana, trying to make conversation with the ones who hadn't wandered off to the dining room, and the fireplace there, to get warm.

"Who is everyone again?" said Kit. "And where are they from?"

"Dane and Samantha Larkspear," said Livvy, indicating two dark-haired Centurions. "Atlanta."

"Twins," said Ty.

"How dare they," said Livvy, with a grin. Kit had been worried she wouldn't be thrilled with Ty's plan to absorb Kit into his detecting plans, but she'd just given a wry smile when they'd come over to her in the training room and said, "Welcome to the club."

Livvy pointed. "Manuel Casales Villalobos. From Madrid. Rayan Maduabuchi, Lagos Institute. Divya Joshi, Mumbai Institute. Not everyone's connected with an Institute, though. Diego's not, Zara isn't, or her friend Jessica, who's French, I think. And there's Jon

Cartwright and Gen Whitelaw, and Thomas Aldertree, all Academy graduates." She tilted her head. "And not one of them has the sense to come in out of the rain."

"Tell me again why you think they're up to something?" said Kit.

"All right," said Ty. Kit had noticed already that Ty responded directly to what you said to him, and much less so to tone or intonation. Not that he couldn't use a refresher on why they were halfway up a building, staring at a bunch of jerks. "I was sitting in front of your room this morning when I saw Zara go into Diana's office. When I followed her, I saw that she was going through papers there."

"She could have had a reason," said Kit.

"To be sneaking through Diana's papers? What reason?" said Livvy, so firmly that Kit had to admit that if it looked scurrilous, it probably was scurrilous.

"I texted Simon Lewis about Cartwright, Whitelaw, and Aldertree," said Livvy, resting her chin on the lower crossbar of the railing. "He says Gen and Thomas are solid, and Cartwright is kind of a lunk, but basically harmless."

"They might not all be involved," said Ty. "We have to figure out which of them are, and what they want."

"What's a lunk?" said Kit.

"Sort of a combination of hunk and lump, I think. As in, large but not that smart." Livvy grinned her quick grin as a shadow rose up over them—Cristina, her hands on her hips, her eyebrows quirked.

"What are you three doing?" she asked. Kit had a healthy respect for Cristina Rosales. Sweet as she looked, he'd seen her throw a balisong fifty feet and hit her target exactly.

"Nothing," said Kit.

"Making rude comments about the Centurions," said Livvy.

For a moment, Kit thought Cristina was going to scold them. Instead she sat down next to Livvy, her mouth curling up into a smile. "Count me in," she said.

Ty was resting his forearms on the crossbar. He flicked his storm-cloud-gray eyes in Kit's direction. "Tomorrow," he said quietly, "we follow them to see where they go."

Kit was surprised to find he was looking forward to it.

It was an uncomfortable evening—the Centurions, even after drying off, were exhausted and reluctant to talk about what they'd done that day. Instead they descended on the dining room and the food laid out there like ravenous wolves.

Kit, Ty, and Livvy were nowhere to be seen. Emma didn't blame them. Meals with the Centurions were an increasingly uncomfortable affair. Though Divya, Rayan, and Jon Cartwright tried their best to hold up a friendly conversation about where everyone planned to spend their travel year, Zara soon interrupted them with a long description of what she'd been doing in Hungary before she'd arrived at the Institute.

"Bunch of Shadowhunters complaining that their steles and seraph blades stopped working during a fight with some faeries," she said, rolling her eyes. "We told them it was just an illusion—faeries fight dirty, and they should be teaching that at the Academy."

"Faeries don't fight dirty, actually," said Mark. "They fight remarkably cleanly. They have a strict code of honor."

"Honor?" Samantha and Dane laughed at the same time. "I doubt you know what that means, ha—"

They paused. It had been Dane who was speaking, but it was Samantha who flushed. The word unspoken hung in the air. *Half-breed.*

Mark shoved his chair back and walked out of the room.

"Sorry," Zara said into the silence that followed his departure. "But he shouldn't be sensitive. He's going to hear a lot worse if he goes to Alicante, especially at a Council meeting."

Emma stared at her incredulously. "That doesn't make it all right," she said. "Just because he's going to hear something ugly from the bigots on the Council doesn't mean he should hear it first at home."

"Or ever at home," said Cristina, whose cheeks had turned dark red.

"Stop trying to make us feel guilty," Samantha snapped. "We're the ones who've been out all day trying to clean up the mess *you* made, trusting Malcolm Fade, like you could trust a Downworlder. Didn't you people learn anything from the Dark War? The faeries stabbed us in the back. That's what Downworlders do, and Mark and Helen will do it to you, too, if you're not careful."

"You don't know anything about my brother or my sister," said Julian. "Please refrain from saying their names."

Diego had been sitting beside Zara in stony silence. He spoke finally, his lips barely moving. "Such blind hatred does no credit to the office or the uniform of Centurions," he said.

Zara lifted her glass, her fingers curled tightly around the slender stem. "I don't hate Downworlders," she said, and there was cool conviction in her voice. It was more chilling, somehow, than passion would have been. "The Accords haven't worked. The Cold Peace doesn't work. Downworlders don't follow our rules, or any rules that aren't in their interest to follow. They break the Cold Peace when they feel like it. We are warriors. Demons should fear us. And Downworlders should fear us. Once we were great: We were feared, and we ruled. We're a shadow now of what we were then. All I'm saying is that when the systems aren't working, when they've brought us down to the level we're at now, then we need a new system. A better one."

Zara smiled, tucked a stray bit of hair back into her immaculate bun, and took a sip of water. They finished dinner in silence.

"She lies. She just sits there and lies like her opinions are facts," said Emma furiously. After dinner, she'd retreated with Cristina to the other girl's room; they were both sitting on the bed, Cristina worrying her dark hair between her fingers.

"I think they are, to her and those like her," said Cristina. "But we should not waste time on Zara. You said on the way upstairs that you had something to tell me?"

As concisely as she could, Emma caught Cristina up on the visit from Gwyn. As Emma talked, Cristina's face grew more and more pinched with worry. "Is Mark all right?"

"I think so—he can be really hard to read, sometimes."

"He's one of those people with a lot going on in his head," said Cristina. "Has he ever asked—about you and Julian?"

Emma shook her head violently. "I don't think it would ever cross his mind we had anything but *parabatai* feelings for each other. Jules and I have known each other so long." She rubbed at her temples. "Mark assumes Julian feels the same way about me that he does—brotherly."

"It's strange, the things that blind us," said Cristina. She drew her knees up, her hands looped around them.

"Have you tried to reach Jaime?" Emma asked.

Cristina leaned her cheek on the tops of her knees. "I sent a fire-message, but I haven't heard anything."

"He was your best friend," Emma said. "He'll respond." She twisted a piece of Cristina's woven blanket between her fingers. "You know what I miss most? About Jules? Just—being *parabatai*. Being Emma and Julian. I miss my best friend. I miss the person I told everything to, all the time. The person who knew everything about me. The good things and the bad things." She could see Julian in her mind's eye as she spoke, the way he had looked during the Dark War, all thin shoulders and determined eyes.

The sound of a knock on the door echoed through the room. Emma glanced at Cristina—was she expecting someone?—but the other girl looked as surprised as she did.

"*Pasa*," Cristina called.

It was Julian. Emma looked at him in surprise, the younger Julian of her memory blurring back into the Julian standing in front of her: a nearly grown-up Julian, tall and muscular, his curls unruly, a hint of stubble prickling along his jawline.

"Do you know where Mark is?" he asked, without preamble.

"Isn't he in his room?" Emma said. "He left during dinner, so I thought—"

Julian shook his head. "He's not there. Could he be in your room?"

It cost him visible effort to ask, Emma thought. She saw Cristina bite her lip and prayed Julian wouldn't notice. He could never find out how much Cristina knew.

"No," Emma said. "I locked my door." She shrugged. "I don't completely trust the Centurions."

Julian ran a hand distractedly through his hair. "Look—I'm worried about Mark. Come with me and I'll show you what I mean."

Cristina and Emma followed Julian to Mark's room; the door was propped wide open. Julian went in first, and then Emma and Cristina, both of them glancing around carefully as if Mark might be found hiding in a closet somewhere.

Mark's room had changed a great deal since he'd first come back from Faerie. Then it had been dusty, a clearly unused space kept empty for the sake of memory. All his things had been cleared out and put into storage, and the curtains, filmed with dust, had been always drawn.

It was very different now. Mark had folded his clothes in neat stacks at the foot of his bed; he'd told Emma once that he didn't see the point of a wardrobe or a dresser, since all they did was hide your clothes from you.

The windowsills were covered with small items from nature— flowers in various stages of drying, leaves and cactus needles, shells from the beach. The bed was made neatly; clearly he hadn't slept in it once.

Julian looked away from the too-orderly bed. "His boots are gone," he said. "He only had the one pair. They were supposed to ship more from Idris, but they haven't yet."

"His jacket, too," Emma said. It had been his only heavy one, denim lined with shearling. "His bag . . . he had a duffel bag, didn't he?"

Cristina gave a gasp. Emma and Julian both swung to look at her as she reached up for a piece of paper that had just appeared, floating at shoulder height. Glowing runes sealed it shut; they faded as she caught the fire-message out of the air. "Addressed to me," she said, tearing it open. "From Mark." Her eyes scanned the page; her cheeks paled, and she handed over the paper without a word.

Julian took the message, and Emma read over his shoulder as he studied it.

> *My dear Cristina,*
> *I know you will show this to the right people at the right time. I can always trust you to do what is necessary when it needs to be done.*
> *By now you know what has happened with Kieran's arrest. Though things ended badly between us, he was my protector for many Faerie years. I owe him and cannot leave him to die in the grim Court of his father. I take the moon's road for Faerie tonight. Tell my brothers and sisters I will return to them as soon as I can. Tell Emma I will be back. I returned to them from the Land Under the Hill once before. I will do it again.*
> *Mark Blackthorn*

Julian crumpled the paper viciously between unsteady fingers. "I'm going after him."

Emma started to reach for his arm before remembering, and dropping her hand to her side. "I'm going with you."

"No," Julian said. "Do you understand what Mark's trying to do? He can't invade the Unseelie Court by himself. The King of Shadows will have him killed before you can blink."

"Of course I understand," said Emma. "That's why we need to get to Mark before he makes it to an entrance to Faerie. Once he enters the Fair Folk's Lands, it'll be practically impossible to intercept him."

"There is also the issue of time," said Cristina. "Once he crosses the border, time will be different for him. He could come back in three days, or three weeks—"

"Or three years," said Emma grimly.

""Which is why I should go after him now," said Julian. "Before he makes it into Faerie and time starts being our enemy—"

"I can help with that," Cristina said.

Faeries had been Cristina's special field of study when she was growing up. She'd once confessed to Emma that this had been partly because of Mark, and what she'd learned about him as a child. He'd fascinated her, the Shadowhunter boy taken by faeries during the Dark War.

Cristina touched the pendant at her throat, the golden pendant that bore an image of Raziel. "This is a faerie-blessed charm. My family has . . ." She hesitated. "Many of them. Years ago, they were close with the Fair Folk. We still have many tokens of their regard. We speak of it little, though, as the Clave's attitude toward those who befriend Fair Folk is . . ." She glanced around Mark's room. "As you know it to be."

"What does the charm do?" said Emma.

"It keeps time from passing too quickly for mortals in the Fair Folk's realm." Cristina held the pendant between her fingers, gazing at Jules with quiet inquiry as if to say she had many more surprises up her neat sleeves, if he cared to hear them.

"It's only one pendant," said Julian. "How can it protect us all?"

"If I wear it into the realm, the protection will extend to you and Emma, and Mark, too, as long as you do not go too far away from me."

Julian leaned against the wall and sighed. "And I suppose you're not going to consider just giving it to me, so I can wear it into Faerie? By myself?"

"Absolutely not," Cristina said primly. "It's a family heirloom."

Emma could have kissed Cristina. She settled for winking at her. The corner of Cristina's lip curled up slightly.

"Then the three of us will go," Emma said, and Julian seemed to realize there would be no point in disagreement. He nodded at her, and there was a little of the old *parabatai* look in his eye, the look that said that he expected the two of them to enter into danger. Together.

"The pendant will also allow us take the moon's road," said Cristina. "Usually only those with faerie blood can access it." She squared her shoulders. "Mark will not imagine that we could follow him; that is why he sent the note."

"The moon's road?" Julian said. "What is that, exactly?"

At that, Cristina did smile. It was an odd smile—not quite a look of happiness, and Emma expected that she was too worried for that—but there was a little bit of wonder in it, the look of someone who was getting to experience something they never thought they'd get a chance to do.

"I'll show you," she said.

They gathered their things swiftly. The house was dark, unusually alive with the untidy breathing of multiple sleepers. As Julian moved down the hallway, sliding the straps of his pack over his shoulders, he saw Ty asleep in front of Kit's room, half-sitting up, his chin in his hand. A book was open beside him on the floor.

Julian paused at the door to the attic. He hesitated. He could leave a note, walk away. That would be the easier thing to do. There wasn't much time; they had to get to Mark before he got to Faerie. It wouldn't be cowardly. Just practical. Just—

He shoved the door open and pounded up the stairs. Arthur was where he had left him, at his desk. Moonlight streamed in, angular, through the skylight.

Arthur dropped his pen and turned to look at Julian. Gray hair framed his tired Blackthorn eyes. It was like looking at a blurred picture of Julian's father, something that had been flawed in the development process, pulling the angles of his face out of familiar alignment.

"I have to leave for a few days," Julian said. "If you need anything, talk to Diana. Not to anyone else. Just Diana."

Arthur's eyes seemed glazed. "You are—where are you going, Julian?"

Julian considered lying. He was good at lying, and it came easily to him. But for some reason, he didn't want to.

"Mark went—back," he said. "I'm going to get him, hopefully before he crosses over into Faerie."

A shudder went through Arthur's body. "You're going after your brother in Faerie?" he said hoarsely, and Julian remembered the shreds of what he knew of his uncle's story—that he had been trapped with Julian's father, Andrew, in Faerie for years, that Andrew had fallen in love with a gentry woman and fathered Helen and Mark on her, but Arthur had been separated from him, locked away, tortured with enchantments.

"Yes." Julian shifted his pack to one shoulder.

Arthur reached his hand out, as if he meant to take Julian's, and Julian flinched back, startled. His uncle never touched him. Arthur dropped his hand. "In the republic of Rome," he said, "there was always a servant assigned to every general who won a war. When the general rode through the streets, accepting the thanks of the grateful people, the servant's task was to whisper in his ear, 'Respice post te. Hominem te esse memento. Memento mori.'"

"Look behind you," Julian translated. "Remember that you are a man. Remember that you will die." A faint shiver went up his spine.

"You're young, but you're not immortal," Arthur said. "If you find yourself in Faerie, and I pray that you do not, for it is Hell there if there ever was a Hell—if you find yourself there, listen to nothing the faeries tell you. Listen to none of their promises. Swear to me, Julian."

Julian exhaled. He thought of that long-ago general, being exhorted not to let the glory go to his head. To remember that everything passed. Everything went. Happiness went, and so did loss and pain.

Everything but love.

"I swear," he said.

"We have to wait for the moment," said Cristina. "Where the moon on the water seems solid. You can see it if you look—like the green flash."

She smiled at Emma, who stood between Jules and Cristina, the three of them in a line at the edge of the ocean. There was little wind and the ocean stretched out before them thick and black, edged with white where the water met the sand. Surges of sea foam where the waves had broken and spent themselves on the tideline pushed seaweed and bits of shells farther up the beach.

The sky had cleared from the earlier storm. The moon was high, casting a perfect, unbroken line of light across the water, reaching toward the horizon. The waves made a soft noise like whispers as they spilled around Emma's feet, the surf lapping at her water-proofed boots.

Jules had his gaze on his watch—it had been his father's, a large old-fashioned mechanical watch, gleaming on his wrist. Emma saw with a slight lurch that the sea-glass bracelet she'd fashioned for him once was still on his wrist beside it, shining in the moonlight.

"Almost midnight," he said. "I wonder how much of a head start Mark has."

"It depends how long he had to wait for the right moment to step on the path," said Cristina. "Such moments come and go. Midnight is only one of them."

"So how are we planning on capturing him?" Emma said. "Just your basic chase and tackle, or are we going to try to distract him with the power of dance, and then lasso his ankles?"

"Jokes not helping," said Julian, staring at the water.

"Jokes always help," said Emma. "Especially when we're not doing anything else but waiting for water to solidify—"

Cristina squeaked. "Go! *Now!*"

Emma went first, leaping over a small wave crashing at her feet. Half her brain was still telling her that she was throwing herself into water, that she'd splash down into it. The impact when her boots struck a hard surface was jarring.

She took a few running steps and spun around to face the beach. She was standing on a gleaming path that looked as if it were made of hard rock crystal, cut thin as glass. The moonlight on the water had become solid. Julian was already behind her, balanced on the shimmering line, and Cristina was leaping up onto the path behind him.

She heard Cristina gasp as she landed. As Shadowhunters, they had all seen wonders, but there was something distinctly Faerie about this kind of magic: It seemed to take place in the interstices of the normal world, between light and shadow, between one minute and another. As Nephilim they existed in their own space. This was *Between.*

"Let's move," Julian said, and Emma began to walk. The path

was wide; it seemed to flex and curl under her feet with the motion and ripple of the tide. It was like walking on a bridge held suspended over a chasm.

Except that when she looked down, she didn't see empty space; she saw what she feared much more. The deep darkness of the ocean, where her parents' dead bodies had floated before they washed up on the shore. For years she had imagined them struggling, dying, underwater, miles of sea all around, totally alone. She knew more now about how they'd died, knew they'd been dead when Malcolm Fade had consigned their bodies to the sea. But you couldn't speak to fear, couldn't tell it the truth: Fear lived in your bones.

This far out, Emma would have expected the water to be so deep it was opaque. But the moonlight made it glow as if from within. She could gaze down into it as if into an aquarium.

She saw the fronds of seaweed, moving and dancing with the push and pull of the tides. The flutter of schools of fish. Darker shadows, too, bigger ones. Flickers of movement, heavy and enormous—a whale, perhaps, or something bigger and worse—water demons could grow to the size of football fields. She imagined the path breaking up suddenly, giving way, and all of them plunging into the darkness, the enormity all around them, cold and deathly and filled with blind-eyed, shark-toothed monsters, and the Angel knew what else rising up out of the deep. . . .

"Don't look down." It was Julian, approaching on the path. Cristina was a little behind them, looking around in wonder. "Look straight ahead at the horizon. Walk toward that."

She raised her chin. She could feel Jules next to her, feel the warmth coming off his skin, raising the hair along her arms. "I'm fine."

"You're not." He said it flatly. "I know how you feel about the ocean."

They were far out from shore now—it was a shining line in the distance, the highway a ribbon of moving lights, the houses and restaurants along the coastline glimmering. "Well, as it turns out, my parents didn't die in the ocean." She took a shuddering breath. "They didn't drown."

"Knowing that doesn't wipe out years of bad dreams." Julian glanced toward her. The wind blew soft tendrils of his hair against his cheekbones. She remembered what it felt like to have her hands in that hair, how holding him had anchored her not just to the world, but to herself.

"I hate feeling like this," she said, and for a moment even she wasn't sure what she was talking about. "I hate being afraid. It makes me feel weak."

"Emma, everyone's afraid of something." Julian moved slightly closer; she felt his shoulder bump hers. "We fear things because we value them. We fear losing people because we love them. We fear dying because we value being alive. *Don't* wish you didn't fear anything. All that would mean is that you didn't feel anything."

"Jules—" She started to turn toward him in surprise at the intensity in his voice, but paused when she heard Cristina's footsteps quicken, and then her voice, raised in recognition, calling:

"Mark!"

8

NEAR THE RIVER

Emma saw Mark immediately. A shadow out on the gleaming path before them, the moonlight sparking off his pale hair. He didn't seem to have noticed them yet.

Emma began to run, Cristina and Jules at her heels. Though the path surged and dipped under her, she was used to running on the beach where the soft sand gave way under her feet. She could see Mark clearly now: He'd stopped walking, and turned to face them, looking astonished.

His gear was gone. He was wearing clothes similar to the ones he'd come to the Institute in, though clean and undamaged: linen and soft, tanned hide, high laced boots and a duffel bag slung over his back. Emma could see the stars reflected in his wide eyes as she drew closer to him.

He dropped the duffel bag at his feet, looking accusingly at his three pursuers. "What are you doing here?"

"Seriously?" Julian kicked Mark's duffel bag aside, grabbing hold of his brother's shoulders. "What are *you* doing here?"

Julian was taller than Mark, a fact that always struck Emma as odd—Mark had been taller for so many years. Taller and older. But he was neither now. He looked like a slim pale blade in the darkness, against Julian's more solid strength and height. He looked as if he might at any moment turn into moonlight on the waves and vanish.

He turned his gaze to Cristina. "You got my fire-message."

She nodded, tendrils of her dark hair, caught in a jeweled clip at the back of her head, curling around her face. "We all read it."

Mark closed his eyes. "I had not thought you could follow me on the moon's road."

"But we did." Julian tightened his hands on Mark's shoulders. "You're not going anywhere in Faerie, much less alone."

"It's for Kieran," Mark said simply.

"Kieran betrayed you," said Julian.

"They will *kill* him, Jules," said Mark. "Because of me. Kieran killed Iarlath because of me." He opened his eyes to gaze into his brother's face. "I should not have tried to leave without telling you. That was unfair of me. I knew you would try to stop me, and I knew I had little time. I will never forgive Kieran for what happened to you and Emma, but I will not leave him to death and torture, either."

"Mark, the Fair Folk aren't fond of you," said Julian. "They were forced to give you back, and they hate giving back anything they take. If you go into Faerie, they'll keep you there if they can, and it won't be easy, and they will hurt you. I won't let that happen."

"Then you will be my jailer, brother?" Mark held out his hands, palms up. "You will bind my wrists in cold iron, my ankles with thorns?"

Julian flinched. It was too dark to see Mark's Blackthorn features, his blue-green eye, and in the dimness the brothers seemed only a Shadowhunter and a faerie, eternally at odds. "Emma," Julian said, removing his hands from Mark's shoulders. There was a desperate bitterness in his voice. "Mark loves you. *You* convince him."

Emma felt Julian's bitterness like thorns under her skin, and heard Mark's anguished words again: *Will you be my jailer?* "We aren't going to stop you from going. We're going to go with you."

Even in the moonlight, she could see Mark's face lose color. "No. You're obviously Nephilim. You're in gear. Your runes aren't hidden. Shadowhunters are not well-loved in the Land Under the Hill."

"Apparently only Kieran is," said Julian. "He's lucky to have your loyalty, Mark, since we don't."

At that, Mark flushed and turned toward his brother, his eyes glittering angrily. "All right, stop—stop," Emma said, taking a step toward them. The shimmering water bent and flexed beneath her feet. "Both of you—"

"Who walks the path of moonlight?"

A figure approached, its voice a deep boom above the waves. Julian's hand went to the hilt of the dagger at his waist. Emma's seraph blade was out; Cristina had her balisong in hand. Mark's fingers had reached for the place where the elf-bolt Kieran had given him had once rested in the hollow of his throat. It was gone now. His face tightened before relaxing into recognition.

"It's a phouka," he said under his breath. "Mostly, they're harmless."

The figure on the path before them had drawn closer. It was a tall faerie, dressed in ragged trousers held up by a belt of rope. Thin strands of gold were woven into his long dark hair and gleamed against his dark skin. His feet were bare.

He spoke, and his voice sounded like the tide at sunset. "Seek you to enter through the Gate of Lir?"

"Yes," said Mark.

Metallic gold eyes without irises or pupils passed over Mark, Cristina, Julian, and Emma. "Only one of you is fey," the phouka said. "The others are human. No—Nephilim." Thin lips curled into a smile. "That is a surprise. How many of you wish passage through the gate to the Shadow Lands?"

"All of us," said Emma. "The four."

"If the King or Queen finds you, they will kill you," said the phouka. "The Fair Folk are not friendly to the angel-blooded, not since the Cold Peace."

"I am half-faerie," said Mark. "My mother was the Lady Nerissa of the Seelie Court."

The phouka raised his eyebrows. "Her death grieved us all."

"And these are my brothers and sisters," Mark continued, pressing his advantage. "They would accompany me; I will protect them."

The phouka shrugged. "It is not my concern what befalls you in the Lands," he said. "Only that first you must pay a toll."

"No payments," said Julian, his hand tightening on his dagger hilt. "No tolls."

The phouka smiled. "Come here and speak to me a moment, in private, and then decide if you would pay my price. I will not force you."

Julian's expression darkened, but he stepped forward. Emma strained to hear what he was saying to the phouka, but the sound of wind and waves slid between them. Behind them, the air swirled and clouded: Emma thought she could see a shape in it, arched like the shape of a door.

Julian stood motionless as the phouka spoke, but Emma saw a muscle twitch in his cheek. A moment later, he unsnapped his father's watch from around his wrist and dropped it into the phouka's hand.

"One payment," said the phouka loudly, as Julian turned away. "Who would come next?"

"I will," said Cristina, and moved carefully across the path toward the phouka. Julian rejoined Mark and Emma.

"Did he threaten you?" Emma whispered. "Jules, if he threatened you—"

"He didn't," Julian said. "I wouldn't let Cristina near him if he had."

Emma turned to watch as Cristina reached up and pulled the jeweled clip from her hair. It cascaded down over her back and shoulders, blacker than the night sea. She handed the clip over and began to walk back toward them, looking dazed.

"Mark Blackthorn will go last," said the phouka. "Let the golden-haired girl come to me next."

Emma could feel the others watching her as she went toward the phouka, Julian more intensely than the rest. She thought of the painting he'd done of her, where she'd risen above the ocean with a body made of stars.

She wondered what he'd done with those paintings. If he'd thrown them all out. Were they gone, burned? Her heart ached at the thought. Such lovely work of Jules's, every brushstroke a whisper, a promise.

She reached the faerie, who stood slyly smiling as his kind did when they were amused. All around them the sea stretched, black and silver. The phouka bent his head to speak to her; the wind rushed up around them. She stood with him inside a circle of cloud. She could no longer see the others.

"If you're going to threaten me," she said, before he could speak, "understand that I will hunt you down for it, if not now, then later. And I will make you die for a long time."

The phouka laughed. His teeth were also gold, tipped in silver. "Emma Carstairs," he said. "I see you know little about phoukas. We are seducers, not bullies. When I tell you what I tell you, you will wish to go to Faerie. You will wish to give me what I ask for."

"And what do you ask for?"

"That stele," he said, pointing at the one in her belt.

Everything in Emma rebelled. The stele had been given to her by Jace, years ago in Idris, after the Dark War. It was a symbol of everything that had marked her life after the War. Clary had given her words, and she treasured them: Jace had given her a stele, and with it given a grief-stricken and frightened girl a purpose. When she touched the stele, it whispered that purpose to her: *The future is yours now. Make it what you will.*

"What use could a faerie have for a stele?" she asked. "You don't draw runes, and they only work for Shadowhunters."

"No use for a stele," he said. "But for the precious demon bone of the handle, quite a lot."

She shook her head. "Choose something else."

The phouka leaned in. He smelled of salt and seaweed baking in the sun. "Listen," he said. "If you enter Faerie, you will again see the face of someone you loved, who is dead."

"What?" Shock stabbed through Emma. "You're lying."

"You know I cannot lie."

Emma's mouth had gone dry.

"You must not tell the others what I told you, or it will not happen," said the phouka. "Nor can I tell you what it means. I am only a messenger—but the message is true. If you wish to look again upon one you have loved and lost, if you wish to hear their voice, you must pass through the Gate of Lir."

Emma drew the stele from her belt. A pang went through her as she handed it over. She turned away blindly from the phouka, his words ringing in her ears. She was barely aware of Mark brushing past her, the last to speak to the water faerie. Her heart was pounding too hard.

One you have loved and lost. But there were many, so many, lost in the Dark War. Her parents—but she dared not even think of them; she would lose her ability to think, to go on. The Blackthorns' father, Andrew. Her old tutor, Katerina. Maybe—

The sound of wind and waves died down. Mark stood before the phouka in silence, his face pale: All three of the others looked stricken, and Emma burned to know what the faerie had told them. What could compel Jules, or Mark, or Cristina, to cooperate?

The phouka thrust out his hand. "Lir's Gate opens," he said. "Take it now, or flee back toward the shore; the moon's road begins to dissolve already."

There was a sound like shattering ice, melting under spring sunlight. Emma looked down: The shining path below was riven with black where the water was springing up through cracks.

Julian grabbed her hand. "We have to go," he said. Behind Mark, who stood ahead of them on the path, an archway of water had formed. It gleamed bright silver, the inside of it churning with water and motion.

With a laugh, the phouka leaped from the path with an elegant dive and slipped between the waves. Emma realized she had no idea what Mark had given him. Not that it seemed to matter now. The path between them was shattering rapidly: Now it was in pieces, like ice floes in the Arctic.

Cristina was on Emma's other side. The three of them pushed forward, leaping from one solid piece of path to another. Mark was gesturing toward them, shouting, the archway behind him solidifying. Emma could see green grass through it, moonlight and trees. She pushed Cristina forward; Mark caught her, and the two of them vanished through the gate.

She moved to take a step forward, but the path gave way under her feet. For what seemed like much more than seconds she tumbled toward the black water. Then Julian had caught her. His arms around her, they fell together through the arch.

The shadows had lengthened in the attic. Arthur sat motionless, gazing out the window with its torn paper at the moonlight over the sea. He could guess where Julian and the others were now: He knew the moon's road, as he knew the other roads of Faerie. He had been driven down them by hooting packs of pixies and goblins, riding ahead of their masters, the unearthly beautiful princes and princesses of the gentry. Once in a winter forest he had fallen, and his body had shattered the ice of a pond. He recalled watching his blood spray across the pond's silvered surface.

"How pretty," a faerie lady had mused, as Arthur's blood melted into the ice.

He thought of his mind that way sometimes: a shattered surface reflecting back a broken and imperfect picture. He knew his madness was not like human madness. It came and went, sometimes leaving him barely touched so he hoped it was gone forever. Then it would return, crushing him beneath a parade of people no one else could see, a chorus of voices no one else could hear.

The medicine helped, but the medicine was gone. Julian had always brought the medicine, from the time he was a small boy. Arthur wasn't sure how old he was now. Old enough. Sometimes Arthur wondered if he loved the boy. If he loved any of his brother's children. There had been times he had awoken from dreams in which terrible things had happened to them with his face wet with tears.

But that might have been guilt. He had lacked either the ability to raise them, or the bravery to let the Clave replace him with a better guardian. Though who would have kept them together? No one, perhaps, and family should be together.

The door at the foot of the stairs creaked. Arthur turned eagerly. Perhaps Julian had thought better of his mad plan and returned. The moon's road was dangerous. The sea itself was full of treachery. He had grown up near the sea, in Cornwall, and he recalled its monsters. *And bitter as blood is the spray; and the crests are as fangs that devour.*

Or perhaps there had never been monsters.

She appeared at the top of the steps and looked at him coolly.

Her hair was pulled back so tightly her skin seemed stretched. She tilted her head, taking in the cramped, dirty room, the papered-over windows. There was something in her face, something that stirred a flicker of memory.

Something that made cold terror wash through him. He gripped the arms of his chair, his mind chattering with bits of old poetry. *Her skin was white as leprosy, the nightmare Life-in-Death was she—*

"Arthur Blackthorn, I presume?" she said with a demure smile. "I'm Zara Dearborn. I believe you knew my father."

Emma landed hard on thick grass, tangled up in Julian. For a moment he was propped over her, elbows on the ground, his pale face luminous in the moonlight. The air around them was cold, but his body was warm against hers. She felt the expansion of his chest as he inhaled a sharp breath, the current of air against her cheek as he turned his face quickly away from hers.

A moment later he was on his feet, reaching down to pull her up after him. But she scrambled upright on her own, spinning around to see that they were standing in a clearing surrounded by trees.

The moonlight was bright enough for Emma to see that the grass was intensely green, the trees hung with fruit that was vividly colored: purple plums, red apples, star- and rose-shaped fruits that Emma didn't recognize. Mark and Cristina were there too, under the trees.

Mark had pushed the sleeves of his shirt up and was holding his hands out as if he were touching the air of Faerie, feeling it on his skin. He tipped his head back, his mouth slightly open; Emma, looking at him, blushed. It felt like a private moment, as if she were watching someone reconnect with a lover.

"Emma," Cristina breathed. "Look." She pointed upward, at the sky.

The stars were different. They arched and whirled in patterns that Emma didn't recognize, and they had *colors*—icy blue, frost green, shimmering gold, brilliant silver.

"It's so beautiful," she whispered. She saw Julian look over at her, but it was Mark who spoke. He no longer looked quite so abandoned to the night, but he still seemed a little dazed, as if the air of Faerie were wine and he had drunk too much.

"The Hunt rode through the sky of Faerie sometimes," he said. "In the sky the stars look like the crushed dust of jewels—powdered ruby and sapphire and diamond."

"I knew about the stars in Faerie," Cristina said in an awed, quiet voice. "But I never thought I would see them myself."

"Should we rest?" Julian asked. He was prowling the outline of the clearing, peering between the trees. Trust Jules to ask the practical questions. "Gather our energy for traveling tomorrow?"

Mark shook his head. "We can't. We must travel through the night. I know only how to navigate the Lands by the stars."

"Then we're going to need Energy runes." Emma held out her arm to Cristina. It wasn't meant as a deliberate snub to Jules—runes your *parabatai* put on you were always more powerful—but she could still feel where his body had crashed against hers when they'd fallen. She could still feel the visceral twist inside her when his breath had ghosted against her cheek. She needed him not to be close to her right now, not to see what was in her eyes. The way Mark had looked at the sky of Faerie: that was how she imagined she looked at Julian.

Cristina's touch was warm and comforting, her stele swift and skilled, its tip tracing the shape of an Energy rune onto Emma's forearm. Finished, she let Emma's wrist go. Emma waited for the usual alert, searing heat, like a double jolt of caffeine.

Nothing happened.

"It's not working," she said, with a frown.

"Let me see—" Cristina stepped forward. She glanced down at Emma's skin, and her eyes widened. "Look."

The Mark, black as ink when Cristina had placed it on Emma's forearm, was turning pale and silvery. Fading, like melting frost. In seconds it had blended back into Emma's skin and was gone.

"What on earth . . . ?" Emma began. But Julian had already whirled on Mark. "Runes," he said. "Do they work? In Faerie?"

Mark looked astonished. "It never occurred to me that they wouldn't," he said. "No one's ever mentioned it."

"I've studied Faerie for years," Cristina said. "I've never seen it said anywhere that runes do not work in the Lands."

"When was the last time you tried to use one here?" Emma asked Mark.

He shook his head, blond curls falling into his eyes. He shoved them back with narrow fingers. "I can't remember," he said. "I didn't have a stele—they broke it—but my witchlight always worked—" He dug into his pocket and drew out a round, polished rune-stone. They all watched, breathless, as he held it up, waiting for the light to come, to shine brilliantly from his palm.

Nothing happened.

With a soft curse, Julian drew one of his seraph blades from his belt. The *adamas* gleamed dully in the moonlight. He turned it so that the blade lay flat, reflecting the multicolored brilliance of the stars. "*Michael,*" he said.

Something sparked inside the blade—a brief, dull gleam. Then it was gone. Julian stared at it. A seraph blade that could not be brought to life was barely more use than a plastic knife: dull-bladed, heavy, and short.

With a violent jerk of his arm, Julian cast the blade aside. It skidded across the grass. He raised his eyes. Emma could sense how tightly he was holding back. She felt it like a pressure in her own body that made it hard to breathe.

"So," he said. "We're going to have to journey across Faerie, a place where Shadowhunters aren't welcome, using only the stars to navigate, and we can't use runes, seraph blades, or witchlight. Is that the situation, roughly?"

"I would say it's the situation exactly," said Mark.

"Also, we're heading for the Unseelie Court," Emma added. "Which is supposed to be like one of those horror movies Dru likes, but less, you know, fun."

"Then we will travel at night," Cristina said. She pointed into the distance. "There are landmarks that I've seen on maps. Do you see those ridges in the distance, against the sky? I think that those are the Thorn Mountains. The Unseelie Lands lie in their shadow. It is not so far away."

Emma could see Mark relax at the sound of Cristina's sensible voice. It didn't seem to be working on Julian, though. His jaw was clenched, his hands rigid fists at his sides.

It wasn't that Julian didn't get angry. It was that he didn't let himself show it. People thought he was quiet, calm, but that was deceptive. Emma recalled something she had read once: that volcanoes had the lushest green slopes, the loveliest and quietest aspect, because the fire that pulsed through them kept their earth from ever freezing.

But when they erupted, they could rain down devastation for miles.

"Jules," she said. He glanced over at her; fury gleamed behind his eyes. "We might not have witchlight, or runes, but we are still Shadowhunters. With everything that means. We can do this. We *can*."

It felt like a clumsy speech to her, but she saw the fire die in his eyes. "You're right," he said. "Sorry."

"And I'm sorry for bringing you all here," said Mark. "If I had known—about the runes—but it must be something recent, very much so. . . ."

"You didn't bring us here," said Cristina. "We followed you.

And we all came through not just for you but because of what the phouka told each of us; isn't that true?"

One you have loved and lost. "It's true for me," said Emma. She glanced at the sky. "We should get going, though. Morning is probably in just a few hours. And if we don't have Energy runes, we'll have to get our energy the old-fashioned way."

Mark looked puzzled. "Drugs?"

"Chocolate," Emma said. "I brought *chocolate.* Mark, where do you even come up with these things?"

Mark smiled crookedly, shrugging one shoulder. "Faerie humor?"

"I thought faeries mostly made jokes at other people's expense and played pranks on mundanes," said Julian.

"Sometimes they tell very long, rhyming stories they think are hilarious," said Mark. "But I have to admit I never really understood why."

Julian sighed. "That actually sounds worse than anything else I've heard about the Unseelie Court."

Mark shot Julian a grateful look, as if to say that he understood that his brother had mastered his temper in part for him, for all of them, so that they would be all right. So that they could continue on their way, and find Kieran, with Julian leading them as he always did. "Come," Mark said, turning. "It is this way—we should begin walking; it may not be very many more hours until dawn."

Mark headed into the shadows between the trees. Mist clung to the branches, like ropes of white and silver. Leaves rustled softly in the wind above their heads. Julian moved to walk up ahead next to his brother; Emma could hear him asking, "Puns? At least promise me there won't be puns."

"The way that boys tell each other they love each other is so very odd," said Cristina as she and Emma ducked beneath a branch. "Why can't they just say it? Is it so difficult?"

Emma grinned at her friend. "I love you, Cristina," she said. "And I'm glad you're getting to visit Faerie, even if it's under weird circumstances. Maybe you can find a hot faerie guy and forget about Imperfect Diego."

Cristina smiled. "I love you, too, Emma," she said. "And maybe I will."

Kit's list of grievances against the Shadowhunters had now gotten long enough that he'd started writing it down. *Stupid hot people,* he'd written, *won't let me go home and get my stuff.*

They won't tell me anything about what it would mean to actually become a Shadowhunter. Would I have to go somewhere and train?

They won't tell me how long I can stay here, except "as long as you need to." Don't I have to go to school eventually? Some kind of school?

They won't talk about the Cold Peace or how it sucks.

They won't let me eat cookies.

He thought for a while, and then crossed that one out. They did let him eat cookies; he just suspected they were judging him for it.

They don't seem to understand what autism is, or mental illness, or therapy, or medical treatment. Do they believe in things like chemotherapy? What if I get cancer? I probably won't get cancer. But if I did . . .

They won't tell me how Tessa and Jem found my dad. Or why my dad hated Shadowhunters so much.

That one was the hardest to write. Kit had always thought of his father as a small-time con man, a lovable rogue, a sort of Han Solo type, swindling his way across the galaxy. But lovable rogues didn't get torn apart by demons the moment their elaborate protection spells fell apart. And though mostly Kit was confused by what had happened at the Shadow Market, he had learned one thing: His dad had *not* been like Han Solo.

Sometimes, in the dark watches of the night, Kit wondered who he was like himself.

Speaking of the dark watches of the night, he had a new griev-ance to add to his list. *They make me get up early.*

Diana, whose official title was tutor but who seemed to function as a guardian-slash-high school principal, had woken Kit up early in the morning and herded him, along with Ty and Livvy, into a corner office with an expansive view and a massive glass desk. She looked pissed off the way adults sometimes looked pissed off when they were angry at someone else, but they were going to take it out on you.

Kit was correct. Diana was currently furious at Julian, Emma, Mark, and Cristina, who, according to Arthur, had disappeared to Faerie in the dead of night to rescue someone named Kieran who Kit had never met. Further discussion illuminated that Kieran was the son of the Unseelie King and Mark's ex-boyfriend, both of which were interesting pieces of information that Kit filed away for later.

"This is not good," Diana finished. "Any travel to Faerie is entirely off-limits to Nephilim without special permissions."

"But they'll come back, right?" Ty said. He sounded strained. "*Mark* will come back?"

"Of course they'll come back," said Livvy. "It's just a mission. A rescue mission," she added, turning to Diana. "Won't the Clave understand they had to go?"

"Rescuing a faerie—no," Diana said, shaking her head. "They are not entitled to our protection under the Accords. The Centuri-ons can't know. The Clave would be furious."

"I won't tell," said Ty.

"I won't either," agreed Livvy. "Obviously."

They both looked at Kit.

"I don't even know why I'm here," he said.

"You have a point," said Livvy. She turned to Diana. "Why *is* he here?"

"You seem to have a way of knowing everything," Diana said to

Kit. "I thought it would be better to control your information. And get a promise from you."

"That I won't tell? Of course I won't tell. I don't even like the Centurions. They're . . ." *What I always thought Shadowhunters would be like. You're not. You're all . . . different.* "Jerks," he finished.

"I cannot *believe*," Livvy said, "that Julian and them have found a fun adventure to go on and just left the rest of us here to fetch towels for Centurions."

Diana looked surprised. "I thought you'd be upset," she said. "Worried about them."

Livvy shook her head. Her long hair, shades lighter than Ty's, flew around her. "That they're off having fun and getting to see Faerie? While we drudge around here? When they get back, I'm going to have *words* with Julian."

"Which words?" Ty looked confused for a moment, before his face cleared. "Oh," he said. "You're going to curse him out."

"I'm going to use every bad word I know, and look up some other ones," said Livvy.

Diana was biting her lip. "You're really all right?"

Ty nodded. "Cristina has studied Faerie extensively, Mark was a Hunter, and Julian and Emma are clever and brave," he said. "I'm sure they'll be fine."

Diana looked stunned. Kit had to admit he was surprised too. The Blackthorns had struck him as a family so close-knit that "enmeshed" didn't begin to cover it. But Livvy kept up her cheerful annoyance when they went to tell Dru and Tavvy that the others had gone to the Shadowhunter Academy to fetch something—she was quite convincing, too, as she told them how Cristina had gone along because visiting the Academy was now a required part of one's travel year—and they repeated the same story to a glowering Diego and a bunch of Centurions, including his fiancée, who Kit had taken to calling Loathsome Zara in his mind.

"In sum," Livvy finished sweetly, "you may have to launder some of your own towels. Now if you'll excuse us, Ty and I are going to take Kit here on a tour of the perimeter."

Zara arched an eyebrow. "The perimeter?"

"The wards *you* just put up," said Livvy, and marched outside. She didn't actually drag Ty and Kit after her physically, but something about the force of her personality accomplished basically the same thing. The Institute doors fell shut behind them as she was already clattering down the front steps.

"Did you see the look on those Centurions' faces?" she demanded as they made their way around the massive side of the Institute. She was wearing boots and denim shorts that showed off her long, tanned legs. Kit attempted to seem as if he wasn't looking.

"I don't think they appreciated what you said about washing their own towels," said Ty.

"Maybe I should have drawn them a map to where the detergent is," said Livvy. "You know, since they like maps so much."

Kit laughed. Livvy glanced over at him, half-suspicious. "What?"

They'd passed the parking lot behind the Institute and reached a low hedge of sagebrush, behind which was a statuary garden. Greek playwrights and historians stood around in plaster poses, holding wreaths of laurel. It seemed oddly out of place, but then Los Angeles was a city of things that didn't seem like they belonged where they were.

"It was funny," Kit said. "That was all."

She smiled. Her blue T-shirt matched her eyes, and the sunlight found the red and copper threads in her dark brown hair and made them shine. At first Kit had been a little unnerved by how much the Blackthorns all looked like each other—except Ty, of course—but he had to admit, if you had to share family traits, luminous blue-green eyes and wavy dark hair weren't bad ones.

The only things he shared with his father were moodiness and a penchant for burglary.

As for his mother—

"Ty!" Livvy called. "Ty, get down from there!"

They had moved far enough away from the house that they were now in real chaparral desert. Kit had only been in the Santa Monica Mountains a few times, on school trips. He remembered drinking in the air, the mix of salt and sagebrush, the soft breathless heat of the desert. Hasty green lizards bloomed like sudden leaves in between the scrub cactus, and disappeared just as quickly. Large rocks were tumbled everywhere—the castoffs of some fast-moving glacier, a million years ago.

"I will when I'm done with this." Ty was busy climbing one of the largest rocks, expertly finding handholds and footholds. He hauled himself up to the top, totally unself-conscious, arms out to keep his balance. He looked as if he were getting ready to launch himself into flight, his hair blowing back like dark wings.

"Is he going to be all right?" Kit asked, watching him climb.

"He's a really good climber," said Livvy. "It used to freak me out when we were younger. He didn't have any kind of realistic sense of when he was in danger or wasn't. I thought he was going to fall off the rocks at Leo Carillo and smash in his head. But Jules went with him everywhere and Diana showed him how, and he learned."

She looked up at her brother and smiled. Ty had raised himself up on the balls of his feet and was looking down at the ocean. Kit could almost imagine him on a desolate plain somewhere, with a black cloak flapping around him like a hero in a fantasy illustration.

Kit took a deep breath. "You didn't really believe what you told Diana," he said to Livvy. She whipped around to stare at him. "About not being worried about Julian and the others."

"Why do you think that?" Her tone was carefully neutral.

"I've been watching you," he said. "All of you."

"I know." She looked up at him with her bright eyes, half-amused. "It's like you've been taking mental notes."

"Habit. My dad taught me everyone in the world was divided into two categories. Those you could trick and cheat and the ones you couldn't. So you observe people. Try to figure out what they're about. How they tick."

"How do we tick?"

"Like a very complicated machine," said Kit. "You're all intertwined—one of you moves a little and that drives the others. And if you move the other way, that directs what they do too. You're more connected than any family I've seen. And you can't tell me you're not worried about Julian and the others—I know you are. I know what you people think about the Fair Folk."

"That they're evil? It's a lot more complicated than that, believe me."

Livvy's blue gaze darted away, toward her brother. Ty was lying down on his back on the rock now, barely visible. "So why would I lie to Diana?"

"Julian lies to protect all of you," said Kit. "If he's not around, then *you'll* lie to protect the younger ones. Nothing to worry about, Julian and Mark are off to the Unseelie Court, hope they send a postcard, wish we were there."

Livvy seemed poised between irritation and relief—angry that Kit had guessed the truth, relieved there was someone with whom she didn't have to pretend. "Do you think I convinced Diana?" she said finally.

"I think you convinced her *you* weren't worried," said Kit. "*She's* still worried. She's probably pulling whatever strings she's got to pull to figure out how to find them."

"We're pretty low on strings here, you might have noticed," Livvy said. "As Institutes go, we're a weird one."

"I don't really have a lot of points of reference. But I believe you."

"So you didn't actually tell me." Livvy tucked a piece of hair behind her ear. "Are we the kind of people you can trick and cheat, or not?"

"Not," said Kit. "But not because you're Shadowhunters. Because you genuinely seem to care about each other more than you care about yourselves. Which makes it hard to convince you to be selfish."

She took a few steps away, reaching out to touch a small red flower blooming on a silvery-green hedge. When she turned back to Kit, her hair was blowing around her face, and her eyes were unnaturally bright. For a moment, he worried she might be about to cry, or yell at him.

"Kiss me," she said.

Kit didn't know where he'd thought the conversation was going, but definitely not there. He just managed not to start coughing. "*What?*"

"You heard me." She moved back toward him, pacing slowly and deliberately. He tried not to stare at her legs again. "I asked you to kiss me."

"Why?"

She was starting to smile. Behind her, Ty was still balanced on his rock, gazing out to sea. "Haven't you ever kissed anyone before?" she inquired.

"Yes. I'm not sure how that's relevant, though, to you wanting me to kiss you right now, right here."

"Are you sure you're a Herondale? I'm pretty sure a Herondale would lunge at this kind of opportunity." She crossed her arms over her chest. "Is there some reason you don't want to kiss me?"

"For one, you have a terrifying older brother," said Kit.

"I do not have a terrifying older brother."

"That's true," Kit said. "You have *two*."

"Fine," Livvy said, dropping her arms and turning away. "Fine, if you don't want to—"

Kit caught her shoulder. It was warm under his grasp, the heat of her skin tactile through the thin material of her T-shirt. "I do, though."

To his surprise, he meant it. His world was sliding away from him; he felt as if he were falling toward something, a dark unknown, the ragged edge of unwanted choices. And here was a pretty girl offering him something to cling to, a way to forget, something to catch and hold, even if only for a moment.

The pulse fluttered lightly in her neck as she half-turned her head, her hair brushing his hand. "All right," she said.

"But tell me one thing. Why me? Why do you want to kiss *me*?"

"I've never kissed anyone," she said in a low voice. "In my whole life. I hardly ever *meet* anyone. It's us alone, against the whole world, and I don't mind that, I'd do anything for my family, but I feel like I'm missing all the chances I should have. You're my age, and you're a Shadowhunter, and you don't get on my nerves. I don't have that many options."

"You could kiss a Centurion," Kit suggested.

She turned around completely at that, his hand still on her shoulder, her expression indignant.

"Okay, I guess that suggestion was a little out of bounds," he admitted. The urge to kiss her had become overwhelming, so he gave up trying not to, and curved his arm around her shoulder, pulling her closer. Her eyes widened, and then she tilted her head back, her mouth angled toward his and their mouths slanted together surprisingly gently.

It was soft and sweet and warm, and she moved into the circle made by his arm, her hands coming to rest at first hesitantly and then with greater purpose on his shoulders. She gripped tightly, pulling him in, his eyes shutting against the blue dazzle of the ocean in the distance. He forgot the ground under his feet, the world around him, everything but the sense of being comforted by someone holding him. Someone caring.

"Livvy. Ty! *Kit!*"

It was Diana's voice. Kit snapped out of his daze and let Livvy go; she moved away from him looking surprised, one hand rising to touch her lips.

"All of you!" Diana called. "Get back here, now! I need your help!"

"So how was it?" Kit asked. "Okay for your first?"

"Not bad." Livvy lowered her hand. "You really put your back into it. I didn't expect that."

"Herondales don't do perfunctory kisses," said Kit. There was a brief flurry of movement, and Ty was down from the rock he'd climbed, picking his way toward them through the desert scrub.

Livvy gave a short, soft laugh. "I think that's the first time I've heard you call yourself a Herondale."

Ty joined them, his pale oval face unreadable. Kit couldn't tell anything from his expression—whether he'd seen Kit and Livvy kiss or not. Though what reason would he have to care if he had?

"Looks like it's going to be clear tonight," he said. "No clouds coming in."

Livvy said something about better weather for following suspicious Centurions, and she was already moving to walk next to Ty, like she always did. Kit followed after them, hands in the pockets of his jeans, though he could feel the Herondale ring, heavy on his finger, as if he had only now remembered the weight.

The Land Under the Hill. The Delightful Plain. The Place Beneath the Wave. The Lands of the Ever-Young.

As the hours wore on, all the names Emma had ever heard for Faerieland ran through her head. Conversation between the four of them had grown quieter and fallen eventually into an exhausted silence; Cristina trudged along beside Emma wordlessly, her pendant glimmering in the moonlight. Mark led the way, checking their path against the stars every short while. In the distance the Thorn Mountains became clearer and closer, rising stark and unforgettable against a sky the color of blackened sapphire.

The mountains weren't often visible, though. Mostly the path they followed wound through low-hanging trees that grew close together, boughs occasionally intertwining. More than once Emma would catch a glimpse of bright eyes flashing out from between the shadows. When tree branches rustled, she would look up to catch sight of shadows moving quickly above them, laughter trailing behind them like mist.

"These are the places of the wild fey," said Mark, as the road curved around a hill. "The gentry fey stay within the Courts or sometimes town. They like their creature comforts."

Here and there were signs of habitation: crumbled mossy bits of old stone walls, wooden fences cleverly fitted together without the use of nails. They passed through several villages in the hour before dawn: Every one of them was shuttered and dark, windows broken and empty. As they went farther into Faerie they began to see something else, too. The first time they saw it, Emma stopped short and exclaimed—the grass they'd been walking on had suddenly dissolved under her feet, puffing up white and gray like ash around her ankles.

She looked around in astonishment and discovered that the others were staring too. They had wandered into the edge of a ragged circle of diseased-looking land. It reminded Emma of photos she'd seen of crop circles. Everything within the perimeter of the circle was a dull, sickly whitish gray: the grass, the trees, the leaves and plants. The bones of small animals were scattered among the gray vegetation.

"What is this?" Emma demanded. "Some kind of dark faerie magic?"

Mark shook his head. "I have never seen any blight such as this before. I do not like it. Let us make haste away."

No one argued, but as they hurried through the ghost towns and across the hills, they saw several more patches of the ugly blight. At last the sky began to turn light with dawn. All of them were nearly dropping with exhaustion when they left the road behind and found themselves in a place of trees and rolling hills.

"We can rest here," Mark said. He pointed to a rise of ground opposite, whose top was hidden by a number of stone cairns. "Those will give some shelter, and some cover."

Emma frowned. "I hear water," she said. "Is there a stream?"

"You know we can't drink the water here," Julian said, as she picked her way downhill, toward the sound of fluid bubbling over rocks and around tree roots.

"I know, but we could at least wash off in it—" Her voice died. There *was* a stream, of sorts, bisecting the valley between the two low hills, but the water wasn't water. It was scarlet, and thick. It moved sluggishly, slow and red and dripping, between the black trunks of trees.

"'All the blood that's shed on earth, runs through the springs of that country,'" said Mark, at her elbow. "You quoted that to me."

Julian moved to the edge of the blood stream and knelt down. With a quick gesture, he dipped his fingers in. They came out scarlet. "It clots," he said, frowning in mixed fascination and disgust, and wiped his hand off on the grass. "Is it really—human blood?"

"That's what they say," said Mark. "Not all the rivers of faerie are like this, but they claim that the blood of the murdered dead of the human world runs through the streams and creeks and springs here in the woods."

"Who is *they?*" Julian asked, standing up. "Who says that?"

"Kieran," said Mark simply.

"I know the story too," said Cristina. "There are different versions of the legends, but I have heard many and most say that the blood is human, mundane blood." She backed up, took a running jump, and landed on the other side of the bloody stream with some feet to spare.

The rest of them followed her, and trudged up the hill to the flat, grassy top, which commanded a view of the surrounding countryside. Emma suspected the cairns of crumbled stones had once been a watchtower of some sort.

They unrolled the blankets they had and spread out coats, huddling under them for warmth. Mark curled up and immediately fell asleep. Cristina lay down more cautiously, her body wrapped in her dark blue coat, her long hair spilling over the arm on which her head rested.

Emma found a place for herself in the grass, folding her gear jacket up to make a pillow. She had nothing to wrap herself in, and shivered when her skin touched the cold ground as she reached to balance Cortana carefully on a nearby stone.

"Emma." It was Julian, rolling over toward her. He'd been so still she'd thought he was asleep. She didn't even remember lying down this close to him. In the dawn light, his eyes glowed like sea glass. "I've got a spare blanket. Take it."

It was soft and gray, a thin coverlet that used to lie across the foot of his bed. Forcibly, Emma pushed away memories of waking up with it bunched around her feet, yawning and stretching in the sunlight of Julian's room.

"Thanks," she whispered, sliding under the blanket. The grass was dampening with dew. Julian was still watching her, his head resting on his curved arm.

"Jules," Emma whispered. "If our witchlight doesn't work here, and seraph blades don't work here, and runes don't work here—what does that mean?"

He sounded weary. "When I looked into an inn, in one of the towns we passed, I saw an angelic rune someone had scrawled on a wall. It was splattered in blood—scratched and defaced. I don't know what's happened here since the Cold Peace, but I know they hate us."

"Do you think Cristina's pendant will still work?" Emma said.

"I think it's just Shadowhunter magic that's blocked here," Julian said. "Cristina's pendant was a faerie gift. It should be all right."

Emma nodded. "Good night, Jules," she whispered.

He smiled faintly. "It's morning, Emma."

She didn't say anything, only closed her eyes—but not all the way, so she could still see him. She hadn't slept near him since that terrible day Jem had told her about *parabatai* and their curse, and she didn't realize how much she had missed it. She was exhausted, her tiredness seeping out of her bones and into the ground beneath her as her aching body relaxed; she had forgotten what it was like to let consciousness go slowly, as the person she trusted most in the world lay beside her. Even here in Faerie, where Shadowhunters were hated, she felt safer than she had in her own bedroom alone, because Jules was there, so close that if she'd reached out, she could have touched him.

She couldn't reach out, of course. Couldn't touch him. But they were breathing close together, breathing the same breath as consciousness fragmented, as Emma let go of wakefulness and fell, the image of Julian in the dawn light following her down into dreams.

9

THESE LANDS

Kit soon had a new item to add to his list of things he didn't like about Shadowhunters. *They wake me up in the middle of the night.*

It was Livvy who woke him up specifically, shaking him out of a dream of Mantid demons. He sat up, gasping, a knife in his hand—one of the daggers he'd taken from the weapons room. It had been on his nightstand and he had no recollection of picking it up.

"Not bad," Livvy said. She was hovering over his bed, her hair tied back, her gear half-invisible in the darkness. "Fast reflexes."

The knife was about an inch from her chest, but she didn't move. Kit let it clatter back to the nightstand. "You have got to be kidding me."

"Get up," she said. "Ty just saw Zara sneak out the front door. We're Tracking her."

"You're what?" Kit got yawning out of bed, only to be handed a pile of dark clothes by Livvy. She raised her eyebrows at the sight of his boxers but made no other comment.

"Put your gear on," she said. "We'll explain on the way."

She headed out of the room, leaving Kit to change. He had always wondered what Shadowhunter gear would feel like. The boots, pants, shirt, and jacket of sturdy, dark material and heavy weapons belt looked uncomfortable, but—they weren't. The gear was light and flexible on, despite being so tough that when he took the dagger from his bedside and tried to cut the arm of the jacket, the blade didn't even part the material. The boots seemed to fit immediately, like the ring, and the weapons belt sat light and snug around his hips.

"Do I look all right?" he asked, appearing in the hall. Ty was gazing thoughtfully at his closed right hand, a rune glimmering on the back of it.

Livvy gave Kit a thumbs-up. "You absolutely could have been rejected from the yearly Hot Shadowhunters Calendar."

"*Rejected?*" Kit demanded as they started downstairs.

Her eyes were dancing. "For being too young, of course."

"There is no Hot Shadowhunters Calendar," said Ty. "Both of you be quiet; we need to get out of the house without being spotted."

They crept out the back way and down the road toward the beach, careful to avoid the night patrol. Livvy whispered to Kit that Ty was holding a hair clip that Zara had left on a table: It worked as a sort of homing beacon, pulling him in her direction. She seemed to have gone down to the beach and then walked along the sand. Livvy pointed to her footprints, in the process of being washed away by the rising tide.

"It could have been a mundane," said Kit, for argument's sake.

"Following this exact path?" Livvy said. "Look, we're even zigging and zagging where she did."

Kit couldn't really argue. He set his mind to keeping up with Ty, who was practically flying over the dunes of sand and the boulders and uneven rocks that dotted the coastline more thickly as they moved north. He scaled an alarmingly tall wall of pitted rock and dropped down on the other side; Kit, following, almost tripped and landed face-first in the sand.

He managed to regain his footing and was relieved. He wasn't sure who he least wanted to look like a fool in front of, Livvy or Ty. Maybe it was an equal split.

"There," Ty said in a whisper, pointing to where a dark hole opened up in the rocky wall of the bluff that rose to divide the beach from the highway. Tumbled piles of rock jutted out into the ocean, where waves broke around them, casting silvery-white spray high into the air.

The sand had given way to rocky reef. They picked their way carefully across it, even Ty, who bent to examine something in a tide pool. He straightened with a smile and a starfish in his hand.

"Ty," said Livvy. "Put it back, unless you're planning on throwing it at Zara."

"Waste of a perfectly good starfish," muttered Kit, and Ty laughed. The salt air had tangled his arrow-straight black hair, and his eyes glowed like the moonlight on the water. Kit just stared, unable to think of anything else clever to say, as Ty gently placed the starfish back in its tide pool.

They made it to the cave opening without any other stops for wildlife. Livvy went in first, with Ty and Kit following. Kit paused as the darkness of the cave enveloped him.

"I can't see," he said, trying to fight his rising panic. He hated the pitch dark, but then who didn't?

Light burst around him like the sudden appearance of a falling star. It was witchlight; Ty was holding it. "Do you want a Night Vision rune?" Livvy asked, her hand on her stele.

Kit shook his head. "No runes," he said. He wasn't sure why he was insisting. It wasn't as if the *iratze* had hurt. It just seemed like the final hurdle, the last admission that he was a Shadowhunter, not just a boy with Shadowhunter blood who had decided to make the Institute a way station while he figured out a better plan.

Whatever that plan might be. Kit tried not to brood on it as they advanced deeper into the tunnels.

"Do you think this is part of the convergence?" he heard Livvy whisper.

Ty shook his head. "No. The bluffs of the coast are riddled with caves, always have been. I mean, anything could be down here—nests of demons, vampires—but I don't think this has anything to do with Malcolm. And the ley lines are nowhere near here."

"I really wish you hadn't said 'nests of demons,'" said Kit. "It makes them sound like spiders."

"Some demons are spiders," said Ty. "The biggest one ever reported was twenty feet tall and had yard-long mandibles."

Kit thought of the giant praying mantis demons that had ripped his father apart. It was hard to think of anything witty to say about a giant spider when you'd seen the white of your father's rib cage.

"Shh." Livvy held up a hand. "I hear voices."

Kit strained his ears, but heard nothing. He suspected there was another rune he was lacking, something that would give him Superman hearing. He could see lights moving up ahead, though, around the curve of the tunnel.

They moved ahead, Kit staying to the rear of Ty and Livvy. The tunnel opened out into a massive chamber, a room with cracked granite walls, a packed-earth floor, and a smell of mold and decay. The ceiling rose into blackness.

There was a wooden table and two chairs in the middle of the room. The only light came from rune-stones placed on the table; one chair was occupied by Zara. Kit pressed himself instinctively back against the wall; on the other side of the tunnel, Livvy and Ty did the same.

Zara was examining some papers she'd spread on the table. There was a bottle of wine and a glass at her elbow. She wasn't dressed in gear, but in a plain dark suit, her hair drawn back into an impossibly tight bun.

Kit strained to see what she was studying, but he was too far away. He could read some words etched into the table, though: FIRE WANTS TO BURN. He had no idea what they meant. Zara didn't seem to be doing anything interesting, either; maybe she just came here to have privacy for her reading. Maybe she was secretly tired of Perfect Diego and was hiding. Who could blame her?

Zara looked up, her eyebrows creasing. Someone was coming—Kit heard the quick tread of feet, and a tousle-haired figure in jeans appeared at the far end of the room.

"It's Manuel," Livvy whispered. "Maybe they're having an affair?"

"Manu," Zara said, frowning. She didn't sound lovelorn. "You're late."

"Sorry." Manuel grinned a disarming grin and grabbed for the free chair, swinging it around so he could seat himself with his arms folded over the back. "Don't be cross, Zara. I had to wait until Rayan and Jon fell asleep—they were in a chatty mood, and I didn't want to chance anyone seeing me leave the Institute." He indicated the papers. "What have you got there?"

"Updates from my father," Zara said. "He was disappointed about the outcome of the last Council, obviously. The decision to let that half-breed Mark Blackthorn remain among decent Nephilim would offend anyone."

Manuel picked up her glass of wine. Red lights glinted in its depths. "Still, we must look to the future," he said. "Getting rid of Mark wasn't the point of our journey here, after all. He's a minor annoyance, like his siblings."

Ty, Kit, and Livvy exchanged confused looks. Livvy's face was tight with anger. Ty's was expressionless, but his hands moved restlessly at his sides.

"True. The first step is the Registry," Zara said. She patted the papers, making them rustle. "My father says the Cohort is strong in Idris, and they believe the Los Angeles Institute is ripe for the plucking. The incident with Malcolm sowed considerable doubt in the West Coast's ability to make judgments. And the fact that the High Warlock of Los Angeles and the head of the local vampire clan both turned out to be enmeshed in dark magic—"

"That wasn't our fault," Livvy whispered. "There was no way to possibly know—"

Ty shushed her, but Kit had missed the last of what Zara was saying. He was only conscious of her grin like a dark red slash across her face.

"Confidence isn't very high," she finished.

"And Arthur?" said Manuel. "The putative head of the place? Not that I've laid eyes on him once."

"A lunatic," said Zara. "My father told me he suspected as much. He knew him at the Academy. I talked to Arthur myself. He thought I was someone named Amatis."

Kit glanced at Livvy, who gave a puzzled shrug.

"It will be easy enough to put him up in front of the Council and prove he's a madman," said Zara. "I can't say who's been running the Institute in his stead—Diana, I imagine—but if she'd wanted the head position, she'd have taken it already."

"So your father steps in, the Cohort makes sure he carries the vote, and the Institute is his," said Manuel.

"Ours," Zara corrected. "I will run the Institute by his side. He trusts me. We'll be a team."

Manuel didn't seem impressed. He'd probably heard it before. "And then, the Registry."

"Absolutely. We'll be able to propose it as Law immediately, and once it passes, we can begin the identifications." Zara's eyes glittered. "Every Downworlder will wear the sign."

Kit's stomach lurched. This was close enough to mundane history to make him taste bile in the back of his throat.

"We can start at the Shadow Market," said Zara. "The creatures congregate there. If we take enough of them into custody, we should be able to seize the rest for registration soon enough."

"And if they're not inclined to be registered, then they can be convinced easily enough with a little pain," said Manuel.

Zara frowned. "I think you enjoy the torture, Manu."

He leaned forward, elbows on the table, his face open and hand-some and charming. "I think you do too, Zara. I've seen you admiring my work." He flexed his fingers. "You just don't want to admit it in front of Perfect Diego."

"Seriously? They call him that too?" Kit muttered under his breath.

Zara tossed her head, but Manuel was grinning.

"You're going to have to tell him eventually, about the Cohort's full plans," he said. "You know he won't approve. He's a Downworlder-lover if there ever was one."

Zara made a disgusted noise. "Nonsense. He's nothing like that disgusting Alec Lightwood and his stupid Alliance and his repulsive demon-spawn boyfriend. The Blackthorns may be faerie-loving morons, but Diego's just . . . confused."

"What about Emma Carstairs?"

Zara began gathering up the pages of her father's letter. She didn't look at Manuel. "What about her?"

"Everyone says she's the best Shadowhunter since Jace Heron-dale," said Manuel. "A title I know you've long coveted for yourself."

"Vanessa Ashdown says she's a boy-crazy slut," said Zara, and the ugly words seemed to echo off the rock walls. Kit thought of Emma with her sword, Emma saving his life, Emma hugging Cristina and looking at Julian like he hung the moon, and he wondered if he could get away with stomping on Zara's foot the next time he saw her. "And I haven't been particularly impressed by her in person. She's quite, quite ordinary."

"I'm sure she is," said Manuel as Zara rose to her feet, papers in hand. "I still don't understand what you see in Diego."

"You wouldn't. It's a family alliance."

"An arranged marriage? How mundane and medieval." Manuel grabbed for the rune-stones on the table, and for a moment the light in the room seemed to dance, a wild pattern of shine and shadow. "So, are we heading back?"

"We'd better. If anyone sees us, we can say we were checking the wards." Zara crumpled the pages of her father's letter and stuffed them into her pocket. "The Council meets soon. My father will read out my letter to him there, stating Arthur Blackthorn's inability to run an Institute, and then announce his own candidacy."

"They won't know what hit them," said Manuel, sliding his hands into his pockets. "And when it's all over, of course . . ."

"Don't worry," Zara said irritably. "You'll get what you want. Though it would be better if you were more committed to the cause."

She had already turned away; Kit saw Manuel's eyes glint beneath his lashes as he looked after her. There was something in his expression—an unpleasant sort of hunger, though whether it was desire for Zara or something far more arcane, Kit couldn't tell. "Oh, I'm committed," said Manuel. "I'd like to see the world burned clean of Downworlders as much as you, Zara. I just don't believe in doing something for nothing."

Zara glanced back over her shoulder as she moved into the corridor Manuel had used as an entrance. "It won't be nothing, Manu," she said. "I can promise you that."

And they were gone, leaving Kit, Ty, and Livvy to huddle together in the mouth of the tunnel, stunned into silence.

The sound that woke Cristina was so faint she thought at first she might have imagined it. She lay, still tired, blinking against the foggy sunlight. She wondered how long it would be until sundown, when they could navigate by the stars again.

The sound came again, a sweet far-calling cry, and she sat up, shaking her hair back. It was wet with dew. She combed her fingers through it, wishing for something to tie it back with. She hardly ever wore her hair down like this, and the weight against her neck was bothersome.

She could see Julian and Emma, both asleep, hunched figures on the ground. But where was Mark? His blanket was discarded, his boots lying beside it. The sight of the boots made her scramble up to her feet: They'd all been sleeping with their shoes on, just in case. Why would he take his off?

She thought about waking up Emma, but likely she was being ridiculous: He'd probably just gone for a walk. She reached to pull her butterfly knife out of her weapons belt and started down the hill, moving past Jules and Emma as she did. She saw with a sort of pang at her heart that their hands, between them, were clasped: Somehow they'd found their way toward each other in sleep. She wondered if she should reach down, gently separate them. But no, she couldn't do that. There was no way to *gently* separate Jules and Emma. The mere action of separating them at all was like an act of violence, a tear in the fabric of the world.

There was still heavy mist everywhere, and the sun pierced through it dimly in several places, creating a glowing white veil she could see through only in patches. "Mark?" she called softly. "Mark, where are you?"

She caught the sound she had heard before again, and now it was clearer: music. The sound of a pipe, the twang of a harp string. She strained to hear more—and then nearly screamed as something touched her shoulder. She whirled and saw Mark in front of her, holding his hands up as if to ward her off.

"I didn't mean to startle you," he said.

"Mark," she breathed, and then paused. "Are you Mark? Faeries weave illusions, don't they?"

He cocked his head to the side. His blond hair fell across his forehead. She remembered when it had hit his shoulders, as if he were the illustration of a faerie prince in a book. Now it was short, soft and curling. She had given him a modern haircut, and it seemed odd suddenly, out of place in Faerie. "I cannot hear my heart or what it tells me," he said. "I can only hear the wind."

It was one of the first things he had ever said to her.

"It is you," she said, exhaling with relief. "What are you doing? Why aren't you sleeping? We need to rest, if we are to arrive at the Unseelie Court by moon's rise."

"Can't you hear the music?" he said. It *was* louder now, the very clear sounds of fiddles and woodwinds, and the sound of dancing, too—laughter, and the stamp of feet. "It's a revel."

Cristina's heart skipped a beat. Faerie revels were things out of legend. The Fair Folk danced to enchanted music, and drank enchanted wine, and sometimes they would dance for days. The food they ate made you delirious or love-struck or mad . . . it could pierce your dreams. . . .

"You should go back to sleep," Mark said. "Revels can be dangerous."

"I've always wanted to see one." A surge of rebellion went through her. "I'm going to go closer."

"Cristina, *don't*." He sounded breathless as she turned and moved down the hill toward the noise. "It's the music—it's making you want to dance—"

She whirled around, a curl of black hair sticking to her damp cheek. "*You* brought us here," she said, and then she plunged on, toward the music, and it rose up and surrounded her, and she could hear Mark, swearing but following after her.

She reached a field at the foot of the hill and stopped to stare. The field was full of blurred, colorful movement. All around her the music echoed, piercingly sweet.

And everywhere, of course, there were Fair Folk. A troupe of faeries in the center of the dancers, playing their instruments, their heads thrown back, their feet stamping the ground. There were green-skinned wood faeries dancing, with gnarled hands and eyes that glowed yellow as sap. Faeries blue and green and shimmering as water, with hair like transparent netting cascading down to their feet. Beautiful girls with flowers wound through their hair, tied around their waists and throats, whose feet were hooves: pretty boys in ragged clothes with fever-bright eyes who held out their hands as they spun by.

"Come and dance," they called. "Come and dance, beautiful girl, *chica bella*, come and dance with us."

Cristina began to move toward them, toward the music and the dancing. The field was still clouded with fog, carving its streaks of white across the ground and hiding the blue of the sky. The mist glowed as she moved into it, heavy with strange scents: fruit and wine and incense-like smoke.

She began to dance, moving her body to the music's rhythm. Exhilaration seemed to pour into her with every breath she took in. She was suddenly no longer the girl who had let Diego Rosales fool her not once, but twice, not the girl who followed rules and trusted people until they broke her trust as casually as knocking a glass off a table. No longer the girl who stood back and let her friends be wild and crazy and waited to catch them when they fell. Now she was the one falling.

Hands seized her, spinning her around. Mark. His eyes were flashing. He pulled her up close against him, his arms slipping around her, but his grip was unyielding with anger. "What are you doing, Cristina?" he asked in a low voice. "You know about faeries, you know this is dangerous."

"That's why I'm doing it, Mark." She hadn't seen him look so furious since Kieran had come riding up to the Institute with Iarlath and Gwyn. She felt a small, secret pulse of excitement inside her chest, that she could make him that angry.

"They hate Shadowhunters here, don't you remember?" he said.

"They don't know I'm a Shadowhunter."

"Believe me," said Mark, leaning in close so that she could feel his breath, hot, against her ear. "They know."

"Then they don't care," said Cristina. "It's a revel. I've read about these. Faeries lose themselves in the music, like humans. They dance and they forget, just like us."

Mark's hands curved around her waist. It was a protective gesture, she told herself. It didn't mean anything. But her pulse quickened regardless. When Mark had first arrived at the Institute, he'd been stick-thin, hollow-eyed. Now she could feel muscle over his bones, the hard strength of him against her.

"I never asked you," he said, as they moved among the crowd. They were close to two girls dancing together; both of them had their black hair bound up in elaborate crowns of berries and acorns. They wore dresses of russet and brown, ribbons around their slim throats, and swished their skirts away from Mark and Cristina, laughing at the couple's clumsiness. Cristina didn't mind. "Why faeries? Why did you make that the thing you studied?"

"Because of you." She tilted her head back to look up at him, saw the surprise that passed across his expressive face. The beginning of the gentle curves of wonder at the corners of his mouth. "Because of you, Mark Blackthorn."

Me? His lips shaped the word.

"I was in my mother's rose garden when I heard what had happened to you," she said. "I was only thirteen. The Dark War was ending, and the Cold Peace had been announced. The whole Shadowhunter world knew of your sister's exile, and that you had been abandoned. My great-uncle came out to tell me about it. My family always used to joke that I was softhearted, that it was easy to make me cry, and he knew I'd been worrying about you—so he told me, he said, 'Your lost boy will never be found now.'"

Mark swallowed. Emotions passed like storm clouds behind his eyes; not for him Julian's guardedness, his shields. "And did you?"

"Did I what?"

"Did you cry?" he said. They were still moving together, in the dance, but it was almost mechanical now: Cristina had forgotten the steps her feet were taking, she was aware only of Mark breathing, her fingers locked behind Mark's neck, Mark in her arms.

"I did not cry," Cristina said. "But I did decide that I would dedicate myself to eradicating the Cold Peace. It was not a fair Law then. It will never be a fair Law."

His lips parted. "Cristina—"

A voice like doves interrupted them. Soft, feathery, and light, it crooned, "Drinks, madam and sir? Something to cool you after dancing?"

A faerie with a face like a cat's—furred and whiskered—stood before them in the tatters of an Edwardian suit. He held a gold plate on which were many small glasses containing liquid of different colors: blue, red, and amber.

"Is it enchanted?" Cristina said breathlessly. "Will it give me strange dreams?"

"It will cool your thirst, lady," said the faerie. "And all I would ask for in return is a smile from your lips."

Cristina seized up a glass full of amber fluid. It tasted of passionfruit, sweet and tart—she took one swallow, and Mark dashed the glass from her hand. It fell tinkling at their feet, splashing his hand with liquid. He licked the fluid from his skin, glaring at her all the while.

Cristina backed away. She could feel a pleasant warmth spreading in her chest. The drinks seller was snapping at Mark, who pushed him away with a coin—a mundane penny—and started after Cristina.

"Stop," he said. "Cristina, slow down, you're going toward the center of the revel—the music will only be stronger there—"

She stopped, held out a hand to him. She felt fearless. She knew she ought to be terrified: She had swallowed a faerie drink, and anything might happen. But instead she only felt as if she were flying. She was soaring free, only Mark here to tether her to the ground. "Dance with me," she said.

He caught at her. He looked angry, still, but he held her tightly nonetheless. "You've had enough dancing. And drinking."

"Enough dancing?" It was the girls in russet again, their red mouths laughing. Other than their different-colored eyes, they looked nearly identical. One of them pulled the ribbon from around her throat—Cristina stared; her neck was horribly scarred, as if her head had nearly been severed from her body. "Dance *together*," the girl said—nearly spat it, as if it were a curse, and looped the ribbon around Mark's and Cristina's wrists, binding them together. "Enjoy the binding, *Hunter*." She grinned at Mark, and her teeth were black, as if they had been painted that color, and sharp as needles.

Cristina gasped, stumbling back, pulling Mark after her, the ribbon connecting them. It stretched like a rubber band, not breaking or fraying. Mark caught up to her, seizing her hand in his, his fingers threaded through hers.

He drew her after him, fast and sure-footed on the uneven terrain, finding the breaks in the heavy mist. They pushed between dancing couples until the grass under them was no longer trampled and the music was faint in their ears.

Mark veered to the side, making for a copse of trees. He slipped under the branches, holding the low-hanging ones aside to let Cristina in after him. Once she had ducked underneath, he released them, closing them both into a dirt-floored space beneath the trees, hidden from the outside world by long branches, laden with fruit, that touched the ground.

Mark sat down, drawing a knife from his belt. "Come here," he said, and when Cristina came to sit beside him, he took her hand and slashed apart the ribbon binding them.

It made a little shrieking, hurt sound, like a wounded animal, but frayed and gave. He let go of Cristina and dropped the knife. Faint sunlight filtered down through the branches above, and in the dim illumination, the ribbon still around his wrist looked like blood.

The ribbon was looped around Cristina's wrist as well, no longer burning, trailing its lonely end in the dirt. She worried at it with her nails until it came free and fell to the ground. Her fingers kept slipping. Probably the faerie drink, still in her system, she thought.

She glanced over at Mark. His face was drawn, his gold and blue eyes shadowed. "That could have been very bad," he said, casting the rest of his ribbon aside. "A binding spell like that can tie two people together and send one of them mad, make them drown themselves and pull the other in after them."

"Mark," Cristina said. "I'm sorry. I should have listened to you. You know more about revels than I do. You have experience. I only have the books I read."

"No," he said unexpectedly. "I wanted to go too. I liked dancing with you. It was good to be there with someone . . ."

"Human?" Cristina said.

The heat in her chest had turned into a strange pinching feeling, a hot pressure that increased when she looked at him. At the curves of his cheekbones, the hollows of his temples. His loose, wheat-colored shirt was open at the throat, and she could see that place she had always thought was the most beautiful spot on a man's body, the smooth muscle over the clavicle and the vulnerable hollow.

"Yes, human," he said. "We are all human, I know. But I have almost never known anyone as human as you."

Cristina felt breathless. The faerie mist had stolen her breath, she thought, that and the enchantment all around them.

"You are kind," he said, "one of the kindest people I have known. In the Hunt, there was not much kindness. When I think that when the sentence of the Cold Peace was passed, there was someone a thousand miles away from Idris, someone who had never met me but who cried for a boy who had been abandoned . . ."

"I said I didn't cry." Cristina's voice hitched.

Mark's hand was a pale blur. She felt his fingers against her face. They came away wet, shining in the mist-light. "You're crying now," he said.

When she caught at his hand, it was damp with her own tears. And when she leaned toward him through the mist, and kissed him, she tasted salt.

For a moment Mark was startled, unmoving, and Cristina felt a spear of terror go through her, worse than the sight of any demon. That Mark might not want this, that he might be horrified . . .

"Cristina," he said, as she broke away from him, and went up on his knees, his arm coming around her a little awkwardly, his hand burying itself in her hair. "*Cristina*," he said again, with a break in his voice, the rough sound of desire.

She put her hands on either side of his face, her palms in the hollows of his cheeks, and marveled at the softness where Diego had had stubble, rough against her skin. She let him come to her this time, closing her into the circle of his left arm, fitting his mouth to hers.

Stars exploded behind her eyelids. Not just any stars, but the many-colored stars of Faerie. She saw clouds and constellations; she tasted night air on his mouth. His lips moved frantically against hers. He was still whispering her name, incoherent between kisses. His free hand slid over her waist, up her side. He groaned when her fingers found their way into the neck of his shirt and brushed along his collarbone, touched the beating pulse in his throat.

He said something in a language she didn't know, and then

he was flat on the ground and she was over him, and he was pulling her down, hands fierce on her back and her shoulders, and she wondered if this was how it had always been for him with Kieran, fierce and ungentle. She remembered seeing them kiss in the desert behind the Institute, and how it had been a frantic thing, a clash of bodies, and it had sparked desire in her then and did again now.

He arched up and she heard him gasp as she slid down his body, kissing his throat, then his chest through his shirt, and then her fingers were on his buttons and she heard him laugh breathlessly, saying her name, and then, "I never thought you'd even look at me, not someone like you, Shadowhunter royalty— like a princess—"

"It's amazing what a bit of enchanted faerie drink will do." She meant to sound teasing, lighthearted. But Mark went still under her. A moment later he had moved, quick and graceful, and was sitting at least a foot from her, his hands up as if to hold her away.

"Faerie drink?" he echoed.

Cristina looked at him in surprise. "The sweet drink the cat-faced man gave to me. You tasted it."

"There was nothing in it," Mark said, with uncharacteristic sharpness. "I knew the moment I put my lips to my skin. It was only brambleberry juice, Cristina."

Cristina recoiled slightly, both from his anger and from the realization that there had been no blurring cloak of magic over the things she'd just done.

"But I thought—"

"You thought you were kissing me because you were intoxicated," Mark said. "Not because you wanted to, or because you actually like me."

"But I do like you." She rose to her knees, but Mark was already on his feet. "I have since I met you."

"Is that why you got together with Diego?" Mark said, and then shook his head, backing up. "Maybe I can't do this."

"Do what?" Cristina staggered upright.

"Be with a human who lies," Mark said, uninflected.

"But you've lied too," said Cristina. "You've lied about being with Emma."

"And you've taken part in that same lie."

"Because it has to be told," Cristina said. "For both their sakes. If Julian wasn't in love with her, then he wouldn't need to think—"

She broke off, then, as Mark went white in the shadows. "What did you say?"

Cristina put her hand to her mouth. The fact of Emma and Julian's feelings for each other was so rooted in what she knew about them that it was hard to remember others didn't know. It was so clear in their every word and gesture, even now; how could Mark *not* know?

"But they're *parabatai*," he said, bewildered. "It's illegal. The punishment—Julian wouldn't. He just wouldn't."

"I'm so sorry. I shouldn't have said anything. I was just guessing—"

"You weren't guessing," Mark said, and turned away from her, shoving his way out through the branches of the trees.

Cristina went after him. He had to understand he couldn't say anything to Julian. Her betrayal weighted her heart like a stone, her sense of humiliation forgotten in her fear for Emma, her realization of what she'd done. She pushed through the tree branches, the dry-edged leaves scratching at her skin. A moment later, she was outside on the green hill, and she saw Julian.

The music woke Jules, the music and an enveloping sense of warmth. He hadn't been warm in so long, not even at night, bundled in blankets.

He blinked his eyes open. He could hear music in the distance, weaving feathery tendrils across the sky. He turned his head to the side and saw with a jolt of familiarity Emma beside him, her head on her jacket. Their hands were clasped on the grass between them, his tanned fingers wrapped tightly around her smaller ones.

He drew his hand back fast, his heart pounding, and scrambled to his feet. He wondered if he'd reached for her in his sleep, or had she reached for him? No, she wouldn't have reached for him. She had Mark. She might have kissed him, Julian, but it was Mark's name she'd said.

He'd thought he would be all right, sleeping this close to her, but apparently he'd been wrong. His hand still felt as if it were burning, but the rest of his body was cold again. Emma murmured and turned, her blond hair falling over her hand, now curled palm-up on the grass as if she were reaching out for him.

He couldn't stand it. He seized his jacket up off the ground, shrugged it on, and went to look out from the hill. Maybe he could tell how close they were to the foot of the mountains. How long it would take them to reach the Unseelie Court and end this insane mission. Not that he blamed Mark; he didn't. Kieran was like family to Mark, and Julian understood family better than he understood almost anything else.

But he was already worried about the children at the Institute, whether they would be furious, panicked, unforgiving. He'd never left them before. Never.

The wind changed and the music picked up. Julian found himself at the edge of the hill looking down at a vista of green grass, dotted here and there with copses of trees that swept down to a cleared space where a blur of color and movement was visible.

Dancers. They were moving in time to the thrum of a music that seemed to well up from inside the earth. It was insistent, demanding. It called to you to join it, to be swept up and carried the way that a wave might carry you from sea to shore.

Julian felt the pull, though it was distant enough not to be uncomfortable. His fingers ached for his paintbrushes, though. Everywhere he looked he saw an intensity of color and movement that made him wish he was in his studio in front of his easel. He felt as if he were looking at pictures where the colors had been adjusted for maximum saturation. The leaves and grass were intently, almost poisonously green. Fruit was brighter than jewelry. The birds that dipped and dove through the air had plumage so wildly colorful it made Julian wonder if nothing here hunted them—if they had no other purpose but beauty and display.

"What's wrong?" He turned around and saw her just behind him on the ridge of the hill. Emma. Her long hair untied and flying around her like a sheet of metal hammered thin. His heart lurched, feeling a pull far more insistent than that of faerie music.

"Nothing." His voice came out rougher than he'd intended. "Just looking for Mark and Cristina. Once I find them, we should go. We've got a lot more walking to do."

She moved toward him, her expression wistful. The sun was raying down through the clouds, lighting her hair to rich waves of saffron. Julian clenched his hand tightly, refusing to let himself raise his fingers, to bury them in the pale hair that Emma usually undid only at night. That spoke to Julian of the moments of peace between twilight and nightfall when the children were asleep and he was alone with Emma, moments of soft speech and intimacy that far predated any realization on his part that they were anything more than *parabatai*. In the curve of her sleeping face, in the fall of her hair, in the shadows of her lashes against her cheeks, was a peace he had only rarely known.

"Do you hear the music?" she asked, taking a step closer. Close enough to touch. Julian wondered if this was how drug addicts felt. Wanting what they knew they shouldn't have. Thinking, *Just this once won't matter.*

"Emma, don't," he said. He didn't know what he was asking, exactly. *Don't be close to me, I can't bear it. Don't look at me like that. Don't be everything I want and can't have. Don't make me forget you're Mark's and anyway you could never be mine.*

"Please," she said. She looked at him with wide, pained eyes. "Please, I need . . ."

The part of Julian that could never withstand being needed unlocked his clenched hands, his braced feet. He was inside the sphere of her presence in seconds, their bodies almost colliding. He put a hand against her cheek. She wasn't wearing Cortana, he noticed with a distant puzzlement. Why had she left it behind?

Her eyes flashed. She raised herself onto her toes, tilting up her face. Her lips moved, but he couldn't hear what she was saying over the roaring in his own ears. He remembered being knocked down by a wave once, pressed to the bottom of the ocean, breathless and unable to get up. There had been a terror in it, but also a sense of letting go: Something more powerful was carrying him, and he no longer needed to fight.

Her arms were around his neck, her lips on his, and he let go, surrendering. His whole body contracted, his heart racing, exploding, veins thrumming with blood and energy. He caught her up against him, small and strong in his arms. He gasped, unable to breathe, tasting the sweet-sharpness of blood.

But not Emma. He couldn't taste Emma, the familiarity of her, and the scent of her was different too. Gone was the sweetness of sun-warmed skin, of the herbs in her soap and shampoo, the scent of gear and gold and girl.

You didn't grow up with someone, dream of them, let them shape your soul and put their fingerprints on your heart, and not know when the person you were kissing wasn't them. Julian yanked himself away, wiping the back of his hand across his mouth. Blood smeared his knuckles.

He was looking at a faerie woman, her skin smooth and pale, an unmarked, unwrinkled canvas. She was grinning, her lips red. Her hair was the color of cobwebs—it *was* cobwebs, gray and fine and drifting. She could have been any age at all. Her only clothes were a ragged black shift. She was beautiful and also hideous.

"You delight me, Shadowhunter," she crooned. "Will you not come back to my arms for more kisses?"

She reached out. Julian stumbled back. He had never in his life kissed anyone but Emma; he felt sick now, in his heart and guts. He wanted to reach for a seraph blade, to burn the air between them, to feel the familiar heat race up his arm and through his veins and cauterize his nausea.

His hand had only just closed around the hilt of the blade when he remembered: It wouldn't work here.

"Leave him alone!" someone shouted. "Get away from my brother, *leanansídhe!*"

It was Mark. He was emerging from a copse of trees with Cristina just behind him. There was a dagger in his hand.

The faerie woman laughed. "Your weapons will not work in this realm, Shadowhunter."

There was a click, and Cristina's folding knife bloomed open in her hand. "Come and speak your words of challenge to my blade, barrow-woman."

The faerie pulled back with a hiss, and Julian saw his own blood on her teeth. He felt light-headed with sickness and anger. She whirled and was gone in a moment, a gray-black blur racing down the hill.

The music had stopped. The dancers, too, had begun to scatter: The sun was setting, the shadows thick across the ground. Whatever kind of revel it had been, it was one that apparently was not friendly to nightfall.

"Julian, brother." Mark hurried forward, his eyes concerned. "You look ill—sit down, drink some water—"

A soft whistle came from farther up the hill. Julian turned. Emma was standing on the ridge, buckling on Cortana. He saw the relief on her face as she caught sight of them.

"I wondered where you'd gone," she said, hurrying down the hill. Her smile as she looked at them all was hopeful. "I was worried you'd eaten faerie fruit and were running naked around the greensward."

"No nudity," said Julian. "No greensward."

Emma tightened the strap on Cortana. Her hair had been pulled back into a long braid, only a few pale tendrils escaping. She looked around at their tense faces, her brown eyes wide. "*Is* everything okay?"

Julian could still feel the fingerprints of the *leanansídhe* all over him. He knew what *leanansídhe* were—wild faeries who took the shape of whatever you wanted to see, seduced you, and fed on your blood and skin.

At least he was the only one who would have seen Emma. Mark and Cristina would have seen the *leanansídhe* in her true form. That was one humiliation and danger spared them all.

"Everything's fine," he said. "We'd better get going. The stars are just coming out, and we've got a long way still to go."

"All right," Livvy said, pausing in front of a narrow wooden door. It didn't look much like the rest of the Institute, glass and metal and modernity. It seemed like a warning. "Here we go."

She didn't look eager.

They'd decided—with Kit mostly as silent onlooker—to go directly to Arthur Blackthorn's office. Even if it was two in the morning, even if he didn't want to be bothered with Centurion business, he needed to know what Zara was planning.

She was after the Institute, Livvy had explained as they scrambled back along the beach and rocks to where they'd started. Surely that's why she'd said what she had about Arthur—clearly she'd tell any lie.

Kit had never thought about Institutes much—they'd always struck him as something like police stations, buzzy hives of Shadowhunters meant to keep an eye on specific locations. It seemed they were more like small city-states: in charge of a certain area, but run by a family appointed by the Council in Idris.

"There's *seriously* an entire private country that's just Shadowhunters?" Kit demanded as they headed up the road to the Institute, rising like a shadow against the mountains behind it.

"Yes," said Livvy tersely. In other words, *Shut up and listen*. Kit had the feeling she was processing what was happening by explaining it to him. He shut up and let her.

An Institute was run by a head, whose family lived with him or her; they also housed families who'd lost members, or Nephilim orphans— of whom there were many. The head of an Institute had significant power: Most Consuls were chosen from that pool, and they could propose new Laws, which would be passed if a vote went their way.

All Institutes were just as empty as the Los Angeles one. In fact, it was unusually crowded at the moment, due to the Centurion presence. They were meant to be that way, in case they needed to house a battalion of Shadowhunters at any moment. There was no staff, as there was no need of one: Shadowhunters who worked for the Institute, called the Conclave, were spread out all over the city in their own houses.

Not that there were many of *them* either, Livvy added grimly. So many had died in the war five years ago. But if Zara's father were to become the head of the Los Angeles Institute, not only would he be able to propose his bigoted Law, but the Blackthorns would be thrown out on their ears with nowhere to go but Idris.

"Is Idris so bad?" Kit had asked as they went up the stairs. Not that *he* wanted to be shipped off to Idris. He was just getting used to the Institute. Not that he'd want to stay in it if Zara's father took over—not if he was anything like Zara.

Livvy glanced at Ty, who hadn't interrupted her during her tirade. "Idris is fine. Great, even. But this is where we live."

They'd reached the door to Arthur's office then, and everything had gone silent. Kit wondered if he should just lead the way. He didn't care particularly if he annoyed Arthur Blackthorn or not.

Ty looked at the door with troubled eyes. "We're not supposed to bother Uncle Arthur. We promised Jules."

"We have to," Livvy said simply, and pushed the door open.

A narrow set of stairs led to a shadowy room under the eaves of the house. There was a cluster of desks, each with a lamp on it—so many lamps the room was filled with brilliance. Every book, every piece of paper with scrawled writing, every plate with half-eaten food on it, was harshly illuminated.

A man sat at one of the desks. He wore a long bathrobe over a ragged sweater and jeans; his feet were bare. The robe had probably once been blue, but was now a sort of dirty white from many washings. He was clearly a Blackthorn—his mostly gray hair curled like Julian's did, and his eyes were a brilliant blue-green.

They went past Livvy and Ty and fastened on Kit.

"Stephen," he said, and dropped the pen he was holding. It hit the ground, spilling ink in a dark pool over the floorboards.

Livvy's mouth was partly open. Ty was pressed against the wall. "Uncle Arthur, that's Kit," said Livvy. "Kit Herondale."

Arthur chuckled dryly. "Herondale, indeed," he said. His eyes seemed to burn: There was a look of sickness in them, like the heat of a fever. He rose to his feet and came over to Kit, staring down into his face. "Why did you follow Valentine?" he said. "You, who had everything? 'Yea, is not even Apollo, with hair and harpstring of gold, a bitter God to follow, a beautiful God to behold?'" He smelled bitter, of old coffee. Kit took a step back. "What kind of Herondale will you be?" Arthur whispered. "William or Tobias? Stephen or Jace? Beautiful, bitter, or both?"

"*Uncle*," said Ty. He pitched his voice loud, though it shook slightly. "We need to talk to you. About the Centurions. They want to take the Institute. They don't want you to be head of it anymore."

Arthur whirled on Ty with a fierce look—almost a glare, but not quite. Then he began to laugh. "Is that true? Is it?" he demanded. The laughter built and seemed to break in almost a sob. He whirled around and sat heavily down in his desk chair. "What a *joke*," he said savagely.

"It's not a joke," Livvy began.

"They want to take the Institute from *me*," Arthur said. "As if I hold it! I've never run an Institute in my life, children. *He* does everything—writes the correspondence, plans the meetings, speaks with the Council."

"Who does everything?" said Kit, though he knew he had no place in the conversation.

"Julian." The voice was Diana's; she was standing at the top of the attic stairs, looking around the room as if the brightness of the light surprised her. Her expression was resigned. "He means Julian."

10

SO WILLS ITS KING

They were in Diana's office. Through the window, the ocean looked like rippled aluminum, illuminated by black light.

"I'm sorry you had to learn this about your uncle," said Diana. She was leaning back against her desk. She wore jeans and a sweater but still looked immaculate. Her hair was swept back into a mass of curls clipped by a leather barrette. "I had hoped—Julian had hoped—that you'd never know."

Kit was leaning against the far wall; Ty and Livvy sat on Diana's desk. Both of them looked stunned, as if they were recovering from having the wind knocked out of them. Kit had never been more conscious that they were twins, despite the difference in their coloring.

"So all these years it's been Julian," said Livvy. "Running the Institute. Doing everything. Covering up for Arthur."

Kit thought of his drive with Julian to the Shadow Market. He hadn't spent that much time with the second-oldest Blackthorn boy, but Julian had always seemed terrifyingly adult to him, as if he were years older than his calendar age.

"We should have guessed." Ty's hand twisted and untwisted

the slim white cords of the headphones looped around his neck. "I should have figured it out."

"We don't see the things that are closest to us," said Diana. "It's the nature of people."

"But Jules," Livvy whispered. "He was only twelve. It must have been so hard on him."

Her face shone. For a moment, Kit thought it was reflected light from the windows. Then he realized—it was tears.

"He always loved you so much," said Diana. "It was what he wanted to do."

"We need him here," said Ty. "We need him here *now*."

"I should go," Kit said. He had never felt so uncomfortable. Well, maybe not *never*—there had been the incident with the five drunk werewolves and the cage of newts at the Shadow Market—but rarely.

Livvy looked up, her tearstained face baleful. "No, you shouldn't. You need to stay here and help us explain to Diana about Zara."

"I didn't understand half of what she said," Kit protested. "About Institute heads, and registries—"

Ty took a deep breath. "I'll explain," he said. The recitation of what had happened seemed to calm him down: the regular march of facts, one after another. When he was done, Diana crossed the room and double-locked the door.

"Do either of the rest of you remember anything else?" Diana asked, turning back to them.

"One thing," said Kit, surprised he actually had something to contribute. "Zara said the next Council meeting was going to be soon."

"I assume that's the one where they tell everyone about Arthur," said Livvy. "And make their play for the Institute."

"The Cohort is a powerful faction inside the Clave," said Diana. "They're a nasty bunch. They believe in interrogating any Down-worlders they find breaking the Accords with torture. They support the Cold Peace unconditionally. If I'd known Zara's father was one of them . . ." She shook her head.

"Zara can't have the Institute," said Livvy. "She *can't*. This is our home."

"She doesn't care about the Institute," said Kit. "She and her father want the power it can give." He thought of the Downworlders he knew at the Shadow Market, thought of them rounded up, forced to wear some kind of signs, branded or stamped with identification numbers. . . .

"The Cohort has the upper hand, though," said Livvy. "She knows about Arthur, and we can't afford to have anyone find out. She's right: They'll hand the Institute over to someone else."

"Is there anything you know about the Dearborns, or the Cohort? Something that might discredit them?" said Kit. "Keep them from getting the Institute if it was up for grabs?"

"But we'd still lose the Institute," said Ty.

"Yeah," said Kit. "But they wouldn't be able to start registering Downworlders. Maybe it doesn't sound that harmful, but it never stops there. Zara clearly doesn't care if Downworlders live or die— once she knows where they all are, once they have to report to her, the Cohort has power over them." He sighed. "You should really read some mundane history books."

"Maybe we could threaten her by saying we'll tell Diego," said Livvy. "He doesn't know, and—I know he was a jerk to Cristina, but I can't believe he'd be okay with all this. If he knew, he'd dump Zara, and she doesn't want that."

Diana frowned. "It's not our strongest position, but it is something." She turned to her desk, picked up a pen and notepad. "I'm going to write to Alec and Magnus. They head up the Downworlder-Shadowhunter Alliance. If anyone knows about the Cohort, or any tricks we can use to defeat them, they will."

"And if they don't?"

"We try Diego," said Diana. "I wish I believed I could trust him more than I do, but—" She sighed. "I like him. But I liked Manuel, too. People are not what they seem."

"And do we keep telling everyone that Julian and the others went to the Academy?" Livvy asked, sliding off the desk. Her eyes were dark-rimmed with exhaustion. Ty's shoulders drooped. Kit felt a little as if he'd been hit with a sandbag himself. "If anyone finds out they went to Faerie, it won't matter what we do about Zara—we'll lose the Institute anyway."

"We hope they come back soon," Diana said, looking out at the moon's reflection on the ocean water. "And if hoping doesn't work, we pray for it."

The woods had gone, and as the twilight deepened into true night, the four Shadowhunters trekked through a spectral land of green fields, separated by low stone walls. Every once in a while they would see another patch of the strange blighted earth through the mist. Sometimes they would glimpse the shape of a town in the distance and fall silent, not wanting to attract attention.

They had eaten what was left of their food back on the hill, though it wasn't much. Emma wasn't hungry, though. A snarl of misery had taken up residence in her stomach.

She couldn't forget what she'd seen when she'd woken up, alone in the grass.

Rising, she had looked around for Julian. He was gone, even the impression in the grass where he'd lain beside her fading.

The air had been heavy and gray-gold, making her head buzz as she climbed up over the ridge, about to call Julian's name.

Then she'd seen him, standing halfway down the hill, the dank air lifting his sleeves, the edges of his hair. He wasn't alone. A faerie girl in a black, ragged shift was with him. Her hair was the color of burnt rose petals, a sort of gray-pink, drifting around her shoulders.

Emma thought the girl looked up at her for a moment and smiled. She might have imagined it, though. She knew she didn't imagine what happened next, when the faerie girl leaned in to Jules and kissed him.

She wasn't sure what she thought would happen; some part of her expected Jules to push the girl away. He didn't. Instead he put his arms around her and drew her in, his hand tangling in her shimmering hair. Emma's stomach turned itself inside out as he pressed her close. He held the faerie girl tightly, their mouths moving together, her hands sliding from his shoulders down his back.

There was something almost beautiful about the sight, in a horrible way. It stabbed Emma through with the remembrance of what it had been like to kiss Jules herself. And there was no hesitancy in him, no reluctance, nothing held back as if he were reserving any piece of himself for Emma. He gave himself up utterly to the kiss, and he was as beautiful doing it as the realization that she had really lost him now was awful.

She thought she could actually feel her heart break, like a friable piece of china.

The faerie girl had broken away, and then there had been Mark and Cristina there, and Emma hadn't been able to watch what was happening: She'd turned away, crumpling into the grass, trying not to throw up.

Her hands balled into fists against the ground. *Get up,* she told herself fiercely. She owed that much to Jules. He'd hidden whatever pain he'd felt when she'd ended things between them, and she owed it to him to do the same.

Somehow she'd managed to get to her feet, plaster a smile on her face, speak normally when she came down the hill to join the others. Nod as they sat and divided up food, as the stars came out and Mark determined that he could navigate by them. Seem unconcerned as they set off, Julian beside his brother, and she and Cristina behind them, following Mark down the winding, unmarked paths of Faerie.

The sky was radiant now with multicolored stars, each blazing an individual path of pigment across the sky. Cristina was uncharacteristically quiet, kicking at stones with the toe of her boot as she walked. Mark and Julian were up ahead of them, just far enough to be out of earshot.

"¿Qué onda?" Cristina asked, looking sideways at Emma.

Emma's Spanish was bad, but even she understood *what's going on?* "Nothing." She felt awful about lying to Cristina, but worse about her own feelings. Sharing them would only make them seem more real.

"Well, good," Cristina said. "Because I have something to tell you." She took a deep breath. "I kissed Mark."

"Whoa," said Emma, diverted. "Whoa ho *ho*."

"Did you just say 'whoa ho ho'?"

"I did," Emma admitted. "So is this like a high-five-slash-chest-bump situation or an oh-my-God-what-are-we-going-to-do situation?"

Cristina tugged nervously on her hair. "I don't know—I like him very much, but—at first I thought I was only kissing him because of the faerie drink—"

Emma gasped. "You drank faerie wine? Cristina! That's how you black out and wake up the next day under a bridge with a tattoo that says I LOVE HELICOPTERS."

"It wasn't really wine! It was just juice!"

"Okay, okay." Emma lowered her voice. "Do you want me to end things with Mark? I mean, you know, tell the family it's over?"

"But Julian," Cristina said, looking troubled. "What about him?"

For a moment, Emma couldn't speak—she was remembering Julian as the pretty faerie girl had come through the grass toward him, the way she had put her hands on his body, the way his arms had locked across her back.

She had never felt jealousy like that before. It still ached in her, like the scar of an old wound. She welcomed the pain in a strange way. It was pain she deserved, she thought. If Julian hurt, she should hurt too, and she had cut him free—he was free to kiss faerie girls and look for love and be happy. He was doing nothing wrong.

She remembered what Tessa had told her, that the way to make Julian stop loving her was to make him think she didn't love him. To *convince* him. It seemed she had.

"I think my whole charade with Mark has done what it needed to do," she said. "So if you want . . ."

"I don't know," Cristina said. She took a deep breath. "I have to tell you something. Mark and I argued, and I didn't mean to, but I—"

"Stop!" It was Mark, up ahead. He whirled, Julian beside him, and held out a hand toward them. "Do you hear that?"

Emma strained her ears. She wished it was possible to rune herself—she missed the runes that improved speed and hearing and reflex.

She shook her head. Mark had changed into what must have been his Hunt clothes, darker and more ragged, and had even rubbed dirt into his hair and face. His two-colored eyes glittered in the twilight.

"Listen," he said, "it's getting louder," and suddenly Emma could hear it: music. A sort of music she'd never heard before, eerie and tuneless, it made her nerves feel like they were wriggling under her skin.

"The Court is near," Mark said. "Those are the King's pipers." He plunged into the thicker woods alongside the path, turning only to call "Come along!" to the others.

They followed. Emma was conscious of Julian just ahead of her;

he'd taken out a shortsword and was using it to hack away under-growth. Piles of leaves and branches studded with small, blood-colored flowers tumbled at her feet.

The music was louder now, and grew louder still as they passed through thick forest, the trees above them glimmering with will-o'-the-wisp lights. Multicolored lanterns hung from the branches, pointing the way toward the darkest part of the forest.

The Unseelie Court appeared suddenly—a burst of louder music and bright lights that stung Emma's eyes after so long in the dark. She wasn't sure what she'd imagined when she'd tried to picture the Unseelie Court. A massive stone castle, perhaps, with a grim throne room. A dark jewel of a chamber at the top of a tower with a winding gray stair. She recalled the shadowy darkness of the City of Bones, the hush of the place, the chill in the air.

But the Unseelie Court was outside—a number of tents and booths not unlike the ones at the Shadow Market, clustered in a glade in a circle of thick trees. The main part of it was a massive draped pavilion, with banners of velvet on which was displayed the emblem of a broken crown, stamped in gold, flying from every part of the structure.

A single tall throne made of smooth, glimmering black stone sat in the pavilion. It was empty. The back was carved with the two halves of a crown, this time hanging above a moon and a sun.

A few gentry faeries in dark cloaks were milling around in the pavilion near the throne. Their cloaks bore the crown insignia, and they wore thick gloves like the one Cristina had found at the ruins of Malcolm's house. Most were young; some barely looked older than fourteen or fifteen.

"The Unseelie King's sons," whispered Mark. They were crouched behind a tumble of boulders, peering around the edges, weapons in hand. "Some of them, anyway."

"Doesn't he have any daughters?" Emma muttered.

"He has no use for them," said Mark. "They say he has girl children killed at birth."

Emma couldn't prevent a flinch of anger. "Just let me get close to him," she whispered. "I'll show him what use girls are."

There was a sudden blare of music. The faeries in the area began to move toward the throne. They were brilliant in their finery, gold and green and blue and flame-red, the men as brightly clothed as the women.

"It's almost time," said Mark, straining to see. "The King is calling the gentry to him."

Julian straightened, still hidden by the boulders. "Then we should move now. I'm going to see if we can get any closer to the pavilion." His shortsword gleamed in the moonlight. "Cristina," he said. "Come with me."

After a single startled moment, Cristina nodded. "Of course." She took out her knife, sliding a quick apologetic look toward Emma as she and Julian disappeared into the trees.

Mark leaned forward against the massive boulder blocking them from the view of the glade. He didn't look at Emma, only spoke in a low voice. "I can't do this," he said. "I can no longer lie to my brother."

Emma froze. "Lie to him about what?" she asked, though she knew the answer.

"About us," he said. "The lie that we're in love. We must end it."

Emma closed her eyes. "I know. You and Cristina—"

"She told me," Mark interrupted. "That Julian is in love with you."

Emma didn't open her eyes, but she could still see the bright light of the torches surrounding the pavilion and the clearing burning against her eyelids.

"Emma," Mark said. "It was not her fault. It was an accident. But when she spoke the words to me, I understood. None of this ever had anything to do with Cameron Ashdown, did it? You were trying to protect Julian from his own feelings. If Julian loves you, you must convince him it's impossible for you to love him back."

His sympathy almost broke her. She opened her eyes—closing them was cowardice, and the Carstairs were not cowards. "Mark, you know about the Law," she said. "And you know Julian's secrets—about Arthur, the Institute. You know what would happen if anyone found out, what they would do to us, to your family."

"I do know," he said. "And I am not angry at you. I would stand beside you if you found someone else to deceive him. Sometimes we must deceive the ones we love. But I cannot be the instrument that causes him pain."

"But it can only be you. You think if there was anyone else, I would have asked you?" She could hear the desperation in her own voice.

Mark's eyes clouded. "Why only me?"

"Because there isn't anyone else Jules is jealous of," she said, and she saw the astonishment bloom in his eyes just as a twig snapped behind her. She whirled, Cortana flashing out.

It was Julian. "You should know better than to draw steel on your own *parabatai*," he said, with a crook of a smile.

She lowered the blade. Had he heard anything she and Mark had said? It didn't look like it. "You should know better than to make noise when you walk."

"No Soundless runes," said Jules, and glanced from her to Mark. "We've found a position closer to the throne. Cristina's already—"

But Mark had gone still. He was staring at something Emma couldn't see. Julian's gaze met hers, full of unguarded alarm, and then Mark was moving, pushing through the undergrowth.

The other two threw themselves after him. Emma could feel sweat gather in the hollow of her back as she strained herself not to step on a twig that might break, a leaf that might crack. It was painful, humbling almost to realize how much Nephilim relied on their runes.

She came up short quickly, almost bumping into Mark. He hadn't gone that far, only to the very edge of the clearing, where he was still hidden from the view of the pavilion by an overgrowth of ferns.

Their view of the clearing was unobstructed. Emma could see the Unseelie Faeries gathered close in front of the throne. There were likely a hundred of them, maybe more. They were dressed in stunning finery, much more elegant than she'd imagined. A woman with dark skin wore a dress made of the feathers of a swan, stark and white, a necklace of down encircling her slender throat. Two pale men were dressed in rose silk overcoats and waistcoats of shimmering blue bird's wings. A wheat-skinned woman with hair made of rose petals approached the pavilion, her dress an intricate cage of the bones of small animals, fastened together with thread made of human hair.

But Mark was looking at none of them, nor was he looking at the pavilion where the Unseelie princes stood, clearly waiting. Instead he was staring at two of the Unseelie princes, both clothed in black silk. One was tall with deep brown skin, the skull of a raven, dipped in gold, dangling around his throat. The other was pale and black-haired, his face narrow and bearded. Slumped between them was the figure of a prisoner, his clothes bloodstained, his body limp. The crowd parted for them, their voices quiet murmurs.

"Kieran," Mark whispered. He started forward, but Julian caught at the back of his shirt, gripping his brother so tightly that his knuckles turned white.

"Not yet," he hissed under his breath. His eyes were flat, glittering; in them Emma saw the ruthlessness that she had once told him frightened her. Not for herself, but for him.

The princes had reached a tall, white-barked tree just to the left and in front of the pavilion. The bearded prince slammed Kieran up against it, hard. The prince with the raven necklace spoke to him sharply, shaking his head. The other prince laughed.

"The one with the beard is Prince Erec," said Mark. "The King's favorite. The other is Prince Adaon. Kieran says that Adaon does not like to see people hurt. But Erec enjoys it."

It seemed to be true. Erec produced a rope of thorns and held it out toward Adaon, who shook his head and walked away toward the pavilion. Shrugging, Erec commenced binding Kieran to the tree trunk. His own hands were protected with thick gloves, but Kieran was wearing only a torn shirt and breeches, and the thorns cut into his wrists and ankles, and then his throat when Erec pulled a strand of the vicious rope tight against his skin. Through it all, Kieran slumped inertly, his eyes half-closed, clearly beyond caring.

Mark tensed, but Julian held on to him. Cristina had rejoined them and was pressing her hand over her mouth; she stared as Erec finished with Kieran and stepped back.

Blood welled from the lacerations where the thorn bindings cut into Kieran's skin. His head had fallen back against the trunk of the tree; Emma could see his silver eye, and the black one as well, both half-lidded. There were bruises on his pale skin, on his cheek and above his hip where his shirt was torn.

There was a commotion atop the pavilion, and a single blast from a horn shattered the murmuring quiet in the clearing. The gentry looked up. A tall figure had appeared beside the throne. He was all in white, salt-white, with a doublet of white silk and gauntlets of white bone. White horns curled from either side of his head, startling against the blackness of his hair. A gold band encircled his forehead.

Cristina exhaled. "The King."

Emma could see his profile: It was beautiful. Clear, precise, clean like a drawing or painting of something perfect. Emma couldn't have described the shape of his eyes or cheekbones or the turn of his mouth, and she lacked Jules's ability to paint it, but she knew it was uncanny and wonderful and that she would remember the face of the King of the Unseelie Court for all her life.

He turned, bringing his face into full view. Emma heard Cristina gasp faintly. The King's face was divided down the middle. The right side was the face of a young man, luminous with elegance and beauty, though his eye was red as flame. The left side was an inhuman mask, gray skin tight and leathery over bone, eye socket empty and black, mottled with brutal scars.

Kieran, bound to the tree, looked once at the monstrous face of his father and turned his head away, his chin dropping, tangled black hair falling to hide his eyes. Erec hurried toward the pavilion, joining Adaon and a crowd of other princes at their father's side.

Mark was breathing hard. "The face of the Unseelie King," he whispered. "Kieran spoke of it, but . . ."

"Steady," Julian whispered back. "Wait to hear what he says."

As if on cue, the King spoke. "Folk of the Court," he said. "We have gathered here for a sad purpose: to witness justice brought against one of the Fair Folk who has taken up arms and murdered another in a place of peace. Kieran Hunter stands convicted of the murder of Iarlath of the Unseelie Court, one of my own knights. He slew him with his blade, here in the Unseelie Lands."

A murmur ran through the crowd.

"We pay a price for the peace among our folk," said the King. His voice was like a ringing bell, lovely and echoing. Something touched Emma's shoulder. It was Julian's hand, the one that wasn't clasping Mark's arm. Emma looked at him in surprise, but he was staring ahead, toward the clearing. "No Unseelie faerie shall raise hand against another. The price of disobedience is justice. Death is paid with death."

Julian's fingers moved quickly against Emma's skin through her shirt, the age-old language of their shared childhood. S-T-A-Y H-E-R-E.

She whipped around to look at him, but he was already moving. She heard Mark's breath hiss out in a gasp and caught at his wrist, preventing him from going after his brother.

Under the starlight, Julian walked out into the clearing full of Unseelie gentry. Emma, her heart pounding, held tight to Mark's wrist; everything in her wanted to rush out after her *parabatai*, but he had asked her to stay, and she would stay, and hold on to Mark. Because Julian was moving as if he had a plan, and if he had a plan, she owed it to him to trust that it might work.

"What is he *doing*?" Cristina moaned, in an agony of suspense. Emma could only shake her head. Some of the faeries on the edge of the crowd had spotted him now and were gasping, drawing back as he approached. He had done nothing to cover the black, permanent runes on his skin—the Voyance rune on the back of his hand glared like an eye at the Fair Folk in their gaudy finery. The woman in the dress made of bones gave a screech.

"*Shadowhunter!*" she cried.

The King sat bolt upright. A moment later a row of faerie knights in black-and-silver armor—among them the princes who had dragged Kieran to the tree—had surrounded Julian, forming a circle around him. Swords of silver and brass and gold flashed up around him like a grim tribute.

Kieran raised his head and stared. The shock on his face as he recognized Julian was complete.

The King rose. His bifurcated face was grim and terrible. "Bring the Shadowhunter spy to me that I may kill him with my own hand."

"You will not kill me." Julian's voice, calm and confident, rose above the din of voices. "I am no spy. The Clave sent me, and if you kill me, it will mean open war."

The King hesitated. Emma felt a wild half urge to laugh. Julian had spoken the lie so calmly and confidently that she almost believed it herself. Doubt flickered across the King's face.

My parabatai, she thought, looking at Jules, standing with his back straight and his head back, *the only seventeen-year-old boy in the world who could make the King of the Dark Court doubt himself.*

"The Clave sent you? Why not an official convoy?" said the King.

Julian nodded, as if he'd expected the question. Probably he had. "There was no time. When we heard of the threat to Kieran Hunter, we knew we had to move immediately."

Kieran made a choked sound. There was a lash of thorned wire around his throat. Blood trickled down onto his collarbone.

"What cares the Clave or Consul for the life of a boy from the Wild Hunt?" said the King. "And a criminal, at that?"

"He is your own son," said Julian.

The King smiled. It was a bizarre sight, as half his face sprang into light and the other displayed a ghastly grimace. "No one can then," he said, "accuse me of favoritism. The Unseelie Court extends the hand of justice."

"The man he murdered," said Julian. "Iarlath. He was a kin-slayer. He plotted with Malcolm Fade to murder others of the Fair Folk."

"They were of the Seelie Court," said the King. "Not of our people."

"But you say you are the ruler of both Courts," said Julian. "Should not then the people who will one day be yours to rule expect your fairness and clemency?"

There was a murmur in the crowd, this one softer in tone. The King frowned.

"Iarlath also murdered Nephilim," said Julian. "Kieran prevented other Shadowhunter lives from being lost. Therefore we owe him, and we pay our debts. We will not let you take his life."

"What can you do to stop us?" snapped Erec. "Alone, as you are?"

Julian smiled. Though Emma had known him all her life, though he was like another part of herself, the cold surety of that smile sent ice through her veins. "I am not alone."

Emma let go of Mark. He strode forward into the clearing without looking back, and Emma and Cristina came after. None of them drew their weapons, though Cortana was strapped to Emma's back, visible to everyone. The crowd parted to let them pass through and join Julian. Emma realized, as they stepped into the circle of guards, that Mark's feet were still bare. They looked pale as a white cat's paws against the long dark grass.

Not that it mattered. Mark was a formidable warrior even barefoot. Emma had good cause to know.

The King looked at them and smiled. Emma didn't like the look of that smile. "What is this?" he said. "A convoy of children?"

"We are Shadowhunters," said Emma. "We bear the mandate of the Clave."

"So you said," said Prince Adaon. "What is your demand?"

"A good question," said the King.

"We demand a trial by combat," said Julian.

The King laughed. "Only one of the Fair Folk can enter a trial by combat in the Unseelie Lands."

"I am one of the Fair Folk," said Mark. "I can do it."

At that, Kieran began to struggle against his bonds. "No," he said, violently, blood running down his fingers, his chest. "*No.*"

Julian didn't even look at Kieran. Kieran might be who they were there to save, but if they had to torture him to save him, Julian would. *You're the boy who does what has to be done because no one else will,* Emma had told him once. It seemed like years ago.

"You are a Wild Hunter," said Erec. "And half Shadowhunter. You are bound by no laws, and your loyalty is to Gwyn, not to justice. You cannot fight." His lip curled back. "And the others are not faerie at all."

"Not quite true," said Julian. "It has often been said that children and the mad are of the faerie kind. That there is a bond between them. And we are children."

Erec snorted. "That's ridiculous. You are grown."

"The King called us children," said Julian. "'A convoy of children.' Would you call your liege lord a liar?"

There was a collective gasp. Erec went pale. "My Lord," he began, turning to the King. "Father—"

"Silence, Erec, you've said enough," said the King. His gaze was on Julian, the brilliant eye and the dark, empty socket. "An interesting one," he said, to no one in particular, "this boy who looks like a Shadowhunter and speaks like gentry." He rose to his feet. "You will have your trial by combat. Knights, lower your blades."

The flashing wall of bright metal around Emma and her friends vanished. Stony faces regarded them instead. Some were princes, bearing the distinct stamp of Kieran's delicate angular features. Some were badly scarred from past battles. Quite a few had their faces hidden by hoods or veils. Beyond them, the gentry of the Court were milling and exclaiming, clearly excited. The words "trial by combat" drifted through the clearing.

"You will have your trial," the King said again. "Only I shall pick which of you will be the champion."

"We are all willing," Cristina said.

"Of course you are. That is the nature of Shadowhunters. Foolish self-sacrifice." The King turned to glance at Kieran, throwing the skeletal side of his face into sharp relief. "Now how to choose? I know. A riddle of sorts."

Emma felt Julian tense. He wouldn't like the idea of a riddle. Too random. Julian didn't like anything he couldn't control.

"Come closer," said the King, beckoning them with a finger. His hands were pale like white bark. A hook like a short claw extended from each finger just above the knuckle.

The crowd parted to let Emma and the others closer to the

pavilion. As they went, Emma was conscious of a strange scent that hung all around them. Thick and bittersweet, like tree sap. It intensified as they drew close to the throne until they stood looking up at it, the King looming above them like a statue. Behind him stood a row of knights whose faces were covered by masks wrought from gold and silver and brass. Some were in the shape of rats, some golden lions or silver panthers.

"Truth is to be found in dreams," the King said, looking down at them. From this angle, Emma could see that the odd splitting of his face ended at his throat, which was ordinary skin. "Tell me, Shadowhunters: You enter a cave. Inside the cave is an egg, lit from within and glowing. You know that it beats with your dreams—not the ones you have during the day, but the ones you half-remember in the morning. It splits open. What emerges?"

"A rose," said Mark. "With thorns."

Cristina cut her eyes toward him in surprise, but remained motionless. "An angel," she said. "With bloody hands."

"A knife," said Emma. "Pure and clean."

"Bars," Julian said quietly. "The bars of a prison cell."

The King's expression didn't change. The murmurs of the Court around them seemed confused rather than angry or intrigued. The King reached out a long white taloned hand.

"You there, girl with the bright hair," he said. "You will be the champion of your people."

Relief speared through Emma. It would be her; the others would not be risked. She felt lighter, as if she could breathe again.

Cristina turned her face toward Emma, looking stricken; Mark seemed to be holding himself in with main force. Julian caught Emma's arm, moving to whisper in her ear, urgency in every line of his body.

She stood still, her eyes fixed on his face, letting the chaos of the Court flow around her. The coldness of battle was already beginning to descend on her: the chill that dampened emotions, letting everything but the fight fall away.

Julian was part of that, the beginning of battle and the cold of the middle of it and the fierceness of the fighting. There was nothing she wanted to look at more in the moments before a battle than his face. Nothing that made her feel more fully at home in herself, more like a Shadowhunter.

"Remember," Julian whispered into Emma's ear. "You've spilled faerie blood before, in Idris. They would have killed you, killed us all. This is a battle too. Show no mercy, Emma."

"Jules." She didn't know if he heard her say his name. Knights surrounded them suddenly, separating her from the others. Her arm slipped away from Julian's grip. She looked one last time at the three of them before being guided roughly forward. A space was being cleared just in front of the pavilion.

A horn blew, the sharp sound parting the night like a knife. One of the princes strode out from behind the pavilion beside a masked knight. The knight wore thick gray armor like an animal's hide. His helmet covered his face. A crude drawing was painted onto the front of the helmet: wide eyes, a mouth stretched in a grin. Someone had touched the helmet with paint-wet hands, and there were red streaks along the sides that lent an ominous air to what might otherwise have been clownish.

The prince guided the masked knight to his side of the cleared space and left him there, facing Emma. He was armed with a longsword of faerie workmanship, its blade silver traced with gold, its hilt studded with gems. The edges gleamed sharp as razor blades.

A strong sword, but nothing could break Cortana. Emma's weapon would not fail her. She could only fail herself.

"You know the rules," said the King in a bored tone. "Once the battle commences, neither warrior can be helped by a friend. The fight is to the death. The victor is he or she who survives."

Emma drew Cortana. It flashed like the setting sun, just before it drowned in the sea.

There was no reaction from the knight with the painted helmet. Emma focused on his stance. He was taller than her, had greater reach. His feet were carefully planted. Despite the ridiculous helmet, he was clearly a serious fighter.

She moved her own feet into position: left foot forward, right foot back, arcing the dominant side of her body toward her opponent.

"Let it begin," said the King.

Like a racehorse bursting out of the box, the knight rushed toward Emma, sword leaping forward. Caught off guard by his speed, Emma spun out of the way of the blade. But it was a late start. She should have raised Cortana earlier. She'd been counting on the swiftness of her Sure-Strike rune, but it was no longer working. A sharp terror she hadn't known in a long time went through her as she felt the whisper of the tip of the knight's sword gliding inches from her side.

Emma remembered her father's words when she'd first been learning. *Strike at your enemy, not his weapon.* Most fighters went for your blade. A good fighter went for your body.

This was a good fighter. But had she expected anything else? The King had chosen him, after all. Now she just had to hope that the King had underestimated *her.*

Two quick turns brought her to a slightly raised hillock of grass. Maybe she could even their height difference. The grass rustled. Emma didn't need to look to know that the knight was plunging toward her again. She whirled, bringing Cortana around in a slicing arc.

He barely moved backward. The sword cut along the material of his thick leather armor, opening a wide slit. He didn't flinch, though, or seem hurt. He certainly wasn't slowed down. He lunged for Emma, and she slid into a crouch, his blade whistling over her head. He lunged again and she sprang back.

She could hear her own breath, ragged in the cool air of the forest. The faerie knight was good, and she didn't have the benefit of runes, of seraph blades—any of the armaments of a Shadowhunter. And what if she was tiring earlier? What if this dark land was sucking out even the power in her blood?

She parried a blow, leaped back, and remembered, oddly, Zara's sneering voice, *Faeries fight dirty.* And Mark, *Faeries don't fight dirty, actually. They fight remarkably cleanly. They have a strict code of honor.*

She was already bending, striking at the other knight's ankles—he leaped upward, nearly levitating, and brought his own sword down, just as she seized a handful of leaves and dirt and rose, hurling them at the gaps in the faerie warrior's mask.

He choked and stumbled back. It was only a second, but it was enough; Emma slashed at his legs, one-two, and then his torso. Blood soaked his armored chest; his legs went out from under him, and he hit the ground on his back with a crash like a felled tree.

Emma slammed her foot down on his blade, as the crowd roared. She could hear Cristina calling her name, and Julian and Mark. Heart pounding, she stood over the motionless knight. Even now, sprawled in the grass, blackened around him by his own blood, he didn't make a sound.

"Remove his helmet and end it," said the King. "That is our tradition."

Emma took a deep breath. Everything that was Shadowhunter in her revolted against this, against taking the life of someone lying weaponless at her feet.

She thought of what Julian had said to her just before the combat. *Show no mercy.*

The tip of Cortana clanged against the rim of the helmet. She wedged it beneath the edge and pushed.

The helmet fell away. The man lying in the grass beneath Emma was human, not faerie. His eyes were blue, his hair blond streaked with gray. His face was more familiar to Emma than her own.

Her hand fell to her side, Cortana dangling from nerveless fingers.

It was her father.

11

On a Black Throne

Kit sat on the steps of the Institute, looking out at the water.

It had been a long and uncomfortable day. Things were tenser than ever between the Centurions and the inhabitants of the Institute, though at least the Centurions didn't know *why*.

Diana had made a heroic effort to teach lessons, as if everything were normal. No one could concentrate—for once Kit, despite being completely at sea regarding the comparisons of various seraphic alphabets, wasn't the most distracted person in the room. But the point of the lessons was to keep up appearances in front of the Centurions, so they slogged on.

Things didn't get much better at dinner. After a long, wet day during which they hadn't found anything, the Centurions were testy. It didn't help that Jon Cartwright had apparently had some kind of temper tantrum and stalked off, his whereabouts unknown. Judging by Zara's thinly compressed lips, he'd had an argument with her, though about what, Kit could only wonder. The morality of locking warlocks up in camps or escorting faeries to torture chambers, he guessed.

Diego and Rayan did their best to make cheerful conversation, but it failed. Livvy stared at Diego for most of the meal, probably thinking about their plan to use him to stop Zara, but it was clearly making Diego nervous, since he tried twice to cut his steak with a spoon. To make it worse, Dru and Tavvy seemed to pick up on the prickly vibes in the room and spent dinner peppering Diana with questions about when Julian and the others would be back from their "mission."

When it was all over, Kit thankfully slipped away, avoiding the washing-up after dinner, and found himself a quiet spot under the front portico of the house. The air blowing off the desert was cool and spiced, and the ocean gleamed under the stars, a sheet of deep black that ended in a series of unfurling white waves.

For the thousandth time, Kit asked himself what was keeping him here. While it seemed silly to disappear because of awkward dinner conversation, he'd been reminded sharply in the past day that the Blackthorns' problems weren't his, and probably never should be. It was one thing to be Johnny Rook's son.

It was another thing completely to be a Herondale.

He touched the silver of the ring on his finger, cool against his skin.

"I didn't know you were out here." It was Ty's voice; Kit knew it before he looked up. The other boy had come around the side of the house and was looking up at him curiously.

There was something around Ty's neck, but it wasn't his usual earphones. As he came up the stairs, a slim shadow in dark jeans and sweater, Kit realized it had eyes.

He pressed his back against the wall. "Is that a *ferret*?"

"It's wild," said Ty, leaning against the railing around the porch. "Ferrets are domesticated. So technically, it's a weasel, though if it was domesticated, it would be a ferret."

Kit stared at the animal. It blinked its eyes at him and wiggled its small paws.

"Wow," Kit said. He meant it.

The weasel ran down Ty's arm and leaped onto the railing, then disappeared into the darkness. "Ferrets make great pets," Ty said. "They're surprisingly loyal. Or at least, people say it's surprising. I don't know why it would be. They're clean, and they like toys and quiet. And they can be trained to—" He broke off. "Are you bored?"

"No." Kit was jolted; had he looked bored? He'd been enjoying the sound of Ty's voice, lively and thoughtful. "Why?"

"Julian says sometimes people don't want to know as much about some topics as I do," said Ty. "So I should just ask."

"I guess that's true for everyone," said Kit.

Ty shook his head. "No," he said. "I'm different." He didn't sound bothered, or at all upset about it. It was a fact he knew about himself and that was all. Ty had a quiet confidence Kit found to his surprise that he envied. He never thought he would have envied anything about a Shadowhunter.

Ty climbed up onto the porch beside Kit and sat down. He smelled faintly of desert, sand and sage. Kit thought of the way he'd liked the sound of Ty's voice: It was rare to hear someone get that kind of sincere pleasure out of simply sharing information. He guessed it might be a coping mechanism, too—with the unpleasantness of the Centurions, and the worry about Julian and the others, Ty was probably stressed out.

"Why are you outside?" Ty asked Kit. "Are you thinking about running away again?"

"No," Kit said. He wasn't, really. Maybe a little. Looking at Ty made him not want to think about it. It made him want to discover a mystery so he could present it to Ty for solving, the way you might give someone who loved candy a box of See's.

"I wish we all could," Ty said, with disarming frankness. "It took us a long time to feel safe here, after the Dark War. Now it feels as if the Institute is full of enemies again."

"The Centurions, you mean?"

"I don't like having them all here," said Ty. "I don't like crowds of people in general. When they're all talking at the same time, and making noise. Crowds are the worst—especially places like the Pier. Have you ever been there?" He made a face. "All the lights and the shouting and the people. It's like broken glass in my head."

"What about fighting?" asked Kit. "Battles, killing demons, that must be pretty noisy and loud?"

Ty shook his head. "Battle is different. Battle is what Shadow-hunters *do*. Fighting is in my body, not my mind. As long as I can wear headphones—"

He broke off. In the distance, Kit heard a delicate shattering, like a window being blown in by a hurricane.

Ty exploded into a standing position, almost stepping on Kit, and drew a seraph blade from his weapons belt. He gripped it, staring out toward the ocean with a look as set as the glares on the statues in the garden behind the Institute.

Kit scrambled up after him, his heart hammering. "What's wrong? What was that?"

"Wards—the wards the Centurions put up—that's the sound of them breaking," said Ty. "Something's coming. Something dangerous."

"I thought you said the Institute was safe!"

"It usually is," Ty said, and raised the blade in his hand. "*Adriel*," he said, and the blade seemed to burn up from within. The glow lit the night, and in its illumination Kit saw that the road leading up to the Institute was packed with moving shapes. Not human ones—a surge of dark things, slippery and dank and undulating, and a stink rolled up toward them from below, one that almost made Kit gag. He remembered having been on Venice Beach once and passing the rotting corpse of a seal, festooned in maggoty seaweed—it stank like that, but worse.

"Hold this," Ty said, and a second later Kit found that Ty had shoved his blazing seraph blade into Kit's hand.

It was like holding a live wire. The sword seemed to pulse and writhe, and it was all Kit could do to hang on to it. "I've never held one of these before!" he said.

"My brother always says you have to start somewhere." Ty had detached a dagger from his belt. It was short and sharp and seemed altogether less fearsome a weapon than the seraph blade.

Which brother? Kit wondered, but he didn't have a chance to ask—he could hear shouts now, and running feet, and he was glad because the dark tide of *things* was nearly at the top of the road. He had turned his wrist a way he wouldn't have thought was possible, and the blade seemed steadier in his hand—it glowed without heat, as if it were composed of whatever made stars or moonlight.

"So now that everyone's awake," Kit said, "I don't suppose that means we retreat inside?"

Ty was pulling his headphones out of his pocket, bracing his black-sneakered feet just above the top step. "We're Shadowhunters," he said. "We don't run."

The moon came out from behind the cloud then, just as the door behind Kit and Ty flew open, and Shadowhunters poured out. Several of the Centurions carried witchlights: The night lit up, and Kit *saw* the things coming up the road, spilling onto the grass. They clamored toward the Institute, and on the porch the Shadowhunters raised their weapons.

"Sea demons," he heard Diana say grimly, and Kit knew suddenly that he was about to be in his first real battle, whether he liked it or not.

Kit whirled around. The night was full of light and noise. The brilliance of seraph blades illuminated the darkness, which was a blessing and a curse.

Kit could see Livvy and Diana with their weapons, followed by

Diego, a massive ax in his hand. Zara and the other Centurions were just behind.

But he could also see the sea demons, and they were much worse than he'd imagined. There were things that looked like prehistoric lizards, scaled with stone, their heads a mass of dripping needle teeth and dead black eyes. Things that looked like pulsing jelly with fanged mouths, in which hideous organs hung: misshapen hearts, transparent stomachs in which Kit could discern the outlines of what one of them had just eaten—something with human arms and legs ... Things like huge squids with leering faces and tentacles dotted with suckers from which green acid dripped to the ground, leaving seared holes in the grass.

The demons who'd killed his father were looking pretty attractive by comparison.

"By the Angel," Diana breathed. "Get behind me, Centurions."

Zara shot her a nasty look, though the Centurions were mostly clustered on the porch, gaping. Only Diego looked as if he literally couldn't wait to hurl himself into the fray. Veins stood out on his forehead, and his hand trembled with hatred.

"We are Centurions," Zara said. "We don't take orders from you—"

Diana whirled on her. "Shut up, you stupid child," she said in a voice of cold fury. "As if the Dearborns didn't cower in Zurich during the Dark War? You've never been in a real battle. I have. Don't speak another word."

Zara reeled back, rigid with shock. Not a one of her Centurions, not even Samantha or Manuel, moved to argue for her.

The demons—squawking, flapping, and sliding across the grass—had nearly reached the porch. Kit felt Livvy edging toward him and Ty, moving to stand in front of him. They were trying to block him, he realized suddenly. To protect him. He felt a wave of gratitude, and then a wave of annoyance—did they think he was a helpless mundane?

He'd fought demons before. Deep down in his soul, something was stirring. Something that made the seraph blade blaze brighter in his hand. Something that made him understand the look on Diego's face as he turned to Diana and said, "Orders?"

"Kill them all, obviously," Diana said, and the Centurions began to pour down the stairs. Diego plunged his ax into the first one he saw; runes gleamed along the blade as it slashed through jelly, spraying gray-black blood.

Kit threw himself forward. The space in front of the steps had become a melee. He saw the full power of seraph blades as Centurions plunged and stabbed, and the air filled with the stench of demon blood, and the blade in his hand blazed and blazed and something caught his wrist, trapping him at the top of the steps.

It was Livvy. "No," she said. "You're not ready—"

"I'm fine," he protested. Ty was halfway down the steps; he drew his hand back and flung the dagger he was still holding. It sank into the wide, flat flounder-eye of a rearing fish-headed demon, which blinked into oblivion.

He turned back to look at Kit and his sister. "Livvy," he said. "Let him—"

The door slammed open again, and to Kit's surprise, it was Arthur Blackthorn, still in jeans with his bathrobe over them, but he had jammed his feet into shoes at least. An ancient, tarnished sword dangled from his hand.

Diana, locked in combat with a lizard-demon, looked up in horror. "Arthur, no!"

Arthur was panting. There was terror on his face, but something else as well, a sort of fierceness. He hurtled down the steps, flinging himself at the first demon he saw—a fringed, reddish thing with a single massive mouth and a long stinger. As the stinger came down, he sliced it in half, sending the creature bobbing and shrieking through the air like a deflating balloon.

Livvy released Kit. She was staring at her uncle in amazement. Kit turned to descend the stairs, just as the demons began to draw back—retreating, but why? The Centurions had started to cheer as the space before the Institute cleared, but to Kit, it seemed too soon. The demons hadn't been losing. They hadn't been winning, but it was too early for a retreat.

"Something's going on," he said, looking between Livvy and Ty, both of whom were poised on the steps with him. "Something's wrong—"

Laughter pierced the air. The demons froze in a semicircle, blocking the way to the road, but not moving forward. In the middle of their semicircle walked a figure out of a horror movie.

It had once been a man; he still had the blurred shape of one, but his skin was fish-belly gray-green, and he limped because most of one arm and his side had been chewed away. His shirt hung in rags, showing where the white bones of his ribs had been picked clean, the drained gray skin around his terrible wounds.

His hair was mostly gone, though what remained of it was bone-white. His face was drowned and bloated, his eyes gone milky, bleached by seawater. He smiled with a mouth that was mostly lipless. In his hand he clutched a black sack, its fabric stained wet and dark.

"Shadowhunters," he said. "How I've missed you."

It was Malcolm Fade.

In the silence that followed the unmasking of the Unseelie champion, Julian could hear his own heart slamming against his chest. He felt the burning of his *parabatai* rune, a clear searing pain. Emma's pain.

He wanted to go to her. She stood like a knight in a painting, her head bowed and her sword at her side, blood splattering her gear, her hair half-torn out of its bindings, floating down around her. He saw her lips move: He knew what she was saying, even if he couldn't hear her. It cut through him with memories of the Emma he had known what seemed like a thousand years ago, a little girl reaching out her arms for her father to lift her up.

Daddy?

The King laughed. "Cut his throat, girl," he said. "Or can't you kill your own father?"

"*Father?*" Cristina echoed. "What does he mean?"

"That's John Carstairs," said Mark. "Emma's father."

"But how—"

"I don't know," Julian said. "It's impossible."

Emma dropped to her knees, sliding Cortana back into its scabbard. In the moonlight she and her father were shadows as she bent over him.

The King began to laugh, his eerie face split by a wide grin, and the Court laughed with him, howls of mirth exploding around them.

No one was paying attention to the three Shadowhunters in the center of the clearing.

Julian wanted to go to Emma. He wanted it desperately. But he was someone who was used to not doing, or getting, what he wanted. He spun toward Mark and Cristina. "Go to her," he said to Cristina. Her dark eyes widened. "Go to *him*," he said to Mark, and Mark nodded and slipped into the crowd, a shadow into shadows.

Cristina disappeared after him, plunging the opposite way into the crowd. The courtiers were still laughing, the sound of their ridicule rising up, painting the night. *Human emotions are so foolish to them, and human minds and hearts so fragile.*

Julian slid a dagger from his belt. Not a seraph blade, or even a runed one, but it was cold iron, and fit comfortably into his palm. The princes among the knights were looking toward the pavilion, laughing. It took Julian only a few steps to reach them, to throw his arms around Prince Erec from the back and press the edge of his dagger to his throat.

Kit's first, distracted thought was, *So that's why they haven't been able to find Malcolm's body.*

His second was a memory. The High Warlock had been a fixture of the Shadow Market, and friendly with Kit's father—though he had only learned later that they had been more than acquaintances, but partners in crime. Still, the lively, purple-eyed warlock had been popular at the Market, and had sometimes produced interesting candy for Kit that he claimed came from faraway places he had traveled to.

It had been strange for Kit to realize that the friendly warlock he knew was a murderer. It was even stranger now to see what Malcolm had become. The warlock moved forward, stripped of all his previous grace, lurching over the grass. The Shadowhunters snapped into formation, like a Roman legion: They faced Malcolm in a line, shoulder to shoulder, their weapons out. Only Arthur stood alone. He stared at Malcolm, his mouth working.

The grass in front of them all was seared black and gray by demon blood.

Malcolm smirked, as well as he could with his ruined face. "Arthur," he said, gazing at the shrinking man in his bloodstained bathrobe. "*You* must miss me. You don't look as if you're doing well without your medication. Not at all."

Arthur flattened himself against the Institute wall. There was a murmur among the Centurions, cut off when Diana spoke. "Malcolm," she said. She sounded remarkably calm, considering. "What do you want?"

He came to a stop, close to the Centurions, though not close enough for them to strike. "Have you been enjoying looking for my body, Centurions? It's been a real treat to watch you. Splashing around in your invisible boat, no idea what you're looking for or how to find it. But then you never have been much use without warlocks, have you?"

"Silence, filth," said Zara, vibrating like an electrical wire. "You—"

Divya elbowed her. "Don't," she whispered. "Let Diana talk."

"Malcolm," said Diana, in the same cold tone. "Things aren't like they were before. We have the might of the Clave on our side. We know who you are, and we will find out where you are. You are a fool to have come here and shown your hand."

"My hand," he mused. "Where is my hand again? Oh, right. It's inside this bag. . . ." He plunged his hand into the sack he'd been carrying. When he drew it out, he was carrying a severed human head.

There was a horrified silence.

"*Jon!*" Diego said hoarsely.

Gen Whitelaw seemed about to collapse. "Oh God, poor Marisol. Oh—"

Zara was staring with openmouthed horror, though she made no move to go forward. Diego took a step, but Rayan caught his arm as Diana snapped, "Centurions! Remain in formation!"

There was a gagging sound as Malcolm threw Jon Cartwright's severed head onto the bare grass. Kit realized he'd made the noise himself. He was staring at Jon's exposed spinal column. It was very white against the dark ground.

"I suppose you're right," Malcolm said to Diana. "It's rather time to give up our pretenses, isn't it? You know my weaknesses— and I know yours. Killing this one"—he gestured at Jon's remains— "took seconds, and taking down your wards took less. Do you think it will take much longer for me to get something I actually want?"

"And what is that?" said Diana. "What is it you want, Malcolm?"

"I want what I've always wanted. I want Annabel and what it will take to get her back." Malcolm laughed. It was a gurgling sort of sound. "I want my Blackthorn blood."

Emma couldn't remember dropping to her knees, but she was kneeling.

Churned ground and dead leaves were all around her. The faerie knight—her father—was on his back in a pool of spreading blood. It soaked into the already dark earth and turned it nearly black.

"Daddy," she whispered. "Daddy, please look at me."

She hadn't said the word "daddy" in years. Probably since she was seven years old.

Blue eyes opened in his scarred face. He looked just as Emma remembered him—blond whiskers where he'd forgotten to shave, lines of kindness around his eyes. Dried blood spattered his cheek. He stared at her, wide-eyed.

The King laughed. "Cut his throat," he said. "Or can't you kill your own father, girl?"

John Carstairs's lips moved, but no sound came out.

You will see again the face of someone you loved, who is dead, the phouka had said. But Emma had never dreamed this, not this.

She caught hold of her father's arm, covered in leathery faerie armor. "I concede," she said raggedly, "I concede, I concede, just help him—"

"She has conceded," said the King.

The Court began to laugh. Laughter rose up around Emma, though she barely heard it. A voice in the back of her head was telling her that this wasn't right, there was a fundamental wrongness here, but the sight of her father was roaring in her head like the sound of a crashing wave. She reached for a stele—he was still a Shadowhunter after all—but dropped her hand; no *iratze* would work here.

"I won't leave you," she said. Her head was buzzing. "I won't leave you here." She gripped his arm tighter, crouching at the foot of the pavilion, aware of the King's gaze on her, the laughter all around. "I'll stay."

It was Arthur who moved. He burst away from the wall, careening toward Livvy and Ty. He seized each of them by an arm and propelled them toward the Institute door.

They both struggled, but Arthur seemed shockingly strong. Livvy half-turned, calling Kit's name. Arthur kicked the front door open and shoved his niece and nephew through. Kit could hear Livvy shouting, and the door slammed behind them.

Diana arched an eyebrow at Malcolm. "Blackthorn blood, you said?"

Malcolm sighed. "Mad dogs and Englishmen," he said. "And sometimes you encounter someone who's both. He can't think that would *work*."

"Are you saying you can get into the Institute?" Diego demanded.

"I'm saying it doesn't matter," said Malcolm. "I set this all up before Emma killed me. My death—and I am dead, though not for long, isn't the Black Volume wonderful?—released the sea demons along this coast. What you see with me tonight is a tiny fraction of the numbers I control. Either you bring me a Blackthorn, or I send them up on land to murder and destroy mundanes."

"We will stop you," Diana said. "The Clave will stop you. They will send Shadowhunters—"

"There aren't *enough* of you," said Malcolm, with glee. He had begun to pace up and down in front of the wall of sea demons that slavered behind him. "That's the beauty of the Dark War. You simply can't hold off every demon in the Pacific, not with your current numbers. Oh, I'm not saying you might not win eventually. You would. But think of the death toll in the meantime. Is one measly Blackthorn really worth it?"

"We're not going to give you one of our own to murder, Fade," said Diana. "You know better than that."

"You don't speak for the Clave, Diana," said Malcolm. "And they are not above sacrifices." He tried to grin. One rotted lip split, and black fluid spilled down his chin. "One for many."

Diana was breathing hard, her shoulders rising and falling angrily. "And then what? All that death and destruction and what will you gain?"

"You will have also suffered," said Malcolm. "And that is enough for me, for now. That the Blackthorns suffer." His eyes raked the group in front of him. "Where are my Julian and Emma? And Mark? Too cowardly to face me?" He chuckled. "Too bad. I would have liked to see Emma's face when she laid eyes on me. You may tell her I said I hope the curse consumes them both."

Consumes who? Kit thought, but Malcolm's gaze had dipped to focus on him, and he saw the warlock's milky eyes glitter. "Sorry about your father, Herondale," said Malcolm. "It couldn't be helped."

Kit raised Adriel over his head. The seraph blade was hot under his grip, starting to flicker, but it cast a glow all around him, one he hoped illuminated him enough that the warlock could see it when he spat in his direction.

Malcolm's gaze flattened. He turned back to Diana. "I will give you until tomorrow night to decide. Then I will return. If you do not provide a Blackthorn to me, the coast will be ravaged. In the meantime—" He snapped his fingers, and a dim purple fire flickered in the air. "Enjoy amusing yourselves with my friends here."

He vanished as the sea demons surged forward toward the Centurions.

12

BY THE MOUNTAINS

Mark shoved his way through the Unseelie Court. He had been among these people before only for revels: the Court was not always in the same place, but moved around the Unseelie Lands. Mark could smell blood on the night air now as he darted among the close-packed gentry. He could smell panic and fear and hate. Their hate of Shadowhunters. The King was calling to the Court to be quiet, but the crowd was shouting for Emma to spill her father's blood.

No one was guarding Kieran. He slumped on his knees, the weight of his body pulling against the thorned ropes that held him as if they were barbed wire. Blood oozed sluggishly around the lacerations on his wrists, neck, and ankles.

Mark pushed past the last of the courtiers. This close, he could see that Kieran wore something around his neck on a chain. An elf-bolt. *Mark's* elf-bolt. Mark's stomach tightened.

"Kieran." He put his hand against the other boy's cheek.

Kieran's eyes fluttered open. His face was gray with pain and hopelessness, but his smile was gentle. "So many dreams," he said. "Is this the end? Have you come to bear me to the Shining Lands? You could not have chosen a better face to wear."

Mark ran his hands along the ropes of thorns. They were tough. A seraph blade could have cut them, but seraph blades did not work here, leaving him only ordinary daggers. An idea sparked in Mark's mind, and he reached up to gently unfasten the elf-bolt from Kieran's throat.

"Whatever gods have done this," Kieran whispered, "they are gracious to bring me the one my soul loves, in my last moments." His head fell back against the tree, exposing the scarlet gashes around his throat where the thorns had cut in. "My Mark."

"Hush." Mark spoke through a tightened throat. The elf-bolt was sharp, and he drew the blade of it against the ropes that bound Kieran's throat and then his wrists. They fell away, and Kieran gave a gasp of pain relieved.

"It is true, as they say," said Kieran. "The pain leaves you as you die."

Mark slashed away the ropes binding Kieran's ankles, and straightened up. "That is enough," he said. "I am Mark, not an illusion. You are not dying, Kieran. You are living." He took Kieran by the wrist and helped him to his feet. "You are escaping."

Kieran's gaze seemed dazzled by moonlight. He reached for Mark and laid his hands on Mark's shoulders. There was a moment where Mark could have drawn away, but he didn't. He stepped toward Kieran just as Kieran did toward him, and he could smell blood and cut vines on Kieran, and they were kissing.

The curve of Kieran's lips under his own was as familiar to Mark as the taste of sugar or the feel of sunlight. But there was no sugar or sunlight here, nothing bright or sweet, only the dark pressure of the Court all around them and the scent of blood. And still his body responded to Kieran's, pressing the other boy up against the bark of the tree, gripping him, hands sliding on his skin, scars and fresh wounds under his fingertips.

Mark felt himself lifted up and out of his body, and he was in the Hunt again, hands gripped in Windspear's mane, leaning low into the wind that tore his hair and seared his throat and carried away his laughter. Kieran's arms were around him, the only warm thing in a cold world, and Kieran's lips against his cheek.

Something sang by his ear. He jerked away from Kieran. Another object whistled by and he instinctively crowded Kieran against the tree.

Arrows. Each arrow tipped with flame, they ripped their way through the Court like deadly fireflies. One of the Unseelie princes was racing toward Mark and Kieran, raising a bow as he came.

They had been noticed after all, it seemed.

The grass in front of the Institute seemed to boil, a mass of sea demons and Centurions, whipping tentacles and slashing seraph blades. Kit half-threw himself down the stairs, almost knocking into Samantha, who, alongside her twin, was battling furiously with a grotesque gray creature covered with sucking red mouths.

"Look where you're going!" she yelled, and then shrieked as a tentacle snaked around her chest. Kit whipped Adriel forward, severing the tentacle just above Samantha's shoulder. The demon shrieked from all its mouths and vanished.

"Disgusting," said Samantha, who was now covered in thick grayish demon-blood. She was frowning, which seemed ungrateful to Kit, but he hardly had time to worry about it; he was already turning to raise his sword against a spiny-looking creature with nubbly, stony skin like a starfish.

He thought of Ty on the beach with the starfish in his hand, smiling. It filled him with rage—he hadn't realized before how much demons seemed like the beautiful things of the world had been warped and sickened and made revolting.

The blade came down. The demon shrieked and flinched back—and arms were suddenly around Kit, dragging him backward.

It was Diana. She was half-drenched in blood, some human and some demon. She seized hold of Kit's arm, pulling him back toward the stairs, the Institute.

"I'm fine—I don't need help—" he panted, wrenching at her grip.

She plucked Adriel out of his hand and threw it toward Diego, who caught the blade and spun to drive it into the thick body of a jellyfish demon, bringing his ax down with the other hand. It was very impressive, but Kit was too angry to care.

"I don't *need help!*" he shouted again, as Diana hauled him up the steps. "I don't need to be saved!"

She spun him around to look at her. One of her sleeves was bloody, and there was a red mark on her throat where her necklace had been ripped away. But she was as imperious as always. "Maybe you don't," she said. "But the Blackthorns do, and you are going to help them."

Stunned, Kit stopped fighting. Diana let go of him and shouldered the doors of the Institute open, stalking inside; after one last glance back, he followed.

The moments after Julian seized Erec and put his knife to his throat were chaotic. Several of the faeries near the pavilion howled; the knights fell back, looking terrified. The Unseelie King was shouting.

Julian kept his mind focused: *Hold your prisoner. Keep the knife to his throat. If he gets away, you have nothing. If you kill him too quickly, you have nothing. This is your advantage. Take it.*

At a command from the King, the knights moved aside, forming a sort of tunnel for Julian to walk down, marching Erec ahead of him. The tunnel ended below the King's throne. The King was standing at the edge of the pavilion, his white cloak snapping in the breeze.

Erec didn't struggle, but when they reached the pavilion, he craned his head back to look up at his father. Julian could feel them lock eyes.

"You won't cut my son's throat," said the Unseelie King, gazing down at Julian with a look of disdain. "You're a Shadowhunter. You have a code of honor."

"You're thinking of Shadowhunters the way they used to be," said Julian. "I came of age in the Dark War. I was baptized in blood and fire."

"You are soft," said the King, "gentle as angels are gentle."

Julian settled the knife more firmly into the curve of Erec's throat. The faerie prince smelled like fear and blood. "I killed my own father," he said. "You think I won't kill your son?"

A look of surprise passed over the King's face. Adaon spoke. "He is telling the truth," he said. "Many were in the Hall of Accords during the war. It was witnessed. He is a ruthless one, that one."

The King frowned. "Adaon, be silent." But he was clearly troubled. Shadows moved behind his eyes. "The price you would pay for spilling the blood of my family in my Court would be unspeakable," he said to Julian. "Not just you would pay it. All the Clave would pay it."

"Then don't make me," Julian said. "Let us depart in peace. We will take Erec with us, for the distance of a mile, then let him go. No one is to follow us. If we sense we are being followed, we will kill him. *I* will kill him."

Erec cursed and spat. "Let him kill me, Father," he said. "Let my blood begin the war we know is coming."

The King's eyes rested for a moment on his son. *He is the King's favorite*, Mark had said. But Julian couldn't help but wonder if the King was more concerned about the war to come, controlling how and when it began, than he was about Erec's fate.

"You think angels are gentle," said Julian. "They are anything but. They bring justice in blood and heavenly fire. They take vengeance with fists and iron. Their glory is such it would burn out your eyes if you looked at them. It is a cold and brutal glory." He met the King's gaze: his angry eye, and his empty one. "Look at me, if you doubt what I say I will do," said Julian. "Look at my eyes. Faeries see much, they say. Do you think I am someone who has anything to lose?"

They were in the entryway: Ty, Livvy, Arthur, and the younger ones, Dru holding Tavvy in her arms.

They lit up when Diana and Kit came in, though Kit didn't know if that was for him, or for her. Arthur was sitting on the stairs, silent and staring in his bloodstained bathrobe. He lunged to his feet at the sight of them, though he clung to the banister with one hand.

"We heard everything," Livvy said. She was gray with shock, her hand in Ty's. "Malcolm wants Blackthorn blood and he has an army of demons—"

"When he says 'Blackthorn blood,' there isn't any chance he just means, like, an ounce?" said Kit. "Maybe a pint?"

Everyone glared at him except Ty. "I thought of that too," Ty said, looking delightedly at Kit. "But spells are written in archaic language. 'Blackthorn blood' means a Blackthorn life."

"He isn't getting what he wants," said Diana. She shrugged off her blood-soaked jacket and threw it on the floor. "We need a Portal. Now." She dug around for her phone in her jeans pocket, found it, and began to dial.

"But we can't just disappear," said Livvy. "Malcolm will release all those demons! People will be killed!"

"You can't bargain with Malcolm," said Diana. "He lies. He could get the Blackthorn blood he wants and still release the demons. Getting you safe and then striking against him is the better bet."

"But—"

"She's right," said Kit. "Malcolm promised all sorts of things to my dad, including keeping him safe. In the end, it turned out he'd made sure that if anything happened to him, my father would die too."

"Catarina?" Diana turned aside, the phone pressed to her ear. "I need a favor. A big one."

"We'll be seen as cowards," said Dru unhappily. "Running away like this—"

"You are children," said Arthur. "No one would expect you to stand and fight." He went across the room to the window. No one moved to join him. The sounds coming from outside were enough. Tavvy had his face pressed against his sister's shoulder.

"To London?" said Diana. "That's fine. Thanks, Catarina." She hung the phone up.

"*London?*" said Livvy. "Why London?"

"Why don't we go to Idris?" said Dru. "Where Emma and Jules are."

"Catarina can't open up a Portal to Idris," said Diana, not meeting Dru's gaze. "But she has an arrangement with the London Institute."

"Then we should contact the Clave!" said Dru. She jumped back as the air in front of her began to shimmer.

"We need to get our things," said Tavvy, looking at the growing shimmer with worry. It was spreading, a sort of pinwheel now of whirling colors and moving air. "We can't go with nothing."

"We don't have time for any of that," said Diana. "And we don't have time to contact the Clave. And there are Blackthorn houses in London, safe places, people you know—"

"But why?" Livvy began. "If the Clave—"

"It's entirely possible the Clave would prefer to trade one of you to Malcolm," said Arthur. "Isn't that what you mean, Diana?"

Diana said nothing. The whirling pinwheel was resolving into a shape: the shape of a door, tall and broad, surrounded by glowing runes.

"As would the Centurions, at least some of them," said Diana. "We are running from them, as much as from anyone else. They are already vanquishing the sea demons. There is little time."

"Diego would never—" Dru began indignantly.

"Diego isn't in charge," said Diana. The Portal had resolved into a steadily wavering door, which was open; through it, Kit could see a living room of sorts, with faded, flowered wallpaper. It seemed incongruous in the extreme. "Now, come—Drusilla, you first—"

With a look of despairing anger, Drusilla crossed the room and stepped through the Portal, still holding Tavvy. Kit watched in stunned amazement as they spun away, vanishing.

Livvy moved toward the Portal next, hand in hand with Ty. She paused in front of it, the force of the magic that pulsed through it lifting her hair. "But we can't leave this place to Zara and the Cohort," she protested, turning toward Diana. "We can't let them have it—"

"Better than any of you dying," Diana said. "Now, *go*."

But it was Ty who hesitated. "Kit's coming, right?"

Diana looked at Kit. He felt his throat hurt; he didn't know why.

"I'm coming," he said. He watched as Livvy and Ty stepped into the colorful void, watched as they vanished. Watched as Diana followed. Stepped up to the Portal himself, and paused there, looking at Arthur.

"Did you want to go first?" he said.

Arthur shook his head. There was an odd look on his face—odd even for Arthur. Though Arthur hadn't been that odd tonight, Kit thought. It was as if the emergency had forced him to hold himself together in a way he normally couldn't.

"Tell them," he said, and the muscles in his face twitched. Behind him, the front door shook; someone was trying to open it. "Tell them—"

"You'll be able to tell them yourself, in a minute," said Kit. He could feel the force of the Portal pulling at him. He even thought he could hear voices through it—Ty's voice, Livvy's. Yet he stood where he was.

"Is something going on?" he said.

Arthur moved toward the Portal. For a moment, Kit relaxed, thinking Arthur was going to step into it beside him. Instead he felt a hand on his shoulder.

"Tell Julian thank you," Arthur said, and shoved, hard.

Kit fell into the whirling, soundless nothingness.

The faerie prince let fly his arrow.

Kieran moved faster than Mark would have thought possible. He swung his body around, covering Mark's. The arrow whistled through the air, singing like a deadly bird. Mark only had time to grab for Kieran to push him away when the arrow struck, burying itself in Kieran's back just below his shoulder blade.

He slumped against Mark's shoulder. With his free hand, Mark pulled a dagger from his belt and threw it; the prince fell, screaming, the blade in his thigh.

Mark began to drag Kieran from the clearing. The arrows had stopped, but fire was blooming from the banners with their mark of the broken crown. They had caught fire. The gentry faeries were screaming and milling, many breaking free to run.

Still holding Kieran, Mark vanished into the forest.

"Emma," Cristina whispered. The clearing was thick with noise; laughter, hoots and jeers. In the distance she could see Julian with his knife to Erec's throat; gasps rose up as he pushed his way toward the King's pavilion, though the King, distracted by Emma, had not yet seen.

Emma was kneeling on the ground, gripping the arm of the wounded Faerie champion. She looked up and saw Cristina, and her eyes brightened.

"Help me with my dad," Emma said. She was tugging at her

father's arm, trying to get it looped around her neck. He lay motionless, and for a moment Cristina feared he was dead.

He pulled away from Emma and lumbered to his feet. He was a slender man, tall, and the family resemblance was clear: He had Emma's features, the shape of her eyes. His were blank, though, their blue dulled to milkiness.

"Let me go," he said. "Bitch Nephilim girl. Let me go. This has gone far enough."

Cristina's blood froze at his words. The King burst out into another round of laughter. Cristina caught at Emma, pulling her toward her. "Emma, you can't believe everything you see here."

"*This is my father*," said Emma. Cristina was holding her wrist; she could feel the pulse pounding in Emma's veins. Emma held her free hand out. "Dad," she said. "Please. Come with me."

"You are Nephilim," said Emma's father. Faintly, on his throat, the white scars of old Marks were visible. "If you touch me, I will drag you to the feet of my King, and he will have you killed."

The faeries all around them were giggling, uproarious, clutching at each other, and the thought that it was Emma's horror and confusion that was making them chuckle sent spikes of murderous rage through Cristina's veins.

It was one thing to study faeries. One thing to read about how their emotions were not like human emotions. How the Unseelie Court faeries were raised to find pleasure in the pain of others. To wrap you in a net of words and lies and watch smiling while you choked on their tricks.

It was another thing to see it.

There was a sudden commotion. The Unseelie King ran to the opposite edge of the pavilion; he was shouting orders, the knights in sudden disarray.

Julian, Cristina thought. And yes, she could see him, Julian holding Erec in front of him, at the foot of the King's pavilion. He had deliberately drawn the King away from Emma and Cristina.

"It will be easy enough to decide this," Cristina said. She took her balisong from her belt and held it out to the champion. "Take this," she said.

"Cristina, what are you doing—?" Emma said.

"It is cold iron," said Cristina. She took another two steps toward the champion. His face was changing even as she watched, less and less like Emma's, more and more like something else—something grotesque living under the skin. "He's a Shadowhunter. Cold iron shouldn't bother him."

She moved closer—and the champion who had looked like John Carstairs changed completely. His face rippled and his body flexed and changed, his skin growing mottled and gray-green. His lips pushed outward as his eyes sprang horrifyingly wide and yellow, his hair receding to show a slick, lumpy pate.

Where Emma's father had stood was a faerie knight with a squat body and the head of a toad. Emma stared, white-faced. Its wide mouth opened and it spoke in a croaking voice.

"At last, at last, free to slough the illusion of the disgusting Nephilim—"

It didn't finish its sentence. Emma had seized up Cortana and lunged forward, slamming the blade into the knight's throat.

It made a wet, squelching sound. Pus-colored blood sprayed from its wide mouth; it staggered back, but Emma followed, twisting the hilt of the knife. The stench of blood and the sound of wetly tearing flesh almost made Cristina vomit.

"Emma!" Cristina shouted. "*Emma!*"

Emma drew the sword back and stabbed again, and again, until Cristina grabbed her shoulders and yanked her back. The faerie knight sank to the ground, dead.

Emma was shaking, spattered with foul blood. She swayed on her feet.

"Come on." Cristina grabbed her friend's arm, started to pull her away from the pavilion. Just then the air exploded with a rustling, singing sound. Arrows. They were tipped with fire, lighting the clearing with an eerie, moving glow. Cristina automatically ducked, only to hear a loud *clang* a few inches from her head. Emma had whipped Cortana to the side and an arrow had struck the blade, crumbling instantly into pieces.

Cristina picked up her pace. "We have to get out of here—"

A flaming arrow shot by them and struck a banner dangling from the King's pavilion. The banner caught alight in crackling flames. It illuminated the princes running from the pavilion, dropping off the edges into shadow. The King still stood before his throne, though, staring down into emptiness. Where was Jules? Where had he and Erec gone?

As they neared the edge of the clearing, the faerie woman in the bone dress loomed up in front of them. Her eyes were fish-green, without pupils, shimmering like oil in the starlight. Cristina brought her foot down hard on the faerie woman's; her screams were drowned in the Court's howls as Cristina elbowed her aside. She crashed into the pavilion, small bones raining down from her gown like misshapen snow.

Emma's hand was in Cristina's. Her fingers felt like ice. Cristina tightened her grip. "Come *on*," she said, and they plunged back into the trees.

Mark didn't dare go far. Julian, Emma, and Cristina were still in the Court. He pulled Kieran behind a thick oak tree and drew him down to sit leaning against it.

"Are you all right? Are you in pain?" Mark demanded.

Kieran looked at him with clear exasperation. Before Mark could stop him, he reached back, grasped the arrow, and yanked it out. Blood came with it, a welter that soaked the back of his shirt.

"Christ, Kieran, what the hell—"

"What foreign gods do you call on now?" Kieran demanded. "I thought you said I wasn't dying."

"You weren't." Mark pulled off his linen vest, wadding up the material to press it to Kieran's back. "Except now I might kill you for being so stupid."

"Hunters heal fast," said Kieran with a gasp. "Mark. It really is you." His eyes were luminous. "I knew you would come for me."

Mark said nothing. He was concentrating on holding the cloth against Kieran's wound, but a sense of anxiety pressed against the inside of his rib cage. He and Kieran had hardly ended things on good terms. Why would Kieran think Mark would come for him, when Mark very nearly hadn't?

"Kier," he said. He moved the vest away; Kieran was right about the healing. The blood had slowed to a sluggish trickle. Mark dropped the blood-wet linen and touched the side of Kieran's face. It was furnace hot. "You're burning up." He reached up to sling the elf-bolt necklace back around Kieran's throat, but the other boy stopped him.

"Why do I have your necklace?" he said, frowning. "It should be yours."

"I gave it back to you," Mark said.

Kieran gave a hoarse laugh. "I would remember that." His eyes went wide then. "I don't remember killing Iarlath," he said. "I know that I did. They told me that much. And I believe it; he was a bastard. But I don't remember it. I don't remember anything after I saw you through the window of the Institute, in the kitchen, talking to that girl. *Cristina.*"

Mark went cold all over. Automatically, he slung the elf-bolt necklace over his head, feeling it thump against his chest. *Kieran didn't remember?*

That meant he didn't remember betraying Mark, telling the

Wild Hunt that Mark had shared faerie secrets with Nephilim. He didn't remember the punishment, the whippings Julian and Emma had borne.

He didn't remember that Mark had broken things off between them. Given him his necklace back.

No wonder he'd thought Mark would come for him.

"*That girl* Cristina is right here," said a voice above them. Cristina had joined them in the shadows. She looked disheveled, though not nearly as much as Emma, who was splattered with faerie blood and bleeding from a long scratch on her cheek. Mark sprang up.

"What's going on? Are either of you hurt?"

"I—I think we're all right," Emma said. She sounded bewildered and worryingly blank.

"Emma killed the King's champion," said Cristina, and then closed her mouth. Mark sensed there was more to it, but didn't press.

Emma blinked, slowly focusing on Mark and Kieran. "Oh, it's *you*," she said to Kieran, sounding more like her old self. "Weasel Face. Committed any acts of monstrous personal betrayal lately?"

Kieran looked stunned. People didn't usually talk to Unseelie princes that way, and besides, Mark thought, Kieran no longer remembered why Emma might be angry with him or accuse him of betrayal. "You brought her here with you to rescue me?" he said to Mark.

"We *all* came to rescue you." It was Julian, only partly visible behind Erec, who he was shoving ahead of him. Emma exhaled, an audible sound of relief. Julian looked over at her quickly, and they shared a glance. It was what Mark had always thought of as the *parabatai* glance: the quick once-over to make sure the other person was all right, that they were beside you, safe and living. Though now that he knew of Julian's true feelings for Emma, he couldn't help but wonder if there was a layer more to what they shared.

Erec's throat was bleeding where the dagger had likely slipped; he was glaring out from beneath black brows, his face contorted into a snarl.

"Blood traitor," he said to Kieran. He spat past the knife. "Kin-slayer."

"Iarlath was no kin of mine," said Kieran, in an exhausted voice.

"He was more your kin than these monsters," said Erec, glaring around at the Shadowhunters surrounding him. "Even now, you betray us for them."

"As you betrayed me to the King our father?" said Kieran. He was huddled among the tree roots, looking surprisingly small, but when he tipped his face back to look at Erec, his eyes were hard as gems. "You think I do not know who told the King I killed Iarlath? You think I do not know at whose feet I can lay the blame for my exile to the Hunt?"

"Arrogant," said Erec. "You have always been arrogant, whelp, thinking you belonged in the Court with the rest of us. I am the King's favorite, not you. You earned no special place in his heart or the hearts of the Court."

"Yet they liked me better," Kieran said quietly. "Before—"

"Enough," Julian said. "The Court is on *fire*. Knights will be coming after us as soon as the chaos dies down. It's madness to stay here and gossip."

"Important Court business is not gossip," snarled Erec.

"It is to me." Julian peered through the woods. "There must be a quick way out of here, toward Seelie Lands. Can you lead us?"

Erec was silent.

"He can," said Kieran, rising unsteadily to his feet. "He can't lie and say it's not possible; that's why he's not talking."

Emma raised an eyebrow at Kieran. "Weasel Face, you're surprisingly helpful when you want to be."

"I wish you would not be so familiar," Kieran said disapprovingly.

Erec made a grunting noise—Julian was digging the knife into his neck. There was a slight tremble to Julian's hand, his grip on the blade. Mark imagined it must be a physical strain to keep Erec contained, but he suspected there was more to it than that. Julian did not have a torturer's nature, for all that he could and would be ruthless in protecting those he loved.

"I will kill you if you don't take us in the right direction," he said now. "I will do it slowly."

"You promised my father—"

"I am not a faerie," said Julian. "I can lie."

Erec looked darkly furious, in a way that alarmed Mark. Faeries could hold grudges for a very long time. He began to walk, though, and the others followed him, leaving behind the orange light glowing from the clearing.

They headed into the dark fastness of the forest. The trees grew close together, and there were thick roots snaking up through the dark soil. Clusters of flowers in deep colors, blood-reds and poison-greens, clustered around the low boughs of the trees. They passed a giggling tree faerie who sat in the fork of a branch, naked except for an elaborate net of silvery wires, and winked at Mark as he went by. Kieran was leaning heavily against his shoulder; Mark kept a hand splayed in the small of Kieran's back. Were the others puzzled or wondering what was going on between them? He saw Cristina glance back toward him, but couldn't read her expression.

Emma and Cristina walked close together. Julian was in front, letting Erec guide them. Mark still felt uneasiness. It seemed as if they had gotten away too easily. For the King of the Unseelie Court to have let them go, and to have them take his favorite son . . .

"Where are the others?" Erec asked as the trees thinned out

and the sky, multicolored in all its glory, became visible. "Your friends?"

"Friends?" Mark said, in a puzzled tone.

"The archers," said Erec. "Those flaming arrows in the Court—clever, I'll grant you. We wondered how you would cope with weapons once we took your angel powers away."

"How did you do that?" Mark asked. "Did you unhallow all this land?"

"That wouldn't make a difference," said Emma. "Runes work even in demon realms. This is something stranger."

"And the blight," said Mark. "What is the meaning of the blighted land? It is everywhere in the Unseelie Lands, like cancer in a sick body."

"As if I would speak of it," snapped Erec. "And it is no use threatening me—it would be worth my life to tell you."

"Believe me, I'm tired of threatening you myself," said Julian.

"Then let me go," said Erec. "How long do you plan to keep me? Forever? For that is how long you'd have to use me for protection to keep my father and his knights from finding you and cutting your throats."

"I said I was tired of threatening you, not that I was going to stop doing it," said Jules, tapping the knife blade. They'd come to the edge of the forest, where the trees ended and fields began. "Now, which way?"

Erec set off into the field, and they followed. Kieran was leaning more heavily on Mark. His face was very pale in the moonlight. The stars picked out the blue and green in his hair—his mother had been an ocean faerie, and a little of the shimmering loveliness of water remained in the colors of Kieran's hair and eyes.

Mark's arm curved around him unconsciously. He was angry at Kieran, yes, but here in Faerie, under the brilliant polychromatic stars, it was hard not to remember the past, not to think of all the times he'd clung to Kieran for warmth and companionship. How it had been just them, and he had thought perhaps it always would be. How he'd thought himself lucky that someone like Kieran, a prince, and beautiful, would ever look at him.

Kieran's whisper was a light caress against Mark's neck. "Windspear."

Windspear was Kieran's horse, or had been. He had come with him from the Court when Kieran had joined the Hunt.

"What about him? Where is he?"

"With the Hunt," said Kieran, and coughed, hard. "He was a gift from Adaon, when I was very young."

Mark had never before met Kieran's half brothers, the dozens of princes by different mothers who vied for the Unseelie Throne. Adaon, he knew from Kieran's tales, was one of the kinder ones. Erec was the opposite. He had been brutal to Kieran for most of his life. Kieran rarely spoke of him without anger.

"I thought I heard his hoofbeats," Kieran said. "I hear them still."

Mark listened. At first he heard nothing. His hearing was not as sharp as Kieran's or any true faerie's, at least not when his runes weren't working. He had to strain his ears to finally hear the sound. It *was* hoofbeats, but not Windspear's. Not any one horse's. This was a thunder of hoofbeats, dozens of them, coming from the forest.

"Julian!" he cried.

There was no keeping the panic from his voice; Jules heard it and turned, fast, his grip on Erec loosening. Erec tore away, exploding into motion. He streaked across the field, his black cloak flying behind him, and plunged into the forest.

"And he was such awesome company, too," Emma muttered. "All that 'Nephilim, you will die in a welter of your own blood' stuff was really refreshing." She paused. She had heard the horses. "What's that—?"

Cortana seemed to fly into her hand. Julian was still holding his dagger; Cristina had reached for her balisong.

"The King's cavalry," said Kieran, with surprising calm. "You cannot fight them."

"We must run," Mark said. "Now."

No one argued. They ran.

They tore through the field, leaped a stone wall on the far side, Mark half-carrying Kieran over. The ground had begun to tremble by then with the force of distant hoofbeats. Julian was swearing, a low steady stream of curses. Mark guessed he didn't get to swear all that much back at the Institute.

They were moving fast, but not fast enough, unless they could find more woods, some kind of cover. But nothing was visible in the distance, and looking up at the stars told Mark little. He was exhausted enough that they dizzied him. Half his strength felt as if it were going to Kieran: not just dragging him along but willing him upright.

They reached another wall, not high enough to stop faerie horses but high enough to be annoying. Emma leaped it; Julian sprang after her, his fingers lightly brushing the top of the wall as he sailed over.

Kieran shook his head. "I cannot do it," he said.

"Kier—" Mark began angrily, but Kieran had his head down, like a beaten dog. His hair fell, sweat-tangled, into his face, and his shirt and the waist of his breeches were soaked in blood. "You're bleeding again. I thought you said you were healing."

"I thought I was," Kieran said softly. "Mark, leave me here—"

A hand touched Mark's shoulder. Cristina. She had put her knife away. She looked at him levelly. "I'll help you get him over the wall."

"Thanks," Mark said. Kieran didn't seem to even have the energy to look at her angrily. She scrambled to the wall's top and reached her hands down; together she and Mark hauled Kieran up over the barrier. They jumped down, into the grass beside Emma and Julian, who were waiting, looking worried. Kieran landed beside them and collapsed to the ground.

"He can't keep running," said Mark.

Julian glanced over the wall. The hoofbeats were loud now, like thunder overhead. The leading edge of the Unseelie cavalry was in view, a dark and moving line. "He has to," he said. "They'll kill us."

"Leave me here," said Kieran. "Let them kill me."

Julian dropped to one knee. He put a hand under Kieran's chin, forcing the prince's face up so their eyes met. "You called me ruthless," he said, his fingers pale against Kieran's bloodied skin. "I have no pity for you, Kieran. You brought this on yourself. But if you think we came all the way here to save your life just to let you lie down and die, you're more foolish than I thought." His hand fell from Kieran's face to his arm, hauling him upright. "Help me, Mark."

Together they lifted Kieran between them and started forward. It was a blindingly hard task. Panic and the strain of holding up Kieran threw off Mark's hunting senses; they stumbled over rocks and roots, plunged into a thick copse of trees, its branches reaching down to tear at their skin and gear. Halfway through the copse, Kieran went limp. He had finally fainted.

"If he dies—" Mark began.

"He won't die," Julian said grimly.

"We could hide him here, come back to get him—"

"He's not a spare pair of shoes. We can't just leave him somewhere and expect him to be there when we get back," Julian hissed.

"Would you two stop—" Emma began, and then broke off with a gasp. "Oh!"

They had burst out of the small patch of trees. In front of them rose a hill, green and smooth. They could climb it, but it would demand digging in with hands and feet, scrambling over the top. It would be impossible to do and keep Kieran with them.

Even Julian stopped dead. Kieran's arm had been looped around Julian's neck; now it swung free, dangling at his side. Mark had the distant horrible feeling he was already dead. He wanted to lay Kieran down in the grass, check for his heartbeat, hold him as a Hunter should be held in his last moments.

Instead he turned his head and looked behind them. Cristina had her eyes closed; she was holding her pendant, her mouth moving in silent prayer. Emma held Cortana the same way, her eyes watchful and glittering. She would defend them to the last, Kieran too; she would go down under the hooves of the dark cavalry.

And they were coming. Mark could see them, shadows between the trees. Horses like black smoke, blazing eyes like red coals, shod in silver and burning gold. Fire and blood gave them life: They were murderous, and brutal.

Mark thought he could see the King, riding at their head. His battle helmet was etched with a pattern of screaming faces. Its face-plate covered only that half of the King's face that was human and beautiful, leaving the dead gray skin exposed. His single eye burned like red poison.

The sound of their coming was like the sound of a glacier breaking apart. Deafening, deadly. Mark wished suddenly that he could hear what Cristina was saying, the words of her quiet prayer. He watched her lips move. *Angel, provide for us, bless us, save us.*

"Mark." Julian turned his head toward his brother, his blue-green eyes suddenly unguarded, as if he were about to say something he had been desperate to say for a long time. "If you—"

The hill seemed to crack apart. A large square in the front of it peeled away from the rest and swung open like a door. Mark's mouth fell open. He had heard of such things, hills with doors in the sides, but he had never seen one.

Light glowed from the opening. It seemed to be a corridor, winding into the heart of the hill. A young faerie woman with gently pointed ears, her pale hair bound back with ropes of flowers, stood in the entryway, holding a lamp. She reached out a hand toward them.

"Come," she said, and her voice had the undeniable accent of the Seelie Court. "Come quickly, before they reach you, for the King's riders are savage and they will not leave you alive."

"And you?" Julian said. "Do you mean us well?"

Only Julian would argue with providence, Mark thought. But then Julian trusted no one but his family. And sometimes, not even them.

The woman smiled. "I am Nene," she said. "I will aid you and not harm you. But come, now, quickly."

Mark heard Cristina whisper a thank-you. Then they were all racing again, not daring to look behind them. One by one they leaped through the door and onto the packed earth inside. Mark and Julian came last, carrying Kieran. Mark caught one last glimpse of the dark riders behind them, and heard their screams of disappointed rage. Then the door slammed shut behind them, sealing up the hill.

13

DREAMLAND

Emma looked around in wonder. The entranceway bore no traces of having been carved out of a hillside. It was made of smooth ash-colored stone, the roof of blue marble patterned with gilded stars. A shadowed corridor led deeper into the hill.

The faerie woman, Nene, raised her lamp. It was filled with darting fireflies that cast a limited glow over their small group. Emma saw Julian with his mouth set in a hard line, Cristina holding her pendant tightly. Mark was lowering Kieran to the ground, his hands gentle. It took her a moment to realize Kieran was unconscious, his head lolling back, clothes dappled in blood.

"We are on Seelie Lands now," said Nene. "You can use your runes and witchlights." Her gaze on Kieran was troubled. "You can heal your friend."

"We can't." Julian flipped his witchlight out of his pocket. Its illumination rushed over Emma like the relief of water in the desert. "He's not a Shadowhunter."

Nene drifted closer, her pale eyebrows arched in consternation. Mark was on the ground, holding Kieran, whose face was drained icy-white, his closed eyes pale crescents in his blanched face. "Is he a Hunter?" she asked.

"We both—" began Mark.

"Is there anything you can do for him?" Emma interrupted, before Mark said too much.

"Yes." Nene knelt down, setting her lamp on the floor beside her. She took a vial from the inside of the sleeveless white fur jacket she wore over her dress. She hesitated, looking at Mark. "You do not need this? You are not injured?"

He shook his head, puzzled. "No, why?"

"I brought it for you." She uncorked it. Setting it to Kieran's lips, she crooned something under her breath in a language unfamiliar to Emma.

Kieran's lips parted and he swallowed. Pale gold liquid ran from the corners of his mouth. His eyes fluttered open and he pulled himself upright, swallowing a second mouthful and a third. His eyes met Nene's over the rim of the bottle and he turned his face away, wiping his mouth with his sleeve. "Save the rest," he said hoarsely. "It's enough."

He staggered to his feet, Mark helping him. The others had put away their steles. A new Healing rune burned on Emma's arm, an Energy rune beside it. Still, her body ached, and her heart hurt. She kept seeing her father, over and over, looking up at her from the grass.

It hadn't been him, not really, but that didn't make the image less painful.

"Come," said Nene, putting the vial away. "The drink will only sustain him a short time. We must hurry to the Court."

She started down the corridor and the others followed, Mark supporting the staggering Kieran. Julian had his witchlight stone out, and the hall was bright. The walls looked like intricate mosaic from a distance, but up close Emma could see that they were clear resin, behind which the petals of flowers and wings of butterflies were pressed flat.

"My lady," said Cristina. Her hair, like Emma's, was tangled with leaves and burrs. "What did you mean you brought that drink for Mark? How did you know he would come here?"

"We had guests, here in the Court," said Nene. "A Shadowhunter girl with red hair and a blond boy."

"Jace Herondale and Clary Fairchild," guessed Emma.

"They told me of the Blackthorns. That was a name I knew. My sister Nerissa loved a Blackthorn man, and had two of his children, and died of her love of him when he left her."

Mark stopped in his tracks. Kieran gave a slight hiss of pain. "You're my mother's sister?" he said incredulously.

"I think they usually call that your aunt," said Emma.

Mark gave her a dark look.

"I am the one who carried you and your sister to your father's doorstep and left you there for him to raise," said Nene. "You are my blood."

"I am beginning to wonder if any of you do not have a long-lost relative in Faerie," said Kieran.

"I don't," said Cristina, sounding regretful.

"Half Mark's relatives *are* faeries," pointed out Emma. "Where else would they be?"

"How did you know I would need saving?" said Mark to the faerie woman.

"The phouka who let you through the moon gate is an old friend," Nene said. "He told me of your journey, and I guessed your mission. I knew you would not survive the Lord of Shadows' tricks without aid."

"The burning arrows," Julian said. The corridor had now turned from stone and tile to packed earth. Roots dangled from the ceiling, each one twined with glimmering flowers that lit the darkness. Veins of minerals in the rock shimmered and changed as Emma looked at them. "That was you."

Nene nodded. "And a few others, of the Queen's Guard. Then I had only to stay a few steps ahead of you and open this door. It was not simple, but there are many doors to Seelie, all over the King's Lands. More than he knows." She cast a sharp look at Kieran. "You will not speak of this, will you, Hunter?"

"I thought you imagined me Nephilim," said Kieran.

"That was before I saw your eyes," she said. "Like my nephew, you are a servant of Gwyn." She sighed softly. "If my sister Nerissa had known her son would grow to be so cursed, it would have broken her heart."

Julian's face darkened, but before he could speak, a figure loomed up in front of them. They had reached a place where the corridor opened into a circular room, with other hallways leading off it in a dizzying array of directions.

Blocking their forward progress was a faerie knight. A tall, wheat-skinned man with a somber expression, he wore robes and a doublet of brilliant multicolored fabric. "Fergus," said Nene. "Let us go by."

He arched a dark brow and replied with a torrent of words in an odd, birdlike language—not angry, but clearly annoyed. Nene held up a hand, her voice sharp in response. As Emma watched her, she thought she could detect some resemblance to Mark. Not just the pale blond hair, but the delicacy of her bones, the deliberateness of her gestures.

The knight sighed and stepped aside. "We can go now, but we will be called to an audience with the Queen at first light," said Nene, hurrying forward. "Come, help me get the Hunter to a room."

Emma had quite a few questions—how they could tell when it was first light down here, why Nene seemed to dislike the Wild Hunt so much, and, of course, where they were going. She kept them to herself, though, and eventually they reached the end of a corridor where the walls were polished rock, gleaming with semiprecious stones: tiger's-eye, azurite, jasper. Gaps in the rock were covered with long velvet hangings, embroidered with glimmering thread.

Nene swept one of the hangings aside, revealing a room whose walls were smooth and curved in toward a domed ceiling. White hangings drifted down, half-covering a bed made of thick branches wound with flowers.

Nene set down her lamp. "Lay the Hunter down," she said.

Kieran had gone quiet since they'd entered the Seelie Court proper. He let Mark lead him over to the bed. He looked pretty awful, Emma thought, as Mark helped Kieran settle onto the mattress. She wondered how many times Mark had done this sort of thing for Kieran when Kieran was exhausted after a hunt—or how many times Kieran had done it for Mark. Being a Hunter was a risky job; she couldn't imagine how much of each other's blood they'd seen.

"Is there a healer in this Court?" Mark asked, straightening up.

"I am the healer," said Nene. "Though I rarely work alone. Usually I am assisted, but the hour is late and the Court half-empty." Her gaze fell on Cristina. "You will help me."

"Me?" Cristina looked startled.

"You have a healing air about you," said Nene, bustling up to a wooden cabinet and throwing the doors open. In it were jars of herbs, dangling strings of dried flowers, and vials of different-colored liquids. "Can you name any of these?"

"Foamflower," said Cristina promptly, as if they were in class. "Miner's lettuce, false lily, queen's cup."

Nene looked impressed. She pulled a stack of linens, including strips cut neatly into bandage size, from a drawer and handed them to Cristina. "Too many people in the room will slow a patient's healing. I will take these two next door; you must remove Kieran's clothes."

Cristina's cheeks flamed. "Mark can do that."

Nene rolled her eyes. "As you like." She turned toward the bed, where Kieran was collapsed back against the pillows. There were rusty smears of blood all over Mark's shirt and skin, but he didn't seem to notice. "Crush some foamflower, give it to him with water. Do not bandage him yet. We must inspect the wound."

She hurried from the room, and Emma and Julian dashed after her. They went only a few steps down the corridor, to where a dark red curtain hid an open door. Nene pushed it aside and gestured the two of them to come in.

Once inside, Emma had to suppress a gasp. This room was much grander than the other. The roof was lost in shadows. The walls were silvery quartz, and glowed from within, lighting the room with a soft radiance. Creamy white and ivory flowers cascaded down the walls, perfuming the air with the scent of a garden. A massive bed stood on a platform, steps leading up to it. It was piled with velvet cushions and a rich coverlet.

"Will this do?" Nene asked.

Emma could only nod. A hedge atop which grew a lattice of roses stretched across one end of the room, and behind it a cascade of water rushed down the rocks. When she glanced around the hedge, she saw that it emptied into a rock pool, lined with green and blue stones that formed the shape of a butterfly.

"Not as fancy as the Institute," she heard Julian say, "but it'll do."

"Whose room is this?" Emma asked. "Is it the Queen's?"

Nene laughed. "The Queen's chambers? Certainly not. This is Fergus's—actually, he has two. He is much favored in Court. He won't mind if you sleep here; he has night watch."

She turned to walk away, but stopped at the curtain and glanced back at them. "You are my nephew's brother and sister?"

Emma opened her mouth, then closed it again. Mark was more of a brother to her than anything else. Certainly more of a brother than Julian.

"Yes," Julian said, sensing her hesitation.

"And you love him," said Nene.

"I think you will find, if you take the time to get to know him, that he is easy to love," said Jules, and Emma's heart expanded, yearning for him, for him and Mark together, happy and laughing as brothers should be, and for the challenge in Julian's eyes when he looked at Nene. *You owe my brother the love he deserves; show it, or I turn my back on you.*

Nene cleared her throat. "And my niece? Alessa?"

"Her name is Helen now," said Julian. He paused for a moment, and Emma could see him weighing the mention of Helen's situation and dismissing it—he did not trust Nene enough, not yet. "Yes, she is my sister; yes, I love her as I love Mark. They are both easy to love."

"Easy to love," echoed Nene, in a musing voice. "There are few of our people I would ever have said were easy to love." She ducked back through the door. "I must hurry back, before that Hunter boy expires," she said, and was gone.

Julian looked at Emma with arched eyebrows. "She's very . . ."

"Yes," agreed Emma, not needing the rest of the words to know what he meant. She and Julian almost always agreed on people. She felt her mouth curve up as she smiled at him, despite everything, despite the incredible, impossible strain of the night.

And it wasn't as if the risk was over, she thought, turning to gaze at the room. She had hardly ever been in such a beautiful space. She had even heard of cave hotels, places in Cappadocia and Greece where gorgeous rooms were dug out of rocks and draped with silks and velvets. But it was the flowers, here, that tugged at her heart—those white flowers that smelled like cream and sugar, like the white flowers that grew in Idris. They seemed to radiate light.

And then there was the bed. With a sort of belated shock, she realized that she and Julian had been left alone together in a wildly romantic room with only one, very large and very plush, bed.

Definitely, the night's worries were not over, at all.

When Nene returned, she cleaned Kieran's wound gently with damp linens, pressing the edges of the cut carefully with her fingers. He sat upright and rigid on the edge of the bed, not moving or acknowledging what was going on, but Cristina could see from the deep crescent marking his lower lip that he was in pain.

Mark sat quietly beside him. He seemed wrung out, exhausted, and did not move to hold Kieran's hand, only sat with his shoulder touching the other boy's. But then, they had never been the hand-holding type, Cristina thought. The Wild Hunt had not been a place where such gentle expressions of affection were welcome.

"There was monkshood on the Unseelie's arrow," Nene said when she was done cleaning the wound. She held her hand out for a bandage and began wrapping Kieran's slender torso. He had been undressed and re-dressed in clean trousers, a shirt folded on the bed next to him. There were scars on Kieran's back, not unlike the ones on Mark's, and they stretched to the tops of his arms and down his forearms, too. He was thin but strong-looking, with clear lines of muscles in his arms and across his chest. "If you were a human or even ordinary fey, it would have killed you, but Hunters have their own protection. You will live."

"Yes," Kieran said, an arrogant tilt to his chin. But Cristina wondered. He didn't say, *Yes, I knew I would live.* He had doubted, she suspected. He had feared he would die.

She rather admired his bravery. She couldn't help it.

Nene rolled her eyes, finishing with the bandages. She tapped Cristina's shoulder as Kieran shrugged his shirt on, doing the buttons up with slow, shaking fingers, and indicated a shallow marble dish on the nightstand, filled with damp cloths swimming in a greenish liquid. "Those are poultices to prevent infection. Put a new one on the wound every two hours."

Cristina nodded. She wasn't sure how she would set an alarm or wake up every two hours, or if she was simply meant to stay awake through the night, but she would manage, either way.

"Here," Nene said, leaning down to Kieran with another vial. "Drink this. It will not harm you, only help you."

After a moment, Kieran drank. Suddenly he pushed the vial away, coughing. "How dare you—" he began, and then his eyes rolled back and he sank down to the pillows. Mark caught him before his wounded back could touch the bed, and helped Nene carefully roll him onto his side.

"Don't feel bad," Mark said, noticing Nene's set jaw. "He always falls asleep yelling that."

"He needed to rest," was all Nene said. She swept from the room.

Mark watched her go, his face troubled. "She is not what I imagined, when I dreamed that I might have family in Faerie," he said. "For so many years I looked and asked, and there was no sign of them. I had given up."

"She went out of her way to find you and save you," said Cristina. "She clearly cares for you."

"She doesn't know me," said Mark. "Faeries feel very strongly about blood. She could not leave me to fall into the hands of the Unseelie King. What happens to one member of a family reflects upon the others of that bloodline."

She touched your hair, Cristina wanted to say. She had seen it only very quickly: As Nene had reached to bandage Kieran's back, her fingers had brushed the fine edges of Mark's pale hair. He hadn't noticed, and Cristina wondered now, if she told him, if he would even believe her.

Cristina sat down on the foot of the bed. Kieran had curled up, his dark hair tangled beneath his restless head. Mark was leaning back against the headboard. His bare feet were on the bed, only a few inches from Cristina; his arm lay outstretched, his fingers nearly touching hers.

But his gaze was on Kieran. "He doesn't remember," he said.

"Kieran? What doesn't he remember?"

Mark pulled his knees up to his chest. In his torn and bloody shirt and trousers, he looked more like the ragged figure he'd been when the Wild Hunt had let him go. "The Unseelie Court beat him and tortured him," he said. "I expected it. It's what they do to their prisoners. After I untied him, as soon as I got him out of the clearing, I realized they'd done him some kind of damage that meant he didn't remember killing Iarlath. He doesn't remember anything since that night he saw us talking in the kitchen."

"He doesn't remember the whipping, what happened with Jules and Emma—?"

"He doesn't remember it happening, or that I left him over it," Mark said grimly. "He said he knew I would come for him. As if we were still—what we were."

"What *were* you?" Cristina realized she'd never asked. "Did you exchange promises? Did you have a word for it, like *novio*?"

"Boyfriend?" Mark echoed. "No, nothing like that. But it was something and then it was nothing. Because I was angry." He looked at Cristina wretchedly. "But how can I be angry at someone who doesn't even remember what he did?"

"Your feelings are your feelings. Kieran did do those things. He did them even if he does not remember them." Cristina frowned. "Do I sound harsh? I don't mean to. But I sat with Emma, after. I helped bandage her whip cuts."

"Now you've helped bandage Kieran." Mark took a deep breath. "I'm sorry, Cristina. This must seem— I can't even imagine what you're thinking. Having to sit here with me, with him—"

"You mean because of—" Cristina blushed. *Because of the way we kissed at the revel?* She searched inside her heart, looking for jealousy, for bitterness, for anger at Mark. There was nothing. Not even the fury she'd felt at Diego at the appearance of Zara.

How far away that seemed now. How distant and how unimportant. Zara was welcome to Diego; she could have him.

"I'm not angry," she said. "And you shouldn't be worrying about what I'm feeling, anyway. We should be concentrating on the fact that Kieran is safe, that we can return."

"I can't stop worrying about what you're feeling," Mark said. "I can't stop thinking about you at all."

Cristina felt her heart thump.

"It would be a mistake to think of the Seelie Court as safe ground where we can rest. There is an old saying that the only difference between Seelie and Unseelie is that the Unseelie do evil in the open, and the Seelie hide it." Mark glanced down. Kieran was breathing softly, evenly. "And I don't know what we will do with Kieran," he said. "Send him back to the Hunt? Call for Gwyn? Kieran will not understand why I would want to be parted from him now."

"Do you? Want to be parted from him now?"

Mark said nothing.

"I understand," she said. "I do. You have always needed Kieran so badly, you never had the chance to think about what you *wanted* with him before."

Mark made a short noise under his breath. He took her hand and held it, still looking at Kieran. His grip was tight, but she didn't pull away.

Julian sat on Fergus's massive bed. He could see nothing of Emma behind the high hedge that blocked the rock pool, but he could hear her splashing, a sound that echoed off the shining walls.

The sound made his nerves crank tighter. When she was done with the pool, she'd come out, and she'd get in bed with him. He'd shared beds with Emma a hundred times. Maybe a thousand. But it had meant nothing when they were children, and later, when they weren't, he had told himself it still meant nothing, even when he was waking up in the middle of the night to watch the way strands of her hair tickled her cheek while she slept. Even when she started to leave early in the morning to run on the beach, and he'd curl up in the warmth she left against the sheets and inhale the rose-water scent of her skin.

Breathe. He dug his hands into the velvet pillow he'd pulled onto his lap. *Think about something else.*

It wasn't as if he didn't have plenty of other things to think about. Here they were in the Seelie Court, not quite prisoners and not quite guests. Faerie was just as hard to escape as it was to enter, and yet they had no plan for how to leave.

But he was exhausted; this was the first time he'd been alone in a bedroom with Emma since she'd ended things, and for this rare instant, his heart was doing the thinking, not his brain.

"Jules?" she called. He remembered the brief days when she had called him *Julian*, the way the sound of the word in her mouth had made his heart shatter with pleasure. "Nene left me a dress, and it's . . ." She sighed. "Well, I guess you'd better see."

She came out from behind the hedge that hid the pool, her hair down, wearing the dress. Faerie clothes were usually either very ornate or very simple. This dress was simple. Thin straps criss-crossed her shoulders; it was made of a silky white material that clung to her wet body like a second skin, outlining the curves of her waist and hips.

Julian felt his mouth go dry. Why had Nene left her a dress? Why couldn't Emma be coming to bed in filthy gear? Why did the universe hate him?

"It's white," she said, frowning.

For death and mourning, the color's white. White was funerals for

Shadowhunters: There was white gear for state funerals, and white silk was placed over the eyes of dead Shadowhunters when their bodies were burned.

"White doesn't mean anything to faeries," he said. "To them, it's the color of flowers and natural things."

"I know, it's just . . ." She sighed and began to pad barefoot up the stairs to the dais where the bed was centered. She stopped to examine the enormous mattress, shaking her head in wonderment. "Okay maybe I didn't immediately warm to Fergus when we met," she said. Her face was glowing from the heat of the water, her cheeks pink. "But he would run an awesome bed-and-breakfast, you have to admit. He'd probably slip a mint tenderly under your pillow every night."

The gown fell away slightly as she climbed onto the bed, and Julian realized to his horror that it was slit up the side almost to her hip. Her long legs flashed against the material as she settled herself onto the bedspread.

The universe didn't just hate him, it was trying to kill him.

"Give me some more pillows," Emma demanded, and snatched several of them from beside Julian before he could move. He kept firm hold of the one on his lap and looked at Emma levelly.

"No stealing the covers," he said.

"I would never." She pushed the pillows behind her, making a pile she could lean against. Her damp hair adhered to her neck and shoulders, long locks of pale wet gold.

Her eyes were red-rimmed, as if she'd been crying. Emma rarely cried. He realized her chatter since she'd come into the bedroom was false cheer, something he ought to have known—he, who knew Emma better than anyone.

"Em," he said, unable to help himself, or the gentleness in his voice. "Are you all right? What happened at the Unseelie Court—"

"I just feel so stupid," she said, the bravado draining from her voice. Under the artifice was Emma, his Emma, with all her force and intelligence and bravery. Emma, sounding shattered. "I know faeries play tricks. I know they lie without lying. And yet the phouka said to me—he said if I came into Faerie, I would see the face of someone I had loved and lost."

"Very Fair Folk," said Julian. "You saw his face, your father's face, but it wasn't him. It was an illusion."

"It was like I couldn't process it," she said. "My whole mind was clouded. All I could think was that I had my father back."

"Your mind probably *was* clouded," said Julian. "There are all sorts of subtle enchantments that can blur your thoughts here. And it happened so quickly. I didn't suspect it was an illusion either. I've never heard of one so strong."

She didn't say anything. She was leaning back on her hands, her body outlined by the white gown. He felt a flash of almost-pain as if there were a key embedded under his flesh, tightening his skin every time it was turned. Memories attacked his mind ruthlessly—what it was like to slide his hands over her body, the way her teeth felt against his lower lip. The arch of her body fitting into the arch of his: a double crescent, an unraveled infinity sign.

He'd always thought desire was meant to be a pleasurable feeling. He'd never thought it could cut like this, like razors under his skin. He'd thought before that night on the beach with Emma that he wanted her more than anyone had ever wanted. He'd thought the wanting might kill him. But now he knew imagination was a pale thing. That even when it bled from him in the form of paint on canvas, it couldn't capture the richness of her skin on his, the sweet-hot taste of her mouth. Wanting wouldn't kill him, he thought, but knowing what he was missing might.

He dug his fingernails into his palms, hard. Unfortunately, he'd bitten them down too far to do much damage.

"Seeing that *thing* turn out not to be my father—it made me realize how much of my life was an illusion," Emma said. "I spent so much time looking for revenge, but finding it didn't make me happy. Cameron didn't make me happy. I thought all these things would make me happy, but it was all an illusion." She turned toward him, her eyes wide and impossibly dark. "You're one of the only real things in my life, Julian."

He could feel his heart beating through his body. Every other emotion—his jealousy of Mark, the pain of separation from Emma, his worry for the children, his fear of what the Seelie Court held for them—faded. Emma was looking at him and her cheeks were flushed and her lips were parted and if she leaned toward him, if she wanted him at all, he would give up and break down and apart. Even if it meant betraying his brother, he would do it. He would pull her toward him and bury himself in her, in her hair and her skin and her body.

It would be a thing he would remember later with agony that felt like white-hot knives. It would be a further reminder of everything he could never really have. And he would hate himself for hurting Mark. But none of that would stop him. He knew how far his willpower went, and he had reached its limit. Already his body was shaking, his breath quickening. He had only to reach out—

"I want to be *parabatai* again," she said. "The way we were before."

The words exploded like a blow inside his head. She didn't want him; she wanted to be *parabatai*, and that was it. He'd been sitting there thinking of what he wanted and how much pain he could take, but it didn't matter if she didn't want him. How had he been so stupid?

He spoke evenly. "We'll always be *parabatai*, Emma. It's for life."

"It's been weird ever since we—ever since I started dating Mark," she said, holding his gaze with her own. "But it's not because of Mark. It's because of us. What we did."

"We'll be fine," he said. "There's no rule book for this, no guidance. But we don't want to hurt each other, so we won't."

"There've been *parabatai* in the past who started hating each other. Think of Lucian Graymark and Valentine Morgenstern."

"That won't happen to us. We chose each other when we were children. We chose each other again when we were fourteen. I chose you, and you chose me. That's what the *parabatai* ceremony is, really, isn't it? It's a way of sealing that promise. The one that says that I will always choose you."

She leaned against his arm, just the lightest touch of her shoulder against his, but it lit up his body like fireworks over the Santa Monica Pier. "Jules?"

He nodded, not trusting himself to speak.

"I will always choose you, too," she said, and, laying her head on his shoulder, shut her eyes.

Cristina woke out of an uneasy sleep with a start. The room was dim; she was curled on the foot of the bed, her legs drawn up under her. Kieran was sleeping a drugged sleep propped against pillows, and Mark was on the floor, tangled in blankets.

Two hours, Nene had said. She had to check on Kieran every two hours. She looked again at Mark, decided she couldn't wake him, sighed, and rose to a sitting position, edging up the bed toward the faerie prince.

Many people looked calm in their sleep, but not Kieran. He was breathing hard, eyes darting back and forth behind his eyelids. His hands moved restlessly over the bedcovers. Still, he did not wake when she leaned forward to push up the back of his shirt with awkward fingers.

His skin was fever-hot. He was achingly lovely so close, though:

His long cheekbones matched his long eyes, their thick lashes feathering down, his hair a deep blue-black.

She quickly changed out the poultice; the old one was half-soaked with blood. As she leaned forward to pull his shirt back down, a hand clamped around her wrist like a vise.

Black and silver eyes gazed up at her. His lips moved; they were chapped and dry.

"Water?" he whispered.

Somehow, one-handedly, she managed to pour water from a pitcher on the nightstand into a pewter cup and give it to him. He drank it without letting go of her.

"Maybe you do not remember me," she said. "I am Cristina."

He put the cup down and stared at her. "I know who you are," he said, after a moment. "I thought—but no. We are in the Seelie Court."

"Yes," she said. "Mark is asleep," she added, in case he was worried.

But his mind seemed far away. "I thought I would die this night," he said. "I was prepared for it. I was ready."

"Things do not always happen when we think they will," Cristina said. It didn't seem that convincing a remark to her, but Kieran appeared comforted. Exhaustion was sweeping over his face, like a curtain sliding across a window.

His grip tightened on her. "Stay with me," he said.

Jolted by surprise, she would have replied—perhaps even refused—but she did not get the chance. He was already asleep.

Julian lay awake.

He wanted to sleep; exhaustion felt as if it had soaked into his bones. But the room was full of dim light and Emma was maddeningly close to him. He could feel the heat from her body as she slept. She had pushed away part of the bedspread that covered her, and he could see her bare shoulder where the dress she wore had slipped down, and the shape of the *parabatai* rune on her arm.

He thought of the storm clouds outside the Institute, the way she'd kissed him on the Institute steps before Gwyn had come. No, best to be truthful with himself. Before she'd pulled away and said his brother's name. That had been what ended it.

Perhaps it was just too easy to fall back into inappropriate emotion when they were already so close. Part of him wanted her to forget him and be happy. Part of him wanted her to remember the way he remembered, as if the memory of what they had been like together were a living part of his blood.

He ran his hands restlessly through his hair. The more he tried to bury such thoughts, the more they bubbled up, like water in the rock pool. He wanted to reach down and draw Emma toward him, capture her mouth with his—kiss the *real* Emma and erase the memory of the *leanansídhe*—but he would have settled for curling her close against his side, holding her through the night and feeling her body expand and contract as she breathed. He would have settled for sleeping through the night with only their smallest fingers touching.

"Julian," said a soft voice. "Awaken, son of thorns."

He sat up straight. Standing at the foot of the bed was a woman. Not Nene or Cristina: a woman he'd never seen before in person, though she was familiar from pictures. She was thin to the point of gauntness, but still beautiful, with full lips and glass-blue eyes. Red hair rippled to her waist. Her dress looked as if it had been made for her in a time before she had been so starved, but it was still lovely: deep blue and white, patterned with a delicate tracery of feathers, it wrapped her body in a downed softness. Her hands were long and white and pale, her mouth red, her ears slightly pointed.

On her head was a golden circlet—a crown, of intricate faerie-work.

"Julian Blackthorn," said the Queen of the Seelie Court. "Wake now and come with me, for I have something to show you."

14

THROUGH DARKENED GLASS

The Queen was silent as she walked, and Julian, barefoot, hurried to keep up with her. She moved purposefully down the long corridors of the Court.

It was hard to wrap one's mind around the geography of Faerie, with its ever-changing terrain, the way huge spaces fitted inside smaller ones. It was as if someone had taken the philosopher's question of how many angels could fit on the head of a pin and turned it into a landscape.

They passed other members of the gentry as they went. Here in the Seelie Court, there was less dark glamour, less viscera and bone and blood. Green livery echoed the color of plants and trees and grass. Everywhere there was gold: gold doublets on the men, long gold dresses on the women, as if they were channeling the sunshine that couldn't reach them below the earth.

They turned at last from the corridor into a massive circular room. It was bare of any furniture, and the walls were smooth stone, curving up toward a crystal set into the peak of the roof. Directly below the crystal was a great stone plinth, with a golden bowl resting on top of it.

"This is my scrying glass," said the Queen. "One of the treasures of the fey. Would you look into it?"

Julian hung back. He didn't have Cristina's expertise, but he did know what a scrying glass was. It allowed you to gaze into a reflective surface, usually a mirror or pool of water, and see what was happening somewhere else in the world. He itched to use it to check on his family, but he would take no gifts from a faerie unless he had to.

"No, thank you, my lady," he said.

He saw anger flash in her eyes. It surprised him. He would have thought her better at controlling her emotions. The anger was gone in a moment, though, and she smiled at him.

"A Blackthorn is about to put their own life in grave danger," she said. "Is that not a good enough reason for you to look in the glass? Would you be ignorant of harm coming to your family, your blood?" Her voice was almost a croon. "From what I know of you, Julian, son of thorns, that is not in your nature."

Julian clenched his hands. A Blackthorn putting themselves in danger? Could it be Ty, throwing himself into a mystery, or Livvy, being willful and reckless? *Dru? Tavvy?*

"You are not easily tempted," she said, and now her voice had grown softer, more seductive. Her eyes gleamed. She liked this, he thought. The chase, the game. "How unusual in one so young."

Julian thought with an almost despairing amusement of his near breakdown just now around Emma. But that was a weakness. Everyone had them. Years of denying himself anything and everything he wanted for the sake of his family had forged his will into something that surprised even him sometimes.

"I can't reach through and change what happens, can I?" he said. "Wouldn't it just be torture for me to watch?"

The Queen's lips curved. "I cannot tell you," she said. "I do not know what will happen myself. But if you do not look, you will never know either. And it is not my experience of humans or Nephilim that they can bear not knowing." She glanced down into the water. "Ah," she said. "He arrives at the convergence."

Julian was beside the plinth before he could stop himself, gazing down into the water. What he saw shocked him.

The water was like sheer glass, like the screen of a television onto which a scene was projected with an almost frightening clarity. Julian was looking at night in the Santa Monica Mountains, a sight familiar enough to send a dart of homesickness through him.

The moon rose over the ruins of the convergence. Boulders lay tumbled around a plain of dry grass that stretched to a sheer drop toward the ocean, blue-black in the distance. Wandering among the boulders was Arthur.

Julian couldn't remember the last time he had seen his uncle out of the Institute. Arthur had put on a rough jacket and boots, and in his hand was a witchlight, dimly glowing. He had never looked quite so much like a Shadowhunter, not even in the Hall of Accords.

"Malcolm!" Arthur called out. "Malcolm, I demand you come to me! Malcolm Fade! I am here, with Blackthorn blood!"

"But Malcolm's dead," Julian murmured, staring at the bowl. "He *died*."

"It is a weakness of your kind, to regard death as so final," said the Queen with glee, "especially when it comes to warlocks."

Fear tore through Julian like an arrow. He had been sure when they'd left the Institute that they were leaving his family safe. But if Malcolm was there—still hunting for Blackthorn blood—though, if Arthur was offering it, Malcolm must still not have acquired it— but then, Arthur could hardly be trusted—

"Hush," said the Queen, as if she could hear the clamor of his thoughts. "Watch."

"*Malcolm!*" Arthur cried, his voice echoing off the mountains.

"I am here. Though you are early." The voice belonged to a shadow—a twisted, misshapen shadow. Julian swallowed hard as Malcolm stepped out into the moonlight and what had been done to him, or what he had done to himself, was clearly revealed.

The water in the bowl blurred. Julian almost reached for the image before checking himself and jerking his hand back. "Where are they?" he said, in a harsh voice. "What are they doing?"

"Patience. There is a place they must go. Malcolm will take your uncle there." The Seelie Queen gloated. She thought she had Julian in the palm of her hand now, he thought, and hated her. She dipped her long fingers into the water, and Julian saw a brief swirl of images—the doors of the New York Institute, Jace and Clary asleep in a green field, Jem and Tessa in a dark, shadowy place—and then the images resolved again.

Arthur and Malcolm were inside a church, an old-fashioned one with stained-glass windows and carved pew-ends. Something covered in a black cloth lay on the altar. Something that moved ever so slightly, restlessly, like an animal waking from sleep.

Malcolm stood watching Arthur, with a smile playing on his ruined face. He looked like something dragged up from some watery Hell dimension. Cracks and runnels in his skin leaked seawater. His eyes were milky and opaque; half his white hair was gone, and his bald skin was patchy and scabbed. He wore a white suit, and the raw fissures in his skin disappeared incongruously under expensive collar and cuffs.

"For any blood ritual, willing blood is better than unwilling," said Arthur. He stood in his usual slumped posture, hands in the pockets of his jeans. "I'll give you mine willingly if you'll swear to leave my family alone."

Malcolm licked his lips; his tongue was bluish. "That's all you want? That promise?"

Arthur nodded.

"You don't want the Black Volume?" Malcolm said in a taunting voice, tapping the book tucked into the waistband of his trousers. "You don't want assurance I'll never harm a single Nephilim?"

"Your revenge only matters to me inasmuch as my family remains unharmed," said Arthur, and relief weakened Julian's knees. "The Blackthorn blood I give you should slake your thirst for it, warlock."

Malcolm smiled. His teeth were twisted and sharp, like a shark's. "Now, if I make this agreement, am I taking advantage of you, given that you are a madman?" he mused aloud. "Has your shaky mind mistaken the situation? Are you confused? Bewildered? Do you know who I am?" Arthur winced, and Julian felt a pang of sympathy for his uncle, and a flash of hate for Malcolm.

Kill him, he thought. *Tell me you brought a seraph blade, Uncle, and run him through.*

"Your uncle will not be armed," said the Queen. "Fade would have seen to that." She was watching with an almost avaricious delight. "The mad Nephilim and the mad warlock," she said. "It is like a storybook."

"You are Malcolm Fade, betrayer and murderer," said Arthur.

"Quite an ungrateful thing to say to someone who's been providing you with your cures all these years," Malcolm murmured.

"*Cures?* More like temporary lies. You did what you had to do to continue to deceive Julian," said Arthur, and Julian started to hear his own name. "You gave him medicine for me because it made him trust you. My family loved you. More than they ever did me. You twisted a knife in their hearts."

"Oh," Malcolm murmured. "If only."

"I would rather be mad my way than yours," said Arthur. "You had so much. Love once, and power, and immortal life, and you have thrown it away as if it were trash by the side of the road." He glanced toward the twitching thing on the altar. "I wonder if she will still love you, the way you are now."

Malcolm's face contorted. "Enough," he said, and a quick look of triumph passed over Arthur's tired, battered features. He had outwitted

Malcolm, in his own way. "I agree to your promise. Come here."

Arthur stepped forward. Malcolm seized him and began to propel him toward the altar. Arthur's witchlight was gone, but candles burned in brackets fastened to the walls, casting a flickering, yellowish light.

Malcolm held Arthur with one hand, bending him over the altar; with the other he drew the dark covering away from the altar. Annabel's body was revealed.

"Oh," breathed the Queen. "She was lovely, once."

She was not now. Annabel was a skeleton, though not the clean white down-to-the-bones type one usually saw in art and pictures. Her skin was leathery and dried, and pocked with holes where worms had crawled in and out. Nausea rose in Julian's stomach. She was covered with white winding-sheets, but her legs were visible, and her arms: There were places the skin had peeled away, and moss grew on the bones and dried tendons.

Brittle dark hair spilled from her skull. Her jaw worked as she saw Malcolm, and a moan issued from her destroyed throat. She seemed to be shaking her head.

"Don't worry, darling," said Malcolm. "I've brought you what you need."

"No!" Julian cried, but it was as he had feared: He could not halt the events unfolding before him. Malcolm snatched up the blade from beside Annabel and sliced open Arthur's throat.

Blood fountained over Annabel, over her body and the stone she lay on. Arthur groped at his neck, and Julian gagged, clutching the sides of the bowl with his fingers.

Annabel's winding-sheets had turned crimson. Arthur's hands dropped slowly to his sides. He was upright now only because Malcolm was holding him. Blood soaked Annabel's brittle hair and dried skin. It turned the front of Malcolm's white suit to a sheet of scarlet.

"Uncle Arthur," Julian whispered. He tasted salt on his lips. For a moment he was terrified that he was crying, and in front of the Queen—but to his relief he had only bitten his lip. He swallowed the metal of his own blood as Arthur went limp in Malcolm's grasp, and Malcolm shoved his body impatiently away. He crumpled to the ground beside the altar and lay still.

"Annabel," Malcolm breathed.

She had begun to stir.

Her limbs moved first, her legs and arms stretching, her hands reaching for nothing. For a moment Julian thought there was something wrong with the water in the bowl, an odd reflection, before he realized that it was actually Annabel herself. A white glow was creeping over her—no, it was skin, rising to cover bare bones and stripped tendons. Her corpse seemed to swell up and out as flesh filled out the shape of her, as if a smooth, sleek glove had been drawn over her skeleton. Gray and white turned to pink: Her bare feet and her calves looked human now. There were even clear half-moons of nails at the tips of her toes.

The skin crawled up her body, slipping under the winding-sheets, rising to cover her chest and collarbones, spreading down her arms. Her hands starfished out, each finger splayed as she tested the air. Her neck arched back as black-brown hair exploded from her skull. Breasts rose under the sheets, her hollow cheeks filled, her eyes snapped open.

They were Blackthorn eyes, shimmering blue-green as the sea.

Annabel sat up, clutching the rags of her bloody winding-sheets to her. Under them she had the body of a young woman. Thick hair cascaded around a pale oval face; her lips were full and red; her eyes shimmered in wonder as she stared at Malcolm.

And Malcolm was transformed. Whatever the vicious damage done to him, it seemed to fade away, and for a moment Julian saw him as he must have been when he was a young man in love. There was a wondering sweetness about him; he seemed frozen in place, his face shining in adoration as Annabel slid down from the altar. She landed on the stone floor beside Arthur's crumpled body.

"Annabel," Malcolm said. "My Annabel. I have waited so long for you, done so much to bring you back to me." He took a stumbling step toward her. "My love. My angel. Look at me."

But Annabel was looking down at Arthur. Slowly, she bent down and picked up the knife that had fallen by his body. When she straightened up, her gaze fixed on Malcolm, tears streaked her face. Her lips formed a soundless word—Julian craned forward, but it was too faint to hear. The surface of the scrying glass had begun to roil and tremble, like the surface of the sea before a storm.

Malcolm looked stricken. "Do not weep," he said. "My darling, my Annabel." He reached for her. Annabel stepped toward him, her face lifting to his. He bent down as if to kiss her just as she swept her arm up, driving the knife she held into his body.

Malcolm stared at her in disbelief. Then he cried out. It was a cry of more than pain—a howl of utter, despairing betrayal and heartbreak. A howl that seemed to rip through the universe, tearing apart the stars.

He staggered back, but Annabel pursued him, a wraith of blood and terror in her white-and-scarlet grave clothes. She slashed at him again, opening his chest, and he fell to the ground.

Even then he didn't raise a hand to fend her off as she moved to stand over him. Blood bubbled from the corner of his lips when he spoke. "*Annabel,*" he breathed. "Oh, my love, my love—"

She stabbed down viciously with the blade, driving it into his heart. Malcolm's body jerked. His head fell back, his eyes rolling to whites. Expressionless, Annabel bent over him and snatched the Black Volume from his belt. Without another glance at Malcolm, she turned and strode from the church, disappearing from the view of the scrying glass.

"Where did she go?" Julian said. He barely recognized his own voice. "Follow her, use the glass—"

"The scrying glass cannot find its way through so much dark magic," said the Queen. Her face was shining as if she'd just seen something wonderful.

Julian flinched away from her—he couldn't help it. He wanted nothing more than to stagger off to a corner of the room and be sick. But the Queen would see that as weakness. He found his way to a wall and leaned against it.

The Queen stood with one hand on the edge of the golden bowl, smiling at him. "Did you see how Fade never raised a hand to defend himself?" she said. "That is love, son of thorns. We welcome its cruelest blows and when we bleed from them, we whisper our thanks."

Julian braced himself against the wall. "Why did you show me that?"

"I would bargain with you," she said. "And there are things I would not have you be ignorant of when we do."

Julian tried to steady his breathing, forcing himself deeper into his own head, his own worst memories. He was in the Hall of Accords, he was twelve years old and he had just killed his father. He was in the Institute, and he had just found out that Malcolm Fade had kidnapped Tavvy. He was in the desert, and Emma was telling him that she loved Mark; Mark, and not him.

"What kind of bargain?" he said, and his voice was as steady as a rock.

She shook her head. Her red hair rayed out around her gaunt and hollowed face. "I would have all of your group there when the bargain is made, Shadowhunter."

"I will not bargain with you," said Julian. "The Cold Peace—"

She laughed. "You have shattered the Cold Peace a thousand times, child. Do not pretend that I know nothing of you or your family. Despite the Cold Peace, despite all I have lost, I am still the Queen of the Seelie Court."

Julian couldn't help but wonder what *despite all I have lost* meant—what had she lost, exactly? Did she only mean the strain of the Cold Peace, the shame of losing the Dark War?

"Besides," she said, "you don't know what I am offering yet. And neither do your friends. I think they might be quite interested, especially your lovely *parabatai*."

"You have something for Emma?" he demanded. "Then why did you bring me here alone?"

"There was something I wished to say to you. Something that you might not wish her to know that you knew." A tiny smile played across her lips. She took another step toward him. He was close enough to see the detail of the feathers on her dress, the flecks of blood that showed they had been torn by the roots from the bird. "The curse of the *parabatai*. I know how to break it."

Julian felt as if he could not catch his breath. It was what the phouka had said to him at the Gate: *In Faerie, you will find one who knows how the* parabatai *bond might be broken.*

He had carried that knowledge in his heart since they had arrived here. He had wondered who it would be. But it was the Queen—of course it was the Queen. Someone he absolutely should not trust.

"The curse?" he said, keeping his voice mild and a little puzzled, as if he had no idea why she'd called it that.

Something indefinable flashed in her eyes. "The *parabatai* bond, I should say. But it is a curse to you, is it not?" She caught his wrist, turning his hand over. The crescents he'd dug into his palms with his bitten nails were faint but visible. He thought of the scrying glass. Of her watching him with Emma in Fergus's room. Of course she had. She'd known when Emma fell asleep. When he was vulnerable. She knew he loved Emma. It might be something he could conceal from his family and friends, but to the Queen of the Seelie Court, accustomed to seeking out weakness and vulnerability and cruelly attuned to unpleasant truths, it would be as clear as a beacon. "As I said," she told him, smiling, "we welcome the wounds of love, do we not?"

A wave of rage went through him, but his curiosity was stronger. He drew his hand from hers. "Tell me," he said. "Tell me what you know."

Faerie knights in green and gold and red came to fetch Emma and bring her to the throne room. She was a little bewildered at Julian's absence, though reassured when she met Mark and Cristina in the hall, similarly escorted, and Mark told her in a low voice that he'd heard one of the guards say that Julian was already waiting for them in the throne room.

Emma cursed her own exhaustion. How could she not have noticed him leave? She'd forced herself to sleep, unable to bear another second of being so physically close to Jules without being able to even hug him. And he'd been so calm, so totally calm; he'd looked at her with distant friendliness—kindness, even, when he reassured her their friendship was intact—and it hurt like hell and all she wanted was for exhaustion to wipe it all away.

She reached to touch Cortana, strapped across her back. She carried the rest of her and Julian's things in her pack. She felt silly wearing a weapon over a filmy dress, but she hadn't been about to change in front of the Queen's Guard. They'd offered to carry the sword for her, but she'd refused. No one touched Cortana but her.

Cristina was nearly twitching with excitement. "The throne room of the Seelie Queen," she whispered. "I have read about it but never thought to actually see it. The look of it is meant to change with the moods of the Queen, as she changes."

Emma remembered Clary telling her stories of the Court, of a room of ice and snow where the Queen wore gold and silver, of a curtain of fluttering butterflies. But it was not quite like that when they arrived. Just as Mark had said, Julian was already in the throne room. It was a bare oval place, filled with grayish smoke. Smoke drifted across the floor and crackled along the ceiling, where it was forked with small darts of black lightning. There were no windows, but the gray smoke formed patterns against the walls—a field of dead flowers, a crashing wave, the skeleton of a winged creature.

Julian was sitting on the steps that led up to the great stone block where the Queen's throne stood. He wore a piecemeal mix of gear and ordinary clothes, and over his shirt was thrown a jacket he could only have found here in Faerie. It shimmered with bright thread and bits of brocade, the sleeves turned back to expose his forearms. His sea-glass bracelet glittered on his wrist.

He looked up when they came in. Even against the colorless background, his blue-green eyes shone.

"Before you say anything, I have something to tell you," he said. Only half of Emma's mind was on his words as he began to speak; the other was on how strangely at ease he seemed.

He looked calm, and when Julian was calm was always when he was at his most frightening. But he spoke on, and she began to realize what he was saying. Waves of shock went through her. Malcolm: dead, alive, and dead again? Arthur, murdered? Annabel risen from the grave? The Black Volume gone?

"But Malcolm was dead," she said, numbly. "I killed him. I saw his body float away. He was *dead*."

"The Queen cautioned me against thinking death was final," said Julian. "Especially in the case of warlocks."

"But Annabel is alive," said Mark. "What does she want? Why did she take the Black Volume?"

"All good questions, Miach," said a voice from across the room. They all turned in surprise, save Julian.

She came out of the gray shadows wrapped in more gray: a long gray gown made of moth wings and ashes, dipped low in front so that it was easy to see the jutting bones of her clavicle. Her face was pinched, triangular, dominated by burning blue eyes. Her red hair was bound back tightly in a silver net. The Queen. There was a glitter in her eye: malice or madness, it would be hard to be sure.

"Who's Miach?" Emma asked.

The Queen indicated Mark with the sweep of her hand. "Him," she said. "The nephew of my handmaiden Nene."

Mark looked stunned.

"Nene called Helen 'Alessa,'" said Emma. "So—Alessa and Miach are their fey names?"

"Not their full names, which would give power. No. But much more harmonious than Mark and Helen, don't you agree?" The Queen moved toward Mark, one hand holding up her skirt. She reached to touch his face.

He didn't move. He seemed frozen. Fear of the faerie gentry, and the monarchs in particular, had been bred into him for years. It was Julian's eyes that narrowed as the Queen put a hand against Mark's cheek, her fingers stroking down his skin.

"Beautiful boy," she said. "You were wasted on the Wild Hunt. You could have served here in my Court."

"They kidnapped me," Mark said. "You didn't."

Even the Queen seemed a bit nonplussed. "Miach—"

"My name is Mark." He said it without any hostility or resistance. It was a simple fact. Emma saw the spark in Julian's eyes: pride in his brother, as the Queen dropped her hand. She walked back toward her throne, and Julian rose and came down the steps, joining the others below her as she took her seat.

The Queen smiled down at them, and the shadows moved around her as if commanded: curling into wisps and shapes like flowers. "So now Julian has told you all there is to know," she said. "Now we can bargain."

Emma didn't like the way the Queen said Jules's name: the possessive, almost languid *Julian*. She also wondered where the Queen had been while Julian had told them what happened. Not out of earshot, of that she was sure. Somewhere close, where she could overhear him, could gauge their reactions.

"You have brought us all here, my lady, though we do not know why," said Julian. It was clear from his expression that he didn't know what the Queen planned to ask of them. But it was also clear that he had not made up his mind to refuse her. "What do you want from us?"

"I want you to find Annabel Blackthorn for me," she said, "and retrieve the Black Volume."

They all looked at each other; whatever they had expected, that had not been it.

"You just want the Black Volume?" said Emma. "Not Annabel?"

"Just the book," said the Queen. "Annabel does not matter, save that she has the book. Having been brought back so long after her death, she is likely quite mad."

"Well, that does make looking for her so much more fun," said Julian. "Why can't you send your Court to search the mundane world for her yourself?"

"The Cold Peace makes that difficult," the Queen said dryly. "I or my folk will be seized on sight. You, on the other hand, are the darlings of the Council."

"I wouldn't say 'darlings,'" Emma said. "That might be over-stating things."

"So tell us, what does the Queen of Faerie want with the Black Volume of the Dead?" said Mark. "It is a warlock's toy."

"Yet dangerous in the wrong hands, even when those hands are faerie hands," said the Queen. "The Unseelie King grows in power since the Cold Peace. He has blighted the Lands of Unseelie with evil and filled the rivers with blood. You have seen yourself that no works of the Angel can survive in his land."

"True," said Emma. "But what do you care if he's made the Unseelie Lands off-limits to Shadowhunters?"

The Queen looked at her with a smile that didn't reach her eyes. "I do not," she said. "But the King has taken one of my people. A member of my Court, very dear to me. He holds that person captive in his land. I want them back."

Her voice was cold.

"How will the book help you with that?" Emma asked.

"The Black Volume is more than necromancy," said the Queen. "It contains spells that will allow me to retrieve the captive from the Unseelie Court."

Cristina shook her head. "My lady," she said. She sounded very sweet and firm and not at all anxious. "While we are sympathetic to your loss, that is a great deal of danger and work for us, just to assist you. I think you would have to offer something quite special to gain our help."

The Queen looked amused. "You are very decided, for one so young." Rings sparkled on her fingers as she gestured. "But our interests are aligned, you see. You do not want the Black Volume in the King's hands, and neither do I. It will be safer here in my Court than it will ever be out in the world—the King will be looking for it, too, and only in the heart of Seelie can it be protected from him."

"But how do we know you won't also use it to work against Shadowhunters?" said Emma, uneasily. "It wasn't such a long time ago that Seelie soldiers attacked Alicante."

"Times change and so do alliances," said the Queen. "The King is now a greater threat to me and mine than the Nephilim. And I will prove my loyalty." She leaned her head back, and her crown shimmered. "I offer the end of the Cold Peace," she said, "and the return of your sister, Alessa, to you."

"That is beyond your power," said Mark. But he had not been able to control his reaction to his sister's name; his eyes were overly bright. So were Julian's. *Alessa. Helen.*

"It is not," said the Queen. "Bring me the book, and I will offer my Lands and arms to the Council that we might defeat the King together."

"And if they say no?"

"They will not." The Queen sounded supremely confident. "They will understand that only by allying themselves with us will they be able to defeat the King, and that to make such an alliance means they must first end the Cold Peace. It is my understanding your sister was punished with the Nephilim punishment of exile because she is part faerie. It is in the Inquisitor's power to overturn such a sentence of exile. With the end of the Cold Peace, your sister will be free."

The Queen couldn't lie, Emma knew. Still, she felt that somehow they were being tricked. Looking around, she could tell from the uneasy expression of the others that she wasn't the only one with that thought. And yet . . .

"You wish to seize the Unseelie Lands?" said Julian. "And you wish the Clave to help you do it?"

She waved a lazy hand. "What use have I for the Unseelie Lands? I am not driven by conquest. Another shall be placed on the throne to replace the Shadow Lord, one more friendly to the concerns of Nephilim. That should interest your kind."

"Have you someone in mind?" said Julian.

And now the Queen smiled, really smiled, and one could forget how thin and wasted she looked. Her beauty was glorious when she smiled. "I do." She turned toward the shadows behind her. "Bring him in," she said.

One of the shadows moved and detached itself. It was Fergus, Emma saw, as he slipped through an arched doorway and returned a moment later. Emma didn't think anyone was surprised to see who he had with him, blinking and startled and sullen-looking as ever.

"Kieran?" said Mark, in amazement. "Kieran, King of the Unseelie Court?"

Kieran managed to look frightened and insulted all at once. He had been put into new clothes, linen shirt and breeches and a fawn-colored jacket, though he was still very pale and the bandages wrapping his torso were visible through his shirt. "No," he said. "Absolutely not."

The Queen began to laugh. "Not Kieran," she said. "His brother. Adaon."

"Adaon will not want that," Kieran said. Fergus was holding the prince firmly by the arm; Kieran seemed to be pretending it wasn't happening, as a way to retain his dignity. "He is loyal to the King."

"Then he doesn't sound very friendly to Nephilim," said Emma.

"He hates the Cold Peace," said the Queen. "All know it; all know as well that he is loyal to the Unseelie King and accepts his decisions. But only as long as the King lives. If the Unseelie Court is defeated by an alliance of Shadowhunters and Seelie folk, it will be easy to place our choice on the throne there."

"You make it sound so simple," Julian said. "If you do not plan on putting Kieran on the throne, why drag him in here?"

"I have another use for him," said the Queen. "I require an envoy. One whose identity they know." She turned to Kieran. "You will be my messenger to the Clave. You will swear loyalty to one of these Shadowhunters, here. Because of that, and because you are the Shadow King's son, when you speak to the Council, they will know you are speaking from me, and that they will not be tricked again as they were with the liar Meliorn."

"Kieran must agree to this plan," said Mark. "It must be his choice."

"Well, it is his choice, certainly," said the Queen. "He can agree, or he can most likely be murdered by his father. The King does not like it when condemned captives escape him."

Kieran muttered something under his breath and said, "I will swear loyalty to Mark. I will do as he bids me do, and follow the Nephilim for his sake. And I shall argue with Adaon for your cause, though it is his choice in the end."

Something flickered in Julian's eyes. "No," he said. "You will not do this for Mark."

Mark looked at his brother, startled; Kieran's expression tensed. "Why not Mark?"

"Love complicates things," said Julian. "An oath should be free of entanglements."

Kieran looked as if he might explode. His hair had gone completely black. With an angry look at Julian, he strode toward the Shadowhunters—and knelt in front of Cristina.

Everyone looked surprised, none more than Cristina. Kieran tossed his dark hair back and looked up at her, a challenge in his eyes. "I swear fealty to you, Lady of Roses."

"Kieran Kingmaker," said Mark, looking at Kieran and Cristina with an absolutely unreadable look in his eyes. Emma couldn't blame him. He must be constantly waiting for Kieran to remember what he had forgotten. She knew he would be dreading the pain the memories would bring them both.

"I am not doing this because of Adaon or the Cold Peace," said Kieran. "I am doing it because I want my father dead."

"Reassuring," muttered Julian, as Kieran rose to his feet.

"It is settled, then," said the Queen, looking satisfied. "But so that you understand: You may promise my assistance and my goodwill to the Council. But I will not make war on the Shadow Throne until I hold the Black Volume."

"What if he makes war on you?" Julian said.

"He will make war on you first," said the Queen. "That much I know."

"What if we don't find it?" said Emma. "The book, I mean."

The Queen sliced her hand lazily through the air. "Then the

Clave will still have my goodwill," she said. "But I will not add my folk to their army until I have the Black Volume."

Emma looked at Julian, who shrugged, as if to say he hadn't expected the Queen to say anything else.

"There is one last thing," said Julian. "Helen. I don't want to wait for the Cold Peace to be over to get her back."

The Queen looked briefly annoyed. "There are things I cannot do, little Nephilim," she snapped, and it was the first thing she'd said that Emma really believed.

"You can," he said. "Swear that you will insist to the Clave that Helen and Aline be your ambassadors. Once Kieran has finished his duty and given your message to the Council, his role is ended. Someone else will have to go back and forth from Faerie for you. Let it be Helen and her wife. They will have to bring them back from Wrangel Island."

The Queen hesitated a moment, and then inclined her head. "You understand, they have no reason to do as I say unless they are awaiting aid from me and mine," she said. "So when you have the Black Volume, yes, you may make that a condition of my assistance. Kieran, I authorize you to make such a demand, when the time comes."

"I will make it," said Kieran, and looked at Mark. Emma could almost read the message in his eyes. *Though not for you.*

"Lovely," said the Queen. "You could be heroes. The heroes who ended the Cold Peace."

Cristina stiffened. Emma remembered the other girl saying to her, *It has always been my hope that one day I might be part of brokering a better treaty than the Cold Peace. Something more fair to Downworlders and those Shadowhunters who might love them.*

Cristina's dream. Mark and Julian's sister. Safety for the Blackthorns when Helen and Aline returned. The Queen had offered them all their desperate hopes, their secret wishes.

Emma hated to be afraid, but at that moment, she was afraid of the Queen.

"Is it finally settled, fussing children?" asked the Queen, her eyes glowing. "Are we agreed?"

"You know we are." Julian almost flung the words. "We'll start looking, though we have no idea where to begin."

"People go to the places that mean something to them." The Queen cocked her head to the side. "Annabel was a Blackthorn. Learn about her past. Know her soul. You have access to the Blackthorn papers, to histories no one else can touch." She rose to her feet. "Some of my folk visited them once when they were young and happy. Fade had a house in Cornwall. Perhaps it still stands. There could be something there." She began to descend the steps. "And now it is time to speed your journey. You should return to the mundane world before it is too late." She had reached the foot of the steps. She turned, magnificent in her finery, her imperiousness. "Come in!" she called. "We have been awaiting you."

Two figures appeared in the doorway of the room, flanked on either side by knights in the Queen's livery. One Emma recognized as Nene. There was a look on her face, one of respect and even a little fear, as she came in. She was escorting beside her the formidable figure of Gwyn ap Nudd. Gwyn wore a formal doublet of dark velvet, against which his massive shoulders strained.

Gwyn turned to Mark. His eyes, blue and black, fixed on him with a look of pride. "You saved Kieran," he said. "I should not have doubted you. You did everything I could have asked of you, and more. And now, for one last time, you will ride with me and the Wild Hunt. I shall take you to your family."

The five of them followed the Queen, Nene, and Gwyn down a series of tangled corridors until one ended in a sloping tunnel down which blew fresh, cool air. It opened into a green space: There was no sign of trees, only grass studded with flowers, and above them the night sky whirling with multicolored clouds. Emma wondered if it was still the same night that they'd arrived at the Seelie Court, or if a whole day had passed underground. There was no way of knowing. Time in Faerie moved like a dance whose steps she didn't know.

Five horses stood in the clearing. Emma recognized one as Windspear, Kieran's mount, who he had ridden into battle with Malcolm. He whinnied when he caught sight of Kieran, and kicked at the sky.

"This is what the phouka promised me," Mark said in a low voice. He stood behind Emma, his eyes fixed on Gwyn and the horses. "That if I came to Faerie, I would ride with the Wild Hunt again."

Emma reached out and squeezed his hand. At least for Mark, the phouka's promise had come true without a bitter sting in its tail. She hoped the same for Julian and Cristina.

Cristina was approaching a red roan, which skittishly kicked at the dirt. She murmured softly to the horse until it calmed, and swung herself up onto its back, reaching to stroke the horse's neck. Julian pulled himself onto a black mare whose eyes were an eerie green. He looked unfazed. Cristina's eyes were glowing with delight. She met Emma's gaze and grinned as if she could barely contain herself. Emma wondered how long Cristina must have dreamed of riding with a faerie host.

She hung back, waiting to hear Gwyn call her name. Why were there only five horses, not six? She got her answer when Mark swung himself up onto Windspear and reached down to pull Kieran up after him. The elf-bolt around Mark's throat gleamed in the multicolored starlight.

Nene came up to Windspear then, and reached for Mark's hands, ignoring Kieran. Emma couldn't hear what she was whispering to him, but there was deep pain on her face; Mark's fingers clung to hers for a moment before he released them. Nene turned and went back into the hill.

Silent, Kieran settled himself into place behind Mark, but he didn't touch the other boy.

Mark half-turned in his seat. "Are you worried?" he asked Kieran.

Kieran shook his head. "No," he said. "Because I am with you."

Mark's face tightened. "Yes," he said. "You are."

Beside Emma, the Queen laughed softly. "So many lies in just three words," she said. "And he did not even say 'I love you.'"

A dart of anger went through Emma. "You would know lies," she said. "In fact, if you ask me, the biggest lie the Fair Folk have ever told is that they *don't* tell them."

The Queen drew herself up. She seemed to be looking down at Emma from a great height. The stars wheeled behind her, blue and green, purple and red. "Why are you angry, girl? I have offered you a fair bargain. Everything you might desire. I have given you fair hosting. Even the clothes on your back are Faerie clothes."

"I don't trust you," Emma said flatly. "We bargained with you because we had no choice. But you have manipulated us every step of the way—even the dress I'm wearing is a manipulation."

The Queen arched an eyebrow.

"Besides," Emma said, "you allied yourself with Sebastian Morgenstern. You helped him wage the Dark War. Because of the war, Malcolm got the Black Volume and my parents died. Why shouldn't I blame you?"

The Queen's eyes raked Emma, and now Emma could see in them what the Queen had been at pains to hide before: her anger, and her viciousness. "Is that why you have set yourself as the protector of the Blackthorns? Because you could not save your parents, you will save them, your makeshift family?"

Emma looked at the Queen for a long moment before she spoke. "You bet your ass it is," she said.

Without another glance at the ruler of the Seelie Court, Emma stalked off toward the horses of the Hunt.

Julian had never much liked horses, though he'd learned to ride them, as most Shadowhunters did. In Idris, where cars didn't work, they were still the main form of transportation. He'd learned on a crabby pony that kept blowing out its sides and darting under low-hanging branches, trying to knock him off.

The horse Gwyn had given him had a dark look in its ghastly green eyes that didn't bode much better. Julian had braced himself for a lurching plunge upward, but when Gwyn gave the order, the horse simply glided up into the air like a toy lifted on a string.

Julian gasped out loud with the shock of it. He found his hands plunging into the horse's mane, gripping hard, as the others shot up into the air around him—Cristina, Gwyn, Emma, Mark and Kieran. For a moment they hovered, shadows under the moonlight.

Then the horses shot forward. The sky blurred above them, the stars turning to streaks of shimmering, multicolored paint. Julian realized that he was grinning—truly grinning, the way he rarely had since he was a child. He couldn't help it. Buried in everyone's soul, he thought as they spun forward through the night, must be the yearning desire to fly.

And not the way mundanes did, trapped inside a metal tube. Like this, exploding up through clouds as soft as down, the wind caressing your skin. He glanced over at Emma. She was leaning down over her horse's mane, long legs curved around its sides, her brilliant hair flying like a banner. Behind her rode Cristina, who had her hands in the air and was shrieking with happiness. "Emma!" she shouted. "Emma, look, no hands!"

Emma glanced back and laughed aloud. Mark, who rode

Windspear with an air of familiarity, Kieran clinging to his belt with one hand, was not as amused. "Use your hands!" he yelled. "Cristina! It's not a roller coaster!"

"Nephilim are insane!" shouted Kieran, pushing his wildly blowing hair out of his face.

Cristina just laughed, and Emma looked at her with a wide smile, her eyes glowing like the stars overhead, which had turned to the silver-white stars of the mundane world.

Shadows loomed up in front of them, white and black and blue. The cliffs of Dover, Julian thought, and felt an ache inside that it might be over so quickly. He turned his head and looked at his brother. Mark sat astride Windspear as if he'd been born on a horse's back. The wind tore his pale hair, revealing his sharply pointed ears. He was smiling too, a calm and secret smile, the smile of someone doing what they loved.

Far below them the world spun by, a patchwork of silver-black fields, shadowy hills, and luminous, winding rivers. It was beautiful, but Julian could not take his eyes off his brother. *So this is the Wild Hunt,* he thought. This freedom, this expanse, this ferocity of joy. For the first time, he understood how and why Mark's choice to stay with his family might not have been an easy one. For the first time he thought in wonder of how much his brother must love him after all, to have given up the sky for his sake.

PART TWO

Thule

———◀❖▶———

15

FRIENDS LONG GIVEN

Kit had never thought he'd set foot in one Shadowhunter Institute. Now he had eaten and slept in two. If this kept up, it was going to become a habit.

The London Institute was exactly the way he would have imagined it, if he'd ever been asked to imagine it, which he admittedly hadn't. Housed in a massive old stone church, it lacked the glossy modernity of its Los Angeles counterpart. It looked as if it hadn't been renovated for eighty years—the rooms were painted in Edwardian pastels, which had faded over the decades into soft and muddied colors. The hot water was irregular, the beds were lumpy, and dust limned the surfaces of most of the furniture.

It sounded, from bits and snatches Kit had overheard, as if the London Institute had once had many more people in it. It had been attacked by Sebastian Morgenstern during the Dark War, and most of the former inhabitants had never returned.

The head of the Institute looked nearly as ancient as the building. Her name was Evelyn Highsmith. Kit got the sense that the Highsmiths were a big deal in Shadowhunter society, though not as big a deal as the Herondales. Evelyn was a tall, imperious, white-haired

woman in her eighties who wore long 1940s-style dresses, carried a
silver-headed walking stick, and sometimes talked to people who
weren't there.

Only one other person seemed to live in the Institute: Evelyn's
maid, Bridget, who was just as ancient as her mistress. She had
bright dyed-red hair and a thousand fine wrinkles. She was always
popping up in unexpected places, which was inconvenient for Kit,
who was once again on the lookout for anything he might steal. It
wasn't a quest that was going well—most of what appeared valuable was furniture, and he couldn't imagine how he was supposed
to creep away from the Institute carrying a sideboard. The weapons
were carefully locked away, he didn't know how to sell candlesticks
on the street, and though there were valuable first editions of books
in the enormous library, most of them had been scribbled in by
some idiot named Will H.

The dining room door opened and Diana came in. She was
favoring one arm: Kit had found out that some Shadowhunter injuries, especially those that involved demon poison or ichor, healed
slowly despite runes.

Livvy perked up at the sight of her tutor. The family had gathered for dinner, which was served at a long table in a massive Victorian dining room. Angels had once been painted on the ceiling, but
they had long ago been nearly completely covered by dust and the
stains of old burns. "Did you hear anything from Alec and Magnus?"

Diana shook her head, taking the seat opposite Livvy. Livvy
wore a blue dress that looked like it had been stolen from the set
of a BBC period piece. Though they'd fled the L.A. Institute with
none of their belongings, it turned out there were years' worth of
clothes stored in London, though none of them looked as if they'd
been purchased after 1940. Evelyn, Kit, and the Blackthorn family
sat around the table in an odd assortment of clothes: Ty and Kit
in trousers and long-sleeved shirts, Tavvy in a striped cotton shirt

and shorts, and Drusilla in a black velvet gown that had delighted her with its Gothic appeal. Diana had rejected all the garments and simply hand washed her own jeans and shirt.

"What about the Clave?" said Ty. "Have you talked to the Clave?"

"Are they ever useful?" Kit muttered under his breath. He didn't think anyone had heard him, but someone must have, because Evelyn burst out laughing. "Oh, *Jessamine*," she said to no one. "Come now, that isn't in good taste at all."

The Blackthorns all raised their eyebrows at each other. No one commented, though, because Bridget had appeared from the kitchen, carrying steaming plates of meat and vegetables, both of which had been boiled to the point of tastelessness.

"I just don't see why we can't go *home*," Dru said glumly. "If the Centurions defeated all the sea demons, like they said . . ."

"It doesn't meant Malcolm won't come back," said Diana. "And it's Blackthorn blood he wants. You're staying within these walls, and that's final."

Kit had passed out during the horrible thing they called a Portal journey—the terrible whirl through absolutely icy nothingness—so he'd missed the scene that must have occurred when they'd appeared in the London Institute—minus Arthur—and Diana had explained they were there to stay.

Diana had contacted the Clave to tell them about Malcolm's threats—but Zara had been there first. Apparently she'd assured the Council that the Centurions had it all under control, that they were more than a match for Malcolm and his army, and the Clave had been only too happy to take her word for it.

And as if Zara's assurance had in fact effected a miracle, Malcolm didn't turn up again, and no demons visited the Western Seaboard. Two days had passed, and there had been no news of disaster.

"I *hate* Zara and Manuel being in the Institute without us there to watch them," said Livvy, throwing her fork down. "The longer they're there, the better claim they have for the Cohort taking it over."

"Ridiculous," said Evelyn. "Arthur runs the Institute. Don't be paranoid, girl." She pronounced it *gel*.

Livvy flinched. Though everyone, even Dru and Tavvy, had finally been brought up to speed on the situation—including Arthur's illness and the facts about where Julian and the others really were—it had been decided it was better for Evelyn not to know. She wasn't an ally; there was no reason she'd side with them, though she seemed patently uninterested in Council politics. In fact, most of the time she didn't seem to be listening to them at all.

"According to Zara, Arthur's been locked in his office with the door shut since we left," said Diana.

"I would be too, if I had to put up with Zara," said Dru.

"I still don't see why Arthur didn't come with you," sniffed Evelyn. "He used to live in this Institute. You'd think he wouldn't mind paying a visit."

"Look on the bright side, Livvy," Diana said. "When Julian and the others return from—from where they are—they're most likely to go straight to Los Angeles. Would you want them to find an empty Institute?"

Livvy poked at her food and said nothing. She looked pale and drawn, purple shadows under her eyes. Kit had gone down the corridor the night after they'd arrived in London, wondering if she wanted to see him, but he'd heard her crying through her door when he put his hand on the knob. He'd turned around and left, a strange, pinching feeling in his chest. No one crying like that wanted anyone to come near them, especially not someone like him.

He got the same pinching feeling when he looked across the table at Ty and remembered how the other boy had healed his hand. How cool Ty's skin had been against his. Ty was tense in his own way—the move to the London Institute had constituted a major disruption in his daily routine and it was clearly bothering him. He spent a lot of time in the training room, which was almost identical in layout to its Los Angeles counterpart. Sometimes when he was especially stressed, Livvy would take his hands in hers and rub them matter-of-factly. The pressure seemed to ground him. Still, at the moment Ty was tense and distracted, as if he'd folded in on himself somehow.

"We could go to Baker Street," Kit said, without even knowing he was going to say it. "We *are* in London."

Ty looked up at that, his gray eyes aglow. He had shoved his food away: Livvy had told Kit that Ty took a long time to warm up to new foods and new flavors. For the moment, he was almost solely eating potatoes. "To 221B Baker Street?"

"When everything with Malcolm is cleared up," Diana interrupted. "No Blackthorns out of the Institute until then, and no Herondales, either. I didn't like the way Malcolm glared at you, Kit." She stood up. "I'll be in the parlor. I need to send a fire-message."

As the door closed behind her, Tavvy—who was staring at the air next to his chair in a way Kit found frankly alarming—giggled. They all turned to look in surprise. The youngest Blackthorn hadn't been laughing much lately.

He supposed he didn't blame the kid. Julian was all Tavvy had in the way of a father. Kit knew what missing your father was like, and he wasn't seven years old.

"Jessie," Evelyn scolded, and for a moment Kit actually looked around, as if the person she was addressing was in the room with them. "Leave the child alone. He doesn't even know you." She glanced around the table. "Everyone thinks they're good with children. Few know when they are not." She took a bite of carrot. "I am not," she said, around the food. "I have never been able to stand children."

Kit rolled his eyes. Tavvy looked at Evelyn as if he was considering throwing a plate at her.

"You might as well take Tavvy to bed, Dru," said Livvy hastily. "I think we're all done with dinner here."

"Sure, why not? It's not like I didn't find clothes for him this morning or put him to bed last night. I might as well be a *servant*," Dru snapped, then snatched Tavvy out of his chair and stalked out of the room, dragging her younger brother behind her.

Livvy put her head into her hands. Ty looked over at her and said, "You don't have to take care of everyone, you know."

Livvy sniffled and looked sideways at her twin. "It's just— without Jules here, I'm the oldest. By a few minutes, anyway."

"Diana's the oldest," said Ty. Nobody mentioned Evelyn, who had placed a pair of spectacles on her nose and was reading a newspaper.

"But she's got so much more to do than look after us—I mean, look after the little things," said Livvy. "I never really thought about it before, all the stuff Julian does for us, but it's so much. He always holds it together and takes care of us and I don't even get how—"

There was a sound like an explosion overhead. Ty's face drained. It was clear he was hearing a noise he'd heard before.

"Livvy," Ty said. "The Accords Hall—"

The noise sounded less like an explosion now, and more like thunder, a rushing thunder that was taking over the sky. A sound like clouds being ripped apart as if cloth were tearing.

Dru burst into the room, Tavvy just behind her. "It's them," she said. "You won't believe it, but you have to come, quickly. I saw them flying—I went up to the roof—"

"Who?" Livvy was on her feet; they all were, except Evelyn, who was still reading the paper. "Who's on the roof, Dru?"

Dru swept Tavvy up into her arms.

"*Everyone*," she said, her eyes shining.

The roof of the Institute was shingle, stretching out wide and flat to a waist-high wrought-iron railing. The finials of the railings were tipped with iron lilies. In the distance, Kit could see the glimmering dome of St. Paul's, familiar from a thousand movies and TV shows.

The clouds were heavy, iron-colored, surrounding the top of the Institute like clouds around a mountain. Kit could barely see down to the streets below. The air was acrid with summer thunder.

They had all spilled up onto the roof, everyone but Evelyn and Bridget. Diana was here, her arm carefully cradled. Ty's gray eyes were fixed on the sky.

"There," Dru said, pointing. "Do you see?"

As Kit stared, the glamour peeled away. Suddenly it was as if a painting or a movie had come to life. Only movies didn't give you this, this visceral tangle of wonder and fear. Movies didn't give you the smell of magic in the air, crackling like lightning, or the shadows cast by a host of impossibly soaring creatures against the sky above it. They didn't give you starlight on a girl's blond hair as she slid shrieking in excitement and happiness from the back of a flying horse and landed on a roof in London. They didn't give you the look on the Blackthorns' faces as they saw their brothers and friends coming back to them.

Livvy leaped at Julian, hurling her arms around his neck. Mark flung himself from his horse and half-tumbled down to find himself being hugged tightly by Dru and Tavvy. Ty came more quietly, but with the same incandescent happiness on his face. He waited for Livvy to be done nearly strangling her brother and then stepped in to take Julian's hands.

And Julian, who Kit had always thought of as an almost frightening model of control and distance, grabbed his brother and yanked him close, his hands twisting in the back of Ty's shirt. His eyes were shut, and Kit had to look away from the expression on his face.

He had never had anyone but his father, and he was sure beyond any words that his father had never loved him like that.

Mark came up to his brothers then, and Ty turned to look at him. Kit heard him say: "I wasn't sure you would come back."

Mark laid his hand on his brother's shoulder, and spoke gruffly. "I'll always come back to you, Tiberius. I am sorry if I ever led you to believe anything else."

There were two other arrivals as well among the Blackthorns, who Kit didn't recognize: a gorgeously scowling boy with blue-black hair that waved around his angular face, and a wide-shouldered, massive man wearing an alarming helmet with carved antlers protruding from either side. Both of them sat astride their horses silently, without dismounting. A faerie escort, perhaps, to keep the others safe? But how had the Blackthorns and Emma managed to secure a favor like that?

Then again, if anyone could manage to secure such a thing, it would be Julian Blackthorn. As Kit's father used to say about various criminals, Julian was the kind of person who could descend into Hell and come out with the devil himself owing him a favor.

Diana was hugging Emma and then Cristina, tears shining on her face. Feeling awkwardly out of place at the reunion, Kit made his way to the edge of the railing. The clouds had cleared away, and he could see Millennium Bridge from here, lit up in rainbow colors. A train rattled over another bridge, casting its reflection into the water.

"Who are you?" said a voice at his elbow. Kit started and turned around. It was one of the two faeries he had noticed earlier, the scowling one. His dark hair, up close, looked less black than like a mixture of deep greens and blues. He brushed a bit of it away from his face, frowning; he had a full, slightly uneven mouth, but far more interesting were his eyes. Like Mark's, they were two different colors. One was the silver of a polished shield; the other was a black so dark his pupil was barely visible.

"Kit," said Kit.

The boy with the ocean hair nodded. "I'm Kieran," he said. "Kieran Hunter."

Hunter wasn't a real sort of faerie name, Kit knew. Faeries didn't generally give their true names, as names held power; *Hunter* just denoted what he was, the way nixies called themselves *Waterborn*. Kieran was of the Wild Hunt.

"Huh," said Kit, thinking of the Cold Peace. "Are you a prisoner?"

"No," said the faerie. "I'm Mark's lover."

Oh, Kit thought. *The person he went into Faerie to save.* He tried to stifle a look of amusement at the way faeries talked. Intellectually, he knew the word "lover" was part of traditional speech, but he couldn't help it: He was from Los Angeles, and as far as he was concerned, Kieran had just said, *Hello, I have sex with Mark Blackthorn. What about you?*

"I thought Mark was dating Emma," Kit said.

Kieran looked confused. A few of the curls of his hair seemed to darken, or perhaps it was a trick of the light. "I think you must be mistaken," he said.

Kit raised an eyebrow. How close was this guy actually to Mark, after all? Maybe they'd just had a meaningless fling. Though why Mark would then have dragged half his family to Faerie to save him was a mystery.

Before he could say anything, Kieran turned his head, his attention diverted. "That must be the lovely Diana," he said, gesturing toward the Blackthorns' tutor. "Gwyn was most enraptured with her."

"Gwyn's the big guy? Antler helmet?" said Kit. Kieran nodded, watching as Gwyn dismounted his horse to speak with Diana, who looked quite tiny against his bulk, though she was a tall woman.

"Providence has brought us together again," Gwyn said.

"I don't believe in providence," said Diana. She looked awkward, a little alarmed. She was holding her injured arm close against her. "Or an interventionist Heaven."

"'There are more things in heaven and earth,'" said Gwyn, "'than are dreamt of in your philosophy.'"

Kit snorted. Diana looked flabbergasted. "Are you quoting *Shakespeare?*" she said. "I would have thought at least it would have been *A Midsummer Night's Dream.*"

"Faeries can't stand *A Midsummer Night's Dream,*" muttered Kieran. "Gets everything wrong."

Gwyn's lips twitched at the corners. "Speaking of dreams," he said. "You have been in mine, and often."

Diana looked stunned. The Blackthorns had quieted their loud reunion and were watching her and Gwyn with unabashed curiosity. Julian was even smiling a little; he was holding Tavvy, who had his arms hooked around his brother's neck like a clinging koala.

"I would that you would meet me, formally, that I might court you," said Gwyn. His large hands moved aimlessly at his sides, and Kit realized with a shock that he was nervous—this big, muscled man, the leader of the Wild Hunt, nervous. "We could together slay a frost giant, or devour a deer."

"I don't want to do either of those things," said Diana after a moment.

Gwyn looked crestfallen.

"But I *will* go out with you," she said, blushing. "Preferably to a nice restaurant. Bring flowers, and *not* the helmet."

The Blackthorns burst into giggling applause. Kit leaned against the wall with Kieran, who was shaking his head in bemusement. "And thus was the proud leader of the Hunt felled by love," he said. "I hope there will be a ballad about it someday."

Kit watched Gwyn, who was ignoring the applause as he readied his horses to leave.

"You don't look like the other Blackthorns," said Kieran after a moment. "Your eyes are blue, but not like the ocean's blue. More of an ordinary sky."

Kit felt obscurely insulted. "I'm not a Blackthorn," he said. "I'm a Herondale. Christopher Herondale."

He waited. The name Herondale seemed to produce an explosive reaction in most denizens of the supernatural world. The boy with the ocean hair, though, didn't bat an eye. "Then what are you doing here, if you are not family?" he asked.

Kit shrugged. "I don't know. I don't belong, that's for sure."

Kieran smiled a sideways faerie smile. "That makes two of us."

They eventually gathered in the parlor, the warmest room in the house. Evelyn was already there, muttering by the fire burning in the grate; even though it was late summer, London had a damp, chill edge to it. Bridget brought sandwiches—tuna and sweet corn, chicken and bacon—and the newcomers tucked into them as if they were wildly starving. Julian had to eat awkwardly with his left hand, balancing Tavvy on his lap with the other.

The parlor had aged better than a lot of the other rooms in the Institute. It had cheerful flowered wallpaper, only slightly discolored, and gorgeous antique furniture someone had clearly picked out with care—a lovely rolltop desk, a delicate escritoire, plush velvet armchairs and sofas grouped around the fireplace. Even the fire screen was made of delicate wrought iron, patterned with wing-spread herons, and when the fire shone through it, the shadow of the birds was cast against the wall as if they were flying by.

Kieran alone didn't seem thrilled with the sandwiches. He poked at them suspiciously and then pulled them apart, eating only the tomatoes, while Julian explained what had happened in Faerie: their journey to the Unseelie Court, the meeting with the Queen, the blight on the Unseelie Land. "There were burned places, white as ash, like the surface of the moon," Mark said, eyes dark with distress. Kit tried his best to hang on to the story, but it was like trying to ride a roller coaster with faulty brakes—phrases like "scrying glass," "Unseelie champion," and "Black Volume of the Dead" kept hurling him off track.

"How much time passed for them?" he whispered finally to Ty, who was wedged in beside him and Livvy on a love seat too small for the three of them.

"It sounds like a few less days than passed for us," said Ty. "Some time slippage, but not much. Cristina's necklace seems to have worked."

Kit whistled under his breath. "And who's Annabel?"

"She was a Blackthorn," said Ty. "She died, but Malcolm brought her back."

"From the *dead*?" said Kit. "That's—that's necromancy."

"Malcolm was a necromancer," pointed out Ty.

"Shut up." Livvy elbowed Kit, who was lost in thought. Necromancy wasn't just a forbidden art at the Shadow Market, it was a forbidden *topic*. The punishment for raising the dead was death. If the Shadowhunters didn't catch you, other Downworlders would, and the way you died would not be pretty.

Bringing back the dead, Johnny Rook had always said, warped the fabric of life, the same way making humans immortal did. Invite in death, and death would stay. *Could anyone bring back the dead and have it work?* Kit had asked him once. *Even the most powerful magician?*

God, Johnny had said, after a long, long pause. *God could do that. And those who raise the dead may think they are God, but soon enough they will find out the lie they have believed.*

"The head of the Los Angeles Institute is dead?" Evelyn exclaimed, dropping the remains of her sandwich on a likely very expensive antique table.

Kit didn't really blame her for her surprise. The Blackthorns didn't act like a family in grief over the death of a beloved uncle. Rather they seemed stunned and puzzled. But then, they had behaved around Arthur almost as if they were strangers.

"Is that why he wanted to stay behind in Los Angeles?" Livvy demanded, her cheeks flushed. "So he could sacrifice himself—for us?"

"By the Angel." Diana had her hand against her chest. "He hadn't replied to any of my messages, but that wasn't unusual. Still, for Zara not to notice—"

"Maybe she did, maybe she didn't," said Livvy. "But it's better for her plans if he's out of the way."

"What plans?" said Cristina. "What do you mean, Zara's plans?"

It was time for another long explanation, this time of things Kit already knew about. Evelyn had fallen asleep in front of the fireplace and was snoring. Kit wondered how much the silver top of her cane was worth. Was it real silver, or just plated?

"By the Angel," said Cristina, when the explanation was done. Julian said nothing; Emma said something unprintable. Mark leaned forward, a flush on his cheeks.

"Let me get this straight," he said. "Zara and her father want to run the Los Angeles Institute so they can push their anti-Downworlder agenda. The new Laws would likely apply to me and to Helen. Certainly to Magnus, Catarina—every Downworlder we know, no matter how loyal."

"I know of their group," said Diana. "They don't believe in loyal Downworlders."

"What is their group?" Emma asked.

"The Cohort," said Diana. "They are a well-known faction in the Council. Like all groups who exist primarily to hate, they believe that they speak for a silent majority—that everyone despises Downworlders as they do. They believe opposition to the Cold Peace is moral cowardice, or at best, whining from those who feel inconvenienced by it."

"Inconvenienced?" said Kieran. There was no expression in his voice, just the word, hanging there in the room.

"They are not intelligent," said Diana. "But they are loud and vicious, and they have frightened many better people into silence. They do not number an Institute head among them, but if they did . . ."

"This is bad," Emma said. "Before, they would have had to prove Arthur wasn't fit to run an Institute. Now he's dead. The spot's open. All they have to do is wait for the next Council meeting and put their candidate forward."

"And they're in a good place for it." Diana had risen to her feet and begun to pace. "The Clave is enormously impressed with Zara Dearborn. They believe she and her Centurions beat back the sea demon threat on their own."

"The demons vanished because Malcolm died—again, and this time hopefully for good," said Livvy furiously. "None of it's because of Zara. She's taking credit for what *Arthur* did!"

"And there's nothing we can do about it," said Julian. "Not yet. They'll figure out Arthur is dead or missing soon enough—but even abandonment of his post would be cause to replace him. And we can't be seen to know how or why he died."

"Because the only reason we do know is thanks to the Seelie Queen," said Emma in a low voice, eyeing the sleeping Evelyn.

"Annabel is the key to our finding the Black Volume," said Julian. "We need to be the only ones looking for her right now. If the Clave finds her first, we'll never get the book to the Queen."

"When we agreed with the Queen's plan, though, we didn't know about the Cohort," said Mark, looking troubled. "What if there isn't time to find the book before the Cohort makes their move?"

"We'll just have to find the book faster," said Julian. "We can't face the Dearborns in an open Council. What's Zara done wrong, according to the Clave? Arthur *wasn't* qualified to run an Institute. Many Council members do hate Downworlders. She wants to run an Institute so she can pass an evil law. She wouldn't be the first. She's not breaking the rules. *We* are."

Kit felt a faint shudder go up his spine. For a moment, Julian had sounded like Kit's father. *The world isn't the way you want it to be. It's the way it is.*

"So we're just supposed to pretend we don't know what Zara's up to?" Emma frowned.

"No," said Diana. "I'm going to go to Idris. I'm going to speak to the Consul."

They all looked at her, wide-eyed—all except Julian, who didn't seem surprised, and Kieran, who was still glaring at his food.

"What Zara is proposing would mean Jia's daughter would be married to one of the Downworlders being registered. Jia knows what that would lead to. I know she'd meet with me. If I can reason with her—"

"She let the Cold Peace pass," said Kieran.

"She had no choice," said Diana. "If she'd had warning of what was coming, I'd like to think it would have turned out differently. This time, she'll have that warning. Besides—we have something to offer her now."

"That's right," said Julian, gesturing at Kieran. "The end of the Cold Peace. A faerie messenger from the Queen of Seelie."

Evelyn, who had been napping by the fire, bolted upright. "That is enough." She glared daggers at Kieran. "I can accept a Blackthorn into this house, even one with a questionable bloodline. I will always accept a Blackthorn. But a full-blood faerie? Listening to the business of Nephilim? I will not allow it."

Kieran looked briefly startled. Then he rose to his feet. Mark began to rise too. Julian stayed exactly where he was. "But Kieran is part of our plan—"

"Stuff and nonsense. Bridget!" she called, and the maid, who had clearly been lurking in the corridor, stuck her head into the room. "Please lead the princeling to one of the spare bedrooms. I will have your word, faerie, that you will not depart it until you are allowed."

Kieran looked at Cristina. "What is *your* desire, my lady?"

Kit was baffled. Why was Kieran, a prince of the gentry, taking orders from Cristina?

She blushed. "You don't need to swear you won't leave the room," she said. "I trust you."

"*Do* you?" Emma said, sounding fascinated, as Kieran gave a stiff bow and departed.

Bridget's muttering could be heard by all as she led Kieran out the door. "Faeries in the Institute," she muttered. "Ghosts is one thing, warlocks is another thing, but never in all my born days—"

Drusilla looked puzzled. "Why *is* Kieran here?" she said, as soon as he was gone. "I thought we hated him. Like, mostly hated him. I mean, he did save our lives, but he's still a jerk."

There was a murmur of voices. Kit remembered something he'd overhead Livvy say to Dru a day or two ago. More pieces of the Kieran puzzle: Livvy had been angry that Mark would go to Faerie to help someone who had hurt him. Had hurt Emma and Julian. Kit didn't know exactly what had happened, but it had clearly been bad.

Emma had moved to sit on the couch beside Cristina. She'd arrived wearing a pale gossamer dress that looked like something Kit would have seen in the Shadow Market. It made her look delicate and graceful, but Kit remembered the steel in her, the way she'd sliced apart the praying mantis demons in his house with all the calm of a bride cutting slices of wedding cake.

Julian was quietly listening to his family talk. Even though he wasn't looking at Emma, an almost visible energy crackled between them. Kit remembered the way Emma had said *this isn't Julian's kind of place* to his father—one of the first things he'd heard her say, in the Market—and the way her voice had seemed to hug the syllables of his name.

Parabatai were strange. So close, and yet it wasn't a marriage, yet it was more than a best friendship. There was no real analogue in the mundane world. And it drew him, the idea of it, of being connected to someone like that, the way all the dangerous and beautiful things of the Shadowhunter world drew him.

Maybe Ty . . .

Julian stood up, setting Tavvy down in an armchair. He stretched out his arms, cracking the sinews in his wrists. "The thing is, we need Kieran," he said.

Evelyn snorted. "Imagine needing a faerie lord," she said. "For anything."

Julian whispered something in Tavvy's ear. A moment later he was on his feet. "Miss Highsmith," he said. "My little brother is exhausted, but he says he doesn't know where his bedroom is. Can you show him?"

Evelyn looked irritably from Julian to Tavvy, who smiled angelically at her, showing off his dimples. "Can't you escort the child?"

"I've only just arrived," said Julian. "I don't know where the room is." He added his own smile to Tavvy's. Julian could radiate charm when he wanted to; Kit had nearly forgotten.

Evelyn looked around to see if there were any volunteers to take over for her; no one moved. Finally, with a disgusted snort, she snapped her fingers at Tavvy, said, "Well, come on then, child," and stalked from the room with him in tow.

Julian's smile turned crooked. Kit couldn't help the feeling that Julian had used Evelyn to get rid of Kieran, and Tavvy to get rid of Evelyn, and done it so handily no one could ever prove it.

If Julian had ever wanted to turn his hand to cons and crime, Kit thought, he would have excelled at it.

"We need Kieran to bargain with the Clave," said Julian, as if nothing had happened. "When we found him in Faerie, his father was about to have him killed. He escaped, but he'll never be safe as long as the Unseelie King sits on the throne." He ran his hands through his hair restlessly; Kit wondered how Julian kept it all in his head: plans, plots, concealments, truths.

"And the Queen wants the King off the throne," said Emma. "She's willing to help us replace him with Kieran's brother, but Kieran had to promise to convince him."

"Kieran's brother would be better than the King they have right now?" asked Dru.

"He would be better," Emma confirmed. "Believe it or not."

"Kieran will also testify in front of the Council," said Julian. "He will bring the Queen's message that she's willing to ally with us to defeat the King. He can confirm for the Council what the King is doing in the Unseelie Lands—"

"But you could tell them that," said Kit.

"If we wanted to risk the wrath of the Clave for having ventured into Faerie," Julian said. "Not to mention that while we might get out of that, there will be no forgiveness for our having entered into a bargain with the Seelie Queen."

Kit had to admit Julian was right. He knew how much trouble the Blackthorns had nearly gotten in for bargaining with the faerie convoy who had returned Mark to them. The Seelie Queen was a whole other level of forbidden. It was like getting a slap on the wrist for running a red light and then coming back the next day and blowing up the whole street.

"Kieran's your get-out-of-jail-free card," he said.

"It's not just about us," said Emma. "If the Council will listen to him, it could end the Cold Peace. In fact, it would have to. They'll have to believe him—he can't lie—and if the Queen is willing to fight the Unseelie King with the Clave, I don't think they'll be able to turn that down."

"Which means we have to keep Kieran safe," said Julian. "We also have to do what we can not to antagonize him."

"Because he's doing this for Mark?" said Dru.

"But Mark broke up with him," said Livvy, and then looked around, alarmed. Her ponytail brushed Kit's shoulder. "Is that something I wasn't supposed to say?"

"No," Mark said. "It's the truth. But—Kieran doesn't remember. When the Unseelie Court tortured him, he lost some of his memories. He doesn't recall bringing the envoy to the Institute, or Emma and Julian being whipped, or what danger he put us all in with his haste and anger." He looked down at his intertwined hands. "And he must not be told."

"But—Emma," said Livvy. "Are we supposed to pretend that she and Mark aren't . . . ?"

Kit leaned close to Ty. Ty smelled like ink and wool. "I don't understand any of this."

"Neither do I," Ty whispered back. "It's very complicated."

"Mark and I," Emma, said, looking very steadily at Mark. "We broke up."

Kit wondered if Mark had known that. He wasn't able to hide the look of astonishment on his face. "It just didn't work out," Emma went on. "So it's all right, whatever Mark needs to do."

"They're broken *up*?" Livvy whispered. Ty shrugged, baffled. Livvy had gone tense and was glancing from Emma to Mark, clearly worried.

"We have to let Kieran think he and Mark are still dating?" said Ty, looking bewildered. Kit felt the whole thing was beyond him as well, but then Henry VIII *had* beheaded several of his wives for apparently governmental reasons. The personal, the political, and the romantic were often oddly entwined.

"Concealing these things from Kieran isn't ideal," said Julian, hands in his pockets. "And I hate to ask you guys to lie. Probably it's best to avoid the subject. But there's literally no other way to make sure he actually shows up in front of the Clave."

Mark sat, running his fingers through his blond hair in a

distracted manner. Kit could hear him saying, "I'm all right, it's fine," to Cristina. He felt a surge of odd sympathy—not for Mark, but for Kieran. Kieran, who didn't know that his boyfriend wasn't really his boyfriend, that he was sleeping in a house full of people who, however friendly they might seem, would lie to him to get something they needed.

He thought of the coldness he'd seen in Julian back at the Shadow Market. Julian, who would sacrifice Kieran, and perhaps his own brother in a way, to get what he wanted.

Even if it was a good thing to want. Even if it was the end of the Cold Peace. Kit looked at Julian, gazing at the parlor fire with fathomless eyes, and suspected that there was more to it.

That where Julian Blackthorn was concerned, there would always be more to it.

16

PASS THE WANDERER

Mark made his way toward Kieran's room, steeling himself to lie.

Uneasiness and exhaustion had driven Mark from the parlor. The others, equally tired, were scattering to their own bedrooms. Cristina had slipped away without Mark noticing—though he *had* felt her absence, as a sort of pang in his chest, after she was gone. Diana had decided to leave as soon as she could for Idris, and Julian and Emma had gone to see her off.

Mark had been a little shocked by Emma's announcement that the pretense of their relationship was over; he knew what he'd said to her, back in Faerie, and that she'd only done as he asked. Still he felt slightly unmoored, alone, with no idea how to look in Kieran's eyes and tell him untruths.

He didn't like lying; he hadn't done it in the Hunt, and he felt uncomfortable with the rhythms of it. He wanted to talk about it with Cristina, but he couldn't imagine she'd want to hear about his complicated feelings for Kieran. Julian would be focused entirely on what was necessary and had to be done, no matter how painful. And now he could no longer talk to Emma. He hadn't realized how close their relationship, however false, had brought them in actual friendship; he wondered, now, if he would lose that, too.

And as for Kieran—Mark leaned his head against the wall next to Kieran's door. The corridors were papered in dulled gold leaf, trailing vines and trellises, cool against his forehead. Kieran was the person he could talk to least.

Not that banging his head on a wall was going to do any good. He straightened up and pushed the door open quietly; the room they'd set aside for Kieran was far away from the rest of the sleeping quarters, up a small flight of stairs, a room that looked as if it had likely once been used for storage. Narrow, arched windows looked out over the flat walls of other buildings. There was a massive four-poster bed in the middle of the room and an enormous wardrobe—though what they thought Kieran could possibly put in it, Mark had no idea.

The coverlet had been pulled off the bed and Kieran was nowhere to be seen. Mark felt a lurch of unease. Kieran *had* promised Cristina he would stay, in his own way: If he had decided not to honor his pledge to Cristina, there would be trouble.

Mark sighed, and closed his eyes. He felt stupid and vulnerable, standing in the middle of the room with his eyes shut, but he knew Kieran. "Kier," he said. "I can't see anything. Come out and talk to me."

A moment later there were fierce hands on his sides, lifting him, tossing him back on the bed. Kieran's weight pushed Mark down into the mattress; Mark opened his eyes and saw Kieran propped over him, savage and strange in his gentry clothes. The outline of Kieran's bandages pressed against Mark's chest, but otherwise Kieran's weight was a familiar one. To his body, a welcome one.

Kieran was looking down at him, silver and black eyes like the night sky. "I love you," Kieran said. "And I have made promises. But if I am to be constantly shamed and sent away, I will not answer for my actions."

Mark smoothed back a lock of Kieran's hair. The strands slipped through his fingers, heavy silk. "I'll make sure they treat you with more respect. They just have to get used to you."

Kieran's eyes glittered. "I have done nothing to earn their distrust."

Oh, but you have, Mark thought, *you have, and everyone remembers it but you.*

"They helped me rescue you," he said instead. "Don't be ungrateful."

Kieran smiled at that. "I would rather imagine it was only you responsible." He bent down to nuzzle Mark's throat.

Mark half-closed his eyes; he could feel his own lashes tickle his cheeks. He could feel the shift of the weight of Kieran on top of him. Kieran smelled like ocean, as he usually did. Mark remembered a hill in a green country, a damp cairn of stones, tumbling with Kieran to the bottom of it. Hands in his hair and on his body when he hadn't been touched in so long. He had burned and shivered. He shivered now. What was Kieran to him? What was he to Kieran? What had they ever been to each other?

"Kier," Mark said. "Listen—"

"Now is not the time for talking," said Kieran, and his lips were featherlight on Mark's skin, moving along the pulse of his throat, along his jaw, to capture his mouth.

It was a moment that felt stretched out to forever, a moment in which Mark fell through stars that shattered all around him. Kieran's lips were soft and cool and tasted like rain, and Mark clung to him in the dark and broken place at the bottom of the sky.

He tangled his fingers in Kieran's hair, curled his fingertips in, heard Kieran exhale harshly against his mouth. His body pressed harder against Mark's, and then Kieran's fingers slid against the back of Mark's neck and knotted in the chain that held his elf-bolt necklace.

It was like being shaken awake. Mark rolled over, taking Kieran with him, so they were lying side by side on the bed. The movement broke the kiss, and Kieran stared at him, half-annoyed and half-dazed. "Miach," he said. His voice took the word and turned it into a beckoning caress, an invitation to faerie pleasures unimaginable.

"No," said Mark. "Don't call me that."

Kieran inhaled. "There is something wrong between us, is there not? Mark, please tell me what it is. I sense the distance but do not understand its cause."

"You don't remember, but we had an argument. About me staying with my family. It's why I gave you my elf-bolt necklace back."

Kieran looked bewildered. "But I always knew you might stay with your family. I did not want it, but I must have come to accept it. I remember waking in the Unseelie Court. I do not remember feeling any anger toward you."

"It wasn't a bad fight." Mark swallowed. "But I wasn't expecting this—you, in my world. All the complications of these politics."

"You don't want me here?" Kieran's face didn't change, but his hair was suddenly streaked with white where it curled against his temples.

"It's not that," Mark said. "In the Wild Hunt, I thought I might die any night. Every night. I wanted everything, always, and risked anything, because no one depended on me. And then there was you, and we depended on each other, but . . ." He thought of Cristina. Her words came to him, and he couldn't help using them, though it almost felt like a betrayal. Cristina, who he had kissed with joyous abandon for those few moments near the revel, before he had realized what she thought of him . . . someone she would only kiss when drunk or out of her mind . . .

"I have always needed you, Kieran," he said. "I have needed you to live. I've always needed you so much, I never had a chance to think about whether we were good for each other or not."

Kieran sat up. He was silent, though Mark saw—to his relief—that the white streaks in his hair had gone back to their more normal blue-black color. "That is honest," he said finally. "I cannot fault you there."

"Kieran—"

"How much time do you need?" Kieran had drawn himself up, and he was all proud prince of Faerie now. Mark thought of the times he'd seen Kieran at revels, at a distance; seen the smaller faeries scatter in front of him. Girls and boys who hung on his arms, hoping for a word or look, because the favor of even a disgraced prince was currency. And Kieran, granting neither those words nor those looks, because his words and looks were all for Mark. All for what they had between them when the Wild Hunt was looking away . . .

"Maybe a few days," Mark said. "If you can be patient for that long."

"I can be patient for a few days."

"Why did you choose Cristina?" Mark said abruptly. "When you had to swear fealty to one of us. Why her? Did you do it to unsettle me?"

Kieran grinned. "Not everything is, as they say, about you, Mark." He leaned back; his hair was very black against the stark white linens. "Shouldn't you be going?"

"Don't you want me to stay here?" Mark said. "With you?"

"While you weigh my merits as if I were a horse you were considering buying? No," Kieran said. "Go back to your own room, Mark Blackthorn. And if loneliness keeps you from your rest, do not seek me out. Surely there must be a rune for sleeplessness."

There wasn't, but Mark didn't feel like it would be a good idea to say so. Kieran's eyes were glittering dangerously. Mark left, wondering if he'd made a horrible mistake.

* * *

Cristina's room in the London Institute was much like the rooms she'd seen in pictures of other Institutes all over the world: plainly furnished with a heavy bed, wardrobe, dresser, and desk. A small bathroom, clean, with a shower that she'd already used. Now she lay on the lumpy mattress, the blankets pulled up to her chest, her arm aching.

She wasn't sure why. She'd loved every moment of flying with the Wild Hunt; if she'd injured herself somehow, she had no memory of it. Not when she'd mounted the horse, or when they'd ridden, and surely she'd recall pain like that? And how could she have hurt herself any other way?

She rolled to the side and reached to touch her witchlight, on the nightstand table. It flared to a soft glow, illuminating the room—the enormous English bed, the heavy oak furniture. Someone had scrawled the initials JB+LH into the paint by the window.

She stared down at her right arm. Around her wrist was a band of paler skin, slightly reddened at the edges, like the scar left by a fiery bracelet.

"You'll be all right?" Diana said. It was half declaration, half question.

Diana, Julian, and Emma stood in the entryway of the London Institute. The Institute doors were open and the dark courtyard was visible; it had rained earlier, and the flagstones were washed clean. Julian could see the arch of the famous metal gate that closed off the Institute, and the words worked into it: WE ARE DUST AND SHADOWS.

"We'll be fine," Julian said.

"Malcolm's dead, again. No one's trying to kill us," said Emma. "It's practically a vacation."

Diana hoisted her bag higher on her shoulder. Her plan was to take a taxi to Westminster Abbey, where a secret tunnel accessible only to Shadowhunters led to Idris.

"I don't like leaving you."

Julian was surprised. Diana had always come and gone according to her own lights. "We'll be fine," he said. "Evelyn's here, and the Clave is a phone call away."

"Not a phone call you want to make," said Diana. "I sent another message to Magnus and Alec, and I'll keep in touch with them from Alicante." She paused. "If you need them, send a fire-message and they'll come."

"I can handle this," Julian said. "I've handled a lot worse for a lot longer."

Diana's eyes met his. "I would step in, if I could," she said. "You know that. I'd take the Institute if it was possible. Put myself up against the Dearborns."

"I know," Julian said, and oddly enough, he did. Even if he didn't know what prevented Diana from putting herself forward as a candidate, he knew it was something important.

"If it would make *any* difference," Diana said. "But I wouldn't even get through the interview. It would be futile, and then I wouldn't be able to stay with you, or help you."

She sounded as if she were trying to convince herself, and Emma reached her hand out, impulsive as always.

"Diana, you know we'd never let them take you away from us," she said.

"Emma." Julian's voice was sharper than he'd intended. The anger he'd been shoving down since Emma had said she and Mark had broken up was rising again, and he didn't know how long he could control it. "Diana knows what she's talking about."

Emma looked startled by the coldness in his tone. Diana flicked her eyes between them. "Look, I know it's incredibly stressful, being kept from your home like this, but try not to fight," she said. "You're going to have to hold everything together until I get back from Idris."

"It's only a day or two," said Emma, not looking at Julian. "And nobody's fighting."

"Stay in touch with us," Julian said to Diana. "Tell us what Jia says."

She nodded. "I haven't been back to Idris since the Dark War. It'll be interesting." She leaned forward then, and kissed first Jules and then Emma, quickly, on the cheek. "Take care of yourselves. I mean it."

She flipped the hood up on her jacket and stepped outside, swallowed up almost instantly by shadows. Emma's arm pressed briefly against Julian's as she raised her hand to wave good-bye. In the distance, Julian heard the clang of the front gate.

"Jules," she said, without turning her head. "I know you said Diana refused to try to take the Institute, but do you know why . . . ?"

"No," he said. It was a single word, but there was venom in it. "On the topic of confessions, were you planning on telling the rest of Mark's family *why* you dumped their brother with no warning?"

Emma looked astonished. "You're angry that Mark and I broke up?"

"I guess you've dumped two of their brothers, if we're really counting," he said as if she hadn't spoken. "Who's next? Ty?"

He knew immediately he'd gone too far. Ty was her little brother, just as he was Julian's. Her face went very still.

"Screw you, Julian Blackthorn," she said, spun on her heel, and stalked back upstairs.

Neither Julian nor Emma slept well that night, though each of them thought they were the only one troubled, and the other one was probably resting just fine.

"I think it's time for you to get your first real Mark," said Ty.

Only the three of them—Livvy, Ty, and Kit—were left in the

parlor. Everyone else had gone to bed. Kit guessed from the quality of the darkness outside that it was probably three or four in the morning, but he wasn't tired. It could be jet lag, or Portal lag, or whatever they called it; it could be the contagious relief of the others that they were all reunited again.

It could be an approximate six hundred cups of tea.

"I've had Marks," said Kit. "You put that *iratze* on me."

Livvy looked mildly curious but didn't ask. She was sprawled in an armchair by the fire, her legs hooked over one side.

"I meant a permanent one," said Ty. "This is the first real one we all get." He held up his long-fingered right hand, the back toward Kit, showing him the graceful eye-shaped rune that identified all Shadowhunters. "Voyance. It clarifies Sight."

"I can already see the Shadow World," Kit pointed out. He took a bite out of a chocolate digestive biscuit. One of the few great foods England had to offer, in his opinion.

"You probably don't see everything you could," Livvy said, then held up her hands to indicate neutrality. "But you do what you want."

"It's the most painful rune to get," said Ty. "But worthwhile."

"Sure," said Kit, idly picking up another biscuit—Livvy had sneaked a whole package from the pantry. "Sounds great."

He looked up in surprise a moment later when Ty's shadow fell across him; Ty was standing behind him, his stele out, his eyes bright. "Your dominant hand is your right," he said, "so put that one out, toward me."

Surprised, Kit choked on his cookie; Livvy sat bolt upright. "Ty," she said. "Don't; he doesn't *want* one. He was just kidding."

"I—" Kit started, but Ty had gone the color of old ivory and stepped back, looking dismayed. His eyes darted away from Kit's. Livvy was starting to get up out of her chair.

"No—No, I do want one," Kit said. "I *would* like the Mark. You're right, it's time I got a real one."

The moment hung suspended; Livvy was half out of her chair. Ty blinked rapidly. Then he smiled, a little, and Kit's heart resumed its normal beating. "Your right hand, then," Ty said.

Kit put his hand out, and Ty was right: The Mark hurt. It felt like what he imagined getting a tattoo was like: a deep burning sting. By the time Ty was done, his eyes were watering.

Kit flexed his fingers, staring at his hand. He'd have this forever, this eye on the back of his hand, this thing that *Ty* had put there. He could never erase it or change it.

"I wonder," Ty said, sliding his stele back into his belt, "where that house of Malcolm's, in Cornwall, might be."

"I can tell you exactly where it is," said the girl standing by the fireplace. "It's in Polperro."

Kit stared. He was absolutely sure she hadn't been standing there a moment ago. She was blond, very young, and—translucent. He could see the wallpaper right through her.

He couldn't help himself. He yelled.

Bridget had led Emma to a bedroom she seemed to have picked out ahead of time, and Emma soon found out why: There were two height charts scribbled on the plaster, the kind you got by standing someone against a wall and drawing a line just above their head, with the date. One was marked *Will Herondale*, the other, *James Carstairs*.

A Carstairs room. Emma hugged her elbows and imagined Jem: his kind voice, his dark eyes. She missed him.

But that wasn't all; after all, Jem and Will could have done their height charts in any room. In the nightstand drawer, Emma found a cluster of old photographs, most dating from the early 1900s.

Photographs of a group of four boys, at various stages of their lives. They seemed a lively bunch. Two of them—one blond, one dark-haired—were together in almost every photo, their arms slung around each other, both laughing. There was a girl with brown hair who looked a great deal like Tessa, but wasn't Tessa. And then there *was* Tessa, looking exactly the same, with a gorgeously handsome man in his late twenties. The famous Will Herondale, Emma guessed. And there was a girl, with dark red hair and brown skin, and a serious look. There was a golden sword in her hands. Emma recognized it instantly, even without the inscription on the blade: *I am Cortana, of the same steel and temper as Joyeuse and Durendal.*

Cortana. Whoever the girl was in the photograph, she was a Carstairs.

On the back, someone had scrawled what looked like a line from a poem. *The wound is the place where the Light enters you.*

Emma stared at it for a long time.

"There's really no need for you to yell," said the girl crossly. Her accent was very English. "I'm a ghost, that's all. You act as if you haven't seen one before."

"I haven't," Kit said, nettled.

Livvy was on her feet. "Kit, what's going on? Who are you talking to?"

"A ghost," said Ty. "Who is it, Kit?"

"My name is Jessamine," said the girl. "And just because you didn't see me before doesn't mean I wasn't *trying.*"

"Her name is Jessamine," Kit reported. "She says she's been trying to get our attention."

"A ghost," said Ty, looking toward the fireplace. It was clear he couldn't see Jessamine, but also clear he had a good idea where she was standing. "They say a ghost saved the London Institute during the Dark War. Was that her?"

Kit listened and repeated. "She says she did. She looks very smug about it."

Jessamine glared.

"She also says she knows where Malcolm lived," said Kit.

"She *does?*" Livvy moved over to the desk, grabbing a pen and a notebook. "Will she tell us?"

"Polperro," said Jessamine again. She was very pretty, with blond hair and dark eyes. Kit wondered if it was weird to think a ghost was attractive. "It's a small town in southern Cornwall. Malcolm used to talk about his house plans sometimes, when he was in the Institute." She waved a translucent hand. "He was very proud of the house—right on top of some famous caves. Dreadful he's turned out to be a villain. And *poor* Arthur," she added. "I used to look after him sometimes when he slept. He had the most awful nightmares about Faerie and his brother."

"What's she saying?" Livvy asked, her pen poised over her paper.

"Polperro," said Kit. "Southern Cornwall. He was very proud of the location. She's sorry he turned out to be an asshole."

Livvy scribbled it down. "I bet she didn't say asshole."

"We need to go to the library," Ty said. "Find an atlas and train schedules."

"Ask her something for me," said Livvy. "Why didn't she just tell Evelyn where Malcolm's house was?"

After a moment, Kit said, "She says Evelyn can't really hear her. She often just makes things up and pretends Jessamine's said them."

"But she knows Jessamine's here," said Ty. "She must be a faint spirit, if none of the rest of us can see her."

"Humph!" said Jessamine. "Faint spirit indeed; it's clear none of you have practice observing the undead. I have done everything to get your attention outside of smacking one of you in the head with a Ouija board."

"I just saw you," said Kit. "And I've never practiced being a Shadowhunter at all."

"You're a Herondale," said Jessamine. "They can see ghosts."

"Herondales can usually see ghosts," said Ty, at the same time. "That's why I wanted you to get the Voyance Mark."

Kit swiveled to look at him. "Why didn't you say so?"

"It might not have worked," said Ty. "I didn't want you to feel bad if it didn't."

"Well, it did work," said Livvy. "We should go wake up Julian and tell him."

"The older boy, with the brown curly hair?" said Jessamine. "He's awake." She chuckled. "It's nice to see those lovely Blackthorn eyes again."

"Julian's up," Kit said, deciding not to mention that the ghost might have crush on him.

Ty joined Livvy at the door. "Are you coming, Kit?"

Kit shook his head, surprising himself. If you'd asked him a few weeks ago if he'd be pleased to be left alone with a ghost, he would have said no. And he wasn't pleased, exactly, but he wasn't bothered, either. There was nothing terrifying about Jessamine. She seemed older than she looked, a little wistful, and not at all dead.

She was, though. She drifted in the waft of air from the closing door, her long white fingers resting on the mantel. "You needn't stay," she said to Kit. "I'll probably disappear in a minute. Even ghosts need rest."

"I had a question," Kit said. He swallowed hard; now that it had come to the moment, his throat was dry. "Have you—have you ever seen my father? He just died a little while ago."

Her brown eyes filled with pity. "No," she said. "Most people don't become ghosts, Christopher. Only those with unfinished business on earth, or who have died feeling they owe someone something."

"My father never thought he owed anyone anything," muttered Kit.

"It's better that I haven't seen him. It means he's gone on. He's at peace."

"Gone on where?" Kit raised his head. "Is he in Heaven? I mean, it seems so unlikely."

"*Christopher!*" Jessamine sounded shocked.

"Seriously," said Kit. "You didn't know him."

"I don't know what comes after death," Jessamine said. "Tessa used to come and ask me too. She wanted to know where Will was. But he didn't linger—he died happy and at peace, and he went on." Her hands fluttered helplessly. "I am not like Charon. I am no ferryman. I cannot say what lies on the other side of the river."

"It could be awful," said Kit, making a fist, feeling his new Mark sting. "It could be torture forever."

"It could be," Jessamine said. There was wisdom in her feather-light voice. "But I don't think so."

She bent her head. The firelight glinted off her pale blond hair, and then she was gone, and Kit was alone in the room. There was something in his hand, though, something that crackled when he moved.

It was a folded piece of paper. He opened it, scanning the words quickly; they had been sketched in a delicate, feminine hand.

If you steal any of the books from the library, I will know, and you'll be sorry.

It was signed, with several flourishes: *Jessamine Lovelace.*

When Livvy came into Julian's room, he was lying flat on the bed, like a dropped piece of toast. He hadn't even bothered to change his clothes or get under the covers.

"Jules?" Livvy said, hovering in the doorway.

He sat up, fast. He'd been trying to sort through his thoughts, but the sight of his younger sibling—in his room, this late at night—banished everything but immediate, atavistic panic. "Is everything all right? Did something happen?"

Livvy nodded. "It's good news, actually. We figured out where Malcolm's house is—the one in Cornwall."

"What?" Julian scrubbed his hands through his hair, rubbing at his eyes to wake himself up. "Where's Ty?"

"In the library." She sat down on the corner of Julian's bed. "Turns out there's a house ghost. Jessamine. Anyway, she remembered Malcolm and knew where his house was. Ty's checking on it, but there's no reason to think she wouldn't be right. Evelyn's been talking to her for days, we just didn't think she really existed, but Kit—"

"Can see ghosts. Right," said Julian. He felt more alert now. "All right. I'll go tomorrow, see what I can find out."

"And we'll go to Blackthorn Hall," Livvy said. Blackthorn Hall was one of the Blackthorn family's two land properties: They had a manor in Idris, and a large home in Chiswick, on the Thames. It had once belonged to the Lightwoods, a long time ago. "See if there's any papers, anything about Annabel. Kieran can't really leave the Institute, so Mark can stay here with him and Cristina and they can look in the library."

"No," said Julian.

Livvy set her jaw. "Jules—"

"You can go to Blackthorn Hall," he said. "You've certainly earned that much, you and Ty, and Kit, too. But Mark goes with you. Kieran can amuse himself weaving daisy chains or making up a ballad."

Livvy's mouth twitched. "It seems wrong to make fun of the Fair Folk."

"Kieran's fair game," said Julian. "He's annoyed us in the past."

"I guess Cristina can watch him."

"I was going to ask her to come to Cornwall," said Julian.

"You and Cristina?" Livvy looked baffled. Julian couldn't blame her. It was true that their group fell into established patterns based on age and acquaintance. Jules and Emma, or Jules and Mark, made sense. Jules and Cristina didn't.

"And Emma," Julian added, cursing silently. The thought of extended time with Emma, especially now, was—terrifying. But it would be considered bizarre if he went without her, his *parabatai*. Never mind that Emma wouldn't sit still for it. Not a chance.

Bringing Cristina would help, though. Cristina would be a buffer. Having to put someone between himself and Emma made him feel sick, but the memory of the way he'd snapped at her in the entryway made him feel sicker.

It had been like watching someone else talking to the person he loved the most in the world; someone else, hurting his *parabatai* on purpose. He had been able to do *something* with his feelings while she'd been with Mark—twist and crumple them, shove them far underneath his skin and consciousness. He had felt them there, bleeding, like a tumor slicing open his internal organs, but he hadn't been able to *see* them.

Now they were there again, laid out before him. It was terrifying to love someone who was forbidden to you. Terrifying to feel something you could never speak of, something that was horrible to almost everyone you knew, something that could destroy your life.

It was in some ways more terrifying to know that your feelings were unwanted. When he had thought Emma loved him back, he had not been completely alone in his hell. When she was with Mark, he could tell himself that it was Mark keeping them apart. Not that she would rather be with no one than be with him.

"Cristina knows a great deal about the Black Volume," Julian said. He had no idea if this was true or not. Graciously, Livvy didn't pursue it. "She'll be helpful."

"Blackthorn Hall, here we come," said Livvy, and slid off the bed. She looked to Julian like a little girl from an old illustration in a picture book, in her puffed-sleeve blue dress. But maybe Livvy would always look like a little girl to him. "Jules?"

"Yes?"

"We know," she said. "We know about Arthur, and what was wrong with him. We know you ran the Institute. We know it was you doing all of it since the Dark War."

Julian felt as if the bed were tilting under him. "Livia . . ."

"We're not angry," she said quickly. "I'm here by myself because I wanted to talk to you alone, before Ty and Dru. There was something I wanted to say to you."

Julian still had his fingers in the bedspread. He suspected he was in some kind of shock. He'd thought of how this moment might go for so many years that now that it was happening, he had no idea what to say.

"Why?" he managed finally.

"I realized something," she said. "I want to be like you, Jules. Not this second, not right now, but someday. I want to take care of people, other Shadowhunters, people who need me. I want to run an Institute."

"You'd be good at it," he said. "Livvy—I didn't tell you because I couldn't. Not because I didn't trust you. I didn't even tell Emma. Not until a few weeks ago."

She only smiled at him, and came around the side of the bed to where he was sitting. She bent down, and he felt her kiss him softly on the forehead. He closed his eyes, remembering when she'd been small enough for him to lift her in his arms, when she'd followed him, holding her hands out to him: *Julian, Julian, carry me.*

"There's nobody else I'd rather be like than you," she said. "I want you to be proud of me."

He opened his eyes at that and hugged her awkwardly, one-armed, and then she pulled away and ruffled his hair. He complained, and she laughed and headed for the door, saying she was exhausted. She flipped off the light as she went out of the room, leaving him in darkness.

He rolled under the blanket. Livvy knew. They knew. They knew, and they didn't hate him. It was a weight off him he had almost forgotten he'd been carrying.

17

HAUNTED

It was a perfect English day. The sky was the color of Wedgwood china, smooth and blue. The air was warm and sweet and full of possibilities. Julian stood on the front step of the Institute, trying to prevent his smallest brother from choking him to death.

"Don't go," Tavvy wailed. "You were already gone. You can't go *again*."

Evelyn Highsmith sniffed. "In my time, children were seen and not heard, and they certainly did not *complain*."

She was standing in the arch of the door, hands folded primly over the head of her cane. She had put on an amazing outfit in order to see them off to the train station: There was a sort of riding habit involved, and possibly jodhpurs. Her hat had a bird on it, though to Ty's disappointment, the bird was definitely dead.

The ancient black car that belonged to the Institute had been unearthed, and Bridget was waiting beside it with Cristina and Emma. Their backpacks were stashed in the trunk—Mark had been amused to find out that in England, they called it a boot—and they were talking excitedly. Both were in jeans and T-shirts, since they'd have to pass as mundane on the train, and Emma's hair was tied back into a braid.

Still, Julian was glad Cristina was going. In the back of his mind, he clung to the idea that she would be a buffer between him and Emma. Emma hadn't betrayed any hint of being angry that morning, and the two of them had functioned well together, mapping their route to Polperro, figuring out the train schedules and raiding the storage room for clothes. They planned to get a room in a bed-and-breakfast, preferably one with a kitchen they could cook in, to minimize exposure to mundanes. They'd even purchased their train tickets from Paddington ahead of time. All the planning had been easy and simple: They were a *parabatai* team; they still worked, they still functioned better together than alone.

But even with the most iron self-control imposed on himself, the sheer force of love and yearning when he looked at her was like being hit unexpectedly by a train, over and over. Not that he imagined being hit expectedly by a train would be much better.

Best to be buffered against that, until it stopped happening. If it stopped happening. But he wouldn't let himself think that way.

It had to end someday.

"Jules!" Tavvy wailed. Julian gave his brother a last hug and set him down. "Why can't I come with you?"

"Because," Julian explained. "You have to stay here and help Drusilla. She needs you."

Tavvy looked as if he doubted that. Drusilla, wearing an overly long cotton skirt that reached her toes, rolled her eyes. "I can't believe you're going," she said to Julian. "The minute you leave, Livvy and Ty start treating me like a servant."

"Servants get paid," Ty observed.

"See? *See* what I mean?" Dru poked Julian in the chest with an index finger. "You'd better hurry back so they don't maltreat me."

"I'll try." Julian met Mark's look over Dru's head; they shared a smile. Emma and Mark's good-bye had been bizarre, to say the least.

Emma had given him a quick, absentminded hug before descending the stairs; Mark hadn't looked bothered until he'd noticed Julian and the others staring at him. He'd run down the steps after Emma, caught her hand, and spun her to face him.

"It is better that you go," he said, "that I might forget your fair, cruel face, and heal my heart."

Emma had looked stunned; Cristina, saying something in a low voice to Mark that sounded like *unnecessary*, had hauled Emma off toward the car.

Ty and Livvy were the last to come to say good-bye to Jules; Livvy embraced him fiercely, and Ty gave him a soft, shy smile. Julian wondered where Kit was. He'd been glued to Ty's and Livvy's sides the whole time they'd been in London, but he appeared to have vanished for the family farewell.

"I've got something for you," Ty said. He held out a box, which Julian took with some surprise. Ty was absolutely punctual about Christmas and birthday presents, but he rarely gave gifts spontaneously.

Curious, Julian popped open the top of the box to find a set of colored pencils. He didn't know the brand, but they looked pristine and unused. "Where did you get these?"

"Fleet Street," said Ty. "I went out early this morning."

An ache of love pressed against the back of Julian's throat. It reminded him of when Ty was a baby, serious and quiet. He hadn't been able to go to sleep for a long time without someone holding him, and though Julian had been very small himself, he remembered holding Ty while he fell asleep, all round wrists and straight black hair and long lashes. He'd felt so much love for his brother even then it had been like an explosion in his heart.

"Thanks. I've missed drawing," Julian said, and tucked the box into his duffel bag. He didn't fuss; Ty didn't like fuss, but Julian made his tone as warm as he could, and Ty beamed.

Jules thought of Livvy, the night before, the way she'd kissed his forehead. Her thank-you. This was Ty's.

"Be careful at Blackthorn Hall," he said. He was nervous that they were going but tried not to show it; he knew he was being unreasonable. "Go during the day. During the *day*," he insisted, when Livvy made a face. "And try not to get Drusilla and Tavvy into trouble. Remember, Mark is in charge."

"Does he know that?" said Livvy.

Julian sought Mark in the crowd on the steps. He was standing with his hands behind his back, exchanging a mistrustful look with a carved stone gnome. "Your pretense does not fool me, gnome," he muttered. "My eye will be upon you."

Julian sighed. "Just do what he says."

"Julian!" Emma called. She was standing beside the car, Cortana—glamoured to be invisible to mundanes—glittering just over her right shoulder. "We're going to miss the train."

Julian nodded and held up two fingers. He made his way across the steps to Mark and gripped his shoulder. "You going to be okay?"

Mark nodded. Julian thought about asking where Kieran was, but decided there was no point. It would probably just stress Mark out more. "Thanks for trusting me to be in charge," said Mark. "After what happened before, with the kitchen."

In Los Angeles, Julian had left Mark for a night to look after their siblings. Mark had managed to destroy the kitchen, cover Tavvy in sugar, and almost give Jules a nervous breakdown.

"I do trust you." Unspeaking, Julian and Mark looked at each other. Then Julian grinned. "Besides," he added, "this isn't my kitchen."

Mark laughed softly. Julian headed down the stairs as Emma and Cristina piled into the car. He went around the back to toss his bag into the trunk and came to a stop. Wedged into the space beside the luggage was a small figure in a smudged white T-shirt.

Tavvy looked up at him, wide-eyed. "I want to go too," he announced.

Julian sighed and began to roll up his sleeves. A brother's work was never done.

One of the benefits of being a Shadowhunter that was rarely talked about, Emma thought, was easy parking at places like train stations and churches. Often a place had been set aside for Shadowhunters to leave their cars, glamoured to appear to mundanes as something they would ignore—a construction site or a pile of trash bins. Bridget pulled the rattling black Austin Metro to a stop on Praed Street, mere feet from Paddington Station, and the Shadowhunters piled out to retrieve their bags while she locked up the vehicle.

They'd packed fast and light, just enough for a few days. Weapons, gear, and few clothes besides the ones on their backs, though Emma had no doubt that Cristina would look elegant all the time anyway. Demurely, Cristina tucked her knife into her pocket and bent to sling her backpack over her shoulder. She winced.

"Are you all right?" Emma asked, sliding into step beside her. She was enormously glad to have Cristina there between her and Jules, something to smooth the prickly and dangerous roads of their conversations.

They passed into the station, which was brightly lit and modern, the walkways lined with stores like the Body Shop and Caffè Nero. She glanced ahead at Julian, but he was deep in discussion with Bridget. Julian had an amazing ability to make conversation with literally anyone. She wondered what he could possibly find to talk to Bridget about. Evelyn's odd habits? London history?

"Have you gotten a chance to talk to Mark at all about, you know, the kiss?" asked Emma as they passed an Upper Crust bakery that smelled like butter and cinnamon, mixed with the smoke of the station. "Especially with the whole Kieran thing going on now."

Cristina shook her head. She looked drawn and pale, as if she hadn't slept well. "Kieran and Mark have history. Like Diego and me. I can't find fault with Mark for being drawn to his history. It was the reason I was drawn to Diego, and I did that without all the pressures that are on Mark now."

"I don't know how it'll play out. Mark's not much of a liar," said Emma. "I say this as someone who isn't great at it myself."

Cristina gave a pained smile. "You are terrible. Watching you and Mark pretend to be in love was like watching two people who kept falling over and then hoping nobody noticed."

Emma giggled. "Very flattering."

"I am only saying that for the good of us all, Kieran must believe in Mark's feelings," said Cristina. "A faerie who thinks they have been scorned or spited can be very cruel."

She gasped suddenly, bending almost double. Emma caught her as she sank down. In a blind panic, she dragged Cristina into a corner between two shops. She didn't dare scream; she wasn't glamoured, mundanes would hear her. But she glanced toward Julian and Bridget, still deep in conversation, and *thought* as hard as she could.

Jules, Julian, I need you, right now, come right now, please!

"Emma—" Cristina had her arms crossed, hugging her stomach as if it pained her, but it was the blood on her shirt that terrified Emma.

"Cristina—sweetheart—let me see, let me see." She pulled frantically at Cristina's arms until the other girl let go.

There was blood on her right hand and sleeve. Most of it seemed to be coming from her arm and to have transferred itself to her shirt. Emma breathed a little easier. A wound to the arm was less serious than one to the body.

"What's going on?" It was Julian's voice. He and Bridget had reached them; Jules was white-faced. She saw the terror in his eyes and realized what had caused it: He'd thought something had happened to *Emma.*

"I'm all right," Emma said mechanically, shocked by the look on his face.

"Of course you are," said Bridget impatiently. "Let me get to the girl. Stop clinging to her, for goodness' sake."

Emma detached herself and watched as Bridget knelt and peeled Cristina's sleeve back. Cristina's wrist was banded with a bracelet of blood, her skin puffy. It was as if someone was tightening an invisible wire around her arm, cutting into the flesh.

"What are you two just sitting there for?" Bridget demanded. "Put a healing rune on the girl."

They both reached for steles; Julian got to his first and drew a quick *iratze* on Cristina's skin. Emma leaned forward, holding her breath.

Nothing happened. If anything, the skin around the bleeding circle seemed to swell more. A fresh gush of blood welled up, spattering Bridget's clothes. Emma wished she still had her old stele; she'd always superstitiously believed she could draw stronger runes with it. But it was in faerie hands now.

Cristina didn't whimper. She was a Shadowhunter, after all. But her voice shook. "I don't think an *iratze* will help this."

Emma shook her head. "What is it—?"

"It looks like a faerie charm," said Bridget. "While you were in the Lands, did any fey seem to cast a spell on you? Were your wrists ever tied?"

Cristina pushed herself up on her elbows. "That—I mean, that couldn't be it. . . ."

"What happened?" Emma demanded.

"At the revel, two girls tied my wrist and Mark's together with a ribbon," Cristina said reluctantly. "We sliced it off, but there may have been a stronger magic there than I guessed. It could be a sort of binding spell."

"This is the first time you've been away from Mark since we were in Faerie," Julian said. "You think that's it?"

Cristina looked grim. "The farther I go from him, the worse it becomes. Last night was almost the first time I'd left his side, and my arm burned and ached. And as we drove away from the Institute, the pain got worse and worse—I hoped it would go away, but it didn't."

"We need to get you back to the Institute," said Emma. "We'll all go. Come on."

Cristina shook her head. "You and Julian should still go to Cornwall," she said, and gestured with her uninjured hand overhead, toward the board on which the schedules for the trains were posted. The train for Penzance left in less than five minutes. "You need to. This is necessary."

"We could wait a day," Emma protested.

"This is faerie magic," said Cristina, letting Bridget help her to her feet. "There's no assurance it will be fixed in a day."

Emma hesitated. She hated the thought of leaving Cristina.

Bridget spoke in a sharp voice, surprising them all. "Go," she said. "You are *parabatai*, the most powerful team the Nephilim can offer. I have seen what *parabatai* can do. Stop hesitating."

"She's right," Julian said. He shoved his stele back into his belt. "Come on, Emma."

A blur followed, of Emma hugging Cristina hurriedly goodbye, Julian catching at her hand, drawing her away, of the two of them running haphazardly through the train station, nearly knocking over the ticket barriers, and flinging themselves into the empty coach of a Western Railway train just as it pulled out of the station with a loud screeching of released brakes.

With every mile she and Bridget covered that brought them closer to the Institute, Cristina's pain faded. At Paddington, her arm had screamed with agonizing pain. Now it was a dull ache that seemed to push down into her bones.

I have lost something, the ache seemed to whisper. *There is something I am missing.* In Spanish, she might have said, *Me haces falta.* She had noticed early on when she learned English that a direct translation of that phrase didn't really exist: English speakers said *I need you*, where *me haces falta* meant something closer to, *You are lacking to me.* That was what she felt now, a lack like a missing chord in a song or a missing word on a page.

They pulled up in front of the Institute with a squeal of brakes. Cristina heard Bridget call her name, but she was already out of the car, cradling her wrist as she ran toward the front steps. She couldn't help herself. Her mind revolted at the thought of being controlled by something outside herself, but it was as if her body was dragging her along, pushing her toward what it needed to make itself whole.

The front doors banged open. It was Mark.

There was blood on his arm, too, soaking through the light blue sleeve of his sweater. Behind him was a chatter of voices, but he was only looking at Cristina. His light hair was disarrayed, his blue and gold eyes burning like banners.

Cristina thought she had never seen anything so beautiful.

He ran down the steps—he was barefoot—and caught at her hand, pulling her against him. The moment their bodies slammed together, Cristina felt the ache inside her vanish.

"It's a binding spell," Mark whispered into her hair. "Some kind of binding spell, tying us together."

"The girls at the revel—one tied our wrists together and the other laughed—"

"I know." He brushed his lips across her forehead. She could feel his heart pounding. "We'll figure it out. We'll fix it."

She nodded and closed her eyes, but not before she saw that

several others had spilled out onto the front step and were staring at them. In the center of the group was Kieran, his elegant face pale and set, his eyes unreadable.

The tickets they had bought were first class, so Emma and Julian had a compartment to themselves. The gray-brown of the city had been left behind, and they were rolling through green fields, studded with wildflowers and copses of green trees. Charcoal stone farmers' walls ran up and down the hills, dividing the land into puzzle pieces.

"It looks a bit like Faerie," said Emma, leaning against the window. "You know, without the rivers of blood or the high-body-count dance parties. More scones, less death."

Julian glanced up. He had his sketchbook on his knees and a black box of colored pencils on the seat next to him. "I think that's what it says on the front gate of Buckingham Palace," he said. He sounded calm, entirely neutral. The Julian who had snapped at her in the entryway of the Institute was gone. This was polite Julian, gracious Julian. Putting-up-a-front-for-strangers Julian.

There was absolutely no way she could handle interacting only with that Julian for however long they were in Cornwall. "So," she said. "Are you still angry?"

He looked at her for a long moment and set his sketchbook aside. "I'm sorry," he said. "What I said—that was unacceptable and cruel."

Emma stood up and leaned against the window. The countryside flew by: gray, green, gray. "Why did you say it?"

"I was angry." She could see his reflection in the window, looking up at her. "I was angry about Mark."

"I didn't know you were that invested in our relationship."

"He's my brother." Julian touched his own face as he spoke, unconsciously, as if to connect with those features—the long cheekbones and eyelashes—that were so like Mark's. "He's not—he gets hurt easily."

"He's fine," she said. "I promise you."

"It's more than that." His gaze was steady. "When you were together, at least I could feel like you were both with someone I cared about and could trust. You loved someone I loved too. Is that likely to happen again?"

"I don't know what's likely to happen," she said. *I know you have nothing to worry about. I wasn't in love with Mark. I'll never be in love with anyone again who isn't you.* "Just that there are things we can and can't control."

"Em," he said. "This is me we're talking about."

She turned away from the window, pressed her back to the cold glass. She was looking at Julian directly, not just his reflection. And though his face betrayed no anger, his eyes at least were open and honest. It was real Julian, not pretend Julian now. "So you admit you're a control freak?"

He smiled, the sweet smile that went straight to Emma's heart because it recalled for her the Julian of her childhood. It was like sun, warmth, the sea, and the beach all rolled up in one punch to the heart. "I admit nothing."

"Fine," she said. She didn't have to say she forgave him and knew he forgave her; they both knew it. Instead she sat down in the seat opposite him and gestured toward his art supplies. "What are you drawing?"

He picked up the sketchbook, turning it so she could see his work—a gorgeous rendition of a stone bridge they'd passed, surrounded by the drooping boughs of oak trees.

"You could sketch me," said Emma. She flung herself down onto her seat, leaning her head on her hand. "'Draw me like one of your French girls.'"

Julian grinned. "I hate that movie," he said. "You know I do."

Emma sat up indignantly. "The first time we watched *Titanic*, you cried."

"I had seasonal allergies," Jules said. He'd started to draw again, but his smile still lingered. This was the heart of her and Julian, Emma thought. This gentle joking, this easy amusement. It almost surprised her. But this was what they always returned to, the comfort of their childhood—like birds returning and returning in migratory patterns toward their home.

"I wish we could get in touch with Jem and Tessa," Emma said. Green fields flashed by the window in a blur. A woman was pushing a refreshment cart up and down the narrow train corridor. "And Jace and Clary. Tell them about Annabel and Malcolm and everything."

"The whole Clave knows about Malcolm's return. I'm sure they have their ways of finding out, too."

"But only we really know about Annabel," said Emma.

"I drew her," Julian said. "I thought somehow if we could look at her, it might help us find her."

He turned his sketch pad. Emma suppressed a small shudder. Not because the face looking out was hideous—it wasn't. It was a young face, oval and even-featured, almost lost in a cloud of dark hair. But an air of something haunted and almost feral burned in Annabel's eyes; she clutched her hands at her throat, as if trying to wrap herself in a covering that had vanished.

"Where could she be?" Emma wondered aloud. "Where would you go, if you were so sad?"

"Do you think she looks sad?"

"Don't you?"

"I thought she seemed angry."

"She *did* kill Malcolm," said Emma. "I don't understand why she'd do that—he brought her back. He loved her."

"Maybe she didn't want to be brought back." He was still looking down at the sketch. "Maybe she was happy where she was. Strife, agony, loss—those are things the living experience." He closed the sketchbook as the train pulled into a small white station whose sign read LISKEARD. They had arrived.

"Was this planned?" Kieran said. His expression was stony. "It cannot be a coincidence."

Mark raised his eyebrows. Cristina was sitting on the edge of one of the beds in the infirmary, her wrist bandaged; Mark's injury was hidden by the sleeve of his sweater. There was no one else in the room. Tavvy had been upset by the sight of blood on Mark and Cristina, and Dru had taken him away to calm him down. Livvy and the other two boys had left for Blackthorn Hall while Cristina was at the train station.

"What the hell is that supposed to mean?" Mark said. "You think Cristina and I planned to spray blood all over London for fun?"

Cristina looked at him in surprise; he sounded more human than she'd ever heard him.

"Such a binding spell," said Kieran. "You must have held your wrists out for it. You would have to have remained still while you were bound."

He sounded bewildered, hurt. He looked enormously out of place in his breeches and linen shirt, now very crumpled, in the heart of the Institute. All around them were hospital-style beds, glass and copper jars of tinctures and powders, stacks of bandages and runed medical tools.

"It happened at a revel," said Mark. "We couldn't expect it—we didn't expect it. And no one would want this, no one would set it up on *purpose*, Kieran."

"A faerie would," Kieran said. "It is just the sort of thing one of us would do."

"I am not a faerie," said Mark.

Kieran flinched, and Cristina saw the hurt in his eyes. She felt a wave of sympathetic pain for him. It must be horrible to be so alone.

Even Mark looked stricken. "I didn't mean that," he said. "I am not *only* a faerie."

"And how glad you are," said Kieran, "how you brag of it at every opportunity."

"Please," said Cristina, "please, don't fight. We need to be on the same side in this."

Kieran turned puzzled eyes on her. Then he stepped close to Mark; he put his hands on Mark's shoulders. They were nearly the same height. Mark didn't avert his gaze. "There is only one way I know that you cannot lie," Kieran said, and kissed Mark on the mouth.

A pulse of pain went through Cristina's wrist. She had no idea if it was random or some reflection of the intensity of what Mark was feeling. There was no way he could reject the kiss, not without rejecting Kieran and severing the delicate chain of lies that kept the faerie prince bound here.

If, indeed, Mark didn't want to kiss Kieran back. Cristina couldn't tell; he returned the kiss with a fierceness like the fierceness Cristina had seen in him the first time she'd glimpsed him with Kieran. But there was more anger in it now. He gripped Kieran's shoulders, his fingers digging in; the force of the kiss angled Kieran's head back. He sucked at Kieran's bottom lip and bit it, and Kieran gasped.

They broke apart. Kieran touched his mouth; there was blood on his lip, and hot triumph in his eyes. "You did not look away," he said to Cristina. "Was it that interesting?"

"It was for my benefit." Cristina felt odd and shivery and hot, but refused to show it. She sat with her hands in her lap and smiled at Kieran. "It would have seemed rude not to watch."

At that Mark, who had been looking furious, laughed. "She understands you, Kier."

"It was very well-done kissing," she said. "But we should talk practically now, about the spell."

Kieran was still staring at Cristina. He looked at most people with disgust or fury or consideration, but when he looked at Cristina, he seemed bewildered, as if he were trying to put her together like a puzzle and couldn't.

Abruptly, he spun on his heel and stalked out of the room. The door slammed behind him. Mark looked after him, shaking his head.

"I don't think I've ever seen anyone aggravate him like that," he said. "Not even me."

Diana had hoped to see Jia the moment she arrived in Idris, but the bureaucracy of the Clave was worse than she had recalled. There were forms to fill out, messages to be given and carried up the chain of command. It didn't help that Diana refused to state her business: For the delicate matter of Kieran and what was happening in Faerie, Diana didn't dare trust the information to anyone other than the Consul herself.

Her small apartment in Alicante was above the weapons shop on Flintlock Street that had been in her family for years. She'd closed it up when she went to live in Los Angeles with the Blackthorns. Impatience jittering her nerves, she went downstairs into the store and threw open the windows, letting in light, making the dust motes dance in the bright summer air. Her sore arm still ached, though it had nearly healed.

The shop was musty inside, dust on the formerly bright blades and rich leather of sheaths and ax handles. She took down a few of her favorite weapons and put them aside for the Blackthorns.

The children deserved new weapons. They'd earned them.

When a knock came on the door, she'd successfully managed to distract herself and was sorting sword blades by the hardness of the metal. She set down one of her favorites—a weapon of Damascus steel—and went to open the door.

Smirking on the doorstep was Manuel, who Diana had last seen fighting sea demons on the front lawn of the Institute. He was out of his Centurion gear, wearing a fashionable black sweater and jeans, his hair gelled into curls. He smiled sideways at her.

"Miss Wrayburn," he said. "I've been sent to bring you up to the Gard."

Diana locked up the store and fell in beside Manuel as he made his way up Flintlock Street toward the northern part of Alicante. "What are you doing here, Manuel?" she asked. "I thought you'd be in Los Angeles."

"I was offered a post at the Gard," he said. "I couldn't pass up the chance for advancement. There are plenty of Centurions still in Los Angeles, guarding the Institute." He looked at Diana sideways; she said nothing. "It's a pleasure to see you in Alicante," Manuel went on. "The last time we were together, I believe, you were fleeing for London."

Diana gritted her teeth. "I was taking the children who were in my charge to safety," she said. "They're all fine, by the way."

"I assumed I would have heard if it had been otherwise," said Manuel airily.

"I'm sorry about your friend," she said. "Jon Cartwright."

Manuel was silent. They had reached the gate to the path leading up to the Gard. Once it had closed only with a latch. Now Diana watched as Manuel passed his hand over it and it clicked open.

The path was as rough as it had been when Diana was a child, snaked with the roots of trees. "I didn't know Jon well," said Manuel as they began the climb. "I understand his girlfriend, Marisol, is very upset."

Diana said nothing.

"Some people cannot manage their grief as Shadowhunters should," added Manuel. "It's a shame."

"Some people do not show the empathy and tolerance a Shadowhunter should," said Diana. "That's also a shame."

They had reached the upper part of the path, where Alicante spread out before them like a map, and the demon towers rose to pierce the sun. Diana remembered walking this path with her sister, when they were both children, and her sister's laughter. She missed her so much sometimes it felt as if her heart were being clutched by talons.

In this place, she thought, looking out over Alicante, *I was lonely. In this place I had to hide the person I knew I was.*

They reached the Gard. It rose up above them, a mountain of gleaming stone, sturdier than ever since its rebuilding. A path lined with witchlights led to the front gate. "Was that a jab at Zara?" Manuel looked amused. "She's very popular, you know. Especially since she killed Malcolm. Something the Los Angeles Institute couldn't manage."

Shocked out of her reverie, Diana could only stare at him. "Zara didn't kill Malcolm," she said. "That's a lie."

"Is it?" Manuel said. "I'd like to see you prove that." He grinned his beaming grin and walked away, leaving Diana to stare after him, squinting her eyes in the sunlight.

"Let me see your wrist," Cristina said to Mark. They were sitting side by side on the infirmary bed. His shoulder was warm against hers.

He drew his sweater up and held his arm out silently. Cristina folded back her bandage and put her wrist against his. They looked in silence at their identical wounds.

"I know nothing about this kind of magic," said Mark. "And we cannot go to the Clave or the Silent Brothers. They can't know we were in Faerie."

"I'm sorry about Kieran," she said. "That he's angry."

Mark shook his head. "Don't be—it's my fault." He took a deep breath. "I am sorry I was angry with you, in Faerie, after the revel. People are complicated. Their situations are complicated. I know why you hid Julian's feelings from me. I know you and Emma had little choice."

"And I am not angry at you now," she hastened to assure him. "About Kieran."

"I am changed," said Mark, "because of you. Kieran can sense that my feelings for him have altered in some way, though he doesn't know why. And I cannot tell him." He looked up at the ceiling. "He is a prince. Princes are spoiled. They cannot bear to be thwarted."

"He must feel so alone," said Cristina. She remembered the way she had felt with Diego, that what they'd had once had was gone, and she couldn't understand how to get it back. It had been like trying to catch smoke that had dissolved into the air. "You are his only ally here, and he cannot understand why his connection to you feels broken."

"He did swear to you," said Mark. He ducked his head, as if he were ashamed of what he was saying. "It is possible that if you order him to do something, he'll have to do it."

"I don't want to do that."

"Cristina."

"No, Mark," she said firmly. "I know this binding spell affects you, too. And upsetting Kieran affects the chances he'll testify. But I won't force him into anything."

"Aren't we already?" Mark said. "Lying to him about the situation so he'll talk to the Clave?"

Cristina's fingers crept to her injured wrist. The skin felt odd under her fingertips: hot and swollen. "And after he testifies? You'll tell him the truth, right?"

Mark rose to his feet. "By the Angel, yes. What do you take me for?"

"Someone in a difficult situation," said Cristina. "As we all are. If Kieran doesn't testify, innocent Downworlders may die; the Clave may sink further into corruption. I understand the need for deception. That doesn't mean I like it—or that you do either."

Mark nodded, not looking at her. "I had better search for him," he said. "If he'll agree to be helpful, he's our best way to fix this." He indicated his wrist.

Cristina felt a slight ache inside. She wondered if she had hurt Mark; she hadn't meant to. "Let's see what kind of range this has," she said. "How far from each other we can go without it hurting."

Mark stopped in the doorway. The clean, sharp planes of his face looked cut from glass. "It already hurt me to be away from you," he said. "Perhaps that was meant to be the joke."

He was gone before Cristina could answer.

She got to her feet and went to the counter where the powders and medicines were. She had a rough idea of medicinal Shadowhunter work: Here were the leaves that had anti-infection properties, here the poultices that kept swelling down.

The door of the infirmary opened while she was unscrewing a jar. She looked up: It was Kieran. He looked flushed and windblown, as if he'd been outside. There were patches of color on his high cheekbones.

He looked as discomfited to see her as she was to see him. She set the jar down carefully and waited.

"Where is Mark?" he said.

"He went to find you." Cristina leaned against the counter. Kieran was quiet. A faerie sort of quiet: inward, considering. She had a feeling many people would feel compelled to fill that silence. She let him have it; let him draw the silence into himself, shape and decipher it.

"I should apologize," he said finally. "It was uncalled for to accuse you and Mark of having arranged the binding spell. Foolish, too. You have nothing to gain from it. If Mark did not want to be with me, he would say so."

Cristina said nothing. Kieran took a step toward her, carefully, as if afraid of frightening her. "Might I see your arm again?"

She held her arm out. He took it—she wondered if he had ever touched her deliberately before. It felt like the touch of cool water in summer.

Cristina felt a slight shiver up her spine as he studied her injury. She wondered what he had looked like when both of his eyes had been black. They were even more startling now than Mark's, the contrast between the dark and the shimmering silver, like ice and ash.

"The shape of a ribbon," he said. "You say you were tied together during a revel?"

"Yes," said Cristina. "By two girls. They knew we were Nephilim. They laughed at us."

Kieran's grip on her tightened. She remembered the way he'd clung to Mark in the Unseelie Court. Not as if he were weak and needed help. It was a grip of strength, a grip that held Mark in place, that said, *Stay with me, it is my command.*

He *was* a prince, after all.

"That sort of binding spell is one of the oldest," he said. "Oldest and strongest. I do not know why someone would play such a prank on you. It is quite vicious."

"But do you know how to undo it?"

Kieran dropped Cristina's hand. "I was an unwanted son of the Unseelie King. I received little schooling. Then I was thrown into the Wild Hunt. I am no expert on magic."

"You're not useless," Cristina said. "You know more than you think you do."

Kieran looked as if she'd startled him once again. "I could speak to my brother, Adaon. I am meant to ask him about taking the throne. I could inquire of him as to whether he knows anything of binding spells or how to end them."

"When do you think you will talk to him?" asked Cristina. An image came into her mind of the way Kieran, asleep, had clung to her hand in the Seelie Court. Trying not to blush, she glanced down at her bandage, tugging it back into place.

"Soon," he said. "I have tried to reach him already, but not yet with success."

"Tell me if there is anything I can do to help you," she said.

His eyebrow quirked. He bent down then and lifted her hand, this time to kiss it, not seeming to mind the blood or the bandage. It was a gesture of courts long past in this world, but not in Faerie. Startled, Cristina did not protest.

"Lady Mendoza Rosales," he said. "Thank you for your kindness."

"I'd rather you called me Cristina," she said. "Honestly."

"*Honestly,*" he echoed. "Something we faeries never say. Every word we speak is an honest word."

"I wouldn't go that far," said Cristina. "Would you?"

A thunderclap shook the Institute. At least, it felt like a thunderclap: It rattled the windows and walls.

"Stay here," Kieran said. "I will go find out what that was."

Cristina almost laughed. "Kieran," she said. "Really, you don't need to *protect* me."

His eyes flashed; the infirmary door flew open and Mark was there, wide-eyed. He only grew more so when he saw Kieran and Cristina standing at the counter together.

"You'd better come," he said. "You won't believe who's just Portaled into the parlor."

The town of Polperro was tiny, whitewashed, and picturesque. It was nestled into a quiet harbor, with miles of blue sea spreading out where the harbor opened into the ocean. Small houses in different pale colors clambered up and down the hills that rose steeply on either side of the port. Cobblestoned streets wound among shops selling pastries and soft-serve ice cream.

There were no cars. The bus from Liskeard had let them off outside the town; nearing the harbor, they crossed a small bridge at the bottom of the marina. Emma thought of her parents. Her father's gentle smile, the sun on his blond hair. He'd loved the sea, living near the ocean, any kind of beach holiday. He would have loved a town like this, where the air smelled like seaweed and burnt sugar and sunscreen, where fishing boats traced white trails across the blue surface of the distant sea. Her mother would have loved it too—she had always liked to lie in the sun, like a cat, and watch the ocean dance.

"What about here?" Julian said. Emma blinked back to reality, realizing they'd been talking about finding something to eat before they'd passed over the bridge and her mind had wandered.

Julian was standing in front of a half-timbered house with a restaurant menu pasted up in the diamond-paned window. A group of girls passed by, in shorts and bikini tops, on their way to the sweetshop next door. They giggled and nudged each other when they saw Julian.

Emma wondered what he looked like to them—handsome, with all that windblown brown hair and luminous eyes, but surely odd as well, a little unearthly maybe, Marked and scarred as he was.

"Sure," she said. "This is fine."

Julian was tall enough to need to duck under the low-hanging doorframe to get into the inn. Emma followed, and a few moments later they were being shown to a table by a cheerful, plump woman in a flowered dress. It was nearly five o'clock and the place was mostly deserted. A sense of history hung lightly about it, from the uneven floorboards to the walls decorated with smuggling memorabilia, old maps, and cheerful illustrations of Cornish piskies, the mischievous Fair Folk native to the area. Emma wondered how much the locals believed in them. Not as much as they should, she suspected.

They ordered—Coke and fries for Jules, sandwich and lemon-ade for Emma—and Julian spread his map out over the table. His phone was next to it; he flipped through the photos he'd been tak-ing with one hand, poking at the map with the other. Smears of colored pencil decorated his hand, familiar smudges of blue and yellow and green.

"The east side of the harbor is called the Warren," he said. "Lots of houses, and a lot of them are old, but most of them are rented out now to tourists. And none of them are on top of any caves. That leaves the area around Polperro and to the west."

Their food had arrived. Emma started wolfing her sandwich; she hadn't realized how hungry she was. "What's this?" she asked, pointing at the map.

"That's Chapel Cliff, love," said the waitress, setting down Emma's drink. She pronounced it *chaypel*. "Start of the coastal path. From there, you can walk all the way to Fowey." She glanced over at the bar, where two tourists had just sat down. "Oi! Be right there!"

"How do you find the path?" Julian said. "If we were to walk it today, where would we start?"

"Oh, it's a long way to Fowey," said the waitress. "But the path starts up behind the Blue Peter Inn." She pointed out the window, across the harbor. "There's a walking trail that goes up the hill. You turn onto the coastal path at the old net loft, it's all broken down now, you'll see it easy. It's just above the caves."

Emma raised her eyebrows. "The caves?"

The waitress laughed. "The old smugglers' caves," she said. "I guess you came in at high tide, didn't you? Or you'd have seen them for sure."

Emma and Julian exchanged a single look before scrambling to their feet. Heedless of the waitress's startled protests, they spilled out into the street beside the inn.

She'd been right, of course: The tide had come down and the

harbor looked very different now, the boats beached on rises of muddy sand. Behind the harbor rose a narrow spit of land shingled with gray rocks. It was easy to see why it was called Chapel Cliff. The spit was tipped with gray rocks, which twisted narrowly up into the air like the spires of a church cathedral.

The water had lowered enough so that a great deal of the cliff was revealed. The sea had been pounding against the rocks when they'd arrived; now it sloshed quietly in the harbor, retreating to reveal a small, sandy beach, and behind it, the dark openings of several cave mouths.

Above the caves, perched on the steep slope of the cliff, was a house. Emma had barely spared it a glance when they'd first arrived—it had simply been one of many small houses that dotted the side of the harbor across from the Warren, though she could see now that it was farther out along the spit of land than any of the others. In fact, it was quite distant from them, standing small and alone between the sea and the sky.

Its windows were boarded up; its whitewash had peeled away in gray strips. But if Emma looked with her Shadowhunter eyes, she could see more than an abandoned house: She could see white lace curtains in the windows, and new shingles on the roof.

There was a mailbox nailed to the fence. A name was painted onto the box, in sloppy white letters, barely visible from this distance. They certainly wouldn't have been visible to a mundane, but Emma could see them.

FADE.

18

MEMORIES OF THE PAST

Jia Penhallow was seated behind the desk in the Consul's office, illuminated by the rays of the sun over Alicante. The spires of the demon towers glittered outside the window: red, gold, and orange, like shards of bloody glass.

She had the same warmth in her face Diana remembered, but she looked as if much more time had passed since the Dark War than five years. There was white in her black hair, which was pinned up elegantly on top of her head.

"It's good to see you, Diana," she said, inclining her head toward the chair opposite her desk. "We've all been very curious about your mysterious news."

"I imagine." Diana sat down. "But I was hoping what I had to say would stay between the two of us."

Jia didn't look surprised. Not that she would show it if she was. "I see. I'd wondered if you'd come about the Los Angeles Institute head position. I assumed you'd want to take over now that Arthur Blackthorn is dead." Her graceful hands fluttered as she shuffled and stacked papers, slotted pens into their holders. "It was very brave of him to approach the convergence alone. I was sorry to hear he was slain."

Diana nodded. For reasons none of them knew, Arthur's body had been found near the destroyed convergence site, covered in blood from his cut throat and in stains of ichor that Julian told her grimly were Malcolm's blood. There was no reason to contradict the official assumption that he had waged a solo assault on the convergence and been killed by Malcolm's demons.

At least Arthur would be remembered as brave, though it gave her a pang that he had been burned and buried without his nieces and nephews there to mourn him. That in fact, no one in the wider world would know he had sacrificed himself for his family. Livvy had said to her that she hoped they would be able to have a remembrance ceremony for him when they all went to Idris. Diana hoped so too.

Jia didn't seem nonplussed by Diana's silence. "Patrick remembers Arthur from when they were boys," she said, "though I'm afraid I never knew him. How are the children coping?"

The children? How did you explain that the Blackthorns' second father had been their older brother since he was twelve years old? That Julian and Emma and Mark weren't children at all, really, having suffered enough for most adults' entire lifetimes? That Arthur Blackthorn had never, really, run the Institute, and the whole idea that he needed to be replaced was like an elaborate and terrible joke?

"The children are devastated," Diana said. "Their family has been fragmented, as you know. What they want is to return to Los Angeles, their home."

"But they cannot return while there is no one to head the Institute. Which is why I thought you—"

"I don't want it to be me," Diana said. "I'm not here to ask for that job. But neither do I want it to go to Zara Dearborn and her father."

"Really," said Jia. Her tone was neutral but her eyes glittered with interest. "If not the Dearborns, and not you, then who?"

"If Helen Blackthorn was allowed to return—"

Jia sat up straight. "And run the Institute? You know the Council would never allow—"

"Then let Aline run the Institute," said Diana. "Helen could simply remain in Los Angeles as her wife, and be with her family."

Jia's expression was calm, but her hands gripped the desk tightly. "Aline is my daughter. You think I don't want to bring her home?"

"I've never known what you thought," Diana said. It was true. She had no children, but if it had been her sister who had been exiled, she couldn't imagine not fighting tooth and claw to have her released.

"When Helen was first exiled, and Aline chose to go with her, I thought about resigning as Consul," said Jia, her hands still taut. "I knew I had no power to reverse the Clave's decision. The Consul is not a tyrant who can impose her choices on the unwilling. Usually I would say that was a good thing. But I will tell you, for a long time, I wished I could be a tyrant."

"Why not resign, then?"

"I didn't trust who might come after me," said Jia simply. "The Cold Peace was very popular. If the Consul who followed me wished to, they could separate Aline from Helen—and though I want my daughter home, I don't want her heart broken. They could do worse, too. They could try Aline and Helen as traitors, turn Helen's sentence of exile into one of death. Maybe Aline's as well. Anything was possible." Her gaze was dark and heavy. "I remain where I am to stand between my daughter and the Clave's darker forces."

"Then aren't we on the same side?" Diana said. "Don't we want the same thing?"

Jia gave a flat smile. "What separates us, Diana, is five years. Five years of my trying everything to get the Council to reconsider.

Helen is their example. Their way of saying to the Fair Folk: Look, we take the Cold Peace so seriously we even punish our own. Every time the issue comes up for a vote, I am voted down."

"But what if other circumstances presented themselves?"

"What other circumstances did you have in mind?"

Diana rolled her shoulders back, feeling the tension prickle along her spine. "Jace Herondale and Clary Fairchild were dispatched to Faerie for a mission," she said. It was half a guess— while the two of them had been at the Institute, she had glimpsed the contents of their bags: Both had been packed with iron and salt.

"Yes," said Jia. "We have received several messages since they left."

"Then they've told you," said Diana. "About the blight on the Unseelie King's Lands."

Jia sat arrested, one hand hovering over her desk. "No one knows what they told me but the Inquisitor and myself," she said. "How do you know . . . ?"

"It doesn't matter. I'm telling you because I need you to believe that I know what I'm talking about," said Diana. "I know that the Unseelie King hates Nephilim, and that he has uncovered some force, some magic, that renders our powers useless. He has made it so that there are parts of his kingdom where runes do not work, where seraph blades will not light."

Jia frowned. "Jace and Clary didn't mention anything so specific. And they've had no contact with anyone but me since they entered Faerie—"

"There is a boy," said Diana. "A faerie, a messenger from the Seelie Court. Kieran. He's also a prince of Unseelie. He knows some of what his father plans. He's willing to testify in front of the Council."

Jia looked bewildered. "An Unseelie prince would testify for the Seelie Court? And what is the Seelie Court's interest?"

"The Seelie Queen hates the Unseelie King," said Diana. "More, apparently, than she hates Shadowhunters. She is willing to commit the forces of her army to defeating the Unseelie King. To wiping out his power and reversing the blight on his Lands."

"Out of the kindness of her heart?" Jia raised an eyebrow.

"In exchange for the end of the Cold Peace," said Diana.

Jia gave a short bark of laughter. "No one will agree to that. The Clave—"

"Everyone is sick of the Cold Peace except the most extreme bigots," said Diana. "And I don't think either of us want to see them gain power."

Jia sighed. "You mean the Dearborns. And the Cohort."

"I spent quite a bit of time with Zara Dearborn and her Centurion friends at the Institute," said Diana. "Her views are not pleasant."

Jia stood up, turning toward the window. "She and her father seek to return the Clave to a lost golden age. A time that never was, when Downworlders knew their place and Nephilim ruled in harmony. In truth, that past was a violent time, when Downworlders suffered and those Nephilim who possessed compassion and empathy were tormented and punished along with them."

"How many of them are there?" Diana asked. "The Cohort?"

"Zara's father, Horace Dearborn, is the unofficial leader," said Jia. "His wife is dead and he has raised his daughter to follow in his footsteps. If he succeeds in placing himself at the head of the Los Angeles Institute, she will rule from beside him. Then there are other families—the Larkspears, the Bridgestocks, the Crosskills—they're scattered around the world."

"And their goal is to continue restricting Downworlder rights. Registering them all, giving them numbers—"

"Forbidding their marriages to Shadowhunters?"

Diana shrugged. "It's all part of a piece, isn't it? First you number people, then you restrict their rights and break up their marriages. Then—"

"No." Jia's voice was gritty. "We can't let this happen. But you don't understand—Zara's being put forth as the great new Shadowhunter of her generation. The new Jace Herondale. Since she killed Malcolm—"

Diana bolted out of her chair. "That—that lying girl did not kill Malcolm."

"We know Emma didn't," said Jia. "He returned."

"I am aware of exactly how he died," said Diana. "He raised Annabel Blackthorn from the dead. *She* killed him."

"*What?*" Jia sounded shocked.

"It's the truth, Consul."

"Diana. You would need proof that what you're saying is true. A trial by Mortal Sword—"

Diana's greatest fear. "No," she said. *It wouldn't be just my secrets I'd be revealing. It would be Julian's. Emma's. They'd all be ruined.*

"You must see how this looks," Jia said. "As if you're seeking a way to keep the Los Angeles Institute under your control by discrediting the Dearborns."

"They discredit themselves." Diana looked hard at Jia. "You know Zara," she said. "Do you really think she killed Malcolm?"

"No," Jia said, after a pause. "I don't." She went to an ornate carved cabinet against one wall of her office. She slid open a drawer. "I need time to think about this, Diana. In the meantime—" She drew out a thick, cream-colored folder full of papers. "This is Zara Dearborn's report on the death of Malcolm Fade and the attacks on the L.A. Institute. Perhaps you can find some discrepancies that might discredit her story."

"Thank you." Diana took the folder. "And the Council meeting? A chance for Kieran to give testimony?"

"I'll discuss it with the Inquisitor." Jia suddenly looked even older than she had before. "Go home, Diana. I'll summon you tomorrow."

* * *

"We should have brought Dru," Livvy said, standing inside the gates of Blackthorn Hall. "This is every horror-movie fantasy she's ever had come true."

Blackthorn Hall turned out to be in a suburb of London not far from the Thames River. The area around it was ordinary: redbrick houses, bus stops plastered with movie posters, kids riding by on bicycles. After days trapped in the Institute, even the foreignness of London felt to Kit like waking up to reality after a dream.

Blackthorn Hall was glamoured, which meant that mundanes couldn't see it. Kit had a sort of double vision when he glanced at it for the first time: He could see a pleasant but dull-looking private park, superimposed over a massive house with towering walls and gates, its stones blackened by years of rain and neglect.

He squinted hard. The park vanished, and only the house remained. It loomed overhead. It looked to Kit a little like a Greek temple, with columns holding up an arched portico in front of a set of double doors, massive and made of the same metal as the fence that ran all the way around the property. It was high, tipped with sharp points; the only entrance was a gate, which Ty had made short work of with one of his runes.

"What's that one mean?" Kit had asked, pointing, as the gate creaked open with a puff of rust.

Ty looked at him. "*Open.*"

"I was going to guess that," Kit muttered as they headed inside. Now within the property, he gazed around in wonder. The gardens might have fallen into disrepair now, but you could see where there had been rose arbors, and marble balustrades holding up massive stone jugs spilling flowers and weeds. There were wildflowers everywhere—it was beautiful in its own odd, ruined way.

The house was like a small castle, the circlet of thorns that Kit recognized as the Blackthorn family symbol stamped into the metal front doors and onto the tops of the columns.

"Looks haunted," said Livvy, as they went up the front steps. In the distance, Kit could see the pitch-black circle of an old ornamental pond. Around it were set marble benches. A single statue of a man in a toga regarded him with blank, worried eyes.

"There used to be a whole collection of statues of different Greek and Roman playwrights and poets here," said Livvy, as Ty went to work on the doors. "Uncle Arthur had most of them shipped to the L.A. Institute."

"The open rune's not working," said Ty, straightening up and looking at Kit as if he knew everything Kit was thinking. As if he knew everything Kit had *ever* thought. There was something about being the focus of Tiberius's gaze that was frightening and thrilling all at once. "We'll have to figure another way in."

Ty pushed past Kit and his sister, heading down the stairs. They made their way around the side of the Hall, down a pebbled path. Hedges that had probably once been neat and clipped curved away in explosions of leaves and flowers. In the far distance, the water of the Thames shimmered.

"Maybe there's a way in through the back," Livvy said. "The windows can't be that secure either."

"What about this door?" Kit pointed.

Ty turned around, frowning. "What door?"

"Here," Kit said, puzzled. He could see the door very clearly: a tall, narrow entrance with an odd symbol carved into it. He placed his hand on the old wood: It felt rough and warm under his fingers. "Don't you see it?"

"I see it *now*," Livvy said. "But—I swear it wasn't there a second ago."

"Some kind of doubled glamour?" said Ty, coming up beside Kit. He had pulled up the hood on his sweater, and his face was a pale oval in between the black of his hair and the darkness of his collar. "But why would Kit be able to see it?"

"Maybe because I'm used to seeing glamours at the Shadow Market," said Kit.

"Glamours that aren't made by Shadowhunters," said Livvy.

"Glamours that aren't meant for Shadowhunters to see *through*," said Kit.

Ty looked thoughtful. There was an opaqueness to him sometimes that made it hard for Kit to tell whether Ty agreed with him or not. He did, however, put his stele to the door and begin to draw the Open rune.

It wasn't the lock that clicked, but the hinges that popped open. They jumped out of the way as the door half-fell, half-sagged to the side, slamming into the wall with an echoing sound.

"Don't press down so hard when you draw," Livvy said to Ty. He shrugged.

The space beyond the door was dark enough for the twins to need to spark up their witchlights. The glow of them had a pearlescent whitish tint that Kit found strangely beautiful.

They were in an old hallway, filled with dust and the webs of scuttling spiders. Ty went ahead of Kit and Livvy behind him; he suspected they were protecting him, and resented it, but knew that they wouldn't understand his protest if he lodged one.

They went down the hall and up a long, narrow staircase, at the end of which was the rotted remains of a door. Through that door was a massive room with a hanging chandelier.

"Probably a ballroom," Livvy said, her voice echoing oddly in the space. "Look, this part of the house is better taken care of."

It was. The ballroom was empty but clean, and as they moved through other rooms, they found furniture shrouded in drop cloths, windows boarded carefully to protect the glass, boxes stacked in the halls. Inside the boxes were cloths and the strong smell of mothballs. Livvy coughed and waved a hand in front of her face.

"There's got to be a library," Ty said. "Somewhere they would keep family documents."

"I can't believe our dad might have visited here when he was growing up." Livvy led the way down the hall, her body casting an elongated shadow. Long hair, long legs, shimmering witchlight in her hand.

"He didn't live here?" Kit asked.

Livvy shook her head. "Grew up in Cornwall, not London. But he went to school in Idris."

Idris. Kit had read more about Idris in the London Institute library. The fabled homeland of Shadowhunters, a place of green forests and high mountains, icy-cold lakes and a city of glass towers. He had to admit that the part of him that loved fantasy movies and *Lord of the Rings* yearned to see it.

He told that part of himself to be quiet. Idris was Shadowhunter business, and he hadn't yet decided he wanted to be a Shadowhunter. In fact, he was quite—nearly totally—sure he didn't.

"Library," Ty said. It occurred to Kit that Ty never used five words when one would do. He was standing in front of the door to a hexagonal room, the walls beside him hung with paintings of ships. Some were cocked at odd angles as if they were plunging up or down waves.

The library walls were painted dark blue, the only art in the room a marble statue of a man's head and shoulders sitting atop a stone column. There was a massive desk with multiple drawers that turned out to be disappointingly empty. Forays behind the bookshelves and under the rug also turned up nothing but dust balls.

"Maybe we should try another room," Kit said, emerging from under an escritoire with dust in his blond hair.

Ty shook his head, looking frustrated. "There's something in here. I have a feeling."

Kit wasn't sure Sherlock Holmes operated on *feelings*, but he didn't say anything, just straightened up. As he did, he caught sight of a piece of paper sticking out of the edge of the small writing desk. He pulled at it, and it came away.

It was old paper, worn almost to transparency. Kit blinked. On it was written his name—not his name, but his last name, *Herondale*, over and over, entwined with another name, so that the two words formed looping patterns.

The other word was *Blackthorn*.

A deep sense of unease shot through him. He tucked the paper quickly into his jeans pocket just as Ty said, "Move, Kit. I want to get a closer look at that bust."

To Kit, *bust* only meant one thing, but since the only breasts in the room belonged to Ty's sister, he stepped aside with alacrity. Ty strode over to the small statue on the marble column. He'd pulled his hood down, and his hair stood up around his head, soft as the downy feathers of a black swan.

Ty touched a small placard below the carving. "'The difficulty is not so great to die for a friend, as to find a friend worth dying for,'" he said.

"Homer," said Livvy. Whatever kind of education the Shadowhunters got, Kit had to admit, it was thorough.

"Apparently," said Ty, pulling a dagger out of his belt. A second later he'd driven the blade into the carved eye socket of the statue. Livvy yelped.

"Ty, what—?"

Her brother yanked the blade back out and repeated the action on the statue's second eye socket. This time something round and glimmering popped out of the hole in the plaster with an audible crack. Ty caught it in his left hand.

He grinned, and the grin changed his face completely. Ty when he was still and expressionless had an intensity that fascinated Kit; when he was smiling, he was extraordinary.

"What did you find?" Livvy darted across the room and they

gathered around Tiberius, who was holding out a many-faceted crystal, the size of a child's hand. "And how'd you know it was in there?"

"When you said Homer's name," said Ty, "I recalled that he was blind. He's almost always depicted with his eyes shut or with a cloth blindfold. But this statue had open eyes. I looked a little closer and saw that the bust was marble but the eyes were plaster. After that, it was . . ."

"Elementary?" said Kit.

"You know, Holmes never says, 'Elementary, my dear Watson,' in the books," said Ty.

"I swear I've seen it in the movies," Kit said. "Or maybe on TV."

"Who would ever want movies or TV when there are books?" said Ty with disdain.

"Could someone here pay attention?" Livvy demanded, her ponytail swinging in exasperation. "What is that thing you found, Ty?"

"An *aletheia* crystal." He held it up so that it caught the glow of his sister's witchlight. "Look."

Kit glanced at the faceted surface of the stone. To his surprise, a face flashed across it, like an image seen in a dream—a woman's face, clouded around with long dark hair.

"Oh!" Livvy clapped her hand over her mouth. "She looks a little like me. But how—?"

"An *aletheia* crystal is a way of capturing or transporting memories. I think this one is of Annabel," said Ty.

"*Aletheia* is Greek," Livvy said.

"She was the Greek goddess of truth," said Kit. He shrugged when they stared at him. "Ninth-grade book report."

Ty's mouth crooked at the corner. "Very good, Watson."

"Don't call me Watson," said Kit.

Ty ignored this. "We need to figure out how to access what's trapped in this crystal," he said. "As quickly as possible. It could help Julian and Emma."

"You don't know how to get into it?" Kit asked.

Ty shook his head, clearly disgruntled. "It's not Shadowhunter magic. We don't learn other kinds. It's forbidden."

This struck Kit as a stupid rule. How were you ever supposed to know how your enemies operated if you made it forbidden to learn about them?

"We should go," Livvy said, hovering in the doorway. "It's starting to get dark. Demon time."

Kit glanced toward the window. The sky was darkening, the stain of twilight spreading across the blue. The shadows were coming down over London.

"I have an idea," he said. "Why don't we take it to the Shadow Market here? I know my way around the Market. I can find a warlock or even a witch to help us get at whatever's in this thing."

The twins glanced at each other. Both were clearly hesitant. "We're not really supposed to go to Shadow Markets," said Livvy.

"So tell them I ran off there and you had to catch me," said Kit. "If you even ever have to explain, which you won't."

Neither of them spoke, but Kit could see curiosity in Ty's gray eyes.

"Come on," he said, pitching his voice low, the way his father had taught him, the tone you used when you wanted to convince people you really meant something. "When you're home, Julian never lets you go anywhere. Now's your chance. Haven't you always wanted to see a Shadow Market?"

Livvy broke first. "Okay," she said, casting a quick look at her brother to see if he agreed with her. "Okay, if you know where it is."

Ty's pale face lit with excitement. Kit felt the same spark transfer to him. The Shadow Market. His home, his sanctuary, the place he'd been raised.

Trailing around after demons and artifacts with Livvy and

Ty, they were the ones who knew everything while he knew nothing. But at the Shadow Market, he could shine. He'd shock them. Impress them.

And then, maybe, he'd cut and run away.

The shadows were lengthening by the time Julian and Emma finished their lunch. Julian bought some food and supplies at a small grocer's shop, while Emma darted next door to pick up pajamas and T-shirts at a small New Age shop that sold tarot cards and crystal gnomes. When she emerged, she was grinning. She produced a blue-and-purple T-shirt emblazoned with a smiling unicorn for Jules, who stared at it in horror. She tucked it into his pack carefully before they started across the town to find the beginning of the path that led up and around the coast.

The hills sloped up steeply from the water; it wasn't an easy climb. Marked only as TO THE CLIFFS, the path wound up through the outskirts of the town and the precariously perched houses, all of which looked as if they might at any moment tumble down into the half-moon harbor.

Shadowhunters were trained for much more than this kind of exertion, though, and they made good time. Soon they were out of the town proper and walking along a narrow path, the hill rising farther on their right, falling down toward the sea on their left.

The sea itself was a luminous deep blue, glowing like a lamp. Clouds the color of seashells twined across the sky. It was beautiful in a completely different way than sunset over the Pacific. Instead of the stark colors of sea and desert, everything here was soft pastels: greens and blues and pinks.

What was stark was the cliffs themselves. They were climbing closer to the Chapel part of Chapel Cliff, the rocky promontory that jutted out into the ocean, the spikes of gray stone that crowned it ominously black against the rosy sky. The hill was gone; they were out on the spit of land itself: Long gray slate shingles that looked like a pack of playing cards shuffled and then scattered tumbled steeply away on either side, down toward the sea.

The house they had seen from town was nestled among the rocks, the spiked crown of the stone chapel rising behind it. As Emma neared it, she felt the force of its glamour almost as a wall, pushing her back.

Jules had slowed too. "There's a placard here," he said. "Says this place belongs to the National Trust. No trespassers."

Emma made a face. "No trespassers usually means the local kids have made it into a hangout and the whole place is covered with empty candy wrappers and booze bottles."

"I don't know. The glamour here is really strong—it's not just visual, but emotional. You can feel it, right?"

Emma nodded. The cottage was giving off waves of *stay away* and *danger* and *nothing here you want to see*. It was a bit like being shouted at by an angry stranger on the bus.

"Take my hand," Julian said.

"What?" She turned in surprise: He was holding his hand out. She could see the faint smatter of colored pencil on his skin. He flexed his fingers.

"We can get through this better together," he said. "Concentrate on pushing it back."

Emma took his hand, accepting the shock that went through her at his touch. His skin was warm and soft, rough where there were calluses. He tightened his fingers around hers.

They moved forward, past the gate and onto the path leading up to the front door. Emma imagined the glamour as a curtain, as something she could touch. She imagined drawing it aside. It was hard, like lifting a weight with her mind, but strength flowed through her from Julian, through her fingers and wrist, up her arm, into her heart and lungs.

Her concentration snapped into focus. Almost casually, she let herself draw the glamour away, lifting it lightly aside. The cottage sprang into clearer view: The windows weren't boarded up at all, but clean and whole, the front door freshly painted a bright blue. Even the knob looked recently polished to a shiny bronze. Julian took hold of it and pushed and the door swung open, welcoming them inside.

The sense of something ordering them away from the cottage was gone. Emma let go of Julian's hand and stepped inside; it was too dark to see. She took her witchlight out of her pocket and let its light rise up and around them.

Julian, behind her, gave a low whistle of surprise. "This doesn't look deserted. Not by a long shot."

It was a small, pretty room. A wooden four-poster bed stood beneath a window with a view out to the village below. Furniture that looked as if it had been hand-painted in blues, grays, and soft seaside colors was scattered about among a profusion of rag rugs.

Two walls were taken up by a kitchen with all the modern conveniences: a coffeemaker, a stove, a dishwasher, and granite-topped counters. Neat stacks of firewood rose on either side of a stone-bound fireplace. Two doors led off the main room: Emma investigated and found a small office with a hand-painted desk, and a blue-tiled bathroom with a tub and shower and a basin sink. She turned the shower faucets half in disbelief and yelped as water sprayed her. Everything seemed to be completely in working order, as if someone who lived in the cottage and took loving care of it had only just left.

"I guess we might as well stay here," Emma said, returning to the living room, where Julian had flicked on the electric lights.

"Way ahead of you, Carstairs," he said, opening a kitchen cabinet and starting to put the groceries away. "Nice place, no rent, and it'll be easier to search if we're here anyway."

Emma set her witchlight down on the table and looked around wonderingly. "I know this seems far-fetched," she said, "but do you think Malcolm had a secret second life as a renter of adorably furnished holiday cottages?"

"Or," Julian said, "there's an even stronger glamour on this place than we realized and it only *looks* like an adorably furnished holiday cottage, while actually it's a hole in the ground full of rats."

Emma threw herself down on the bed. The blanket felt like a cloud, and the mattress was heavenly after the lumpy one in the London Institute. "Best rats *ever*," she announced, glad they weren't going to have to stay in a bed-and-breakfast after all.

"Imagine their tiny, furry bodies wiggling around you." Julian had turned back and was facing her, a half grin on his face. When Emma had been small, she'd been horrified by rats and rodents.

She sat up and glared at him. "Why are you trying to ruin my good time?"

"Well, to be fair, this isn't a holiday. Not for us. This is a mission. We're supposed to be looking for anything that might give us an idea where Annabel might have gone."

"I don't know," Emma said. "This place looks like it's been stripped down and totally renovated. It was built so long ago, how do we know what's left of the original house? And wouldn't Malcolm have taken anything that was important to him to his house in L.A.?"

"Not necessarily. I think this cottage was special to him." Julian hooked his thumbs through the belt loops of his jeans. "Look at the way he's taken care of it. This house is personal. It feels like a home. Not like that glass-and-steel thing he lived in in L.A."

"Then I guess we should start looking around." Emma tried to sound excited at the prospect, but she felt exhausted. No sleep the night before, the long trip on the train, her worry about Cristina, had all sapped her energy.

Julian looked at her critically. "I'll make tea," he said. "That'll help."

She crinkled her nose at him. "Tea? *Tea* is your solution? You're not really even British! You spent two months in England! How did they brainwash you?"

"You don't like coffee, and you need caffeine."

"I get my caffeine the way right-thinking people get it." Emma threw up her hands and stalked into the office. "From chocolate!"

She began to pull the drawers out of the desk. They were empty. She examined the bookshelves; nothing interesting there, either. She started to cross the room to the closet and heard something creak. She turned back and knelt down, shoving the rag rug out of the way.

The floor was stripped oak. Just under the rug was a square of lighter wood, and the faint black lines of seaming where the square outline of a trapdoor was visible. Emma took her stele out and placed the tip against it.

"*Open*," she whispered, drawing the rune.

There was a tearing sound. The square of wood ripped away and crumbled into chunks of sawdust, tumbling into the hole she'd uncovered. It was slightly bigger on all sides than she'd thought. In it were several small books, and a large, leather-bound tome that Emma squinted at in puzzlement. Was it some kind of spell book?

"Did you just blow something up?" Julian came in, his cheek smeared with something black. He glanced over Emma's shoulder and whistled. "Your classic secret floor compartment."

"Help me take this stuff out of it. You get the giant book." Emma picked up the three smaller volumes; they were all bound in worn leather with a stamped MFB on the spines, their pages rough-edged.

"It's not a book," Julian said in a slightly odd voice. "It's a portfolio."

He retrieved it and carried it into the living room, Emma

hurrying after him. Two steaming cups of tea stood on the kitchen island, and a fire was blazing away. Emma realized that the black stuff on Julian's face was probably ash. She pictured him kneeling here, starting a fire for them, patient and thoughtful, and felt a wave of overwhelming tenderness for him.

He was already standing at the island, gently opening the portfolio. He caught his breath. The first picture was a watercolor of Chapel Cliff, seen from a distance. The colors and shapes leaped out vividly; Emma could feel cool sea air on her neck, hear the cry of gulls.

"It's lovely," she said, sitting down opposite him on a tall stool.

"Annabel did it." He touched her signature in the right-hand corner. "I had no idea she was an artist."

"I guess art runs in your blood," Emma said. Julian didn't look up. He was turning the pages with careful, almost reverent hands. There were many more seascapes: Annabel seemed to have loved capturing the ocean and the curves of land that bordered it. Annabel had also drawn dozens of pictures of the Blackthorn manor house in Idris, lingering on the softness of its golden stone, the beauty of its gardens, the vines of thorns that wrapped the gates. *Like the mural on the wall of your room*, Emma wanted to say to Julian, but she didn't.

Julian's hand stopped on none of those, though. He paused instead on a sketch that was unmistakably of the cottage they were in at that moment. A wooden fence surrounded it, and Polperro was visible in the distance, the Warren crawling up the opposite hill, crowded with houses.

Malcolm leaned against the fence, looking impossibly young— he clearly had not yet stopped aging. Though it was a pencil sketch, somehow the drawing caught the fairness of his hair, the oddity of his eyes, but they had been rendered in such loving lines that he looked beautiful. He seemed about to smile.

"I think that they lived here two hundred years ago, probably in hiding from the Clave," Julian said. "There's something about a place you've been with someone you love. It takes on a meaning in your mind. It becomes more than a place. It becomes a distillation of what you felt for each other. The moments you spend in a place with someone . . . they become part of its bricks and mortar. Part of its soul."

The firelight touched the side of his face, his hair, turning them gold. Emma felt tears rise in the back of her throat and fought them back.

"There's a reason Malcolm didn't just let this place fall into ruins. He loved it. He cared about it because it was a place he'd been with *her*."

Emma picked up her tea. "And maybe a place he wanted to bring her back to?" she said. "After he raised her?"

"Yes. I think Malcolm raised Annabel's body nearby, that he planned to hide with her here the way he had so long ago." Julian seemed to shake off the intense mood that had come on him, like a wet dog shaking water off its fur. "There're some guidebooks to Cornwall on the shelves—I'll go through them. What have you got there? What's in the books?"

Emma opened the first one. *Diary of Malcolm Fade Blackthorn, Age 8,* was scrawled on the inside cover. "By the Angel," she said. "His diaries."

She began to read out loud from the first page:

> "My name is Malcolm Fade Blackthorn. I chose the
> first two names myself, but the last was given to me to
> use by the Blackthorns, who have kindly taken me in.
> Felix says I am a ward, though I don't know what that
> means. He also says I am a warlock. When he says it, I
> think it is probably not a good thing to be, but Annabel

*says not to worry, that we are all born what we are and
can't change it. Annabel says . . ."*

She broke off. This was the man who'd murdered her parents;
but it was also a child's voice, helpless and wondering, echoing
down through the centuries. Two hundred years—the diary wasn't
dated, but it must have been written in the early 1800s.

"'Annabel says,'" she whispered. "He fell in love with her so *early*."

Julian cleared his throat and stood up. "Looks like it," he said.
"We'll have to search the diary for mentions of places that were
important to both of them."

"It's a lot of diary," Emma said, glancing at the three volumes.

"Then I guess we've got a lot of reading ahead of us," said Julian.
"I'd better make more tea."

Emma's wail of "Not *tea*!" followed him into the kitchen.

The London Shadow Market was located at the southern end of
London Bridge. Kit was disappointed to find that London Bridge
was just a dull concrete edifice without towers. "I thought it would
be like it is in the postcards," he lamented.

"You're thinking of Tower Bridge," Livvy informed him archly
as they began scrambling down a set of narrow stone steps to
reach the space below the London Bridge railway lines, which
crisscrossed overhead. "That's the one in all the pictures. The real
London Bridge was knocked down a long time ago; this one's the
modern replacement."

A sign advertised some kind of daytime fruit and vegetable
market, but that had long since closed. The white-painted stalls
were battened down tightly, the gates locked. The shadow of South-
wark Cathedral loomed over it all, a bulk of glass and stone that
blocked their view of the river.

Kit blinked away the glamour as he reached the bottom of

the steps. The image tore like spiderwebs and the Shadow Market burst into life. They were still using many of the ordinary market's stalls—clever, he thought, to hide in plain sight like that—but they were brightly colored now, a rainbow of paint and shimmer. Tents billowed in between the stalls as well, made of silks and draperies, signs floating beside their openings, advertising everything from fortune-telling to luck charms to love spells.

They slipped into the bustling crowd. Stalls sold enchanted masks, bottles of vintage blood for vampires—Livvy looked like she was going to gag over the RED HOT CHERRY FLAVOUR variety—and apothecaries did a brisk trade in magical powders and tinctures. A werewolf with thin, pale white hair sold bottles of a silvery powder, while across from him a witch whose skin had been tattooed with multicolored scales was hawking spell books. Several stands were taken up with selling Shadowhunter-repelling charms, which made Livvy giggle.

Kit was less amused.

"Push your sleeves down," he said. "And pull your hoods up. Cover your Marks as much as you can."

Livvy and Ty did as they were told. Ty reached for his headphones, too, but paused. Slowly he looped them back around his neck. "I should keep them off," he said. "I might need to hear something."

Livvy squeezed his shoulder and said something to him in a low voice that Kit couldn't hear. Ty shook his head, waving her away, and they pushed farther into the Market. A group of pale-skinned Night's Children had gathered at a stall advertising WILLING VICTIMS HERE. A crowd of humans sat around a deal table, chatting; occasionally another vampire would come up, money would change hands, and one of the humans would be drawn into the shadows to be bitten.

Livvy made a smothered noise. "They're very careful," Kit

assured her. "There's a place like this in the L.A. Market. The vamps never drink enough to hurt anyone."

He wondered if he should say something else reassuring to Ty. The dark-haired boy was pale, with a fine sheen of sweat along his cheekbones. His hands were opening and closing at his sides.

Farther along was a stall advertising a RAW BAR. Werewolves surrounded a dozen fresh carcasses of animals, selling bloody hunks torn off in fistfuls by passing customers. Livvy frowned; Ty said nothing. Kit had noticed before that puns and language jokes didn't interest Ty much. And right now, Ty looked as if he were struggling between trying to take in the details of the Market, and throwing up.

"Put your headphones on," Livvy murmured to him. "It's all right."

Ty shook his head again. His black hair was sticking to his forehead. Kit frowned. He wanted to grab Ty and drag him out of the Market to somewhere it would be calm and quiet. He remembered Ty saying that he hated crowds, that the sheer noise and confusion was "like broken glass in my head."

There was something else, too, something odd and off about this Market.

"I think we've wandered into the food area," said Livvy, making a face. "I wish we hadn't."

"This way." Kit turned more toward the cathedral. Usually there was a section of the Market where warlocks grouped together; so far he'd only seen vampires, werewolves, witches, and . . .

He slowed almost to a stop. "No faeries," he said.

"What?" Livvy asked, nearly bumping into him.

"The Market is usually full of faeries," he said. "They sell everything from invisibility clothes to sacks of food that are never empty. But I haven't seen a single one here."

"I have," said Ty. He pointed.

Nearby was a large stall manned by a tall male witch with long braided gray hair. In front of the stall was a green baize table. Displayed on the table were antique birdcages made of white-painted wrought iron. Each one was quite pretty in its own right, and for a moment Kit thought that they were what was for sale.

Then he looked closer. Inside each cage was a small, trapped creature. An assortment of pixies, nixies, brownies, and even a goblin, whose wide eyes were nearly swollen shut—probably from so much proximity to cold iron. The other faeries were chattering mournfully and softly, their hands seizing at the bars and then falling away with low cries of pain.

Ty was white with distress. His hands trembled against his sides. Kit thought of Ty in the desert, stroking the small lizards, putting mice in his pockets, capturing weasels for company. Ty, whose heart went out to small and helpless living things. "We can't leave them like that."

"They're probably selling them for blood and bones," said Livvy, her voice shaking. "We have to do something."

"You have no authority here, Shadowhunter." A cool, clipped voice spun them around. A woman stood before them. Her skin was dark as mahogany, her hair like bronze and dressed high on her head. The pupils of her eyes were shaped like golden stars. She was dressed in a glacier-white pantsuit with high, sparkling heels. She could have been any age from eighteen to thirty.

She smiled when they looked at her. "Yes, I can recognize a Shadowhunter, even those clumsily hiding their Marks," she said. "I suggest you leave the Market before someone less friendly than I am notices you."

Both the twins had made subtle gestures toward their weapons belts, their hands hovering near the hilts of their seraph blades. Kit knew this was his moment: his moment to show how well he could handle a Market and its denizens.

Not to mention preventing a bloodbath.

"I am an emissary of Barnabas Hale," he said. "Of the Los Angeles Market. These Shadowhunters are under my protection. Who are you?"

"Hypatia Vex," she said. "I co-run this Market." She narrowed her starry eyes at Kit. "A representative of Barnabas, you say? Why should I believe you?"

"The only people who know about Barnabas Hale," said Kit, "are people he wants to know."

She nodded slightly. "And the Shadowhunters? Barnabas sent them, too?"

"He needs me to consult a warlock regarding a peculiar magical object," said Kit. He was flying high now, high on the lies and the trickery and the con. "They have it in their possession."

"Very well, then. If Barnabas sent you to consult a warlock, which warlock was it?"

"It was me." A deep voice spoke from the shadows.

Kit turned to see a figure standing in front of a large dark green tent. It had been a male voice, but otherwise the figure was too covered—massive robe, cloak, hood, and gloves—to discern gender. "I'll take this, Hypatia."

Hypatia blinked slowly. It was like the stars vanishing and then reappearing from behind a cloud. "If you insist."

She made as if to turn and stalk away, then paused, looking back over her shoulder at Livvy and Ty. "If you pity those creatures, those faeries, dying inside their cages," she said, "think of this: If it were not for the Cold Peace your people insisted on, they would not be here. Look to the blood on your own hands, Shadowhunters."

She disappeared between two tents. Ty's expression was full of distress. "But my hands—"

"It's an expression." Livvy put her arm around her twin, hugging him tightly to her side. "It's not your fault, Ty, she's just being cruel."

"We should go," Kit said to the robed and hooded warlock, who nodded.

"Come with me," he said, and slipped into his tent. The rest of them followed.

The inside of the tent was remarkably clean and plain, with a wooden floor, a simple cot bed, and several shelves filled with books, maps, bottles of powder, candles in different colors, and jars of alarming-colored liquids. Ty exhaled, leaning back against one of the tent poles. Relief was printed clearly on his face as he basked in the relative calm and quiet. Kit wanted to go over to Ty and ask him if he was all right after the cacophony of the Market, but Livvy was already there, brushing the sweat-damp hair off her brother's forehead. Ty nodded, said something to her Kit couldn't hear.

"Come," said the warlock. "Sit down with me."

He gestured. In the center of the room was a small table surrounded by chairs. The Shadowhunters sat down, and the hooded warlock settled opposite them. In the flickering light inside the tent, Kit could glimpse the edge of a mask beneath the hood, obscuring the warlock's face.

"You may call me Shade," he said. "It's not my last name, but it will do."

"Why did you lie for us?" Livvy said. "Out there. You don't have any agreement with Barnabas Hale."

"Oh, I have a few," said Shade. "Not regarding you, to be fair, but I do know the man. And I'm curious that you do. Not many Shadowhunters are even aware of his name."

"I'm not a Shadowhunter," said Kit.

"Oh, you are," said Shade. "You're that new Herondale, to be exact."

Livvy's voice was sharp. "How do you know that? Tell us now."

"Because of your face," he said, to Kit. "Your pretty, pretty face. You're not the first Herondale I've met, not even the first with those eyes, like distilled twilight. I don't know why you only have one Mark, but I can certainly make a guess." He templed his hands under his chin. Kit thought he saw a gleam of green skin at his wrist, just below the edge of his glove. "I have to say I never thought I'd have the pleasure of entertaining the Lost Herondale."

"I'm not all that entertained, actually," said Kit. "We could put on a movie."

Livvy leaned forward. "Sorry," she said. "He gets like this when he's uncomfortable. Sarcastic."

"Who knew *that* was an inherited trait?" Shade held out a gloved hand. "Now, show me what you've brought. I assume *that* wasn't a lie?"

Ty reached into his jacket and brought out the *aletheia* crystal. In the candlelight, it glittered more than ever.

Shade chuckled. "A memory-holder," he said. "It looks like you might get your movie, after all." He reached out, and after a moment's hesitation, Ty allowed him to take it.

Shade set the crystal delicately in the center of the table. He passed a hand over it, then frowned and removed his glove. As Kit had thought, the skin of the hand he revealed was deep green. He wondered why Shade would bother covering something like that up, here in the Shadow Market, where warlocks were commonplace.

Shade passed his bare hand over the crystal and murmured. The candles in the room began to gutter. His murmuring increased— Kit recognized the words as Latin, which he'd taken three months of in school before he decided there was no point in knowing a language you couldn't converse in with anyone but the Pope, who he was unlikely to meet.

He had to admit now that it had a weight to it, though, a sense that each word was freighted with a deeper meaning. The candles went out entirely, but the room wasn't dark: The crystal was glowing, brighter and brighter under Shade's touch.

At last a focused beam of light seemed to explode from it, and Kit realized what Shade had meant when he'd joked about a movie. The light worked like the beam of a projector, casting moving images against the dark wall of the tent.

A girl sat bound to a chair inside a circular room filled with benches, a sort of auditorium. Through the windows of the room Kit could see mountains covered in snow. Though it was likely winter, the girl was wearing only a white shift dress; her feet were bare, and her long dark hair hung in tangles.

Her face was remarkably like Livvy's, so much so that to see it twisted in agony and terror made Kit tense.

"Annabel Blackthorn." A slight man with bent shoulders entered the scene. He was dressed in black; he wore a pin not unlike Diego's clasped at his shoulder. His hood was drawn up: Because of that and the angle of the crystal's viewpoint, it was hard to see his face or body in much detail.

"The Inquisitor," muttered Shade. "He was a Centurion, back then."

"You have come before us," the man went on, "accused of consorting with Downworlders. Your family took in the warlock Malcolm Fade and raised him as a brother to you. He repaid their kindness with abject treachery. He stole the Black Volume of the Dead from the Cornwall Institute, and you helped him."

"Where is Malcolm?" Annabel's voice was shaking, but also clear and firm. "Why isn't he here? I refuse to be questioned without him."

"How attached you are to your warlock despoiler," sneered the Inquisitor. Livvy gasped. Annabel looked furious. She had Livvy's stubborn set to her jaw, Kit thought, but there was a little of Ty and the rest in her too. Julian's haughtiness, Dru's look of easy hurt, the thoughtful cast of Ty's mouth and eyes. "So will it disappoint you, then, to hear that he is gone?"

"Gone?" Annabel repeated blankly.

"Disappeared from his cell in the Silent City overnight. Abandoned you to our tender mercies."

Annabel clasped her hands tightly in her lap. "That can't be true," she said. "Where is he? What have you done with him?"

"We have done nothing with him. I would be happy to testify to such under the grip of the Mortal Sword," said the Inquisitor. "In fact, what we want from you now—and we will release you afterward—is Fade's location. Now, why would we want to know that unless he truly had escaped?"

Annabel was shaking her head wildly, her dark hair whipping across her face. "He wouldn't leave me," she whispered. "He wouldn't."

"The truth is better faced, Annabel," said the Inquisitor. "He used you to gain access to the Cornwall Institute, to thieve from it. Once he had what he wanted, he vanished with it, leaving you alone to take the brunt of our wrath."

"He wanted it for our protection." Her voice trembled. "It was so we could begin a new life together where we would be safe—safe from the Law, safe from you."

"The Black Volume does not contain spells of safety or protection," said the Inquisitor. "The only way it could be of help to you would be if you traded it to someone powerful. Who was Fade's powerful ally, Annabel?"

She shook her head, her chin set stubbornly. Behind her someone else was coming into the room: a stern-faced woman carrying what looked like a bundle of black cloth. She sent a shiver up Kit's spine. "I will tell you nothing. Not even if you use the Sword."

"Indeed, we cannot believe what you say under the Sword," said the Inquisitor. "Malcolm has so tainted you—"

"*Tainted?*" Annabel echoed in horror. "As if—as if I am filth now?"

"You were filth from the time you first touched him. And now we do not know how he has changed you; you may well have some protection from our instruments of justice. Some charm we know not of. So we must do this as mundanes do it."

The woman with the stern face had arrived at the Inquisitor's side. She passed him the black bundle. He unrolled it, revealing a variety of sharp instruments—knives and razors and awls. Some of them had blades already stained with rusty red.

"Tell us who has that book now and the pain stops," said the Inquisitor, lifting up a razor.

Annabel began to scream.

Mercifully, the image went dark. Livvy was pale. Ty was leaning forward, his arms clasping his body tightly. Kit wanted to reach out, wanted to put his hands on Ty, wanted to tell him it would be all right, communicate it in a way that startled him.

"There is more," said Shade. "A different scene. Look."

The image on the wall shifted. They were still inside the same auditorium, but it was night, and the windows were dark. The place was lit with torches that burned white-gold. They could see the Inquisitor's face now, where before they had only been able to see the edges of his dark clothes and his hands. He wasn't nearly as old as Kit had thought: a youngish man, with dark hair.

The room was empty except for him and a group of other men of varying ages. There were no women. The other men weren't wearing robes, but Regency-era clothes: buckskin trousers and short, buttoned jackets. Several had sideburns as well, and a few had neat, trimmed beards. They all looked agitated.

"Felix Blackthorn," said the Inquisitor, drawling a bit. "Your daughter, Annabel, was chosen to become an Iron Sister. She was sent to you for a final farewell, but I hear now from the ladies of the Adamant Citadel that she never arrived. Have you any idea of her whereabouts?"

A man with brown hair streaked with gray frowned. Kit stared at him in some fascination: Here was a living ancestor of Ty and Livvy, Julian and Mark. His face was broad and bore the marks of a bad temper.

"If you suggest I am hiding my daughter, I am not," he said. "She fouled herself with the touch of a warlock, and she is no longer a part of our family."

"My uncle speaks the truth," said another of the men, this one younger. "Annabel is dead to us all."

"What a vivid image," said the Inquisitor. "Don't mind me if I find it more than an image."

The younger man flinched. Felix Blackthorn didn't change expression.

"You would not mind a trial by Mortal Sword, would you, Felix?" said the Inquisitor. "Just to ensure that you truly do not know where your daughter is."

"You sent her back to us tortured and half-mad," snapped the younger Blackthorn. "Do not tell us now you care about her fate!"

"She was no more hurt than many Shadowhunters might be in a battle," said the Inquisitor, "but death is another thing entirely. And the Iron Sisters are asking."

"Might I speak?" said another of the men; he had dark hair and an aristocratic look.

The Inquisitor nodded.

"Since Annabel Blackthorn went to join the Iron Sisters," he said, "Malcolm Fade has become a true ally to Nephilim. One of those rare warlocks we can count on our side, and who is indispensable in a battle."

"Your point, Herondale?"

"If he does not think his lady love left him, shall we say, voluntarily, or if he learns of any harm that came to her, I think it unlikely that he will continue to be such a valuable asset to us."

"The ladies of the Adamant Citadel do not leave their island to truck in gossip," said another man, narrow-faced as a ferret. "If the discussion of the fate of unfortunate Annabel ends here, then it ends. After all, perhaps she ran away on the road, or perhaps she fell victim to a demon or a highwayman on the way to the Citadel. We may never know."

The Inquisitor tapped his fingers on the arm of his chair. He was looking at Felix Blackthorn, his eyes hooded; it was impossible for Kit to tell what he might be thinking. Finally he said, "You're damnably clever, Felix, bringing your friends into this. You know I can't punish you all without chaos. And you're right about Fade. There's been a demon uprising near the Scholomance, and we need him." He flung his hands up. "Very well. We'll never discuss this again."

A look of relief passed over Felix Blackthorn's face, mixed with an odd bitterness. "Thank you," he said. "Thank you, Inquisitor Dearborn."

The vision narrowed to a pinpoint of black and vanished.

For a moment Kit sat still. He heard Livvy and Ty speaking in rapid voices, and Shade answering: Yes, the vision was a real memory; no, there was no way of identifying whose it might be. It was probably two hundred years old. They were clearly excited about the mention of an Inquisitor Dearborn. But Kit's brain had snagged on one word like a piece of cloth on a hook:

Herondale.

One of those horrible men had been his ancestor. Herondales and Dearborns and Blackthorns *together* had been complicit in covering up the torture and murder of a young woman whose only crime had been to love a warlock. It had been one thing to think he was related to Jace, who seemed to be universally adored and good at everything. Everyone had spoken of Herondales to him as though they were royalty, world-saving royalty.

He remembered Arthur's words. *What kind of Herondale will you be? William or Tobias? Stephen or Jace? Beautiful, bitter, or both?*

"Rook!" The front of the tent shook. "Kit Rook, come out of there right now!"

The chatter inside the tent stopped. Kit blinked; he *wasn't* Kit Rook, he was Christopher Herondale, he was—

He staggered to his feet. Livvy and Ty leaped up after him, Ty pausing only to pocket the *aletheia* crystal. "Kit, don't—" Livvy started, reaching for him, but Kit had already shoved his way out of the tent.

Someone was calling his real name—or maybe it wasn't his real name—but it was a part of him that he couldn't deny. He stumbled into the lane outside.

Barnabas Hale stood in front of him, his arms crossed over his chest, his scaled white skin gleaming sickly in the torchlight. Behind him loomed a group of werewolves: big, muscular men and women in black leather and spiked bracelets. More than one sported a pair of brass knuckles.

"So, little Rook," Barnabas said, his snake's tongue flickering as he grinned. "What's this I hear about you pretending to be here on business for me?"

19

THE GRAY WOODS

"I told you to stay away from the Shadow Market, Rook," said Barnabas. "Is there a reason you didn't listen? Lack of respect for me, or just a lack of respect for Downworlders overall?"

A crowd had begun to gather, a curious mixture of sneering vampires, grinning werewolves, and wary-looking warlocks.

"You told me to stay out of the Los Angeles Market," said Kit, "not every Shadow Market in the world. You don't have that power and reach, Hale, and it's up to the owner of this Market to decide if I stay or if I go."

"That would be me." It was Hypatia, her smooth face expressionless.

"I thought you were the co-runner?" said Kit.

"Good enough, and watch your impertinence. I don't appreciate being lied to, child. Nor do I appreciate you bringing two Nephilim in here with you."

The crowd gasped. Kit winced internally. This was not going their way.

"They don't support the Cold Peace," he said.

"Did they vote against it?" asked a warlock with a ring of spikes growing from around her throat.

"We were ten years old," said Livvy. "We were too young."

"Children," hissed the man standing behind the counter of caged faeries. It was hard to tell if he said the word with surprise, contempt, or hunger.

"Oh, he didn't just bring Nephilim with him," said Barnabas, with his snakelike grin. "He is one. A Shadowhunter spy."

"What do we do?" Ty whispered. They were now pressed so tightly together that Kit couldn't move his arms, pinned between Ty and Livvy.

"Get your weapons," said Kit. "And get ready to figure out how to run."

To the twins' credit, neither gave so much as an intake of breath. Their hands moved quickly at the periphery of Kit's vision.

"That's a lie," he said. "My father is Johnny Rook."

"And your mother?" said the deep voice of Shade, behind them. A crowd had gathered behind him, too; they couldn't run that way.

"I don't know," said Kit, between his teeth. To his surprise, Hypatia raised her eyebrows, as if she knew something he didn't. "And it doesn't matter—we didn't come here to harm you or spy on you. We needed a warlock's help."

"But Nephilim have their own pet warlocks," said Barnabas, "those willing to betray Downworld as they grub for money in the pockets of the Clave. Though after what all of you did to Malcolm . . ."

"Malcolm?" Hypatia stood up straight. "These are Blackthorns? The ones responsible for his death?"

"He only died halfway," Ty said. "He came back as a sort of sea demon, for a while. He's dead now, obviously," he added, as if realizing that he had somehow put his foot in it.

"This is why Sherlock Holmes lets Watson do the talking," Kit said to him in a hissing whisper.

"Holmes never lets Watson do the talking," Ty snapped. "Watson is backup."

"I'm not backup," said Kit, and drew a knife from his pocket. He heard the werewolves laugh, mocking the dagger's puny dimensions, but it didn't bother him. "Like I said," he told them. "We came here to peacefully speak to a warlock and leave. I've grown up in Shadow Markets. I bear them no ill will, and neither do my companions. But if you attack us, we will fight back. And then there will be others, other Nephilim, who will come to avenge us. And for what? What good will it do?"

"The boy is right," said Shade. "War like this benefits no one."

Barnabas waved him away. His eyes had a fanatical gleam to them. "But setting an example does," he said. "Let the Nephilim know what it is like to find the crumpled bodies of your children dead on your doorstep and for there to be no restitution and no justice."

"Don't do this—" Livvy began.

"Finish them," said Barnabas, and his pack of werewolves, as well as a few of the onlookers, sprang toward them.

Outside the cottage, the lights of Polperro gleamed like stars against the dark hillsides. The sweep of the sea was audible, the soft sound of ocean rising and falling, the lullaby of the world.

It had certainly worked on Emma. Despite Julian's best efforts with the tea, she had fallen asleep in front of the fireplace, Malcolm's diary open beside her, her body curled like a cat's.

She had been reading out loud to him from the diary before she'd fallen asleep. From the very beginning, when Malcolm had been found alone, a confused child who couldn't remember his parents and had no idea what a warlock was. The Blackthorns had taken him in, as far as Julian could tell, because they thought a warlock might be useful to them, a warlock they could control and compel. They had explained to him his true nature, and none too gently at that.

Of all the family, only Annabel had shown kindness to Malcolm. They had explored the cliffs and caves of Cornwall together as children, and she had shown him how they could exchange messages secretly using a raven as a carrier. Malcolm wrote lyrically of the seaside, its changes and tempests, and lyrically of Annabel, even when he did not know his own feelings. He loved her quick wit and her strong nature. He loved her protectiveness—he wrote of how she had defended him angrily to her cousins—and over time he began to marvel at not just the beauty of her heart. His pen skipped and stuttered as he wrote of her soft skin, the shape of her hands and mouth, the times when her hair came out of its plaits and floated around her like a cloud of shadow.

Julian had almost been glad when Emma's voice had trailed off, and she'd lain down—just to rest her eyes, she said—and fallen almost instantly asleep. He had never thought he would sympathize with Malcolm or think of the two of them as alike, but Malcolm's words could have been the story of the ruination of his own heart.

Sometimes, Malcolm had written, *someone you have known all your life becomes no longer familiar to you, but strange in a marvelous way, as if you have discovered a beach you have been visiting all your life is made not of sand but of diamonds, and they blind you with their beauty. Annabel, you have taken my life, my life as dull as the edge of an unused blade, you have taken it apart and put it back together in a shape so strange and marvelous I can only wonder . . .*

There was a loud thud, a sound as if a bird had flown into the glass of one of the windows. Julian sat up straight, reaching for the dagger he'd placed on the low table next to the sofa.

The thud came again, louder.

Julian rose to his feet. Something moved outside the window—the flash of something white. It was gone, and then there was another thud. Something thrown against the glass, like a child throwing pebbles at a friend's window to get their attention.

Julian glanced at Emma. She had rolled onto her back, her eyes closed, her chest rising and falling in a regular rhythm. Her mouth was slightly open, her cheeks flushed.

He went to the door and turned the knob slowly, trying to prevent it from squeaking. It opened, and he stepped out into the night.

It was cool and dark, the moon dangling over the water like a pearl on the end of a chain. Around the house was uneven ground that fell away almost sheerly on one side to the ocean. The surface of the water was darkly transparent, the shape of rocks visible through it as if Julian was looking through black glass.

"Julian," said a voice. "Julian Blackthorn."

He turned. The house was behind him. Ahead of him was Peak Rock, the tip of the cliff, and dark grass growing out of gaps between the gray stones.

He raised his hand, the witchlight rune-stone in it. Light rayed out, illuminating the girl standing in front of him.

It was as if she'd stepped out of his own drawing. Dark hair, straight as a pin, an oval face like a sad Madonna, framed by the hood of an enormous cloak. Beneath the cloak he could see thin, pale ankles and cracked shoes.

"Annabel?" he said.

The knife flew from Kit's hand. It shot across the distance between him and the approaching mob and drove straight into Barnabas Hale's shoulder. The snake-scaled warlock staggered backward and fell, yelling in pain.

"Kit!" Livvy said, in amazement; he could tell she wasn't sure he'd done the right thing, but he'd never forgotten an Emerson quote that was a favorite of his father's: *When you strike at a king, you must kill him.*

One warlock was more powerful than a pack of werewolves, and Barnabas was their leader. Two reasons to take him out of the fight. But there was no more time to think about that, because the Downworlders were on them.

"*Umbriel!*" shouted Livvy. A blazing blade shot from her hand. She was a whirl of motion, her saber training making her fast and graceful. She spun in a deadly circle, her hair whipping around her. She was a gorgeous blur of light and dark, and arcs of blood followed her blade.

Ty, wielding a shortsword, had backed up against the pillar of a stall, which was clever because the stall owner was shouting at the Downworlders to get back even as they advanced.

"Oi! Get away!" yelled the stall owner, and her wares began to fly through the air, bottles of tinctures splattering against the surprised faces of werewolves and vampires. Some of the substances seemed corrosive—at least one werewolf fell back with a yell, clutching a sizzling face.

Ty smiled, and despite everything that was happening, it made Kit want to smile, too. He filed it away as a memory to revisit later, considering that right now a massive werewolf with shoulders like flying buttresses was careening toward him. He reached out and yanked a pole free of Shade's tent, causing the whole structure to tilt.

Kit swung out with the pole. It wasn't the hardest metal, but it was flexible, like a massive whip. He heard the crunch of bone against skin as it slammed the leaping werewolf directly in the sternum. With a grunt of agony, the lycanthrope went sailing past Kit's head.

Kit's body thrummed with excitement. Maybe they could do it. Maybe the three of them could fight their way out of this. Maybe that was what it meant to have Heaven in your blood.

Livvy screamed.

Kit knocked a vampire out of his way with a vicious whack of the pole, and spun to see what had happened. One of the bottles flying through the air had smashed against her side. It was clearly an acidic substance—it was burning through the material of her clothes, and though her hand was clamped against the wound, Kit could see blood between her fingers.

She was still slashing out with her other hand, but the Downworlders, like sharks smelling blood, had turned away from Ty and Kit and were moving toward her. She hit out, spearing two, but without being able to properly shield her body, her circle of protection was shrinking. A vampire stepped nearer, licking his lips.

Kit began to run toward her. Ty was ahead of him, using his shortsword to hack his way through the crowd. Blood was pattering down on the ground at Livvy's feet. Kit's heart tensed with panic. She slumped just as Ty reached her and the two of them went down on the ground, Livvy in her brother's arms. Umbriel clattered from her hand.

Kit staggered toward the two of them. He threw his pole aside, hitting several werewolves, and snatched up Livvy's seraph blade.

Ty had put down the shortsword. He was holding his sister, who was unconscious, her hair spilling across his shoulders and chest. He had his stele out and was tracing a healing rune on her skin, though his hand was shaking and the rune was uneven.

Kit held up the blazing sword. The light of it made the Downworlders cringe back slightly, but he knew it wasn't enough: They would press on, and tear him apart, and then they would tear apart Livvy and Ty. He saw Barnabas, his suit soaked in blood, leaning on the arm of a bodyguard. His eyes, fixed on Kit, were filled with hate.

There would be no mercy here.

A wolf leaped toward Kit. He raised Umbriel, swung it—and connected with nothing. The wolf had tumbled to the ground, as if shoved by an unseen hand.

There was a blast of wind. Kit's gold hair blew across his face;

he pushed it back with a hand stained red. The tents were rattling; more jars and bottles smashed. Blue lightning crackled, and a fork of it stabbed into the ground just in front of Barnabas.

"I see," said a silky voice, "that I seem to have arrived here just in time."

Walking toward them was a tall man with short, black, spiked hair. He was clearly a warlock: His eyes were cat's eyes, with slit pupils, green and gold. He wore a charcoal trench coat dramatically lined with red that swept out behind him when he walked.

"Magnus Bane," said Barnabas, with clear loathing. "The Ultimate Traitor."

"Not my favorite nickname," Magnus said, gently wiggling his fingers in Barnabas's direction. "I prefer 'Our Lord and Master' or maybe 'Unambiguously the Hottest.'"

Barnabas shrank back. "These three Nephilim broke into the Market under false pretenses—"

"Did they break the Accords?"

Barnabas snarled. "One of them stabbed me."

"Which one?" Magnus asked.

Barnabas pointed at Kit.

"Dreadful business," Magnus said. His left hand was down by his side. Surreptitiously, he gave Kit a thumbs-up. "Was that before or after you attacked them?"

"After," Kit said. One of Barnabas's bodyguards started toward him; he jabbed out with his blade. This time the lightning that forked from Magnus's hand snapped like a downed electrical wire between their feet.

"Stop," he said.

"You have no authority here, Bane," said Barnabas.

"Actually, I do," said Magnus. "As the warlock representative to the Council of Shadowhunters, I have a great deal of authority. I imagine you know that."

"Oh, we know entirely how in thrall to the Shadowhunters you are." Barnabas was so furious, saliva flew when he spoke. "Especially the Lightwoods."

Magnus raised a lazy eyebrow. "Is this about my boyfriend? Jealous, Barnabas?"

Kit cleared his throat. "Mr. Bane," he said. He'd heard of Magnus Bane, everyone had. He was probably the most famous warlock in the world. His boyfriend, Alec, helped head up the Downworlder-Shadowhunter Alliance, along with Maia Roberts and Lily Chen. "Livvy lost a lot of blood. Ty used a healing rune, but—"

Magnus's face darkened with real anger. "She's fifteen years old; she's a child," he snarled. "How dare you all."

"Going to report us to the Council, Magnus?" said Hypatia, speaking for the first time. She hadn't joined in the melee; she was leaning against the side of a stall, eyeing Magnus up and down. Shade seemed to have vanished; Kit had no idea where he'd gone.

"It seems to me we have two choices," said Magnus. "You fight me, and you will not win, believe me, because I am very angry and I am older than any of you. And then I tell the Council. Or you let me walk away with these Nephilim children, we don't fight, and I don't report you to the Council. Thoughts?"

"I pick number two," said the woman who'd thrown her bottles at the werewolves.

"She's right, Barnabas," said Hypatia. "Step back."

Barnabas's face was working. He turned abruptly on his heel and strode away, followed by his bodyguards. The other Downworlders began to shuffle away, disappearing into the crowd, shoulders hunched.

Kit dropped down on his knees next to Ty, who had barely moved. His eyes were darting back and forth, his lips almost white; he looked as if he was in shock.

"Ty," Kit said hesitantly, and put a hand on the other boy's arm. "Ty—"

Ty shook him off almost without seeming to register who he was. His arms were around Livvy, his fingers pressed to her wrist; Kit realized he was taking her pulse. It was clear she was alive. Kit could see the rise and fall of her chest. But Ty kept his fingers on her wrist regardless, as if the pulse of her heartbeat steadied him.

"Tiberius." It was Magnus, kneeling down, heedless of the blood and mud spattering his expensive-looking coat. He didn't reach out or try to touch Ty, just spoke in a low voice. "Tiberius. I know you can hear me. You have to help me get Livvy to the Institute. I can take care of her there."

Ty looked up. He wasn't crying, but the gray in his eyes had darkened to a searing charcoal. He looked stunned. "She'll be all right?" he said.

"She'll be fine." Magnus's voice was firm. Kit reached out to help Tiberius lift Livvy, and this time Ty let him do it. As they stood up, Magnus was already creating a Portal, a whirl of blue and green and rose colors, rising up against the shadows of the tents and stalls of the Market.

Ty turned suddenly to Kit. "Can you take her?" he said. "Carry Livvy?"

Kit nodded in astonishment. For Ty to let him carry his twin was a sign of trust that shocked him. He lifted Livvy in his arms, the scent of blood and magic in his nose.

"Come on!" Magnus called. The Portal was wide open now: Kit could see the shape of the London Institute through it.

Ty didn't turn. He had slammed his headphones down over his ears and was running through the empty lane of the Market. His shoulders were hunched, as if he were warding off blows that came from all sides, but his hands were steady when he reached the stall at the end, the one with the caged faeries. He began seizing the cages, yanking them open one by one. The pixies and nixies and hobgoblins inside poured out, yelping with joy at their freedom.

"You! You, stop that!" shouted the stall owner, running back to prevent further destruction, but it was already too late. Ty flung the last cage toward him and it burst open, releasing a furious, clawing hobgoblin, who fastened his teeth into his former captor's shoulder.

"Ty!" Kit called, and Ty ran back toward the open Portal. Knowing Ty was behind him, Kit stepped into it, holding Livvy tight, and let the whirlwind take him.

Annabel came toward him silently, her cracked shoes making no sounds on the rock. Julian couldn't move. He was rooted to the spot with disbelief.

He knew she was alive. He'd watched her kill Malcolm. But somehow he'd never imagined her as so tangible and distinct. So human. She seemed like someone he might meet anywhere: in a movie theater, at the Institute, at the beach.

He wondered where she'd gotten the clothing from. The cloak didn't seem like something you'd find hanging on a washing line, and he doubted she had any money.

The high rocks threw their shadows down as she came closer to him, pushing her hood back. "How did you find this place?" she demanded. "This house?"

He held up his hands and she stopped, only a few feet from him. The night wind picked up strands of her hair and they seemed to dance.

"The piskies told me where you were," she said. "Once they were Malcolm's friends, and still they hold affection for me."

Was she serious? Julian couldn't tell.

"You should not be here," she said. "You should not be looking for me."

"I have no desire to hurt or harm you," Julian said. He wondered; if he moved closer to her, would he be able to grab her? Though the idea of using physical force to try to get the Black Volume sickened him. He realized he hadn't imagined *how* he was going to get it away from her. Finding her had been too much of a priority. "But I saw you kill Malcolm."

"I remember this place two hundred years past," she said as if he hadn't spoken. Her accent was British, but there was an oddness to it, a sound Julian had never heard before. "It looked much the same, though there were fewer houses, and more ships in the harbor." She turned to look back at the cottage. "Malcolm built that house himself. With his own magic."

"Why didn't you come inside?" Julian said. "Why did you wait for me out here?"

"I am barred," she said. "Malcolm's blood is on my hands. I cannot enter his home." She turned to face Julian. "How could you have seen me kill him?"

The moon had come out from behind a cloud. It lit the night up brilliantly, framing the ragged edges of the clouds with light.

"I watched Malcolm raise you," Julian said. "In a scrying glass of the Seelie Queen. She wanted me to see it."

"But why would the Queen want such a thing?" Her lips parted in realization. "Ah. To make you want to follow me. To make you want the Black Volume of the Dead and all its power."

She reached into her cloak and drew out the book. It *was* black, a dense sort of black that seemed to gather shadows into itself. It was tied closed with a leather strap. The words stamped onto its cover had long faded away.

"I remember nothing of my death," Annabel said softly, as Julian stared at the book in her hands. "Not how it was done, nor the time after it when I lay beneath the earth, nor when Malcolm learned of my death and disturbed my bones. I only discovered later that Malcolm had spent many years trying to raise me from the dead, but during that time none of the spells he cast worked. My body rotted and I did not wake." She turned the book over in her hands. "It was the Unseelie King who told him that the Black Volume was the key. The Unseelie King who gave him the rhyme and the spell. And it was the King who told Malcolm when Sebastian Morgenstern's attack on the Institute would come—when it would be empty. All the King asked in return was that Malcolm worked for him on spells that would weaken the Nephilim."

Julian's mind raced. Malcolm hadn't mentioned the Unseelie King's part in all this when he'd told his version of the story to the Blackthorns. But that was hardly surprising. The King was far more powerful than Malcolm, and the warlock would have been reluctant to invoke his name. "In the Unseelie Lands, our powers are useless," said Julian. "Seraph blades don't work there, or witch-light or runes."

"Malcolm's doing," she said. "As it is in his own Lands, so the King wishes it to be all over the world, and in Idris. Shadowhunters made powerless. He would take Alicante and rule from it. Shadow-hunters would become the hunted."

"I need the Black Volume, Annabel," Julian said. "To stop the King. To stop all this."

She only stared at him. "Five years ago," she said, "Malcolm spilled Shadowhunter blood trying to raise me."

Emma's parents, Julian thought.

"It woke my mind but not my body," Annabel said. "The spell had half-worked. I was in agony, you understand, half-alive and trapped beneath the earth. I screamed my pain in silence. Malcolm could not hear me. I could not move. He thought me insensible, unhearing, yet he spoke to me nonetheless."

Five years, Julian thought. For five years she had been trapped in the convergence tomb, conscious but unable to be heard, unable to speak or scream or move.

Julian shuddered.

"His voice filtered down into my tomb. He read me that poem, over and over. 'It was many and many a year ago.'" Her gaze was bleak. "He betrayed me while I lived, and again when I was dead. Death is a gift, you understand. The passing beyond pain and sorrow. He denied me that."

"I'm sorry," Julian said. The moon had started to sink in the sky. He wondered how late it was.

"Sorry," she echoed dismissively, as if the word had no meaning for her. "There will be a war," she said, "between Faerie and Shadowhunters. But that is not my concern. My concern is that you promise to no longer try to obtain the Black Volume. Let it alone, Julian Blackthorn."

He exhaled. He would have lied in a moment and promised, but he suspected a promise to someone like Annabel would hold a terrifying weight. "I can't," he said. "We need the Black Volume. I cannot tell you why, but I swear it will be kept safe and out of the hands of the King."

"I have told you what the book did to me," she said, and for the first time, she seemed animated, her cheeks flushed. "It has no use but evil use. You should not want it."

"I won't use it for evil," Julian said. That much was true, he thought.

"It cannot be used for anything *else*," she said. "It destroys families, people—"

"My family will be destroyed if I don't have the book."

Annabel paused. "Oh," she said. And then, more gently, "But think of what will be destroyed with this book out there, in the world. So much more. There are higher causes."

"Not to me," said Julian. *The world can burn if my family lives*, he thought, and was about to say it when the cottage door flew open.

Emma stood in the doorway. She was shoving her feet into unlaced boots, Cortana in her hand. Her hair was rumpled over her shoulders, but her grip on the sword was unwavering.

Her gaze sought out Julian, then found Annabel; she started, stared incredulously. He saw her mouth shape Annabel's name, as Annabel threw her hood up over her head and bolted.

Julian started after her, Emma only a second behind him. But Annabel was shockingly fast. She flew across the grass and heather-strewn slope to the edge of the cliff; with a last glance back, she flung herself into the air.

"*Annabel!*" Julian raced to the cliff edge, Emma at his side. He stared down into the water, hundreds of feet below, untroubled by even a ripple. Annabel had vanished.

They exploded back into the Institute, appearing in the library. It was like being dropped from a great height, and Kit staggered and fell back against the table, clawing at Livvy so he wouldn't drop her.

Ty had fallen to his knees and was righting himself. Kit glanced at Livvy's face—it was gray, with an eerie yellowish tinge.

"Magnus—" he gasped.

The warlock, who had landed with the ease of long practice, spun around, instantly assessing the situation. "Calm down," he said, "everything's fine," and he started to take Livvy from Kit's grasp. Kit let her go with relief—someone was going to take care of this. Magnus Bane was going to take care of this. He wouldn't let Livvy die.

It took Kit a moment to notice that there was already someone standing in the library. Someone he didn't know, who moved toward Magnus just as the warlock eased Livvy down onto the long table. It was a young man about Jace's age, with straight dark hair that looked as if he had slept on it and not bothered to brush it. He wore a washed-out sweater and jeans. He glared at Magnus. "You woke up the kids," he said.

"Alec, we have kind of an emergency here," said Magnus.

So this was Alec Lightwood. Somehow Kit had expected him to look older.

"Small children who are awake are also an emergency," said Alec. "I'm just saying."

"All right, move the furniture back," Magnus said to Ty and Kit. "I need some working space." He glanced sideways at Alec as the two younger boys moved chairs and small bookcases out of the way. "So where are the kids?"

Magnus was stripping off his coat. Alec held out his hand and caught the coat as Magnus tossed it to him, a practiced move that suggested he was used to the gesture. "I left them with a nice girl named Cristina. She said she likes children."

"You just left our children with strangers?"

"Everyone else is asleep," said Alec. "Besides, she knows lullabies. In Spanish. Rafe is in love." He glanced over at Kit again. "By the Angel, it's uncanny," he said in a sudden burst, as if he couldn't help it.

Kit felt unnerved. "What's uncanny?"

"He means you look like Jace," said Magnus. "Jace Herondale."

"My *parabatai*," said Alec, with love and pride.

"I know Jace," said Kit. He was looking at Ty, who was struggling to move a chair. It wasn't that it was too heavy for him, but that his hands were opening and closing at his sides, making his gestures unusually clumsy and uncoordinated. "He came out to the L.A. Institute after my—after they found out who I was."

"The legendary Lost Herondale," said Magnus. "You know, I was starting to think that was a rumor Catarina made up, like the Loch Ness Monster or the Bermuda Triangle."

"Catarina made up the Bermuda Triangle?" said Alec.

"Don't be ridiculous, Alexander. That was Ragnor." Magnus touched Livvy's arm lightly. She cried out. Ty dropped the chair he'd been struggling with and took a ragged breath.

"You're hurting her," he said. "Don't."

His voice was quiet, but in it Kit could hear steel in it, and see the boy who'd held him at knifepoint in his father's house.

Magnus leaned his hands on the table. "I'll try not to, Tiberius," he said. "But I may have to cause her pain to heal her."

Ty seemed about to answer, just as the door flew open and Mark burst in. He caught sight of Livvy, and blanched. "Livvy. *Livia!*"

He tried to start forward, but Alec caught at his arm. For all Alec's slenderness, he was deceptively strong. He held Mark back while blue fire sparked from Magnus's hand and he passed it down Livvy's side. The sleeve of her jacket and shirt seemed to melt away, revealing a long, ugly cut seeping yellow fluid.

Mark sucked in a breath. "What's going on?"

"Fight at the Shadow Market," Magnus said briefly. "Livia was cut with a piece of glass with orias root on it. Very poisonous, but curable." He moved his fingers over Livvy's arm; as he did, a bluish light seemed to glow under her skin, as if it were pulsing from the inside out.

"The Shadow Market?" Mark demanded. "What the hell was Livvy doing at the Shadow Market?"

Nobody answered. Kit felt as if he was shrinking inward.

"What's going on?" Ty demanded. His hands were still opening at his sides, as if he were trying to shake something off his skin. His shoulders rolled back. It was as if his worry and agitation were expressing themselves through a silent music that made his nerves and muscles dance. "Is that blue light normal?"

Mark said something to Alec, and Alec nodded. He released the other boy's arm, and Mark came around the table to put his hand on Ty's shoulder. Ty leaned into him, though he didn't stop moving.

"Magnus is the best there is," Alec said. "Healing magic is his specialty." Alec's voice was gentle. The voice of someone who wasn't quieting his tone to keep someone calm, but who actually empathized. "Magnus cured me, once," he added. "It was demon poison; I shouldn't have lived, but I did. You can trust him."

Livvy gave a sudden gasp and her back jerked; Ty put his hand to his own arm, his fingers clenching. Then her body relaxed. Color began to come back to her face, her cheeks turning from yellowish-gray to pink. Ty, too, relaxed visibly.

"That's the poison gone," said Magnus matter-of-factly. "Now we have to work on the blood loss and the cut."

"There are runes for both those things," said Ty. "I can put them on her."

But Magnus was shaking his head. "Better not to use them—runes draw some of their strength from the bearer," he said. "If she had a *parabatai*, we could try pulling strength from them, but she doesn't, does she?"

Ty didn't say anything. His face had gone still and completely white.

"She doesn't," Kit said, realizing Ty wasn't going to say anything.

"That's all right. She'll be fine," Magnus reassured them. "Might as well move her to her bedroom, though. No reason for her to sleep on a table."

"I'll help you take her," Mark said. "Ty, why don't you come with us."

"Alec, can you go to the infirmary?" Magnus said, as Mark went to lift his sister into his arms. Poor Livvy, Kit thought; she would hate to be dragged around like a sack of potatoes. "You'll know what I need."

Alec nodded.

"Take Kit with you," said Magnus. "You'll want help carrying everything."

Kit found himself not minding the idea of making conversation with Alec. Alec had a comforting sort of presence—quiet, and contained. As he and Alec headed out of the room, Kit glanced back once at Ty. Kit had never had siblings, never had a mother, had only had Johnny. His father. His father who had died, and he didn't think he'd ever looked the way Ty looked now, as if the possibility of something happening to Livvy was enough to break him inside.

Maybe there was something wrong with him, Kit thought as he followed Alec into the hallway. Maybe he didn't have the right kind of feelings. He'd never wondered that much about his mother, who she was: Wouldn't someone who knew how to feel properly wonder that?

"So you met Jace," said Alec, scuffing his shoes along the carpet as they went. "What did you think?"

"Of Jace?" Kit was puzzled. He didn't know why anyone would solicit his opinion on the head of the New York Institute.

"Just making small talk." Alec had an odd half smile, as if he were keeping a number of thoughts to himself. They passed through a door marked INFIRMARY into a large room, filled with old-fashioned single metal beds. Alec went behind a counter and started rummaging.

"Jace isn't much like you," said Kit. There was a weird dark patch of wall across from him, as if paint had smeared up and across it in almost the shape of a tree.

"That's an understatement." Alec piled bandages on the countertop. "But it doesn't matter. *Parabatai* don't need to be like each other. They just need to complement each other. To work well together."

Kit thought of Jace, all shining gold and confidence, and Alec, all steady, quiet ease. "And you and Jace complement each other?"

"I remember when I met him," Alec said. He'd found two boxes and was dumping bandages into one, jars of powder into another. "When he arrived from Idris. He was skinny and he had bruises and he had these big eyes. He was arrogant, too. He and Isabelle used to fight. . . ." He smiled at the memory. "But to me everything about him said, 'Love me, because nobody ever has.' It was all over him, like fingerprints.

"He was worried about meeting you," Alec added. "He's not used to having living blood relatives. He cared what you thought. He wanted you to like him." He glanced over at Kit. "Here, take a box."

Kit's head was swimming. He thought of Jace, swaggering and amused and proud. But Alec spoke of Jace as if he saw him as a vulnerable child, someone who needed love because he'd never gotten it. "I'm no one, though," he said, taking the box full of bandages. "Why would he care what I think? I don't matter. I'm nothing."

"You matter to Shadowhunters," said Alec. "You're a Herondale. That'll never be nothing."

Holding Rafe in her arms, Cristina sang softly. He was small for five years old, and his rest was fitful. He squirmed and sighed in his sleep, his small brown fingers twisted into a lock of his dark hair. He reminded her a little of her own small cousins, always wanting another hug, another sweet, another song before sleep.

Max, on the other hand, slept like a rock—a dark blue rock, with adorable big navy eyes and a gap-toothed grin. When Cristina, Mark, and Kieran had run down to find Alec, Magnus, and their two children in the Institute parlor, Evelyn had been there, fussing about warlocks in her house and the undesirability of being blue. Cristina hoped most adult Shadowhunters didn't react to Max like that—it would be awfully traumatic for the poor little mite.

It seemed that Alec and Magnus had returned from a trip to

find Diana's messages asking them for help. They had Portaled to the London Institute immediately. On hearing about the binding spell from Mark and Cristina, Magnus had headed for the local Shadow Market to scout out a spell book he hoped might break the enchantment.

Rafe and Max, upon being left in a strange house with only one parent, had wailed. "Sleep," Alec had said glumly to Rafe, carrying him into a spare room. "*Adorno.*"

Cristina giggled. "That means 'ornament,'" she said. "Not 'sleep.'"

Alec sighed. "I'm still learning Spanish. Magnus is the one who speaks it."

Cristina smiled at Rafael, who was sniffling. She'd always sung her little cousins to sleep, just as her mother had with her; maybe Rafe would like that. "*Oh, Rafaelito,*" she said to him, *oh, little Rafael baby.* "*Ya es hora de ir a dormir. ¿Te gustaría que te cante una canción?*"

He nodded vigorously. "*¡Sí!*"

Cristina spent some time teaching Alec all the lullabies she knew while he held Max and she sat with Rafe. Not long after that, Magnus had Portaled back, and there had been a great deal of thumping and bumping from the library, and Alec had raced off, but Cristina had decided to stay where she was unless called on, because the ways of warlocks were mysterious and their charming boyfriends, too.

Besides, it was good to have something as harmless as a child to distract her from her anxiety. She was sure—relatively sure—that the binding spell could be undone. But it bothered her just the same: What if it couldn't? She and Mark would be miserable forever, tied by a bond they didn't want. And where would they go? What if he wanted to return to Faerie? She couldn't possibly go with him.

Thoughts of Diego nagged at her too: she'd thought she would come back from Faerie to a message from him, but there had been nothing. Could someone disappear out of your life like that twice?

She sighed and leaned down to stroke Rafe's hair, singing softly.

> *"Arrorró mi niño,*
> *arrorró mi sol,*
> *arrorró pedazo*
> *de mi corazón.*

> *Hush-a-bye my baby*
> *Hush-a-bye my sun*
> *Hush-a-bye, oh piece*
> *of my heart."*

Alec had come in while she was singing, and was sitting on the bed beside Max, leaning against the wall.

"I've heard that song before." It was Magnus, standing in the doorway. He looked tired, his cat's eyes heavily lidded. "I can't remember who was singing it."

He came over and bent down to take Rafe from her. He lifted the boy in his arms, and for a moment Rafe's head lolled against his neck. Cristina wondered if this had ever happened before: a Shadowhunter with a warlock for a parent.

> *"Sol solecito, caliéntame un poquito,*
> *Por hoy, por mañana, por toda la semana,"*

Magnus sang. Cristina looked at him in surprise. He had a nice singing voice, though she didn't know the melody. *Sun, little sun, warm me a little, for the noon, for the dawning, for all the week long.*

"Are you all right, Magnus?" Alec asked.

"Fine, and Livvy's fine. Healing. Should be back to normal

tomorrow." Magnus rolled his shoulders back, stretching his muscles.

"Livvy?" Cristina sat up in alarm. "What happened to Livvy?"

Alec and Magnus exchanged a look. "You didn't tell her?" Magnus said in a low voice.

"I didn't want to upset the kids," said Alec, "and I thought you could reassure her better—"

Cristina scrambled to her feet. "Is Livvy hurt? Does Mark know?"

She was reassured by both Magnus and Alec that Livvy was fine and that yes, Mark did know, but she was already halfway out the door.

She bolted down the hallway toward Mark's room. Her wrist was throbbing and aching—she'd been ignoring it, but it flared up now as she worried. Was it pain Mark was feeling, transmitted through the connection between them, the way *parabatai* sometimes felt each other's agony? Or was the binding spell getting worse, more intense?

His door was half-open, light spilling out from beneath it. She found him awake inside, lying on his bed. She could see the deep indentation of the binding rune like a bracelet around his left wrist.

"Cristina?" He sat up. "Are you all right?"

"I am not the one who was hurt," she said. "Alec and Magnus told me about Livvy."

He drew his legs up, making room for her to sit on the blanket beside him. The sudden reduction of pain in her wrist made her feel a little dizzy.

He told her what they had done, Kit, Livvy, and Ty: about the crystal they'd found at Blackthorn Hall, their visit to the Shadow Market and how Livvy had been injured. "I cannot help but think," he finished, "that if Julian had been here, if he hadn't left me in charge, none of it would have happened."

"Julian's the one who said they could go to Blackthorn Hall. And most of us are running missions at fifteen. It's not your fault they disobeyed."

"I didn't tell them not to go to the Shadow Market," he said, shivering a little. He pulled the patchwork blanket up around his shoulders, giving him the look of a sad Harlequin.

"You didn't tell them not to stab each other with knives, either, because they know that," she said tartly. "The Market is off-limits. Forbidden. Although—don't be too hard on Kit. The Shadow Market is the world he knows."

"I don't know how to take care of them," he said. "How do I tell them to obey rules when none of us do? We went to Faerie—a much greater breakage of the Law than a visit to the Shadow Market."

"Maybe you should all try taking care of each other," she said.

He smiled. "You're awfully wise."

"Is Kieran all right?" she said.

"Still awake, I think," he said. "He wanders around the Institute at night. He hasn't rested well since we came here—too much cold iron, I think. Too much city."

The neck of his T-shirt was frayed and loose. She could see where the scars on his back started, the marks of old injuries, the memory of knives. The patchwork blanket had begun slipping down his shoulder. Almost absently, Cristina reached to pull it up.

Her hand brushed along Mark's neck, along the bare skin where his throat met the cotton of his shirt. His skin was hot. He leaned in toward her; she could smell the pine of forests.

His face was close enough to hers that she could make out the changing colors in the irises of his eyes. The rise and fall of her own breath seemed to lift her toward him.

"Can you sleep here tonight?" he said hoarsely. "It will hurt less. For both of us."

His inhuman eyes glittered for a moment, and she thought of what Emma had said to her, that when she looked at him sometimes, she saw wildness and freedom and the unending roads of the sky.

"I can't," she whispered.

"Cristina—" He rose up on his knees. It was too cloudy outside for any moonlight or starlight, but Cristina could still see him, his light hair in tangles, his eyes fixed on her.

He was too close, too tangible. She knew if he touched her, she'd crumble. She wasn't even sure what that would mean, only that the idea of such total dissolution frightened her—and that she could see Kieran when she looked at Mark, like a shadow always beside him.

She slid off the bed. "I'm sorry, Mark," she said, and left the room so quickly she was almost running.

"Annabel seems so sad," Emma said. "So very sad."

They were lying in the cottage bed, side by side. It was a lot more comfortable than beds in the Institute, which was a little ironic, considering it was Malcolm's place. Julian guessed even murderers needed regular mattresses and didn't actually sleep on platforms made of skulls.

"She wanted me to leave the Black Volume alone," said Julian. He was lying on his back; they both were. Emma was in a pair of cotton pajamas she'd bought from the village shop, and Julian wore sweats and an old T-shirt. Their shoulders touched, and their feet; the bed wasn't very wide. Not that Julian would have moved away if he could have. "She said it only brings bad things."

"But you don't think we should do that."

"I don't think we have a choice. The book probably really is better off in the Seelie Court than anywhere in our world." He sighed. "She said she's been talking to the piskies in the area. We're going to have to text the others, see if they know any piskie-trapping secrets. Get hold of a piskie and find out what they know."

"Okay." Emma's voice was fading, her eyes closing. Julian felt the same exhaustion tugging at him. It had been an incredibly long day. "You can send the message from my phone if you want."

Julian hadn't been able to plug his phone in due to not having the right adapter. Things Shadowhunters didn't think about.

"I don't think we should tell the others Annabel came," said Julian. "Not yet. They'll freak out, and I want to see what the piskies say first."

"You have to at least tell them the Unseelie King helped Malcolm get the Black Volume," Emma said sleepily.

"I'll tell them he wrote about it in his diaries," said Julian.

He waited to see if Emma would object to the lie, but she was already asleep. And Julian was nearly there. Emma was here, lying beside him, the way things were supposed to be. He realized how badly he'd slept for the past few weeks without her.

He wasn't sure if he'd drifted off, or for how long if he had. When his eyes fluttered open, he could see the dark glow of the fire in the hearth, nearly burned down to embers. And he could feel Emma, beside him, her arm thrown across his chest.

He froze. She must have moved in her sleep. She was curled against him. He could feel her eyelashes, her soft breath, against his skin.

She murmured and turned her head against his neck. Before they climbed into bed, he'd been frightened that if he touched her, he'd feel again the same willpower-smashing desire he'd felt in the Seelie Court.

What he felt now was both better and worse. It was an overpowering and terrible tenderness. Though when awake Emma had a presence that made her seem tall and even imposing, she was small curled against him, and delicate enough to make his heart turn over with thoughts of how to keep the world from breaking something so fragile.

He wanted to hold her forever, to protect her and keep her close.

He wanted to be able to write as freely about his feelings for her as Malcolm had written about his dawning love for Annabel. *You took my life apart and put it back together.*

She sighed softly, settling into the mattress. He wanted to trace the outline of her mouth, to draw it—it was always different, its heart shape changing with her expressions, but this expression, between sleeping and waking, half-innocent and half-knowing, caught at his soul in a new way.

Malcolm's words echoed in his head. *As if you have discovered a beach you have been visiting all your life is made not of sand but of diamonds, and they blind you with their beauty.*

Diamonds might be blinding in their beauty, but they were also the hardest and sharpest gems in the world. They could cut you or grind you down, smash and slice you apart. Malcolm, deranged with love, had not thought of that. But Julian could think of nothing else.

Kit was awoken by the bang of Livvy's door. He sat up, aware he was aching all over, as Ty strode out of her bedroom.

"You're on the floor," Ty said, looking at him.

Kit couldn't deny it. He and Alec had come to Livvy's room once they'd finished in the infirmary. Then Alec had gone off to check on the children, and it had just been Magnus, quietly sitting with Livvy, occasionally examining her to see if she was healing. And Ty, leaning against the wall, staring unblinking at his sister. It had felt like a hospital room to which Kit shouldn't have access.

So he'd gone outside, remembering how Ty had slept in front of his own door his first days in Los Angeles, and he'd curled up on the worn carpeted floor, not expecting to get much sleep. He didn't even remember passing out, but he must have.

He struggled up into a sitting position. "Wait—"

But Ty was walking off down the hall, as if he hadn't heard Kit at all. After a moment, Kit scrambled to his feet and followed him.

He wasn't entirely sure why. He barely knew Tiberius Black-thorn, he thought, as Ty turned almost blindly and started up a set of stairs. He barely knew his sister, either. And they were Shadow-hunters. And Ty wanted to form some kind of detective team with him, which was a ridiculous idea. Definitely one in which he wasn't interested at all, he told himself, as the staircase ended in a short landing in front of a worn-looking old door.

And it was probably cold outside too, he thought, as Ty pushed the door open and, yes, damp chilly air swirled in. Ty disappeared into the chill and the shadows outside, and Kit followed.

They were back on the roof, though it was no longer night, to Kit's surprise; it was early morning—gray and heavy, with clouds gathering over the Thames and the dome of St. Paul's. The noise of the city rose up, the pressure of millions of people going about their daily business, unaware of Shadowhunters, unaware of magic and danger. Unaware of Ty, who had gone to the railing surround-ing the central part of the roof and was staring out over the city, his hands gripping the iron fleur-de-lis.

"Ty." Kit went toward him, and Tiberius turned around, so his back was against the railing. His shoulders were stiff, and Kit stopped, not wanting to invade his personal space. "Are you all right?"

Ty shook his head. "Cold," he said. His teeth were chattering. "I'm cold."

"Then maybe we should go back downstairs," said Kit. "Inside it's warmer."

"I can't." Ty's voice sounded like it was coming from a long way down deep inside him, an echo half-sunk in water. "Being in that room, I couldn't—it was—"

He shook his head in frustration, as if being unable to find the words was torturing him.

"Livvy's going to be fine," said Kit. "She'll be okay by tomorrow. Magnus said."

"But it's my fault." Ty was pressing his back harder against the railing, but it wasn't holding him up. He slid down it until he was sitting on the ground, his knees pulled up to his chest. He was breathing hard and rocking back and forth, his hands up by his face as if to brush away cobwebs or annoying gnats. "If I was her *parabatai*—I wanted to go to the Scholomance, but that doesn't matter; Livvy matters—"

"It's not your fault," Kit said. Ty just shook his head, hard. Kit tried frantically to remember what he'd read online about meltdowns, because he was pretty sure Ty was on his way to having one. He dropped to his knees on the damp roof—was he supposed to touch Ty, or not touch him?

He could only imagine what it was like for Ty all the time: all the world rushing at him at once, blaring sounds and stabbing lights and nobody remembering to modulate their voices. And to have all the ways you usually managed that ripped away by grief or fear, leaving you exposed as a Shadowhunter going into battle without their gear.

He remembered something about darkness, about pressure and weighted blankets and silence. Though he had no idea how he was going to get hold of any of those things up on top of a building.

"Tell me," Kit said. *Tell me what you need.*

"Put your arms around me," said Ty. His hands were pale blurs in the air, as if Kit were looking at a time-lapse photo. "Hold on to me."

He was still rocking. After a moment, Kit put his arms around Ty, not quite knowing what else to do.

It was like holding a loosed arrow: Ty felt hot and sharp in his arms, and he was vibrating with some strange emotion. After what felt like a long time he relaxed slightly. His hands touched

Kit, their motion slowing, his fingers winding themselves into Kit's sweater.

"Tighter," Ty said. He was hanging on to Kit as if he were a life raft, his forehead digging painfully into Kit's shoulder. He sounded desperate. "I need to feel it."

Kit had never been a casual hugger, and no one had ever, that he could remember, come to him for comforting. He wasn't a comforting sort of person. He'd always assumed that. And he barely knew Ty.

But then, Ty didn't do things for no reason, even if people whose brains were differently wired couldn't see his reasons immediately. Kit remembered the way Livvy rubbed Ty's hands tightly when he was stressed and thought: *The pressure is a sensation; the sensation must be grounding. Calming.* That made sense. So Kit found himself holding Ty harder, until Ty relaxed under the tight grip of his hands; held him more tightly than he'd ever held anyone, held him as if they'd been lost in the sea of the sky, and only holding on to each other could keep them afloat above the wreckage of London.

20

Evermore

Diana sat in her small room above the weapons shop and flipped through the file Jia had given her.

She hadn't been in this room since the end of the Dark War, but it felt comfortable and familiar—the blanket her grandmother had made folded at the foot of the bed, the first blunt wooden daggers her father had given her to practice with on the wall, her mother's shawl across the back of a chair. She wore a pair of bright red satin pajamas she'd found in an old trunk and felt amusingly dressed up.

Her amusement faded quickly, though, as she examined the pages inside the cream-colored file. First was Zara's story about how she'd killed Malcolm, which had been signed off on by Samantha and Dane as witnesses. Not that Diana would have believed Samantha or her brother if they'd said the sky was blue.

Zara was claiming that the Centurions had chased Malcolm away the first time he'd attacked, and that the next night she'd fearlessly patrolled the borders of the Institute until she'd found him lurking in the shadows and bested him in a one-on-one swordfight. She claimed his body had then disappeared.

Malcolm was hardly a lurk-in-the-shadows type, and from what Diana had seen on the night he'd returned, his magic was still working. He'd never fight Zara with a blade when he could blast her with fire.

But none of that was hard evidence that she was lying. Diana frowned, turning the pages, and then sat up straight. There was more here than just the report on Malcolm's death. There were pages and pages about Zara. Dozens of reports of her achievements. All together like this, it was an impressive package. And yet . . .

As Diana read through, taking careful notes, a pattern started to emerge. Every success of Zara's, every triumph, took place when no one was around to witness it except those in her inner circle—Samantha, Dane, or Manuel. Often others would arrive in time to see the empty demon nest, or the evidence of a battle, but that was all.

There were no reports of Zara ever being wounded or hurt in any battle. Diana thought of the scars she'd gotten through her life as a Shadowhunter and frowned more deeply. And more deeply yet when she reached Marisol Garza Solcedo's year-old report—Marisol claimed to have saved a group of mundanes from an attacking Druj demon in Portugal. She was knocked unconscious. When she awoke, she said, Zara's destruction of the Druj was being celebrated.

The report had been submitted, along with a signed statement by Zara, Jessica, Samantha, Dane, and Manuel, stating that Marisol was imagining things. Zara, they said, had killed the Druj after a fierce fight; again, Zara had no wounds.

She takes credit for what other people do, Diana thought. Her window rattled, wind probably. *I ought to go to bed*, she thought. The clock in the Gard, new since the Dark War, had rung the early hours of dawn some time ago. But she kept reading, fascinated. Zara would hang back, wait for the battle to be over, and announce the victory as her own. With her group backing her up, the Clave accepted her claims at face value.

But if it could be proved that she hadn't killed Malcolm—in some way that kept Julian and the others protected—then perhaps the Cohort would be disgraced. Certainly the Dearborns' bid to seize the Los Angeles Institute would fail—

Her window rattled again. She looked up and saw Gwyn on the other side of the glass.

She stood up with a yelp of surprise, sending her papers flying. *Get a grip*, she told herself. There was no way that the leader of the Wild Hunt was actually outside her window.

She blinked, and looked again. He was still there, and as she moved toward the window, she saw that he was hovering in the air just below her sill, on the back of a massive gray horse. He wore dark brown leather, and his antlered helmet was nowhere to be seen. His expression was grave and curious.

He gestured for her to open the window. Diana hesitated, then reached to undo the latch and fling up the sash. She didn't have to let him in, she reasoned. They could just talk through the window.

Cool air rushed into her room, and the smell of pine and morning air. His bicolored eyes fixed on her. "My lady," he said. "I had hoped you would accompany me on a ride."

Diana tucked a lock of hair behind her ear. "Why?"

"For the pleasure of your company," Gwyn said. He peered at her. "I see you are richly attired in silk. Are you expecting another guest?"

She shook her head, amused. Well, the pajamas *were* nice.

"You look beautiful," he said. "I am fortunate."

She supposed he wasn't lying. He *couldn't* lie.

"You couldn't have arranged this meeting in advance?" she asked. "Sent me a message, maybe?"

He looked puzzled. He had long eyelashes and a square chin—a pleasant face. A handsome face. Diana often tried not to think about those things, as they only caused trouble, but now she couldn't help it. "I only discovered you were here in Idris this dawn," he said.

"But you're not allowed to be here!" She looked nervously up and down empty Flintlock Street. If anyone saw him . . .

He grinned at that. "As long as my horse's hooves do not touch Alicante ground the alarm will not be raised."

Still, she felt a bubble of tension in her chest. He was asking her on a date—she couldn't pretend otherwise. And though she wanted to go, the fear—that old fear that walked hand in hand with distrust and grief—held her back.

He reached out a hand. "Come with me. The sky awaits."

She looked at him. He wasn't young, but he didn't look old, either. He seemed ageless, as faeries did sometimes, and though he seemed solid and thoughtful in himself, he carried with him the promise of the air and the sky. *When else will you ever have a chance to ride a faerie horse?* Diana asked herself. *When else will you ever fly?*

"You're going to be in so much trouble," she whispered, "if they find out you're here."

He shrugged, hand still outstretched. "Then you had better come quickly," he said.

She began to climb out the window.

Breakfast was late; Kit managed to snag a few hours of sleep and a shower before wandering into the dining room to find everyone else already sitting down.

Well, everyone but Evelyn. Bridget was serving tea, pinched-faced as always. Alec and Magnus each had a child on their lap, and introduced them to Kit: Max was the small, blue warlock who was spilling brown sauce down the front of Magnus's designer shirt, and Rafe was the brown-eyed child who was tearing his toast into pieces.

Kieran was nowhere to be seen, which wasn't unusual at meals. Mark was seated beside Cristina, who was quietly drinking coffee.

She looked neat and self-contained as always, despite the red mark on her wrist. She was an interesting mystery, Kit thought, a non-Blackthorn like himself, but inextricably tied to the Blackthorns nevertheless.

And then there were Livvy and Ty. Ty had the buds of his earphones in. Livvy looked tired but entirely healthy. Only a slight shadow under Ty's eyes let Kit know he hadn't dreamed the whole of last night.

"What we found at Blackthorn Hall was an *aletheia* crystal," Ty was saying as Kit sat down. "In the past the crystals were used by the Clave to hold evidence. The evidence of memories."

There was a babble of curious voices. Cristina's rose above the others—it was an impressive talent of hers, to make herself heard without ever shouting. "Memories of what?"

"A sort of trial," said Livvy. "In Idris, with the Inquisitor there. Lots of familiar families—Herondales, Blackthorns, of course, Dearborns."

"Any Lightwoods?" asked Alec.

"One or two looked like they might be." Livvy frowned.

"The Herondales have always been famous for their good looks," said Bridget, "but if you ask me, the Lightwoods are the more sexually charismatic of the bunch."

Alec spit out his tea. Magnus seemed to be keeping a straight face, but with an effort.

"I should examine the memories," Magnus said. "See if there's anyone I recognize from that era."

"If Annabel is angry at Shadowhunters," said Livvy, "it seems to me she has good reason."

"Many have good reason to be angry with the Nephilim," said Mark. "Malcolm did as well. But those who harmed her are dead, and their descendants blameless. That is the problem with revenge—you wind up destroying the innocent as well as the guilty."

"But does she know that?" Ty frowned. "We don't understand her. We don't know what she thinks or feels."

He looked anxious, the shadows under his eyes more pronounced. Kit wanted to go across the table and put his arms around Ty the way he had the night before, on the roof. He felt intensely protective of the other boy, in a way that was strange and unnerving. He'd cared about people before, mostly his father, but he'd never wanted to protect them.

He wanted to kill anyone who would try to hurt Ty. It was a very peculiar feeling.

"Everyone should watch the scenes in the crystal," Magnus announced. "In the meantime, Alec and I have some news."

"You're getting married," said Livvy, beaming. "I love weddings."

"Nope, still not getting married right now," said Alec. Kit wondered why not; they were clearly a committed couple. But it was none of his business, really.

"Evelyn has left us," said Magnus. Somehow he managed to retain his sangfroid despite having a grizzling toddler on his lap. "According to Jia, the Institute is temporarily in Alec's charge."

"They've been trying to lumber me with an Institute somewhere for years," said Alec. "Jia must be thrilled."

"Evelyn has left us?" Dru's eyes were huge. "You mean she died?"

Magnus started to cough. "Of course not. She went to visit your great-aunt Marjorie, actually, in the countryside."

"Is this like when the family dog dies and they say he's living on a farm now?" Kit asked, curious.

It was Alec's turn to choke. Kit strongly suspected he was laughing and trying not to show it.

"Not at all," said Magnus. "She just decided she'd prefer to miss the excitement."

"She is with Marjorie," Mark confirmed. "I got a fire-message about it this morning. She left Bridget, obviously, to help around the house."

Kit thought of the way Evelyn had reacted to having a faerie in the Institute. He could only imagine how she'd felt about two warlocks added to the situation. She'd probably left tire marks behind when she raced out of the place.

"Does that mean we don't have to eat our porridge?" said Tavvy, eyeing the grayish stuff with dislike.

Magnus grinned. "In fact . . ."

He snapped his fingers, and a bag from the Primrose Bakery appeared in the middle of the table. It tipped over, spilling muffins, croissants, and iced cakes.

There was a great shout of happiness and everyone lunged for the pastries. A small war over the chocolate cookies was won by Ty, who shared them with Livvy.

Max crawled onto the table, reaching for a muffin. Magnus leaned on his elbows, his cat eyes watchful. "And after breakfast," he said, "maybe we can go into the library and discuss what we know about the current situation."

Everyone nodded; only Mark looked at him with a slightly narrow gaze. Kit understood—Magnus had gotten rid of Evelyn for them, he'd brought breakfast, he'd put them in a good mood. Now he was going to see what they knew. A straightforward con.

Looking at the cheerful faces around the table, for a moment Kit hated his own father, for destroying his ability to ever believe someone might be willing to give something for nothing.

Kieran found the whole business of eating dinner and breakfast in a group bizarre and of little interest. Mark had been bringing him plates of food as plain as Bridget could make them—meat and rice and bread, uncooked fruit and vegetables.

But Kieran only picked at them. When Mark came into Kieran's room after breakfast, the prince was looking out at the city through his window with a weary loathing. His hair had paled to blue-white, curling like the break of surf at the edge of the water around his ears and temples.

"Listen to this," Kieran said. He had a book open on his lap.

> *"The land of Faery,*
> *Where nobody gets old and godly and grave,*
> *Where nobody gets old and crafty and wise,*
> *Where nobody gets old and bitter of tongue."*

He glanced up at Mark with his luminous eyes. "That's ridiculous."

"That's Yeats," said Mark, handing over some raspberries. "He was a very famous mundane poet."

"He didn't know anything about faeries. Nobody grows bitter of tongue? Ha!" Kieran swallowed the raspberries and slid off the windowsill. "Where do we journey now?"

"I was going to the library," said Mark. "There's a sort of— meeting—about what we're going to do next."

"Then I would like to go to it," said Kieran.

Mark's mind raced. Was there any reason Kieran shouldn't come? As far as Magnus and Alec knew, his relationship with Kieran was whatever he said it was. Nor was it any good for Kieran, or for their strained relationship, for the faerie prince to spend all his time in a small room, hating seminal Irish poets.

"Well," Mark said. "If you're sure."

When they walked into the library, Magnus was examining the *aletheia* crystal while the others tried to fill him in on what had been going on before he'd arrived. The warlock was lying full-length on one of the tables, holding the crystal delicately above him.

Cristina, Ty, Livvy, and Dru were seated around the long library table. Alec was sitting on the floor of the room with three children clustered around him: his own two boys, and Tavvy, who was delighted to have someone to play with. The seven-year-old was explaining to Max and Rafe how he made towns and cities out of books, showing them how you could make tunnels with books splayed open on their faces for trains to go through.

Magnus gestured Mark over to look into the *aletheia* crystal, which was glowing with an odd light. The sounds in the room around him faded as Mark watched the trial, saw Annabel beg and protest, saw the Blackthorns doom her to her fate.

He felt chilled all over when he finally looked away. It took several moments for the library to come back into focus. To Mark's surprise, Kieran had picked up Max and was holding him in the air, obviously delighted by his blue skin and the buds of his horns.

Max stuck his hand into Kieran's wavy hair and pulled. Kieran just laughed. "That's right, it changes color, little nixie-like warlock," he said. "Look." And his hair went from blue-black to bright blue in an instant. Max giggled.

"I didn't know you could do that on purpose," said Mark, who had always thought of Kieran's hair as a reflection of his moods, uncontrollable as the tides.

"You don't know a lot of things about me, Mark Blackthorn," Kieran said, setting Max down.

Alec and Magnus had exchanged a look at that, the sort of look that made Mark feel as if they had reached a silent and agreed-upon consensus about his relationship with Kieran.

"So," Magnus said, looking at Kieran with some interest. "You're the son of the Unseelie King?"

Kieran had what Mark thought of as his Court face on, blank and superior as befitted a prince. "And you are the warlock Magnus Bane."

"Quite," Magnus said. "Although that was an easy guess, since there's one of me and fifty of you."

Ty looked puzzled.

"Fifty sons of the Unseelie King," explained Livvy. "I think that was a joke."

"Not one of my best," said Magnus to Kieran. "I apologize—I'm not a big fan of your father."

"My father does not have fans." Kieran leaned against the edge of the table. "He has subjects. And enemies."

"And sons."

"His sons are his enemies," said Kieran, without inflection.

Magnus looked at him with a flicker of extra interest. "All right," he said, sitting up. "Diana explained some of this to us, but it's more complicated than I thought. Annabel Blackthorn, who was brought back from the dead by Malcolm, who was sort of dead before but is now very definitely dead, has the Black Volume. And the Seelie Queen wants it?"

"She does," said Mark. "She was very clear about that."

"And she made you a deal," Alec said, from the floor. "She always makes a deal."

"If we give her the Black Volume, she will use it against the Unseelie King," said Mark, and hesitated. YOU CAN TRUST MAGNUS AND ALEC, Julian had texted earlier. TELL THEM ANYTHING. "She has sworn not to try to use it to harm us. In fact, she has promised aid to us. She made Kieran her messenger. He'll testify in front of the Council about the Unseelie King's plans to make war on Alicante. Once the Queen has the Black Volume, she will authorize her Seelie soldiers to fight alongside Shadowhunters against the King—but the Clave will have to end all laws that forbid cooperation with faeries if they want her help."

"Which they will," said Magnus. "Fighting a war against Faerie would be much easier with faeries on your side."

Mark nodded. "We are hoping not just to defeat the King, but also to crush the Cohort and end the Cold Peace."

"Ah, the Cohort," said Magnus, exchanging a look with Alec. "We know them well. Horace Dearborn and his daughter, Zara."

"Horace?" Mark was startled.

"Sadly," said Magnus, "that is his name. Hence his life of evil."

"Not that the Dearborns are all of it," said Alec. "Plenty of bigots in the Clave, happy to gather under the umbrella of tossing out the Downworlders and returning the Clave to its former glory."

"Glory?" Kieran raised an eyebrow. "Do they mean the time of freely killing Downworlders? When our blood ran in the streets and their houses were stuffed with the spoils of their one-sided war?"

"Yes," said Magnus, "though they wouldn't describe it that way."

"Heading up the Alliance, we've heard more than a little about the Cohort," said Alec. "Their pushes to limit warlocks' use of their magic, to centralize blood supply for vampires so it can be monitored by the Clave—those have not gone unnoticed."

"They must not be allowed to get their hands on an Institute," said Magnus. "That could be potentially disastrous." He sighed and swung his legs over the side of the table. "I understand we must give the Black Volume to the Queen. But I don't like it, especially since it seems doubly important here."

"You mean because Annabel and Malcolm stole it from the Cornwall Institute," said Ty. "And then Malcolm stole it again, from the Institute in Los Angeles."

"The first time they were going to trade it to someone who they thought could protect them from the Clave," said Livvy. "The second time was with the Unseelie King's help. At least, according to Emma and Jules."

"And how did they find that out?" asked Magnus.

"It was in one of the books they found," said Cristina. "A diary.

It explains why we found an Unseelie Court glove at the ruins of Malcolm's house. He must have met with the King or one of his sons there."

"Odd thing to write in a diary," Magnus muttered. "'Traitorous plans with the Unseelie King afoot today, what ho.'"

"Odder that Malcolm disappeared from the Silent City after the first theft," said Mark, "and left Annabel to take the blame and the punishment."

"Why odd?" said Livvy. "He was a terrible person."

"But he did love Annabel," Cristina said. "Everything he did, the crimes, the murders, all his choices were made for love of her. And when he found out she hadn't become an Iron Sister, but had been murdered by her family, he went to the King of Faeries and asked for help in bringing her back. Don't you remember?"

Mark did remember, the story in the old book Tavvy had found, which had turned out to be true. "Which explains why Malcolm broke into the Los Angeles Institute to get the book five years ago," he said. "To bring Annabel back. But what did Malcolm want it for, two hundred years ago? Who was he planning to trade it to? Most necromancers couldn't help him with protection. And if it was a warlock, it would have to have been one stronger than Malcolm himself."

"'Fade's powerful ally,'" Ty said, quoting the scene in the crystal.

"We don't think it could have been the Unseelie King?" Livvy said. "Both times?"

"The Unseelie King didn't hate Shadowhunters in 1812," said Magnus. "At least, not that much."

"And Malcolm told Emma that when he went to the Unseelie King after he found out that Annabel wasn't dead, he thought the King might kill him, because he disliked warlocks," said Cristina. "He wouldn't have a reason to dislike warlocks if he'd worked with Malcolm before, would he?"

Magnus stood up. "All right, enough guesswork," he said. "We have two duties to carry out today. First, we shouldn't lose sight of the binding spell on Mark and Cristina. It's more than just a nuisance, it's a danger to them both."

Mark couldn't help glancing at Cristina. She was looking down at the table, not at him. He remembered the night before, the warmth of her body beside him in bed, her breath in his ear.

He came back to reality with a start, realizing that a discussion of where they were going to get the ingredients for an anti-binding spell was underway. "Given what happened at the Shadow Market yesterday," Magnus added, "none of us will be welcomed back there again. There is, however, a shop here in London that sells what I need. If I give you the address, can Kit, Ty, and Livvy find it?"

Livvy and Ty clamored their agreement, clearly thrilled to have a mission. Kit was quieter, but the corner of his mouth quirked up. Somehow, this youngest Herondale had become so attached to the twins, even Magnus thought of them as a team.

"Do you really think it's wise for them to go?" Mark interrupted. "After what happened yesterday, with them sloping off to the Shadow Market and practically getting Livvy killed?"

"But, Mark—" Ty protested.

"Well," said Magnus, "you and Cristina should stay inside the Institute. Binding spells are dangerous, and you shouldn't be too far away from each other. Alec's the Institute head; he should stay here, and anyway—the owner of the shop has a certain, let's say, history with me. Better I don't go."

"I could go," said Dru, in a small voice.

"Not by yourself, Dru," said Mark. "And these three"—he indicated Kit, Ty, and Livvy—"will just get you in trouble."

"I can put a tracking spell on one of them," said Magnus. "If they wander off the path they're supposed to follow, it'll make an awful noise mundanes can hear."

"Delightful," said Mark as the twins protested. Kit didn't say anything—he rarely complained. Mark suspected he was silently plotting to get even instead, possibly with everyone he'd ever met.

Magnus examined a large blue ring on his finger. "We'll do library research. More about the history of the Black Volume. We don't know who created it, but perhaps who owned it in the past, what it was used for, anything that might point to who Malcolm was working with in 1812."

"And remember what Julian and Emma asked us for help with," said Cristina, tapping the phone in her pocket. "It should only take a few minutes to look it up. . . ."

Mark couldn't help staring at her. She was tucking her dark hair behind her ears, and as she did, the sleeve of her sweater slipped down and he saw the red mark on her wrist. He wanted to go to her, to kiss the mark, to take her pain onto himself.

He looked away from her, but not before he caught the edge of a glance from Kieran. Ty and Livvy and Kit were getting out of their chairs, excitedly chattering, eager to go on their trip. Dru was sitting with her arms crossed. And Magnus was looking between Cristina, Mark, and Kieran thoughtfully, his cat eyes slow and considering.

"We shouldn't need to look it up at all," Magnus said. "We have a primary source right here. Kieran, what do you know about catching piskies?"

Emma woke late in the morning, surrounded by warmth. Light was breaking through the unshaded windows and making patterns on the walls like dancing waves. Through the window she could see flashes of blue sky and blue water: a holiday view.

She yawned, stretched—and went still as she realized why she was so warm. She and Julian had somehow wrapped themselves around each other during the night.

Emma froze in horror. Her left arm was thrown across Julian's body, but she couldn't just remove it. He had turned toward her, his own arms curved around her back, securing her. Her cheek brushed the smooth skin of his collarbone. Their legs were tangled together as well, her foot resting on his ankle.

She began to slowly detangle herself. Oh God. If Julian woke up it would be so awkward, and everything had been going so well. Their conversation on the train—finding the cottage—talking about Annabel—everything had been comfortable. She didn't want to lose that, not now.

She edged sideways, slipping her fingers out of his—closer to the edge of the bed—and went over the side with an ungainly tumble. She landed with a thump and a scream that woke Julian, who peered over the side of the bed in confusion.

"Why are you on the floor?"

"I've heard rolling out of bed in the morning helps you build up resistance to surprise attacks," Emma said, lying sprawled on the hardwood.

"Oh yeah?" He sat up and rubbed his eyes. "What does screaming 'holy crap!' do?"

"That part's optional," she said. She got to her feet with as much dignity as she could muster. "So," she said. "What's for breakfast?"

He grinned his low-key grin and stretched. She didn't look at where his shirt rode up. There was no reason to sail down Sexy Thoughts River to the Sea of Perversion when it wasn't going to go anywhere. "You hungry?"

"When am I not hungry?" She went over to the table and rooted in her bag for her phone. Several texts from Cristina. Most were about how Cristina was FINE and Emma had NOTHING TO WORRY ABOUT and she should STOP TEXTING BECAUSE MAGNUS WAS GOING TO FIX THE BINDING SPELL. Emma sent her a worry face and scrolled down.

"Any word on piskie-catching techniques?" Julian asked.

"Not yet."

Julian didn't say anything. Emma stripped down to her boy shorts and tank top. She saw Julian glance away from her, though it wasn't anything he'd never seen before—her clothes covered more than a bikini. She grabbed up her towel and soap. "I'm going to shower."

Maybe she was imagining his reaction. He just nodded and went over to the kitchen, firing up the stove. "No pancakes," he said. "They don't have the right stuff to make them."

"Surprise me," Emma said, and headed to the bathroom. When she emerged fifteen minutes later, scrubbed clean, her hair tied into two damp braids that dripped onto her T-shirt, Julian had set the table with breakfast—toast, eggs, hot chocolate for her and coffee for him. She slid gratefully onto a chair.

"You smell like eucalyptus," he said, handing her a fork.

"There's eucalyptus shower gel in the bathroom." Emma took a bite of eggs. "Malcolm's, I guess." She paused. "I've never really thought of serial killers as having shower gel."

"No one likes a filthy warlock," said Julian.

Emma winked. "Some might disagree."

"No comment," Julian said, spreading peanut butter and Nutella on his toast. "We got a reply to our question." He held up her phone. "Instructions on how to catch piskies. From Mark, but probably really from Kieran. So first, breakfast, and afterward—piskie hunting."

"I am so ready to hunt down those tiny adorable creatures and give them what for," said Emma. "SO READY."

"Emma . . ."

"I may even tie bows on their heads."

"We have to interrogate them."

"Can I get a selfie with one of them first?"

"Eat your toast, Emma."

* * *

Everything sucked, Dru thought. She was lying under the desk in the parlor, arms crossed behind her head. A few feet above her she could see where a message, blurred over time and the years, had been scratched into the wood.

It was quiet in the room, only the clock ticking. The quiet was both a reminder of how lonely she was, and a relief. No one was telling her to go take care of Tavvy, or asking her if she'd play demons and Shadowhunters for the millionth time. No one was demanding she deliver messages or ferry papers back and forth in the library. No one was talking over her, and not listening.

No one was telling her she was too young. In Dru's opinion, age was a matter of maturity, not years, and she was plenty mature. She'd been eight years old when she'd defended her little brother's crib with a sword. She'd been eight when she'd seen Julian kill the creature that wore her father's face, when she'd run through the capital city of Idris as it fell apart in flames and blood.

And she'd stayed calm only a few days ago when Livvy had come to tell her that Uncle Arthur had never run the Institute; it had always been Julian. She'd been very matter-of-fact about it, as if it were no big deal, and she'd glossed over the fact that Diana hadn't even bothered to invite Dru to the meeting where she'd apparently broken this news. As far as Livvy was concerned, it seemed, the news was useful primarily for guilting Dru into further babysitting.

It wasn't so much that she hated looking after Tavvy. She didn't. It was more that she felt she deserved some credit when she made an effort. Not to mention, she'd put up with Great-Aunt Marjorie calling her fat for two months over the summer, and she hadn't murdered her, which in Dru's opinion was an epic sign of maturity and self-restraint.

She glanced down at her own round body and sighed. She had never been thin. Most Shadowhunters were—working out for fourteen hours a day tended to have that effect—but she had always been curved and rounded no matter what she did. She was strong and muscular, her body was fit and capable, but she'd always have the hips, breasts, and softness that she did. She was resigned to it. Unfortunately, the Great-Aunt Marjories of the world weren't.

There was a *clunk*. Something in the room had fallen. Dru froze. Was someone else in here with her? She heard a soft voice swearing—not in English, but in Spanish. It couldn't be Cristina, though. Cristina never swore, and besides, the voice was masculine.

Diego? Her crush-harboring heart skipped a beat, and she popped up from behind the desk.

A yelp of shock burst from her. The other person in the room also yelped, and sat down hard on the arm of the chair.

It wasn't Diego. It was a Shadowhunter boy about Julian's age, tall and rangy, with a shock of black hair that contrasted with his brown skin. He was covered in Marks, and not just Marks but tattoos, too—words ran up and down his forearms and snaked across his collarbone.

"What—what's going on?" Dru demanded, brushing dust bunnies out of her hair. "Who are you? What are you doing here?"

She thought about screaming. Any Shadowhunter could come into any Institute, of course, but usually they at least rang the bell.

The boy looked alarmed. He held up a hand as if to forestall her, and she saw the gleam of the ring on his finger, carved with a pattern of roses. "I—" he began.

"Oh, you're Jaime," she said, relief going through her in a whoosh. "Diego's brother, Jaime."

The boy's face clouded. "You know my brother?"

He had a slight accent, more noticeable than Diego's or Cristina's. It lent a richness to the texture of his voice.

"Sort of," Dru said, and cleared her throat. "I live in the Los Angeles Institute."

"One of the Blackthorns?"

"I'm Drusilla." She stuck out her hand. "Drusilla Blackthorn. Call me Dru."

He gave a dry sort of chuckle and shook her hand. His was warm. "A pretty name for a pretty girl."

Dru felt herself blush. Jaime wasn't as perfectly handsome as Perfect Diego—his nose was a little too big, his mouth too wide and mobile—but his eyes were a brilliant sparkling brown, his lashes wickedly long and black. And there was something about him, a sort of energy that Diego didn't have, handsome as he was.

"Cristina must have told you terrible things about me," he said.

She shook her head, drawing her hand back. "She hasn't said much about you to me at all."

Cristina wouldn't have, Dru thought. She wouldn't think of Dru as old enough to confide in, to share her secrets with. Dru only knew what the other girls had dropped in casual conversation.

Not that she'd admit that to Jaime.

"That's very disappointing," he said. "If I were her, I wouldn't be able to stop talking about me." His eyes crinkled at the corners. "Do you want to sit down?"

Feeling slightly flustered, Dru sat beside him.

"I'm going to confide in you," he said. It seemed like an announcement, as if he'd made up his mind on the spot and felt it was important to publicize as soon as possible.

"Really?" Dru wasn't sure anyone had ever confided in her before. Most of her siblings considered her too young, and Tavvy had no secrets.

"I came here to see Cristina, but she can't know I'm here quite yet. I need to communicate with my brother first."

"Is Diego all right?" Dru said. "The last time I saw him—I mean,

I heard he was all right after the fight with Malcolm, but I haven't seen him or heard from him, and he and Cristina—"

She clammed up.

He laughed softly. "It's all right, I know. *Ellos terminaron.*"

"They broke up," she translated. "Yes."

He looked surprised. "You speak Spanish?"

"I'm learning it. I'd like to go to the Mexico City Institute for my travel year, or maybe to Argentina to help rebuild."

She saw his long eyelashes sweep down as he winked. "Not eighteen yet, then?" he said. "It's all right. Neither am I."

Not even close. But Drusilla just smiled nervously. "What were you going to confide?"

"I'm in hiding. I can't tell you why, only that it's important. Please do not tell anyone I'm here until I can talk to Cristina."

"You haven't committed a crime or something, have you?"

He didn't laugh. "If I said no, but I might know who did, would you believe me?"

He was watching her intently. She probably shouldn't help him, she thought. After all, she didn't know him, and from the few things Diego had said about him, it had been clear he thought Jaime was trouble.

On the other hand, here was someone willing to trust her, to put their plans and safety in her hands rather than shutting her out because she was too young, or because she should be looking after Tavvy.

She exhaled and met Jaime's eyes. "All right," she said. "How were you planning on not being seen until you can talk to Cristina?"

His smile was blinding. She wondered how she'd ever thought he wasn't as good-looking as Diego.

"That's where you can help me," he said.

Having climbed up the side of the cottage and onto the roof, Emma reached out to help Julian up after her. He declined the hand, though, flipping himself easily up onto the shingled surface.

The roof of Malcolm's cottage was tilted at a slight grade, overhanging the front and back of the house. Emma walked down to the edge of the roof where it protruded over the front door.

From here, the trap was visible. Mark had told them what bait was best: Piskies loved milk and bread and honey. They also loved dead mice, but Emma was unwilling to go that far. She liked mice, despite Church's deep-seated antagonism toward them.

"And now we wait," Julian said, sitting down on the edge of the roof. The bowls of milk and honey and the plate of bread were out, shining temptingly on top of a pile of leaves near the path to the door.

Emma sat down beside Jules. The sky was cloudless blue, stretching away to where it met the darker sea on the horizon. Slow mackerel boats traced white patterns on the sea's surface, and the dull booming roar of the waves was a soft counterpoint to the warm wind.

She couldn't help but be reminded of all the times she and Jules had sat on the roof of the Institute, talking and looking at the ocean. An entirely different shore, perhaps, but all seas were connected.

"I'm sure there's some kind of law about not trapping piskies without permission from the Clave," said Emma.

"*Lex malla, lex nulla,*" said Julian with a regretful wave of his hand. It was the Blackthorn family motto: A bad law is no law.

"I wonder what other family mottoes are," Emma mused. "Do you know any?"

"The Lightwood family motto is 'We mean well.'"

"Very funny."

Julian looked over at her. "No, really, it actually is."

"Seriously? So what's the Herondale family motto? 'Chiseled but angsty'?"

He shrugged. 'If you don't know what your last name is, it's probably Herondale'?"

Emma burst out laughing. "What about Carstairs?" she asked, tapping Cortana. "'We have a sword'? 'Blunt instruments are for losers'?"

"Morgenstern," offered Julian. "'When in doubt, start a war'?"

"How about 'Has even one of us ever been any good, like ever, seriously'?"

"Seems long," said Julian. "And kind of on the nose."

They were both giggling almost too hard to talk. Emma bent forward—and gave a gasp, which combined with the giggle into a sort of cough. She slapped her hand over her mouth. "Piskies!" she whispered through her fingers, and pointed.

Julian moved soundlessly to the edge of the roof, Emma beside him. Standing near their trap were a group of scrawny, pallid figures dressed in rags. They had near-translucent skin, pale hair like straw, and bare feet. Huge black pupilless eyes stared from faces as delicate as china.

They looked exactly like the drawings on the wall of the inn where they'd eaten the day before. She hadn't seen a single one in Faerie—indeed, it seemed true that they had been exiled to the mundane world.

Without a word, they fell on the dishes of bread, milk, and honey—and the ground gave way under them. The frail construction of branches and leaves Emma had laid over the mouth of the pit Julian had dug fell away, and the piskies tumbled into their trap.

Gwyn made no attempt at small talk as his horse soared through the air over Alicante and then the woods of Brocelind Forest. Diana was grateful for it. With the wind in her hair, cool and soft, and the forest spread out below her in deep green shadow, she felt freer than she had in what seemed like a long time. Talking would have been a distraction.

Dawn gave way to daylight as she watched the world rushing by under her: the sudden flash of water, the graceful shapes of fir trees and white pine. When Gwyn pointed the horse's head downward, and it began to descend, she felt a pang of disappointment and a sudden flash of kinship with Mark. No wonder he had missed the Hunt; no wonder that even when he was back with his family, he had yearned for the sky.

They landed in a small clearing between linden trees. Gwyn slid from the horse's back and offered Diana his hand to clamber down to the ground: The thick green moss was soft on her bare feet. She wandered among the white flowers and admired the blue sky while he spread out a linen cloth and food unpacked from his saddlebag.

She couldn't quite hold back the urge to laugh—here she was, Diana Wrayburn, of the law-abiding and respectable Wrayburn family, about to have a picnic with the leader of the Wild Hunt.

"Come," he said, when he was done and seated on the ground. His horse had wandered off to crop grass at the edge of the clearing. "You must be hungry."

To Diana's surprise, she found she was—and hungrier when she tasted the food: delicious fruit, cured meat, thick bread and honey, and glasses of wine that tasted the way rubies looked.

Maybe it was the wine, but she found that Gwyn, despite his quiet nature, was easy to talk to. He asked her about herself, though not her past; her passions instead, her interests and her dreams. She found herself telling him of her love for teaching, how she wished to teach at the Academy someday. He asked her about the Blackthorns, and how Mark was settling in, and nodded gravely at her answers.

He was not beautiful in the manner of many faeries, but she found his face more pleasing for it. His hair was thick and brown, his hands wide and capable and strong. There were scars on his skin—at his neck and chest, and on the backs of his palms—but that made her think of her own scars and Shadowhunting. It was comforting in its familiarity.

"Why are there no women in the Wild Hunt?" she asked. It was something she had always wondered.

"Women are too savage," he said with a grin. "We reap the dead. It was discovered that when Rhiannon's Ladies ran with the Hunt, they were unwilling to wait until the dead *were* dead."

Diana laughed. "Rhiannon. The name is familiar."

"The women left the hunt and became Adar Rhiannon. The Birds of Rhiannon. Some call them 'Valkyrie.'"

She smiled at him sadly. "Faerie can be so lovely," she said. "And yet also terrible."

"You are thinking of Mark?"

"Mark loves his family," she said. "And they are happy to have him back. But he does miss the Hunt. Which is hard to understand sometimes. When he came to us, he was so scarred, in body and mind."

"Many Shadowhunters are scarred," he said. "That does not mean they no longer wish to be Shadowhunters."

"I'm not sure it's the same."

"I am not sure it is so different." He leaned back against a large gray boulder. "Mark was a fine Hunter, but his heart was not in it. It is not the Hunt he misses, but the freedom and the open sky, and perhaps Kieran."

"You knew they had fought," said Diana. "But when you came to us, you were so sure Mark would save him."

"Shadowhunters desire to save everyone. And more so when there is love."

"You think Mark still loves Kieran?"

"I think you cannot root out love entirely. I think where there has been love, there will always be embers, as the remains of a bonfire outlast the flame."

"But they die eventually. They become ashes."

Gwyn sat forward. His eyes, blue and black, were grave on hers. "Have you ever loved?"

She shook her head. She could feel the shaking all through her nerves—the anticipation, and the fear. "Not like that." She should tell him why, she thought. But the words didn't come.

"That is a shame," he said. "I think to be loved by you would be a tremendous honor."

"You barely know me at all," Diana said. *I shouldn't be affected by his words. I shouldn't want this.* But she did, in a way she had tried to bury long ago.

"I saw who you are in your eyes the night I came to the Institute," said Gwyn. "Your bravery."

"Bravery," echoed Diana. "The kind that kills demons, yes. Yet there are many kinds of bravery."

His deep eyes flashed. "Diana—"

But she was on her feet, walking to the edge of the glade, more for the relief of movement than anything else. Gwyn's horse whinnied as she neared it, backing away.

"Be careful," Gwyn said. He had risen, but was not following her. "My Wild Hunt horses can be uneasy around women. They have little experience with them."

Diana paused for a moment, then stepped around the horse, giving it a wide berth. As she neared the edge of the wood, she caught a flash of something pale out of the corner of her eye.

She moved closer, realizing suddenly how vulnerable she was, here in the open without her weapons, wearing only pajamas. How had she agreed to this? What had Gwyn said to convince her?

I saw who you are.

She pushed the words to the back of her mind, reaching a hand out to steady herself on the slender trunk of a linden. Her eyes saw before her mind could process: a bizarre sight, a circle of blasted nothingness in the center of Brocelind. Land like ash, trees burned to stumps, as if acid had charred away everything living.

"By the Angel," she whispered.

"It is blight." Gwyn spoke from behind her, his big shoulders taut with tension, his jaw set. "I have seen this before only in Faerie. It is the mark of a great dark magic."

There were burned places, white as ash, like the surface of the moon.

Diana gripped the tree trunk harder. "Take me back," she said. "I need to return to Alicante."

21

THE EYE UNCLOSED

Mark sat on the edge of his bed, examining his wrist. The wound that wrapped it appeared darker, crusted with blood at the edges, and the bruises that radiated out from it shaded from deep red to purple.

"Let me bandage it," Kieran said. He sat on the nightstand, his feet half pulled up under him. His hair was tangled and he was barefoot. It looked as if a wild creature had alighted on some piece of civilization: a hawk balancing on the head of a statue. "At least let me do that for you."

"Bandaging it won't help," Mark said. "Like Magnus said—it won't heal until the spell's off."

"Then do it for me. I cannot bear looking at it."

Mark looked at Kieran in surprise. In the Wild Hunt, they had seen their fair share of injuries and blood, and Kieran had never been squeamish.

"There are bandages in there." Mark indicated the drawer of the nightstand. He watched as Kieran hopped down and retrieved what he needed, then returned to the bed and to him.

Kieran sat down and took Mark's wrist. His hands were clever and capable, blunt-nailed, calloused from years of fighting and riding. (Cristina's hands were calloused, too, but her wrists and fingertips were smooth and soft. Mark remembered the feel of them against his cheek in the faerie grove.)

"You are so distant, Mark," Kieran said. "Further from me now than you were when I was in Faerie and you were in the human world."

Mark looked steadfastly at his wrist, now wrapped in a bracelet of bandage. Kieran tied the knot expertly and set the box aside. "You can't stay here forever, Kier," Mark said. "And when you go, we *will* be separated. I can't not think about that."

Kieran gave a soft, impatient noise and flopped down on the bed, among the sheets. The blankets were already flung onto the floor. With his black hair tangled against the white linen, his body sprawled out with no regard for human modesty—his shirt had ridden up to the bottom of his rib cage, and his legs were flung wide apart—Kieran looked even more of a wild creature. "Come with me, then," he said. "Stay with me. I saw the look on your face when you saw the horses of the Hunt. You would do anything to ride again."

Suddenly furious, Mark leaned down over him. "Not *anything*," he said. His voice throbbed with low anger.

Kieran gave a slight hiss. He caught at Mark's shirt. "There," he said. "Be angry with me, Mark Blackthorn. Shout at me. Feel *something*."

Mark stayed where he was, frozen, just above Kieran. "You think I don't feel?" he said, incredulously.

Something flickered in Kieran's eyes. "Put your hands on me," he said, and Mark did, feeling helpless to stop himself. Kieran clutched at the sheets as Mark touched him, pulling at his shirt, snapping the buttons. He moved his hands over Kieran's body, as he had done on countless nights before, and a slow flame began in his own chest, the memory of desire becoming the immediate present.

It burned in him: a lambent, sorrowful heat, like a signal fire on a distant hill. Kieran's shirt came up and over his head and his arms were tangled in it, so he reached for Mark with his legs, pulling him in, holding him with his knees. Kieran lifted up his mouth to Mark's, and he tasted like the sweet ice of polar expanses under skies streaked with the northern lights. Mark couldn't stop his hands: The shape of Kieran's shoulder was like the rise of hills, his hair soft and dark as clouds; his eyes were stars and his body moved under Mark's like the rush of a waterfall no human eye had ever seen. He was starlight and strangeness and freedom. He was a hundred arrows loosed from a hundred bows at the same time.

And Mark was lost; he was falling through dark skies, silvered with the diamond dust of stars. He was tangling his legs with Kieran's, his hands were in Kieran's hair, they were hurtling through mist over green pastures, they were riding a fire-shod horse over deserts where sand rose up in clouds of gold. He cried out, and then Kieran was rushing away from him as if he had been lifted up off the bed—it was all rushing away, and Mark opened his eyes and he was in the library.

He had fallen asleep, head on his arms, face against the wood of the table. He bolted upright with a gasp and saw Kieran, sitting in the embrasure of the windowsill, looking at him.

The library was otherwise empty, thank the Angel. No one was there except them.

Mark's hand was throbbing. He must have struck it against the edge of the table; the sides of his fingers were already starting to swell.

"A pity," said Kieran, looking at Mark's hand thoughtfully. "Or you wouldn't have woken up."

"Where is everyone?" Mark said. He swallowed against the dryness in his throat.

"Some have gone to find ingredients to dissolve the binding spell," said Kieran. "The children became restive, and Cristina went with them and Magnus's lover."

"You mean Alec," said Mark. "His name is Alec."

Kieran shrugged. "As for Magnus, he went to something called an Internet café to make printings of Emma and Julian's messages. We were left to do research, but you promptly fell asleep."

Mark chewed his lower lip. His body could still feel Kieran's, though he knew Kieran hadn't touched him. He knew it, but he had to ask anyway, despite dreading the answer. "And you made me dream," he said.

It wasn't the first time Kieran had ever done that: He had given Mark pleasant dreams a few times when he could not sleep during the nights of the Hunt. It was a faerie gift.

But this was different.

"Yes," Kieran said. There were white threads in his dark hair, like lines of ore running through a mine shaft.

"Why?" Mark said. Anger was gathering in his veins. He felt it like a pressure in his chest. They'd had terrific fights while they were in the Hunt. The screaming sort you had when everything in the world seemed to be at stake because the other person was all you had. Mark remembered pushing Kieran partway down a glacier and then flinging himself after: catching him as they both rolled into a snowbank, gripping each other in the cold with wet, frozen fingers that slipped and slid on their skin.

The problem was that fights with Kieran usually led to kissing, and that, Mark felt, was not helpful. It probably wasn't all that healthy, either.

"Because you are not truthful with me. Your heart is closed and shrouded. I cannot see it," Kieran said. "I thought, in dreams, perhaps . . ."

"You think I'm lying to you?" Mark felt his heart give a thump of dread.

"I think you are lying to yourself," said Kieran. "You were not born for this life, of politics and plots and lies. Your brother is. Julian thrives at it. But you do not wish to make these kinds of bargains, where you ruin your soul to serve a greater good. You are kinder than that."

Mark let his head fall against the chair back. If only he could tell himself Kieran was wrong, but he wasn't. Mark loathed himself every moment of every day for lying to Kieran, even if the lie was in a good cause.

Kieran said, "Your brother would burn the world if it saved his family. Some are like that. But you are not."

"I understand you cannot believe this matters to me as much as it does, Kieran," Mark said. "But it is the truth."

"*Remember*," Kieran whispered. Even now, in the mundane world, there was something proud and arrogant about Kieran's gestures, his voice. Despite the jeans Mark had lent him, he looked as if he should be at the head of a faerie army, flinging out his arm in sweeping command. "*Remember that none of it is real.*"

And Mark did remember. He remembered a note written on parchment, wrapped in the shell of an acorn. The first message Kieran had sent him after he'd left the Hunt.

"It is real to me," Mark said. "All of this is real to me." He leaned forward. "I need to know you are here in this with me, Kieran."

"What does that mean?"

"It means no more anger," said Mark. "It means no more sending me dreams. I needed you for so long, Kieran. I needed you so much, and that kind of need, it bends you and warps you. It makes you desperate. It makes you not *choose*."

Kieran had frozen. "You're saying you didn't choose me?"

"I'm saying the Wild Hunt chose us. I'm saying if you are finding strangeness in me, and distance, it is because I cannot help but ask myself, over and over: In another world, in another situation, would we still have chosen each other?" He looked hard at the other boy. "You are a gentry prince. And I am half-Nephilim, worse than the lowest chaff, tainted in blood and lineage."

"*Mark.*"

"I am saying the choices we make in captivity are not always the choices we make in freedom. And thus we question them. We cannot help it."

"It is different for me," said Kieran. "After this, I return to the Hunt. You are the one with freedom."

"I will not let you be forced back into the Hunt if you do not wish it."

Kieran's eyes softened. In that moment, Mark thought he would have promised him anything, no matter how rash.

"I would like us both to have freedom," Mark said. "To laugh, to enjoy ourselves together, to love in the ordinary way. You are free here with me, and perhaps we could take that chance, that time."

"Very well," Kieran said, after a long pause. "I will stay with you. And I will help you with your dull books." He smiled. "I am in this with you, Mark, if that is how we will learn what we mean to each other."

"Thank you," Mark said. Kieran, like most faeries, had no use for "you're welcome"; instead he slid off the windowsill and went in search of a book on the shelves. Mark stared after him. He had said nothing to Kieran that was not true, and yet he felt as leaden inside as if every word he had spoken was a lie.

The sky over London was cloudless and blue and beautiful. The water of the Thames, parting on either side of the boat, was *almost* blue. Sort of the color of tea, Kit thought, if you put blue ink into it.

The place they were going—Ty had the address—was on Gill Street, Magnus had explained, in Limehouse. "Used to be a terrible neighborhood," he said. "Full of opium dens and gambling houses. God, it was fun back then."

Mark had looked immediately panicked.

"Don't worry," Magnus had added. "It's very dull now. All fancy condos and gastropubs. Very safe."

Julian would have forbidden this excursion, Kit was fairly sure. But Mark hadn't hesitated—he seemed, far more than his brother, to regard Livvy and Ty as adult Shadowhunters who were simply expected to work like the others.

It was Ty who had hesitated for a moment, looking worriedly at his sister. Livvy seemed absolutely fine now—they were on the top level of the boat, open to the air, and she was raising her face into the wind with unabashed pleasure, letting it lift her hair and whip it around.

Ty was watching everything around them with that absorbed fascination of his, as if he were memorizing every building, every street. His fingers drummed a tattoo on the metal railing, but Kit didn't think that indicated anxiety. He'd noticed that Ty's gestures didn't always correspond to a bad mood. Sometimes they corresponded to a good one: If he was feeling relaxed, he'd watch his own fingers make lazy patterns against the air, the way a meteorologist might watch the movement of clouds.

"If I became a Shadowhunter," Kit said, to neither of the twins specifically, "would I have to do a lot of homework? Or could I just, sort of, start doing it?"

Livvy's eyes sparkled. "You are doing it."

"Yes, but this is a state of emergency," said Ty. "He's right—he'd have to catch up on some classes. It's not as if you're as ignorant as a mundane would be," he added to Kit, "but there are some things you'd probably need to learn—classes of demons, languages, that sort of thing."

Kit made a face. "I was really hoping I could learn on the job."

Livvy laughed. "You could always go in front of the Council and make a case for it."

"The Council?" said Kit. "How are they different from the Clave?"

Livvy laughed harder.

"I can see how your case might not be successful," said Ty. "Though I suppose we could tutor you a bit."

"A bit?" said Kit.

Ty smiled his rare, dazzling smile. "A bit. I do have important things to do."

Kit thought of Ty on the roof the night before, how desperate he had seemed. He was back to his old self now, as if Livvy's restoration had restored him, too. He rested his elbows on the rail as the boat chugged past an imposing fortress-like building that loomed over the riverbank.

"The Tower of London," said Livvy, noticing Kit's gaze.

"The stories say that six ravens must always guard the Tower," said Ty, "or the monarchy will fall."

"All the stories are true," said Livvy in a soft voice, and a chill went up Kit's spine.

Ty turned his head. "Wasn't it a raven that carried Annabel and Malcolm's messages?" he said. "I think that was in Emma and Julian's notes."

"Seems unreliable," said Kit. "What if the raven got bored, or distracted, or met a hot falcon on the way?"

"Or was intercepted by faeries," said Livvy.

"Not all faeries are bad," said Ty.

"Some faeries are good, some are bad, like anyone," said Kit. "But that might be too complicated for the Clave."

"It's too complicated for most people," Ty said.

From anyone else, Kit would have thought that the comment was meant to be reproving. Ty, though, probably just meant it. Which was oddly pleasant to know.

"I don't like what we've been hearing from Diana," said Livvy. "About how Zara's claiming she killed Malcolm."

"My dad used to say that a big lie was often easier to carry off than a small one," said Kit.

"Well, hopefully he was wrong," said Livvy, a little sharply. "I can't stand the idea that anyone thinks Zara and people like her are heroes. Even if they don't know she's lying about Malcolm, the Cohort's plans are despicable."

"It's too bad none of you can just tell the Clave what Julian saw happen in the scrying glass," said Kit.

"If they knew he'd gone to Faerie, he could be exiled," said Livvy, and there was an edge of real fear in her voice. "Or have his Marks stripped."

"I could pretend I'm the one who saw it—it matters a lot less if I get tossed out of the Nephilim," Kit said.

Kit had meant to lighten the mood with an obvious joke, but the twins looked rattled. "Don't you want to stay?" Ty's question was direct and sharp as a knife.

Kit had no answer. There was a clamor of voices, and the boat jerked to a halt. It had docked at Limehouse, and the three of them hurried to get off—they were unglamoured, and as they pushed past several mundanes to get to the exit, Kit heard one of them mutter about kids getting tattooed way too young these days.

Ty had made a face at all the noise, and had his headphones on as they wove through the streets. The air smelled like river water, but Magnus had been right—the docks vanished quickly, replaced by winding roads full of massive old factory buildings that had been turned into lofts.

Ty had the map, and Livvy and Kit walked a little behind him, Livvy with her hand casually at her waist, where her weapons belt was hidden by her jacket. "He uses the headphones less when you're around," she said, her eyes on her brother, though her words were for Kit.

"Is that good?" Kit was surprised.

Livvy shrugged. "It isn't good or bad. It's just something I noticed. It's not magic or anything." She glanced sideways at him. "I think he just doesn't want to miss anything you say."

Kit felt an odd stab of emotion go through him. It surprised him. He glanced sideways at Livvy. Since they'd left Los Angeles, she'd done nothing to indicate she wanted to repeat their one kiss. And Kit had found that he didn't either. Not that he didn't like Livvy, or find her pretty. But something seemed off about it now—as if it were somehow wrong.

Maybe it was the fact that he didn't know if he wanted to be a Shadowhunter at all.

"We're here." Ty had shoved his headphones down, the white band of them stark against his black hair. He alone among all the current Blackthorns had hair like that, though Kit had seen pictures in the Institute of their ancestors, some with the same dark hair and silver-gray eyes. "This should be illuminating. Shops like this have to abide by the Accords, unlike the Shadow Market, but they're also run by specialists." Ty looked enormously happy at the thought of all that specialized knowledge.

They had passed the wider thoroughfare of Narrow Street and were now on what was presumably Gill Street, across from a single open shop. It had dimly lit windows and the owner's name spelled out in brass letters over the door. PROPRIETOR: F. SALLOWS. There was no description of what kind of shop it was, but Kit supposed that those who shopped there knew what they were shopping for.

Ty was already across the street, opening the door. Livvy hurried after him. Kit was last—cautious and a little less than eager. He had grown up around magic-sellers and their patrons, and was wary of both.

The inside of the shop didn't offer much reason to improve his views. The frosted windows let in glare but not light. It was clean at least, with long shelves lined with some things he'd seen before—dragon's teeth, holy water, blessed nails, enchanted beauty powders, luck charms—and quite a few he hadn't. Clocks that ran backward, though he had no idea why. The wire-jointed skeletons of animals he'd never seen before. Shark teeth too big to belong to any shark on earth. Jar after jar of butterfly wings in explosive colors of hot pink, neon yellow, and lime green. Bottles of blue water whose surfaces rippled like tiny seas.

There was a dusty copper bell on the front counter. Livvy picked it up and rang it, while Ty studied the maps on the walls. The one he was staring at was marked with names Kit had never seen before—the Thorn Mountains, Hollow Town, the Shattered Forest.

"Faerie," Ty said in an unusually subdued voice. "Hard to get maps of it, since the geography tends to change, but I looked at quite a few when Mark was missing."

The *tap-tap* of heels on the floor announced the arrival of the shop-keeper. To Kit's surprise, she was familiar—dark-skinned and bronze-haired, dressed today in a plain black sheath dress. Hypatia Vex.

"Nephilim," she said with a sigh. "I hate Nephilim."

"I take it this isn't one of those places where the customer is always right," Livvy said.

"You're not Sallows," said Ty. "You're Hypatia Vex. We met you yesterday."

"Sallows died years ago," said Hypatia. "Killed by Nephilim, as it happens."

Awkward, Kit thought.

"We have a list of things we need." Livvy pushed a paper across the counter. "For Magnus Bane."

Hypatia raised an eyebrow. "Ah, Bane, your great defender. What a pest that man is." She took the paper. "Some of these will take at least a day to prepare. Can you come back tomorrow?"

"Do we have a choice?" said Livvy, with a winsome smile.

"No," said Hypatia. "And you'll pay in gold. I'm not interested in mundane money."

"Just tell us how much," said Ty, and she reached for a pen and began scribbling. "And also—there's something I want to ask you."

He looked over at Kit and Livvy. Livvy got the hint first, and drew

Kit outside the shop until they were standing in the street. The sun was warm on his hair and skin; he wondered what mundanes saw when they looked at the shop. Maybe a dusty convenience store or a place that sold tombstones. Something you'd never want to go into.

"How long are you planning on being friends with my brother?" Livvy said abruptly.

Kit jumped. "I—what?"

"You heard me," she said. Her eyes were much bluer than the Thames. Ty's eyes were really more the river's color.

"People don't really think about friendship that way," said Kit. "It depends how long you know the person—how long you're in the same place."

"It's your *choice*," she said, her eyes darkening. "You can stay with us as long as you want to."

"Can I? What about the Academy? What about learning to be a Shadowhunter? How am I supposed to catch up with you when you're all a million years ahead of me?"

"We don't care about that—"

"Maybe I care about that."

Livvy spoke in a steady voice. "When we were kids," she said, "the Ashdowns used to come over to play. Our parents thought we should see more kids outside our family, and Paige Ashdown was about my age, so she got shoved together with me and Ty. And once he was talking to us about what he was obsessed with—it was cars back then, before Sherlock. And she said sarcastically that he ought to come over and tell her all about it because it was so interesting."

"What happened?"

"He went over to her house to talk to her about cars, and she wasn't there, and when she came home, she laughed at him and told him to go away, she hadn't meant it, and was he stupid?"

Kit felt a slow boil of fury toward a girl he'd never met. "I'd never do that."

"Look," Livvy said. "Since then, Ty's learned so much about the way people say things they don't mean, about tone not matching expression, all that. But he trusts you, he's let you in. He might not always remember to apply that stuff to you. I'm just saying—don't lie to him. Don't lead him on."

"I haven't—" Kit began, when the bell rang and the shop door opened. It was Ty, pulling his hood up against the gentle breeze.

"All done," he said. "Let's get back."

If he noticed any atmosphere of tension, he didn't say anything, and all the way home, they talked about unimportant things.

The piskies sat in an unhappy line on a row of stones at the edge of the cottage garden. After pulling them out of the pit, Emma and Jules had offered them food, but only one had accepted, and was currently facedown in a bowl of milk.

The tallest of the faerie creatures spoke in a piping voice. "Malcolm Fade? Where is Malcolm Fade?"

"Not here," said Julian.

"Gone to visit a sick relative," said Emma, gazing at the piskies in fascination.

"Warlocks don't have relatives," said the piskie.

"No one gets my references," Emma muttered.

"We're friends of Malcolm's," said Julian, after a moment. If Emma didn't know him, she would have believed him. His face was entirely guileless when he lied. "He asked us to look after the place while he was away."

The piskies whispered to each other in small, high voices. Emma strained her ears but couldn't understand them. They weren't speaking a gentry language of Faerie, but something much more simple and ancient-sounding. It had the murmur of water over rocks, the sharp acidity of green grass.

"Are you warlocks too?" said the tallest of the piskies, breaking away from the group. His eyes were marled with gray and silver, like Cornwall rock.

Julian shook his head and held his arm out, turning it so the Insight rune on his forearm was visible, stark against his skin. "We're Nephilim."

The piskies murmured among themselves again.

"We're looking for Annabel Blackthorn," said Julian. "We want to take her home where she'll be protected."

The piskies looked dubious.

"She said you knew where she was," said Julian. "You've been talking to her?"

"We knew her and Malcolm years ago," said the piskie. "It is not often a mortal lives so long. We were curious."

"You might as well tell us," said Emma. "We'll let you go if you do."

"And if we don't?" said the smallest piskie.

"We won't let you go," said Julian.

"She's in Porthallow Church," said the smallest piskie, speaking up for the group. "It's been empty these many years. She knows it and feels safe there, and there are few tallfolk in the area on most days."

"Is Porthallow Church near here?" Julian demanded. "Is it close to the town?"

"Very close," said the tallest piskie. "Killing close." He raised his thin, pale hands, pointing. "But you cannot go today. It is Sunday, when the tallfolk come in groups to study the graveyard beside the church."

"Thank you," said Julian. "You've been very helpful, indeed."

Dru pushed the door of her bedroom open. "Jaime?" she whispered.

There was no answer. She crept inside, shutting the door after her. She was carrying a plate of scones that Bridget had made. When she'd asked for a whole plate of them, Bridget had giggled at something it seemed clear only she remembered, then sharply told Dru not to eat them all or she'd get fatter.

Dru had long ago learned not to eat much in front of people she didn't know, or seem as if she was hungry, or put too much food on her plate. She hated the way they looked at her if she did, as if to say, *oh, that's why she's not thin.*

But for Jaime, she'd been willing to do it. After he'd made himself at home in her room—flinging himself across her bed as if he'd been sleeping there for days, then bolting up and asking if he could use the shower—she'd asked if he was hungry and he'd lowered his eyelashes, smiling up at her. "I didn't want to impose, but . . ."

She'd hurried off to the kitchen and didn't want to return empty-handed. That was something a scared thirteen-year-old might do, but not a sixteen-year-old. Or however old he thought she was. She hadn't been specific.

"Jaime?"

He came out of the bathroom in jeans, pulling his T-shirt on. She caught a glimpse of a black tattoo—not a Mark, but words in Roman letters—snaking across flat brown skin before the T-shirt covered his stomach. She stared at him without speaking as he approached her and grabbed a scone. He winked at her. "Thanks."

"You're welcome," she said faintly.

He sat on the bed, scattering crumbs, black hair damp and curling with the humidity. She placed the scones carefully on the top of the dresser. By the time she turned back around, he was asleep, head pillowed on his arm.

She perched herself on the nightstand table for a moment, her arms around herself. She could see Diego in the colors and curves of Jaime's face. It was as if someone had taken Diego and sharpened him, made all his angles more acute. A tattoo of more script looped around one brown wrist and disappeared up Jaime's shirtsleeve; she wished she knew enough Spanish to translate it.

She started to turn toward the door, meaning to leave him alone to rest. "Don't go," he said. She spun around and saw that his eyes were half-open, his lashes casting shadows on his too-sharp cheekbones. "It's been a long time since I had anyone to talk to."

She sat down on the edge of the bed. Jaime rolled over on his back, his arms folded behind his head. He was all long limbs and black hair and lashes like spider's legs. Everything about him was slightly off-kilter, where everything about Diego had been even lines like a comic book. Dru tried not to stare.

"I was looking at the stickers on your nightstand," he said. Dru had bought them in a store on Fleet Street when she'd been out with Diana picking up sandwiches. "They're all horror movies."

"I like horror movies."

He grinned. Black hair flopped into his eyes. He shoved it back. "You like to be scared?"

"Horror movies don't scare me," said Dru.

"Aren't they supposed to?" He sounded genuinely interested. Dru couldn't remember the last time anyone had seemed genuinely interested in her love for slasher films and vintage horror. Julian had sometimes stayed up to watch *Horror Hotel* with her, but she knew that was just older-brother kindness.

"I remember the Dark War," she said. "I remember watching people die in front of me. My father was one of the Endarkened. He came back, but it wasn't—it wasn't him." She swallowed hard. "When I watch a scary movie, I know whatever happens, I'll be all right when it's over. I know the people in it were just actors and after everything was done, they walked away. The blood was fake and washed off."

Jaime's eyes were dark and fathomless. "It almost lets you believe none of those things exist," he said. "Imagine if they didn't."

She smiled a little sadly. "We're Shadowhunters," she said. "We don't get to imagine that."

"People will do anything to get out of housework," said Julian.

"Not you," Emma said. She was lying on the sofa with her legs hooked over the arm.

Since they couldn't follow Annabel to the church today, they'd decided to spend the afternoon reading through Malcolm's diaries and studying Annabel's drawings. By the time the sun began going down, they had a sizable amount of notes systematically arranged around the cottage in piles. Notes about timeline—when Malcolm had joined Annabel's family, how they, who ran the Cornwall Institute, had adopted him when he was a child. How intensely Annabel had loved Blackthorn Manor, the Blackthorns' ancestral home in the green hills of Idris, and how they had played in Brocelind Forest together. When Malcolm had started planning for their future, and built the cottage in Polperro, and how he and Annabel had hidden their relationship, exchanging all their messages through Annabel's raven. When Annabel's father had discovered them, and thrown his daughter out of the Blackthorn house, and Malcolm had found her the next morning, weeping alone on the beach.

Malcolm had determined then that he would need protection for them from the Clave. He had known of the collection of spell books at the Cornwall Institute. He would need a powerful patron, he had decided. Someone he could trade the Black Volume to, who in turn would keep the Council away from them.

Emma read aloud from the diaries, and Julian took notes. Every once in a while they would stop, take pictures with their phones of their notes and questions, and text them to the Institute. Sometimes they got questions back and scrambled to answer them; sometimes they got nothing. Once they got a picture of Ty, who had found an entire row of first-edition Sherlock Holmes books in the library and was beaming. Once they got a picture of Mark's foot. Neither of them knew what to make of that.

At some point Julian stretched, padded into the kitchen, and made them both toasted cheese sandwiches on the Aga, a massive iron stove that radiated warmth through the room.

This is bad, he thought, looking down at his hands as he settled the sandwiches onto plates and remembered that Emma liked hers with the crusts cut off. He'd made fun of her for it often. He reached for a knife, the gesture mechanical, habit.

He imagined doing this every day. Living in a house he'd designed himself—like this one, it would have a view of the sea. A massive studio where he could paint. A room for Emma to train. He imagined waking up every morning to find her beside him, or sitting at a table in the kitchen with her morning cereal, humming, raising her face to smile at him when he came in.

A wave of desire—not just for the physicality of her but for the dream of that life—swept through him, almost choking him. It was dangerous to dream, he reminded himself. As dangerous as it was for Sleeping Beauty in her castle, where she'd fallen into dreams that had devoured her for a century.

He went to join Emma by the fire. She was bright-eyed, smiling as she took the plate from him. "You know what I'm worried about?"

His heart did a slow curl inside his chest. "What?"

"Church," she said. "He's all alone in the Institute in L.A."

"No, he isn't. He's surrounded by Centurions."

"What if one of them tries to steal him?"

"Then they'll be appropriately punished," said Julian, moving slightly closer to the fire.

"What's the appropriate punishment for stealing a cat?" Emma asked around her sandwich.

"In Church's case, having to keep him," said Julian.

Emma made a face. "If there were any crusts on this sandwich, I'd throw them at you."

"Why don't you just throw the sandwich?"

She looked horrified. "And give up the tasty cheese? I would never, ever give up the tasty cheese."

"My mistake." Julian tossed another log onto the fire. A bubble of happiness swelled in his chest, sweet and unfamiliar.

"Cheese this tasty doesn't just come along every day," she informed him. "You know what would make it even better?"

"What?" He sat back on his heels.

"Another sandwich." She held out her empty plate, laughing. He took the plate, and it was a completely ordinary moment, but it was also everything he'd ever wanted and never let himself imagine. A house, with Emma; laughing by a fire together.

All that would make it better would be his brothers and sisters somewhere nearby, where he could see them every day, where he could fence with Livvy and watch movies with Dru and help Tavvy learn the crossbow. Where he could look for animals with Ty, hermit crabs down by the edge of the water, scuttling under their shells. Where he could cook massive dinners with Mark and Helen and Aline and they'd all eat them together, out under the stars in the desert air.

Where he could hear the sea, as he could hear it now. And where he could see Emma, always Emma, the better, brighter half of him, who tempered his ruthlessness, who forced him to acknowledge the light when he saw only darkness.

But they would all have to be together, he thought. Long ago the pieces of his soul had scattered, and every piece lived in one of his brothers or sisters. Except for the piece that lived in Emma, which had been burned into its home in her by the flame of the *parabatai* ceremony, and the pressure of his own heart.

It was impossible, though. An impossible thing that could never happen. Even if by some miracle his family came through all this unscathed and together—and if Helen and Aline could come back to them—even then, Emma, his Emma, would someday have her own family and her own life.

He wondered if he would be her *suggenes*, if he would give her away at her wedding. It was the usual thing, with *parabatai*.

The thought made him feel as if he was being cut up inside with razor blades.

"Do you remember," she was saying, in her soft, teasing voice, "when you said you could sneak Church into class without Diana noticing, and then he bit you in the middle of the lecture on Jonathan Shadowhunter?"

"Not at all." He settled back on the floor, one of the diaries by his hand. The warmth in the room, the smell of tea and burnt bread, the glow of the firelight on Emma's hair, were making him sleepy. He was as intensely happy as he was miserable, and it exhausted him to be pulled in two such different directions at once.

"You yelled," she said. "And then you told Diana it was because you were really excited to be learning."

"Is there a reason you remember every embarrassing thing that happens to me?" he wondered aloud.

"Someone has to," she said. The curve of her face was rosy in the firelight. The glass bracelet on his wrist glinted, cold against his cheek when he lowered his head.

He had been frightened that without Cristina here, they would fight and argue. That they would be bitter with each other. Instead everything was perfect. And in its own way, that was so much worse.

Pain woke Mark in the middle of the night, the feeling that his wrist was ringed with nails.

They'd worked in the library until late, Magnus fiddling with the recipe for the binding spell antidote and the rest of them poring through old books about the Black Volume. Combining the memories from the *aletheia* crystal and the information from the notes Emma and Julian had sent was beginning to create a more complete picture of Annabel and Malcolm, but Mark couldn't help wondering if it was doing any good. What they needed was the Black Volume, and even if its story was woven in the past, would that help the Blackthorns find it in the present?

On the plus side, he'd managed to convince Kieran to eat almost an entire meal Alec had brought over from a café on Fleet Street, despite the fact that he spent the whole time complaining that the juice wasn't really juice and that chutney didn't exist. "It cannot possibly," he had said, glaring at his sandwich.

He was asleep now, curled in a tangle of blanket under Mark's window, his head propped on a stack of poetry books he'd brought from the library. Almost all of them had been inscribed on the inside cover by a James Herondale, who had neatly written out his favorite lines.

Mark's wrist throbbed again now, and with the pain came a sense of unease. *Cristina,* he thought. They'd barely spoken that day, both of them avoiding each other. It was partly Kieran, but even more the binding spell, the awful reality of it between them.

Mark scrambled to his feet and pulled on jeans and a T-shirt. He couldn't sleep, not like this, not worrying about her. Barefoot, he went down the hall to her room.

But it was empty. Her bed was made, the cover pulled flat, moonlight shining on it.

Perplexed, he moved down the hallway, letting the binding spell lead him. It was like following the music of a revel from a distance. He could almost hear her: She was in the Institute, somewhere.

He passed Kit's door and heard raised voices, and someone laugh—Ty. He thought of the way Ty had seemed to need him when he'd first come back, and now that was gone: Kit had worked an odd sort of magic, rounding out what the twins had into a threesome that balanced itself. Ty no longer looked at Mark the same way, as if he were looking for someone to understand him.

Which was good, Mark thought, as he took the stairs down, two at a time. Because he wasn't in much shape to understand anyone. He didn't even understand himself.

A long corridor took him to two white-painted double doors, one of them standing open. Inside was a massive, dusty, half-lit room.

It clearly hadn't been used in many years, though it was clean other than the dust. White sheets covered most of the furniture. Arched windows looked out onto the courtyard, and a night that sparkled with stars.

Cristina was there, in the middle of the room, looking up at one of the chandeliers. There was a row of three of them, unlit but glittering with crystal drops.

He let the door fall shut behind him and she turned. She didn't look surprised to see him. She was wearing a simple black dress that looked as if it had been cut for someone shorter than her, and her hair was up off her face.

"Mark," she said. "Couldn't you sleep?"

"Not well." He glanced ruefully down at his wrist, though the pain had gone now that he was with Cristina. "Did you feel the same?"

She nodded. Her eyes were bright. "My mother always said that the ballroom in the London Institute was the most beautiful room she'd ever seen." She looked around, at the Edwardian striped wallpaper, the heavy velvet curtains looped back from the windows. "But she must have seen it very much alive and filled with people. It seems like Sleeping Beauty's castle now. As if the Dark War surrounded it with thorns and since then it has slept."

Mark held out his hand, the wound of the binding circling his wrist like Julian's sea-glass bracelet circled his. "Let us wake it up," he said. "Dance with me."

"But there's no music," she said. She swayed a little toward him, though, as she spoke.

"I have danced at many a revel," he said, "where there has been no pipe and no fiddle, where there has been only the music of the wind and stars. I can show you."

She came toward him, the golden pendant at her throat glittering. "How magical," she said, and her eyes were huge and dark and luminous with mischief. "Or I could do this."

She took her phone out of her pocket and thumbed a few buttons. Music poured out of the small speakers: not loud, but Mark could feel it—not a tune he knew, but fast and energetic, thrumming down through his blood.

He held out his hands. Setting her phone down on a windowsill, she took them, laughing as he pulled her toward him. Their bodies touched once, lightly, and she spun away, making him follow her. If he'd thought he would be leading, he realized, he was wrong.

He paced after her as she moved like fire, always just ahead of him, spinning until her hair came down out of its fastening and flew around her face. The chandeliers glittered overhead like rain and Mark seized Cristina's hand in his. He whirled her in a circle; her body brushed his as she turned, and he caught her hips and drew her toward him.

And now she was in his arms, moving, and everywhere her body touched his felt like a lit spark. Everything had been driven out of his head but Cristina. The light on her brown skin, her flushed face, the way her skirt flew up when she twirled, affording him a glimpse of the smooth thighs he'd imagined a hundred times.

He caught her by the waist and she swayed backward in his arms, boneless, her hair brushing the floor. When she rose up again, eyes half-lidded, he could no longer contain himself. He drew her into him and kissed her.

Her hands flew up and fastened in his hair, her fingers tugging and pulling him closer against her. She tasted like cold clear water and he drew on her mouth as if he were incredibly thirsty. His whole body felt like one desperate ache, and when she moved away from him, he groaned softly. But she was laughing, looking at him, dancing lightly backward with her hands held out. His skin felt tight all over; he was desperate to kiss her again, desperate to let his hands go where his eyes had gone earlier: sliding up the outsides of her long legs, under her skirt, along her waist, over her back where the muscles were smooth and long on either side of her spine.

He wanted her, and it was a very human want; not starlight and strangeness, but right here and right now. He strode after her, reaching for her hands. "Cristina—"

She froze, and for a moment of fear he thought it was because of him. But she was looking past him. He turned and saw Kieran in the doorway, leaning against it, gazing very steadily at them both.

Mark tensed. In a moment of delayed clarity he realized he had been stupid, alarmingly stupid to have done what he was doing. But none of it was Cristina's fault. If Kieran brought his temper to bear on her—

But when Kieran spoke, it was lightly. "Mark," he said. "You really have no idea, do you? You should show her how it is properly done."

He walked toward them, a true prince of Faerie in all his grace. He wore a white shirt and breeches and his black hair fell partway to his shoulders. He reached the middle of the room and held a hand out to Cristina. "My lady," he said, and bowed. "Favor me with a dance?"

Cristina hesitated a moment, and then nodded.

"You don't have to," Mark said in a whisper. She only gave him a long look, and then followed Kieran out to the middle of the floor.

"Now," Kieran said, and he began to move.

Mark didn't think he'd ever danced with Kieran before, not at a revel; they had always tried to conceal their relationship in front of the greater world of Faerie. And Kieran, if he could not dance with his chosen partner, would not dance with anyone.

But he was dancing now. And if Cristina had moved like fire, Kieran moved like lightning. After a moment of hesitation, Cristina followed him—he drew her into his arms—caught her, lifted her up into the air with easy faerie strength, whirling her around him. She gasped, and her face lit up with the pleasure of the music and the movement.

Mark stood where he was, feeling awkward and startled in equal measure. What was Kieran doing? What was he thinking? Was this a reproach of some sort? But it didn't seem to be one. How much had Kieran seen? The kissing, or just the dancing?

He heard Cristina laugh. His eyes widened. Incredible. She and Kieran were like stars whirling together, just touching at the edges, but flaring up into a rain of sparks and fire when they did. And Kieran was smiling, actually smiling. It changed his face, made him look as young as he actually was.

The music ended. Cristina stopped dancing, looking suddenly shy. Kieran lifted his hand to touch her long dark hair, sweeping it back over her shoulder so he could lean in and kiss her cheek. Her eyes widened in surprise.

Only then, when he had drawn back, did he look at Mark. "There," he said. "That is how the blood of Faerieland can dance."

"Wake up."

Kit groaned and rolled over. He'd finally been sleeping, and dreaming something pleasant about being at the beach with his dad. Not that his dad had ever actually taken him to the beach, but that was what dreams were for, weren't they?

In the dream, his father had touched his shoulder and said, *I always knew you'd make a good Shadowhunter.*

Never mind that Johnny Rook would rather that his son became a serial killer than one of the Nephilim. Struggling up out of sleep, Kit remembered his father's knowing smile and the last time he had seen it, on the morning when Malcolm Fade's demons had torn Johnny Rook to shreds.

"Didn't you hear me?" The voice rousing Kit out of sleep became more urgent. "Wake up!"

Kit opened his eyes. His room was full of the pale glow of witchlight, and there was a shadow hovering over his bed. With memories of Mantid demons fresh at the edge of his consciousness, he bolted upright.

The shadow moved swiftly backward, barely avoiding colliding with Kit. The witchlight beamed upward, illuminating Ty, his soft black hair a mess, as if he'd rolled out of bed and come to Kit's room without brushing it. He wore a gray hoodie Julian had given him before he left for Cornwall, likely half for convenience and half for comfort. The cord of his headphones trailed from his pocket to wrap around his neck.

"Watson," he said. "I want to see you."

Kit groaned and scrubbed at his eyes. "What? What time is it?"

Ty spun the witchlight in his fingers. "Did you know that the first words ever spoken on the telephone were 'Watson, come here, I want to see you'?"

"Totally different Watson, though," Kit pointed out.

"I know," said Ty. "I just thought it was interesting." He tugged at the cord of his headphones. "I did want to see you. Or at least, I have something I have to do, and I'd rather you came with me. It was actually something you said that gave me the idea to do the research."

Kit kicked the covers off. He'd been sleeping in his clothes anyway, a habit instilled in him during the times when some deal his father had been involved in had gone wrong, and they'd slept fully dressed for days in case they had to pick up and run. "Research?" he asked.

"It's in the library," Ty said. "I can show it to you before we go. If you want."

"I'd like to see it."

Kit slid out of bed and kicked on his shoes, grabbing up a jacket before following Ty down the hall. He knew he ought to feel exhausted, but there was something about Ty's energy, the brightness and concentration of his focus, that worked on Kit like caffeine. It woke him up inside with a sense of promise, as if the moments in front of him suddenly held endless possibilities.

In the library, Ty had taken over one of the tables with the notes Emma and Julian had sent from Cornwall and printouts of Annabel's drawings. It still looked like the same mess to Kit, but Ty glided his witchlight over the pages with confidence.

"Remember when we were talking about how a raven carried messages between Malcolm and Annabel? On the boat? And you said it seemed unreliable?"

"I remember," said Kit.

"It gave me an idea," said Ty. "You're good at giving me ideas. I don't know why." He shrugged. "Anyway. We're going to Cornwall."

"Why? Are you going to exhume the bird and interrogate it?"

"Of course not."

"That was a joke, Ty—" Kit broke off, the impact of Ty's words hitting him belatedly. "What? We're going where?"

"I know it was a joke," said Ty, picking up one of the printouts of the drawings. "Livvy told me that when people tell jokes that aren't that funny, the polite thing is to ignore them. Is that not true?"

He looked anxious, and Kit wanted to hug him, the way he had the other night on the roof. "No, it's true," he said, hurrying after Ty as they left the library. "It's just that humor is subjective. Not everyone agrees the same things are funny, or not funny."

Ty looked at him with sincere friendliness. "I'm sure many people find you hilarious."

"They absolutely do." They were hurrying down a set of steps now, into shadows. Kit wondered why they were going, but it almost didn't matter—he felt excitement sparking at the tips of his fingers, the promise of adventure. "But Cornwall, seriously? How? And what about Livvy?"

Ty didn't turn around. "I don't want to bring her tonight."

They'd reached the bottom of the steps. A door swung out from here into a massive open stone-bound room. The crypt of the cathedral. The floor and walls were made of massive dark slabs of stone, filed to smoothness, and there were brass fixtures attached to stone pillars that had probably once held lamps. Now the light came from Ty's rune-stone, spilling between his cupped fingers.

"What are we doing, exactly?" said Kit.

"Remember when I stayed at the shop to talk to Hypatia Vex?" Ty said. "She told me there's a permanent Portal down here. An old one, maybe one of the first ever, made around 1903. It only goes to the Cornwall Institute. The Clave doesn't know about it or regulate it."

"An unregulated Portal?" said Kit. Ty was moving around the room, shining his witchlight against the walls, into cracks and corners. "Isn't that dangerous?"

Ty didn't say anything. Long tapestries hung against the walls at intervals. He was glancing behind each one, running the light up and down the wall. It bounced off the stone, lighting up the room like fireflies.

"That's why you didn't want Livvy to come," said Kit. "It *is* dangerous."

Ty straightened up. His hair was a mess. "She already got hurt," he said. "Because of me."

"Ty—"

"I need to find the Portal." Ty leaned against the wall, his fingers drumming against it. "I looked behind all the tapestries."

"Maybe look *in* them?" Kit suggested.

Ty gave him a long, considering look, with a tinge of surprise to it. Kit caught just a flash of his gray eyes as he turned back to examine the tapestries again. Each one showed a scene from what looked like a medieval landscape: castles, long stone walls, towers and roads, horses and battle. Ty stopped in front of one that showed a high hedge, in the middle of which was an arched opening. Through the opening the sea was visible.

He put his hand against it, a hesitant, questioning gesture. There was a flare of light. Kit darted forward as the tapestry shimmered, turning glimmering and colorful as a slick of oil.

Ty glanced again at the drawing he held, then turned, his other hand outstretched to Kit. "Don't be so slow."

Kit reached for him. His fingers closed around Ty's, warm and firm under his grasp. Ty stepped forward, into the Portal, the colors parting and re-forming around him—he was half invisible already—and his grip tightened on Kit's, pulling him after.

Kit held on tightly. But somewhere in the whirling chaos of the Portal, his hand ripped free of Ty's. An irrational panic seized him, and he shouted something out loud—he wasn't sure what—before the Portal winds cartwheeled him through a shadowy doorway and spit him out into cold air, onto a slope of damp grass.

"Yes?" Ty was standing over him, witchlight in hand. The sky behind him was high and dark, shimmering with a million stars.

Kit stood up, wincing. He was getting used to Portal travel, but he still didn't like it.

"What is it?" Ty's gaze didn't meet Kit's, but he looked him over, as if checking for injuries. "You were saying my name."

"Was I?" Kit glanced around. Green lawns sloped away in three directions, and rose in the fourth to meet a large gray church. "I think I was worried you were lost in the Portal."

"That's only happened a few times. It's statistically very unlikely." Ty raised his witchlight. "This is the Cornwall Institute."

In the distance, Kit could see the glimmer of moonlight on black water. The sea. Above them the church was a heap of gray stone with broken black windows and a missing front door. The spire of the church stabbed upward into swirling clouds, lit from behind by the moon. He whistled through his teeth. "How long has it been abandoned?"

"Only a few years. Not enough Shadowhunters to man all the Institutes. Not since the Dark War." Ty was glancing between the drawing in his hand and their surroundings. Kit could see the remains of a garden gone to seed: weeds growing up among dead rosebushes, grass far too long and in need of cutting, moss covering the dozens of statues that were scattered around the garden like victims of Medusa. A horse reared into the air beside a boy with a bird perched on his wrist. A stone woman held a dainty parasol. Tiny stone rabbits peeked through weeds.

"And we're going inside?" Kit said dubiously. He didn't like the look of the dark windows. "Wouldn't we be better off coming during the day?"

"We're not going inside." Ty held up the drawing he'd brought. In the witchlight, Kit could see that it was an ink sketch of the Institute and the gardens, done during daylight hours. The place hadn't changed much in the past two hundred years. The same rosebushes, the same statues. It looked as if the drawing had been done in winter, though, as the boughs of the trees were skeletal. "What we need is out here."

"What do we need?" said Kit. "Indulge me. Explain what this has to do with my idle comment about ravens being unreliable."

"It would be unreliable. The thing is, Malcolm didn't say the raven was alive, or a real bird. We just assumed."

"No, but—" Kit paused. He'd been about to say it didn't make any sense to give your messages to a dead raven, but something about the look on Ty's face silenced him.

"It actually makes more sense for them to have just left the messages in a hiding place," said Ty. "One they could both get to easily." He crossed the grass to the statue of the boy with the bird on his wrist.

A little jolt went through Kit. He didn't know much about birds, but this one was carved out of glossy black stone. And it looked a lot like drawings he'd seen of ravens.

Ty reached around to run his fingers over the stone bird. There was a clicking noise, and a squeak of hinges. Kit hurried over to see Ty prying open a small opening in the bird's back. "Is there anything in there?"

Ty shook his head. "It's empty." He reached into his pocket, retrieved a folded-up piece of paper, and dropped it into the opening before sealing it back up again.

Kit stopped in his tracks. "You left a message."

Ty nodded. He'd folded up the drawing and put it in his pocket. His hand swung free at his side, the witchlight in it: Its light was dimmed, the moon providing enough illumination that they could both see.

"For Annabel?" said Kit.

Ty hesitated. "Don't tell anyone," he said finally. "It was just an idea I had."

"It was smart," said Kit. "Really smart—I don't think anyone else would have guessed about the statue. I don't think anyone else *could* have."

"But it might not matter," said Ty. "In which case I would have failed. And I'd rather no one know." He began to murmur under his breath, the way he did sometimes.

"I'll know."

Ty paused in his murmuring. "I don't mind," he said, "if it's you."

Kit wanted to ask him why not, wanted to ask badly, but Ty looked as if he wasn't sure he knew the answer himself. And he was still murmuring, the same soft stream of words that was somewhere between a whisper and a song. "What are you saying?" Kit asked finally, not sure if it was all right to ask, but unable to help his curiosity.

Ty glanced up at the moon through his lashes. They were thick and dark, almost childlike. They gave his face a look of innocence that made him look younger—a strange effect, at odds with his almost frighteningly sharp mind. "Just words I like," he said. "If I say them to myself, it makes my mind—quieter. Does it bother you?"

"No!" Kit said quickly. "I was just curious what words you liked."

Ty bit his lip. For a moment, Kit thought he wasn't going to say anything at all. "It's not the meaning, just the sound," he said. "Glass, twin, apple, whisper, stars, crystal, shadow, lilt." He glanced away from Kit, a shivering figure in his too-large hoodie, his black hair absorbing moonlight, giving none of it back.

"Whisper would be one of mine, too," said Kit. He took a step toward Ty, touched his shoulder gently. "Cloud, secret, highway, hurricane, mirror, castle, thorns."

"Blackthorns," said Ty, with a dazzling smile, and Kit knew, in that instant, that whatever he'd been telling himself about running away for the past few days had been a lie. And maybe it had been that lie that Livvy had been responding to, when she'd snapped at him outside the magic store that day—the kernel inside his own heart that had told him he might still be leaving.

But he knew now that he could reassure her. He wasn't leaving the Shadowhunters. He wasn't going anywhere. Because where the Blackthorns were, was his home now.

22

THE MOST UNHOLY

When Emma woke the next morning, she found she had managed *not* to tie herself in a knot around Julian while sleeping. Progress. Maybe because she'd spent all night having terrible dreams where she saw her father again, and he peeled off his face to reveal that he was Sebastian Morgenstern underneath.

"Luke, I am your father," she muttered, and heard Julian laugh softly. She staggered off to find her gear so she wouldn't have to watch him getting up adorably sleepy-eyed and tousle-haired. She changed in the office while Julian showered and dressed; they met up for a quick breakfast of toast and juice, and were off to find Annabel.

It was nearly noon and the sun was high in the sky by the time they made it to Porthallow Church—apparently what was *close* for piskies wasn't what humans would call nearby. Though Emma kept hearing the high voice of the piskie in her head. *Killing close*, it had said. Whatever that meant, she didn't like the sound of it.

The church had been built on a cliff over a headland. The sea spread out in the distance, a carpet of matte blue. Clouds brushstroked across the sky, like a ball of cotton someone had picked apart and scattered. The air was full of the hum of bees and the scent of late wildflowers.

The area around the church was overgrown, but the building itself was in decent shape despite having been abandoned. The windows had been carefully boarded up, and a KEEP OUT: PRIVATE PROPERTY: YOU ARE TRESPASSING sign was nailed to the front door. Some small distance from the church was a little graveyard, its gray, rain-washed tombstones barely visible among the long grass. The church's single square tower was cast in lonely relief against the sky. Emma adjusted Cortana on her back and glanced over at Julian, who was frowning down at her phone.

"What are you looking at?" she asked.

"Wikipedia. 'Porthallow Church is located above the sea, on the cliff-top at Talland near Polperro in Cornwall. The altar of the church is said to date from the time of King Mark, of Tristan and Isolde fame, and was built at the junction of ley lines.'"

"Wikipedia knows about ley lines?" Emma took her phone back.

"Wikipedia knows about everything. It might be run by warlocks."

"You think that's what they do all day in the Spiral Labyrinth? Run Wikipedia?"

"I admit it seems like a letdown."

Tucking the phone in her pocket, Emma indicated the church. "So this is another convergence?"

Julian shook his head. "A convergence is where every ley line in the area links up. This is a junction—two ley lines crossing. Still a powerful place." In the bright sunshine he drew a seraph blade from his belt, holding it against his side as they approached the church entrance.

"Do you know what you're going to say to Annabel?" Emma whispered.

"Not a clue," Julian said. "I guess I'll—" He broke off. There was something in his eyes: a troubled look.

"Is something wrong?" Emma asked.

They'd reached the church doors. "No," Julian said, after a long moment, and though Emma could tell he didn't mean it, she let it slide. She drew Cortana from her back, just in case.

Julian shouldered the doors open. The small lock holding them shut burst apart, and they were inside, Julian a few steps ahead of Emma. It was pitch-black inside the abandoned church. "*Arariel*," he murmured, and his seraph blade lit like a small bonfire, illuminating the interior.

A stone arcade ran along one side of the church, the pews nestled between the arches. The stone was carved with delicate designs of leaves. The nave and the transept, where the altar was usually located, were deep in shadow.

Emma heard Julian draw in his breath. "This is where Malcolm raised Annabel," he said. "I remember it from the scrying glass. This is where Arthur died."

"Are you sure?"

"Yes." Julian lowered his head. "*Ave atque vale*, Arthur Blackthorn." His voice was full of sorrow. "You died bravely and for your family."

"Jules . . ." She wanted to reach out and touch him, but he had already straightened up, any sorrow he felt cloaked beneath the mantle of being Nephilim.

"I don't know why Annabel would want to stay here," he said, sweeping the light of his seraph blade over the church's interior. It was thick with dust. "It can't be a spot with good memories for her."

"But if she's desperate for a hiding place . . ."

"Look." Julian indicated the altar, propped on a granite slab a few feet thick. It had a wooden top laid over the stone, and something flashed white against the wood. A folded piece of paper, pinned there by a knife.

Julian's name was scrawled on it in a feminine dark hand.

Emma ripped the paper away and handed it to Jules, who flicked it open quickly, holding it where they could both read by the light of Julian's blade.

> Julian,
>
>> You may consider this in the nature of a test. If you are here, reading this note, you have failed it.

Emma heard Julian draw in his breath. They read on:

>> I told the piskies that I was living here, in the church. It is not true. I would not remain where so much blood has spilled. But I knew that you could not leave my whereabouts alone, that you would ask the piskies where I was, that you would search me out.
>>
>> Though I had asked you not to.
>>
>> Now you are here in this place. I wish you were not, for I was not the only thing that was raised by Malcolm Fade and your uncle's blood. But you had to see what the Black Volume can do.
>>
>> —Annabel

Cristina was sitting in the embrasure of the library window, reading, when she glanced out the window and saw a familiar dark figure slipping through the front gates.

She'd been in the library for several hours, dutifully going through the books in the languages she knew best—Spanish, Ancient Greek, Old Castilian, and Aramaic—for mentions of the Black Volume. Not that she could concentrate.

Memories of the night before kept hitting her at odd moments, like when she was passing the sugar to Ty and nearly spilled it in his lap. Had she really kissed Mark? Danced with Kieran? *Enjoyed* dancing with Kieran?

No, she thought, she'd be truthful with herself: She had enjoyed it. It had been like riding with the Wild Hunt. She'd felt drawn out of her own body, spinning through the stars and clouds. It had been like the stories of revels her mother had told her when she was a child, where mortals had lost themselves in the dances of Faerie-kind, and died for the beautiful joy of it.

Of course, afterward they'd all simply gone back to their separate rooms—Kieran calmly, Mark and Cristina both looking shaken. And Cristina had lain there a long time, not sleeping, looking at the ceiling and wondering what she had gotten herself into.

She set down her book with a sigh. It didn't help that she was alone in the library—Magnus was in and out of the infirmary, where Mark was helping him set up equipment to mix the binding spell cure, and Dru was helping Alec look after the children in one of the spare rooms. Livvy, Ty, and Kit had gone to pick up the supplies from Hypatia Vex's shop. Bridget had been in and out with trays of sandwiches and tea, muttering that she was worked off her feet and that the house was more crowded than a train station. Kieran was . . . nowhere.

Cristina had grown used to a certain amount of controlled chaos in Los Angeles, but she found herself longing for the quiet of the Mexico City Institute, the silence of her mother's rose garden, and even the dreamy afternoons she'd spent with Diego and sometimes Jaime in the Bosque de Chapultepec.

And she missed Emma. Her thoughts were a whirl of confusion—everything was—and she wanted Emma to talk to her, Emma to braid her hair and tell her stupid jokes and make her laugh. Maybe Emma would be able to make some sense out of what had happened the night before.

She reached for her phone, and then drew her hand back. She wasn't going to start texting Emma all her problems, not when they were in the middle of so much. She glanced resolutely out the window instead—and saw Kieran, crossing the courtyard.

He was all in black. She didn't know where he'd gotten the clothes, but they made him look like a slender shadow under the gray and rainy sky that had replaced the morning's blue. His hair was blue-black, his hands hidden by gloves.

There was no rule that Kieran wasn't supposed to leave the Institute, not really. But he hated the city, Mark had said. Cold iron and steel everywhere. And besides, they were meant to keep him safe with them, not let him slip away before he could testify in front of the Clave. Not let anything happen to him.

And maybe he was upset. Maybe he was angry at Mark, jealous, though he hadn't shown it the night before. She slid off the windowsill. Kieran was already slipping through the opening of the gate, into the rainy shadows beyond, where he seemed to flicker and vanish, as faeries did.

Cristina dashed out of the library. She thought she heard someone call after her as she ran down the hallway, but she didn't dare pause. Kieran was fast. She'd lose him.

There was no time to stop to put on a Soundless rune, no time to look for her stele. She hurried down the stairs and grabbed up a jacket hanging on a peg in the entryway. She slid her arms into it and ducked out into the courtyard.

A throb went through her wrist, a warning ache that she was leaving Mark behind. She ignored it, following Kieran through the gate.

Maybe he wasn't doing anything wrong, she told herself, trying to be fair. He wasn't a prisoner in the Institute. Maybe Mark knew about this.

Kieran was hurrying down the narrow street, slipping from shadow to shadow. There was something furtive about the way he moved. Cristina was sure of it.

She kept to the side of the road as she followed him. The streets were deserted, damp with a sprinkling of rain. Without a glamour rune, Cristina was intensely conscious of not being spotted by a mundane—her runes were very visible, and she couldn't be sure they wouldn't react in a way that would tip Kieran off.

She worried that eventually they'd reach a busier street, and she'd be seen. Her arm was more than throbbing now; a sharp pain was lancing through it, as if a steel wire was being tightened around her wrist.

Yet as Kieran moved deeper into the heart of the city, the streets seemed to grow narrower rather than wider. The electric lights dimmed. The small iron fences around the trees vanished, and the branches above her began to reach together across the roads, forming a green canopy.

Kieran walked ahead of her steadily, a shadow among shadows.

Finally they reached a square of brick buildings facing inward, their fronts covered in ivy and green trellises. In the center of the square was a small patch of ordinary city greenery: a few trees, flat, well-cared-for grass, and a stone fountain in the middle. The faint splashing of water was audible as Cristina slipped behind a tree, pressing herself against the bark, and peered around the side at Kieran.

He had paused by the fountain, and a figure in a green cloak was approaching him, leisurely, from the far side of the small park. His face was familiar: He had soft brown skin and eyes that gleamed even in the darkness. His hands were long and slender; under the cloak, he wore a doublet worked with the broken crown of the Unseelie Court. It was Adaon.

"Kieran," he said wearily. "Why did you summon me?"

Kieran gave a small bow. Cristina could sense that he was nervous. It was surprising, that she knew Kieran enough to know when he was nervous. She would have said he was a near stranger.

"Adaon, my brother," he said. "I need your help. I need what you know of spells."

Kieran's brother arched an eyebrow. "I would not set to casting spells in the mundane world, were I you, little dark one. You are among Nephilim, and they will disapprove, as will the warlocks and witches of this place."

"I do not want to cast a spell. I want to undo one. A binding spell."

"Ah," said Adaon. "Who does it bind?"

"Mark," said Kieran.

"*Mark,*" Adaon echoed, a little mockingly. "What is so special about him, that you care if he is bound? Or should he be bound only to you?"

"I would not want that," Kieran said fiercely. "I would never want that. He should love me freely."

"Binding is not love, though it can reveal feelings otherwise buried." Adaon looked thoughtful. "I had not imagined I would hear you speak so, little dark one. When you were a child, you took what you wanted with no thought of the cost."

"No one in the Wild Hunt remains a child," said Kieran.

"It is a pity you were sent away," said Adaon. "You would have made a good King after our father, and the Court loved you."

Kieran shook his head. "I would not want to be King."

"Because you would have to give up Mark," said Adaon. "But every king gives up something. It is the nature of kings."

"But kings are not in my nature." Kieran tilted his head back to look up at his taller brother. "I think you are the one who would make a ruler, brother. Someone to bring peace back to the Lands."

"This is not just about a binding spell, is it?" said Adaon. "There is something else to all of this. Our father believes you have taken refuge with Shadowhunters to escape his wrath; I admit, I assumed the same. Is there more?"

"There might be," said Kieran. "I know you will not move against our father, but I also know you do not like him, or find his rule fair. If the throne were open, would you take it?"

"*Kieran*," said Adaon. "These are not things of which we speak."

"There has been bloodshed for so long, and no hope," said Kieran. "This is not about my safety alone. You must believe that."

"What are you planning, Kieran?" said Adaon. "What trouble have you gotten yourself into now?"

A hand clapped itself across Cristina's mouth. Another arm whipped around her, securing her. Her body jackknifed in surprise and she felt the grip on her loosen. She jerked her head backward, felt her skull connect with someone's face, and heard a yowl of pain.

"Who's there?" Adaon spun, hand on the hilt of his blade. "Show yourself!"

Something dug into Cristina's throat—something long and sharp. The blade of a knife. She froze.

"We should go," Emma whispered. She didn't ask Julian what Annabel had meant. She suspected they both knew.

Something dark and slippery flashed by across the transept, something that moved with a grotesque fluidity. The room seemed to darken. Emma wrinkled her nose—the rotten smell of demonic presence was suddenly all around, as if she'd opened a box full of a horrible potpourri.

Julian's face was luminous-pale in the shadows. He crumpled up the letter in his hand and they began to back out of the church, taking careful steps, the seraph blade offering flickering illumination. They were halfway to the exit when there was an enormous crash—the two big front doors of the church had slammed shut.

Faintly, Emma heard the giggle of a piskie.

They spun around as the altar overturned. It hit the ground with a shattering thud.

"You go left," Emma whispered. "I'll go right."

Julian slipped away noiselessly. Emma could still sense him there, his presence nearby. They had paused to rune each other halfway from the town to the church, looking out over Tal-land Bay and the blue ocean. Her runes prickled alive now as she slipped down the row of a pew and made her way along the inside wall of the church.

She had reached the nave. Shadows gathered thickly here, but her Night Vision rune was sparking and she was finding it easier to see in the dark. She could see the overturned altar, the huge blot of dried blood that stained the stone floor. There was a bloody handprint on one of the nearby pillars. It looked wrong and hor-rible, inside a church like this; it made Emma think of an Institute defiled.

Of Sebastian, spilling blood at the threshold of the Los Angeles stronghold of the Shadowhunters.

She flinched, and for just that moment of memory, her focus was diverted. Something flickered at the edge of her vision, just as Julian's voice exploded in her ears: *"Emma, look out!"*

Emma flung herself sideways, away from the flickering shadow. She landed on the overturned altar and spun around to see a rip-pling horror rising in front of her. It was scarlet-black, the color of blood—it *was* blood, formed of clotted, sludgy scarlet, with two burning white eyes. Its hands ended in flat points like the tip of a shovel, each with a single black, curved talon protruding from it. The talons dripped with a thin, lucent slime.

It spoke. Blood poured from its mouth, a black slash in its scar-let face. *"I am Sabnock of Thule. How dare you stand before me, ugly human?"*

Emma was surprised not to be called Shadowhunter—most demons knew the Nephilim. But she didn't show it. "How per-sonal," she said. "I'm hurt."

"I do not understand your words." Sabnock slipped toward her. Emma edged backward on the altar. She could feel Julian some-where behind her; she knew he was there, without looking.

"Most don't," she said. "It's a burden, being sarcastic."

"Blood drew me here," it said. *"Blood is what I am. Blood spilled in hate and anger. Blood spilled in frustrated love. Blood spilled in despair."*

"You're a demon," Emma said, holding Cortana out, straight and level. "I don't really need to know why or how. I just need you to go back where you came from."

"I came from blood, and to blood I will return," said the demon, and leaped, talons and teeth bared. Emma hadn't even realized it *had* teeth, but there they were, like shards of red glass.

She flipped backward, somersaulting away from the creature. It hit the altar with the sound of fluid smacking against something solid. The world spun around Emma as she turned. She felt utterly cold down to her bones, the freezing calm of battle that slowed everything in the world around her.

She landed, straightening. The demon was crouched at the edge of the altar, snarling. It leaped again, and this time she slashed at it, a swift upward thrust.

Cortana met no resistance. It slid through the creature's shoulder; blood splashed onto Emma's wrist and forearm. Slimy, clotted, foul blood. She gagged as the thing spun like a tornado, whipping out at her with its glassine claw. They twirled across the floor of the church in a sort of dance, Cortana flashing and gleaming. It was impossible to wound the thing—hacking and slashing at it only opened up a temporary gap, like a dent in water, that closed up immediately.

She didn't dare take her eyes off the demon long enough to look around for Julian. She knew he was there, but he felt farther away, as if he'd gone to the other side of the church. She couldn't see the distant, flashing star of his seraph blade, either. *Jules,* she thought. *A little help now would be good.*

With a frustrated growl, the demon charged again. Emma swung, an overhead two-fisted slash, and the demon howled; she'd smashed a few of its teeth in. A sharp pain lanced up her arm. She twisted the sword, grinding it into the demon's head, breathing in the pleasure of its screams.

Light exploded into the world. She staggered back, her eyes burning. A square was opening in the roof above, like the sunroof of a car peeling back. She saw a shadow against the sun; Julian, perched on one of the church's highest rafters, and then the sunlight speared down through the gap and the demon began to burn.

It shrieked as it burned. Its edges blackening, it staggered back. The room stank of boiling blood. Julian dropped from the rafters, landing on the altar: His stele was in one hand, his seraph blade in the other.

She held out her free hand, the one that wasn't clasping Cortana, toward him. He knew what she wanted, without asking. The seraph blade arced through the air toward her like a firework. Emma caught it, spun, and drove the blade into the weakened, burning demon.

With a last shriek, it vanished.

The silence that came after was stunning. Emma gasped, her ears ringing, and turned to Jules. "That was *awesome*—"

Jules flung himself down from the altar, grabbing the ichor-smeared seraph blade out of her hand. It was already starting to warp out of shape, choked with demon blood. He hurled it aside and grabbed Emma's hand, flipping it over so he could see the long scratch that ran from the back of her palm up her forearm.

He was stark white. "What happened? Did it bite you?"

"Not exactly. I sliced myself on its teeth."

He ran his fingers up her arm. She winced. It was a long and narrow cut, but not shallow. "It doesn't burn? Or sting?"

"I'm fine," she said. "Jules. I'm fine."

He stared at her for a moment. His eyes were fierce and tearless in the harsh light from above. He turned away without another word and stalked down the aisle of the church, toward the doors.

Emma looked down at her hand. Her wound was quite ordinary,

she thought; it would need to be cleaned, but it wasn't anything out of the usual in terms of injuries sustained in battle. She slid Cortana back into its sheath and followed Julian out of the church.

For a moment, she didn't see him at all. It was as if he'd vanished, and all that was left was the view from the church. Green fields fading away into a wash of blue: blue sea, blue sky, the blue haze of distant hills.

She heard a cry, thin and faint, and ran toward it, toward the graveyard where headstones thinned and faded by time tilted back and forth like a pack of scattered playing cards.

There was a loud squeak. "Let me go! Let me *go!*" Emma spun around and saw the grass moving; the smallest piskie was wriggling madly, pinned to the ground by Jules, whose bleakly cold expression sent a shiver through Emma.

"You locked us in with that thing," Julian said, his arm across the piskie's throat. "Didn't you?"

"Didn't know it was there! Didn't know!" squeaked the piskie, twisting under Julian's hold.

"What's the difference?" Emma protested. "Julian. Don't—"

"Necromancy happened in that church. It tore open a hole between dimensions that let a demon through. It could have ripped us to shreds."

"Didn't know!" the piskie whined.

"Who didn't know?" Julian demanded. "Because I'll bet anything *you* did."

The piskie went limp, boneless. Julian pinned it with a knee. "The lady said to tell you to go there. She said you were dangerous. Would kill faeries."

"I might now," said Julian.

"It's all right, Jules," Emma said. She knew the piskie wasn't the innocent, childlike creature it appeared to be. But something about seeing it twist and whimper made her feel sick.

"It's not all right. You were hurt," Julian said, and the cold tone in his voice made her remember the look on his face when Anselm Nightshade was led away. *Julian, you scared me a little,* she'd said at the time.

But then, Nightshade had been guilty. Clary had said so.

"Leave him alone!" It was another one of the piskies, wavering palely in the grass. A female piskie, judging from clothes and hair length. She waved her hands ineffectually at Julian. "He doesn't know anything!"

Julian didn't move. He stared icily down at the faerie. He looked like a statue of an avenging angel, something blank and pitiless.

"Don't come near us again," he said. "Speak of this to no one. Or we will find you, and I will make you pay."

The piskie nodded jerkily. Julian stood up, and the piskies vanished as if the ground had swallowed them up.

"Did you have to scare them so much?" Emma said, a little hesitantly. Julian still had that frighteningly blank expression on his face, as if his body was here but his mind was a million miles away.

"Better scared than making trouble." Julian turned to her. A little of the color was coming back to his skin. "You need an *iratze.*"

"It's all right. It doesn't hurt that much, and besides, I want to clean it first." *Iratzes* could heal skin over any wound, but sometimes that meant sealing in infection or dirt.

Concern flickered in his eyes. "Then we should go back to the cottage. But first, I need your help with something."

Emma thought of the broken altar, the spilled blood, and groaned. "Don't say cleaning up."

"We're not going to clean the church up," said Julian. "We're going to burn it down."

Whoever was holding Cristina was strong, stronger than a mundane human.

"Now step forward, and do as I say," said the voice behind her, breathless but low and confident. She found herself shoved ahead into the center of the park. She was hauled toward the fountain, and the two faeries standing there. Both of them stared—Kieran at her, his brother a little above her head.

"Erec," Adaon said, sounding weary. "What are you doing here?"

"I followed you." Erec's voice echoed behind Cristina. She remembered him with a flare of hate, remembered him in Faerie, Julian's knife against his throat as his was against her own now. "I was curious as to your purpose here. And I wanted to see our little brother, too."

"Let her go," Kieran said, with a gesture toward Cristina. He didn't meet her eyes. "She's nothing to do with this. Just a Shadowhunter spying without my knowledge."

"You said she's nothing to do with you," Erec sneered. "Not that you don't care." Hot silver pain flashed at Cristina's throat. She felt the warmth of blood. She stiffened her spine, refusing to flinch.

"Leave her be." Kieran's face was a pale mask of rage. "Do you want the Nephilim after you, Erec? Are you a fool? I *know* you're a torturer—you used to torture me." He took a step toward Cristina and Erec. "Do you remember? You made these." He shoved his loose black sleeves up, and Cristina saw the long scars on his arms. "And the ones on my back."

"You were a soft child," said Erec. "Too soft to be the son of a King. Kindness has no place in the court of a broken crown." He chuckled. "Besides, I come with news. Father has sent the Seven."

Kieran paled even further. "Mannan's Seven? Sent them where?"

"Here. To the mundane world. They are tasked to retrieve the Black Volume, now that the death of Malcolm Fade is known. They *will* find it, and before you do."

"The Black Volume is nothing to do with me," said Kieran.

"But it is to do with our father," said Adaon. "He has wanted it since the First Heir was stolen."

"Longer than he has hated the Nephilim?" Kieran said.

Erec spat. "Those Nephilim you love so. They are a doomed race. You are wasting yourself, Kieran, when you could be much more."

"Let him be, Erec," Adaon said. "What do you imagine Father would do if Kieran came home, besides kill him?"

"If Father was still alive to kill anyone."

"Enough scheming!" roared Adaon. "Enough, Erec!"

"Then let him prove he's loyal!" Erec removed the knife from Cristina's throat with a sudden gesture; she spluttered and coughed. Her wrist was searing pain and Erec's hands were iron bands around her upper arms. He shoved her forward, toward his brothers, without releasing his grip. "Kill the Shadowhunter," he shouted at Kieran. "Adaon, give him your blade. Run it through her heart, Kieran. Show you are loyal and I will intercede for you with Father. You can be welcomed back at Court instead of killed or exiled to the Hunt."

Adaon put his hand to his side, to sieze his sword, but Kieran had already seized it. Cristina struggled, kicking out, but she couldn't dislodge Erec's grip. Terror rose up in her as Kieran came toward them both, the faerie sword glimmering in his hand, his eyes flat as mirrors.

Cristina began to pray. *Angel, keep me safe. Raziel, help me.* She kept her eyes open. She wouldn't close them. That was a coward's way to die. If the Angel wanted her to die now, she'd die on her feet with her eyes open like Jonathan Shadowhunter. She would—

Kieran's eyes flickered, minutely, his head tilting. She followed the movement, suddenly understanding, as he lifted the sword in his hand. He swung it forward—and she ducked her head.

The sword sliced through the air cleanly above her. Something hot and wet and copper-smelling spilled across her back. She cried out, pivoting away as Erec's arms released her, his throat severed to the spine, his body crumpling to the pebbled path.

"*Kieran,*" Adaon breathed in horror. Kieran stood over Erec's body, the blood-smeared sword in his hand. "What have you done?"

"He would have killed her," Kieran said. "And she is my—and Mark—"

Cristina caught at the fountain to hold herself up. Her legs felt numb. The pain in her arm was fire.

Adaon strode forward and snatched the sword from Kieran's hand. "Iarlath was not your blood," he said. His skin looked tight with shock. "But Erec was. You will be denounced a kin-slayer if anyone discovers what you have done."

Kieran raised his head. His eyes burned into his brother's. "Will *you* tell them?"

Adaon jerked the hood up over his face. Wind had begun to blow through the square—a cold, sharp squall of it. Adaon's cloak flapped like wings. "Go, Kieran. Seek the safety of the Institute."

Adaon bent over Erec's body. It was twisted at a violent angle, blood running among the pebbles and grass. As he knelt, Kieran started to walk out of the park—and stopped.

Slowly, he turned back and looked at Cristina. "Aren't you coming?"

"Yes." She was surprised at the steadiness of her own voice, but her body betrayed her—when she stood upright, agony shot through her arm, down into her side, and she doubled over, gasping.

A moment later there were hands on her, none too gentle, and she felt herself lifted off the ground. She started in surprise—Kieran had picked her up and was carrying her from the park.

She let her arms dangle, not knowing what else to do. She was speechless. Despite the dancing the night before, it was bizarre to be held by Kieran like this. Mark had been there, then—and now they were alone.

"Do not be foolish," said Kieran. "Put your arms around me. I do not want to drop you and then have to explain matters to Mark."

He would have killed her. And she is my—and Mark—

She wondered what he'd meant to say. *Mark would have been angry? Mark would have been disappointed? She is my friend?*

No, he couldn't have meant that. Kieran didn't like her. She was sure of it. And maybe that hadn't been what he'd said at all. Her memories were becoming blurred with pain.

They were passing down a street whose lights seemed to change from gas to electric as they went. Illumination blinked on in windows overhead. Cristina raised her arms and put them around Kieran's neck. She laced her fingers together, biting her lip against the pain of the binding spell.

Kieran's hair tickled her fingers. It was soft, surprisingly so. His skin was incredibly fine-grained, more so than any human's, like the surface of polished porcelain. She remembered Mark kissing Kieran against a tree in the desert, hands on his hair, pushing the neck of his sweater down to get at his skin, his bones, his body. She blushed.

"Why did you follow me?" Kieran said stiffly.

"I saw you through the library window," said Cristina. "I thought you were running away."

"I went to see Adaon, as I promised I would, that is all. Besides"—he laughed shortly—"where have I to go?"

"People often run even when they have nowhere to go," said Cristina. "It is all about what you can bear in the place where you are."

There was a long silence, long enough that Cristina assumed Kieran wasn't planning to answer. Then he spoke. "I have the sense," he said, "that I have done Mark some kind of wrong. I do not know what it was. But I see it in his eyes when he looks at me. He thinks he is hiding it, but he is not. Though he can lie with his mouth, he has never learned to conceal the truth in his eyes."

"You'll have to ask Mark," said Cristina. They had reached the street that led to the Institute. Cristina could see the spire of it rising in the distance. "When Adaon said that if you became King, you'd have to give up Mark, what did he mean?"

"A King of Faerie can have no human consort." He looked down at her with his eyes like stars. "Mark lies about you. But I have seen the way he looks at you. Last night, when we danced. He more than desires you."

"Do—do you mind?" Cristina said.

"I do not mind you," said Kieran. "I thought I would, but I do not. It is something about you. You are beautiful, and you are kind, and you are—good. I do not know why that should make a difference. But it does."

He sounded almost surprised. Cristina said nothing. Her blood was getting on Kieran's shirt. It was a surreal sight. His body was warm, not cold as marble as she'd always imagined. He smelled faintly of night and woods, a clean smell untouched by the city.

"Mark needs kindness," Kieran said, after a long pause. "And so do I."

They'd reached the Institute, and Kieran went quickly up the stairs—and paused at the top. His arms tautened around her.

Cristina looked at him, puzzled. Then the light dawned. "You can't open the door," she said. "You're not a Shadowhunter."

"That is the case." Kieran blinked at the doors as if they'd surprised him.

"What if you'd come back without me?" Cristina had the most bizarre urge to laugh, though nothing that had happened had been funny, and Erec's blood still stiffened the back of her clothes. She wondered how many times she'd have to shower before she felt even a little clean. "I really would have imagined you'd thought further ahead."

"I seem to have absorbed some of your human impulsiveness," Kieran said.

He sounded shocked at himself. Taking pity on him, Cristina began to unknot her fingers from around his neck.

She reached for the door, but it swung inward. Light blazed out of the entryway, and on the threshold stood Mark, staring from one of them to the other in astonishment.

"Where were you?" he demanded. "By the Angel—Kieran, Cristina—" He reached out as if to take her from Kieran's arms.

"It's all right," Cristina said. "I can stand."

Kieran gently lowered her to the ground. The pain in her arm was already beginning to fade, though looking at Mark's wrist— red, puffy, ringed with blood—filled her with guilt. It was so hard to believe, even now, that the pain she felt was his pain too; her bleeding, his bleeding.

Mark drew his hand down her sleeve, already hardening as Erec's blood dried. "All this blood—it's not just your wrist—and why would you go out, either of you—?"

"It is not her blood," said Kieran. "It is my brother's."

They were all in the entryway now. Kieran reached behind him and deliberately shut the massive front doors with a loud clang. Above them, Cristina could hear footsteps, someone hurrying downstairs.

"Your brother's?" Mark echoed. Against Kieran's dark clothes the blood hadn't been very visible, but Mark seemed to look more closely now and see the thin spatters of scarlet against Kieran's neck and cheek. "You mean—Adaon?"

Kieran looked dazed. "I went to meet him, to speak of the binding spell and of his possible accession to the throne."

"And blood was spilled? But why?" Mark touched Kieran's cheek gently. "If we had known there might be a fight, we never would have suggested you talk to him on our behalf. And why did you go alone? Why did you not tell me, or bring me with you?"

Kieran closed his eyes for just a moment, turning his cheek into the cup of Mark's palm. "I did not want to risk you," he said in a low voice.

Mark met Cristina's eyes, over Kieran's shoulder. "It wasn't Adaon who wanted a fight," she said, rubbing her wrist. "It was Erec."

Kieran opened his eyes, gently drawing Mark's hand away from his face, lacing his fingers through Mark's as he did. "He must have followed Adaon to our meeting place," he said. "I never even had the chance to tell Adaon of our plans for him, and the throne." His eyes darkened. "Mark, there is something you must know—"

Magnus burst into the vestibule, Alec behind him. They were both out of breath. "What's going on?" Alec asked.

"Where are the children?" Kieran said. "The little ones, and the blue child with the small horns?"

Alec blinked. "Bridget's watching them," he said. "Why?"

"I will explain in more detail when I can," said Kieran. "For now, you must know this. The King my father has sent the Seven Riders to find the Black Volume, and they are here in London. I imagine he believes the location of the Black Volume is known by those in this Institute. The danger is great. We are safe within these walls for now, but—"

Mark had gone white. "But Livvy and Ty aren't within these walls," he said. "They went with Kit to get the ingredients for the binding spell. They're somewhere in the city."

There was a babble of voices, Alec snapping out a question, Magnus gesturing. But the pain and shock—not just hers, but Mark's—was graying out Cristina's vision, however much she tried to cling onto consciousness. She tried to say something but the words disappeared, everything sliding up and away from her as she tumbled into the shadows.

She wasn't sure whether it was Mark or Kieran who caught her as she fell.

* * *

Rain clouds had replaced blue sky over London. Ty, Kit, and Livvy had decided to walk back from Hypatia's after picking up Magnus's ingredients, rather than wait in the fussy, damp line for the riverboat.

Kit was enjoying himself kicking his way through puddles on the Thames Path, which wound like a granite snake along the side of the river. They'd passed the Tower of London again, and Ty had pointed out Traitor's Gate, where condemned criminals had once entered the tower to have their heads chopped off.

Livvy had sighed. "I wish Dru was with us. She would have liked that. She's hardly come out of her room lately."

"I think she's afraid someone will make her babysit if she does," said Kit. He wasn't sure he had a clear impression of Dru yet—more a blurred sense of a round face, flushed cheeks, and a lot of black clothes. She had the Blackthorn eyes, but they were usually focused on something else.

"I think she's keeping a secret," Livvy said. They'd passed Millennium Bridge, a long iron line stretching across the river, and were nearing an older-looking bridge, painted a dented red and gray.

Ty was humming to himself, lost in thought. The river was the same color as his eyes today, a sort of steely-gray, touched with bits of silver. The white band of his headphones was around his neck, trapping his unruly black hair under it. He looked puzzled. "Why would she do that?"

"It's just a feeling I have," said Livvy. "I can't *prove* it. . . ." Her voice trailed off. She was squinting into the distance, her hand up to shield her face from the gray afternoon light. "What's that?"

Kit followed her glance and felt a coldness pass through him. Shapes were moving through the sky, a line of racing figures, silhouetted against the clouds. Three horses, clear as paper outlines, with three riders on their backs.

He looked around wildly. Mundanes were all around, paying

little to no attention to the three teenagers in jeans and hooded raincoats hurrying along with their bags full of magic powders.

"The Wild Hunt?" Kit said. "But why—?"

"I don't think it's the Wild Hunt," said Livvy. "They ride at night. It's broad daylight." She put her hand to her side, where her seraph blades hung.

"I don't like this." Ty sounded breathless. The figures were incredibly close now, skimming the top of the bridge, angling downward. "They're coming toward us."

They turned, but it was too late. Kit felt a breeze ruffle his hair as the horses and their riders passed overhead. A moment later there was a clatter as the three landed in a neat pattern around Kit, Livvy, and Ty, cutting off their retreat.

The horses were a glimmering bronze in color, and their riders were bronze-skinned and bronze-haired, wearing half masks of gleaming metal. They were beautiful, bizarre and unearthly, entirely out of place in the shadows of the bridge as the water taxis skated by and the road above hummed with traffic.

They were clearly faeries, but nothing like the ones Kit had seen before in the Shadow Market. They were taller and bigger, and they were armed, despite the edicts of the Cold Peace. Each wore a massive sword at his waist.

"Nephilim," said one, in a voice that sounded like glaciers breaking apart. "I am Eochaid of the Seven Riders, and these are my brothers Etarlam and Karn. Where is the Black Volume?"

"The Black Volume?" Livvy echoed. The three of them had squeezed tighter against the wall of the path. Kit noticed people giving them odd glances as they passed by, and he knew they looked as if they were staring at nothing.

"Yes," said Etarlam. "Our King seeks it. You will give it up."

"We don't have it," said Ty. "And we don't know where it is."

Karn laughed. "You are but children, so we are inclined to be lenient," he said. "But understand this. The Riders of Mannan have done the bidding of the Unseelie King for a thousand years. In that time many have fallen to our blades, and we have spared none for any reason, not for age or weakness or infirmity of body. We will not spare you now." He leaned over the mane of his horse, and Kit saw for the first time that the horse had a shark's eyes, inky and flat and deadly. "Either you know where the Black Volume is, or you will make useful prisoners to tempt those who do. Which will it be, Shadowhunters?"

23

SKIES OF FIRE

"I win again." Jaime threw down his cards: all hearts. He grinned triumphantly at Dru. "Don't feel bad. Cristina used to say I had the devil's luck."

"Wouldn't the devil have bad luck?" Dru didn't mind losing to Jaime. He always seemed pleased, and she didn't care one way or the other.

He'd slept on the floor at the side of her bed the night before, and when she'd woken up, she'd rolled over and looked down at him, her chest full of happiness. Asleep, Jaime looked vulnerable, and more like his brother, though she thought now that he was better-looking than Diego.

Jaime was a secret, her secret. Something important she was doing, whether the others knew it or not. She knew he was on an important mission, something he couldn't talk much about; it was like having a spy in her room, or a superhero.

"I will miss you," he said frankly, linking his fingers together and stretching out his arms like a cat stretching in the sun. "This is the most fun, and the most rest, I have had in a long time."

"We can stay friends after this, right?" she said. "I mean, when you're done with your mission."

"I don't know when I'll be done." A shadow crossed his face. Jaime was much quicker of mood than his brother: He could be happy, then sad, then thoughtful, then laughing in a five-minute period. "It could be a long time." He looked at her sideways. "You may come to resent me. I've made you keep secrets from your family."

"They keep secrets from me," she said. "They think I'm too young to know anything."

Jaime frowned. Dru felt a little pinch of worry—they'd never discussed how old she was; why would they have? Usually, though, people thought she was at least seventeen. Her curves were bigger than other girls' her age, and Dru was used to boys staring at them.

So far Jaime hadn't stared, at least not the way other boys did, as if they had a right to her body. As if she ought to be grateful for the attention. And she'd discovered she desperately didn't want him to know she was only thirteen.

"Well, Julian does," she went on. "And Julian's pretty much in charge of everything. The thing is, when we were all younger, we were all just 'the kids.' But after my parents died, and Julian basically brought us all up, we split into groups. I got labeled 'younger' and Julian was suddenly older, like a parent."

"I know what that is like," he said. "Diego and I used to play like puppies when we were children. Then he grew up and decided he had to save the world and started ordering me around."

"Exactly," she said. "That's exactly right."

He reached down to pull his duffel bag onto the bed. "I can't stay much longer," he said. "But before I go—I have something for you."

He pulled a laptop computer out of the bag. Dru stared at him— he wasn't going to give her a laptop, was he? He flipped it open, a grin spreading across his face. It was a Peter Pan sort of grin, one that said that he would never be done with mischief. "I downloaded *The House That Dripped Blood*," he said. "I thought we could watch it together."

Dru clapped her hands together and scrambled up onto the mattress beside him. He scooted over, giving her plenty of room. She watched him as he tilted the screen toward them so they could both see. She could read the words that curled up his arm, though she didn't know what they meant. *La sangre sin fuego hierve.*

"And yes," he said, as the first images began to unroll across the screen. "I hope we will in the future be friends."

"Jules," Emma said, leaning against the wall of the church. "Are you sure this is a good idea? Doesn't there seem something kind of sacrilegious about burning down a church?"

"It's abandoned. Unhallowed." Julian pushed his jacket sleeves up. He was marking himself with a Strength rune, neatly and precisely, on the inside of his forearm. Behind him Emma could see the curve of the bay, the water dashing itself in blue curls against the shore.

"Still—we respect all religions. Every religion tithes to Shadowhunters. That's how we live. This seems—"

"Disrespectful?" Julian smiled with little humor. "Emma, you didn't see what I saw. What Malcolm did. He ripped apart the fabric of what made this church a hallowed place. He spilled blood, and then his blood was spilled. And when a church becomes a slaughterhouse like that, it's worse than if it was some other kind of building." He raked a hand through his hair. "Remember what Valentine did with the Mortal Sword? When he took it from the Silent City?"

Emma nodded. Everyone knew the story. It was part of Shadowhunter history. "He changed its alliance from seraphic to infernal. Changed it from good to evil."

"And this church has been changed too." He craned his head back to look up at the tower. "As sacrosanct a place as it once was, it's that unholy now. And demons will keep being attracted to it, and keep coming through, and they won't stay put here—they'll come to the village. They'll be a danger to the mundanes who live there. And to us."

"Tell me this isn't just you wanting to burn down a church because you want to make a statement."

Julian smiled at her blandly—the sort of smile that made everyone love him and trust him, that made him seem harmless. Forgettable even. But Emma saw through it to the razor blades beneath. "I don't think anyone wants to hear any statements I have to make."

Emma sighed. "It's a stone building. You can't just draw a Fire rune on it and expect it to go up like matches."

He looked at her levelly. "I remember what happened in the car," he said. "When you healed me. I know what a rune that's made when we draw on each other's energy can do."

"You want my help for this?"

Julian turned so he was facing the wall of the church, a gray sheet of granite, punctuated by boarded-up windows. Grass grew out of control around their feet, starred with dandelions. In the far distance Emma could hear the cries of children on the beach.

He reached out with his stele and drew on the stone of the wall. The rune flickered, tiny flames lapping at its edge. *Fire.* But the flames died down quickly, absorbed into the stone.

"Put your hands on me," Julian said.

"What?" Emma wasn't sure she'd heard him right.

"It would help if we were touching," he said in a matter-of-fact manner. "Put your hands on my back, maybe, or my shoulders."

Emma moved up behind him. He was taller than her; lifting her hands to his shoulders would mean stretching her body into an awkward position. This close to him, she could feel the expansion of his rib cage when he breathed, see the tiny freckles on the back of his neck where the wind had blown his hair sideways. The arc of broad shoulders into narrower waist and hips, the length of his legs.

She placed her hands on his waist, as if she were riding behind him on a motorcycle, under his jacket but on top of his T-shirt. His skin was warm through the cotton.

"All right," she said. Her breath moved his hair; a shiver went over his skin. She could *feel* it. She swallowed. "Go ahead."

She half-closed her eyes as the stele scratched against the wall. He smelled like cut grass, which wasn't surprising, considering he'd been rolling in it with the struggling piskie.

"Why wouldn't anyone want to hear them?" she asked.

"Hear what?" Julian reached up. His T-shirt rose, and Emma found her hands on bare skin, taut over oblique muscles. Her breath caught.

"Any statements you had to make about, you know, anything," Emma said, as his feet settled back onto the ground. Her hands were tangled in the fabric of his shirt now. She looked up to see a second Fire rune: This one was deeper, darker, and the flames at its edges shone brightly. The stone around it began to crack—

And the fire went out.

"It might not work," Emma said. Her heart was pounding. She wanted this to work, and at the same time she didn't. Their runes ought to be more powerful when created together; that was the case for all *parabatai*. But there was a limit to that power. Unless two *parabatai* were in love with each other. Jem had made it sound as if their power, then, could be almost infinite—that it might grow until it destroyed them.

Julian no longer loved her; she'd seen it in the way he'd kissed that faerie girl. Still, it would be hard to have to watch the proof.

But maybe it would be the best thing for her. She'd have to face reality sooner rather than later.

She slid her arms around Julian, clasping them together across his stomach. The act pressed her body up against his, her chest flush against his back. She felt him tense in surprise.

"Try one more time," she said. "Go slowly."

She heard his breathing quicken. His arm went up, and the stele began to scratch out another rune against the stone.

Instinctively, her hands moved up his chest. She heard the stele hitch and skip. Her palm settled over his heart. It was hammering, slamming against the inside of his rib cage.

Julian's heartbeat. The hundred thousand other times she had heard or felt it crashed into her like an express train. Six years old, she had fallen off a wall she was balanced on and Julian had caught her; they had fallen together, and she had heard his heartbeat. She remembered the pulse in his throat as he held the Mortal Sword in the Council Hall. Racing each other up the beach, putting her fingers to his wrist and counting the beats per minute of his heart afterward. The syncopated rhythm as their heartbeats matched during the *parabatai* ceremony. The sound of the roar of his blood when he carried her out of the ocean. The steady beat of his heart as she'd laid her head on his chest that night.

Her body shuddered with the force of memory, and she felt its strength pulse through her, and into Julian, driving the force of the rune like a whip up through his arm, his hand, the stele. *Fire.*

Julian drew in his breath sharply, dropping his stele; the tip was glowing red. He reeled back and Emma's hands fell away from him; she nearly stumbled, but he caught her, pulling her away from the building, into the churchyard. Both panting, they stared: The rune Julian had drawn on the wall of the church had seared its way straight through the stone. The boards over the windows cracked, and orange tongues of flame leaped out.

Julian looked at Emma. The fire sparkled and crackled in his eyes, more than a reflection. "We did that," he said, his voice rising. "*We* did that."

Emma stared back at him. She was clutching his arms, just above the elbows, muscle hard under her fingers. Jules seemed lit from within, burning with excitement. His skin was hot to the touch.

Their eyes met. And it was Julian, her Julian, no shutters down over his expression, nothing hidden, only the clear brilliance of his eyes and the heat in his gaze. Emma felt as if her heart was tearing apart her chest. She could hear the hard crackle of the flames all around them. Julian moved toward her, closer, splintering her awareness of the need to keep him distant, of anything else but him.

The sound of sirens echoed in Emma's ears, the howl of the fire brigade, hurtling toward the church. Julian drew away from her, only far enough to clasp her hand. They fled from the church just as the first of the fire engines arrived.

Mark didn't really know how they'd all gotten into the library. He vaguely remembered going to check on Tavvy—who was building an elaborate tower of blocks with Rafe and Max—and then to knock on Dru's door; she was in her room, and disinclined to come out, which seemed like a good situation. There was no reason to frighten her before it was necessary.

Still, Mark would have liked to see her. With Julian and Helen gone, and now Ty and Livvy somewhere in London, in danger, he felt like a house whose foundations had been ripped out from under it. He was desperately grateful that Dru and Tavvy were both safe, and also that at the moment, they didn't need him. He didn't know how Julian had done it all those years: how you were supposed to be strong for other people when you didn't know how to be strong for yourself. He knew it was faintly ridiculous for him, an adult, to want the company of his thirteen-year-old sister to fortify his resolve, but there it was. And he was ashamed of it.

He was conscious of Cristina, speaking in rapid-fire Spanish to Magnus. Of Kieran, leaning on one of the tables, his head hanging down: His hair was a purple-black color, like the darkest part of water. Alec returning from the hallway with a pile of clothes in his hands. "These are Ty's, Livvy's, and Kit's," he said, handing them to Magnus. "I got them from their rooms."

Magnus looked over at Mark. "Still nothing on the phone?"

Mark tried to breathe deeply. He'd called Emma and Julian as well as sending texts, but there had been no reply. Cristina had said she'd heard from Emma while she was in the library, and they both seemed to be fine. Mark knew that Emma and Julian were smart and careful, and that there was no better warrior than Emma. Worry pinched at his heart just the same.

But he had to focus on Livvy and Ty and Kit. Kit had next to no training, and Livvy and Ty were so young. He knew he'd been the same age when he was taken by the Hunt, but they were children to him nonetheless.

"Nothing from Emma and Jules," he said. "I've tried Ty a dozen, two dozen times already. No answer." He swallowed back the dread. There were a million reasons Ty might not pick up his phone that didn't have to do with the Riders.

The Riders of Mannan. Even though he knew he was in the library of the London Institute, watching as Magnus Bane began passing his hands over the clothes, beginning the tracking spell, part of him was in Faerie, hearing the tales of the Riders, the murderous assassins of the Unseelie Court. They slept beneath a hill until they were wakened, usually in times of war. He'd heard them called the King's Hounds, for once they had a whiff of their prey, they could follow them across miles of sea, earth, and sky in order to take their lives.

The King must want the Black Volume very badly, to have brought his Riders into it. In old days, they had hunted giants and monsters. Now they were hunting the Blackthorns. Mark felt cold all over.

Mark could hear Magnus speaking in a low voice, also explaining the Seven: who they were and what they did. Alec had given Cristina a gray shirt that was probably Ty's; she was holding it, a Tracking rune on the back of her hand, but she was shaking her head even as she clutched it tighter. "It isn't working," she said. "Maybe if Mark tries—give him something of Livvy's—"

A black flounced dress was shoved into Mark's hands. He couldn't picture his sister wearing something like it, but he didn't imagine that was the point. He held it tightly, sketching a clumsy Tracking rune onto the back of his right hand, trying to remember the way Shadowhunters did this—the way you blanked your mind, reached out into the nothingness, trying to find the spark of the person you sought at the other end of your own reaching imagination.

But there was nothing there. The dress felt like a dead thing to his touch. There was no *Livvy* in it. There was no Livvy anywhere.

He opened his eyes on a gasp. "I don't think this is going to work."

Magnus looked confused. "But—"

"Those are not their garments," said Kieran, lifting his head. "Do you not recall? Clothes were lent to them when they arrived here. I heard them complaining of it."

Mark wouldn't have thought Kieran had been paying enough attention to what the Blackthorns had been saying to take note of such details. Apparently he had.

But that was the way of Hunters, wasn't it? *Seem as if you are paying no attention, but absorb every detail,* Gwyn had often said. *A Hunter's life can depend on what he knows.*

"Is there really nothing of theirs?" Magnus demanded, a slight edge of panic in his voice. "The clothes they were wearing when they got here—"

"Bridget threw them away," said Cristina.

"Their steles—"

"They would have with them," said Mark. "Other weapons would be borrowed." His heart was hammering. "Isn't there anything you can do?"

"What about Portaling to the Los Angeles Institute?" said Alec. "Grabbing some of their things from there—"

Magnus had begun to pace. "It's barred from Portaling right now. Security concerns. I could look for a new spell, we could send someone to dismantle the block on the California Institute, but any of those things takes time—"

"There is no time," said Kieran. He straightened up. "Let me go after the children," he said. "I pledge my life I will do everything I can to find them."

"No," Mark said, rather savagely, and saw the stricken look that passed over Kieran's face. There was no time to explain or clarify, though. "Diana—"

"Is in Idris and cannot help," said Kieran. Mark had slipped his hand into his pocket. His fingers closed on something small, smooth, and cold.

"It might be time to summon the Silent Brothers," said Magnus. "Whatever the consequences."

Cristina winced. Mark knew she was thinking of Emma and Jules, of the Clave meeting in Idris, of the ruination and danger the Blackthorns faced. A ruination that would have taken place on Mark's watch. Something that Julian would never have allowed to happen. Disasters did not happen on Jules's watch—not ones he couldn't fix.

But Mark couldn't think of that. His whole mind, his heart, was filled with the image of his brother and sister in danger. And they were more than his brother and sister at that moment: He understood what Julian felt when he looked at them. These were his children, his responsibility, and he would die to save them.

Mark drew his hand out of his pocket. The gold acorn glittered in the air as he threw it. It struck the opposite wall and broke open.

Cristina whirled. "Mark, what are you—?"

There was no visible change in the library, but a scent filled the room, and for a moment it was as if they stood in a glade in Faerie—Mark could smell fresh air, dirt and leaves, earth and flowers, copper-tinged water.

Kieran had tensed all over, eyes full of a mixture of hope and fear.

"Alec," Magnus said, reaching out a hand, and his voice was less a warning than a sort of stripped-down urgency—the uncanniness of Faerie had come into the room, and Magnus was moving to protect what he loved. Alec didn't move, though, only watched with steady blue eyes as a shadow rose against the far wall. A shadow with nothing to cast it.

It stretched upward. The shadow of a man, head bent, broad shoulders slumped. Cristina put her hand to the pendant at her throat and murmured something—a prayer, Mark guessed.

The light in the room increased. The shadow was no longer a shadow. It had taken on color and form and was Gwyn ap Nudd, arms crossed over his thick chest, two-colored eyes gleaming from beneath heavy brows. "Mark Blackthorn," he said, his voice a rumble. "I did not give that token to you, nor was it meant for you to use."

"Are you really here?" Mark demanded, fascinated. Gwyn seemed solid enough, but if Mark looked closely, he thought he could see the edges of the window frames through Gwyn's body. . . .

"He's a Projection," said Magnus. "Greetings, Gwyn ap Nudd, escort of the grave, father of the slain." He bowed very slightly.

"Magnus Bane," said Gwyn. "It has been a long time."

Alec kicked Magnus in the ankle—probably, Mark suspected, to keep Magnus from saying something about how it hadn't been long enough.

"I need you, Gwyn," said Mark. "We need you."

Gwyn looked disgruntled. "If I had wanted you to be able to call on me at your will, I would have given the acorn to *you*."

"You called on *me*," Mark said. "You came to me to ask me to help Kieran, and so I rescued him from the Unseelie King, and now the Riders of Mannan are hunting my brothers and sisters, who are only children."

"I have carried the bodies of countless children from the battle-field," said Gwyn.

He did not mean to be cruel, Mark knew. Gwyn simply had his own reality, of blood and death and war. There was never a time of peace for Gwyn or the Wild Hunt: Somewhere in the world, there was always war, and it was their duty to serve it.

"If you do not help," said Mark, "then you make yourself a ser-vant of the Unseelie King, protecting his interests, his plans."

"Is *that* your gambit?" Gwyn said softly.

"It's no gambit," said Kieran. "The King my father means to wage a war; if you do not move to position yourself against him, he will presume you are with him."

"The Hunt stands with no one," said Gwyn.

"And that's precisely who will believe that is true, if you do not act now," said Mark. "No one."

"The Hunt can find Livvy and Ty and Kit," said Cristina. "You are the greatest seekers the world has ever known, much greater than the Seven Riders."

Gwyn gave her a slightly incredulous look, almost as if he couldn't believe she'd spoken at all. He looked half-amused, half-exasperated by her flattery. Kieran, on the other hand, looked impressed.

"Very well," Gwyn said. "I will attempt it. I promise nothing," he added darkly, and vanished.

Mark stood staring at the place Gwyn had vanished from, the blank wall of the library, unmarked by shadows.

Cristina offered him a worried smile. Cristina was always

a revelation, he thought. Gentle and honest, but astonishingly capable of plying faerie tricks if necessary. Her words to Gwyn had sounded utterly sincere.

"He might sound reluctant, but if Gwyn says he will attempt something, he will leave no stone unturned," Magnus said. He looked absolutely exhausted in a way Mark didn't remember ever having seen him look before. Exhausted, and grim. "I'm going to need your help, Alec," he said. "It's time for me to Portal to Cornwall. We need to find Emma and Julian before the Riders do."

The Council Hall clock was ringing through the Gard, sounding like the tolling of a huge bell. Diana, having finished her story some minutes ago, folded her hands atop the Consul's desk. "Please, Jia," she said. "Say something."

The Consul rose from her seat behind the desk. She wore a flowing dress whose sleeves were edged with brocade. Her back was very straight. "It sounds like the work of demons," she said in a strained voice. "But there are no demons in Idris. Not since the Mortal War."

The previous Consul had died in that war. Jia had remained in power since, and no demons had entered Idris. But demons were not the only beings who ever meant harm to Shadowhunters.

"Helen and Aline would know had there been demon activity in Brocelind," Jia added. "There are all sorts of maps and charts and sensitive instruments at Wrangel Island. They saw when Malcolm broke the wards around your Institute and reported it to me even before you did."

"This was not the work of demons," said Diana. "It did not have that feeling, the stench of demons—it was the death of growing things, a blight on the earth. It was what—what Kieran has described as happening in the Unseelie Lands."

Be careful, Diana told herself. She had almost said it was what

Julian had described. Jia would be an ally, she hoped, but she had not yet proved herself one. And she was still part of the Clave—its highest representative, in fact.

There was a knock on the door. It was Robert Lightwood, the Inquisitor. He was pulling riding gloves from his hands. "What Miss Wrayburn says is true," he said, without preamble. "There is a blighted space in the center of the forest, perhaps a mile from Herondale Manor. Sensors confirm no demon presence."

"Were you alone when you went to look at it?" Diana demanded.

Robert looked faintly surprised. "A few others were with me. Patrick Penhallow, some of the younger Centurions."

"Let me guess," said Diana. "Manuel Villalobos."

"I didn't realize this was meant to be a confidential mission," said Robert, raising his eyebrows. "Does it matter if he was there?"

Diana said nothing, only looked at Jia, whose dark gaze was weary.

"I hope you took some samples, Robert," Jia said.

"Patrick has them. He's taking them to the Silent Brothers now." Robert stuffed his gloves in his pocket and glanced sideways at Diana. "For what it's worth, I considered your request, and I believe a Council meeting regarding the issues of the Cohort and the faerie messenger would be useful."

He inclined his head toward Diana and left the room.

"It's better that he took Manuel and the others along," said Jia in a low voice. "They cannot deny what they have seen, should it come to that."

Diana rose from her chair. "What do you think they've seen?"

"I don't know," said Jia candidly. "Did you attempt to use your seraph blade, or a rune, when you were in the forest?"

Diana shook her head. She hadn't told Jia what she'd been doing in Brocelind at dawn—certainly not that she'd been there on a semi-date with a faerie in her pajamas.

"You are going to argue this is a sign of the Unseelie Court's incursion into our lands," said Jia.

"Kieran said the Unseelie King would not stop at his own lands. That he would come for ours. That is why we need the Seelie Queen's help."

Which was contingent on finding the Black Volume, Diana knew, though she had not told Jia that. Getting rid of the Cohort was too important.

"I read the file you gave me," Diana added. "I think you may have forgotten to remove some papers regarding Zara's history from it."

"Oh, dear," said Jia, without inflection.

"You gave me those papers because you know it's true," said Diana. "That Zara has lied to the Council. That if she is considered a hero, it is because of those lies."

"Can you prove that?" Jia had moved to the window. The harsh sunlight illuminated the lines in her face.

"Can you?"

"No," Jia said, still looking through the glass. "But I can tell you something that I should not tell you. I spoke of Aline and Helen and their knowledge. Some time ago, they reported that they had seen *something* troubling the maps of Alicante, in the area of Brocelind. Something very odd, dark spots as if the very trees had been practicing evil magic. We rode out but saw nothing—perhaps the patches had not yet grown large enough to be visible. It was put down to a malfunction of equipment."

"They'll have to double-check," Diana said, but her heart was pounding in excitement. Another piece of proof that the Unseelie King was a threat. A clear and present danger to Idris. "If their dark spots match up to the areas of blight, then they must come testify— show the Clave—"

"Slow down, Diana," said Jia. "I've been thinking a great deal about you. I know there are things you are not telling me. Reasons you are so sure Zara didn't kill Malcolm. Reasons you know so much about the Unseelie King's plans. Since the first time I invited Julian Blackthorn and Emma Carstairs into my office, they have confounded me and hidden things from the Clave. As you are hiding things now." She touched her fingers to the glass. "But I am weary. Of the Cold Peace that keeps my daughter from me. Of the Cohort and the climate of hate they breed. What you offer me now is a thin thread on which to tie all our hopes."

"But it is better than nothing," said Diana.

"Yes." Jia turned back to her. "It is better than nothing."

When Diana stepped out of the Gard some minutes later into the gray-white daylight, her blood was singing. She'd done it. There was going to be a meeting; Kieran would testify; they would have their chance to win the Institute back, and perhaps crush the Cohort.

She thought of Emma and Julian and the Black Volume. So much weight on shoulders too young to be forced to bear it. She remembered the two of them as children in the Accords Hall, their swords out as they ringed the younger Blackthorns, ready to die for them.

At the edge of her vision, a bright glint shone momentarily. Something tumbled to the ground at her feet. There was a flutter overhead, a disturbance among the heavy clouds. As Diana bent down and quickly pocketed the small, hollowed acorn, she already knew who the message was from.

Still, she waited until she was halfway down the path to Alicante to read it. To bring her a message in the middle of the day, even under cloud cover, Gwyn must have something serious to say.

Inside the acorn was a tiny piece of paper on which was written: *Come to me now, outside the city walls. It is important. The Blackthorn children are in danger.*

Flinging the acorn aside, Diana bolted down the hill.

* * *

The rain started up as Julian and Emma made their way back from Porthallow Church in silence. Julian seemed to remember the way perfectly, even cutting across the headlands on a path that led them directly down into the Warren.

The sunbathers on the dock and out by the pools under Chapel Rock were hurrying to gather up their things as the first drops of rain splashed down, mothers yanking clothes back onto their unwilling, swimsuited toddlers, bright towels being folded up, beach umbrellas put away.

Emma remembered the way her own father had loved storms on the beach. She recalled being held in his arms as thunder rolled out over the Santa Monica Bay, and he had told her that when lightning struck the beach, it fused sand into glass.

She could hear that roaring in her ears now, louder than the sound of the sea as it rose and began to pound against the rocks on either side of the harbor. Louder than her own breathing as she and Jules hurried up the slippery-wet path to the cottage and ducked inside just as the sky opened up and water came down like the spill through a breaking dam.

Everything inside the cottage seemed almost terrifying in its ordinariness. The kettle silent on the stove. Teacups and coffee mugs and empty plates scattered around the rag rug in front of the fireplace. Julian's sweatshirt on the floor, where Emma had wadded it up and made a pillow out of it the night before.

"Emma?" Julian was leaning against the kitchen island. Water droplets had spattered his face; his hair was curling the way it always did in the humidity and damp. He had the expression of someone who was braced for something, some kind of awful news. "You haven't said anything since we left the church."

"You're in love with me," Emma said. "Still."

Whatever he had been expecting, it hadn't been that. He had

been moving to unzip his jacket. His hands froze in midmotion, fingers reaching. She saw his throat move as he swallowed. He said, "What are you talking about?"

"I thought you didn't love me anymore," she said. She pulled off her coat, reached to hang it on the peg by the door, but her hands were shaking and it fell to the floor. "But that isn't true, is it?"

She heard him inhale, slow and hard. "Why are you saying that? Why now?"

"Because of the church. Because of what happened. We burned a church down, Julian, we *melted stone*."

He yanked the zipper on his jacket down with a vicious jerk and threw it. It bounced off a kitchen cabinet. Underneath, his shirt was wet with sweat and rain. "What does that have to do with anything?"

"It has everything to do with—" She broke off, her voice shaking. "You don't understand. You can't."

"You're right." He stalked away from her, turned in the middle of the room, and kicked out suddenly, violently, at one of the mugs on the floor. It flew across the room and shattered against a wall. "I don't understand. I don't understand *any* of it, Emma, I don't understand why you suddenly decided you didn't want me, you wanted Mark, and then you decided you didn't want him either and you dropped him like he was nothing, in front of everyone. What the hell were you thinking—"

"What do you care?" she demanded. "What do you care how I feel about *Mark*?"

"Because I needed you to love him," Julian said. His face was the color of the ashes in the grate. "Because if you threw me away and everything we had, it had better be for something that meant *more* to you, it had better be for something real, but maybe none of this is ever real to you—"

"Not real to *me*?" Emma's voice tore out of her throat with such force it hurt. Her body felt as if electric sparks were running under her veins, shocking her, pushing her rage higher and higher, and she wasn't even angry at Jules, she was angry at herself, she was angry at the world for doing this to them, for making her the only one who knew, the guardian of a poisonous, poisoning secret. "You don't know what you're talking about, Julian Blackthorn! You don't know what I've given up, what my reasons are for anything, you don't know what I'm trying to do—"

"What you're *trying* to do? How about what you did do? How about breaking my heart and breaking Cameron's and breaking Mark's?" His face twisted. "What, am I missing someone else, some other person whose life you want to wreck forever?"

"Your life isn't wrecked. You're still alive. You can *have a good life!* You kissed that faerie girl—"

"She was a *leanansídhe!* A shape-changer! I thought she was *you!*"

"Oh." Emma stood for a moment, arrested in mid-motion. "Oh."

"Yes, *oh*. You really think I'm going to fall in love with someone *else?*" Julian demanded. "You think I get to do that? I'm not you, I don't get to fall in love every week with someone different. I wish it wasn't you, Emma, but it is, it'll always be you, so don't tell me my life isn't wrecked when you don't know the first thing about it!"

Emma slammed her hand against the wall. The plaster cracked, spidering out from the impact point. She felt the pain only distantly. A roiling black wave of despair rose, threatening to overwhelm her. "What do you want from me, Jules?" she demanded. "What do you want me to *do?*"

Julian took a step forward; his face looked as if it had been carved out of marble or something even harder, even more unyielding. "What do I want?" he said. "I want you to know what it's like. To be tortured all the time, night and day, desperately wanting what you know you should never want, what doesn't even want you *back*. To know how it feels to understand that a decision you made when you were twelve years old means you can never have the one thing that would make you truly happy. I want you to dream about only one thing and want only one thing and obsess about only one thing like I do—"

"Julian—" she gasped, desperate to stop him, to stop all this before it was too late.

"—*like I do with you!*" he finished, the words spat out almost savagely. "Like I do with you, Emma." The rage seemed to have gone out of him; he was shaking now instead, as if in the grip of shock. "I thought you loved me," he said, almost in a whisper. "I don't know how I got that so wrong."

Her heart cracked. She twisted away, away from the look in his eyes, away from his voice, away from the shattering of all her carefully made plans. She clawed the door open—she heard Julian call her name, but she had already plunged out of the cottage and into the storm.

24

LEGION

The crest of Chapel Cliff was a tower in a maelstrom: slick rock rising toward the sky, surrounded on three sides by the boiling cauldron of the ocean.

The sky above was gray, streaked with black, hanging heavy as a rock over the small town and the sea beyond. The water was high in the harbor, raising the fishing boats to the level of the windows of the dockside houses. The small craft tossed and turned on the crests of the waves.

More waves crashed up against the cliff, spraying whitecaps into the air. Emma stood within a whirlwind of swirling water, the smell of the sea all around, the sky exploding above her, lightning forking through the clouds.

She spread her arms out wide. She felt as if the lightning were exploding down through her, into the rocks at her feet, into the water that slammed up in gray-green sheets, almost vertical against the sky. All around her the granite spires that gave Chapel Cliff its name rose like a stone forest, like the points of a crown. The rock under her feet was slippery with wet moss.

All her life, she had loved storms—loved the explosions tearing through the sky, loved the soul-baring ferocity of them. She hadn't thought when she'd burst out of the cottage, at least not logically; she'd been desperate to get away before she told Julian everything he could never know. Let him think she'd never loved him, that she'd broken Mark's heart, that she had no feelings. Let him hate her, if that meant he would live and be all right.

And maybe the storm could wash her clean, could wash what felt like both their hearts' blood off her hands.

She moved down the side of the cliff. The rock grew slipperier, and she paused to apply a new Balance rune. The stele slid on her wet skin. From the lower point, she could see where the caves and tide pools were covered by curling white water. Lightning cracked against the horizon; she lifted her face to taste the salt rain and heard the distant, winding sound of a horn.

Her head jerked up. She'd heard a sound like that before, once, when the convoy of the Wild Hunt had come to the Institute. It was no human horn. It sounded again, deep and cold and lonely, and she started to her feet, scrambling back up the path toward the top of the cliff.

She saw clouds like massive gray boulders colliding in the sky; where they parted, weak golden light shafted down, illuminating the churning surface of the ocean. There were black dots out over the harbor—birds? No, they were too big to be seabirds, and none would be out in this weather anyway.

The black dots were coming toward her. They were closer now, resolving, no longer dots. She could see them for what they were: riders. Four riders, cloaked in glimmering bronze. They hurtled through the sky like comets.

They were not the Wild Hunt. Emma knew that immediately, without knowing how she knew it. There were too few of them, and they were too silent. The Wild Hunt rode with a fierce clamor. The bronze riders glided silently toward Emma, as if they had been formed out of the clouds.

She could run back toward the cottage, she thought. But that would draw them toward Julian, and besides, they had angled themselves to cut her off from the path back toward Malcolm's house. They were moving with incredible speed. In seconds, they would be on the cliff.

Her right hand closed on the hilt of Cortana. She drew it almost without conscious thought. The feel of it in her hand grounded her, slowed her heartbeat.

They soared overhead, circling. For a moment Emma was struck by their odd beauty—up close, the horses seemed barely real, as transparent as glass, formed out of wisps of cloud and moisture. They spun in the air and dove like gulls after their prey. As their hooves struck the solid earth of the cliff, they exploded into ocean whitecaps, each horse a spray of vanishing water, leaving the four riders behind.

And between Emma and the path. She was cut off, from everything but the sea and the small piece of cliff behind her.

The four Riders faced her. She braced her feet. The very top of the ridge was so narrow that her boots sank in on either side of the cliff's spine. She raised Cortana. It flashed in the storm light, rain sliding off its blade. "Who's there?" she called.

The four figures moved as one, reaching to push back the hoods of their bronze cloaks. Beneath was more shining stuff—they were three tall men and a woman, each of them wearing bronze half masks, with hair that looked like metallic thread wound into thick braids that hung halfway down their backs.

Their armor was metal: breastplates and gauntlets etched all over with the designs of waves and the sea. The eyes they fixed on her were gray and piercing.

"Emma Cordelia Carstairs," said one of them. He spoke as if Emma's name were in a foreign language, one his tongue had a hard time wrapping itself around. "Well met."

"In your opinion," Emma muttered. She kept a tight grip on

Cortana—each of the faeries (for she knew they were faeries) that she was facing was armed with a longsword, hilts visible over their shoulders. She raised her voice. "What does a convoy from the Faerie Courts want from me?"

The faerie raised an eyebrow. "Tell her, Fal," said one of the others, in the same accented voice. Something about the accent raised the hairs on Emma's arms, though she couldn't have said what it was.

"We are the Riders of Mannan," said Fal. "You will have heard of us."

It wasn't a question. Emma desperately wished Cristina were with her. Cristina was the one with vast knowledge of faerie culture. If the words "Riders of Mannan" were supposed to mean something to Shadowhunters, Cristina would know it.

"Are you part of the Wild Hunt?" she asked.

Consternation. A low mutter vibrated among the four of them, and Fal leaned to the side and spat. A faerie with a sharply chiseled jaw and an expression of disdain replied for him.

"I am Airmed, son of Mannan," he said. "We are the children of a god, you see. We are much older than the Wild Hunt, and much more powerful."

Emma realized then what it was that she'd heard in their accents. It wasn't distance or foreignness; it was age, a terrifying age that stretched back to the beginning of the world.

"We seek," said Fal. "And we find. We are the searchers. We have been under the waves to search and above them. We have been in Faerie, and in the realms of the damned, and on battlefields and in the dark of night and the bright of day. In all our lives there has only been one thing we have sought and not found."

"A sense of humor?" Emma suggested.

"She should shut her mouth," said the female Rider. "You should shut it for her, Fal."

"Not yet, Ethna," said Fal. "We need her words. We need to know the location of what we seek."

Emma's hand felt hot and slippery on the hilt of Cortana. "What do you seek?"

"The Black Volume," said Airmed. "We seek the same object you and your *parabatai* seek. The one taken by Annabel Blackthorn."

Emma took an involuntary step back. "*You're* looking for Annabel?"

"For the *book*," said the fourth Rider, his voice harsh and deep. "Tell us where it is and we will leave you be."

"I don't have it," Emma said. "Neither does Julian."

"She is a liar, Delan," said the woman, Ethna.

His lip curled. "They are all liars, Nephilim. Do not treat us as fools, Shadowhunter, or we will string your innards from the nearest tree."

"Try it," said Emma. "I'll ram the tree down your throat until branches start poking out of your—"

"Ears?" It was Julian. He must have applied a Soundless rune, because even Emma hadn't heard him approach. He was perched on a wet boulder by the side of the path toward the cottage as if he'd simply appeared there, summoned out of the rain and clouds. He was in gear, his hair wet, an unlit seraph blade in his hand. "I'm sure you were going to say ears."

"Definitely." Emma grinned at him; she couldn't help it. Despite the fight they'd had, he was here, having her back, being her *parabatai*. And now they had the Riders hemmed in, pinned between the two of them.

Things were looking up.

"Julian Blackthorn," drawled Fal, barely glancing at him. "The famous *parabatai*. I hear the two of you gave a most impressive performance at the Unseelie Court."

"I'm sure the King couldn't stop singing our praises," Julian said. "Look, what makes you think we know where Annabel or the Black Volume are?"

"Spies are in every Court," said Ethna. "We know the Queen sent you to find the book. The King must have it before the Queen possesses it."

"But we have promised the Queen," said Julian, "and a promise like that cannot be broken."

Delan growled, his hand suddenly at the hilt of his sword. He had moved so fast it was a blur. "You are humans and liars," he said. "You can break any promise you make, and will, when your necks are on the line. As they are now." He jerked his chin toward the cottage. "We have come for the warlock's books and papers. If you will not tell us anything, then give them to us and we will be gone."

"Give them to you?" Julian looked puzzled. "Why didn't you just . . ." His eyes met Emma's. She knew what he was thinking: *Why didn't you break in and take them?* "You can't get in, can you?"

"The wards," Emma confirmed.

The faeries said nothing, but she could tell by the angry set of their jaws that she was right.

"What will the Unseelie King give us in return for the book?" said Julian.

"*Jules,*" Emma hissed. How could he be scheming at a time like this?

Fal laughed. Emma noted for the first time that the clothes and armor of the faeries were dry, as if the rain didn't fall on them. His glance toward Julian was full of contempt. "You have no advantage here, son of thorns. Give us what we have come for, or when we find the rest of your family, we shall put red-hot pokers through their eyes down to even the smallest child."

Tavvy. The words went through Emma like an arrow. She felt the impact, felt her body jerk, and the cold came down over her, the cold ice of battle. She lunged for Fal, bringing Cortana down in a vicious overhand swipe.

Ethna screamed, and Fal moved faster than a current on the ocean, ducking Emma's blow. Cortana whistled through the air. There was a clamor as the other faeries reached for their swords.

And a glow as Julian's seraph blade burst into light, illuminating the rain. It wove around Emma like bright strings as she twirled, fending off a blow from Ethna, Cortana slamming into the faerie sword with enough force to send Ethna stumbling back.

Fal's face twisted with surprise. Emma gasped, wet, inhaling rain but not feeling the cold. The world was a spinning gray top; she ran toward one of the stone spires and clambered up it.

"Coward!" Airmed cried. "How dare you run away?"

Emma heard Julian laugh as she reached the top of the spire and leaped from it. The descent gave her speed, and she slammed into Airmed with enough force to knock him to the ground. He tried to roll away, but froze when she smashed the hilt of Cortana into his temple. He choked with pain.

"Shut up," Emma hissed. "Don't you dare touch the Blackthorns, don't you even talk about them—"

"Let him be!" Ethna called, and Delan leaped toward them, only to be stopped by Julian and the sweep of his seraph blade. The cliff exploded with light, the rain seeming to hang still in the air, as the blade swung down and slammed against the faerie warrior's breastplate.

And shattered. It broke as if it had been made out of ice, and Julian was thrown back by the recoiling force of it, lifted off his feet and slammed down among the rocks and wet earth.

Delan laughed, striding toward Julian. Emma abandoned Airmed where he lay and leaped after the faerie warrior as he raised his sword over Jules, and brought it down—

Julian rolled fast to the right, swung around, and drove a dagger into the unguarded skin of Delan's calf. Delan yelled with pain and anger, spinning to drive the tip of the sword down toward Julian's body. But Jules had flung himself upward; he was on his feet, dagger in hand.

Light shafted down suddenly through the clouds, and Emma saw the shadows on the ground before her shift; there was someone behind her. She spun away just as a blade came down, barely missing her shoulder. She spun around to find Ethna behind her: Fal was leaning over Airmed on the ground, helping haul him to his feet. For a moment it was just Emma and the faerie woman, and Emma grabbed the hilt of Cortana with both hands and swung.

Ethna darted back, but she was laughing. "You Nephilim," she sneered. "You call yourselves warriors, ringed round with your protective runes, your angel blades! Without them you would be nothing—and you will be without them soon enough! You will be nothing, and we will take everything from you! Everything you have! *Everything!*"

"Did you want to say that again?" Emma asked, evading a slice of Ethna's sword with a twist of her body. She leaped up onto a boulder, looking down. "The *everything* part? I don't think I got it the first time."

Ethna snarled and leaped for her. And for a long series of moments it was only the battle, the glowing vapor of the rain, the sea crashing and thundering in the pools below the cliff, and everything slowing down as Emma knocked Ethna to the side and leaped for Airmed and Fal, her sword clanging against theirs.

They were good: better than good, fast and blindingly strong. But Cortana was like a live thing in Emma's hands. Rage powered her, an electric current that shot through her veins, driving the sword in her hand, hammering the blade against those raised against hers, the clang of metal drowning out the sea. She tasted salt in her mouth, blood or ocean spray, she didn't know. Her wet hair whipped around her as she spun, Cortana meeting the other swords of the faeries, blow after blow.

An ugly laugh cut through the violent dream that gripped her. She looked up to see that Fal had Julian backed up to the edge of the cliff. It fell away sheer behind him; he stood framed against the gray sky, his hair plastered darkly to his head.

Panic blasted through her. She pushed off from the side of a granite facing with a kick that connected solidly against Airmed's body. The faerie fell back with a grunt, and Emma was racing, seeing Julian in her mind's eye run through with a sword or toppled from the cliff's edge to shatter on the rocks or drown in the maelstrom below.

Fal was still laughing. He had his sword out. Julian took another step backward—and ducked down, swift and nimble, to catch up a crossbow from where it had been hidden behind a tumble of rocks. He lifted it to his shoulder just as Emma collided with Fal, her sword out; she didn't slow, didn't pause, just slammed Cortana point-first between Fal's shoulder blades.

It pierced his armor and slid home. She felt the point burst out of the other side of his body, slicing through the metal breastplate.

There was a shriek from behind Emma. It was Ethna. She had her head thrown back, her hands clawing at her hair. She was wailing in a language Emma didn't know, but she could hear that Ethna was shrieking her brother's name. *Fal, Fal.*

Ethna began to sink to her knees. Delan reach to catch her, his own face bone-white and shocked. With a roar, Airmed lifted his sword and lunged toward Emma, who was struggling to free Cortana from Fal's limp body. She tensed and pulled; the sword came free in a gout of blood, but she had no time to turn—

Julian released the bolt from his crossbow. It whistled through the air, a softer sound than the rain, and struck the sword in Airmed's hand, knocking it out of his grip. Airmed howled. His hand was scarlet.

Emma turned, planted her feet, raised her sword. Blood and rain ran down Cortana's blade. "Who wants to try me?" she shouted, her words half-torn out of her mouth by wind and water. "Who wants to be next?"

"Let me kill her!" Ethna struggled in Delan's grip. "She slew Fal! Let me cut her throat!"

But Delan was shaking his head, he was saying something, something about Cortana. Emma took a step forward—if they wouldn't come to her to be killed, she would be happy enough to go to them.

Airmed raised his hand; she saw light flicker from his fingers, pale green in the gray air. His face was twisted into a sneer of concentration.

"*Emma!*" Jules caught her from behind before she could take another step, hauling her back and against him just as the rain exploded into the shapes of three horses, swirling creatures of wind and spray, snorting and pawing at the air between Emma and the rest of the Riders. Fal lay with his blood soaking into the Cornwall dirt as his brothers and sister vaulted onto the bare backs of their steeds.

Emma began to shiver violently. Only one of the Riders paused long enough to look back at her before their horses shot forward into the sky, losing themselves among the clouds and rain. It was Ethna. Her eyes were murderous, disbelieving.

You have slain an ancient and primitive thing, her gaze seemed to say. *Be prepared for a vengeance just as ancient. Just as primitive.*

"*Run,*" Livvy said.

It was the last thing Kit had expected. Shadowhunters didn't run. That was what he'd always been told. But Livvy took off like a bullet out of a gun, flashing past the Rider on the path in front of her, and Ty followed.

Kit ran after them. They tore past the faeries and into the throng of pedestrians on the Thames Path. Kit pulled alongside Livvy and Ty, though he was breathing hard and they weren't.

He could hear thunder behind him. Hoofbeats. *We can't outrun them*, he thought, but he didn't have the breath to say it. The leaden gray air felt heavy as he pulled it into his lungs. Livvy's dark hair streamed on the wind as she flung herself over a gate set into the railing separating the path from the river.

For a moment she seemed to hang suspended in the air, her arms upraised, her coat flapping—and then she soared straight down, vanishing out of sight. And Ty followed her, vaulting sideways over the gate, disappearing as he fell.

Into the river? Kit thought hazily, but he didn't pause; his muscles were already beginning the now-familiar burning, his mind tightening and focusing. He grabbed hold of the top of the gate and pushed himself up and over it.

He fell only a few feet to land in a crouch on a cement platform that stretched out into the Thames, surrounded by a low iron railing that was broken in several places. Ty and Livvy were already there, jackets yanked off to free their arms, seraph blades in hand. Livvy tossed a shortsword toward Kit as he straightened up, realizing why she'd run—not to get away, but to clear them some space to fight.

And hopefully to contact the Institute. Ty had his phone out in his hand, was thumbing at the keypad even as he raised his seraph blade, its light bursting dully against the clouds.

Kit turned just as the three Riders sailed over the gate to join them, flashing bronze and gold as they landed. Their swords whipped free with blinding speed.

"Stop him!" snarled Karn, and his two brothers launched themselves at Ty.

Livvy and Kit moved as one to throw themselves in front of Tiberius. The cold, hard blur of fighting was on Kit, but the Riders were faster than demons, and stronger, too. Kit whipped his shortsword toward Eochaid, but the faerie was no longer there: He'd leaped all the way to the far side of the platform. He laughed at the expression on Kit's face, even as Etarlam slashed out with a blow that knocked the phone out of Ty's hand. It skittered across the concrete and splashed into the river.

A shadow fell over Kit. He responded instantaneously, driving upward with his shortsword. He heard a gasp, and Karn fell back, dark drops of blood spattering on the ground at his feet. Kit flung himself up and forward, lunging for Eochaid, but Livvy and Ty were ahead of him, blurs of light as their seraph blades cut the air around the Riders.

But only the air. Kit couldn't help but notice that the angel blades didn't seem to be cutting through the Riders' armor, or even slicing their skin as he'd managed to do with his shortsword. There was puzzlement on Ty's face, rage on Livvy's as she stabbed at Eochaid's heart with her seraph blade.

The weapon snapped off at the hilt, the force of the rebound sending her staggering back almost into the river. Ty whipped around as he looked after her—Eochaid raised his sword and brought it down in a sweeping arc toward Ty—and Kit lunged across the platform, knocking Tiberius flat.

Ty's blade went flying, splashing down into the Thames, sending up a flurry of fiery droplets. Kit had landed half across Ty, banging his head hard on a jutting piece of wood; he felt Ty try to shove him off, and rolled over to see Eochaid standing over them both.

Livvy had engaged the other two Riders, was fighting them desperately, a whirl of flashing weaponry. But she was on the other side of the platform. Kit fought to get his breath back, raised his sword—

Eochaid stood arrested, his eyes glittering behind the holes of his mask. The irises, too, were bronze-colored. "I know you," he said. "I know your face."

Kit gaped at him. A second later, Eochaid was raising his sword, mouth twisting into a grin—and a shadow fell over them all. The Rider looked up, astonishment crossing his face as a burly arm reached down from above and seized hold of him. A second later he was flying up into the air, yelling. Kit heard a splash; the Rider had been tossed into the river.

Kit struggled to sit up, Ty beside him. Livvy had turned to face them, her mouth open; both the Riders were similarly agape, their swords dangling by their sides as a thunderous, whirling mass landed in the center of the platform.

It was a horse, and on the horse's back was Gwyn, massive in his helmet and bark-like armor. It was his gauntleted arm that had flung Eochaid into the river—but now the Rider had swum back to the platform and was climbing onto it, his movements slowed by his heavy armor.

Clinging to the man's waist was Diana, her dark hair a mass of curls pulling free of their restraints, her eyes wide.

Ty got to his feet. Kit scrambled up after him. There was some blood staining the collar of Ty's hoodie; Kit realized he didn't know if it was Ty's or his own.

"*Riders!*" Gwyn said, in a thunderous voice. There was a wide cut across his arm where Eochaid must have gotten in a blow. "Stop."

Diana slid from the horse's back and stalked across the concrete platform to where Eochaid was clambering out of the water. She unhitched her sword from its scabbard, spun it, and pointed it directly at his chest. "Don't move," she said.

The Rider subsided, teeth bared in a silent snarl.

"This is none of your concern, Gwyn," said Karn. "This is Unseelie business."

"The Wild Hunt bends to no law," said Gwyn. "Our will is the wind's will. And my will now is to send you away from these children. They are under my protection."

"They are *Nephilim*," spat Etarlam. "The architects of the Cold Peace, vicious and cruel."

"You are no better," said Gwyn. "You are the King's hunting dogs, and never have you shown any mercy."

Karn and Etarlam stared at Gwyn. Eochaid, kneeling, dripped on the concrete. The moment stretched out like rubber, seemingly extending forever.

Eochaid shot suddenly to his feet with a gasp, seemingly heedless of Diana's sword, tracking him unerringly as he moved. *"Fal,"* he said. "He is dead."

"That is impossible," said Karn. "Impossible. A Rider cannot die."

But Etarlam let out a loud, keening cry, his sword falling to the ground as his hand flew to cover his heart. "He is gone," he wailed. "I feel it. Our brother is gone."

"A Rider has passed into the Shadow Lands," said Gwyn. "Would you like me to sound the horn for him?"

Though Gwyn had sounded sincere enough to Kit, Eochaid snarled and made as if to lunge for the Hunter, but Diana's sword kissed his throat as he moved, drawing blood. Thick, dark drops ran down her blade.

"Enough!" said Karn. "Gwyn, you will pay for this treachery. Etar, Eochaid, to my side. We go to our brothers and sister."

Diana lowered her sword as Eochaid shouldered past her, joining the other two Riders. They leaped from the platform into the air, long soaring leaps that took them high above, where they caught the manes of their gleaming bronze horses and swung themselves up to ride.

As they hurtled past above the water, Eochaid's voice echoed in Kit's ringing ears.

I know you. I know your face.

Emma was shaking by the time they got back into the cottage. A combination of cold and reaction had set in. Her hair and clothes were plastered to her, and she suspected she looked like a drowned rat.

She propped Cortana against the wall and began wearily to shuck off her drenched jacket and shoes. She was aware of Julian locking the door behind them, aware of the sounds of him moving around the room. Warmth, too. He must have built up the fire earlier.

A moment later something soft was being pressed into her hands. Julian stood in front of her, his expression unreadable, offering a slightly worn bath towel. She took it and began to dry off her hair.

Jules was still wearing his damp clothes, though he was barefoot and he'd thrown on a dry sweater. Water gleamed at the edges of his hair, the tips of his eyelashes.

She thought of the clang of swords on swords, the beauty of the turmoil of the battle, the sea and sky. She wondered if that was how Mark had felt in the Wild Hunt. When there was nothing between you and the elements, it was easy to forget what weighed you down.

She thought of the blood on Cortana, the blood ribboning out from under Fal's body, mixing with the rainwater. They'd rolled his corpse under an overhang of stones, not wanting to leave him there, exposed to the weather, even though he was long past caring.

"I killed one of the Riders," she said now, in a near whisper.

"You had to." Julian's hand was strong on her shoulder, fingers digging in. "Emma, it was a fight to the death."

"The Clave—"

"The Clave will understand."

"The Fair Folk won't. The Unseelie King won't."

The faintest ghost of a smile passed over Julian's face. "I don't think he likes us anyway."

Emma took a tense breath. "Fal had you backed up against the edge of the cliff," she said. "I thought he was going to kill you."

Julian's smile faded. "I'm sorry," he said. "I'd hidden the crossbow there earlier—"

"I didn't know," Emma said. "It's my job to sense what's going on with you in battle, to understand it, to anticipate you, but I didn't know." She threw the bath towel; it landed on the kitchen floor. The mug Julian had broken earlier was gone. He must have cleaned it up.

Despair bubbled up inside her. Nothing she'd done had worked. They were in exactly the same place they'd been before, only Julian didn't know it. That was all that had changed.

"I tried so hard," she whispered.

His face crinkled in confusion. "In the battle? Emma, you did everything you could—"

"Not in the battle. To make you not love me," she said. "I tried."

She felt him recoil, not so much outwardly as inwardly, as if his soul had flinched. "Is it that awful? Having me love you?"

She had started trembling again, though not from the cold. "It was the best thing in the world," she said. "And then it was the worst. And I didn't even have a chance—"

She broke off. He was shaking his head, scattering water droplets. "You're going to have to learn to live with it," he said. "Even if it horrifies you. Even if it makes you sick. Just like I'm going to have to live with whatever other boyfriends you have, because we are forever no matter how, Emma, no matter what you want to call what we have, we will *always* be us."

"There won't be any other boyfriends," she said.

He looked at her in surprise.

"What you said before, about thinking and obsessing and wanting only one thing," she said. "That's how I feel about you."

He looked stunned. She put her hands up to gently cup his face, brushing her fingers over his damp skin. She could see the pulse hammering in his throat. There was a scratch on his face, a long one that went from his temple to his chin. Emma wondered if he'd just gotten it in the fight outside, or if he'd had it before and she hadn't noticed because she'd been trying so hard not to look at him. She wondered if he was ever going to speak again.

"*Jules,*" she said. "Say something, please—"

His hands tightened convulsively on her shoulders. She gasped as his body moved against hers, walking her backward until her back hit the wall. His eyes gazed down into hers, shockingly bright, radiant as sea glass. "Julian," he said. "I want you to call me Julian. Only ever that."

"Julian," she said, and then his mouth came down over hers, dry and burning hot, and her heart seemed to stop and start again, an engine revved into an impossibly high gear.

She clutched him back with the same desperation, clinging on as he drank the rain from her mouth, her lips parting to taste him: cloves and tea. She reached to yank his sweater off over his head. Under it was a T-shirt, the thin wet cloth not much of a barrier when he pressed her back against the wall. His jeans were wet too, molded to his body. She felt how much he wanted her, and wanted him just as much.

The world was gone: There was only Julian; the heat of his skin, the need to be closer to him, to fit herself against him. Every movement of his body against hers sent lightning through her nerves.

"Emma. God, Emma." He buried his face against her, kissing her cheek, her throat as he slid his thumbs under the waistband of her jeans and pushed down. She kicked the wet heap of denim away. "I love you so much."

It felt as if it had been a thousand years since that night on the beach. Her hands rediscovered his body, the hard planes of it, his scars rough under her palms. He had once been so skinny—she could still see him as he had been even two years ago, awkward and gangly. She had loved him then even if she hadn't known it, loved him from the center of his bones to the surface of his skin.

Now those bones were clothed and covered in smooth muscle, hard and unyielding. She ran her hands up under his shirt, relearning him, tracing him, embedding the feel and the texture of him in her memory.

"Julian," she said. "I—"

I love you, she was about to say. *It wasn't ever Cameron, or Mark, it was always you, it will always be you, the marrow of my bones is made up of you, like cells make up our blood.* But he cut her off with a hard kiss. "Don't," he whispered. "I don't want to hear anything reasonable, not now. I don't want logic. I want this."

"But you need to know—"

He shook his head. "I don't." He reached down, grabbed the hem of his shirt, dragged it off. His wet hair showered droplets on them both. "I've been broken for weeks," he said unsteadily, and she knew what that cost him, that admission of lack of control. "I need to be whole again. Even if it doesn't last."

"It can't last," she said, staring at him, because how could it, when they could never keep what they had? "It'll break our hearts."

He caught her by the wrist, brought her hand to his bare chest. Splayed her fingers over his heart. It beat against her palm, like a fist punching its way through his sternum. "Break my heart," he said. "Break it in pieces. I give you permission."

The blue of his eyes had almost disappeared behind the expanding rims of his pupils.

She hadn't known, before, on the beach, what was going to happen. What it would be like between them. Now she did. There were things in life you couldn't refuse. No one had that much willpower.

No one.

She was nodding her head, without even knowing she was going to do it. "Julian, yes," she said. "Yes."

She heard him make an almost anguished sound. Then his hands were on her hips; he was lifting her so she was pinned between his body and the wall. It felt desperate, world-ending, and she wondered if there would ever be a time when it wouldn't, when it could be soft and slow and quietly loving.

He kissed her fiercely and she forgot gentleness or any desire for it. There was only this, his whispering her name as they pushed aside the clothes that needed to be pushed aside. He was gasping, a faint sheen of sweat on his skin, damp hair plastered to his forehead; he lifted her higher, pressed toward her so fast his body collided with hers. She heard the ragged moan dragged out of his throat. When he lifted his face, eyes black with desire, she stared at him, wide-eyed.

"You're all right?" he whispered.

She nodded. "Don't stop."

His mouth found hers, unsteady, his hands shaking where they held her. She could tell he was fighting for every second of control. She wanted to tell him it was fine, it was all right, but coherence had deserted her. She could hear the waves outside, smashing brutally against the rocks; she closed her eyes and heard him say that he loved her, and then her arms were around him, holding him as his knees gave way and they sank to the floor, clutching each other like the survivors of a ship that had run aground on some distant, legendary shore.

* * *

Tavvy, Rafe, and Max were easy enough to locate. They'd been in the care of Bridget, who was amusing them by letting them annoy Jessamine so that she knocked things off high shelves, thus sparking a "Do not tease ghosts" lecture from Magnus.

Dru, on the other hand, was nowhere to be found. She wasn't in her bedroom any longer, or hiding in the library or the parlor, and the kids hadn't seen her. Possibly Jessamine could have helped them more, but Bridget had reported that she had flounced off after the children were done bothering her, and besides, she only liked talking to Kit.

"Dru wouldn't have left the Institute, would she?" Mark said. He was stalking down the corridor, shoving doors open left and right. "Why would she do something like that?"

"Mark." Kieran took the other boy by his shoulders and turned him so that they faced each other. Cristina felt a throb in her wrist, as if Mark's distress were communicating itself to her through the binding.

Of course, Mark and Kieran shared another kind of binding. The binding of shared experience and emotion. Kieran was holding Mark by the shoulders, concentrating on nothing but him in that way that faeries had. And Mark was relaxing slowly, some of the tension leaving his body.

"Your sister is here," said Kieran. "And we will find her."

"We'll split up and look," said Alec. "Magnus—"

Magnus swung Max up into his arms and headed down the hallway, the other two kids trailing behind him. The rest of them agreed to meet back in the library in twenty minutes. Each of them got a quadrant of the Institute to search. Cristina wound up with west, which took her downstairs to the ballroom.

She wished it hadn't—the memories of dancing there with Mark and then with Kieran were confusing and distracting. And she didn't need to be distracted now; she needed to find Dru.

She headed down the stairs—and froze. There, on the landing, was Drusilla, all in black, her brown braids tied with black ribbon. She turned a pale, anxious face to Cristina.

"I was waiting for you," she said.

"Everyone's looking for you!" Cristina said. "Ty and Livvy—"

"I know. I heard. I was listening," said Dru.

"But you weren't in the library—"

"Please," Dru said. "You have to come with me. There's not a lot of time."

She turned and hurried up the stairs. After a moment, Cristina followed her.

"Dru, Mark's worried. The Riders are terribly dangerous. He needs to know you're all right."

"I'll go and tell him I'm fine in a second," Dru said. "But I need you to come with me."

"Dru—" They'd made it to the hallway where most of the spare bedrooms were.

"Look," said Dru. "I just need you to do this, okay? If you try yelling for Mark, I promise you there are places in this Institute I can hide where you won't find me for days."

Cristina couldn't help being curious. "How do you know the Institute so well?"

"You would too if every time you showed your face, someone tried to make you babysit," said Dru. They'd reached her bedroom. She stood hesitating, with her hand on the knob of her door.

"But we looked in your bedroom," Cristina protested.

"I'm telling you," said Dru. "Hiding places." She took a deep breath. "Okay. You go in here. And don't freak out."

Dru's small face was set and determined, as if she were nerving herself to do something unpleasant.

"Is everything all right?" Cristina said. "Are you sure you wouldn't rather talk to Mark than me?"

"It isn't me who wants to talk to you," Dru said, and pushed her bedroom door open. Cristina stepped inside, feeling more puzzled than ever.

She only saw a shadow first, a figure in front of the windowsill. Then he stood up and her heart caught in her throat.

Brown skin, tangled black hair, sharp features, long lashes. The faint slouch to the shoulders she remembered, that she used to tell him always made him look as if he was walking into a high wind.

"Jaime," she breathed.

He reached out his arms, and a moment later she was hugging him tightly. Jaime had always been skinny, but now he felt positively prickly with pointed collarbones and sharp elbows. He hugged her back, tightly, and Cristina heard the bedroom door close quietly, the lock clicking.

She pulled back and looked up into Jaime's face. He looked like he always did—bright-eyed, edged with mischief. "So," he said. "You really missed me."

All the nights she'd stayed up sobbing because of him—because he was missing, because she hated him, because he'd been her best friend and she hated hating him—burst. Her left palm cracked across his cheek, and then she was hitting him on the shoulders, the chest, wherever she could reach.

"Ow!" He writhed away. "That hurts!"

"*¡Me vale madre!*" She hit him again. "How dare you disappear like that! Everyone was worried! I thought maybe you were dead. And now you turn up hiding in Drusilla Blackthorn's bedroom, which by the way if her brothers find out they will kill you dead—"

"It wasn't like that!" Jaime windmilled his arms as if to fend off her blows. "I was looking for you."

She put her hands on her hips. "After all this time avoiding me, suddenly you're looking for me?"

"It wasn't you I was avoiding," he said. He took a crumpled

envelope out of his pocket and held it out to her. With a pang, she recognized Diego's handwriting.

"If Diego wants to write to me, he doesn't need the message hand-delivered," she said. "What does he think you are, a carrier pigeon?"

"He can't write to you," said Jaime. "Zara watches all his mail."

"So you know about Zara," Cristina said, taking the envelope. "How long?"

Jaime slouched back against a large oak desk, hands propped behind him. "How long have they been engaged? Since you two broke up the first time. But it's not a real engagement, Cristina."

She sat down on Dru's bed. "It seemed real enough."

Jaime ran a hand through his black hair. He looked only a little like Diego, maybe in the set of his mouth, the shape of his eyes. Jaime had always been playful where Diego was serious. Now, tired and skinny, he resembled the glum, style-conscious boys who hung around coffee shops in the Colonia Roma. "I know you probably hate me," he said. "You've got every reason. You think I wanted our branch of the family to take over the Institute because I wanted power and didn't care about you. But the fact is I had a good reason."

"I don't believe you," Cristina said.

Jaime made an impatient noise. "I'm not self-sacrificing, Tina," he said. "That's Diego, not me. I wanted our family out of trouble."

Cristina dug her hands into the bedspread. "What kind of trouble?"

"You know we've always had a connection with faeries," said Jaime. "It's where that necklace of yours comes from. But there's always been more than that. Most of it didn't matter, until the Cold Peace. Then the family was supposed to turn everything over to the Clave—all their information, anything the faeries had ever given them."

"But they didn't," Cristina guessed.

"They didn't," Jaime said. "They decided the relationship with the *hadas* was more important than the Cold Peace." He shrugged fluidly. "There's an heirloom. It has power even I don't understand. The Dearborns and the Cohort demanded it, and we told them only a Rosales could make the object work."

Realization came to Cristina with a hard shock. "So the fake engagement," she said. "So Zara could think she was becoming a Rosales."

"Exactly," said Jaime. "Diego ties himself to the Cohort. And I—I take the heirloom and run. So Diego can blame me—his bad little brother ran off with it. And the engagement drags on and they don't find the heirloom."

"Is that your only plan?" Cristina said. "Delay forever?"

Jaime frowned at her. "I don't think you entirely appreciate that I've been very bravely on the run for months now," he said. "Very bravely."

"We are Nephilim, Jaime. It's our job to be brave," Cristina said.

"Some of us are better at it than others," Jaime said. "Anyway. I would not say our whole plan is to delay, no. Diego works to find out what the Cohort's weaknesses are. And I work to find out what the heirloom does exactly."

"You don't know?"

He shook his head. "I know it helps you enter Faerie undetected."

"And the Cohort wants to be able to enter Faerie so they can start a war?" Cristina guessed.

"That would make sense," said Jaime. "To them, anyway."

Cristina sat on the bed in silence. Outside it had begun to rain. Water streaked the windowpanes. She thought of rain on the trees in the Bosque, and sitting there with Jaime, watching him eat bags of Dorilocos and lick the salt off his fingers. And talking—talking for hours, about literally everything, about what they would do when they were *parabatai* and could travel anywhere in the world.

"Where are you going to go?" she said finally, trying to keep her voice steady.

"I can't tell you." He pulled himself away from the desk. "I can't tell anyone. I am a good escape artist, Cristina, but only if I never tell where I'm hiding."

"You don't know, do you," she said. "You're going to improvise."

He smiled sideways. "No one knows me better than you."

"And Diego?" Cristina's voice shook. "Why didn't he ever tell me any of this?"

"People do stupid things when they're in love," said Jaime, in the voice of someone who never had been. "And besides, I asked him not to."

"So why are you telling me now?"

"Two things," he said. "In Downworld, they say the Blackthorns are going up against the Cohort. If it comes to a fight, I want to be in it. Send me a fire-message. I will come." His tone was earnest. "And secondly, to deliver Diego's message. He said you might be too angry to read it. But I was hoping that now—you would not be."

She looked down at the envelope in her hand. It had been bent and folded many times.

"I'll read it," she said quietly. "Won't you stay? Eat a meal with us. You look starved."

Jaime shook his head. "No one can know I was here, Tina. Promise me. On the fact that we were once going to be *parabatai*."

"That isn't fair," she whispered. "Besides, Drusilla knows."

"She won't tell anyone—" Jaime began.

"Cristina!" It was Mark's voice, echoing down the hallway. "Cristina, where are you?"

Jaime's arms were around her suddenly, wiry-strong as he

hugged her hard. When he let go, she touched his face lightly. There were a million things she wanted to say—*ten cuidado* more than anything: Be safe, be careful. But he was already turning away from her, toward the window. He threw it open and ducked outside like a shadow, vanishing into the rain-streaked night.

25
START AND SIGH

Gwyn wouldn't come into the Institute.

Kit didn't know if it was principle or preference, but despite the fact that his arm was bleeding, soaking the side of his gray armor, the Wild Hunt leader only shook his head when Alec invited him cordially into the Institute.

"I am the head of the London Institute, however temporarily," Alec said. "I am empowered to invite whoever I want inside."

"I cannot linger," Gwyn demurred. "There is much to be done."

It had begun to rain. Alec was on the roof along with Mark, who had greeted Livvy and Ty with a mixture of terror and relief. The twins were still standing close to their brother, his arm around Livvy's shoulder, his hand clasping Ty's sleeve.

There was no one to greet Kit that way. He stood off a little to the side, watching. The ride on horseback from the river—Gwyn seemed to be able to summon horses out of the air, like a magician conjuring pennies—had been a blur; Ty and Livvy had ridden with Diana, and Kit had wound up behind Gwyn, clinging desperately to his belt and trying not to fall off the horse into the Thames.

"I cannot stay among all this cold iron," Gwyn said, and he did look fairly peaked, in Kit's opinion. "And you, Blackthorns—you should get yourself inside the Institute. Within its walls you are safe."

"What about Emma and Jules?" Livvy said. "They could be outside, the Riders could be looking for them—"

"Magnus went to find them," Alec reassured her. "He'll make sure they're all right."

Livvy nodded gravely, but she still looked worried.

"We might need some help from you, Diana," said Alec. "We're sending the children to Alicante as soon as Magnus returns."

"Which children?" asked Diana. She had a soft, low voice; now it was rough with tiredness. "Just yours, or . . ."

"Tavvy and Drusilla as well," Alec said. He eyed Livvy and Ty: Kit guessed that if he had his druthers, Alec would bring the twins along, too, but knew they'd never stand for it.

"Ah," said Diana. "Might I suggest that rather than taking up residence with the Inquisitor in Alicante, you stay with me on Flintlock Street? It would be good if the Cohort didn't know you were there."

"My thought exactly," said Alec. "Better to stay under the radar of the Dearborns and their ilk, especially just before the Council meeting." He frowned. "And hopefully we'll be able to get the binding spell off Mark and Cristina before we need to leave. Otherwise they might not be able to—"

"One of the Riders was killed," Kit said.

Everyone stared at him. He wasn't sure why he'd spoken, himself. The world seemed to be swaying around him, and strange things were important.

"You remember," he said. "It's why they fled, in the end. One of them had died, and the others could feel it. Maybe Julian and Emma fought them and won."

"No one can kill one of the Riders of Mannan," said Gwyn.

"Emma could," said Livvy. "If Cortana—"

Kit's knees gave out. It was very sudden and he hadn't expected it at all. One moment he was standing, the next he was kneeling in a cold puddle, wondering why he couldn't get up.

"Kit!" Diana cried. "Alec, he hit his head during the fight—he said it didn't hurt, but—"

Alec was already striding over to Kit. He was stronger than he looked. His arms braced Kit, lifting him; a hot dart of pain went through Kit's head as he moved, and a merciful grayness closed in.

They lay on the bed afterward in the twilight dark, Emma with her head on Julian's chest. She could hear his heart beating through the soft material of his T-shirt.

They had toweled their hair and put on dry clothes and curled up together under one layer of blankets. Their feet were tangled together; Julian was running a slow, thoughtful hand through her loose hair.

"Tell me," he said. "You said there was something I needed to know. And I stopped you." He paused. "Tell me now."

She folded her arms on his chest, resting her chin on them. There was relaxation in the curve of his body around hers. But his expression was more than curious; she could see the intensity in the back of his eyes, his need to know. To make sense out of all the pieces that didn't make sense now.

"I was never dating Mark," she said. "That was all a lie. I asked him to pretend to be dating me, and he had said he owed me his life before, so he agreed. It was never real."

His fingers stilled in her hair. Emma swallowed. She had to get through all this without thinking of whether Julian would hate her at the end. Otherwise she'd never be able to finish.

"Why would you do that?" he said carefully. "Why would Mark agree to hurt me?"

"He didn't know it was hurting you," Emma said. "He never knew there was anything between us—not until we went to Faerie. He found out then, and he told me we had to end it. That's why I stopped things in London. Mark didn't mind. We didn't feel that way about each other."

"So Mark didn't know," he said. "Why did you do it, then?" He held up a hand. "Never mind. I know the answer: to stop me loving you. To break us up. I even know why you picked Mark."

"I wish it could have been anyone else—"

"No one else would have made me hate you," he said flatly. "Nobody else would have made me give you up." He propped himself up on his elbow, looking down at her. "Make me understand," he said. "You love me and I love you, but you wanted to wreck all that. You were so determined you brought Mark into it, which I know you'd never do if you weren't desperate. So what made you so desperate, Emma? I know being in love with your *parabatai* is forbidden, but it's a stupid Law—"

"It's not," she said, "a stupid Law."

He blinked. His hair was dry now. "Whatever you know, Emma," he said in a low voice, "it's time to tell me."

So she did. Leaving nothing out, she told him what Malcolm had said to her about the *parabatai* curse, how he was showing her mercy, killing her, when otherwise she and Julian would watch each other die. How the Nephilim hated love. What Jem had confirmed for her: the terrible fate of *parabatai* who fell in love; the death and destruction they would bring down around them. How she knew that neither of them could ever become mundanes or Downworlders to break the bond: how being Shadowhunters was part of their souls and their selves, how the exile from their families would destroy them.

The light from the fire threw a dark gold glow across his face, his hair, but she could see how pale he was, even under that, and the starkness that took over his expression as she spoke, as if the shadows were growing harsher. Outside, the rain poured steadily down.

When she was done, he was silent a long time. Emma's mouth was dry, as if she'd been swallowing cotton. Finally she could stand it no longer and moved toward him, knocking the pillow onto the floor. "Jules—"

He held a hand up. "Why didn't you tell me any of this?"

She looked at him miserably. "Because of what Jem said. That finding out that what we had was forbidden for good reason would just make it worse. Believe me, knowing what I know hasn't made me love you any less."

His eyes were such a dark blue in the dim light they looked like Kit's. "So you decided to make me hate you."

"I tried," she whispered. "I didn't know what else to do."

"But I could never hate you," he said. "Hating you would be like hating the idea of good things ever happening in the world. It would be like death. I thought you didn't love me, Emma. But I never hated you."

"And I thought you didn't love me."

"And it didn't make any difference, did it? We still loved each other. I understand why you were so upset about what we did to Porthallow Church, now."

She nodded. "The curse makes you stronger before it makes you destructive."

"I'm glad you told me." He touched her cheek, her hair. "Now we know nothing we can do will change how we feel about each other. We'll have to find another solution."

There were tears on Emma's face, though she didn't remember starting to cry. "I thought if you stopped loving me, you'd be sad for a while. And if I was sad forever, that would be okay. Because you'd be all right, and I'd still be your *parabatai*. And if you could be happy eventually, then I could be happy too, for you."

"You're an idiot," Julian said. He put his arms around her and rocked her, his lips against her hair, and he whispered, the way he whispered when Tavvy had nightmares, that she was brave to have done what she did, that they'd fix it all, they'd find a way. And even though Emma could still see no way out for them, she relaxed against his chest, letting herself feel the relief of having shared the burden, just for this moment. "But I can't be angry. There's something I should have told you, as well."

She drew away from him. "What is it?"

He was fiddling with his glass bracelet. Since Julian rarely expressed any anxiety in a visible way, Emma felt her heart thump.

"Julian," she said. "Tell me."

"When we were going into Faerie," he said in a low voice, "the phouka told me that if I entered the Lands, I would meet someone who knew how to break the *parabatai* bond."

The thumping of Emma's heart became a rapid tattoo beating against the inside of her rib cage. She sat up straight. "Are you saying you know how to break it?"

He shook his head. "The wording was correct—I met someone who did know how to break it. The Seelie Queen, to be precise. And she told me she knew it could be done, but not *how*."

"Is that part of returning the book?" Emma said. "We give her the Black Volume, she tells us how to end the bond?"

He nodded. He was looking at the fire.

"You didn't tell me," she said. "Is that because you thought I wouldn't care?"

"Partially," he said. "If you didn't want the bond broken, then neither did I. I'd rather be your *parabatai* than nothing."

"Jules—*Julian*—"

"And there's more," he said. "She told me there would be a cost."

Of course, a cost. There is always a cost when faeries are involved.

"What kind of cost?" she whispered.

"Breaking the bond involves using the Black Volume to dig out the root of all *parabatai* ceremonies," said Julian. "It would break our bond, yes. But it would also destroy every *parabatai* bond in the world. They'd all be snapped. There'd be no more *parabatai*."

Emma stared at him in absolute shock. "We couldn't possibly do that. Alec and Jace—Clary and Simon—there are so many others—"

"You think I don't know that? But I couldn't not tell you. You have a right to know."

Emma felt as if she could barely breathe. "The Queen—"

A sharp bang echoed through the room, as if someone had set off a firecracker. Magnus Bane appeared in their kitchen, wrapped in a long black coat, his right hand sparking blue fire, his expression thunderous. "Why in the names of the nine princes of Hell are neither of you answering your phone?" he demanded.

Emma and Julian gaped at him. After a moment, he gaped back.

"My God," he said. "Are you . . . ?"

He didn't finish the question. He didn't have to.

Emma and Julian scrambled out of the bed. They were both mostly dressed, but Magnus was looking at them as if he'd caught them in flagrante.

"Magnus," Julian said. He didn't follow up his greeting by saying it wasn't like that, or Magnus was getting the wrong idea. Julian didn't say things like that. "What's going on? Is something wrong at home?"

Magnus looked, at that moment, like he was feeling his age. "*Parabatai*," he said, and sighed. "Yes, something's wrong. We need to get you back to the Institute. Grab your things and get ready to leave."

He leaned back against the kitchen island, crossing his arms. He was wearing a sort of greatcoat with several layers of short capes in the back. He was dry—he must have Portaled from inside the Institute.

"There's blood on your sword, Emma," he said, looking at where Cortana was propped against the wall.

"Faerie blood," said Emma. Julian was yanking on a sweater and running his fingers through his wild hair.

"When you say faerie blood," Magnus said, "you mean the Riders, don't you?"

Emma saw Julian start. "They were looking for us—how would you know?"

"They weren't just looking for you. The King sent them to find the Black Volume. He instructed them to hunt all of you—all the Blackthorns."

"To *hunt* us?" Julian demanded. "Is anyone hurt?" He strode across the room to Magnus, almost as if he meant to grab the warlock by his shirt and shake him. *"Is anyone in my family hurt?"*

"Julian." Magnus's voice was firm. "Everyone's fine. But the Riders did come. They attacked Kit, Ty, and Livvy."

"And they're all right?" Emma demanded anxiously, shoving her feet into boots.

"Yes—I got a fire-message from Alec," Magnus said. "Kit got a bump on the head. Ty and Livvy, not a scratch. But they were lucky—Gwyn and Diana intervened."

"Diana and Gwyn? Together?" Emma was baffled.

"Emma killed one of the Riders," Julian said. He was gathering up Annabel's portfolio, Malcolm's diaries, shoving them into his bag. "We hid his body up on the cliff, but we probably shouldn't leave it there."

Magnus whistled between his teeth. "No one's killed one of Mannan's Riders in—well, in all the history I know."

Emma shuddered, remembering the cold feeling as the blade had gone into Fal's body. "It was horrible."

"The rest of them are not gone forever," said Magnus. "They will come back."

Julian zipped his bag and Emma's. "Then we need to take the children somewhere safe. Somewhere the Riders won't find them."

"Right now, the Institute is the safest place outside Idris," said Magnus. "It's warded, and I'll ward it again."

"The cottage is safe too," Emma said, hoisting her bag over her shoulder. It was twice as heavy as it had been before with the addition of Malcolm's books. "The Riders can't come near it; they said so."

"Thoughtful of Malcolm," said Magnus. "But you'd be trapped in the house if you stayed, and I can't imagine you'd want to be unable to leave these four walls."

"No," Julian said, but he said it quietly. Emma could see Magnus raking his gaze over the interior of the cottage—the mess of teacups they hadn't cleaned up, the signs of Julian's cooking, the disarray of the bedcovers, the remains of the fire in the grate. A place built by and for two people who loved each other yet weren't allowed to, and that had sheltered two more such people two hundred years later. "I suppose we wouldn't."

There was sympathy in Magnus's eyes when he looked back at Julian, and at Emma, too. "All dreams end when you wake," he said. "Now, come. I'll Portal us home."

Dru watched the rain streak her bedroom windows. Outside, London was a blur, the glow of streetlights expanding in the rain to become yellow dandelion clocks of light perched on elongated metal posts.

She had been in the library long enough to tell Mark that she was fine, before he'd gotten worried about Cristina and gone looking for her. When they'd both returned, Dru's stomach had tightened with fear. She'd been sure Cristina was going to tell—tell everyone about Jaime, spill her secret, spill *his*.

The expression on Cristina's face wasn't comforting, either. "Can I talk to you in the hall, Dru?" she had said.

Dru nodded and put her book down. She hadn't been reading it anyway. Mark had gone over to Kieran and the children, and Dru followed Cristina out into the hall.

"Thank you," Cristina said, as soon as the door was shut. "For helping Jaime."

Dru cleared her throat. Being thanked seemed like a good sign. At least a sign that Cristina wasn't mad. Maybe.

Cristina smiled. She had dimples. Dru immediately wished she had them too. Did she? She'd have to check. Though smiling at herself in the mirror sounded a little bizarre. "Don't worry, I won't tell anyone he was here, or that you helped him. It must not have been easy, putting up with him as you did."

"I didn't mind," Dru said. "He listened to me."

Cristina's dark eyes were sad. "He used to listen to me, once, too."

"Is he going to be all right?" Dru asked.

"I think so," Cristina said. "He has always been smart and careful." She touched Dru's cheek. "I'll let you know if I hear from him."

And that was that. Dru had gone back to her bedroom, feeling hollow. She knew she'd been supposed to stay in the library, but she needed to be where she could think.

She'd sat on the edge of her bed, kicking her legs listlessly. She wanted Jaime to be there so she'd have someone to talk to. She wanted to talk about the fact that Magnus looked tired, that Mark was stressed, that she was worried about Emma and Jules. She wanted to talk about how she missed home, the smell of the ocean and desert.

She swung her legs harder—and her heel collided with

something. Bending down, she saw with surprise that Jaime's duffel bag was still stuffed under her bed. She pulled it out from under the mattress, trying not to spill the contents. It was already unzipped.

He must have shoved it there in a hurry when Cristina came in, but why would he leave it? Did it mean he was planning on coming back? Or had he just left behind the stuff he didn't need?

She didn't mean to look inside, or at least that was what she told herself later. It wasn't that she needed to know if he was coming back. It was just an accident.

Stuffed inside were a jumble of boy's clothes, a bunch of jeans and shirts, and a few books, spare steles, unactivated seraph blades, a balisong not unlike Cristina's, and some photographs. And something else, something that shone so brightly that she thought for a moment it was a witchlight—but the illumination was less white than that. It glowed with a dim, deep gold color, like the surface of the ocean. Before she knew it, her hand was on it—

She felt herself jerked off her feet, as if she were being sucked into a Portal. She yanked her hand back, but she was no longer touching anything. She was no longer in her room at all.

She was underground, in a long corridor dug out of the earth. The roots of trees grew down into the space, like the curling ribbon on expensively wrapped gifts. The corridor stretched away on either side of her into shadows that deepened like no shadows above ground.

Dru's heart was pounding. A terrible sense of unreality choked her. It was as if she'd traveled through a Portal, but with no idea where she'd gone, with no sense of familiarity. Even the air in the place smelled like something strange and dark, some kind of scent she'd never breathed before.

Dru reached automatically for the weapons at her belt, but

there was nothing there. She'd come here completely unprepared, in only jeans and a black T-shirt with cats on it. She choked back a hysterical laugh and moved to press herself against the wall of the underground corridor, keeping to the depth of the shadows.

Lights appeared at the end of the hall. Dru could hear high, sweet voices in the distance. Their chatter was like the chatter of birds. *Faeries.*

She moved blindly in the other direction, and nearly fell backward when the wall gave way behind her and became a curtain of fabric. She stumbled through and found herself in a large stone room.

The walls were squares of green marble, veined with thick black lines. Some of the squares were carved with golden patterns—a hawk, a throne, a crown divided into two pieces. There were weapons in the room, ranged around on the surfaces of different tables—swords and daggers of copper and bronze, hooks and spikes and maces of all sorts of metal except iron.

There was also a boy in the room. A boy her age, maybe thirteen. He had turned around when she came in, and now he stared at her in astonishment.

"How dare you come into this room?" His voice was sharp, imperious.

He wore rich clothing, silk and velvet, heavy leather boots. His hair was white-blond, the color of witchlight. It was cut short, and a pale band of metal encircled it at his brow.

"I didn't mean to." Dru swallowed. "I just want to get out of here," she said. "That's all I want."

His green eyes burned. "Who are you?" He took a step forward, snatching a dagger up off the table beside him. "Are you a *Shadowhunter?*"

Dru raised her chin and stared back at him. "Who are *you?*" she demanded. "And why are you so rude?"

To her surprise, he smiled, and there was something familiar about it. "I'm called Ash," he said. "Did my mother send you?" He sounded hopeful. "Is she worried about me?"

"Drusilla!" said a voice. "Dru! *Dru!*"

Dru looked around in confusion: Where was the voice coming from? The walls of the room were starting to darken, to melt and merge. The boy in the rich clothes with his sharp faerie's face looked at her in confusion, raising his dagger, as more holes began to open around her: in the walls, in the floor. She shrieked as the ground gave way beneath her and she fell into darkness.

The whirling air caught her again, the cold spinning almost-Portal, and then she slammed back to reality on the floor of her bedroom. She was alone. She gasped and choked, trying to pull herself to her knees. Her heart felt as if it was going to rip its way out of her chest.

Her mind spun—the terror of being underground, the terror of not knowing if she'd ever return home, the terror of an alien place—and yet the images slipped away from her, as if she were trying to hold on to water or wind. *Where was I? What happened?*

She raised herself to her knees, feeling sick and nauseated. She blinked away the dizziness—there were green eyes in the back of her vision, green eyes—and saw that Jaime's duffel bag was gone. Her window was propped open, the floor damp below the window. He must have come in and out while she was . . . gone. But where had she been? She didn't remember.

"Dru!" The voice came again. Mark's voice. And another impatient knock on her door. "Dru, didn't you hear me? Emma and Jules are back."

"There," Diana said, checking the bandage on Gwyn's arm one last time. "I wish I could give you an *iratze*, but . . ."

She let her voice trail off, feeling silly. She was the one who had insisted they go to her rooms in Alicante so she could bandage his wound, and Gwyn had been quiet ever since.

He had slapped his horse's flank after they'd climbed from it into her window, sending it soaring into the sky.

She'd wondered as he looked around her room, his bicolored eyes taking in all the visible traces of her life—the used coffee mugs, the pajamas thrown into a corner, the ink-stained desk—whether she'd made the right decision bringing him here. She had let so few people into her personal space for so many years, showing only what she wanted to show, controlling access to her inner self so carefully. She had never thought the first man she allowed into her room in Idris would be an odd and beautiful faerie, but she knew when he winced violently as he sat down on her bed that she had made the right call.

She'd gritted her teeth in sympathetic pain as he started to peel away his barklike armor. Her father had always kept extra bandages in the bathroom; when she returned from her trip there, gauze in hand, she found Gwyn shirtless and grumpy-looking on her rumpled blanket, his brown hair almost the same color as her wooden walls. His skin was several shades paler, smooth and taut over bones that were just a shade alien.

"I do not need to be ministered to," he said. "I have always bandaged my own wounds."

Diana didn't answer, just set about making a field dressing. Sitting behind him as she worked, she realized it was the closest she'd ever been to him. She'd thought his skin would feel like bark, like his armor, but it didn't: It felt like leather, the very softest kind that was used to make scabbards for delicate blades.

"We all have wounds that are sometimes better cared for by someone else," she said, setting the box of bandages aside.

"And what of your wounds?" he said.

"I wasn't injured." She got to her feet, ostensibly to prove to him that she was fine, walking and breathing. Part of it was also to put some distance between them. Her heart was skipping beats in a way she didn't trust.

"You know that is not what I meant," he said. "I see how you care for those children. Why do you not just offer to head the Los Angeles Institute? You would make a better leader than Arthur Blackthorn ever did."

Diana swallowed, though her mouth was dry. "Does it matter?"

"It matters in that I wish to know you," he said. "I would kiss you, but you draw away from me; I would know your heart, but you hide it in shadow. Is it that you do not like or want me? Because in that case I will not trouble you."

There was no intention to cause guilt in his voice, only a plain statement of fact.

If he had made a more emotional plea, perhaps she would not have responded. As it was, she found herself crossing the room, picking up a book from the shelf by the bed. "If you think there's something I'm hiding, then I suppose you're right," she said. "But I doubt it's what you think." She raised her chin, thinking of her namesake, goddess and warrior, who had nothing to apologize for. "It's nothing I did wrong. I'm not ashamed; I've no reason to be. But the Clave—" She sighed. "Here. Take this."

Gwyn took the book from her, solemn-faced. "This is a book of law," he said.

She nodded. "The laws of investiture. It details the ceremonies by which Shadowhunters take on new positions: how one is sworn in as Consul, or Inquisitor, or the head of an Institute." She leaned over him, opening the book to a well-examined page. "Here. When you're sworn in as the head of an Institute, you must hold the Mortal Sword and answer the Inquisitor's questions. The questions are law. They never change."

Gwyn nodded. "Which of the questions is it," he said, "that you do not want to answer?"

"Pretend you are the Inquisitor," Diana said, as if he hadn't spoken. "Ask the questions, and I will answer as if I'm holding the Sword, entirely truthfully."

Gwyn nodded. His eyes were dark with curiosity and something else as he began to read aloud. "Are you a Shadowhunter?"

"Yes," said Diana.

"Were you born a Shadowhunter, or did you Ascend?"

"I was born a Shadowhunter."

"What is your family name?"

"Wrayburn."

"And what was the name you were given at birth?" asked Gwyn.

"David," said Diana. "David Laurence Wrayburn."

Gwyn looked puzzled. "I do not understand."

"I am a woman," said Diana. "I always have been. I always knew I was a girl, whatever the Silent Brothers told my parents, whatever the contradiction of my body. My sister, Aria, knew too. She said she'd known it from the moment I could talk. But my parents—" She broke off. "They weren't unkind, but they didn't know the options. They told me I should live as myself at home, but in public, be David. Be the boy I knew I wasn't. Stay under the radar of the Clave.

"I knew that would be living a lie. Still, it was a secret the four of us kept. Yet with every year my crushing despair grew. I withdrew from interaction with other Shadowhunters our age. At every moment, waking and sleeping, I felt anxious and uncomfortable. And I feared I would never be happy. Then I turned eighteen. My sister was nineteen. We went to Thailand together to study at the Bangkok Institute. I met Catarina Loss there."

"Catarina Loss," said Gwyn. "She knows. That you are—that you were—" He frowned. "I'm sorry. I don't know how to say it. That you were named David by your parents?"

"She knows," Diana said. "She didn't know at the time. In

Thailand, I lived as the woman I am. I dressed as myself. Aria introduced me as her sister. I was happy. For the first time I felt free, and I chose a name for myself that embraced that freedom. My father's weapons shop had always been called Diana's Arrow, after the goddess of the hunt, who was proud and free. I named myself Diana. I am Diana." She took a ragged breath. "And then my sister and I went out to explore an island where it was rumored there were Thotsakan demons. It turned out not to be demons at all, but revenants—hungry ghosts. Dozens of them. We fought them, but we were both injured. Catarina rescued us. Rescued me. When I woke up in a small house not far away, Catarina was caring for us. I knew she had seen my injuries—that she had seen my body. I knew she knew . . ."

"Diana," said Gwyn in his deep voice, and stretched out a hand. But Diana shook her head.

"Don't," she said. "Or I won't be able to get through it." Her eyes were burning with unshed tears. "I pulled the rags of my clothes around my body. I screamed for my sister. But she was dead, had died while Catarina ministered to her. I broke down completely then. I had lost everything. My life was destroyed. That's what I thought." A tear slipped down her face. "Catarina nursed me back to health and sanity. I was in that cottage with her for weeks. And she talked to me. She gave me words, which I'd never had, as a gift. It was the first time I heard the word 'transgender.' I broke into tears. I had never realized before how much you can take from someone by not allowing them the words they need to describe themselves. How can you know there are other people like you, when you've never had a name to call yourself? I know there must have been other transgender Shadowhunters, that they must have existed in the past and exist now. But I have no way to search for them and it would be dangerous to ask." A flicker of anger at the old injustice sharpened her voice. "Then Catarina told me of transitioning. That

I could live as myself, the way I needed to and be acknowledged as who I am. I knew it was what I wanted.

"I went with Catarina to Bangkok. But not as David. I went as Diana. And I did not go as a Shadowhunter. I lived with Catarina in a small apartment. I told my parents of Aria's death and that I was Diana now: They replied that they had told the Council that David was the one who had died. That they loved me and understood, but that I must live in the mundane world now, for I was seeing mundane doctors and that was against the law.

"It was too late for me to stop them. The Clave was told that David had died out on the island, fighting revenants. They gave David my sister's death, a death with honor. I wished they had not lied, but if they had to wear white for the boy who was gone, even if he'd never really existed, I couldn't deny them that.

"Catarina had worked as a nurse for years. She knew mundane medicine. She brought me to a clinic in Bangkok. I met others like myself there. I wasn't alone any longer. I was there for three years. I never planned to be a Shadowhunter again. What I was gaining was too precious. I couldn't risk being discovered, having my secrets flayed open, being called by a man's name, having who I was denied.

"Through the years, Catarina guided me through the mundane medical procedure that gave me the body in whose skin I felt comfortable. She hid my unusual test results from the doctors so they would never be puzzled by my Shadowhunter blood."

"Mundane medicine," Gwyn echoed. "It is forbidden, is it not, for a Shadowhunter to seek out mundane medical treatment? Why did Catarina not simply use magic to aid you?"

Diana shook her head. "I wouldn't have wanted that," she said. "A magic spell can always be undone by another spell. I will not have the truth of myself be something that can be dissolved by a stray enchantment or passing through the wrong magical gate.

My body is *my body*—the body I have grown into as a woman, as all women grow into their bodies."

Gwyn nodded, though Diana couldn't tell if he understood. "So that is what you fear," was all he said.

"I'm not afraid for myself," said Diana. "I'm afraid for the children. As long as I'm their tutor, I feel like I can protect them in some way. If the Clave knew what I'd done, that I'd sought out mundane doctors, I'd wind up in prison under the Silent City. Or in the Basilias, if they were being kind."

"And your parents?" Gwyn's face was unreadable. Diana wished he would give her some kind of sign. Was he angry? Would he mock her? His calmness was making her pulse race. "Did they come to you? You must have missed them."

"I feared to expose them to the Clave." Diana's voice hitched. "Each time they spoke of a clandestine visit to Bangkok, I put them off. And then the news came that they had died, slain in a demon attack. Catarina was the one who told me. I wept all night. I could not tell my mundane friends of my parents' deaths because they would not understand why I didn't return home for a funeral.

"Then news came of the Mortal War. And I realized I was still a Shadowhunter. I could not let Idris suffer peril without a fight. I returned to Alicante. I told the Council that I was the daughter of Aaron and Lissa Wrayburn. Because that was the truth. They knew there had been a brother and a sister and the brother had died: I gave my name as Diana. In the chaos of war, no one questioned me.

I rose up as Diana in battle. I fought as myself, with a sword in my hand and angel fire in my veins. And I knew I could never go back to being a mundane. Among my mundane friends I had to conceal the existence of Shadowhunters. Among the Shadowhunters I had to hide that I had once used mundane medicine. I knew either way I would have to hide a part of myself. I chose to be a Shadowhunter."

"Who else has known all this? Besides Catarina?"

"Malcolm knew. There is a medicine I must take, to maintain the balance of my body's hormones—I usually get it from Catarina, but there was a time she couldn't do it, and had Malcolm make it. After that, he knew. He never directly held it over my head, but I was always aware of his knowledge. That he could hurt me."

"That he could hurt you," Gwyn murmured. His face was a mask. Diana could hear her heart beating in her ears. It was as if she had come to Gwyn with her heart in her hands, raw and bleeding, and now she waited for him to produce the knives.

"All my life I've tried to find the place to be myself and I'm still looking for it," said Diana. "Because of that, I have hidden things from people I loved. And I have hidden this from you. But I have never lied about the truth of myself."

What Gwyn did next surprised Diana. He rose from the bed, took a step forward, and went down on his knees in front of her. He did it gracefully, the way a squire might kneel to a knight or a knight to his lady. There was something ancient in the essence of the gesture, something that went back to the heart and core of the folk of Faerie.

"It is as I knew," he said. "When I saw you upon the stairs of the Institute, and I saw the fire in your eyes, I knew you were the bravest woman ever to set foot on this earth. I regret only that such a fearless soul was ever hurt by the ignorance and fear of others."

"Gwyn . . ."

"May I hold you?" he asked.

She nodded. She couldn't speak. She knelt down opposite the leader of the Wild Hunt and let him take her into his broad arms, let him stroke her hair and murmur her name in his voice that still sounded like the rumble of thunder—but now it was thunder heard from inside a warm, closed house, where everyone was safe inside.

Tavvy was the first one to sense Emma and Julian's return when they Portaled back into the Institute library with Magnus. He had been sitting on the floor, systematically dismantling some old toys with the assistance of Max. The moment Julian felt the floor solid under his feet, Tavvy bounded upright and careened toward him, crashing into him like a train that had gone off its tracks.

"*Jules!*" he exclaimed, and Julian swung him up into his arms and crushed him in a hug as Tavvy clung to him and babbled about what he'd seen and eaten and done in the past few days, and Jules ruffled his brother's hair and felt a tension he hadn't even known he was carrying go out of him.

Cristina had been sitting with Rafe, talking to him quietly in Spanish. Mark was at a library table with Alec, and—to Julian's surprise—Kieran, a mass of books open in front of them.

Cristina jumped to her feet and ran to hug Emma. Livvy came barreling into the room, Ty following more quietly after, and Julian lowered Tavvy to the ground—where he remained by Julian's side, gripping his leg—while he greeted the rest of his family in a blur of hugs and exclamations.

Emma was hugging the twins, a sight that sent a dart of familiar pain through Julian's rib cage. The dread of separation, of pulling apart what belonged together: the dream of his family, Emma as his partner, the children their responsibility.

A hand touched his shoulder, jolting him out of imagination. It was Mark, who looked at him with uneasiness. "Jules?"

Of course. Mark didn't realize Julian knew the truth about him and Emma. He looked worried, hopeful, like a puppy who had come begging for scraps but half-expected to be slapped away from the table.

Was I that bad? Julian wondered, guilt spearing through him. Mark hadn't even known, hadn't imagined Julian loving Emma. Had been horrified when he found out. Mark and Emma loved each other, but not romantically, which was what Julian would have wanted. His heart swelled with tenderness toward both of them for everything they had given up to protect him, for being willing to let him hate them if that was what it took.

He drew Mark with him into a corner of the room. The hubbub of greeting went on all around them as Julian lowered his voice. "I know what you did," he said. "I know you were never really dating Emma. I'm grateful. I know it was for me."

Mark looked surprised. "It was Emma's idea," he said.

"Oh, believe me, I know." Julian put his hand on his brother's shoulder. "And you did a good job with the kids. Magnus told me. Thank you."

Mark's face lit up. It made Julian's heart ache even harder. "I didn't— I mean, they got in so much trouble—"

"You loved them and you kept them alive," said Julian. "Sometimes that's the best anyone can do."

Julian pulled his brother toward him into a hard hug. Mark made a muffled noise of surprise before his own arms went around Julian, half-crushing the breath out of him. Julian could feel his brother's heart hammering against his, as if the same relief and joy were beating through their shared blood.

They drew apart after a moment. "So you and Emma . . . ?" Mark began, half-hesitantly. But before Julian could reply, Livvy had thrown herself at them, somehow managing to hug Julian and Mark at the same time, and the conversation vanished into laughter.

Ty came more diffidently after her, smiling and touching Julian on the shoulder and then the hand as if to make sure he was really there. Tactile expression sometimes meant as much to Ty as what he could observe with his eyes.

Mark was telling Emma that Dru was still in her room, but she'd be coming shortly. Magnus had gone to Alec, and the two were talking quietly by the fireplace. Only Kieran remained where he was, so silent and still at the table that he could have been a decorative plant. The sight of him flicked a memory in Julian's mind, though, and he looked around for blond hair and a sarcastic expression. "Where's Kit?"

A flood of cross-explanations followed: the story of the Riders at the riverside, the way Gwyn and Diana had saved them, Kit's injury. Emma described the four Riders they'd encountered in Cornwall, though it was Julian who detailed the way Emma had killed one of them, which prompted a great deal of exclaiming.

"I've never heard of anyone killing a Rider before," said Cristina, hurrying to the table to pick up a book. "But someone must have."

"No." It was Kieran, his voice even and quiet. There was something in the timbre of it that reminded Julian of the Unseelie King's voice. "No one ever has. There have only ever been seven, the children of Mannan, and they have lived almost since the beginning of time. There must be something very special about you, Emma Carstairs."

Emma flushed. "There isn't."

Kieran was still looking at Emma curiously. He was wearing jeans and a cream-colored sweater. He looked alarmingly human, until you really examined his face and the uncanniness of his bone structure. "What was it like to kill something so old?"

Emma hesitated. "It was like—have you ever held ice so long in your hand that the coldness hurt your skin?"

After a pause, Kieran nodded. "It is a deathly pain."

"It was like that."

"So we're safe here," Julian said to Magnus, partly to forestall any further questions about the dead Rider. "In the Institute."

"The Riders can't reach us here. They are warded away," said Magnus.

"But Gwyn was able to land on the roof," Emma said. "So Fair Folk can't be completely shut out—"

"Gwyn is Wild Hunt. They're different." Magnus reached down to pick up Max, who giggled and pulled on his scarf. "Also I've doubled the wards around the Institute since this afternoon."

"Where's Diana?" asked Julian.

"She went back to Idris. She says she has to keep Jia and the Council happy and calm and expecting this meeting to take place with no hiccups."

"But we don't have the Black Volume," Julian said.

"Well, we still have a day and a half," said Emma. "To find Annabel."

"Without leaving these hallowed walls?" Mark said. He sat down on the arm of one of the chairs. "We are kind of trapped."

"I don't know if the Riders realize Alec and I are here," Magnus said. "Or perhaps we could prevail on Gwyn."

"The danger seems pretty severe," said Emma. "We wouldn't feel right, asking for that kind of help."

"Well I'm going back to Idris with the kids—I can certainly see what I can do from there." Alec flung himself down in a chair near Rafe and ruffled the boy's dark hair.

Maybe Alec could get into Blackthorn Manor, Julian thought. He was exhausted, nerves frayed from one of the best and worst days of his life. But Blackthorn Manor was probably the place on earth Annabel had loved the most. His mind began to tick over the possibilities.

"Annabel cared about Blackthorn Manor," he said. "Not Blackthorn Hall, here in London—the family didn't own that yet. The one in Idris. She loved it."

"So you think she might be there?" said Magnus.

"No," said Julian. "She hates the Clave, hates Shadowhunters. She'd be too afraid to go to Idris. I was just thinking that if it was in danger, if it was threatened, she might be called out of where she's hiding."

He could tell Emma was wondering why he wasn't mentioning that he'd seen Annabel in Cornwall; he wondered it a bit himself, but his instincts told him to keep it secret a little longer.

"You're suggesting we burn down Blackthorn Manor?" said Ty, his eyebrows up around his hairline.

"Oddly," Magnus muttered, "you wouldn't be the first people ever to have *that* idea."

"Ty, don't sound so excited," Livvy said.

"Pyromania interests me," said Ty.

"I think you have to burn down several buildings before you can consider yourself to be an actual maniac for pyro," Emma said. "I think before that you're just an enthusiast."

"I think setting a large fire in Idris will attract attention we don't want," said Mark.

"I think we don't have a lot of choices," said Julian.

"And I think we should eat," Livvy said hastily, patting her stomach. "I'm *starving*."

"We can discuss what we know, especially regarding Annabel and the Black Volume," said Ty. "We can pool our information."

Magnus glanced fleetingly at Alec. "After we eat we need to send the children to Idris. Diana's standing by on the other side to help us keep the Portal open, and I don't want her to have to wait too long."

It was kind of him, Julian thought, to phrase it as if sending the children to Alicante was a favor Magnus was doing Diana, rather than a precaution taken to protect them. Tavvy skipped along with Rafe and Max to the dining room and Julian felt a pang, realizing how much his little brother had missed having friends close to his own age, even if he hadn't known it.

"Jules?" He glanced down and saw that Dru was walking beside him. Her face was pale in the corridor's witchlight.

"Yeah?" He resisted the urge to pat her cheek or pull her braids. She'd stopped appreciating that when she was ten.

"I don't want to go to Alicante," she said. "I want to stay here with you."

"Dru . . ."

She hunched her shoulders up. "You were younger than me in the Dark War," she said. "I'm thirteen. You can send the babies where it's safe, but not me. I'm a Blackthorn, just like you."

"So is Tavvy."

"He's *seven*." Dru took a shaky breath. "You make me feel like I'm not part of this family."

Julian stopped dead. Dru stopped with him, and they both watched as the others went into the dining room. Julian could hear Bridget scolding them all; apparently she'd been holding dinner for them for hours, though it had never occurred to her to find them and tell them so.

"Dru," he said. "You really want to stay?"

She nodded. "I really want to."

"Then that's all you had to say. You can stay with us."

She threw herself into his arms. Dru wasn't a huggy sort of person, and for a moment Julian was too surprised to move; then he put his arms around his sister and tightened them against the flood of memories—baby Dru sleeping in his arms, taking her first toddling steps, laughing as Emma held her over the water at the beach, barely getting her toes wet.

"You're the heart of this family, baby girl," he said in the voice that only his brothers and sisters ever heard. "I promise you. You're our heart."

* * *

Bridget had somewhat haphazardly set out cold chicken, bread, cheese, vegetables, and banoffee pie. Kieran picked at the vegetables while the rest of them talked over each other to lay out what they knew.

Emma sat beside Julian. Every once in a while their shoulders would bump or their hands collide as they reached for something. Each touch sent a shower of sparks through him, like a small explosion of fireworks.

Ty, his elbows on the table, took point on the discussion, explaining how he, Kit, and Livvy had found the *aletheia* crystal and the memories trapped within it. "Two hundred years ago Malcolm and Annabel broke into the Cornwall Institute," he explained, his graceful hands slicing through the air as he talked. Something seemed different about Ty, Julian thought, though how could his brother have changed in the few short days he'd been away? "They stole the Black Volume, but they were caught."

"Do we know why they wanted it?" Cristina asked. "I do not see how necromancy would have helped them."

"They planned to trade it to someone else, it looks like," said Emma. "The book wasn't for them. Someone had promised to trade them protection from the Clave for it."

"It was a time when a relationship between a Shadowhunter and a Downworlder could have meant a death sentence for both of them," said Magnus. "Protection would have been a very attractive offer."

"They never got that far," Ty said. "They were caught and thrown in prison in the Silent City, and the Black Volume was taken from them and returned to the Cornwall Institute. Then something weird happened." He frowned. Ty didn't like not knowing things. "Malcolm disappeared. He left Annabel to be questioned and tortured."

"He wouldn't have done that willingly," said Julian. "He loved her."

"People can betray even those they love," said Mark.

"No, Julian's right," said Emma. "I hate Malcolm more than anyone, but he absolutely would never have left Annabel. She was his whole life."

"It's still what happened," said Ty.

"They tortured Annabel for information until she pretty much lost her mind," said Livvy. "Then they released her to her family. And they killed her and told everyone she'd become an Iron Sister. But it wasn't true."

There was a tightness in Julian's throat. He thought of Annabel's drawings, the lightness in them, the hope, the love for Blackthorn Manor in Idris and for Malcolm.

"Fast-forward almost a hundred years," said Emma. "Malcolm goes to the Unseelie King. He's found out that Annabel wasn't an Iron Sister, that she was murdered. He's out for bloody vengeance." She paused, combing her fingers back through her hair, still tangled from Cornish wind and rain. "The Unseelie King tells him how to raise Annabel, but there's a catch—Malcolm needs the Black Volume to do it, and now he doesn't have it. It's in the Cornwall Institute. He broke in there once, he doesn't dare do it again. So there it stays until the Blackthorns who run the Institute move to Los Angeles, and they take it with them."

Ty's eyes lit up. "Right. And Malcolm sees his chance when Sebastian Morgenstern attacks, and takes the book. He starts to raise Annabel, and finally he succeeds."

"Except she's pissed off and kills him," said Emma.

"How ungrateful," said Kieran.

"Ungrateful?" Emma said. "He was a murderer. She was right to kill him."

"He may have been a murderer," said Kieran, "but it sounds as if he became one for her. He killed to give her life."

"Maybe she didn't want life," said Alec. He shrugged. "He never did ask her what she wanted, did he?"

As if sensing the tense atmosphere at the table, Max began to wail. With a sigh, Alec picked him up and carried him out of the room.

"I'm sure it's useful to know all this," said Magnus. "But does it bring us closer to the Black Volume?"

"Maybe if we had more time, and the Riders weren't after us," said Julian.

"I think," said Kieran slowly, his gaze unfocused, "that it was my father."

Apparently it was his day for startling pronouncements. Everyone stared at him again. To Julian's surprise, it was Cristina who spoke.

"What do you mean, it was your father?"

"I think he was the one who wanted the book all those years ago, when Malcolm first stole it," said Kieran. "He is the thread that ties all this together. He wanted the book then and he wants it now."

"But why do you think he wanted it then?" Julian said. He kept his voice low and gentle. What Emma thought of as his leading-the-witness voice.

"Because of something Adaon said." Kieran was looking down at his hands. "He said my father had wanted the book since the First Heir was stolen. It is an old story in Faerie, the theft of my father's first child. It happened more than two hundred years ago."

Cristina looked stunned. "I didn't realize that's what he meant."

"The First Heir." Magnus's eyes looked unfocused. "I have heard that tale, or heard of it. The child was not just stolen, but murdered."

"So the story goes," said Kieran. "Perhaps my father wished to use necromancy to raise the child. I could not speak of his motives. But he could have offered Fade and Annabel protection in the Unseelie Lands. No Shadowhunter could touch them if they were safe in Faerie."

Emma set her fork down with a clang. "Pretentious hair prince is right."

Kieran blinked. "What did you call me?"

"I'm trying it out," Emma said, with a wave. "And I said you were right. Enjoy it, because I doubt I'll say it again."

Magnus nodded. "The King is one of the few beings on this earth who could have kidnapped Malcolm from the prisons of the Silent City. He must not have wanted him to reveal their connection to the Council."

"But why didn't he take Annabel, too?" Livvy asked, a forkful of pie halfway to her mouth.

"Maybe because Malcolm had disappointed him by getting caught," said Mark. "Maybe he wanted to punish them both."

"But Annabel could have told on them," said Livvy. "She could have said Malcolm was working for the King."

"Not if she didn't know," said Emma. "There was nothing in the diaries Malcolm kept that mentioned *who* he was stealing the book for, and I bet he didn't tell Annabel, either."

"They tortured her," said Ty, "and she still couldn't say who it was, just that she had no idea. It must have been the truth."

"That explains why when he found out Annabel wasn't an Iron Sister, that he'd been lied to, Malcolm went to the Unseelie King," said Julian. "Because he *knew him.*"

"So once the King wanted the book for necromancy," Cristina said. "Now he wants it so he can destroy Shadowhunters?"

"Not all necromancy is raising the dead." Magnus was gazing at the glass of wine by his plate as if there was some kind of secret hidden in its depth. "One moment," he said, and scooped up Rafe from the chair beside him. He turned to Tavvy. "Would you like to come with us? And play with Alexander and Max?"

After a glance at Julian, Tavvy nodded. The group of them left the room, Magnus gesturing that he would be right back.

"This is just one meeting," said Emma. "First we need to get the Council to believe that the Unseelie Court is an immediate threat.

Right now they can't tell good faeries from bad and aren't interesting in trying."

"Which is where Kieran's testimony comes in," said Mark. "And there is some evidence—there's the blight Diana said she saw in Brocelind Forest, and the report from the Shadowhunters who said they fought a band of faeries but their weapons malfunctioned."

"It's not a lot to go on," said Livvy. "Especially considering Zara and her nasty little band of bigots. They *are* going to try to seize power at this meeting. They're going to try to grab the Institute. They couldn't care less about some vague faerie threat."

"I can make the Clave fear my father," said Kieran. "But it may take all of us to make them understand that if they do not wish for a new era of darkness, they must abandon their dreams of extending the Cold Peace."

"No registering warlocks," said Ty. "No putting werewolves into camps."

"The Downworlders who have seats on the Council all know about the Cohort," said Magnus, returning without the children. "If it actually comes down to a vote about who heads the Los Angeles Institute, they'll have to bring in Maia and Lily, as well as me. We're entitled to vote." He threw himself down in the chair at the head of the table.

"That's still just three votes, even if you vote against the Cohort," said Julian.

"It's a tricky business," Magnus agreed. "According to Diana, Jia doesn't want Zara heading up the Los Angeles Institute any more than we do. She'll be hard to discredit at the moment—with her lie about killing Malcolm, she's pretty popular right now."

Emma made a growling noise low in her throat. Cristina patted her hand.

"Meanwhile what we have is the promise that the Queen will fight with us against a threat the Council is unlikely to believe in, and even then only if she gets a book that we don't currently have and wouldn't be allowed to give her if we did," Magnus said.

"Our bargain with the Seelie Queen is our business," said Julian. "Right now, we say that she's shown herself willing to cooperate under the right circumstances. Kieran's empowered to promise she'll help. He doesn't need to go into details."

"Brother, you think like a faerie," said Mark, in a tone that made Julian wonder if that was a good thing or not.

"Maybe the King wants to raise an army of the dead," said Dru hopefully. "I mean, it is a book of necromancy."

Magnus sighed, tapping a fingernail against his glass thoughtfully. "Necromancy is about doing magic that uses the energy of death to power it. All magic needs fuel. Death energy is incredibly powerful fuel. It's also incredibly destructive. The destruction of the land that you saw in Faerie, the blight in Brocelind—they are the scars left by terrible magic. The question remains—what is his ultimate goal?"

"You mean he needs more energy to spread those spells," said Julian. "The ones that Malcolm helped with, that cancel out Shadowhunter magic."

"I mean your magic is angelic in its nature," said Magnus. "It comes from light, from energy and life. The opposite of that is Sheol, Hell, whatever you want to call it. The absence of light and life. Of any kind of hope." He coughed. "When the Council voted for the Cold Peace, they were voting for a time that never existed. Just as the Cohort wishes everything to return to a lost Golden Age when Shadowhunters walked the world like gods and Downworlders and mundanes bowed before them." Everyone stared at him. This was a Magnus Bane people rarely saw, Julian thought. A Magnus whose good cheer and casual optimism had deserted him. A Magnus who was remembering the darkness of all he had seen over the centuries: the death and the loss; the same Magnus Julian had seen in the Hall of Accords when he was twelve, begging the

Council in vain not to pass the Cold Peace, knowing that they would. "The King wants the same. To unite two kingdoms that have always been separate but in his mind were one land once. We must stop the King, but in a way he is only doing what the Cohort would do. What we have to hope the Clave would not do."

"You mean," said Julian, "this is vengeance?"

Magnus shrugged. "It is the whirlwind," he said. "Let us hope we can stop it."

26
WALK IN SHADOW

Emma sat on Cristina's bed, brushing her friend's hair. She was beginning to understand why her mother had loved brushing her hair so much when she was a little girl: There was something oddly soothing about the smooth dark locks slipping through her fingers, the repetitive motion of the brush.

It soothed the ache in her head, her chest. The one that felt not just her own pain, but Julian's. She knew how much he hated saying good-bye to Tavvy, even if it was for Tavvy's own good, and she felt a hollowness inside herself where Julian was parting from his smallest brother now.

Being with Cristina helped. Emma had spilled everything that happened in Cornwall while clucking over Cristina's wrist and rubbing a mundane cream called Savlon into the red mark from the binding rune. Cristina ouched and complained that it stung, and handed Emma the hairbrush and told her to do something actually useful.

"So does anything help the binding?" said Emma. "Like if Mark came in here and lay down directly on top of you, would the pain go away?"

"Yes," Cristina said, sounding a bit muffled.

"Well, it's very inconsiderate of him not to, if you ask me."

Cristina gave a little wail that sounded like "Kieran."

"Right, Mark has to pretend he still cares about Kieran. I guess lying on top of you wouldn't do much for that."

"He does care about Kieran," Cristina said. "It's just—I think he cares about me, too." She half-turned to look at Emma. Her eyes were big and dark and worried. "I danced with him. With Mark. And we kissed."

"That's good! That is good, right?"

"It was, but then Kieran came in—"

"What?"

"But he wasn't angry, he just told Mark that he should dance better, and he danced with me. It was like dancing with fire."

"Whoa, sexy weirdness," said Emma. "This may be more sexy weirdness than I can handle."

"It is not weird!"

"It is," said Emma. "You are headed for a faerie threesome. Or some kind of war."

"Emma!"

"Hot faerie threesome," said Emma cheerfully. "I can say I knew you when."

Cristina groaned. "Fine. What about you and Julian? Do you have a plan, after what happened in Cornwall?"

Emma sighed and put the hairbrush down. It was a lovely old silver-backed Victorian object. She wondered if it had been in the room when Cristina got here or if she'd found it somewhere else in the Institute. Already Cristina's London room bore signs of her personality—pictures had been cleaned and straightened, she'd found a colorful coverlet for her bed somewhere, and her balisong hung on a new hook by the fireplace.

Emma began to braid Cristina's hair, plaiting the thick strands between her fingers. "We don't have a plan," she said. "It's always the same thing—we're together and we feel like we're invincible. And then we start to realize it's still all the same choices and they're all bad ones."

Cristina looked troubled. "It is always the same choices, isn't it? Separation from each other or ceasing to be Shadowhunters."

Emma had finished the braid. She leaned her chin on Cristina's shoulder, thinking about what Julian had learned from the Seelie Queen. The terrifying possibility of ending all *parabatai* bonds. But it was too horrible a thing to even voice aloud. "I used to think it would help, physical distance from Julian," she said. "But now I don't think it would. Nothing else has. I think no matter where I went, or for how long, I would always feel like this."

"Some loves are strong, like cords. They bind you," Cristina said. "The Bible says love is as strong as death. I believe that."

Emma scooted around to peer closer into her friend's face. "Cristina," she said. "There's something else going on, isn't there? Something about Diego, or Jaime?"

Cristina looked down. "I can't say."

"Let me help you," Emma said. "You're always so strong for everyone else. Let me be strong for you."

There was a knock on the door. They both looked up in surprise. *Mark*, Emma thought. There was something about the look on Cristina's face. It must be Mark.

But it was Kieran.

Emma froze in surprise. Though she'd grown somewhat used to Kieran being around, he still made the fine hairs on Emma's arms rise with tension. It wasn't that she blamed him, specifically, for the injuries she'd suffered at Iarlath's hands. But the sight of him still brought it back to her, all of it: the hot sun, the sound of the whip, the copper scent of blood.

It was true that he looked enormously different now. His black hair was a little wilder, more untidy, but otherwise he cut an incongruously human figure in his jeans. The wild hair hid the tops of his pointed ears, though his black and silver eyes were still startling.

He gave a small, courtly bow. "My ladies."

Cristina looked puzzled. Clearly she hadn't expected this visit either.

"I came to speak with Cristina, if she will permit it," Kieran added.

"Go ahead, then," Emma said. "Speak."

"I think he wishes to speak to me alone," said Cristina, in a whisper.

"Yes," said Kieran. "That is my request."

Cristina looked at Emma. "I'll see you in the morning, then?"

Humph, Emma thought. She'd missed Cristina, and now a brash faerie princeling was kicking her out of her friend's room. Kieran barely spared her a glance as she climbed off the bed and headed to the door.

As she passed Kieran on her way out, Emma paused, her shoulder almost touching his. "If you do anything to hurt or upset her," she said, in a voice low enough that she doubted Cristina could hear it, "I will pull off your ears and turn them into lock picks. Get it?"

Kieran glanced at her with his night-sky eyes, unreadable as clouds. "No," he said.

"Let me spell it out," Emma said sharply. "I love her. Don't mess around with her."

Kieran put his long, delicate hands in his pockets. He looked absolutely unnatural in his modern clothes. It was like seeing Alexander the Great in a biker jacket and leather pants. "She is easy to love."

Emma looked at him in surprise. It hadn't been what she'd expected him to say at all. Easy to love. Nene had behaved as if the concept was bizarre. But then what did the Fair Folk know about love, anyway?

* * *

"Would you like to sit down?" Cristina inquired. Then she wondered if she was turning into her mother, who had always claimed that the first thing one did with a guest was offer them a seat. *Even if they are a murderer?* Cristina had asked. *Yes, even murderers,* her mother had insisted. *If you didn't want to offer a murderer a seat, you shouldn't have invited him in the first place.*

"No," Kieran said. He moved across the room, hands in his pockets, his body language restless. Not unlike Mark's, Cristina thought. They both moved as if they had energy trapped beneath their skin. She wondered what it would be like to contain so much movement, and yet be forced to stay still.

"My lady," he said. "Because of what I swore to you in the Seelie Court, there is a bond between us. I think you have felt its force."

Cristina nodded. It wasn't the enchanted bond she had with Mark. But it was there anyway, a shimmering energy when they danced, when they spoke.

"I think that force can help us do something together I could not do alone." Kieran came closer to the bed, drawing his hand out of his pocket. Something glimmered in his palm. He held it out to Cristina, and she saw the acorn there that Mark had used earlier, to summon Gwyn. It looked slightly dented, but it was whole, as if it had been sealed back together after breaking open.

"You want to summon Gwyn again?" Cristina shook her head. Her hair fell completely out of its unfastened braid, spilling down her back. She saw Kieran glance at it. "No. He won't interfere again. You want to speak to someone else in Faerie. Your brother?"

"As I thought." He inclined his head slightly. "You guess my intentions exactly."

"And you can do it? The acorn won't just call Gwyn?"

"The magic is a fairly simple one. Remember, you are not of the blood than can cast spells, but I am. It should bring a Projection of my brother to us. I will ask him of our father's plans. I shall ask him as well if he can stop the Riders."

Cristina was astonished. "Can anyone stop the Riders?"

"They are servants of the Court, and under its command."

"Why are you telling me this?" Cristina asked.

"Because to summon my brother, I must reach out with my mind into Faerie," said Kieran. "And it would be safer, should I wish to keep my mind intact, for me to have a connection here in the world. Something—someone—to keep me anchored while I seek my brother."

Cristina slid off the bed. Standing straight, she was only a little shorter than Kieran. Her eyes were level with his mouth. "Why me? Why not Mark?"

"I have asked enough of Mark," he said.

"Perhaps," she said, "but even if that is true, I do not think it is the whole truth."

"Few of us are lucky enough ever to know the whole truth of anything." She knew Kieran was young, but there was something ancient in his eyes when he spoke. "Will you put your hand in mine?"

She gave him the hand whose wrist bore the red mark of her bond with Mark. It seemed fitting, somehow. His fingers closed around hers, cool and dry, light as the touch of a leaf.

With his other hand, Kieran dashed the golden acorn against the wall beside the fireplace mantel.

For a moment, there was silence. Cristina could hear his ragged breathing. It seemed strange for a faerie—everything they did was at such a remove from ordinary human emotion, it was odd to hear Kieran gasp. But then she remembered his arms around her, the uneven thud of his heart. They were flesh and blood after all, weren't they? Bone and muscle, just as Shadowhunters were. And the flame of angelic blood burned in them, too. . . .

Darkness spread across the wall like a stain. Cristina sucked in her breath, and Kieran's hand tightened on hers. The darkness moved and shivered, trembled and re-formed. Light danced within it, and Cristina could see the multicolored night sky of Faerie. And within the shadow, a darker shadow. A man, wrapped in a dark cloak. As the darkness lightened, Cristina saw his grin before she saw anything else, and her heart seemed to stop.

It was a grin of bones set within a skeletal half face, beautiful on one side, deathly on the other. The cloak that wrapped him was ink-black and bore the insignia of a broken crown. He stood straight and broad, grinning his lopsided grin down at Kieran.

They had not summoned Adaon at all. It was the Unseelie King.

"No. NO!" Tavvy wept, his face buried in Julian's shoulder. He'd taken the news that he was going to Idris with Alec, Max, and Rafe worse than Mark had expected. Did all children cry like this, like everything in the world was ruined and their hearts were broken, even at the news of a short parting?

Not that Mark blamed Tavvy, of course. It was only that he felt as if his own heart was being shredded into pieces inside his chest as he watched Julian walk up and down the room, holding his small brother in his arms as Tavvy sobbed and pounded his back.

"Tavs," Julian said in his gentle voice, the voice Mark could hardly reconcile with the boy who had faced down the Unseelie King in his own Court with a knife to a prince's throat. "It's only going to be a day, two days at most. You'll get to see the canals in Alicante, the Gard. . . ."

"You keep leaving," Tavvy choked against his brother's shirt-front. "You can't leave again."

Julian sighed. He dipped his chin, rubbing his cheek against his brother's unruly curls. Over Tavvy's head, his eyes met Mark's. There was no blame in them, and no self-pity, only a terrible sadness.

Yet Mark felt as if guilt were crushing his rib cage. *If only* were wasted words, Kieran had once said, when Mark had speculated on whether the two of them would ever have met if they had never joined the Hunt. But he couldn't stop the flood of *if only*s now: if only he had been able to stay with his family, if only Julian hadn't needed to be mother and father and brother to all the younger ones, if only Tavvy hadn't grown up in the shadow of death and loss. Perhaps then, every parting would not feel like the last one.

"It's not your fault," said Magnus, who had appeared noiselessly at Mark's side. "You can't help the past. We grow up with losses, all of us except the supremely lucky."

"I cannot help wishing my brother had been one of the supremely lucky," said Mark. "You can understand."

Magnus glanced toward Jules and Tavvy. The little boy had cried himself out and was clinging to his older brother, his face mashed against Julian's shoulder. His small shoulders were slumped in exhaustion. "Which brother?"

"Both of them," said Mark.

Magnus reached out and, with curious fingers, touched the glimmering arrowhead slung around Mark's neck. "I know this material," he said. "This arrowhead once tipped the weapon of a soldier in the King's Guard of the Unseelie Court."

Mark touched it—cool, cold, smooth under his fingers. Unyielding, like Kieran himself. "Kieran gave it to me."

"It is precious," said Magnus. He turned as Alec called him, and let the pendant fall back against Mark's chest.

Alec stood with Max in his arms and Rafe by his side, along with a small duffel bag of their things. It occurred to Mark that Alec was close to the same age Mark would have been if only he had never been kidnapped by the Hunt. He wondered if he would be as mature as Alec seemed, as self-collected, as able to take care of other people as well as himself.

Magnus kissed Alec and ruffled his hair with infinite tenderness. He bent to kiss Max, too, and Rafe, and straightened up to begin to create the Portal. Light sparked from and between his fingers, and the air before him seemed to shimmer.

Tavvy had sagged into a bundle of hopelessness against Julian's chest. Jules held him closer, the muscles in his arms tensing, and murmured soothing words. Mark wanted to go over to them but couldn't seem to make his feet move. They seemed, even in their unhappiness, a perfect unit who needed no one else.

The melancholy thought vanished a moment later as pain shot up Mark's arm. He grabbed at his wrist, his fingers encountering agonizing soreness, the slickness of blood. *Something's wrong*, he thought, and then, *Cristina*.

He bolted. The Portal was growing and shimmering in the center of the room; through its half-formed door, Mark could see the outline of the demon towers as he darted by and into the corridor.

Some sense in his blood told him he was getting closer to Cristina as he ran, but to his surprise, the pain in his wrist didn't fade. It pulsed again and again, like the warning beam from a lighthouse.

Her door was closed. He set his shoulder against it and shoved without bothering to try the knob. It flew open and Mark half-fell inside.

He choked, eyes stinging. The room smelled as if something inside it had been burning—something organic, like dead leaves or rotted fruit.

It was dark. His eyes adjusted quickly and he made out Cristina and Kieran, both standing by the foot of the bed. Cristina was clutching her balisong. A massive shadow loomed over them—no, not a shadow, Mark realized, moving closer. A Projection.

A Projection of the King of the Unseelie Court. Both sides of his face seemed to gleam with unnatural humor, both the beautiful, kingly side, and the hideous, defleshed skull.

"You thought to summon your brother?" the King sneered, his gaze on Kieran. "And you thought I would not feel you reaching into Faerie, searching for one of my own? You are a fool, Kieran, and always have been."

"What have you done to Adaon?" Kieran's face was bloodless. "He knew nothing. He had no idea I planned to summon him."

"Worry not about others," said the King. "Worry about your own life, Kieran Kingson."

"I have been Kieran Hunter for a long time," said Kieran.

The King's face darkened. "You should be Kieran Traitor," he said. "Kieran Betrayer. Kieran Kin-Slayer. All are better names for you."

"He acted in self-defense," said Cristina sharply. "If he hadn't killed Erec, he would have been killed himself. And he acted to protect me."

The King gave her a brief look of scorn. "And that in itself is a traitorous act, foolish girl," he said. "Placing the lives of Shadow-hunters above the lives of your own people—what could be worse?"

"Selling your son to the Wild Hunt because you worried that people liked him better than they liked you," said Mark. "That's worse."

Cristina and Kieran looked at him in astonishment; it was clear they hadn't heard him come in. The King, though, evinced no sur-prise. "Mark Blackthorn," he said. "Even in his choice of lovers, my son gravitates to the enemies of his people. What does that say about him?"

"That he knows better than you who his people are?" Mark said. Very deliberately, he turned his back on the King. It would have been a hanging offense in the Court. "We must get rid of him," he said, in a low voice, to Kieran and Cristina. "Should I get Magnus?"

"He is only a Projection," Kieran said. His face was drawn. "He cannot hurt us. Nor can he remain forever. It is an effort for him, I think."

"Do not turn your back on me!" the King roared. "Do you think I do not know your plans, Kieran? Do you think I do not know you plan to stand up and betray me before the Council of Nephilim?"

Kieran turned his face away, as if he couldn't bear to look at his father. "Then cease to do what I know you are doing," he said, in a shaking voice. "Parlay with the Nephilim. Do not make war on them."

"There is no parlay with those who can lie," snarled the King. "And have done, and will do again. They will lie and spill the blood of our people. And once they are done with you, do you think they will let you live? Treat you like one of them?"

"They have treated me better than my own father has." Kieran raised his chin.

"Have they?" The King's eyes were dark and empty. "I took some memories from you, Kieran, when you came to my Court. Shall I give them back?"

Kieran looked confused. "What use could you possibly have for my memories?"

"Some of us would know our enemies," said the King.

"Kieran," Mark said. The look in the King's eyes made fear roil in the pit of his stomach. "Do not listen. He seeks to hurt you."

"And what do you seek?" the King demanded, turning toward Mark. Only the fact that Mark could see through him, could see the outline of Cristina's bed, her wardrobe, through the transparent frame of his body, kept him from darting toward the fireplace poker and swinging it at the King. If only . . .

If only the King had been any sort of father, if only he hadn't thrown his son to the Hunt like a bone to a pack of hungry wolves, if only he hadn't sat complacently by while Erec tortured Kieran . . .

How different would Kieran be? How much less afraid of losing love, how much less determined to hold on to it at all costs, even if it meant trapping Mark in the Hunt with him?

The King's lip curled, as if he could read Mark's thoughts. "When I looked into my son's memories," he said, "I saw you, Blackthorn. Lady Nerissa's son." His smile was malignant. "Your mother died of sorrow when your father left her. My son's thoughts were half of you, of the loss of you. Mark, Mark, Mark. I wonder what it is in your bloodline that has the power to enchant our people and make fools of them?"

A small line had appeared between Kieran's brows. *The loss of you.* Kieran didn't remember losing Mark. The cold fear in Mark's stomach had spread to his veins.

"Those who cannot love do not understand it," said Cristina. She turned toward Kieran. "We will protect you," she said. "We won't let him harm you for testifying at the Council."

"Lies," said the King. "Well-intentioned, perhaps, but still lies. If you testify, Kieran, there will be no place on this earth or in Faerie where you will be safe from me and from my warriors. I will hunt you forever, and when I find you, you will wish you had died for what you did to Iarlath, to Erec. There is no torment you can imagine that I will not visit on you."

Kieran swallowed hard, but his voice was steady. "Pain is just pain."

"Oh," said his father, "there is all manner of pain, little dark one." He did not move or make any gesture the way warlocks did when they cast spells, but Mark felt an increase in the weight of the atmosphere in the room, as if the air pressure had risen.

Kieran gasped and reeled back as if he'd been shot. He hit the bed, grasping at the footboard to keep himself from sliding to the floor. His hair fell over his eyes, changing from blue to black to white. "Mark?" He raised his face slowly. "I remember. I *remember.*"

"Kieran," Mark whispered.

"I told Gwyn you had betrayed a law of Faerie," said Kieran. "I thought they would only bring you back to the Hunt."

"Instead they punished my family," said Mark. He knew Kieran hadn't meant it to happen, hadn't anticipated it. But the words still hurt to say.

"That's why you weren't wearing your elf-bolt." Kieran's eyes fixed on a point below Mark's chin. "You did not want me. You turned me away. You hated me. You must hate me now."

"I didn't hate you," Mark said. "Kier—"

"Listen to him," murmured the King. "Listen to him lie."

"Then why?" Kieran said. He backed away from Mark, just a step. "Why did you lie to me?"

"Consider it, child," said the King. He looked as if he were enjoying himself. "What did they want from you?"

Kieran breathed in hard. "Testimony," he said. "Witnessing in front of the Council. You—you planned this, Mark? This deception? Does everyone in the Institute know? Yes, they must. They must." His hair had gone black as oil. "And the Queen knows, too, I suppose. She planned to make a fool of me, with you?"

The agony on his face was too much; Mark couldn't look at it, at Kieran. It was Cristina who spoke for him. "Kieran, no," she said. "It wasn't like that—"

"And you knew?" Kieran turned a look on her that was hardly less betrayed than the one he'd turned on Mark. "You knew as well?"

The King laughed. Rage went through Mark then, a blinding fury, and he seized up the poker from the fireplace. The King continued laughing as he stalked toward him, raised the poker, and swung it—

It slammed against the golden acorn where it lay on the hearth before the fireplace, shattering it into powder. The King's laughter cut off abruptly; he turned a look of pure hatred on Mark and vanished.

"Why did you do that?" Kieran demanded. "Were you afraid of what else he'd tell me?"

Mark threw the poker against the grate with a loud clang. "He gave you back your memories, didn't he?" he said. "Then you know everything."

"Not everything," said Kieran, and his voice cracked and broke; Mark thought of him hanging in the thorn manacles at the Unseelie Court, and how the same despair showed in his eyes now. "I don't know how you planned this, when you decided you would lie to me to get me to do what you wanted. I don't know how much it sickened you every time you had to touch me, to pretend to want me. I don't know when you planned to tell me the truth. After I testified? Did you plan to mock me and laugh at me before all the Council, or wait until we were alone? Did you tell everyone what a monster I am, how selfish and how heartless—"

"You are not a monster, Kieran," Mark interrupted. "There is nothing wrong with your heart."

There was only hurt in Kieran's eyes as he regarded Mark across the small space that separated them. "That cannot be true," he said, "for you were my heart."

"Stop." It was Cristina, her voice small and worried, but firm. "Let Mark explain to you—"

"I am done with human explanations," said Kieran, and stalked from the room, slamming the door behind him.

The last of the shimmering Portal disappeared. Julian and Magnus stood, almost shoulder to shoulder, watching Alec and the children until they vanished.

With a sigh, Magnus tossed the end of his scarf over his shoulder and stalked across the room to fill a glass from the decanter of wine that rested dustily on a table by the window. It was nearly dark outside, the sky over London the color of pansy petals. "Do you want some?" he asked Julian, recapping the decanter.

"I should probably stay sober."

"Suit yourself." Magnus picked up his wineglass and examined it; the light shining through it turned the liquid ruby red.

"Why are you helping us so much?" Julian asked. "I mean, I know we're a likable family, but no one's that likable."

"No," Magnus agreed, with a slight smile. "No one is."

"Then?"

Magnus took a sip of the wine and shrugged. "Jace and Clary asked me to," he said, "and Jace is Alec's *parabatai*, and I have always had a fatherly feeling toward Clary. They're my friends. And there is little I wouldn't do for my friends."

"Is that really all of it?"

"You might remind me of someone."

"Me?" Julian was surprised. People rarely said that to him. "Who do I remind you of?"

Magnus shook his head without answering. "Years ago," he said, "I had a recurring dream, about a city drowned in blood. Towers made of bone and blood running in the streets like water. I thought later that it was about the Dark War, and indeed the dream vanished in the years after the war was fought." He drained his glass and set it down. "But lately I've been dreaming it again. I can't help but think something is coming."

"You warned them," said Julian. "The Council. The day they decided to exile Helen and abandon Mark. The day they decided on the Cold Peace. You told them what the consequences would be." He leaned against the wall. "I was only twelve, but I remember it. You said, 'The Fair Folk have long hated the Nephilim for their harshness. Show them something other than harshness, and you will receive something other than hate in return.' But they didn't listen to you, did they?"

"They wanted their revenge, the Council," said Magnus. "They didn't see how revenge begets more revenge. 'For they sow the wind, and they shall reap the whirlwind.'"

"From the Bible," said Julian. He had not grown up around

Uncle Arthur without learning more classic quotes than he'd ever know what to do with. "But then there's a difference between revenge and vengeance," he added. "Between punishing the guilty, and punishing at random. 'Justly we rid the earth of human fiends, who carry hell for pattern in their souls.'"

"I suppose one can find a quote to justify anything," Magnus said. "Look—I don't tattle to the Clave, whatever the warlocks of the Shadow Market might think to the contrary. But I've known *parabatai*, dozens of them, what they're supposed to be like, and you and Emma are different. I can't imagine that if it hadn't been for the chaos of the Dark War they would even have allowed you to go through with it."

"And now, because of a ceremony that was supposed to bind us forever, we have to figure out how to separate," Julian said bitterly. "We both know it. But with the Riders out there—"

"Yes," said Magnus. "You are forced together for the moment."

Julian exhaled through his teeth. "Just confirm something for me," he said. "There's no such thing as a spell that cancels out love?"

"There are a few temporary charms," said Magnus. "They don't last forever. Real love and the complexities of the human heart and brain are still beyond the tinkering of most magic. Maybe an angel or a Greater Demon . . ."

"So Raziel could do it," said Julian.

"I wouldn't hold your breath," said Magnus. "Have you really already looked this up? Spells to cancel out love?"

Julian nodded.

"You *are* ruthless," said Magnus. "Even with yourself."

"I thought Emma didn't love me anymore," said Julian. "And she thought the same about me. Now we know the truth. It's not just that it's forbidden by the Clave. It's cursed."

Magnus winced. "I wondered if you knew about that."

Julian felt cold all over. No chance it was some kind of mistake of Jem's, then. Not that he'd really thought it might be. "Jem told Emma. But he didn't say exactly how it worked. What would happen."

There was a slight tremor in Magnus's hand as he passed it over his eyes. "Look up the story of Silas Pangborn and Eloisa Ravenscar. There are other stories too, though the Silent Brothers do their best to keep it quiet." His cat's eyes were bloodshot. "You go mad yourself, first," he said. "You become unrecognizable as a human being. And after you become a monster, you are no longer able to tell friend from enemy. As your family run toward you to save you, you will rip the hearts from their chests."

Julian felt as if he were going to throw up. "That—I'd never hurt my family."

"You won't know who they are," said Magnus. "You won't know love from hate. And you'll destroy what's around you, not because you want to, any more than a crashing wave wants to shatter the rocks it breaks on. You'll do it because you won't know not to." He looked at Julian with an ancient sympathy. "It doesn't matter if your intentions are good or bad. It doesn't matter that love is a positive force. Magic doesn't take note of small human concerns."

"I know," Julian said. "But what can we do? I can't become a mundane or a Downworlder and leave my family. It would kill me and them. And not being a Shadowhunter anymore would be like suicide for Emma."

"There is exile," Magnus said. His gaze was fathomless. "You would still be Shadowhunters, but you'd be stripped of some of your magic. That's what exile means. That's the punishment. And because *parabatai* magic is some of the most precious and most ingrained in what you are, exile deadens its power. All the things the curse intensifies—the power your runes give each other, the ability to feel what the other is feeling or know if they're hurt—exile takes those away. If I understand magic, and I know I do, then that means exile would slow the curse down immeasurably."

"And exile would also take me away from the children," said Julian, in despair. "I might never see them again. I might as well become a mundane. At least then I could try to sneak around and maybe watch them from a distance." Bitterness corroded his voice. "The terms of exile are determined by the Inquisitor and the Clave. It would be totally out of our control."

"Not necessarily," said Magnus.

Julian looked at him sharply. "I think you'd better tell me what you mean."

"That you have only one choice. And you won't like it." Magnus paused, as if waiting for Julian to refuse to hear it, but Julian said nothing at all. "All right," said Magnus. "When you get to Alicante, tell the Inquisitor everything."

"Kit . . ."

Something cool touched his temple, brushed back his hair. Shadows surrounded Kit, shadows in which he saw faces familiar and unfamiliar: the face of a woman with pale hair, her mouth forming the words of a song; his father's face, the angry countenance of Barnabas Hale, Ty looking at him through eyelashes as thick and black as the soot covering the London streets in a Dickens novel.

"Kit."

The cool touch became a tap. His eyelids fluttered, and there was the ceiling of the infirmary in the London Institute. He recognized the strange tree-shaped burn on the plastered wall, the view of rooftops through the window, the fan that spun its lazy blades over his head.

And hovering over him, a pair of anxious blue-green eyes. Livvy, her long brown hair spilling down in tangled curls. She exhaled a relieved sigh as he frowned.

"Sorry," she said. "Magnus said to shake you awake every few hours or so, to make sure your concussion doesn't get worse."

"Concussion?" Kit remembered the rooftop, the rain, Gwyn and Diana, the sky full of clouds sliding up and away as he fell. "How did I wind up with a concussion? I was fine."

"It happens, apparently," she said. "People get hit on the head; they don't realize it's serious until they pass out."

"Ty?" he said. He started to sit up, which was a mistake. His skull ached as if someone had taken a bludgeon to it. Bits and pieces of memory flashed against the backs of his eyes: the faeries in their terrifying bronze armor. The concrete platform by the river. The certainty that they were going to die.

"Here." Her hand curved around the back of his neck, supporting him. The rim of something cold clinked against his teeth. "Drink this."

Kit swallowed. Darkness came down, and the pain went away with it. He heard the singing again, down in the deepest part of everything he'd ever forgotten. *The story that I love you, it has no end.*

When he opened his eyes again, the candle by his bed had guttered. There was light, though, in the room—Ty sat by the side of his bed, a witchlight in his hand, looking up at the rotating blades of the fan.

Kit coughed and sat up. This time it hurt a little bit less. His throat felt like sandpaper. "Water," he said.

Ty drew his gaze away from the fan blades. Kit had noticed before that he liked to look at them, as if their graceful motion pleased him. Ty found the water pitcher and a glass, and handed it to Kit.

"Do you want more water?" Ty asked, when Kit's thirst had emptied the pitcher. He'd changed clothes since Kit had seen him last. More of the odd old-fashioned stuff from the storage room. Pinstriped shirt, black pants. He looked like he ought to be in an old advertisement.

Kit shook his head. He held tightly to the glass in his hand. A strange sense of unreality had settled over him—here he was, Kit Rook, in an Institute, having gotten his head bashed in by large faeries for defending Nephilim.

His father would have been ashamed. But Kit felt nothing but a sense of rightness. A sense that the piece that had always been missing from his life, that had made him anxious and uneasy, had been returned to him by chance and fate.

"Why did you do it?" Ty said.

Kit propped himself up. "Why'd I do what?"

"That time I came out of the magic shop and you and Livvy were arguing." Ty's gray gaze rested on a point around Kit's collarbone. "It was about me, wasn't it?"

"How did you know we were arguing?" Kit said. "Did you hear us?"

Ty shook his head. "I know Livvy," he said. "I know when she's angry. I know the things she does. She's my twin. I don't know those things about anyone else, but I know them about her." He shrugged. "The argument was about me, wasn't it?"

Kit nodded.

"Everyone always tries to protect me," said Ty. "Julian tries to protect me from everything. Livvy tries to protect me from being disappointed. She didn't want me to know that you might leave, but I've always known it. Jules and Livvy, they have a hard time imagining that I've grown up. That I might understand that some things are temporary."

"You mean me," Kit said. "That I'm temporary."

"It's your choice to stay or leave," said Ty. "In Limehouse, I thought maybe it would be leaving."

"But what about you?" said Kit. "I thought you were going to the Scholomance. And I could never go there. I don't even have basic training."

Kit set his water glass down. Ty immediately picked it up and began turning it in his hands. It was made of milky glass, rough on the outside, and he seemed to like the texture.

Ty was silent, and in that silence, Kit thought of Ty's headphones, the music in his ears, the whispered words, the way he touched things with such total concentration: smooth stones, rough glass, silk and leather and textured linen. There were people in the world, he knew, who thought human beings like Ty did those things for no reason—because they were inexplicable. Broken.

Kit felt a wash of rage go through him. How could they not understand everything Ty did had a reason? If an ambulance siren blared in your ears, you covered them. If something hit you, you doubled up to protect yourself from hurt.

But not everyone felt and heard exactly the same way. Ty heard everything twice as loud and fast as everyone else. The headphones and the music, Kit sensed, were a buffer: They deadened not just other noises, but also feelings that would otherwise be too intense. They protected him from hurt.

He couldn't help but wonder what it would be like to live so intensely, to feel things so much, to have the world sway into and out of too-bright colors and too-bright noises. When every sound and feeling was jacked up to eleven, it only made sense to calm yourself by concentrating all your energy on something small that you could master—a mass of pipe cleaners to unravel, the pebbled surface of a glass between your fingers.

"I don't want to tell you not to go to the Scholomance if it's what you want," said Kit. "But I would just say that it isn't always about people trying to protect you, or knowing what's best for you, or thinking they do. Sometimes they just know they'd miss you."

"Livvy would miss me—"

"Your whole family would miss you," said Kit, "and I would miss you."

It was a bit like stepping off a cliff, far scarier than any con Kit had ever run for his dad, any Downworlder or demon he'd ever met. Ty looked up in surprise, forgetting the glass in his hands. He was blushing. It was very visible against his pale skin. "You would?"

"Yeah," said Kit, "but like I said, I don't want to stop you from going if you want to—"

"I don't," Ty said. "I changed my mind." He set the glass down. "Not because of you. Because the Scholomance appears to be full of assholes."

Kit burst out laughing. Ty looked even more astonished than he had when Kit had said he'd miss him. But after a second, he started to laugh too. They were both laughing, Kit doubled up over the blankets, when Magnus came into the room. He looked at the two of them and shook his head.

"Bedlam," he said, and went over to the counter where the glass tubes and funnels had been set up. He gave them a pleased look. "Not that anyone here probably cares," he said, "but the antidote to the binding spell is ready. We should have no problem leaving for Idris tomorrow."

Cristina felt as if a tornado had blown through the room. She set her balisong down on the mantel and turned to Mark.

He was leaning against the wall, his eyes wide but not focused on anything. She remembered an old book she had read when she was a girl. There had been a boy in it whose eyes had been two different colors, a knight in the Crusades. One eye for God, the book had said, and one for the devil.

A boy who had been split down the middle, part good and part evil. Just as Mark was split between faerie and Nephilim. She could see the battle raging in him now, though all his anger was for himself.

"Mark," she began. "It is not—"

"Don't say it's not my fault," he said tonelessly. "I couldn't stand it, Cristina."

"It is not only your fault," said Cristina. "We all knew. It is all our fault. It was not the right thing to do, but we had very few choices. And Kieran did wrong you."

"I still shouldn't have lied to him."

A ragged dark crack across the plaster of Cristina's wall, bulging through the paint, was the only sign of what had happened. That, and the crushed golden acorn on the hearth. "I am only saying that if you can forgive him, you should forgive yourself as well," she said.

"Can you come here?" Mark said, in a strangled sort of voice.

Mark had his eyes closed and was clenching and unclenching his hands. She nearly tripped getting to him across the room. He seemed to sense her approach; without opening his eyes, he reached for her and caught her hand in a bone-crushing grip.

Cristina glanced down. He held her hand so tightly it should have hurt, but all she saw was the red marks around both of their wrists. This close together, they had faded to almost nothing.

She felt again what she had felt that night in the ballroom, as if the binding spell amplified their nearness into something else, a thing that dragged her mind back to that hill in Faerie, the memory of being wrapped up in Mark.

Mark's mouth found hers. She heard him groan: He was kissing her hard and desperately; her body felt as if fire was pouring through it, turning her light as ashes.

Yet she could not forget Kieran kissing Mark in front of her, forceful and deliberate. It seemed she could not think of Mark now without thinking of Kieran, too. Could not see blue and gold eyes without seeing black and silver.

"Mark." She spoke against his lips. His hands were on her, stirring her blood to soft heat. "This is not the right way to make yourself forget."

He drew away from her. "I want to hold you," he said. "I want it very badly." He let go of her slowly, as if the motion were an effort. "But it would not be fair. Not to you or Kieran or myself. Not now."

Cristina touched the back of his hand. "You must go to Kieran and make things right between you. He is too important a part of you, Mark."

"You heard what the King said." Mark let his head fall back against the wall. "He'll kill Kieran for testifying. He'll hunt him forever. That's our doing."

"He agreed to it—"

"Without knowing the truth! He agreed to it because he thought he loved me and I loved him—"

"Isn't that true?" Cristina said. "And even if it wasn't, he didn't just forget that you fought. He forgot what he did. He forgot what he owes. He forgot his own guilt. And that is part of why he is so angry. Not at you, but at himself."

Mark's hand tightened on hers. "We owe each other now, Kieran and I," he said. "I have endangered him. The Unseelie King knows he plans to testify. He's sworn to hunt Kieran. Cristina, what do we do?"

"We try to keep him safe," Cristina said. "Whether he testifies or not, the King won't forgive him. We need to find a place Kieran will be protected." Her chin jerked up as realization hit her. "I know exactly where. Mark, we must—"

There was a knock on the door. They stepped away from each other as it swung open; both of them had been expecting Kieran, and Mark's disappointment when it turned out to be Magnus was clear.

Magnus was carrying two etched metal flasks and raised an eyebrow when he saw Mark's expression. "I don't know who you were waiting for, and I'm sorry I'm not it," he said dryly. "But the antidote is ready."

Cristina had expected a thrill of relief to go through her. Instead she felt nothing. She touched her left hand to her sore wrist and glanced toward Mark, who was staring at the floor.

"Don't rush to thank me or anything," said Magnus, handing them each a flask. "Profuse expressions of gratitude only embarrass me, though cash gifts are always welcome."

"Thank you, Magnus," Cristina said, blushing. She unscrewed the flask: A dark and bitter scent wafted from it, like the smell of *pulque*, a drink that Cristina had never liked.

Magnus held up a hand. "Wait until you're in separate rooms to drink it," he said. "In fact, you should spend at least a few hours apart so that the spell can settle properly. All the effects should be gone by tomorrow."

"Thank you," said Mark, and headed for the door. He paused there and looked back at Cristina. "I agree with you," he said to her. "About Kieran. If there's anything you can do to guarantee his safety—do it."

He was gone noiselessly, with cat-soft footsteps. Magnus glanced at the cracked wall, and then at Cristina.

"Do I want to know?" he asked.

Cristina sighed. "Can a fire-message get outside the wards you put up?"

Magnus stared at the wall again, shook his head, and said, "You'd better give it to me. I'll get it sent."

She hesitated.

"I won't read it, either," he added irritably. "I promise."

Cristina set down her flask, found paper, pen, and stele, and scribbled a message with a rune-signature before folding it and handing it to Magnus, who gave a low whistle when he saw the name of the recipient across the top. "Are you sure?"

She nodded with a resolution she didn't feel. "Absolutely."

27

ILL ANGELS ONLY

"Emma." Julian rapped on her door with the back of his knuckles. At least he was fairly sure it was Emma's door. He'd never been inside her room at the London Institute. "Emma, are you awake? I know it's late."

He heard her call for him to come in, her voice muffled through the thick wooden door. Inside, the room was much like his own, small with heavy blocks of Victorian-looking furniture. The bed was a solid four-poster with silk hangings.

Emma was lying on the covers, wearing an overwashed T-shirt and pajama bottoms. She rolled onto her side and grinned at him.

An overwhelming feeling of love hit him like a punch to the chest. Her hair was tied messily back and she was lying on a rumpled blanket with a plate of pastries next to her, and he had to stop in the middle of the room for a moment and catch his breath.

She waved a tart at him cheerily. "Banoffee," she said. "Want some?"

He could have crossed the room in a few steps. Could have picked her up and swung her into his arms and held her. Could have told her how much he loved her. If they were any other couple, it would be that easy.

But nothing for them would ever be easy.

She was looking at him in puzzlement. "Is everything all right?"

He nodded, a little surprised at his own feelings. Usually he kept better control over himself. Maybe it was the conversation he'd had with Magnus. Maybe it had given him hope.

If there was one thing Julian's life had taught him, it was that nothing was more dangerous than hope.

"*Julian*," she said, setting the tart down and brushing the crumbs off her hands. "Would you please say something?"

He cleared his throat. "We need to talk."

She groaned and flopped back against her pillows. "Okay, not that."

Julian sat down at the foot of her bed as she cleared off her covers, setting aside the food and a few things she'd been looking at—he saw an old photograph of a girl carrying a blade that looked like Cortana, and another one of four boys in Edwardian clothes by the side of a river.

When she was done, she brushed off her hands again and turned a set face to his.

"How soon do we have to separate?" she said. Her voice was shaking a little. "As soon as the meeting is over in Alicante? What will we tell the kids?"

"I talked to Magnus," Julian said. "He said we should go to the Inquisitor."

Emma made an incredulous noise. "The *Inquisitor*? As in, the Council leader who enforces Laws?"

"Pretty sure Magnus knows who the Inquisitor is," said Julian. "He's Alec's dad."

"Did he mean it as a sort of threat? Like, either we turn ourselves in to Robert Lightwood or he does it for us? But Magnus wouldn't—I can't see him doing that. He's much too loyal."

"That's not it," Julian said. "Magnus wants to help us. He

remembers other *parabatai* like us and he—he pointed out that no *parabatai* have ever gone to the Clave for help."

"Because it's the Clave's Law—!"

"But that's not the problem," said Julian. "We could handle the Law. It's the curse, which is the reason the Law exists—even if the Clave doesn't know it. But *we* know it."

Emma only looked at him.

"Every other *parabatai* have feared the Law more than the curse," Julian said. "They've always either separated, left the Clave, or hidden what was happening to them until they were caught or the curse killed them. Magnus said we'd be the first, and that would count for something with Robert. And he pointed out something else, too. Robert was exiled, because he was in the Circle years ago. The exile temporarily suspended his bond with his *parabatai*. Magnus said Alec told him about it—that it cut their bond enough that Robert didn't even realize his *parabatai* was dead."

"Exile?" Emma's voice shook. "Exile means the Clave sends you away—you have no choice about it—"

"But the Inquisitor is the one who chooses terms of exile," said Julian. "Robert is the one who decided Aline could stay with Helen when she was exiled; the Clave was against it."

"If one of us has to be exiled, it'll be me," said Emma. "I'll go be with Cristina in Mexico. You're indispensable to the children. I'm not."

Her voice was firm, but her eyes were glimmering with tears. Julian sensed the same wave of desperate love he'd felt before threatening to overwhelm him and forced it back.

"I hate the idea of being separated too," Julian said, running his hand over the blanket, the rough texture comforting against his fingers. "The way I love you is fundamental to me, Emma. It's who I am. No matter how far we are from each other."

The glimmer in her eyes had become liquid. A tear spilled down her cheek. She didn't move to wipe it away. "Then—?"

"Exile will deaden the bond," he said. He tried to keep his voice steady. There was still a part of him that hated the idea of not being Emma's *parabatai*, despite everything, and hated the thought of exile, too. "Magnus is sure of it. Exile will do something separation can't, Emma, because exile is deep Shadowhunter enchantment. The ceremony of exile lessens some of your Nephilim abilities, your magic, and having a *parabatai* is part of that magic. It means the curse will be postponed. It means we can have time—and I can stay with the kids. I'd have to leave them otherwise. The curse doesn't just hurt us, Emma, it hurts the people *around* us. I can't stay near the kids thinking I might be some kind of threat to them."

She nodded slowly. "So if it gives us time, then what?"

"Magnus has promised to bring everything he has to bear on figuring out how to break the bond or end the curse. One or the other."

Emma raised her hand to rub at her wet cheek, and he saw the long scar on her forearm that had been there since he'd handed her Cortana in a room in Alicante, five years ago. *How we have left our marks on each other*, he thought.

"I hate this," she whispered. "I hate the idea of being away from you and the kids."

He wanted to take her hand, but held himself back. If he let himself touch her, he might crumble and fall apart and he had to stay strong and reasonable and hopeful. He was the one who'd listened to Magnus, who'd agreed to this. It was on him.

"I hate it, too," he said. "If there was any way it could be me going into exile, I would do it, Emma. Look, we'll only agree to it if the terms are what we want—if the exile period is short, if you can live with Cristina, if the Inquisitor promises no dishonor will accrue to your family name."

"Magnus really thinks Robert Lightwood is going to be that willing to help us? To basically let us dictate the terms of our exile?"

"He really does," said Julian. "He didn't say why exactly—maybe because Robert was exiled himself once, or because his *parabatai* died."

"But Robert doesn't know about the curse."

"And he doesn't need to," said Julian. "Just being in love breaks the Law long before the curse is triggered. And the Law says we'll have to be separated or have our Marks stripped anyway. That's not good for the Clave. They're hurting for Shadowhunters, certainly ones as good as you. He'll *want* a solution that keeps you Nephilim pretty badly. And besides—we have leverage."

"What leverage?"

Julian drew in a long breath. "We know how to cut the bond. We've been acting like we don't, but we do."

Emma went rigid all over. "Because we can't even *consider* the idea," she said. "It's not something we could ever do."

"It still exists," Julian said. "We still know about it."

Her hand shot out and grabbed the front of his shirt. Her grip was incredibly strong. "Julian," she said. "It would be an *unforgivable* sin to use whatever magic it is the Seelie Queen was talking about. We wouldn't just be hurting Jace and Alec, Clary and Simon. All the people we don't know that we'd be harming—destroying this thing that's as fundamental to them as how you love me and I love you—"

"*They* are not *us*," Julian said. "This isn't just about you and me, this is about the children. About my family. Our family."

"Jules." The dismay in her eyes was stark. "I've always known you'd do anything for the kids. We've always said we both would. But when we talk about *anything*, we still mean there are things we *wouldn't* do. Don't you know that?"

Julian

You scared me

"Yes, I know that," he said, and she relaxed slightly. Her eyes were wide. He wanted to kiss her even more than he had before, partly because she was Emma and that meant she was good and honest and thoughtful.

Ironic, really.

"It's just a threat," he added. "Leverage. We wouldn't do it, but Robert doesn't need to know that."

Emma let go of his shirt. "It's too much of a threat," she said. "Destroying *parabatai* as a thing that exists could rip the whole fabric of Nephilim apart."

"We're not going to destroy anything." He took her face in his hands. Her skin was soft against his palms. "We're going to fix it all. We're going to be together. Exile will give us the time we need to find out how to break the bond. If it can be done the Seelie Queen's way, it can be done some other way. The curse was like a monster at our heels. This gives us breathing room."

She kissed his palm. "You sound so sure."

"I am sure," he said. "Emma, I am totally sure."

He couldn't stand it any longer. He pulled her into his lap. She let her weight fall against his body, her face pressed to the crook of his neck. Her hand traced the collar of his T-shirt, just where his skin touched the cotton.

"Do you know why I'm sure?" he whispered, kissing her temple, her cheek where it tasted like salt. "Because when this universe was born, when it blasted into existence in fire and glory, everything that would ever exist was created. Our souls are made of that fire and glory, of the atoms of it, the fragments of stars. Everyone's are, but I believe ours, yours and mine, are made from the dust of the same star. That's why we've always been drawn to each other like magnets, all our lives. All the pieces of us belong together." He held her tighter. "Your name, Emma, means *universe*, you know," he said. "Doesn't that prove I'm right?"

She gave a sobbing half-laugh, lifted her face, and kissed him hard. His body jumped as if he'd touched an electrified wire. His mind went blank, just the sound of their breathing in his ears and the feel of her hands on his shoulders and the taste of her mouth.

He couldn't stand it; holding her, he rolled sideways, taking her with him so they lay crossways on the coverlet. His hands moved under her oversize shirt, cupped her waist, thumbs tracing the angles of her hips. They were still kissing. He felt raw, cut open, every nerve a bleeding edge of desire. He licked sugar off her lips and she moaned.

Everything about the fact that this was forbidden was wrong, he thought. Nobody belonged together more than he and Emma did. He almost felt as if their connection scorched its way through their *parabatai* Marks, winding them closer, amplifying every sensation. Just his hand tangling in the soft strands of her hair was enough to make his bones feel as if they were turning to liquid, to fire. When she arched up against him he thought he might actually die.

And then she drew away, taking a long and shuddering breath. She was shaking. "Julian—we can't."

He rolled away from her. It felt like ripping off a limb. His hands dug into the blanket, gripping hard enough to hurt.

"Emma," he said. It was all he *could* say.

"I want to," she said, raising herself up on an elbow. Her hair was a mess of golden tangles, her expression earnest. "You have to know I want to. But while we're still *parabatai*, we can't."

"It won't make me love you any more or differently," he said, his voice hoarse. "I love you either way. I love you if we never touch."

"I know. But it seems like tempting fate." She reached to stroke his face, his chest. "Your heart's beating so fast."

"It always does," he said, "when it's you." He kissed her, a kiss that accepted that tonight, there would be no more than kisses. "Only you. No one but you."

It was true. He had never desired anyone before Emma, and never anyone since. There had been times when he was younger that it had puzzled him—he was a teenager, he was supposed to be full of inchoate longings and wantings and yearnings, wasn't he? But he never wanted *anyone*, never fantasized or dreamed or longed at all.

And then there had been one day on the beach, when Emma had been laughing next to him and she had reached up to undo her barrette, and her hair had spilled down over her fingers and against her back like liquid sunlight.

His whole body had reacted. He remembered it even now, the driving pain as if something deadly had struck him. It had made him understand why the Greeks had believed love was an arrow that tore through your body and left a blazing trail of longing behind.

In French, falling suddenly in love was the *coup de foudre*. The bolt of lightning. The fire in your veins, the destructive power of a thousand million volts. Julian hadn't fallen suddenly in love: He always had been in love. He had only just that moment realized it.

And after that, he longed. Oh, how he longed. And wished for the time he'd thought he was missing something by not longing, because the longing was like a thousand cruel voices that whispered to him that he was a fool. It was only six months after their *parabatai* ceremony, and it had been the biggest mistake he'd ever made, and totally irrevocable. And every time he saw Emma after that it was like a knife in his chest, but a knife whose pain he welcomed. A blade whose hilt he held in his own hand, pressed against his own heart, and nothing and no one could have taken it away from him.

"Sleep," he said. He gathered her in his arms and she curled up against him, closing her eyes. His Emma, his universe, his blade.

"You see," Diana said. "It's exactly what we thought it was."

The silver-black moon shone down on Brocelind Forest as Jia Penhallow stepped out of the blighted circle of ashy trees and burned grass. As she did, the seraph blade in her hand blazed with light, as if a switch had been flipped.

She stepped back into the circle. The seraph blade went dark.

"I sent photos to Kieran," said Diana, looking at the Consul's grim face. "They—Kieran said these were the same kind of circles of blight he has seen in the Unseelie Lands." Most of what Kieran had recently seen in the Unseelie Lands had been the inside of a cage.

Jia shuddered. "It is awful to stand inside this circle," she said. "It feels as if the ground is made of ice and despair is in the very air."

"These circles," Diana said. "They are in the places that Helen and Aline said were dark on their map, aren't they?"

Jia didn't have to look. She nodded. "I had not wanted to bring my daughter into this."

"If she and Helen can be present during the Council meeting, they can speak up as candidates for the Institute."

Jia said nothing.

"It is what Helen desperately wants," said Diana. "What they both want. The best place to be is not always the safest. No one is content in a prison."

Jia cleared her throat. "The time it would take to have the Council clear the request—Portals to Wrangel Island are tightly regulated—the meeting would be over—"

"You leave that to me," Diana said. "In fact, the less you know, the better."

Diana couldn't believe she had just said *the less you know, the better* to the Consul. Deciding she was unlikely to come up with a better exit line, she turned and strode from the clearing.

Dru dreamed of underground tunnels split by roots like the bulging knuckles of a giant. She dreamed of a room of glittering weapons and a boy with green eyes.

She woke to find the dim light of dawn illuminating her mantel, where a gold hunting dagger inscribed with roses pinned a note to the wood.

For Drusilla: Thank you for all your help. Jaime.

Sometime in the night Kit woke, the *iratze* softly burning on his arm. The infirmary was lit with warm yellow light, and outside the window he could see the rooftops of London, sturdy and Victorian under a waning moon.

And he could hear music. Rolling onto his side, he saw that Ty was asleep on the bed next to Kit's, his headphones on, the faint sound of a symphony coming from them.

A memory teased the edge of Kit's consciousness. Being very young, sick with the flu, feverish in the night, and someone sleeping by the side of his bed. His father? It must have been. Who else could it have been but his father, but certainty eluded him.

No. He wouldn't think about it. It had been a part of his earlier life; he was someone now who had friends who would sleep by his bed if he was sick. For however long that lasted, he would appreciate it.

The high doors of the Sanctuary were made of iron and carved with a symbol Cristina had known since birth, the four interconnected Cs of Clave, Council, Covenant, and Consul.

The doors opened noiselessly at a push onto a large room. Her spine tightened as she stepped inside, remembering the Sanctuary in the Mexico City Institute. She had played there sometimes as a child, enjoying the vastness of the space, the silence, the smooth cold tiles. Every Institute had a Sanctuary.

"Kieran?" she whispered, stepping inside. "Kieran, are you here?"

The London Sanctuary dwarfed the Mexico City and Los Angeles ones in size and impressiveness. Like a vast treasure box of marble and stone, every surface seemed to gleam. There were no windows, for the protection of vampire guests: Light came from a number of witchlight torches. In the center of the room rose a fountain; in it stood a stone angel. Its eyes were open holes from which rivers of water poured like tears and spilled into the basin below. Words were inscribed around the base: *A fonte puro pura defluit aqua.*

A pure fountain gives pure water.

Silvery tapestries hung from the walls, though their designs had faded with age. Between two large pillars a circle of tall, straight-backed chairs were tumbled on their sides, as if someone had knocked them down in a rage. Cushions were strewn across the floor.

Kieran stepped noiselessly out from behind the fountain. His chin was raised defiantly, his hair the darkest black Cristina had ever seen it. Even the glare of the witchlight torches seemed to sink into it and vanish without reflecting off the strands.

"How did you get the doors open?" Cristina asked, glancing over her shoulder at the massive iron wedges. When she turned back, Kieran had raised his hands, open-palmed: They were scored all over with dark red marks, as if he had picked up red-hot pokers and held them tightly.

Iron burns.

"Does it please you?" Kieran said. He was breathing hard. "Here I am, in your Nephilim iron prison."

"Of course it doesn't please me." She frowned at him. She couldn't help the small voice inside that asked her why she'd come. She hadn't been able to stop herself—she'd kept thinking of Kieran alone, betrayed and lost. Perhaps it was the bond between them, the one he'd spoken of in her room. But she'd felt his presence and his unhappiness like a whisper at the back of her mind until she'd gone to look for him.

"What are you to Mark?" he demanded.

"Kieran," she said. "Sit down. Let's sit down and talk."

He only stared at her, watchful and tense. Like an animal in the woods, ready to break away if she moved.

Cristina sat down slowly on the scattered cushions. She smoothed her skirt down, tucking her legs under her.

"Please," she said, holding out her hand to indicate the cushion across from hers, as if she were inviting him to tea. He lowered himself onto it like a cat settling, fur ruffled with tension. "The answer is," she said, "that I don't know. I don't know what I am to Mark, or he to me."

"How can that be?" Kieran said. "We feel what we feel." He gazed down at his hands. They were faerie hands, long-jointed, scarred with many small nicks. "In the Hunt," he said, "it was real. We loved each other. We slept by each other's sides, and we breathed each other's breath and we were never apart. It was always real. It was never false." He looked at Cristina challengingly.

"I never thought that. I always knew it was real," she said. "I saw the way Mark looked at you." She looped her hands together to keep them from shaking. "You know Diego?"

"The very handsome stupid one," Kieran said.

"He's not stupid. Not that it matters," Cristina added hastily. "I loved him when I was younger, and he loved me. There was a time when we were always together, like you and Mark. Later he betrayed me."

"Mark spoke of it. In Faerie he would have been killed for such disrespect of a lady of your rank."

Cristina wasn't entirely sure what Kieran thought her rank was. "Well, the result was that I thought that what we'd had was never real. It hurt more to think that than it did to think that he'd simply stopped loving me—for I had stopped loving him that way too. We had grown out of what we had. But that is a natural thing and happens often. It is much more painful to believe that your love was always a lie."

"What else am I meant to believe?" Kieran demanded. "When Mark is willing to lie to me for the Clave he despises—"

"He didn't do it for the *Clave*," said Cristina. "Have you been listening to anything the Blackthorns have been saying? This is for his family. His sister is in exile because she is part faerie—this is to bring her back."

Kieran's expression was opaque. She knew family meant little to him in the abstract; it was hard to blame him for that. But the Blackthorns, in all their concrete realness, their messy and honest and total love for each other . . . did he see it?

"So do you no longer believe your love with the Rosales boy was a lie?" he said.

"It was not a lie," she said. "Diego has his reasons for what he's doing now. And when I look back, it is with pleasure at the happiness we had. The bad things can't matter more than the good things, Kieran."

"Mark told me," he said, "that when you went into Faerie, you were each made a promise by the phouka who guards the gate that you would find something you wanted there. What was it you wanted?"

"The phouka told me I would be given a chance to bring the Cold Peace to an end," said Cristina. "It is why I agreed when it was decided to cooperate with the Queen."

Kieran looked at her, shaking his head. For a moment she thought he considered her foolish, and her heart sank. He reached to touch her face. The glide of his fingers was featherlight, as if she had been brushed by the calyx of a flower. "When I swore fealty to you in the Court of the Queen," he said, "it was to annoy and anger Mark. But now I think I made a wiser decision than I could have imagined."

"You know I'll never hold you to that oath, Kieran."

"Yes. And that is why I say you are nothing like I thought you'd be," he said. "I have lived in this small world of the Wild Hunt and Faerie Courts, yet you make me feel the world is bigger and full of possibility." He dropped his hand. "I have never known someone so generous in their heart."

Cristina felt as if her face were on fire. "Mark is also all those things," she said. "When Gwyn came to tell us you were in danger in Faerie, Mark went to get you immediately regardless of the cost."

"That was a kind thing to tell me," he said. "You have always been kind."

"Why do you say that?"

"Because you could always have taken Mark from me, but you didn't."

"No," Cristina said. "It is as you told Adaon—you would not want Mark's love if it did not come freely. Neither would I. I would not pressure or influence him. If you think I would, and that it would work if I did—then you don't know me at all. Nor Mark. Not as he really is."

Kieran's lips parted. He didn't speak, though, because the Sanctuary doors had opened, and Mark had come in.

He was all in black and looked exhausted. The red ring around his wrist drew Cristina's eye; involuntarily, she touched her own wrist, the healing skin of the binding wound.

"I followed you here," he said to Cristina. "There's still enough of the binding spell left to allow me to do that. I thought you'd be with Kieran."

Kieran said nothing. He looked like a faerie prince in a painting: remote, unassailable, distant.

"My lord Kieran," Mark said formally. "Can we talk?"

They looked like a painting, both of them kneeling, Cristina's dark hair falling to hide her face. Kieran, opposite her, was a study in contrasts of black and white. Mark stood in the doorway of the

Sanctuary for a moment, just watching them, his heart feeling as if it were being compressed inside his chest.

He really did have a thing for dark hair, he thought.

At that moment he heard Cristina say his name and realized he was eavesdropping. Coming into the Sanctuary felt like entering a cold, harsh place: It was bound all around with iron. Kieran must have felt it too, though the look on his face gave no sign. It gave no sign he felt anything at all.

"My lord Kieran," Mark said. "Can we talk?"

Cristina rose to her feet. "I should go."

"You need not." Kieran had leaned back to lounge among the spilled cushions. Faeries did not lie with their words, but they lied with their faces and voices, the gestures of their hands. Right now anyone looking at Kieran would think he felt nothing but boredom and dislike.

But he hadn't left. He was still in the Institute. Mark clung to that.

"I must," Cristina said. "Mark and I are not meant to be near each other as the binding spell wears off."

Mark moved closer to her, though, as she went to the door. Their hands brushed. Had he thought she was beautiful the moment he met her? He remembered coming awake to the sound of her voice, seeing her sitting on the floor of his room with her knife open. How grateful he had been that she was someone he had never known before the Hunt, someone who would have no expectations of him.

She looked at him once and was gone. He was alone with Kieran.

"Why are you here?" Kieran demanded. "Why lower yourself to come before someone you hate?"

"I don't hate you. None of this was because I hated you or wanted to hurt you. I was angry with you—of course I was. Can't you understand why?"

Kieran didn't meet Mark's eyes. "This is why Emma dislikes me," he said. "And Julian."

"Iarlath whipped them both. The whipping he gave Emma would have killed a mundane human."

"I remember," said Kieran miserably, "and yet it seems distant." He swallowed. "I knew I was losing you. I was afraid. There was more to it, as well. Iarlath had hinted you would not be safe in the Shadowhunters' world. That they were planning to lure you back, only to execute you on some trumped-up charge. I was a fool to believe him. I know it now."

"Oh," said Mark. The knowledge unfolded in him, realization edged with relief. "You thought you were saving my life."

Kieran nodded. "It makes no difference, though. What I did was wrong."

"You will have to make your own apology to Emma and Julian," said Mark. "But for my sake, Kieran, I have forgiven you. You returned when you did not have to—you helped us save Tavvy—"

"When I sought refuge here, I was blinded by rage," Kieran said. "All I could think was that you had lied to me. I thought you had come to the Court to save me because you—" His voice cracked. "Because you *loved* me. I cannot bear to think on my own stupidity."

"I do love you," Mark said. "But it is not an easy or restful sort of love, Kier."

"Not like what you feel for Cristina."

"No," said Mark. "Not like what I feel for Cristina."

Kieran's shoulders sagged slightly. "I am glad you admit it," he said. "I could not tolerate a lie now, I think. When first I loved you, I knew I was loving something that could lie. I told myself it would not matter. But it matters more than I ever thought."

Mark closed the distance between them. He was half-certain that Kieran would back away from him, but the other boy didn't move. Mark approached until there were only inches of space between them, until Kieran's eyes had widened, and then Mark knelt, cold marble against his knees.

It was a gesture he had seen before, in the Hunt and at revels. One faerie kneeling to another. Not submission, but an apology. *Forgive me.* Kieran's eyes were like saucers.

"It does matter," Mark said. "I wish that I could not lie, so that you would believe me: All these days, I have not held back from affection with you because I was angry at you, or sickened. I wanted you just as I did in the Hunt. But I could not be with you, touch you, with all of it shadowed by lies. It would not have felt true or honest. It would not have felt as if you were choosing me, because to make a true choice, we must have true knowledge."

"Mark," Kieran whispered.

"I do not love you as I love Cristina. I love you as I love *you*," said Mark. He bent his head. "I wish that you could see my heart. Then you would understand."

There was a rustling sound. Kieran had sunk to his own knees, level with Mark. "Would you have told me?" he said. "After the testimony?"

"Yes. I couldn't have stood it otherwise."

Kieran half-closed his eyes. Mark could see crescents of black and silver beneath his lids, fringed by his dark lashes. His hair had paled to almost a pewter color. "I believe you." He opened his eyes, looked directly into Mark's. "Do you know why I trust you?"

Mark shook his head. He could hear the water rushing in the fountain behind them, reminding him of a thousand rivers they had ridden over together, a thousand streams they had slept beside.

"Because of Cristina," said Kieran. "She would not have agreed to a dishonorable plan. I understand you were trying to help your family, your sister. I understand why you were desperate. And I believe you would not have deceived me longer than you needed." Something behind his eyes suddenly seemed very old. "I will testify," he said.

Mark started up. "Kieran, you don't—"

Kieran's hands came up to cup Mark's face. His touch was

gentle. "I am not doing it for you," he said. "This will be what I do for Emma and the others. Then that debt will be paid. You and I, our debts are paid already." He leaned forward and brushed his lips against Mark's. Mark wanted to chase the kiss, the warmth of it, the familiarity. He felt Kieran's hand come down to splay itself over his chest—over the elf-bolt that hung there, below his collarbone. "We will be done with each other."

"*No*," Mark whispered.

But Kieran was on his feet, the warmth of his hands gone from Mark's skin. His eyes were dark, his whole body tense. Mark shot to his feet after, meaning to demand that Kieran explain what he had meant by *done*—just as a terrible noise split the air.

It was a noise that came from outside the Institute, though not very far at all. Not nearly far enough. A memory flashed through Mark's mind, of watching from horseback as a forest of trees was destroyed by lightning. Fire had flashed beneath him, the wrenching crash of branches and trunks like shrieks in his head.

Kieran sucked in a breath. His eyes had gone distant, unfocused. "They have come," he said. "They are near."

A crash ripped Emma out of sleep and out of Julian's arms. A crash that wasn't quite a crash; she thought at first that it sounded like two cars slamming into each other on the highway, the screech of brakes and the explosion of glass. It seemed to be coming from right outside; she bolted up and hurtled across the room to the window.

There were five of them in the courtyard. They gleamed bronze in the morning light, both horses and riders. The steeds seemed metallic, their eyes bound with bronze silk, their hooves gleaming with a high polish. The faeries who sat astride them were just as shimmering and beautiful, their armor without visible jointure so that it looked like liquid bronze. Their faces were masked, their hair long and metallic. Somehow, here in the heart of London, they looked far more terrifying than they had the first time Emma had seen them.

Julian was awake, sitting on the edge of the bed, reaching for the weapons belt that hung on the wall over the nightstand.

"They came," she said. "It's the Riders."

They raced to the library, all of them but Kit and Bridget, as Magnus had instructed. Magnus, Cristina, Ty, and Livvy were already there when Emma came bursting in with Cortana in her hand.

Julian was a few paces behind her. They'd agreed it was better not to seem as if they'd been together.

Everyone was standing at the windows, from which the curtains had been thrown back to provide an uninterrupted view of the courtyard and the front of the Institute. Magnus was leaning against the glass, arm extended, hand flat against the pane, his expression grim. There were black hollows under his eyes and he looked worryingly gaunt and exhausted.

Mark and Kieran came in as Emma hooked her sword over her back and hurried to the windows. Julian slid in beside her and stared through the glass.

The five Riders hadn't moved from the courtyard. They remained where they were, like statues. Their horses had no reins or bridles, nothing for them to hold. They sat with their swords unsheathed, held out ahead of them like a row of gleaming teeth.

Kieran came forward before Mark, crossing the room to the window, and after a moment Mark followed. They stood in a line: the Shadowhunters, the warlock, and the faerie prince, staring grimly down at the courtyard. Kieran was silent and sick-looking, his hair a pale white, the color of bones.

"They can't get inside the Institute," said Ty.

"No," Magnus said. "The wards keep them out."

"Nonetheless, we should get away as soon as we can," said Kieran. "I do not trust the Riders. They will think of some way in."

"We need to contact Alicante," said Livvy. "Get them to open their side of a Portal so we can get out of here."

"We can't do that without revealing that the Riders are here, and why," said Julian. "But—we could still Portal away from here, even if we didn't go straight to Idris." He glanced sideways at Magnus.

"The thing is, I can't make my side of a Portal right now," said Magnus. He spoke with some effort. "We need to hold out a few hours. I've exhausted my energy—I wasn't expecting to need to heal Kit, or to need to send Alec and the children away."

There was an awful silence. It had never occurred to any of them that there were things Magnus couldn't do. That he had weaknesses, like anyone else.

"There's a Portal in the crypt," said Ty. "But it only goes to the Cornwall Institute."

No one asked him how he knew that. "That Institute is abandoned, though," said Julian. "The protections are probably stronger here."

"We'd just be trading Institute for Institute," said Magnus. "We'd still be trapped inside, and with weaker protections. And believe me, they'd be able to follow us. There have never been greater hunters than the Riders of Mannan."

"What about Catarina Loss?" said Livvy. "She got us out of the Los Angeles Institute."

Magnus took a shaky breath. "The same wards keeping the Riders out also prevent anyone from trying to make a Portal from outside."

"What about the Seelie Queen?" Emma said. "Might she be willing to help us fight the Riders?"

"The Queen isn't on our side," said Julian. "She's only on her own side."

There was a long silence. Magnus broke it. "I have to hand it to you," he said. "I never thought Jace and Clary would be topped by anyone else in terms of insane, self-destructive decisions, but you all are giving them a run for their money."

"I really had nothing to do with this," Kieran pointed out stiffly.

"I think you will find many poor decisions led you here, my friend," Magnus said. "All right, there are a few things I can do to try to bring my energy up. You—all of you—wait here. And don't do anything stupid."

He strode out of the room on long, black-clad legs, swearing under his breath.

"He's getting more and more like Gandalf," said Emma, watching him go. "I mean, a hot, younger-looking Gandalf, but I keep expecting him to start stroking his long white beard and muttering darkly."

"At least he's willing to help us," said Julian. His gaze sharpened. A Rider was coming through the gates. The sixth rider, this one with a slighter build, a spill of long bronze hair. *Ethna*, Emma thought. The sister.

Then her thoughts dissolved into a buzz of shock. A small figure was propped on the bronze horse's back in front of her. A little human girl, with short black hair. She dangled limply in the faerie woman's one-handed grip, but she was blinking, her face twisted in terror. She couldn't have been more than four years old—she wore leggings with a cheerful print of bees, and bright pink sneakers.

In her other hand, Ethna held a dagger, the point of it against the back of the girl's neck.

Julian had gone rigid as marble, his face white. Voices rose around Emma in the room, but they were only noise. She couldn't distinguish the words. She was staring at the little girl, and in her mind she saw Dru, Tavvy, even Livvy and Ty; they had all been that tiny once, that helpless.

And Ethna was strong. All she had to do was drive that dagger forward, and she'd sever the child's head from her neck.

"Get back from the window," said Julian. "Everyone, get back from the window. If they don't think we're watching them, they're less likely to hurt the girl."

His hand was on Emma's arm. She staggered back with the others. She could hear Mark protesting. They should go down, he was saying. Fight off the Riders.

"We *can't*," said Julian in anguish. "We'll be slaughtered."

"I killed one of them before," said Emma. "I—"

"They were caught off guard, though." Julian's voice reached her partially distorted through shock. "They didn't expect it— didn't think it was possible—this time they'll be prepared—"

"He is right," said Kieran. "Sometimes the most ruthless heart speaks the most truth."

"What do you mean?" Mark was flushed, his right hand gripping his wrist; Emma realized, distantly, that the mark of the binding spell was gone from his skin, and from Cristina's, too.

"The children of Mannan have never been defeated," Kieran said. "Emma is the first ever to slay one. They have taken the child to lure us out, because they know they will have us in their power when we do."

"They'll kill her," Emma said. "She's a *baby*."

"Emma—" Julian reached out for her. She could read his face. Julian would do anything, brave anything, for his family. There was nothing and no one he wouldn't sacrifice.

That was why this had to be her.

She bolted. She heard Julian shout her name but she was out the library door; she slammed it behind her and took off running down the hall. She was already in gear, already had Cortana; she barreled down the steps, skidded through the entryway, and burst through the front doors of the Institute.

She saw the blur of bronze that was the Riders, before she swung around and shoved the doors closed, whipping her stele from her pocket. She slashed a Locking rune across them just as she heard the dull thumps of bodies striking the other side, voices calling out to her not to be reckless, to open the doors, open them, *Emma*—

She put her stele in her pocket, raised Cortana, and descended the steps.

28

THE SAD SOUL

"That's her!" Ethna cried, her voice rich and sweet. She drew the child in her grip closer to her, raised the blade in her hand. "That is the murderer who slew Fal."

"It was a battle," Emma said. "He would have killed me." She looked at the other Riders. They stood in their row, facing her, a line of grim statuary. "I would think warriors would know the difference."

"You should be killed like your parents," hissed one of the other Riders. Delan. "Tortured and carved with knives, like they were."

Emma's heart lurched in her chest. Her fear for the girl was still there, but rage was starting to mix with it. "Let the girl go," she said. "Let her go and you can fight me. Revenge yourselves on me like you want to."

She could hear pounding on the doors behind her. Soon enough they'd get them open; she didn't have any illusions of the locking rune holding forever. Her runes had surprising power now, because of Julian—but Julian would be a match for their capability.

Emma raised Cortana, the morning sun sliding down the blade like melted butter.

"I killed your brother with this sword," she said. "You want revenge? Let the girl go, and I'll fight you. Threaten her a moment longer and I'll go back inside the Institute." Her eyes flicked from one of them to the other. She thought of her parents, of their bodies, stripped and left on the beach for gulls to pick at. "We despoiled Fal's corpse," she lied. "Tore his armor from him, broke his weapon, left him for the rats and crows—"

Ethna gave a high screech and shoved the small girl away from her. The girl toppled to the ground—Emma gasped—but she found her feet and ran, sobbing, for the road. She looked back over her shoulder only once, mouth wide in her tearstained face as she sprinted through the gate and disappeared.

Relief shot through Emma. The girl was safe.

And then Ethna charged, her horse's hooves silent on the courtyard stone. She was like a thrown spear hurtling through the air, noiseless and deadly; Emma bent her knees and sprang, using the height of the steps and the force of her fall to give the swing of her sword power.

Their blades clanged together in midair. The shock rattled Emma's bones. Ethna's arm flew wide; Emma landed in a crouch and drove her sword upward, but the faerie woman had already flung herself from the back of her horse. She was on her feet, laughing; the other Riders had dismounted as well. Their horses vanished, as if absorbed into the air as the children of Mannan surged toward Emma, blades raised.

She lifted herself out of her crouch, Cortana describing a wide arc above her head, striking each sword aside—Emma was reminded of a hand sliding across piano keys, hitting each note in turn.

But it was close. The last sword, Delan's, caught Emma's shoulder. She felt her gear rip, her skin sting. Another scar to add to the map of them.

She whirled, and Ethna was behind her. She held two shortswords, gleaming bronze, and slashed at Emma with first one and then the other. Emma leaped back, barely in time. If she hadn't been wearing gear, she knew, she'd be dead, her guts spilled out on the flagstones. She felt her jacket tear, and even in the cold of battle, a hot spike of fear went down her spine.

This was impossible. No one person could fight six Riders. She'd been mad to try, but she thought of the little girl's feet in their pink sneakers and couldn't be sorry. Not even when she turned to find three Riders blocking the way back into the Institute.

The door of the Institute had stopped shaking. *Good*, Emma thought. The others should stay safely inside; it was the wise thing to do, the smart thing.

"Your friends have abandoned you," sneered one of the Riders blocking her way. His bronze hair was short and curling, giving him the look of a Greek kouros. He was lovely. Emma hated his guts. "Give yourself up now and we will make your death quick."

"I could give myself a quick death, if that was what I wanted," Emma said, her sword outstretched to hold off the other three faeries. "As it happens."

Ethna was glaring at her. The other Riders—she recognized Airmed, if not the others—were whispering; she caught the last few words of a sentence. "—is the sword, as I told you."

"But runed work cannot harm us," said Airmed. "Nor seraph blades."

Emma dove for Ethna. The faerie woman spun, bringing her blades across in a whip-fast slashing gesture.

Emma leaped. It was a move she had practiced over and over with Julian in the training room, using a bar that they raised just a little bit every day. The blades whipped by beneath her feet, and in her mind's eye she saw Julian, his arms raised to catch her.

Julian. She landed on the other side of Ethna, whirled, and drove her blade into the faerie woman's back.

Or tried, at least. Ethna spun at the last moment, and the blade sliced open her bronze armor, opening a gash in her side. She shrieked and staggered back and Emma jerked Cortana free, blood spattering from the blade onto the flagstones.

Emma raised the sword. "This is Cortana," she gasped, her chest heaving. "Of the same steel and temper as Joyeuse and Durendal. There is nothing Cortana cannot cut."

"A blade of Wayland the Smith," cried the Rider with the bronze curls, and to Emma's amazement, there was fear in his voice.

"Silence, Karn," snapped one of the others. "It is yet only one blade. Kill her."

Karn's beautiful face contracted. He lifted his weapon—a massive battle-ax—and started for Emma; she raised Cortana—

And the front door of the Institute burst open, disgorging Shadowhunters.

Julian. Emma saw him first, a blur of gear and sword and dark hair. Then Mark, Cristina. Kieran, Ty, Livvy. And Kit, who must have come from the infirmary, since he seemed to have thrown gear on over his pajamas. At least he was wearing boots.

They drove back the Riders on the steps, Julian and Mark first, their swords flashing in their hands. Neither of them carried seraph blades, Emma saw—they had taken only plain-bladed weapons, unruned, meant for slaying Downworlders. Even Kieran carried one, a sword whose pommel and grip gleamed with gold and silver instead of steel.

One of the Riders let out a roar of rage when he saw Kieran. "Traitor!" he snarled.

Kieran dropped a courtly little bow. "Eochaid," he said, by way of greeting. "And Etarlam." He winked at the sixth Rider, who made a sour face. "Well met."

Eochaid lunged for him. Kieran dropped into a half crouch, swinging his sword with a lightness and skill that surprised Emma.

The clash of their blades seemed to signal the beginning of a much larger battle. Julian and Mark had forced the Riders from the steps in the first surprise of their appearance. Now the others poured after them, hounding and worrying at them with blades. Mark, carrying a double-edged straight sword, went for Delan; the twins harried Airmed while Cristina, looking beyond furious, engaged Etarlam.

Julian began to move through the blur of battle, slashing to either side of him, cutting his way toward Emma. His eyes suddenly widened. *Behind you!*

She spun. It was Ethna, her face twisted into a mask of hatred. Her blades made a scissoring motion—Emma raised Cortana just in time, and Ethna's double blades closed on it with savage force.

And shattered.

The faerie woman gasped in surprise. A second later she was scrambling back, her hands moving in the air. Julian changed course and leaped after her, but another weapon was taking shape in her grasp, this one with a curved blade like a Persian *shamshir.*

Julian's sword slammed against Ethna's. Emma felt the collision between their weapons. It forked through her like lightning. Suddenly everything was happening very fast: Julian twisted gracefully away from the blade, but the edge of it caught him across the top of the arm. Emma felt the pain of it, her *parabatai's* pain, just as she had felt his blade strike Ethna's. She launched herself at the two of them, but Eochaid rose up in front of her and the point of a sword hurtled toward her face, a silver blur cutting the air.

It fell away to the side. Eochaid howled, a brutal, angry sound, and whirled from her to strike savagely at the figure who had come up behind him, whose blade had pierced his shoulder. Blood stained Eochaid's bronze armor.

It was Kieran. His hair was a mass of black and white strands, sticky with blood over his temple. His clothes were stained with red, his lip split. He stared at Emma, breathing hard.

Eochaid leaped for him and they began to fight savagely. The world seemed a din of clashing blades: Emma heard a cry and saw Cristina fighting to get to Kit, who had been knocked to the ground by Delan. The Riders had swarmed up to the steps to block the Institute doors. Julian was holding off Ethna; the twins were fighting back-to-back, trying to hack their way up the steps alongside Mark.

Emma began to shove blindly toward Kit, a coldness at her heart. The Riders were too fierce, too strong. They wouldn't tire.

Delan was standing over Kit, his blade high in the air. Kit was scrambling back on his elbows. A sword flashed in front of Emma; she knocked it away with Cortana, heard someone swear. Delan was staring at Kit intently, as if his face held a mystery. "Who are you, boy?" the Rider demanded, his blade stilled.

Kit wiped blood from his face. There was a dagger near him on the flagstones, just out of reach of his hand. "Christopher Herondale," he said, his eyes flashing arrogantly. He *was* a Shadowhunter, Emma thought, through and through; he would never beg for his life.

Delan snorted. *"Qui omnia nomini debes,"* he said, and began to swing his sword down, just as Emma ducked and rolled under the blade, Cortana flashing up, shearing through Delan's wrist.

The faerie warrior screamed, an echoing howl of rage and pain. The air was full of a mist of blood. Delan's hand thumped to the ground, still gripping his sword; a second later Kit was on his feet, snatching up the weapon, his eyes blazing. Emma was beside him; together they began to back Delan up, his blood painting the flagstones beneath them as he retreated.

But Delan was laughing. "Slay me if you think you can," he sneered. "But look around you. You have already lost."

Kit had his blade up, pointed directly at Delan's throat. "You look," he said steadily. "I'll stab."

Emma's head snapped around. Airmed had backed Ty and Livvy against a wall. Ethna had her weapon at Julian's throat. Cristina had been driven to her knees by Etarlam. Mark was looking at her in horror but couldn't move—Eochaid had his sword against Mark's back, just where he could sever his spine.

Karn stood at the top of the steps, his blade out, grinning across his cruel and lovely face.

Emma swallowed. Kit swore softly under his breath. Karn spoke, his teeth flashing white with his smile. "Give us the Black Volume," he said. "We will let you go."

Kieran stood frozen, staring from Mark to Cristina. "Do not listen!" he cried. "The Riders are wild magic—they can lie."

"We don't have the book," Julian said steadily. "We've never had it. Nothing has changed."

He looked calm, but Emma could see beneath the surface of him, behind his eyes. She could hear the noise of his thundering heart. He was looking at her, at Mark, at Ty and Livvy, and he was mortally terrified.

"You are asking for something we cannot do," said Julian. "But maybe we can make a deal. We can swear to you that we will bring you the book when we find it—"

"Your oaths mean nothing," snarled Ethna. "Let us kill them now and send a message to the Queen, that her tricks will not be countenanced!"

Karn laughed. "Wise words, sister," he said. "Ready your blades—"

Emma's hand clamped down on Cortana. Her mind whirled—she couldn't kill them all, couldn't prevent what they were going to do, but by the Angel she'd take some of them with her—

The gates of the courtyard burst open. They hadn't been locked, but they were flung wide now with such force that despite their weight, they flew to the sides, slamming into the stone walls of the yard, rattling like sundered chains.

Beyond the gate was fog—thick and incongruous on such a sunny day. The violent tableau in the courtyard remained still, arrested in shock, as the fog cleared and a woman stepped into the yard.

She was slight and of medium height, her hair a deep brown, falling to her waist. She wore a torn shift over a long skirt that didn't fit her well, and a pair of low boots. The bare skin of her arms and shoulders proclaimed her a Shadowhunter, with a Shadowhunter's scars. The Voyance rune decorated her right hand.

She held no weapons. Instead she hugged a book to herself—an old volume, bound in dark leather, scuffed and worn. A folded piece of paper was stuck between two pages, like a bookmark. She raised her head and looked steadily before her at the scene in the courtyard; her expression was unsurprised, as if she'd expected nothing else.

Emma's heart began to thump. She'd seen this woman before, though it had been a dark night in Cornwall. She knew her.

"I am Annabel Blackthorn." The woman spoke in a clear, even tone, slightly accented. "The Black Volume is mine."

Eochaid swore. He had a fine-boned, cruel face, like an eagle. "You lied to us," he snarled at Emma and the rest. "You told us you had no idea where the book was."

"Nor did they," said Annabel, still with the same composure. "Malcolm Fade had it, and I took it from his dead body. But it is mine and always has been mine. It belonged in the library of the house I grew up in. The book has always been Blackthorn property."

"Nevertheless," said Ethna, though she was looking at Annabel with a dubious respect. One due the undead, Emma suspected. "You will give it to us, or face the wrath of the Unseelie King."

"The Unseelie King," murmured Annabel. Her face was placid in a way that chilled Emma—surely no one could be placid in this situation, no one who wasn't insane? "Give him my regards. Tell him I know his name."

Delan blanched. "His *what*?" The true name of a faerie gave anyone who knew it power over them. Emma couldn't imagine what it would mean for the King to have his name revealed.

"His name," Annabel said. "Malcolm was very close to him for many years. He learned your monarch's name. I know it too. If you do not clear off now, and return to the King with my message, I will tell it to everyone on the Council. I will tell every Downworlder. The King is not loved. He will find the results most unpleasant."

"She lies," said Airmed, his hawk's eyes slitted.

"Risk it with your King, then," she said. "Let him find out you are the ones responsible for the revelation of his name."

"It would be easy enough to silence *you*," said Etarlam.

Annabel did not move as he strode toward her, raising his free hand as if he meant to strike her across the face. He swung, and she caught his wrist, as lightly as a debutante taking her waltz partner's arm during a dance.

And she flung him. He sailed across the courtyard and slammed into a wall with the clang of armor. Emma gasped.

"Etar!" Ethna cried. She started toward her brother, abandoning Jules—and froze. Her curved sword was rising out of her hand. She reached for it, but it was floating above her head. More cries came from the other Riders—their swords were being jerked out of their grasps, gliding into the air above their heads. Ethna glared at Annabel. "You fool!"

"That wasn't her," came a drawling voice from the doorway. It was Magnus, leaning heavily on Dru's shoulder. She seemed to be half-supporting him. Blue fire sparked from the fingers of his free hand. "Magnus Bane, High Warlock of Brooklyn, at your service."

The Riders exchanged glances. Emma knew they could make new weapons easily, but what good would it do them if Magnus just snatched them out of their hands? Their eyes narrowed; their lips curled.

"This is not finished," said Karn, and he looked across the courtyard directly at Emma as he said it. *This is not finished between us.*

Then he vanished, and the remaining Riders followed. One

moment they were there, the next gone, winking out of existence like vanishing stars. Their swords crashed to the ground with the loud clang of metal against stone.

"Hey," muttered Kit. "Free swords."

Magnus gave a low grunt and sagged backward; Dru caught at him, worry in her wide eyes. "Get inside, now. All of you."

They scrambled to obey, the intact pausing to help those who had been injured, though none of the injuries were serious. Emma found Julian without even needing to look for him—her *parabatai* senses were still humming, her body's interior knowledge that he had been cut, would need healing. She slid her arm around him as gently as she could, and he winced. His eyes met hers, and she knew he was feeling her own wound, the cut at the top of her shoulder.

She wanted to throw her arms around him, wanted to wipe the blood from his face, kiss his closed eyes. But she knew how that would look. She held herself back with a control that hurt more than her injury did.

Julian squeezed her hands and drew away reluctantly. "I have to go to Annabel," he said in a low voice.

Emma started. She'd nearly forgotten Annabel, but she was still there, in the center of the courtyard, the Black Volume hugged to her chest. The others stood around her uncertainly—after all the time spent looking for Annabel, it was clear no one had ever imagined she'd come to them.

Even Julian paused before he reached her, hesitating as if deciding how to break the silence. Near him, Ty stood between Livvy and Kit, all of them staring at Annabel as if she were an apparition and not really there at all.

"Annabel." It was Magnus. He had limped down the steps to the bottom; he had only a light hand on Dru's shoulder now, though there were dark crescents of exhaustion below his eyes. He sounded sad, that depthless sort of sadness that came out of a time, a life, that Emma could not even imagine. "Oh, Annabel. Why did you come here?"

Annabel drew the folded piece of paper from the Black Volume. "I received a letter," she said, in a voice so soft it was barely audible. "From Tiberius Blackthorn."

Only Kit didn't look surprised. He put his hand on Ty's arm as Tiberius scanned the ground furiously.

"There was something in it," she said. "I had thought the world's hand turned against me, but as I read the letter, I imagined there was a chance it was not so." She raised her chin, that characteristic, defiant Blackthorn gesture that broke Emma's heart every time. "I have come to speak with Julian Blackthorn about the Black Volume of the Dead."

"There is an undead person in our library," said Livvy. She was sitting on one of the long beds in the infirmary. They'd all gathered there—all but Magnus, who had closed himself into the library with Annabel. They were in various stages of being runed and patched up and cleaned. There was a small pile of bloody cloths growing on the counter.

Ty was on the same bed as Livvy, his back to the headboard. As always after a battle, Emma noticed, he had withdrawn a bit, as if he needed time to recuperate from the clang and shock of it. He was twisting something between his fingers in regular rhythmic motions, though Emma couldn't see what it was. "It's not our library," he said. "It's Evelyn's."

"Still strange," Livvy said. Neither she nor Ty had been injured in the fight, but Kit had, and she was finishing an *iratze* on his back. "All done," she said, patting his shoulder, and he drew his T-shirt down with a wince.

"She isn't undead, not exactly," said Julian. Emma had given him an *iratze*, but some part of her had become afraid of drawing runes on him, and she'd stopped there, bandaging the wound instead. He'd had a long cut running down his upper arm, and even after he'd pulled his shirt back on, the bandages were visible through the fabric. "She's not a zombie or a ghost."

One of the glasses of water on a nightstand fell over with a crash.

"Jessamine didn't appreciate that," said Kit.

Cristina laughed—she wasn't injured either, but she was worrying at the pendant around her throat as she watched Mark tend to Kieran's injuries. Hunters healed faster, Emma knew, but they also bruised easily, it seemed. A map of blue-black spread over Kieran's back and shoulders, and one of his cheekbones was darkening. With a cloth that Cristina had wet down in one of his hands, Mark was gently sponging away the blood.

The elf-bolt gleamed around Mark's neck. Emma didn't know what was going on with Mark and Kieran and Cristina exactly—Cristina had been remarkably reluctant to explain—but she knew Kieran had learned the truth about his and Mark's relationship. Still, Kieran hadn't taken his elf-bolt back, so that was something.

She realized with a small jolt of surprise that she was hoping things worked out for them. She hoped that wasn't disloyal to Cristina. But she was no longer angry at Kieran—he might have made a mistake, but he'd made up for it many times over since then.

"Where was Jessamine earlier?" said Julian. "Isn't she supposed to protect the Institute?"

Another crash of glass.

"She says she can't leave the Institute. She can only protect inside of it." Kit paused. "I don't know if I should repeat the rest of what she said." After a moment, he smiled. "Thank you, Jessamine."

"What did she say?" Livvy asked, picking up her stele.

"That I'm a true Herondale," he said. He frowned. "What did that metal guy say to me when I told him my name? Was it faerie language?"

"Oddly, it was Latin," said Julian. "An insult. Something Mark Antony once said to Augustus Caesar—'you, boy, who owe everything to a name.' He was saying he would never have amounted to anything if he hadn't been a Caesar."

Kit looked annoyed. "I've been a Herondale for like three weeks," he said. "And I'm not sure what I've gotten out of it."

"Do not pay too much attention to the pronouncements of faeries," said Kieran. "They will get under your skin in any way they can."

"Does that include you?" asked Cristina, with a smile.

"Obviously," said Kieran, and he smiled too, just slightly.

Theirs might be the weirdest friendship she'd ever seen, Emma thought.

"We're off topic," said Livvy. "*Annabel Blackthorn* is in our library. That's weird, right? Doesn't anyone else think it's weird?"

"Why is that weirder than vampires?" said Ty, clearly perplexed. "Or werewolves?"

"Well, of course *you* wouldn't think it was," said Kit. "You're the one who told her to come."

"Yes, about that," Julian began. "Is there a particular reason you didn't tell any of us—"

Ty was saved from a brotherly chastisement by the infirmary door opening. It was Magnus. Emma didn't like the way he looked—he seemed grimly pale, his eyes shadowed, his movements stiff, as if he were bruised. His mouth was set in a serious line.

"Julian," he said. "If you could come with me."

"What for?" asked Emma.

"I've been trying to talk to Annabel," Magnus said. "I thought she might be willing to open up to someone who wasn't a Shadowhunter if she had the option, but she's stubborn. She's stayed polite, but she says she'll only speak to Julian."

"Does she not remember you?" Julian asked, getting up.

"She remembers me," said Magnus. "But as a friend of Malcolm's. And she's not his biggest fan these days."

Ungrateful, Emma remembered Kieran saying. But he was silent now, rebuttoning his torn shirt, his bruised eyes cast downward.

"Why doesn't she want to talk to Ty?" said Livvy. "He sent her the message."

Magnus shrugged an *I couldn't tell you* shrug.

"All right, I'll be right back," said Julian. "We're leaving for Idris as soon as possible, so everyone grab anything they might need to take with them."

"The Council meeting is this afternoon," Magnus said. "I'll have the strength to make a Portal in a few hours. We'll be sleeping in Alicante tonight."

He sounded relieved about it. He and Julian headed out into the hallway. Emma meant to hang back, but she couldn't—she darted after them before the door closed.

"Jules," she said. He had already started down the corridor with Magnus; at the sound of her voice, they both turned.

She couldn't have done it in the infirmary, but it was just Magnus, and he already knew. She went up to Julian and put her arms around him. "Be *careful*," she said. "She sent us into a trap in that church. This could be a trap too."

"I'll be right there, outside the room," Magnus said, subdued. "I'll be ready to intervene. But Julian, under no circumstances should you try to take the Black Volume from her, even if she isn't holding it. It's tied to her with pretty powerful magic."

Julian nodded, and Magnus disappeared down the hallway, leaving them alone. For long moments, they held each other in silence, letting the anxiety of the day dissipate: their fear for each other in the battle, their fear for the children, their worry over what was going to happen in Alicante. Julian was warm and solid in her arms, his hand tracing a soothing line down her back. He smelled of cloves, as always, as well as antiseptic and bandages. She felt his chin nudge her hair as his fingers flew across the back of her shirt.

D-O-N-T W-O-R-R-Y.

"Of course I'm worried," said Emma. "You saw what she did to Etarlam. Do you think you can convince her to just give you the book?"

"I don't know," Julian said. "I'll know when I talk to her."

"Annabel's been lied to so much," said Emma. "Don't promise anything we can't deliver."

He kissed her forehead. His lips moved against her skin, his voice so low that no one who didn't know him as well as Emma did could have understood him at all. "I will do," he said, "whatever I need to do."

She knew he meant it. There was nothing more to say; she watched him go down the corridor toward the library with troubled eyes.

Kit was in his room packing his meager belongings when Livvy came in. She'd dressed for the trip to Idris, in a long black skirt and a round-collared white shirt. Her hair was loose down her back.

She looked at Ty, sitting on Kit's bed. They'd been discussing Idris and what Ty remembered of it. "It's not like any place else," he'd told Kit, "but when you get there, you'll feel like you've been there before."

"Ty-Ty," Livvy said. "Bridget says you can take one of the old Sherlock Holmes books from the library and *keep* it."

Ty's face lit up. "Which one?"

"Whichever you want. Your choice. Just hurry up; we're going to leave as soon as we can, Magnus said."

Ty bounded to the door, seemed to remember Kit, and swung back around. "We can talk more later," he said, and darted off down the hallway.

"Only one book! *One!*" Livvy called after him with a laugh. "Ouch!" She reached up to fiddle with something at the back of her neck, her face crinkled in annoyance. "My necklace is caught on my hair—"

Kit reached up to untangle the thin gold chain. A locket dangled from it, kissing the hollow of her throat. Up close, she smelled like orange blossoms.

Their faces were very close together, and the pale curve of her mouth was near his. Her lips were light rose pink. Confusion stirred in Kit.

But it was Livvy who shook her head. "We shouldn't, Kit. No more kissing. I mean, we only did it once anyway. But I don't think that's how we're meant to be."

The necklace came free. Kit drew his hands away quickly, confused.

"Why?" he asked. "Did I do something wrong?"

"Not even a little." She looked at him for a moment with her wise and thoughtful eyes; there was a soft happiness in Livvy that drew Kit, but not in a romantic way. She was right, and he knew it. "Everything's great. Ty even says he thinks we should be *parabatai*, after all this is cleared up." Her face glowed. "I hope you'll come to the ceremony. And you'll always be my friend, right?"

"Of course," he said, and only later did he stop to think that she had said *my friend*, and not *our friend*, hers and Ty's. Right now he was just relieved that he didn't feel hurt or bothered by her decision. He felt instead a pleasant anticipation of getting through this Council meeting and going home—back to Los Angeles—where he could start his training and have the twins to help him through the rough parts. "Friends always."

Julian felt a twist of apprehension in his stomach as he entered the library. Part of him half-expected Annabel to have vanished, or to be drifting around the stacks of books like a long-haired ghost in a horror movie. He'd seen one once where the ghost of a girl had crawled out of a well, her pale face hidden behind masses of wet, dark hair. The memory gave him shivers even now.

The library was well illuminated by its rows of green banker's lamps. Annabel sat at the longest table, the Black Volume in front of her, her hands clasped in her lap. Her hair was long and dark, and half-hid her face, but it wasn't wet and there wasn't anything obviously uncanny about her. She looked—ordinary.

He sat down across from her. Magnus must have brought her something to wear from the storage room: She was in a very plain blue dress, a little short in the sleeves. Jules guessed she had been around nineteen when she died, maybe twenty.

"That was quite a trick you pulled," he said, "with the note in the church. And the demon."

"I didn't expect you to burn the church down." That pronounced accent was back in her voice, the strangeness of a way of speaking long outdated now. "You surprised me."

"And you've surprised me, coming here," Julian said. "And saying you'd only talk to me. You don't even like me, I thought."

"I came because of this." She drew the folded paper from the book and held it out to him. Her fingers were long, the joints strangely misshapen. He realized he was looking at evidence that her fingers had been broken, more than once, and that the bones had knit back together oddly. The visible remnants of torture. He felt a little sick as he took the letter and opened it.

> To: Annabel Blackthorn
>
> Annabel,
>   You might not know me, but we are related. My name is Tiberius Blackthorn.
>   My family and I are looking for the Black Volume of the Dead. We know you have it, because my brother Julian saw you take it from Malcolm Fade.
>   I'm not blaming you. Malcolm Fade is not our friend. He tried to hurt our family, to destroy us if he could. He's a monster. But the thing is, we need the book now. We need it so that we can save our family. We're a good family. You

*would like us if you knew us. There's me—I'm going to be
a detective. There is Livvy, my twin, who can fence, and
Drusilla, who loves everything scary, and Tavvy, who likes
stories read to him. There is Mark, who is part faerie. He's
an excellent cook. There is Helen, who was exiled to guard
the wards, but not because she did anything wrong. And
Emma, who isn't strictly a Blackthorn but is like our extra
sister anyway.*

 *And there is Jules. You might like him the best. He is the
one who takes care of us all. He is the reason we're all okay
and still together. I don't think he knows we know that, but
we do. Sometimes he might tell us what to do or not listen,
but he would do anything for any of us. People say we're
unlucky because we don't have parents. But I think they're
unlucky because they don't have a brother like mine.*

Julian had to stop there. The pressure behind his eyes had built
to a shattering intensity. He wanted to put his head down on the
table and burst into unmanly, undignified tears—for the boy he
had been, scared and terrified and twelve years old, looking at his
younger brothers and sisters and thinking, *They're mine now.*

For them, their faith in him, their expectation his love would be
unconditional, that he wouldn't need to be told he was loved back
because of course he was. Ty thought this about him and probably
thought it was obvious. But he had never guessed.

He forced himself to stay silent, to keep his face expressionless.
He laid the letter down on the table so that the shaking of his hand
was less visible. There was only a little writing left.

 *Don't think I'm asking you to do us a favor for nothing
in return. Julian can help you. He can help anyone.
You can't want to be running and hiding. I know what*

happened to you, what the Clave and Council did. Things
are different now. Let us explain. Let us show you how you
don't have to be exiled or alone. You don't have to give us
the book. We just want to help.

We're at the London Institute. Whenever you want to
come, you'd be welcome.

Yours,

Tiberius Nero Blackthorn

"How does he know what happened to me?" Annabel didn't sound angry, only curious. "What the Inquisitor and the others did to me?"

Julian got to his feet and went across the room to where the *aletheia* crystal rested on a bookcase. He brought it back and gave it to her. "Ty found this in Blackthorn Hall," he said. "These are someone's memories of your—trials—in the Council chamber."

Annabel raised the crystal to eye level. Julian had never seen the expression of someone looking into an *aletheia* crystal before. Her eyes widened, tracking back and forth as she gazed at the scene moving before her. Her cheeks flushed, her lips shook. Her hand began to jerk uncontrollably, and she flung the crystal away from her; it hit the table, denting the wood without breaking.

"Oh God, is there to be no mercy?" she said in an empty voice. "Will there never be any mercy or forgetfulness?"

"Not while this is still an injustice." Julian's heart was beating hard, but he knew he showed no outward signs of agitation. "It will always hurt as long as they haven't recompensed you for what they did."

She raised her eyes to his. "What do you mean?"

"Come with me to Idris," Julian said. "Testify in front of the Council. And I will see to it that you get justice."

She turned pale and swayed slightly. Julian half-rose from his chair. He reached for her and stopped; maybe she wouldn't want to be touched.

And there was some part of him that didn't want to touch her. He'd seen her when she was a skeleton held together with a fragile cobwebbing of yellowed skin and tendon. She looked real and solid and alive now, but he couldn't help but feel his hand would pass through her skin and strike crumbling bone beneath.

He drew his hand back.

"You cannot offer me justice," she said. "You cannot offer me anything I want."

Julian felt cold all over, but he could not deny the excitement sparking through his nerves. He saw the plan, suddenly, in front of him, the strategy of it, and the excitement of that overrode even the chill of the razor's edge he was walking.

"I never told anyone you were in Cornwall," he said. "Even after the church. I kept your secret. You can trust me."

She looked at him with wide eyes. This was why he had done it, Julian thought. He had kept this information to himself as possible leverage, even when he hadn't known for sure that there would ever be a moment he could use it. Emma's voice whispered in his head.

Julian, you scared me a little.

"I wanted to show you something," Julian said, and drew from his jacket a rolled-up paper. He handed it across the table to Annabel.

It was a drawing he had done of Emma, on Chapel Cliff, the sea breaking under her feet. He had been pleased with the way he had captured the wistful look on her face, the sea thick as paint below her, the weak sun gray-gold on her hair.

"Emma Carstairs. My *parabatai*," said Julian.

Annabel raised grave eyes. "Malcolm spoke of her. He said she was stubborn. He spoke of all of you. Malcolm was afraid of you."

Julian was stunned. "Why?"

"He said what Tiberius said. He said you would do anything for your family."

You have a ruthless heart. Julian pushed away the words Kieran had said to him. He couldn't be distracted. This was too important. "What else can you tell from the picture?" he said.

"That you love her," said Annabel. "With all of your soul."

There was nothing suspicious in her gaze; *parabatai* were meant to love each other. Julian could see the prize, the solution. Kieran's testimony was one piece of the puzzle. It would help them. But the Cohort would object to it, to any alliance with faeries. Annabel was the key to destroying the Cohort and ensuring the safety of the Black-thorns. Julian could see the image of his family safe, Aline and Helen returned, in front of him like a shimmering city on a hill. He went toward it, thinking of nothing else. "I saw your sketches and paint-ings," he said. "I could tell from them what you loved."

"Malcolm?" she said, with her eyebrows raised. "But that was a long time ago."

"Not Malcolm. Blackthorn Manor. The one in Idris. Where you lived when you were a child. All your drawings of it were *alive*. Like you could see it in your mind. Touch it with your hand. Be there in your heart."

She laid his sketch down on the table. She was silent.

"You could get that back," he said. "The manor house, all of it. I know why you ran. You expected that if the Clave caught you, they'd punish you, hurt you again. But I can promise you they won't. They're not perfect, they're far from perfect, but this is a new Clave and Council. Downworlders sit on our Council."

Her eyes flew open. "Magnus said that, but I didn't believe him."

"It's true. Marriage between a Downworlder and a Shadowhunter isn't illegal anymore. If we bring you before the Clave, they won't just not hurt you—you'll be reinstated. You'll be a Shadowhunter again. You could live in Blackthorn Manor. We'd give it to you."

"Why?" She rose to her feet and began to pace. "Why would you do all that for me? For the book? Because I will not give it to you."

"Because I need you to stand up in front of the Council and say that you killed Malcolm," he told her. She had left the Black Volume on the table before him. She was still pacing, not looking at him. Recalling Magnus's warning—*under no circumstances should you try to take the Black Volume from her, even if she isn't holding it*—Julian opened it cautiously, peered at a page of cramped, unreadable lettering. An idea was beginning to unfurl inside his mind, like a cautious flower. He reached into his pocket.

"That I killed Malcolm?" She spun to stare at him. He had his phone out, but he suspected it meant nothing to her—she'd probably seen mundanes wandering around with cell phones, but she'd never think of it as a camera. In fact, a camera wouldn't mean anything to her either.

"Yes," he said. "Believe me, you'll be hailed as a hero."

She'd begun pacing again. Julian's shoulders ached. The position he was in, both hands occupied and leaning forward, was an awkward one. But if this worked, it would be more than worth the pain.

"There is someone who is lying," he said. "Taking credit for Malcolm's death. She is doing it so that she can get control of an Institute. *Our* Institute." He took a deep breath. "Her name is Zara Dearborn."

The name electrified her, as he had suspected it would. "Dearborn," she breathed.

"The Inquisitor who tortured you," said Julian. "His descendants are no better. They will all be there now, carrying their signs shaming Downworlders, shaming those who stand up to the Clave. They would bring an awful darkness down on us. But you can prove them liars. Discredit them."

"Surely you could tell them the truth—"

"Not without revealing how I know. I saw you kill Malcolm in the Seelie Queen's scrying glass. I'm telling you this because I am desperate—if you heard Malcolm speaking of the Cold Peace, you must know contact with faeries is forbidden. What I did would be considered treason. I'd take the punishment for it, but—"

"Your brothers and sisters couldn't bear that," she finished for him. She turned back toward him just as he leaned away from the book. Were her eyes more like Livvy's or Dru's? They were blue-green and depthless. "I see things have not changed as much as all that. The Law is still hard, and is still the Law."

Julian could hear the hate in her voice, and knew he had her.

"But the Law can be circumvented." He leaned across the table. "We can trick them. And shame them. Force them to confront their lies. The Dearborns will pay. They'll all be there—the Consul, the Inquisitor, all those who have inherited the power that was abused when they hurt you."

Her eyes glittered. "You will make them acknowledge it? What they did?"

"Yes."

"And in return—?"

"Your testimony," he said. "That's all."

"You wish me to come to Idris with you. To stand before the Clave and Council, and the Inquisitor, as I did before?"

Julian nodded.

"And if they call me mad, if they declare I am lying, or under Malcolm's duress, you will stand for me? You will insist I am sane?"

"Magnus will be with you every step of the way," Julian said. "He can stand beside you on the dais. He can protect you. He is the warlock representative on the Council, and you know how powerful he is. You can trust him even if you don't trust me."

It was not a real answer, but she took it for one. Julian had known she would.

"I do trust you," she said with wonder. She came forward and picked up the Black Volume, hugging it to her chest. "Because of your brother's letter. It was honest. I had not thought of an honest Blackthorn before. But I could hear the truth in how he loves you. You must be worthy of such love and trust, to have inspired it in one so truthful." Her eyes bored into him. "I know what you want—what you need. And yet now that I have come to you, you have not once asked for it. That should count for something. Though you failed my trial, I understand it now. You were acting for your family." He could see her swallow, the muscles moving in her thin, scarred throat. "You swear that if the Black Volume is given to you, you will keep it hidden from the Lord of Shadows? You will use it only to help your family?"

"I swear on the Angel," said Julian. He knew how powerful an oath on the Angel was, and Annabel would know it too. But he was speaking only the truth, after all.

His heart was beating in swift and powerful hammer-blows. He was blinded by the light of what he could imagine, what the Queen could do for them if they gave her the Black Volume: *Helen, Helen could come back, and Aline, and the Cold Peace could end.*

And the Queen knows. She knows . . .

He forced the thought back. He could hear Emma's voice, a whisper in the back of his mind. A warning. But Emma was good in her heart: honest, straightforward, a terrible liar. She didn't understand the brutality of need. The absoluteness of what he would do for his family. There was no end to its depth and breadth. It was total.

"Very well," Annabel said. Her voice was strong, forceful: He could hear the unbreakable cliffs of Cornwall in her accent. "I will come with you to the City of Glass and speak before the Council. And if I am acknowledged, then the Black Volume will be yours."

29

ULTIMA THULE

The sun was shining in Alicante.

The first time Emma had been in Idris, it had been winter, cold as death, and there had been death all around—her parents had just been killed, and the Dark War had ravaged the city. They hadn't been able to burn the bodies of Shadowhunters killed in the streets fast enough, and the corpses had stacked up in the Hall like discarded children's toys.

"Emma." Julian was pacing the long corridor in the Gard, lined with doors, each leading to the office of a different official. Alternating between the doors were windows letting in the bright light of late summer, and tapestries depicting significant events in Shadowhunter history. Most had small woven banners across the tops, describing what they were: THE BATTLE OF THE BUND, VALENTINE'S LAST STAND, THE PARIS ENGAGEMENT, THE UPRISING. "Do you remember . . . ?"

She did remember. They'd stood in this exact place five years ago, listening to Lucian Graymark and Jia Penhallow discuss the exile of Mark and Helen, before Emma had thrown open the door to shout at them. It was one of the few times she'd seen Julian lose control. She could hear his voice in her head, even now. *You promised the Clave would never abandon Mark while he was living—you promised!*

"Like I could forget," she said. "This is where we told the Consul we wanted to be *parabatai*."

Julian touched her hand with his. It was only a brush of fingers—they were both conscious anyone could come down the corridor at any moment.

Getting to Alicante had been difficult—Magnus had managed the Portal, though it seemed to have taken the last of his energy in a way that frightened Emma. He had been kneeling by the time the familiar swirling lights had formed, and he'd had to lean on Mark and Julian to rise.

Still he had brushed off all concerns and informed them that they needed to go through the Portal quickly. Idris was warded and Portaling there was a complex business, since someone had to be on the other side to receive you. It was doubly complex now since Kieran was with them, and though Jia had waived the anti-Faerie protections on the Gard temporarily, the window for safe travel was short.

Then the Portal had terrified Annabel.

She had never seen one before, and despite everything she had been through, despite all the awful magic she had seen Malcolm wreak, the sight of the whirling chaos inside the doorway made her scream.

In the end, after the Shadowhunters had all entered the Portal, she went through with Magnus, clutching the Black Volume in her hands, her face hidden against his shoulder.

Only to be met on the other side by a crowd of Council members and the Consul herself. Jia had blanched when she saw Annabel and said in an astonished voice, "Is that really her?"

Magnus had locked eyes with the Consul for a moment. "Yes," he said firmly. "It is. *She* is."

There was a babble of questions. Emma couldn't blame the assembled Council members. There had been quite a few questions for Julian when he'd emerged from the library and told a waiting

Magnus and Emma that Annabel was coming with them to Idris.

As he'd outlined his plan, Emma had caught sight of the expression on Magnus's face. The warlock had looked at Julian with a mixture of astonishment, respect, and something that might have looked a little like horror.

But it had probably just been surprise. After all, Magnus had seemed sanguine enough, and had immediately set about sending a fire-message to Jia to let her know what to expect.

Emma had drawn Julian aside while blue sparks flew from Magnus's fingers. "What about the book?" she'd whispered. "What about the Queen?"

Julian's eyes glittered. "If this works, Annabel will give us the Black Volume," he'd replied in a whisper, and he'd been looking at the library door as if Annabel, behind it, were the answer to all their prayers. "And if not—I have a plan for that, too."

There'd been no chance to ask him what the plan was: Annabel had stepped out of the library, looking fearful and shy. She looked even more fearful now as the hubbub rose around her: Kieran drew some of the fire by stepping up to announce himself as the envoy of the Seelie Queen, sent to speak on the behalf of the Seelie Court to the Council of Shadowhunters. He'd been expected, but there was still a burst of more excited talking.

"Put the wards back up," said the Consul, inclining her head to Kieran. Her expression was polite, but the message was clear: Though Kieran was there to help them, all full-blood faeries were still going to be treated with extreme suspicion by the Clave.

Mark and Cristina moved to Kieran's side protectively, while Magnus spoke quietly with the Consul. After a moment, she nodded, and gestured at Emma and Julian.

"If you want to speak to Robert, go ahead," she said. "But keep it short—the meeting is soon."

Emma was unsurprised, as she and Julian headed toward the

Gard's offices, to see that Livvy, Ty, Kit, and Dru had flanked Annabel protectively. Ty, especially, had his chin jutting out, his hands in fists. Emma wondered if he felt responsible for Annabel because his letter had brought her to them, or if he felt some kind of kinship for those at odds with the Clave's standards for "normalcy."

A door swung open. "You can come in now," said a guard. It was Manuel Villalobos, wearing his Centurion uniform. His start of surprise at seeing them was quickly hidden by a smirk. "An unexpected pleasure," he said.

"We're not here to see you," said Julian. "Though nice to know you're opening doors for the Inquisitor these days. Is he here?"

"Let them in, Centurion," Robert called, which was all the permission needed for Emma to shove by Manuel and stalk down the hallway. Julian followed her.

The short hall ended in the Inquisitor's office. He was sitting behind his desk, looking much the same as he had the last time Emma had seen him at the Los Angeles Institute. A big man only now beginning to show the marks of age—his shoulders were a little hunched, his dark hair woven thickly with gray—Robert Lightwood cut an imposing figure behind his massive mahogany desk.

The room was largely unfurnished aside from the desk and two chairs. There was an unlit fireplace, above whose mantel hung one of the series of tapestries on display in the hall outside. This one said THE BATTLE OF THE BURREN. Figures in red clashed with figures in black—Shadowhunters and the Endarkened Ones—and above the melee, a dark-haired archer was visible standing on a tipped boulder, holding a drawn bow and arrow. To anyone who knew him, it was very clearly Alec Lightwood.

Emma wondered what thoughts went through Robert Lightwood's mind as he sat each day in his office and looked at the portrait of his son, a hero of a now-famous battle. Pride, of course, but there must also be some wonder, that he had created this person—these people, really, for Isabelle Lightwood was no slouch in the heroics department—who had become so fierce and amazing in their own right.

Someday Julian would have that pride, she thought, in Livvy and Ty and Tavvy and Dru. But her parents had never had a chance to feel it. She'd never had a chance to make them proud. She felt the familiar wave of bitterness and resentment, pressing against her heart.

Robert gestured for them to be seated. "I hear you wanted to talk to me," he said. "I hope this isn't meant to be some sort of distraction."

"Distraction from what?" Emma asked, settling herself into the uncomfortable wing-backed chair.

"Whatever you're up to." He sat back. "So what is it?"

Emma's heart seemed to flip. Was this a good idea, or a terrible one? It felt as if everything in her had been armoring against this moment, against the idea that she and Julian would have to spread their feelings out under the feet of the Clave for them to tread on.

She watched Julian as he leaned forward and began to speak. He seemed absolutely calm as he spoke of his and Emma's early friendship, their affection for each other, their decision to be *parabatai*, brought on by the Dark War and the loss of their parents. He made it sound like a reasonable decision—no one's fault—who could have blamed them, any of them? The Dark War had stricken them all with loss. No one could be at fault for overlooking details. For mistaking their feelings.

Robert Lightwood's eyes began to widen. He listened in silence as Julian spoke of his and Emma's growing feelings for each other. How they both had realized what they felt separately, struggled in silence, confessed their emotions, and finally decided to seek the Inquisitor's assistance and even the exercise of the Law.

"We know we've broken the Law," Julian finished, "but it was not intentional, or under our control. All we want is your help."

Robert Lightwood got to his feet. Emma could see the glass towers through his window, glimmering like burning banners. She could hardly believe that just that morning they'd been fighting the Riders in the courtyard of the London Institute. "No one's ever asked me if they could be exiled before," he said, finally.

"But you were exiled yourself, once," said Julian.

"Yes," Robert said. "With my wife, Maryse, and Alec, when he was a toddler. And for good reason. It's a lonely thing, exile. And for someone as young as Emma . . ." He glanced at them. "Does anyone else know about you?"

"No." Julian's voice was calm and firm. Emma knew he was trying to protect those who had guessed or been told—but it unnerved her anyway, the way he could sound so absolutely sincere when he was lying.

"And you're sure? This isn't a crush, or just—*parabatai* feelings can be very intense." Robert sounded awkward as he clasped his hands behind his back. "They're easy to misconstrue."

"We," said Julian, "are absolutely sure."

"The usual measure would be separation, not exile." Robert looked from one of them to the other as if he still couldn't quite believe what was in front of him. "But you don't want that. I can see that already. You wouldn't have come to me if you thought I could only offer you the standard measures—separation, stripping of your Marks."

"We can't risk breaking the Law, and the punishments that entails." Julian's voice was still calm, but Emma could see his hands, white-knuckled, gripping his chair arms. "My family needs me. My brothers and sisters are still young, and they have no parents. I've raised them and I can't leave them. It's out of the question. But Emma and I know we can't trust ourselves just to stay away from each other."

"So you want to be separated by the Clave," said Robert. "You want exile, but you don't want to wait to be caught. You've come to me so you can choose which of you leaves, and for how long, and what punishment the Clave, directed by me, will decide on."

"Yes," said Julian.

"And though you're not saying it, I think you want some of what exile will do for you," said Robert. "It'll deaden your bond. Maybe you think it'll make it easier for you to stop loving each other."

Neither Emma or Julian spoke. He was uncomfortably close to the truth. Julian was expressionless; Emma tried to school her features to match his. Robert was tapping his fingertips together.

"We just want to be able to be normal *parabatai*," said Julian finally, but Emma could hear the silent words beneath the audible ones: *We will never give each other up, never.*

"It's quite something to ask." Emma strained to hear anger or reproach or disbelief in the Inquisitor's voice, but he sounded neutral. It frightened her.

"You had a *parabatai*," she said in desperation. "Didn't you?"

"Michael Wayland." Robert's tone was wintry. "He died."

"I'm so sorry." Emma had known that, but the sympathy was sincere. She could imagine little more horrible than Julian dying.

"I bet he would have wanted you to help us," Julian said. Emma had no idea if he spoke from knowledge of Michael Wayland or just intuition, that skill he had of reading the look in people's eyes, the truth in the way they frowned or smiled.

"Michael would have—yes," Robert murmured. "He would have. By the Angel. Exile will be a heavy burden for Emma. I can try to limit the terms of the punishment, but you'll still lose some of your Nephilim powers. You'll need permission to enter Alicante. There will be some Marks you can't use. Seraph blades won't light for you."

"I have Cortana," said Emma. "That's all I need."

There was sadness in Robert's smile. "If there's a war, you can't fight in it. That's why my exile was lifted—because Valentine returned and began the Mortal War."

Julian's expression was so tight that his cheekbones seemed to stand out like knife blades. "We won't accept the exile unless Emma's allowed to keep enough of her Nephilim power to be safe," he said. "If she's hurt because of this exile—"

"The exile is your idea," said Robert. "Are you sure you'll be able to fall out of love?"

"Yes," Julian lied. "Separation would be the first move, anyway, wouldn't it? We're just asking for a little extra surety."

"I've heard things," Robert said. "The Law against *parabatai* falling in love exists for a reason. I don't know the reason, but my guess is that it's significant. If I thought you knew what it was—" He shook his head. "But you can't possibly. I could speak with the Silent Brothers. . . ."

No, Emma thought. They'd risked so much already, but if Robert learned of the curse, they'd be in very dangerous waters. "Magnus said you would help us," she said, in a soft voice. "He said we could trust you and that you'd understand and keep it secret."

Robert looked up at the tapestry that hung over his mantel. At Alec. He touched the Lightwood ring on his finger; a likely unconscious gesture. "I trust Magnus," he said. "And I owe him a great deal."

His gaze was distant. Emma wasn't sure if he was thinking about the past or considering the future; she and Julian sat tensely while he considered. Finally, he said, "All right. Give me a few days—the two of you will have to remain in Alicante while I look into managing the exile ceremony, and you must stay in separate houses. I need to see a good faith effort to avoid each other. Is that clear?"

Emma swallowed hard. The exile ceremony. She hoped Jem could be there: Silent Brothers were the ones who presided over ceremonies, and even though he no longer was one, he had been at her *parabatai* ceremony with Julian. If he could be there for this, she would feel a little less alone.

She could see Julian's expression: He looked much as she felt, as if relief and dread were warring inside him. "Thank you," he said.

"Thank you, Inquisitor," she echoed, and Robert looked surprised. She suspected no one had ever thanked him for a sentence of exile before.

Cristina had never been in the Gard's Council Hall before. It was a horseshoe-shaped space, rows of benches marching toward a slightly raised dais; a second balcony level, containing more benches and seats, rose high above. Above the dais hung a huge golden clock, gorgeously made with delicate scrollwork and a repeated Latin phrase, ULTIMA THULE, marching around the rim. Behind the dais was an incredible wall of windows, giving out onto a view of Alicante below. She raised herself a little bit on tiptoe, to see the winding streets, the blue slashes of the canals, the demon towers rising like clear needles against the sky.

The Hall was beginning to fill. Annabel and Kieran had been taken to a waiting room, along with Magnus. The rest of them had been allowed in early and had claimed two rows of benches near the front. Ty, Kit, and Livvy were sitting, engaged in conversation. Dru sat quietly on her own, seeming lost in thought. Cristina was about to start toward her when she felt a light tap on her shoulder.

It was Mark. He had dressed carefully for the Council visit, and she felt a pang as she looked at him—he was so gorgeous in his pressed, old-fashioned clothes, like a marvelously colored old photograph. The dark jacket and waistcoat fit him well, and he had brushed his blond hair so that it covered the tips of his ears.

He had even shaved, and nicked himself slightly on the chin— which was ridiculous because Mark had no facial hair to speak of. He looked to Cristina like a little boy wanting to make a good impression on the first day of school. Her heart went out to him— he cared so much about the good opinion of a group of people who had agreed to abandon him to the Wild Hunt despite the pleas of his family, just because of who he was.

"Do you think Kieran will be all right?" Mark said. "They ought to treat an envoy from the Court with more honor. Instead they practically ran to put the wards back up as soon as we arrived."

"He'll be fine," Cristina reassured him. Both Kieran and Mark, she thought, were stronger than the other one could believe, maybe because they'd been so vulnerable in the Hunt. "Though I can't imagine Annabel is much of a conversationalist. At least Magnus is with them."

Mark gave a strained smile as a low murmur swept through the room. The Centurions had arrived in full dress. They wore their uniforms of red, gray, and silver, with their silver pins on display. Each carried a staff of solid *adamas*. Cristina recognized some from Los Angeles, like Zara's friend Samantha, with her thin, nasty face, and Rayan, looking around the room with an expression of concern.

Zara led the procession, her head held high, her mouth a slash of bright red. Her lips curled in distaste as she passed Mark and Cristina. But why wasn't Diego beside her? Had he not come with them? But no, there he was, almost at the end of the line, looking gray and tired, but definitely present.

He paused in front of Mark and Cristina as the other Centurions passed by. "I got your message," he said to Cristina, in a low voice. "If it's what you want—"

"What message?" Mark said. "What's going on?"

Zara appeared at Diego's side. "A reunion," she said. "How nice." She smiled at Cristina. "I'm sure you'll all be pleased to hear how well everything went in Los Angeles after you left."

"Very impressive of you, killing Malcolm," said Mark. His eyes were flat and glittering. "It seems to have resulted in quite a bit of advancement. Well-earned, I'm sure."

"Thank you." Zara laughed breathlessly, laying her hand on Diego's arm. "Oh," she said, with a sharply artificial enthusiasm. "Look!"

More Shadowhunters had entered the room. They were a mix of ages, from old to young. Some wore Centurion uniforms. Most wore gear or ordinary clothes. What was unusual about them was that they were carrying placards and signs. REGISTER ALL WARLOCKS. DOWNWORLDERS MUST BE CONTROLLED. PRAISE THE COLD PEACE. APPROVE THE REGISTRY. Among them was a stolid brown-haired man with a bland sort of face, the kind of face where you could never really remember the features later. He winked at Zara.

"My father," she said proudly. "The Registry was his idea."

"What *interesting* signs," said Mark.

"How wonderful to see people expressing their political views," said Zara. "Of course the Cold Peace has truly created a generation of revolutionaries."

"It is unusual," said Cristina, "for a revolution to call for fewer rights for people, not more."

For a moment Zara's mask slipped, and Cristina saw through the artifice of politeness, the breathy little-girl voice and demeanor. There was something cold behind it all, something without warmth or empathy or affection. "People," she said. "What people?"

Diego took hold of her arm. "Zara," he said. "Let's go sit down."

Mark and Cristina watched them go in silence.

"I hope Julian's right," Livvy said, staring at the empty dais.

"He usually is," Ty said. "Not about everything, but about this sort of thing."

Kit sat between the twins, which meant they were talking over him. He wasn't entirely sure how he'd ended up in this position.

Not that he minded or even noticed at the moment. He was stunned into near silence—something that never happened—by where he was: in Alicante, the heart of the Shadowhunters' country, gazing at the legendary demon towers.

He'd fallen in love with Idris at first sight. He hadn't expected that at all.

It was like walking into a fairy tale. And not the sort he'd grown used to at the Shadow Market, where faeries were another kind of monster. The kind he'd seen on TV and in books when he was little, a world of magnificent castles and lush forests.

Livvy winked at Kit. "You've got that look on your face."

"What look?"

"You're impressed by Idris. Admit it, Mr. Nothing Impresses Me."

Kit was going to do no such thing. "I like the clock," he said, pointing up at it.

"There's a legend about that clock." She wiggled her eyebrows at him. "For a second, when it chimes the hour, the gates to Heaven open." Livvy sighed; a rare wistfulness flashed across her face. "As far as I'm concerned, Heaven is just the Institute being ours again. And all of us going home."

That surprised Kit; he'd been thinking of this trip to Idris as the end of their chaotic adventure. They'd return to Los Angeles and he'd start his training. But Livvy was right: Things weren't that assured. He glanced over at Zara and her immediate circle, bristling with their ugly signs.

"There's still the Black Volume, too," said Ty. He looked formal and neat-haired in a way he didn't usually; Kit was used to him being casual in his hoodies and jeans, and handsome, older-looking Ty left him a bit tongue-tied. "The Queen still wants it."

"Annabel will give it to Jules. I believe in his ability to charm anything out of anyone," Livvy said. "Or trick anything out of anyone. But yeah, I wish they didn't have to actually meet with the

Queen afterwards. I don't like the sound of her."

"I think there's a saying about this," said Kit. "Something about bridges and crossing them when you get there."

Ty had gone rigid, like a hunting dog spotting a fox. "*Livvy.*"

His sister followed his gaze, and so did Kit. Coming toward them through the crowd was Diana, a smile breaking across her face, her koi fish tattoo shimmering across one dark cheekbone.

With her were two young women in their early twenties. One resembled Jia Penhallow more than a little; she also had dark hair and a decided chin. The other looked incredibly like Mark Blackthorn, down to the curling, pale blond hair and pointed ears. They were both bundled in unseasonably warm clothes, as if they'd come from a cold climate.

Kit realized who they were a moment before Livvy's face lit like the sun. "Helen!" she screamed, and bolted into her sister's arms.

The clock in the Council Hall was chiming through the Gard, signaling that all Nephilim were to gather for the meeting.

Robert Lightwood had insisted on leading Julian from his office to the room where Magnus, Kieran, and Annabel were waiting. Unfortunately for Emma, that meant she was stuck with Manuel as her escort to the Council Hall.

Emma had wished she could have a moment alone with Julian, but it wasn't going to happen. They exchanged a wry look before going their separate ways.

"Looking forward to the meeting?" Manuel asked. He had his hands in his pockets. His dirty-blond hair was artfully tousled. Emma was surprised he wasn't whistling.

"No one looks forward to meetings," said Emma. "They're a necessary evil."

"Oh, I wouldn't say *no one*," said Manuel. "Zara loves meetings."

"She seems in favor of all forms of torture," Emma muttered.

Manuel spun around, walking backward down the corridor. They were in one of the larger hallways that had been built after the Gard burned in the Dark War. "You ever thought about becoming a Centurion?" he said.

Emma shook her head. "They don't let you have a *parabatai*."

"I always figured that was kind of a pity thing, you and Julian Blackthorn," said Manuel. "I mean, look at you. You're hot, you're skilled, you're a Carstairs. Julian—he spends all his time with little kids. He's an old man at seventeen."

Emma wondered what would happen if she threw Manuel through a window. Probably it would delay the meeting.

"I'm just saying. Even if you don't want to go to the Scholomance, the Cohort could use someone like you. We're the future. You'll see." His eyes glittered. For a moment, they weren't amused or joking. It was the glitter of real fanaticism, and it made Emma feel hollow inside.

They had reached the doors of the Council Hall. There was no one in view; Emma kicked her leg out and swept Manuel's feet out from under him. He went over in a blur and hit the ground; he pushed up instantly on his elbows, looking furious. She doubted she'd hurt him, except maybe where his dignity was located—which had been the point.

"I appreciate your offer," she said, "but if joining the Cohort means I have to spend my life stuck halfway up a mountain with a bunch of fascists, I'll take living in the past."

She heard him hiss something not very nice in Spanish as she stepped over him and walked into the Hall. She reminded herself to ask Cristina for a translation when she got a chance.

"You don't need to be here, Julian," said Jia firmly.

They were in a massive room whose picture window gave out

onto views of Brocelind Forest. It was a surprisingly fancy room—Julian had always thought of the Gard as a place of dark stone and heavy wood. This room had brocade wallpaper and gilt furniture upholstered in velvet. Annabel sat in a wing-backed armchair, looking ill at ease. Magnus was leaning against a wall, seemingly bored. He looked exhausted, too—the shadows under his eyes were nearly black. And Kieran stood by the picture window, his attention fixed on the sky and the trees outside.

"I would like him to be with me," said Annabel. "He is the reason I came."

"We all appreciate that you're here, Annabel," said Jia. "And we appreciate that you had past bad experiences with the Clave." She sounded calm. Julian wondered if she'd have sounded so calm if she'd seen Annabel rise from the dead, covered in blood, and stab Malcolm through the heart.

Kieran turned away from the window. "We know Julian Blackthorn," he said to Jia. He sounded much more human to Julian than he had when they'd first met, as if his Faerie accent was fading. "We don't know you."

"By which you mean you and Annabel?" Jia said.

Kieran made an expressive faerie gesture that seemed to encompass the room in general. "I am here because I am the messenger of the Queen," he said. "Annabel Blackthorn is here for her own reasons. And Magnus is here as he puts up with all of you because of Alec. But do not think that makes it a good idea for you to order us around."

"Annabel is a Shadowhunter," Robert began.

"And I am a prince of Faerie," said Kieran. "Son of the King, Prince of the Frost Court, Keeper of the Cold Way, Wild Hunter, and Sword of the Host. Do not annoy me."

Magnus cleared his throat. "He has a point."

"About Alec?" said Robert, raising an eyebrow.

"More generally," said Magnus. "Kieran is a Downworlder. Annabel suffered a fate worse than death at the Clave's hands because she cared for Downworlders. Out there in the Council Hall is the Cohort. Today is their grab for power. Preventing them from taking it is more important than rules about where Julian should or shouldn't be standing."

Jia looked at Magnus for a moment. "And you?" she said, surprisingly gently. "You're a Downworlder, Bane."

Magnus gave a slow, tired shrug. "Oh," he said. "Me, I'm—"

The glass he was holding slipped out of his hand. It hit the floor and broke, and a moment later Magnus followed it. He seemed to fold up like paper, his head striking the stone with an ugly thump.

Julian lunged forward, but Robert had already grabbed him by the arm. "Go to the Council Hall," he said. Jia was kneeling next to Magnus, her hand on his shoulder. "Get Alec."

He turned Julian free, and Julian ran.

Emma fought her way through the Council Hall in a state of numb horror. Any pleasure she'd felt over knocking Manuel on his butt had dissolved. The whole room seemed to be a whirlwind of ugly shouting and waving signs: MAKE THE CLAVE PURE and WEREWOLF CONTAINMENT IS THE ANSWER and KEEP DOWNWORLDERS CONTROLLED.

She pushed past a knot of people, Zara at the center, heard someone saying, "Can't *believe* you had to kill that monster Malcolm Fade yourself, after the Clave failed!" There was a chorus of agreement. "Shows what comes of letting warlocks do what they like," said someone else. "They're too powerful. It doesn't make practical sense."

Most of the faces in the room were unfamiliar to Emma. She should have known more of them, she thought, but the Blackthorns had lived a life of isolation in their way, rarely leaving the L.A. Institute.

Among the cluster of unfamiliar faces, she caught sight of Diana, tall and regal as always. She was striding through the crowd, and hurrying along in her wake were two familiar figures. Aline and Helen, both of them pink-cheeked, wrapped in massive coats and shawls. They must have just arrived from Wrangel Island.

Now Emma could see the rest of the Blackthorns—Livvy, Ty, and Dru were spilling out of the seats, running to Helen, who bent down to open her arms and gather them all in, hugging them tightly.

Helen was brushing back Dru's hair, hugging the twins, tears sliding down her face. Mark was there too, striding toward his sister, and Emma watched with a smile as they threw their arms around each other. In a way, it hurt—she would never have that with her parents, never hug them or squeeze their hands again—but it was a good sort of pain. Mark lifted his sister off her feet, and Aline watched smiling as the two embraced.

"Manuel Villalobos is limping," said Cristina. She had come up behind Emma and wrapped her arms around her from behind, resting her chin on her friend's shoulder. "Did you do that?"

"I might have," Emma murmured. She heard Cristina giggle. "He was trying to talk me into joining the Cohort."

She turned around and squeezed Cristina's hand. "We're going to take them down. They won't win. Right?" She glanced at Cristina's pendant. "Tell me the Angel is on our side."

Cristina shook her head. "I am worried," she said. "Worried for Mark, for Helen—and for Kieran."

"Kieran's a witness for the Clave. The Cohort can't touch him."

"He's a prince of Faerie. Everything they hate. And I do not think I realized, until we arrived here, how *much* they hate. They will not want him to speak, and they will absolutely not want the Council to listen."

"That's why we're here to make them listen," Emma began, but Cristina was looking past her, a startled expression on her face.

Emma turned to see Diego, miraculously without Zara, beckoning to Cristina from an empty row of seats.

"I must go and talk to him," Cristina said. She squeezed Emma's shoulder, looking suddenly hopeful. Emma wished her luck and Cristina disappeared into the crowd, leaving Emma looking around for Julian.

She didn't see her *parabatai* anywhere. But what she did see was a tight group of Shadowhunters, Mark among them, and the sudden silver flash of weapons. Samantha Larkspear had pulled a wicked-looking blade. Emma headed toward the raised voices, her hand already reaching for Cortana's hilt.

Mark loved all his brothers and sisters, none more than the others. Still, Helen was special. She was *like him*—half-faerie, drawn to its temptations. Helen even claimed she could remember their mother, Nerissa, though Mark couldn't.

He set Helen down on her feet, ruffling her pale hair. Her face—she looked different, older. Not in lines around her eyes or coarsening skin, just in a certain cast of her features. He wondered if she had named the stars through the years, as he did: *Julian, Tiberius, Livia, Drusilla, Octavian.* And she would have added another, that he never had: *Mark.*

"I would speak to you," he said. "Of Nene, our mother's sister."

An echo of faerie formality was in her voice when she replied. "Diana told me you met her in Faerie. I knew of her, but not where she could be found. We should speak of her, and of other matters as pressing." She looked up at him and sighed, touching her hand to his cheek. "Such as when you got so tall."

"I think it happened when I was in the Hunt. Should I apologize?"

"Not at all. I was worried—" She stepped back to look at him quizzically. "I think I may owe Kieran Kingson some thanks for his care of you."

"As I owe Aline, for her care of you."

Helen smiled at that. "She is the light of my days." She glanced up at the large clock over the dais. "We have little time now, Mark. If all goes as we hope, we will have forever to confer with one another. But either way, Aline and I will remain this night in Alicante, and from what Jia says, so will you. It will give us a chance to talk."

"That depends how tonight goes, doesn't it?" A sharp voice interrupted them. It was Samantha Larkspear. Mark vaguely remembered that she had a brother who looked a great deal like her.

She wore Centurion gear and carried a placard that said THE ONLY GOOD FAERIE IS A DEAD FAERIE. There was a blob of what looked like black paint at the bottom of the sign.

"Pithy," Mark said. But Helen had paled with shock, staring at the words on the placard.

"After this afternoon's vote, if scum like you are allowed in Alicante, I'd be very surprised," Samantha said. "Enjoy it while you can."

"You're talking to the wife of the Consul's daughter," said Aline, her nostrils flaring. "Watch your mouth, Samantha Larkspear."

Samantha made an odd, gulping, hissing noise, and reached for her weapons belt, flashing a dagger with a thick knuckle-guard hilt. Mark could see her brother, pale and black-haired as she was, pushing toward them through the crowd. Helen had her hand on the seraph blade in her belt. Moving instinctively, Mark reached for the blade at his own hip, tensed for violence.

Kit looked up when Julian's hand fell on his shoulder.

He'd been slouching in his chair, mostly looking at Alicante through the big glass window behind the wooden stagelike thing at the front of the room. He'd been deliberately not looking at Livvy and Ty greeting their sister. Something about the tight knot of Blackthorns hugging and exclaiming over each other reminded him exactly how much he wasn't one of them in a way he hadn't been reminded since Los Angeles.

"Your sister's here," he said to Julian. He pointed. "Helen."

Julian glanced over at his siblings briefly; Kit had the feeling he already knew. He looked tense and sparking at the edges, like snapped electrical wire.

"I need you to do something," he said. "Alec's guarding the east doors to the Hall. Go find him and bring him to Magnus. Tell him Magnus is in the Consul's guest quarters; he'll know where that is."

Kit swung his legs off the chair in front of him. "Why?"

"Just trust me." Julian stood up. "Make it look like it's your idea, like you need Alec to show you something or help you find someone. I don't want anyone's curiosity stirred up."

"You're not *really* thinking about fighting in the middle of the Council Hall, are you?" said Emma. "I mean, considering that would be illegal and all that." She clicked her tongue against her teeth. "Not a good idea, Samantha. Put that dagger away."

The small group—Helen, Aline, Mark, and Samantha—turned to stare at Emma as if she'd appeared in a puff of smoke. They'd all been too angry to notice her approach.

The gold clock overhead began to chime urgently. The crowd started to unknot itself, Shadowhunters searching for empty seats in the rows facing the dais. Dane Larkspear, who'd been coming toward his sister, had halted in the middle of an aisle; Emma saw to her surprise that Manuel was blocking his way.

Maybe Manuel didn't think a Centurion brawling on the floor of the Council Hall would be a great idea either. Zara was looking over too, her red mouth set in an angry line.

"You don't get to pull rank on me, Aline Penhallow," said Samantha, but she shoved her dagger back into its sheath. "Not when you're married to that—that *thing*."

"Did you draw that?" Emma interrupted, pointing at the blobby sketch on Samantha's placard. "Is that supposed to be a dead faerie?"

She was pretty sure it was. The sketch had arms and legs and dragonfly wings, sort of.

"Impressive," said Emma. "You've got talent, Samantha. Real talent."

Samantha looked surprised. "You think so?"

"God, no," said Emma. "Now go and sit down. Zara's waving at you."

Samantha hesitated and then turned away. Emma grabbed hold of Helen's hand. She started to walk toward the long bench where the Blackthorns were seated. Her heart was thumping. Not that Samantha was much danger, but if they'd started something, and the rest of Zara's friends had joined in, it could have been a real fight.

Aline and Mark were on either side of them. Helen's fingers curled around Emma's arm. "I remember this," she said in a low voice. Her fingertips brushed the scar that Cortana had made years ago, when Emma had clutched the blade to her body after her parents' death.

It was Helen who had been there when Emma woke up in a world where her parents were gone forever, though it was Julian who had placed the sword in Emma's arms.

But now Cortana was strapped to her back. Now was their chance to right the wrongs of the past—the wrongs done to Helen and Mark and those like them by the Clave, the wrong the Clave had done to the Carstairs in ignoring their deaths. It made the knowledge that she would soon be exiled hurt even more, the thought that she would not be with the Blackthorns when they were reunited.

They sped up as they got close to the other Blackthorns, and there was Julian, standing among his siblings. His eyes met Emma's. She could see even across the distance between them that his had turned nearly black.

She knew without having to ask: Something was very wrong.

* * *

Alec Lightwood was very hard to keep up with. He was older than Kit, and he had longer legs, and he'd taken off flat-out running the moment Kit told him that Magnus needed him.

Kit wasn't sure their cover story that he wanted Alec to show him around the Gard was going to hold up if anyone stopped them. But no one did; the loud chiming was still sounding, and everyone was hurrying toward the main Council Hall.

When they burst into the high-ceilinged Consul's quarters, they found Magnus lying on a long sofa. Kieran and Annabel were at opposite ends of the room, staring like cats just introduced to a new environment.

Jia and Robert stood by the sofa; Alec started toward it, and his father moved to put a hand on his shoulder.

Alec stopped where he was, his whole body tense. "Let me go," he said.

"He's fine," said Robert. "Brother Enoch was just here. His magic's depleted and he's weak, but—"

"I know what's wrong with him," Alec said, pushing past the Inquisitor. Robert watched his son as Alec knelt down by the side of the long couch. He brushed Magnus's hair back from his forehead, and the warlock stirred and murmured.

"He hasn't been well for a while," said Alec, half to himself. "His magic gets depleted so fast. I told him to go to the Spiral Labyrinth, but there hasn't been time."

Kit stared. He'd heard of Magnus even before he'd met him, of course; Magnus was famous in Downworld. And when he had met Magnus, the warlock had been so full of kinetic energy, a whirl of dry wit and blue fire. It hadn't even occurred to him that Magnus might get sick or tired.

"Isn't there any way to make him better?" said Annabel. She was vibrating with tension, her hands working at her sides. He noticed for the first time that she was missing a finger on her right hand. He hadn't looked at her too closely before. She gave him the creeps. "I—I need him."

Admirably, Alec didn't lose his temper. "He needs rest," he said. "We could delay the meeting—"

"Alec, we can't." Jia spoke gently. "Obviously Magnus should rest. Annabel, you'll be taken care of. I promise."

"No." Annabel shrank back against the wall. "I want Magnus with me. Or Julian. Get Julian."

"What's going on?" Kit recognized her voice even before he turned to see Zara in the doorway. Her lipstick looked like a harsh slash of blood against her pale skin. She was looking at Magnus, the corner of her mouth twisted in a smirk. "Consul," she said, and bowed to Jia. "Everyone is assembled. Should I tell them the meeting will be delayed?"

"No, Miss Dearborn," said Jia, smoothing down her embroidered robe. "Thank you, but we don't need you to handle this for us. The assembly will go as planned."

"Dearborn," Annabel echoed. Her gaze was fixed on Zara. Her eyes had gone flat and glittering like a snake's. "You're a Dearborn."

Zara looked merely puzzled, as if wondering who Annabel might be. "Zara is quite an advocate for restricting the rights of Downworlders," Jia said neutrally.

"We're interested in safety," Zara said, clearly stung. "That's all."

"We had better go," said Robert Lightwood. He was still looking at Alec, but Alec wasn't looking at him; he was sitting by Magnus, his hand against Magnus's cheek. "Alec, if you need me, send for me."

"I'll send Kit," Alec said, without looking around.

"I'll return for you," Robert said to Kieran, who had remained silently by the window, barely a shadow in the room's shadows. Kieran nodded.

Robert squeezed Alec's shoulder briefly. Jia extended a hand to

Annabel, and after a moment of staring at Zara, Annabel followed the Consul and the Inquisitor from the room.

"Is he sick?" Zara said, looking at Magnus with a distant interest. "I didn't think warlocks got sick. Wouldn't it be funny if he died before you? I mean, what with him being immortal, you must have thought it would go the other way."

Alec raised his head slowly. "*What?*"

"Well, I mean since Magnus is immortal and you, you know, *aren't*," she clarified.

"He's immortal?" Alec's voice was colder than Kit had ever heard it. "I wish you'd told me before. I would have turned back time and found myself a nice mortal husband to grow old with."

"Well, wouldn't that be better?" Zara said. "Then you could get old and die at the same time."

"At the same time?" Alec echoed. He had barely moved or raised his voice, but his rage seemed to fill the room. Even Zara was starting to look uneasy. "How would you suggest we arrange that? Jump off a cliff together when one of us started feeling sickly?"

"Maybe." Zara looked sulky. "You have to agree the situation you're in is a tragedy."

Alec rose to his feet and in that moment was the famous Alec Lightwood Kit had heard about, the hero of past battles, the archer boy with deadly aim. "This is what I want and what I've chosen," he said. "How dare you tell me it's a tragedy? Magnus never pretended, he never tried to fool me into thinking it would be easy, but choosing Magnus is one of the easiest things I've ever done. We all have a lifetime, Zara, and none of us know how long or short it might be. Surely even you know that. I expect you mean to be rude and cruel, but I doubt you *meant* to sound stupid as well."

She flushed. "But if you die of old age and he lives forever—"

"Then he'll be there for Max, and that makes both of us happy," said Alec. "And I will be a uniquely lucky person, because there will be someone who always remembers me. Who will always love me. Magnus won't always mourn, but until the end of time he will remember me and love me."

"What makes you so sure?" said Zara, but there was an edge of uncertainty in her voice.

"Because he's three thousand times the human being you'll ever be," said Alec. "Now get out of here before I risk his life by waking him up so he can turn you into a garbage fire. Something that would match your personality."

"Oh!" said Zara. "So *rude!*"

Kit thought it was more than rude. He thought Alec meant it. He kind of hoped Zara would stick around to test the theory. Instead she stalked toward the door and paused there, glancing back at them both with dislike.

"Come on, Alec," she said. "The truth is that Shadowhunters and Downworlders aren't *meant* to be together. You and Bane are a disgrace. But you can't just be content with the Clave letting you pervert your angelic lineage. No, you have to force it on the rest of us."

"Really?" said Kieran, who Kit had nearly forgotten was there. "You *all* have to sleep with Magnus Bane? How exciting for you."

"Shut up, faerie dirt," said Zara. "You'll learn. You've picked the wrong side, you and those Blackthorns and Jace Herondale and that ginger bitch Clary—" She was breathing hard, her face flushed. "I'll enjoy watching you all go down," she said, and flounced from the room.

"Did she really say 'pervert your angelic lineage'?" said Alec, looking stupefied.

"Faerie dirt," mused Kieran. "That is, as Mark would say, a new one."

"Unbelievable." Alec sat down next to the sofa again, drawing up his knees.

"Nothing she said surprised me," said Kieran. "That is how they are. That is how the Cold Peace has made them. Afraid of what is new and different, and filled with hatred like ice. She may seem ridiculous, Zara Dearborn, but do not make the mistake of underestimating her and her Cohort." He looked back at the window. "Hate like that can tear down the world."

"This is a very strange request," said Diego.

"You're the one in a fake relationship," said Cristina. "I am sure you've been asked for stranger things."

Diego laughed, not with much humor. They were sitting a row away from the Blackthorns in the Council Hall. The clock had stopped chiming to announce the meeting's beginning and the room was full, though the dais was still empty.

"I am glad Jaime told you," he said. "Selfishly. I could bear that you hated me, but not that you despised me."

Cristina sighed. "I am not sure I ever really did despise you," she said.

"I should have told you more," he said. "I wanted to keep you safe—and I denied to myself that the Cohort and their plans were your problem. I didn't know they had designs on the Los Angeles Institute until too late. And I was mistaken in Manuel, as much as anyone. I trusted him."

"I know," Cristina said. "It is not that I blame you for anything. I—for such a long time, we were Cristina-and-Diego. A pair, together. And when that was over, I felt half myself. When you came back, I thought we could be as we were before, and I tried, but—"

"You don't love me like that anymore," he finished.

She paused for a moment. "No," she said. "I don't. Not like that. It was like trying to return to a place in your childhood you remember as perfect. It will always have changed, because you have changed."

Diego's Adam's apple moved as he swallowed. "I can't blame you. I don't like myself much right now."

"Maybe this could help you like yourself a little more. It would be a great kindness, Diego."

He shook his head. "Trust you, I suppose, to take pity on a lost faerie."

"It isn't pity," said Cristina. She glanced back over her shoulder; Zara had left the room some moments earlier and hadn't returned yet. Samantha was glaring at her, though, apparently in the belief that Cristina was trying to steal Zara's fiancé. "They frighten me. They will kill him after he testifies."

"The Cohort is frightening," Diego said. "But the Cohort is not the Centurions, and not all Centurions are like Zara. Rayan, Divya, Gen are good people. Like the Clave, it is an organization that has a cancer at its heart. Some of the body is sick and some healthy. Our mission is to discover a way to kill the sickness without killing all of the body."

The doors of the Council Hall opened. The Consul, Jia Penhallow, entered, her silver-flecked dark robes sweeping around her.

The room, which had been full of lively chatter, sank to hushed murmurs. Cristina sat back as the Consul began to climb the stairs to the dais.

"Thank you all for coming on such short notice, Nephilim." The Consul stood in front of a low wooden podium, its base decorated with the sigil of four Cs. There was gray in her black hair now that Emma didn't remember seeing before, wrinkles at the corners of her eyes. It couldn't be easy, being the Consul during a time of unspoken war. "Most of you know about Malcolm Fade. He was one of our closest allies, or so we thought. He betrayed us some weeks ago, and even now we are still learning of the bloody and terrible crimes he committed."

The murmur that went around the room sounded to Emma like the rush of the tide. She wished Julian was next to her so that she could bump his shoulder with hers, or squeeze his hand, but—mindful of the Inquisitor's instruction—they had sat at the opposite end of the long bench after he'd told her Magnus had collapsed.

"I promised Annabel Magnus would be with her," he'd said in a low voice, not wanting the younger Blackthorns to hear and be panicked. "I gave my word."

"You couldn't have guessed. Poor Magnus. There was no way to know he was sick."

But she remembered herself, saying, *Don't promise what you can't deliver.* And she felt cold, all over.

"There is a longer story to Fade's betrayal, one you might not know," Jia said. "In 1812 he fell in love with a Shadowhunter girl, Annabel Blackthorn. Her family deplored the idea of her marrying a warlock. In the end, she was murdered—by other Nephilim. Malcolm was told she had become an Iron Sister."

"Why didn't they kill him, too?" called someone from the crowd.

"He was a powerful warlock. A valuable asset," said Jia. "In the end it was decided to leave him alone. But when he discovered what had actually happened to Annabel, he lost his mind. This past century he has spent seeking revenge against Shadowhunters."

"My lady." It was Zara, upright and very prim; she'd just come in through the Hall doors and was standing in the aisle. "You tell us this story as if you mean for us to have sympathy for the girl and the warlock. But Malcolm Fade was a monster. A murderer. Some girl's infatuation with him doesn't excuse what he did."

"I find," said Jia, "that there is a difference between an excuse and an explanation."

"Then why are we being treated to this explanation? The warlock is dead. I hope this is not some attempt to wring reparations out of the Council. No one associated with that monster deserves any recompense for his death."

Jia's look was like the edge of a blade. "I understand that you've been very active in Council affairs lately, Zara," she said. "That does not mean you can interrupt the Consul. Go and sit down."

After a moment, Zara sat, looking angry. Aline pumped her fist. "Go, Mom," she whispered.

However, someone else had risen up to take Zara's place. Her father. "Consul," he said. "We're not ignorant; we were told this meeting would involve significant testimony by a witness that would impact the Clave. Isn't it about time you brought that witness out? If indeed, they exist?"

"Oh, she exists," Jia said. "It is Annabel. Annabel Blackthorn."

Now the murmur that went through the room sounded like the crash of a wave. A moment later Robert Lightwood appeared, wearing a grim expression. Behind him came two guards, and between them walked Annabel.

Annabel seemed quite small as she came up on the dais beside the Inquisitor. The Black Volume was hanging from a strap over her back, which made her look even younger, like a girl on her way to school.

A hiss went through the room. *Undead*, Emma heard, and *Unclean*. Annabel shrank back against Robert.

"This is an outrage," sputtered Zara's father. "Did we not all suffer enough from the corrosive filth of the Endarkened? Must you bring this *thing* in front of us?"

Julian sprang to his feet. "The Endarkened were not undead," he said, turning to face the Hall. "They were Turned by the Infernal Cup. Annabel is exactly who she was in life. She was tortured by Malcolm, kept in a half-alive state for years. She wants to help us."

"Julian Blackthorn," sneered Dearborn. "My daughter told me about you—your uncle was mad, your whole family's mad, only a madman would find this a good idea—"

"Do not," said Annabel, and her voice rang out clear and strong, "speak that way to him. He is my blood kin."

"Blackthorns," said Dearborn. "Seems they're all mad, dead, or both!"

If he'd expected a laugh, he didn't get one. The room was silent.

"Sit," the Consul said to Dearborn coldly. "It appears your family has an issue with the way Nephilim are meant to comport themselves. Interrupt me again and you'll be thrown out of the Hall."

Dearborn sat, but his eyes gleamed with rage. He wasn't the only one. Emma scanned the room quickly and saw clusters of hateful glares directed at the dais. She choked back her nerves; Julian had pushed his way into the aisle and was standing facing the front of the room. "Annabel," he said, his voice low and encouraging. "Tell them about the King."

"The Unseelie King," Annabel said softly. "The Lord of Shadows. He was in league with Malcolm. It is important you all know this, because even now, he plans the destruction of all Shadowhunters."

"But the Fair Folk are weak!" A man in an embroidered *gandora* was on his feet, dark eyes sparking with concern. Cristina murmured into Emma's ear that he was the head of the Marrakech Institute. "Years of the Cold Peace have weakened them. The King cannot hope to stand against us."

"Not in a clash of equal armies, no," Annabel said in her small voice. "But the King has harnessed the power of the Black Volume, and he has learned how to destroy the power of the Nephilim. How to cancel out runes, seraph blades, and witchlight. You would be fighting his forces with no more power than mundanes—"

"This absolutely cannot be true!" It was a thin, dark-haired man Emma remembered from the long-ago discussion of the Cold Peace. Lazlo Balogh, head of the Budapest Institute. "She is lying."

"She has no reason to lie!" Diana was on her feet now too, her shoulders set back in a fighting stance. "Lazlo, of all the people—"

"Miss Wrayburn." The Hungarian man's expression hardened. "I think we all know *you* should recuse yourself from the discussion."

Diana froze.

"You fraternize with faeries," he went on, smacking his lips as he spoke. "You've been *observed*."

"Oh, by the Angel, Lazlo," said the Consul. "Diana has nothing to do with this other than having the bad fortune to disagree with you!"

"Lazlo's right," said Horace Dearborn. "The Blackthorns are faerie sympathizers, betrayers of the Law—"

"But we're not liars," said Julian. His voice was steel edged in ice.

Dearborn took the bait. "What's that supposed to mean?"

"Your daughter didn't kill Malcolm Fade," said Julian. "Annabel did."

Zara popped to her feet like a puppet jerked upward on strings. "That's a lie!" she shrieked.

"It is not a lie," said Annabel. "Malcolm raised me from the dead. He used the blood of Arthur Blackthorn to do it. And for that, and for his torture and abandonment of me, I killed him."

Now the room exploded. Shouts echoed off the walls. Samantha and Dane Larkspear were on their feet, shaking their fists. Horace Dearborn was roaring that Annabel was a liar, that all Blackthorns were.

"Enough!" shouted Jia. "Silence!"

"*La Spada Mortale.*" A small olive-skinned woman rose from a place near the back. She wore a plain dress, but her thick necklace sparkled with jewels. Her hair was a deep gray, worn nearly to her hips, and her voice carried enough authority to cut through the noise in the room.

"What did you say, Chiara?" Jia demanded. Emma knew her name—Chiara Malatesta, head of the Rome Institute in Italy.

"The Mortal Sword," said Chiara. "If there is a question of whether this person—if that's what she can be called—is telling the truth, ply her with Maellartach. Then we can dispense with pointless arguments about whether she's lying."

"No." Annabel's eyes darted around the room in a panic. "Not the Sword—"

"See, she's lying," said Dane Larkspear. "She fears the Sword will reveal the truth!"

"She fears the Sword because she was tortured by the Council!" Julian said. He started toward the dais, but two of the Council guards seized him, holding him back. Emma started to rise, but Helen pressed her firmly back into her seat.

"Not yet," Helen whispered. "It will make things worse—she has to at least try—"

But Emma's heart was racing. Julian was still being restrained from approaching the dais. Every nerve in her body was shrieking as Robert Lightwood moved away and returned carrying something long and sharp and silver. Something that gleamed like dark water. She saw—she *felt*—Julian inhale sharply; he had held the Mortal Sword himself before and knew the pain it caused.

"Don't do this!" he said, but his voice was drowned in the swell of other voices, the clamor in the room as various Shadowhunters rose to their feet, craning for a glimpse of what was going on.

"She's a filthy undead creature!" Zara shouted. "She should be put out of her misery, not standing up in front of the Council!"

Annabel blanched. Emma could feel Julian's tension, knew what he was thinking: If Magnus were here, Magnus could explain: Annabel was *not* a revenant. She had been brought back to life. She was a living Shadowhunter. Magnus was a Downworlder that the Clave trusted, one of the few. None of this would be happening if he'd been able to join the meeting.

Magnus, Emma thought, *oh Magnus, I hope you're all right. I wish you were with us.*

"The Sword will determine Annabel's fitness to give testimony," Jia said in a hard voice that carried to the back of the room. "That is the Law. Stand back and let the Mortal Sword work."

The crowd fell silent. The Mortal Instruments were the highest power the Shadowhunters knew outside of the Angel himself. Even Zara closed her mouth.

"Take your time," Robert said to Annabel. The compassion in his face surprised Emma. She remembered him forcing the blade into Julian's hands, and Julian had been only twelve. She had been angry with Robert for a long time after that, though Julian didn't appear to bear a grudge.

Annabel was panting like a frightened rabbit. She looked at Julian, who gave her an encouraging nod, and reached her hands out slowly.

When she took the Sword, a shudder went through her body, as if she'd touched an electric fence. Her face tensed—but she held the sword unharmed. Jia exhaled with visible relief. The Sword had proved it—Annabel was a Shadowhunter. The Hall remained silent, as everyone stared.

Both the Consul and the Inquisitor stepped back, giving Annabel space. She stood in the center of the dais, a lonely figure in an ill-fitting dress.

"What is your name?" Robert asked her, his tone deceptively mild.

"Annabel Callisto Blackthorn." She spoke between quick breaths.

"And who are you standing on this dais with?"

Her blue-green eyes darted desperately between them. "I don't know you," she breathed. "You are Consul and Inquisitor—but not the ones I knew. You are clearly a Lightwood, but . . ." She shook her head before her face brightened. "Robert," she said. "Julian called you Robert."

Samantha Larkspear laughed derisively, and several of the other placard-bearers joined her. "There isn't enough left of her brain to give decent evidence!"

"Be *silent!*" thundered Jia. "Miss Blackthorn, you knew—you were the lover of Malcolm Fade, High Warlock of Los Angeles?"

"He was only a warlock when I knew him, of no rank." Annabel's voice shook. "Please. Ask me if I killed him. I can't stand much more of this."

"What we discuss here is not your choice." Jia didn't seem angry, but Annabel visibly flinched.

"This is a mistake," Livvy whispered to Emma. "They need to just ask her about Malcolm and end this. They can't make this into an interrogation."

"It'll be fine," Emma said. "It will."

But her heart was racing. The other Blackthorns were watching with visible tension. On her other side, Emma could see Helen, gripping the arms of her seat. Aline was rubbing her shoulder.

"Ask her," Julian said. "Just ask her, Jia."

"Julian. Enough," Jia said, but she turned to Annabel, her dark eyes expectant. "Annabel Callisto Blackthorn. Did you kill Malcolm Fade?"

"Yes." Hate crystallized Annabel's voice, strengthened it. "I cut him open. I watched him bleed to death. Zara Dearborn did nothing. She has been lying to you all."

A gasp ran around the room. For a moment Julian relaxed, and the guards who had been holding him released their grips. Zara, red-faced, gaped from the crowd.

Thank the Angel, Emma thought. *They'll have to listen now.*

Annabel faced the room, the Sword in her hand, and for that moment Emma could see what Malcolm must have fallen in love with. She looked proud, delighted, beautiful.

Something sailed past her head and smashed into the lectern.

A bottle, Emma thought—glass shattered outward from it. There was a gasp, and then a giggle, and then other objects began flying through the air—the crowd seemed to be flinging whatever they had to hand.

Not the whole crowd, Emma realized. It was the Cohort and their supporters. There weren't that many of them—but there were enough. And their hate was bigger than the whole room.

Emma met Julian's eyes; she saw the despair in his. They had expected better. Even after everything that they'd been through, they'd expected better, somehow.

It was true that many Shadowhunters were now on their feet shouting at the Cohort to stop. But Annabel had crumpled to her knees, her head down, her hands still gripping the Sword. She hadn't raised her hands to shield herself from the objects flying at her—they smacked into the floor and the lectern and the window: bottles and bags, coins and stones, even watches and bracelets.

"Stop!" Julian shouted, and the cold rage with which he spoke was enough to shock at least a few into silence. "By the Angel, this is the *truth*. She's telling you the truth! About Malcolm, about the Unseelie King—"

"How are we supposed to know that?" hissed Dearborn. "Who says the Mortal Sword works on that—that *thing*? She is tainted—"

"She is a monster," shouted Zara. "This is a conspiracy to try to drag us into a war with the Unseelie Court! The Blackthorns care about nothing but their lies and their filthy faerie siblings!"

"Julian," Annabel gasped, the Mortal Sword held so tightly in her hands that blood began to bloom on her skin where she gripped the blade. "Julian, help me—Magnus—where's Magnus—"

Julian struggled against the guards' hold. Robert hurried forward, his big hands outstretched. "Enough," he said. "Come with me, Annabel—"

"Leave me alone!" With a hoarse shout, Annabel flinched back from him, raising the blade in her hand. Emma was reminded suddenly and coldly of two things:

The Mortal Sword was not just an instrument of justice. It was a weapon.

And Annabel was a Shadowhunter, with a weapon in her hand.

As if he couldn't believe what was happening, Robert took another step toward Annabel, reaching out for her, as if he could calm her, convince her. He opened his mouth to speak, and she thrust the blade up between them.

It pierced through Robert Lightwood's robes and sliced into his chest.

Kit felt like someone who'd wandered into another family's hospital room by mistake and wasn't allowed to leave. Alec sat by Magnus's side, occasionally touching his shoulder or saying something in a low voice. Kieran stared out the window as if he could transport himself through the glass.

"Do you want . . . I mean, should someone tell the kids? Max and Rafe?" Kit asked finally.

Alec stood up and crossed the room, where a carafe of water rested on a side table. He poured himself a glass. "Not right now," he said. "They're safe in the city with my mother. They don't need—Magnus doesn't need—" He took a drink of water. "I was hoping he'd get better and we wouldn't have to tell them anything."

"You said you knew what was wrong with him," said Kit. "Is it—dangerous?"

"I don't know," Alec said. "But I do know one thing. It isn't just him. It's other warlocks too. Tessa and Jem have been looking for a cause or cure, but she's sick too—"

He broke off. A dull roar was audible; a sound like waves rising, about to crash. Alec blanched. "I've heard that sound before," he said. "Something's happening. In the Hall."

Kieran was off the windowsill in a fluid, single motion. "It is death."

"It might not be," said Kit, straining his ears.

"I can smell blood," Kieran said. "And hear screams." He climbed up on the windowsill and jerked down one of the curtains. He seized up the curtain rod, which had a sharply pointed finial, and leaped to the floor, brandishing it like a spear. His silver-black eyes gleamed. "I will not be found weaponless when they come."

"You should stay here. Both of you. I'll find out what's going on," Alec said. "My father—"

The door flew open. Kieran flung his curtain rod. Diego, who had just appeared in the doorway, ducked as it flew by and slammed into the wall, where it jammed point first.

"¿Que chingados?" said Diego, looking stunned. "What the hell?"

"He thinks you're here to kill us," said Kit. "Are you?"

Diego rolled his eyes. "Things have gone bad in the Hall," he said.

"Has anyone been injured?" Alec asked.

Diego hesitated. "Your father—" he began.

Alec set his glass down and walked across the room to Magnus. He bent and kissed him on the forehead and the cheek. Magnus didn't move, only slept on peacefully, his cat's eyes closed.

Kit envied him.

"Stay here," Alec said to Kit and Kieran. Then he turned and walked out of the room.

Diego looked after him grimly. Kit felt a little sick. He had a feeling that whatever had happened to Alec's father, it hadn't been minor.

Kieran yanked his curtain rod out of the wall and pointed it at Diego. "You have delivered your message," he said. "Now go. I will protect the boy and the warlock."

Diego shook his head. "I am here to get you"—he pointed at Kieran—"and take you to the Scholomance."

"I will not go anywhere with you," said Kieran. "You have no morality. You brought dishonor upon Lady Cristina."

"You've no idea what happened between me and Cristina," added Diego in a frozen voice. Kit noticed that Perfect Diego was looking a little less than perfect. The shadows under his eyes were deep and violet, and his brown skin was sallow. Exhaustion and tension drew his fine features tight.

"Say what you will of faeries," Kieran said. "We have no greater scorn than that we hold toward those who betray a heart given into their keeping."

"It was Cristina," said Diego, "who asked me to come here and bring you to the Scholomance. If you refuse, *you* will be dishonoring her wishes."

Kieran scowled. "You are lying."

"I am not," said Diego. "She feared for your safety. The Cohort's hatred is at a fever pitch and the Hall runs wild. You will be safe if you come with me, but I can promise nothing otherwise."

"How would I be safe at the Scholomance, with Zara Dearborn and her friends?"

"She won't be there," said Diego. "She and Samantha and Manuel plan to remain here, in Idris, at the heart of power. Power is all they have ever wanted. The Scholomance is a place of peaceful study." He held his hand out. "Come with me. For Cristina."

Kit stared, his breath caught. It was a very strange moment. He had learned enough about Shadowhunters now to understand what it meant that Diego was a Centurion, and what laws he was breaking, offering to smuggle Kieran to the Scholomance. And he understood enough of the pride of the Fair Folk to know what Kieran was accepting if he agreed.

There was another roar of noise outside. "If you're here," Kit said cautiously, "and the Cohort attacks you, Mark and Cristina will want to protect you. And they could get hurt doing it."

Kieran set the curtain rod down on the floor. He looked at Kit. "Tell Mark where I have gone," he said. "And give Cristina my thanks."

Kit nodded. Diego inclined his head before stepping forward and taking Kieran awkwardly by the arm. He pressed the fingers of his other hand against the *Primi Ordines* pin on his gear.

Before Kit could speak, Diego and Kieran vanished, a swirl of bright light streaking across the air where they had stood.

The guards surged forward as Jia reached to catch Robert's slumping body. Her face a mask of horror, Jia sank to her knees, reaching for her stele, carving an *iratze* onto Robert's limp, dangling arm.

His blood spread out around them both, a sluggishly moving pool of scarlet.

"*Annabel.*" Julian's voice was barely a whisper of bone-deep shock. Emma could almost see the abyss of guilt and self-blame opening at his feet. He began to struggle frantically against the grip of the guards holding him. "Let me go, let me go—"

"Stay back!" Jia screamed. "All of you, stay back!" She was kneeling beside Robert, her hands wet with his blood as she tried again and again to cut the healing rune into his skin.

Two other guards pounded up the steps and halted uncertainly at her words. Annabel, her blue dress splashed with blood, held the Sword in front of her like a barrier. Robert's blood was already sinking into the blade, as if it were porous stone drinking up water.

Julian tore free of his restraints and leaped onto the bloody dais. Emma shot to her feet, Cristina seizing the back of her shirt, but to no avail: She was already clambering onto the narrow back of the bench.

Thank the Angel for all the hours she'd spent practicing on the rafters in the training room, she thought, and ran, leaping from the end of the bench into the aisle. There were voices shouting at her, to her, a roar like waves; she ignored them. Julian rose slowly to his feet, facing Annabel.

"Stay away!" Annabel shrieked, waving the Mortal Sword. It seemed to be glowing, pulsing even, in her grip, or was that Emma's imagination? "Stay away from me!"

"Annabel, stop." Julian spoke calmly, his hands up to show they were empty—*empty?* Emma fumed, where was his sword, where were his weapons?—his eyes wide and guileless. "This will only make things worse."

Annabel was sobbing harsh breaths. "Liar. Get back, get away from me."

"I never lied to you—"

"You told me they would give me Blackthorn Manor! You told me Magnus would protect me! But look!" She swept her arm in a wide arc, indicating the whole room. "I am *tainted* to them— despised, a criminal—"

"You can still come back." Julian's voice was a marvel of steadiness. "Put the Sword down."

For a moment, Annabel seemed to hesitate. Emma was at the foot of the dais steps; she saw Annabel's grip loosen on the hilt of the Sword—

Jia stood up. Her robes were wet with Robert's blood, her stele limp in her hand. "He's dead," she said.

It was like a key turning in the lock of a cage, freeing the occupants: The guards lunged up the steps, leaping toward Annabel, blades outstretched. She spun with inhuman quickness, striking at them, and the Sword slashed across both their chests. There were screams as they collapsed, and Emma was running up the stairs, drawing Cortana, leaping in front of Julian.

From here, she could see all of the Council Hall. It was a melee. Some were fleeing through the doors. The Blackthorns and Cristina were on their feet, fighting toward the dais, though a line of guards had appeared to hold them back. As Emma watched, Livvy ducked under a guard's arm and began to shove her way toward them. A longsword glimmered in her hand.

Emma looked back at Annabel. It was clear this near to her that something had snapped inside her. She looked blank, her eyes dead and disconnected. Her gaze shifted past Emma. Alec had burst through the doors—he stared up at the dais, his face a mask of grief and shock.

Emma wrenched her eyes away from him as Annabel sprang for Julian like a cat, her sword cutting the air before her. Instead of raising Cortana to meet Annabel's thrust, Emma threw herself to the side, knocking Julian to the polished floor of the dais.

For a moment he was against her; they were together, body to body, and she felt the *parabatai* strength flow through her. The Mortal Sword came down again and they sprang apart, redoubled in strength, as it sliced through the wood at their feet.

The room was full of screaming. Emma thought she heard Alec calling for Robert: *Dad, please, Dad.* She thought of the tapestry of him in Robert's room. She thought of Isabelle. She whirled with Cortana in her hand, and the flat of the blade slammed against Maellartach.

Both swords shuddered. Annabel jerked her sword arm back, her eyes suddenly almost feral. Someone was shouting for Julian. It was Livvy, clambering up the side of the dais.

"*Livvy!*" Julian yelled. "Livvy, get out of here—"

Annabel swung again, and Emma raised Cortana, cutting on the upstroke, pushing closer, slamming her sword against Annabel's with all the force in her body, bringing the blades together with a massive, echoing clang.

And the Mortal Sword shattered.

It cracked jaggedly along the blade, the top half shearing away. Annabel shrieked and stumbled backward, and black fluid spilled from the broken sword like sap from a felled tree.

Emma collapsed to her knees. It was as if the hand that held Cortana had been struck by lightning. Her wrist was humming and a ringing sounded all the way up her bones, making her body shake. She grabbed for Cortana's hilt with her right hand, panicking, desperate not to drop it.

"*Emma!*" Julian was holding his own arm stiffly, Emma saw, as if he had been hurt too.

The humming was receding. Emma tried to get to her feet and stumbled; her teeth bit down into her lip with frustration. How dare her body betray her. "I'm fine—fine—"

Livvy gasped at the sight of the smashed Mortal Sword. She had reached the top of the dais; Julian reached out, and Livvy tossed him the sword she was holding. He caught it neatly and spun to face Annabel, who was staring down at the broken weapon in her hand. The Consul had seen what had happened too, and was striding toward them.

"It's over, Annabel," Julian said. He didn't look triumphant; he looked weary. "It's done."

Annabel gave a growl low in her throat and lunged. Julian raised his blade. But Annabel whipped past him, her black hair seeming to soar around her. Her feet left the ground, and for a moment she was truly beautiful, a Shadowhunter in full flowering glory, just before she landed lightly on the wooden floor at the dais's edge and drove her jagged, broken half blade into Livvy's heart.

Livvy's eyes shot wide. Her mouth formed an O, as if she were astonished by discovering something small and surprising, like a mouse on the kitchen counter. An overturned vase of flowers, a broken wristwatch. Nothing huge. Nothing terrible.

Annabel stepped back, breathing hard. She no longer looked beautiful. Her dress, her arm, was soaked in red and black.

Livvy raised her hand and wonderingly touched the hilt protruding from her chest. Her cheeks flared red.

"Ty?" she whispered. "Ty, I—"

Her knees went out from under her. She thudded hard to the ground on her back. The blade was like an ugly massive insect fastened to her chest, a metal mosquito sucking the blood that ran from her wound, red mixed with the black of the sword, spilling across the floor.

In the aisle of the Council Hall, Ty looked up, his face turning the color of ashes. Emma had no idea if he could see them through the teeming crowd—see his sister, see what had happened—but his hands flew to his chest, pressing over his heart. He pitched to his knees, soundlessly, just as Livvy had, and crumpled to the ground.

Julian made a noise. It was a noise Emma couldn't have described, not as human a sound as a howl or a scream. It sounded like it was ripped out of the inside of him, like something brutal was tearing through his chest. He dropped the longsword Livvy had risked so much to bring him, fell to his knees, and crawled to her, pulling her into his lap.

"Livvy, Livvy, my Livvy," he whispered, cradling her, feverishly stroking her blood-wet hair away from her face. There was so *much* blood. He was covered in it in seconds; it had soaked through Livvy's clothes, even her shoes were drenched in it. "*Livia.*" His hands shook; he fumbled out his stele, put it to her arm.

The healing rune vanished as quickly as he drew it.

Emma felt as if someone had punched her in the stomach. There were wounds that were beyond an *iratze*'s power. Healing runes only vanished from skin when occult poison was involved—or when the person was already dead.

"Livia." Julian's voice rose, cracking and tumbling over itself like a wave breaking far out to sea. "Livvy, my baby, please, sweetheart, open your eyes, it's Jules, I'm here for you, I'm always here for you, please, *please*—"

Blackness exploded behind Emma's eyes. The pain in her arm was gone; she felt nothing at all but rage. Rage that bleached everything else out of the world except the sight of Annabel cringing against the lectern, staring at Julian cradling his sister's dead body. At what she'd done.

Emma whirled and stalked toward Annabel. There was nowhere she could go. The guards had circled the dais. The rest of the room was a seething mass of confusion.

Emma hoped Ty was unconscious. She hoped he was seeing none of this. He would wake up eventually, and the horror of what he would wake up to drove her forward.

Annabel staggered back. Her foot slipped, and she tumbled to the floor. She raised her head as Emma loomed up over her. Her face was a mask of fear.

Emma heard Arthur's voice in her head. *Mercy is better than revenge.* But it was fainter than Julian's whispers or Dru's sobs.

She brought Cortana down, scything the blade through the air—but as it sliced the air, inky smoke erupted from the window behind Annabel. It had the force of an explosion, the concussive wave knocking Emma backward. As she stumbled to her knees she caught sight of a moving shape inside the smoke—the gleam of gold, the flash of a symbol burned onto her brain: a crown, broken in half.

The smoke vanished, and Annabel vanished with it.

Emma curled her body over Cortana, clutching the blade to herself, her soul corroded with despair. All around her she could hear the rising voices in the room, cries and shrieks. She could see Mark bent over Ty, who was crumpled on the floor. Mark's shoulders were shaking. Helen was struggling through the crowd toward both of them. Dru was on the ground, sobbing into her hands. Alec had slumped back against the doors of the Hall, staring at the devastation.

And there in front of her was Julian, his eyes and ears closed to anything but Livvy, her body cradled against his. She seemed a drift of fragile ash or snow, something impermanent that had blown into his arms accidentally: the petal of a faerie flower, the white feather of an angel's wing. The dream of a little girl, the memory of a sister reaching up her arms: *Julian, Julian, carry me.*

But the soul, the spirit that made her Livvy was no longer there: It was something that had gone away to a far and untouchable place, even as Julian ran his hands over her hair again and again and begged her to wake up and look at him just one more time.

High above the Council Hall, the golden clock began to chime the hour.

ACKNOWLEDGMENTS

Rounding up the usual suspects: Holly Black, Maureen Johnson, Leigh Bardugo, Kelly Link, Robin Wasserman, and Sarah Rees Brennan, bringing novelistic and emotional support. Special thanks to Jon Skovron and Anya DeNiro for their guiding light. To Erin, Alyssa, Katie, Manu, Rò & Virna, Julia, Mariane, Thiago, Raissa, Artur, and Laura, for making me smile. Cathrin Langner for remembering everything, and to Viviane Hebel and Gloria Altozano Saiz for assistance with Spanish. And thanks to Karen, on our ten-year anniversary, and to Russ and Danny, special agents. Love and thanks to my parents and especially to Jim Hill. To Emily Houk for going above and beyond. And to Josh, as always, *Aimer, ce n'est pas se regarder l'un l'autre, c'est regarder ensemble dans la même direction.*

Continue Emma and Julian's adventures in

Queen of Air and Darkness,

BOOK THREE OF THE DARK ARTIFICES.

———◆———

There was blood on the Council dais, blood on the steps, blood on the walls and the floor and the shattered remnants of the Mortal Sword. Later Emma would remember it as a sort of red mist. A piece of broken poetry kept going through her mind, something about not being able to imagine people had so much blood in them.

They said that shock cushioned great blows, but Emma didn't feel cushioned. She could see and hear everything: the Council Hall full of guards. The screaming. She tried to fight her way through to Julian. Guards surged up in front of her in a wave. She could hear more shouting. *"Emma Carstairs shattered the Mortal Sword! She destroyed a Mortal Instrument! Arrest her!"*

She didn't care what they did to her; she had to get to Julian. He was still on the ground with Livvy in his arms, resisting all efforts by the guards to lift her dead body away from him.

"Let me through," she said. "I'm his *parabatai*, let me through."

"Give me the sword." It was the Consul's voice. "Give me Cortana, Emma, and you can help Julian."

She gasped, and tasted blood in her mouth. Alec was up on the dais now, kneeling by his father's body. The floor of the Hall was a mass of rushing figures; among them Emma glimpsed Mark, carrying an unconscious Ty out of the Hall, shouldering other Nephilim aside as he went. He looked grimmer than she'd ever seen him. Kit was with him; where was Dru? There—she was alone on the ground; no, Diana was with her, holding her and weeping, and there was Helen, fighting to get to the dais.

Emma took a step back and almost stumbled. The wood floor was slippery with blood. Consul Jia Penhallow was still in front of her, her thin hand held out for Cortana. *Cortana*. The sword was a part of Emma's family, had been a part of her memory for as long as she could recall. She could still remember Julian laying it in her arms after her parents had died, how she'd held the sword to her as if it were a child, heedless of the deep cut the blade left on her arm.

Jia was asking her to hand over a piece of herself.

But Julian was there, alone, bowed in grief, soaked in blood. And he was more of herself than Cortana was. Emma surrendered the sword; feeling it yanked from her grip, her whole body tensed. She almost thought she could hear Cortana scream at being parted from her.

"Go," Jia said; Emma could hear other voices, including Horace Dearborn's, raised, demanding she be stopped, that the destruction of the Mortal Sword and the disappearance of Annabel Blackthorn be answered for. Jia was snapping at the guards, telling them to escort everyone from the Hall: now was a time of grief, not a time for revenge—Annabel would be found—*go with dignity, Horace, or you'll be escorted out, now is not the time*—Aline helping Dru and Diana to their feet, helping them walk from the room . . .

Emma fell to her knees by Julian. The metallic smell of blood was everywhere. Livvy was a crumpled shape in his arms, her skin the color of skimmed milk. He had stopped calling for her to come back and was rocking her as if she were a child, his chin against the top of her head.

"Jules," Emma whispered, but the word sat bitterly on her

tongue: that was her childhood name for him, and he was an adult now, a grieving parent. Livvy had not just been his sister. For years he had raised her as a daughter. "Julian." She touched his cold cheek, then Livvy's colder one. "Julian, love, please, let me help you. . . ."

He raised his head slowly. He looked as if someone had flung a pail full of blood at him. It masked his chest, his throat, spattered his chin and cheeks. "Emma." His voice was barely a whisper. "Emma, I drew so many *iratzes*—"

But Livvy had already been dead when she hit the wood of the dais. Before Julian even lifted her into his arms. No rune, no *iratze*, would have helped.

"Jules!" Helen had finally forced her way past the guards; she flung herself down beside Emma and Julian, heedless of the blood. Emma watched numbly as Helen carefully removed the broken shard of the Mortal Sword from Livvy's body and set it on the ground. It stained her hands with blood. Her lips white with grief, she put her arms around Julian and Livvy both, whispering soothing words.

The room was emptying around them. Magnus had come in, walking very slowly and looking pale. A long row of Silent Brothers followed him. He ascended the dais and Alec rose to his feet, flinging himself into Magnus's arms. They held each other wordlessly as four of the Brothers knelt and lifted Robert Lightwood's body. His hands had been folded over his chest, his eyes carefully closed. Soft murmurs of "*ave atque vale*, Robert Lightwood," echoed behind him as the Brothers carried his body from the room.

The Consul moved toward them. There were guards with her. The Silent Brothers hovered behind them, like ghosts, a blur of parchment.

"You have to let go of her, Jules," Helen said in her gentlest voice. "She has to be taken to the Silent City."

Julian looked at Emma. His eyes were stark as winter skies, but she could read them. "Let him do it," Emma said. "He wants the last person to carry Livvy to be him."

Helen stroked her brother's hair and kissed his forehead before rising. She said, "Jia, please."

The Consul nodded. Julian got slowly to his feet, Livvy cradled against him. He began to move toward the stairs that led down from the dais, Helen at his side and the Silent Brothers following, but as Emma rose too, Jia put a hand out to hold her back.

"Only family, Emma," she said.

I am family. Let me go with them. Let me go with Livvy, Emma screamed silently, but she kept her mouth firmly closed: She couldn't add her own sadness to the existing horror. And the rules of the Silent City were unchangeable. *The Law is hard, but it is the Law.*

The small procession was moving toward the doors. The Cohort had gone, but there were still some guards and other Shadowhunters in the room: a low chorus of "hail and farewell, Livia Blackthorn," followed them.

The Consul turned, Cortana flashing in her hand, and went down the steps and over to Aline, who had been watching as Livvy was carried away. Emma began to shiver all over, a shiver that started deep down in her bones. She had never felt so alone—Julian was going away from her, and the other Blackthorns seemed a million miles away like distant stars, and she wanted her parents with a painful intensity that was almost humiliating, and she wanted Jem and she wanted Cortana back in her arms and she wanted to forget Livvy bleeding and dying and crumpled like a broken doll as the window of the Council Hall exploded and the broken crown took Annabel—had anyone else seen it but her?

"Emma." Arms went around her, familiar, gentle arms, raising her to her feet. It was Cristina, who must have waited through all the chaos for her, who had stayed stubbornly in the Hall as the guards shouted for everyone to leave, stayed to remain by

Emma's side. "Emma, come with me, don't stay here. I'll take care of you. I know where we can go. Emma. *Corazoncita.* Come with me."

Emma let Cristina help her to her feet. Magnus and Alec were coming over to them, Alec's face tight, his eyes reddened. Emma stood with her hand clasped in Cristina's and looked out over the Hall, which seemed to her an entirely different place than it had when they had arrived hours ago. Maybe because the sun had been up then, she thought, dimly hearing Magnus and Alec talking to Cristina about taking Emma to the house that had been set aside for the Blackthorns. Maybe because the room had darkened, and shadows were thick as paint in the corners.

Or maybe because everything had changed, now. Maybe because nothing at all would ever be the same again.

"Dru?" Helen knocked gently on the closed door of the room. "Dru, can I talk to you?"

At least, she was fairly sure it was Dru's room. The canal house next to the Consul's residence on Princewater Street had been prepared for the Blackthorns before the meeting, since everyone had assumed they would spend several nights in Idris. Helen and Aline had been shown it earlier by Diana, and Helen had appreciated the light touch of Diana's loving hands everywhere: There were flowers in the kitchen, and rooms had names taped to the doors—the one with two narrow beds was for the twins, the one for Tavvy full of books and toys Diana had brought from her own home over the weapons shop.

Helen had stopped in front of a small room with flowered wallpaper. "For Dru, maybe?" she'd said. "It's pretty."

Diana had looked dubious. "Oh, Dru isn't like that," she'd said. "Maybe if the wallpaper had bats on it, or skeletons."

Helen had winced.

Aline had taken her hand. "Don't worry," she'd whispered. "You'll get to know them all again." She'd kissed Helen's cheek. "It'll be easy-peasy."

And maybe it would have been, Helen thought, staring at the door with the note that said *Drusilla* on it. Maybe if everything had gone well. Grief's sharp agony flared up in her chest—she felt as she imagined a fish caught on a hook might feel, twisting and turning to get away from the spike of pain driven into its flesh.

She remembered this pain from the death of her father, when only the thought that she had to take care of her family, had to look after the children, had gotten her through. She was trying to do the same now, but it was clear the children—if they could even really be called that; only Tavvy was truly a child, and he was at the Inquisitor's house, having thankfully missed the horror in the Council Hall—felt awkward around her. As if she were a stranger.

Which only made the pain pierce deeper in her chest. She wished Aline was with her, but Aline had gone to be with her parents for a few hours.

"Dru," Helen said again, knocking with more force. "*Please* let me in."

The door flew open and Helen jerked her hand back before she accidentally punched Dru in the shoulder. Her sister stood in front of her, glaring in her ill-fitting black meeting clothes, too tight in the waist and chest. Her eyes were so red-rimmed it looked as if she had smeared scarlet eye shadow across her lids.

"I know you might want to be alone," said Helen. "But I need to know that you're—"

"All right?" Dru said, a little sharply. The implication was clear: *How could I possibly be all right?*

"Surviving."

Dru glanced away for a moment; her lips, pressed tightly

together, trembled. Helen ached to grab her little sister and hug her, to cuddle Dru the way she had years ago when Dru was a stubborn toddler. "I want to know how Ty is."

"He's asleep," said Helen. "The Silent Brothers gave him a sedative potion, and Mark's sitting with him. Do you want to sit with him too?"

"I . . ." Dru hesitated, while Helen wished she could think of something comforting to say about Ty. She was terrified of what would happen when he woke up. He'd fainted in the Council Hall, and Mark had carried him to the Brothers, who were already in the Gard. They'd examined him in eerie silence and stated that physically he was healthy, but they would give him herbs that would keep him sleeping. That sometimes the mind knew when it needed to shut down to prepare itself to heal. Though Helen didn't know how a night of sleep, or even a year of it, would prepare Ty for losing his twin.

"I want Jules," Dru said finally. "Is he here?"

Helen shook her head. "He's still with Livvy," she said. "In the Silent City." She wanted to say he'd be back any moment—Aline had said the ceremony of laying someone out in the City as a preparation for cremation was a short one—but she didn't want to say anything to Dru that would turn out not to be true.

"What about Emma?" Dru's voice was polite but clear: *I want the people I know, not you.*

"I'll go look for her," Helen said.

She had barely turned away from Dru's door when it shut behind her with a small but determined click. She blinked away tears—and saw Mark, standing in the hallway a few feet from her. He had come close so soundlessly that she hadn't heard him approach. He held a crumpled piece of paper in his hand that looked like a fire-message.

"Helen," he said. His voice was rough. After all his years in the Hunt, would he grieve as faeries grieved? He looked rumpled, weary: There were very human lines under his eyes, at the sides of his mouth. "Ty is not alone—Diana and Kit are with him, and he sleeps on, besides. I needed to speak with you."

"I have to get Emma," Helen said. "Dru wants her."

"Her room is just there; we can certainly get her before we leave," Mark said, indicating the farther end of the corridor. The house was paneled in honey-colored wood, the witchlight lamps lighting it to warmth; on another day, it would have been a pretty place.

"Leave?" Helen said, puzzled.

Mark nodded. "I have had a message from Magnus and Alec, at the Inquisitor's house. I must go and fetch Tavvy and tell him our sister is dead." He reached out a hand for her, his face twisting with pain. "Please, Helen. Come with me."

When Diana was young, she had visited a museum in London where the star attraction was a Sleeping Beauty made of wax. Her skin was like pale tallow, and her chest rose and fell as she "breathed" with the help of a small motor implanted in her body.

Something about Ty's stillness and pallor reminded her now of the wax girl. He lay partly covered with the blankets on his bed, his only movement his breath. His hands were loose and open at his sides; Diana longed for nothing more than to see his fingers moving, playing with one of Julian's creations or the cord of his headphones.

"Is he going to be all right?" Kit spoke in a half whisper. The room was papered in cheerful yellow, both twin beds covered in rag bedspreads. Kit could have sat on the empty bed that was meant to be Livvy's, but he hadn't. He was crouched in a corner of the room, his back against the wall, his legs drawn up. He was staring at Ty.

Diana put her hand to Ty's forehead; it was cool. She felt numb throughout her body. "He's fine, Kit," she said. She tugged the

blanket up over Ty; he stirred and mu⟋
windows were open—they'd thoug⟋
Ty—but Diana crossed the room t⟋
had always been obsessed with th⟋
could happen to someone was ca⟋
never forgot what your parents ⟋

Beyond the window she could se⟋
dusk, and the rising moon. She thought of a figu⟋
ing across that vast sky. She wondered if Gwyn knew of this ⟋
events, or if she would have to send him a message. And what woul⟋
he do or say when he received it? He had come to her once before when
Livvy, Ty, and Kit were in danger, but he had been called upon by Mark
then. She still wasn't sure if he'd done it because he was genuinely fond
of the children, or if he had simply been discharging a debt.

She paused, hand on the window curtain. In truth, she knew
little about Gwyn. As the leader of the Wild Hunt he was almost
more mythic than human. She wondered how emotions must be
felt by those so powerful and old they had become part of myths
and stories. How could he really care about any mortal's little life
given the scope of what he had experienced?

And yet he had held her and comforted her in her old bedroom,
when she had told him what she had only ever told Catarina and
her parents before, and her parents were dead. He had been kind—
hadn't he?

Stop it. She turned back to the room; now wasn't the time to
think about Gwyn, even if some part of her hoped he would come
and comfort her again. Not when Ty might wake up any moment
into a world of new and terrible pain. Not when Kit was crouched
against the wall as if he had fetched up on some lonely beach after
a disaster at sea.

She was about to put her hand on Kit's shoulder when he looked
up at her. There were no marks of tears on his face. He had been

his father's death too, she recalled, when he had ⏤oor of the Institute for the first time and realized he ⏤owhunter.

⏤ikes familiar things," said Kit. "He won't know where he is ⏤he wakes up. We should make sure his bag is here, and what- ⏤r stuff he brought from London."

"It's over there." Diana pointed to where Ty's duffel had been placed under the bed that should have been Livvy's. Without looking at her, Kit got to his feet and went over to it. He unzipped it and took out a book—a thick book, with old-fashioned page binding. Silently, he placed it on the bed just next to Ty's open left hand, and Diana caught a glimpse of the title embossed in gold across the cover and realized that even her numb heart could twinge with pain.

The Return of Sherlock Holmes.

The moon had begun to rise, and the demon towers of Alicante glowed in their light.

It had been many years since Mark had been in Alicante. The Wild Hunt had flown over it, and he remembered seeing the land of Idris spread out below him as the others in the Hunt whooped and howled, amused at flying over Nephilim land. But Mark's heart had always beaten faster at the sight of the Shadowhunter homeland; the bright silver quarter of Lake Lyn, the green of Brocelind Forest, the stone manor houses of the countryside, and the glimmer of Alicante on its hill. And Kieran beside him, thoughtful, watching Mark as Mark watched Idris.

My place, my people. My home, he'd thought. But it seemed different from ground level: more prosaic, filled with the smell of canal water in summer, streets illuminated by harsh witchlight. It wasn't far to the Inquisitor's house, but they were walking slowly. It was several minutes before Helen spoke for the first time:

"You saw our aunt in Faerie," she said. "Nene. Only Nene, right?"

"She was in the Seelie Court." Mark nodded, glad to have the silence broken. "How many sisters did our mother have?"

"Six or seven, I think," said Helen. "Nene is the only one who is kind."

"I thought you didn't know where Nene was?"

"She never spoke of her location to me, but she has communicated with me on more than one occasion since I was sent to Wrangel Island," said Helen. "I think she felt sympathy in her heart for me."

"She helped hide us, and heal Kieran," said Mark. "She spoke to me of our faerie names." He looked around; they had reached the Inquisitor's house, the biggest on this stretch of pavement, with balconies out over the canal. "I never thought I would come back here. Not to Alicante. Not as a Shadowhunter."

Helen squeezed his shoulder and they walked up to the door together; she knocked, and a harried-looking Simon Lewis opened the door. It had been years since Mark had seen him, and he looked older now: His shoulders were broader, his brown hair longer, and there was stubble along his jaw.

He gave Helen a lopsided smile. "The last time you and I were here I was drunk and yelling up at Isabelle's window." He turned to Mark. "And the last time I saw you, I was stuck in a cage in Faerie."

Mark remembered: Simon looking up at him through the bars of the fey-wrought cage, Mark saying to him: *I am no faerie. I am Mark Blackthorn of the Los Angeles Institute. It doesn't matter what they say or what they do to me. I still remember who I am.*

"Yes," Mark said. "You told me of my brothers and sisters, of Helen's marriage. I was grateful." He swept a small bow, out of habit, and saw Helen look surprised.

"I wish I could have told you more," Simon said, in a more serious voice. "And I'm so sorry. About Livvy. We're grieving here, too."

Simon swung the door open wider. Mark saw a grand entryway inside, with a large chandelier hanging from the ceiling; off to the left was a family room, where Rafe, Max, and Tavvy sat in front of an empty fireplace, playing with a small stack of toys. Isabelle and Alec sat on the couch: She had her arms around his neck and was sobbing quietly against his chest. Low, hopeless sobs that struck an echo deep inside his own heart, a matching chord of loss.

"Please tell Isabelle and Alec we are sorry for the loss of their father," said Helen. "We did not mean to intrude. We are here for Octavian."

At that moment, Magnus appeared from the entryway. He nodded at them and went over to the children, lifting Tavvy up in his arms. Though Tavvy was getting awfully big to be carried, Mark thought, but in many ways Tavvy was young for his age, as if early grief had kept him more childlike. As Magnus approached them, Helen began to lift her hands, but Tavvy held out his arms to Mark.

In some surprise, Mark took the burden of his little brother in his arms. Tavvy squirmed around, tired but alert. "What's happened?" he said. "Everyone's crying."

Magnus ran a hand through his hair. He looked extremely weary. "We haven't told him anything," he said. "We thought it was for you to do."

Mark took a few steps back from the door, Helen following after him so that they stood in the lighted square of illumination from the entryway. He set Tavvy down on the pavement. This was the way the Fair Folk broke bad news, face-to-face.

"Livvy is gone, child," he said.

Tavvy looked confused. "Gone where?"

"She has passed into the Shadow Lands," said Mark. He was struggling for the words; death in Faerie was such a different thing than it was to humans.

Tavvy's blue-green Blackthorn eyes were wide. "Then we can

rescue her," he said. "We can go after her, right? Like we got you back from Faerie. Like you went after Kieran."

Helen made a small noise. "Oh, Octavian," she said.

"She is *dead*," Mark said helplessly, and saw Tavvy wince away from the words. "Mortal lives are short and—and fragile in the face of eternity."

Tavvy's eyes filled with tears.

"*Mark*," Helen said, and knelt down on the ground, reaching her hands out to Tavvy. "She died so bravely," she said. "She was defending Julian and Emma. Our sister—she was courageous."

The tears began to spill down Tavvy's face. "Where's Julian?" he said. "Where did he go?"

Helen dropped her hands. "He's with Livvy in the Silent City— he'll be back soon—let us take you back home to the canal house—"

"Home?" Tavvy said scornfully. "Nothing here is *home*."

Mark was aware of Simon having come to stand beside him. "God, poor kid," he said. "Look, Mark—"

"Octavian." It was Magnus's voice. He was standing in the doorway still, looking down at the small tearstained boy in front of him. There was exhaustion in his eyes, but also an immense compassion: the kind of compassion that came with great old age.

He seemed as if he would have said more, but Rafe and Max had joined him. Silently they filed down the steps and went over to Tavvy; Rafe was nearly as tall as he was, though he was only five. He reached to hug Tavvy, and Max did too—and to Mark's surprise, Tavvy seemed to relax slightly, allowing the embraces, nodding when Max said something to him in a quiet voice.

Helen got to her feet, and Mark wondered if his face wore the same expression hers did, of pain and shame. Shame that they could not do more to comfort a younger brother who barely knew them.

"It's all right," Simon said. "Look, you tried."

"We did not succeed," said Mark.

"You can't fix grief," said Simon. "A rabbi told me that when my father died. The only thing that fixes grief is time, and the love of the people who care about you, and Tavvy has that." He squeezed Mark's shoulder briefly. "Take care of yourself," he said. "*Shelo ted'u od tza'ar*, Mark Blackthorn."

"What does that mean?" said Mark.

"It's a blessing," said Simon. "Something else the rabbi taught me. 'Let it be that you should know no further sorrow.'"

Mark nodded in gratitude; faeries knew the value of blessings freely given. But his chest felt heavy nonetheless. He could not imagine the sorrows of his family would be ending soon.

See where the adventures begin in

City of Bones,

BOOK ONE OF THE MORTAL INSTRUMENTS.

"You've got to be kidding me," the bouncer said, folding his arms across his massive chest. He stared down at the boy in the red zip-up jacket and shook his shaved head. "You can't bring that thing in here."

The fifty or so teenagers in line outside the Pandemonium Club leaned forward to eavesdrop. It was a long wait to get into the all-ages club, especially on a Sunday, and not much generally happened in line. The bouncers were fierce and would come down instantly on anyone who looked like they were going to start trouble. Fifteen-year-old Clary Fray, standing in line with her best friend, Simon, leaned forward along with everyone else, hoping for some excitement.

"Aw, come on." The kid hoisted the thing up over his head.

It looked like a wooden beam, pointed at one end. "It's part of my costume."

The bouncer raised an eyebrow. "Which is what?"

The boy grinned. He was normal-enough-looking, Clary thought, for Pandemonium. He had electric blue dyed hair that stuck up around his head like the tentacles of a startled octopus, but no elaborate facial tattoos or big metal bars through his ears or lips. "I'm a vampire hunter." He pushed down on the wooden thing. It bent as easily as a blade of grass bending sideways. "It's fake. Foam rubber. See?"

The boy's wide eyes were way too bright a green, Clary noticed: the color of antifreeze, spring grass. Colored contact lenses, probably. The bouncer shrugged, abruptly bored. "Whatever. Go on in."

The boy slid past him, quick as an eel. Clary liked the lilt to his shoulders, the way he tossed his hair as he went. There was a word for him that her mother would have used—*insouciant*.

"You thought he was cute," said Simon, sounding resigned. "Didn't you?"

Clary dug her elbow into his ribs, but didn't answer.

Inside, the club was full of dry-ice smoke. Colored lights played over the dance floor, turning it into a multicolored fairyland of blues and acid greens, hot pinks and golds.

The boy in the red jacket stroked the long razor-sharp blade in his hands, an idle smile playing over his lips. It had been so easy—a little bit of a glamour on the blade, to make it look harmless. Another glamour on his eyes, and the moment the bouncer had looked straight at him, he was in. Of course, he could probably have gotten by without all that trouble, but it was part of the fun— fooling the mundies, doing it all out in the open right in front of them, getting off on the blank looks on their sheeplike faces.

Not that the humans didn't have their uses. The boy's green

eyes scanned the dance floor, where slender limbs clad in scraps of silk and black leather appeared and disappeared inside the revolving columns of smoke as the mundies danced. Girls tossed their long hair, boys swung their leather-clad hips, and bare skin glittered with sweat. Vitality just *poured* off them, waves of energy that filled him with a drunken dizziness. His lip curled. They didn't know how lucky they were. They didn't know what it was like to eke out life in a dead world, where the sun hung limp in the sky like a burned cinder. Their lives burned as brightly as candle flames—and were as easy to snuff out.

His hand tightened on the blade he carried, and he had begun to step out onto the dance floor when a girl broke away from the mass of dancers and began walking toward him. He stared at her. She was beautiful, for a human—long hair nearly the precise color of black ink, charcoaled eyes. Floor-length white gown, the kind women used to wear when this world was younger. Lace sleeves belled out around her slim arms. Around her neck was a thick silver chain, on which hung a dark red pendant the size of a baby's fist. He only had to narrow his eyes to know that it was real—real and precious. His mouth started to water as she neared him. Vital energy pulsed from her like blood from an open wound. She smiled, passing him, beckoning with her eyes. He turned to follow her, tasting the phantom sizzle of her death on his lips.

It was always easy. He could already feel the power of her evaporating life coursing through his veins like fire. Humans were so stupid. They had something so precious, and they barely safeguarded it at all. They threw away their lives for money, for packets of powder, for a stranger's charming smile. The girl was a pale ghost retreating through the colored smoke. She reached the wall and turned, bunching her skirt up in her hands, lifting it as she grinned at him. Under the skirt, she was wearing thigh-high boots.

He sauntered up to her, his skin prickling with her nearness.

Up close she wasn't so perfect: He could see the mascara smudged under her eyes, the sweat sticking her hair to her neck. He could smell her mortality, the sweet rot of corruption. *Got you*, he thought.

A cool smile curled her lips. She moved to the side, and he could see that she was leaning against a closed door. NO ADMITTANCE—STORAGE was scrawled across it in red paint. She reached behind her for the knob, turned it, slid inside. He caught a glimpse of stacked boxes, tangled wiring. A storage room. He glanced behind him—no one was looking. So much the better if she wanted privacy.

He slipped into the room after her, unaware that he was being followed.

"So," Simon said, "pretty good music, eh?"

Clary didn't reply. They were dancing, or what passed for it—a lot of swaying back and forth with occasional lunges toward the floor as if one of them had dropped a contact lens—in a space between a group of teenage boys in metallic corsets, and a young couple cooing affectionately to each other in Japanese, their colored hair extensions tangled together like vines. A boy with a lip piercing and a teddy bear backpack was handing out free tablets of herbal ecstasy, his parachute pants flapping in the breeze from the wind machine. Clary wasn't paying much attention to their immediate surroundings—her eyes were on the blue-haired boy who'd talked his way into the club. He was prowling through the crowd as if he were looking for something. There was something about the way he moved that reminded her of something . . .

"I, for one," Simon went on, "am enjoying myself immensely."

This seemed unlikely. Simon, as always, stuck out at the club like a sore thumb, in jeans and an old T-shirt that said MADE IN BROOKLYN across the front. His freshly scrubbed hair was dark brown instead of green or pink, and his glasses perched crookedly on the end of his nose. He looked less as if he were contemplating the powers of darkness and more as if he were on his way to chess club.

"Mmm-hmm." Clary knew perfectly well that he came to Pandemonium with her only because she liked it, that he thought it was boring. She wasn't even sure why it was that she liked it—the clothes, the music made it like a dream, someone else's life, not her boring real life at all. But she was always too shy to talk to anyone but Simon.

The blue-haired boy was making his way off the dance floor. He looked a little lost, as if he hadn't found whom he was looking for. Clary wondered what would happen if she went up and introduced herself, offered to show him around. Maybe he'd just stare at her. Or maybe he was shy too. Maybe he'd be grateful and pleased, and try not to show it, the way boys did—but she'd know. Maybe—

The blue-haired boy straightened up suddenly, snapping to attention, like a hunting dog on point. Clary followed the line of his gaze, and saw the girl in the white dress.

Oh, well, Clary thought, trying not to feel like a deflated party balloon. *I guess that's that.* The girl was gorgeous, the kind of girl Clary would have liked to draw—tall and ribbon-slim, with a long spill of black hair. Even at this distance Clary could see the red pendant around her throat. It pulsed under the lights of the dance floor like a separate, disembodied heart.

"I feel," Simon went on, "that this evening DJ Bat is doing a singularly exceptional job. Don't you agree?"

Clary rolled her eyes and didn't answer; Simon hated trance music. Her attention was on the girl in the white dress. Through the darkness, smoke, and artificial fog, her pale dress shone out like a beacon. No wonder the blue-haired boy was following her as if he were under a spell, too distracted to notice anything else around him—even the two dark shapes hard on his heels, weaving after him through the crowd.

Clary slowed her dancing and stared. She could just make out that the shapes were boys, tall and wearing black clothes. She couldn't have said how she knew that they were following the other boy, but she did. She could see it in the way they paced him, their careful watchfulness, the slinking grace of their movements. A small flower of apprehension began to open inside her chest.

"Meanwhile," Simon added, "I wanted to tell you that lately I've been cross-dressing. Also, I'm sleeping with your mom. I thought you should know."

The girl had reached the wall, and was opening a door marked NO ADMITTANCE. She beckoned the blue-haired boy after her, and they slipped through the door. It wasn't anything Clary hadn't seen before, a couple sneaking off to the dark corners of the club to make out—but that made it even weirder that they were being followed.

She raised herself up on tiptoe, trying to see over the crowd. The two guys had stopped at the door and seemed to be conferring with each other. One of them was blond, the other dark-haired. The blond one reached into his jacket and drew out something long and sharp that flashed under the strobing lights. A knife. "Simon!" Clary shouted, and seized his arm.

"What?" Simon looked alarmed. "I'm not really sleeping with your mom, you know. I was just trying to get your attention. Not that your mom isn't a very attractive woman, for her age."

"Do you see those guys?" She pointed wildly, almost hitting a curvy black girl who was dancing nearby. The girl shot her an evil look. "Sorry—sorry!" Clary turned back to Simon. "Do you see those two guys over there? By that door?"

Simon squinted, then shrugged. "I don't see anything."

"There are two of them. They were following the guy with the blue hair—"

"The one you thought was cute?"

"Yes, but that's not the point. The blond one pulled a knife."

"Are you *sure*?" Simon stared harder, shaking his head. "I still don't see anyone."

"I'm sure."

Suddenly all business, Simon squared his shoulders. "I'll get one of the security guards. You stay here." He strode away, pushing through the crowd.

Clary turned just in time to see the blond boy slip through the NO ADMITTANCE door, his friend right on his heels. She looked around; Simon was still trying to shove his way across the dance floor, but he wasn't making much progress. Even if she yelled now, no one would hear her, and by the time Simon got back, something terrible might *already* have happened. Biting hard on her lower lip, Clary started to wriggle through the crowd.

"What's your name?"

She turned and smiled. What faint light there was in the storage room spilled down through high barred windows smeared with dirt. Piles of electrical cables, along with broken bits of mirrored disco balls and discarded paint cans, littered the floor.

"Isabelle."

"That's a nice name." He walked toward her, stepping carefully among the wires in case any of them were live. In the faint light she looked half-transparent, bleached of color, wrapped in white like an angel. It would be a pleasure to make her fall. . . . "I haven't seen you here before."

"You're asking me if I come here often?" She giggled, covering her mouth with her hand. There was some sort of bracelet around her wrist, just under the cuff of her dress—then, as he neared her, he saw that it wasn't a bracelet at all but a pattern inked into her skin, a matrix of swirling lines.

He froze. "You—"

He didn't finish. She moved with lightning swiftness, striking out at him with her open hand, a blow to his chest that would have sent him down gasping if he'd been a human being. He staggered back, and now there was something in her hand, a coiling whip that glinted gold as she brought it down, curling around his ankles, jerking him off his feet. He hit the ground, writhing, the hated metal biting deep into his skin. She laughed, standing over him, and dizzily he thought that he should have *known*. No human girl would wear a dress like the one Isabelle wore. She'd worn it to cover her skin—all of her skin.

Discover the origins of Jem and Tessa in

Clockwork Angel,

BOOK ONE OF THE INFERNAL DEVICES.

The demon exploded in a shower of ichor and guts.

William Herondale jerked back the dagger he was holding, but it was too late. The viscous acid of the demon's blood had already begun to eat away at the shining blade. He swore and tossed the weapon aside; it landed in a filthy puddle and commenced smoldering like a doused match. The demon itself, of course, had vanished—dispatched back to whatever hellish world it had come from, though not without leaving a mess behind.

"Jem!" Will called, turning around. "Where are you? Did you see that? Killed it with one blow! Not bad, eh?"

But there was no answer to Will's shout; his hunting partner had been standing behind him in the damp and crooked street a few moments before, guarding his back, Will was positive, but now Will was alone in the shadows. He frowned in annoyance—it was much less fun showing off without Jem to show off *to*. He glanced behind him, to where the street narrowed into a passage that gave onto the black, heaving water of the Thames in the distance. Through the gap Will could see the dark outlines of docked ships, a forest of masts like a leafless orchard. No Jem there; perhaps he had gone back to Narrow Street in search of better illumination. With a shrug Will headed back the way he had come.

Narrow Street cut across Limehouse, between the docks beside the river and the cramped slums spreading west toward Whitechapel. It was as narrow as its name suggested, lined with warehouses and lopsided wooden buildings. At the moment it was deserted; even the drunks staggering home from the Grapes up the road had found somewhere to collapse for the night. Will liked Limehouse, liked the feeling of being on the edge of the world, where ships left each day for unimaginably far ports. That the area was a sailor's haunt, and consequently full of gambling hells, opium dens, and brothels, didn't hurt either. It was easy to lose yourself in a place like this. He didn't even mind the smell of it—smoke and rope and tar, foreign spices mixed with the dirty river-water smell of the Thames.

Looking up and down the empty street, he scrubbed the sleeve of his coat across his face, trying to rub away the ichor that stung and burned his skin. The cloth came away stained green and black. There was a cut on the back of his hand too, a nasty one. He could use a healing rune. One of Charlotte's, preferably. She was particularly good at drawing *iratzes*.

A shape detached itself from the shadows and moved toward Will. He started forward, then paused. It wasn't Jem, but rather a mundane policeman wearing a bell-shaped helmet, a heavy over-coat, and a puzzled expression. He stared at Will, or rather *through*

Will. However accustomed Will had become to glamour, it was always strange to be looked through as if he weren't there. Will was seized with the sudden urge to grab the policeman's truncheon and watch while the man flapped around, trying to figure out where it had gone; but Jem had scolded him the few times he'd done that before, and while Will never really could understand Jem's objections to the whole enterprise, it wasn't worth making him upset.

With a shrug and a blink, the policeman moved past Will, shaking his head and muttering something under his breath about swearing off the gin before he truly started seeing things. Will stepped aside to let the man pass, then raised his voice to a shout: "James Carstairs! Jem! Where *are* you, you disloyal bastard?"

This time a faint reply answered him. "Over here. Follow the witchlight."

Will moved toward the sound of Jem's voice. It seemed to be coming from a dark opening between two warehouses; a faint gleam was visible within the shadows, like the darting light of a will-o'-the-wisp. "Did you hear me before? That Shax demon thought it could get me with its bloody great pincers, but I cornered it in an alley—"

"Yes, I heard you." The young man who appeared at the mouth of the alley was pale in the lamplight—paler even than he usually was, which was quite pale indeed. He was bareheaded, which drew the eye immediately to his hair. It was an odd bright silver color, like an untarnished shilling. His eyes were the same silver, and his fine-boned face was angular, the slight curve of his eyes the only clue to his heritage.

There were dark stains across his white shirtfront, and his hands were thickly smeared with red.

Will tensed. "You're bleeding. What happened?"

Jem waved away Will's concern. "It's not my blood." He turned his head back toward the alley behind him. "It's hers."

Will glanced past his friend, into the thicker shadows of the alley. In the far corner of it was a crumpled shape—only a shadow in the darkness, but when Will looked closely, he could make out the shape of a pale hand, and a wisp of fair hair.

"A dead woman?" Will asked. "A mundane?"

"A girl, really. Not more than fourteen."

At that, Will cursed with great volume and expression. Jem waited patiently for him to be done.

"If we'd only happened along a little earlier," Will said finally. "That bloody demon —"

"That's the peculiar thing. I don't think this is the demon's work." Jem frowned. "Shax demons are parasites, brood parasites. It would have wanted to drag its victim back to its lair to lay eggs in her skin while she was still alive. But this girl—she was stabbed, repeatedly. And I don't think it was here, either. There simply isn't enough blood in the alley. I think she was attacked elsewhere, and she dragged herself here to die of her injuries."

"But the Shax demon—"

"I'm telling you, I don't think it *was* the Shax. I think the Shax was pursuing her—hunting her down for something, or someone, else."

"Shaxes have a keen sense of scent," Will allowed. "I've heard of warlocks using them to follow the tracks of the missing. And it did seem to be moving with an odd sort of purpose." He looked past Jem, at the pitiful smallness of the crumpled shape in the alley. "You didn't find the weapon, did you?"

"Here." Jem drew something from inside his jacket—a knife, wrapped in white cloth. "It's a sort of misericord, or hunting dagger. Look how thin the blade is."

Will took it. The blade was indeed thin, ending in a handle made of polished bone. The blade and hilt both were stained with dried blood. With a frown he wiped the flat of the knife across the rough fabric of his sleeve, scraping it clean until a symbol, burned into the blade, became visible. Two serpents, each biting the other's tail, forming a perfect circle.

"*Ouroboros*," Jem said, leaning in close to stare at the knife. "A double one. Now, what do you think that means?"

"The end of the world," said Will, still looking at the dagger, a small smile playing about his mouth, "and the beginning."

Jem frowned. "I understand the symbology, William. I meant, what do you think its presence on the dagger signifies?"

The wind off the river was ruffling Will's hair; he brushed it out of his eyes with an impatient gesture and went back to studying the knife. "It's an alchemical symbol, not a warlock or Downworlder one. That usually means humans—the foolish mundane sort who think trafficking in magic is the ticket for gaining wealth and fame."

"The sort who usually end up a pile of bloody rags inside some pentagram." Jem sounded grim.

"The sort who like to lurk about the Downworld parts of our fair city." After wrapping the handkerchief around the blade carefully, Will slipped it into his jacket pocket. "D'you think Charlotte will let me handle the investigation?"

"Do *you* think you can be trusted in Downworld? The gambling hells, the dens of magical vice, the women of loose morals . . ."

Will smiled the way Lucifer might have smiled, moments before he fell from Heaven. "Would tomorrow be too early to start looking, do you think?"

Jem sighed. "Do what you like, William. You always do."

Southampton, May.

Tessa could not remember a time when she had not loved the clock-work angel. It had belonged to her mother once, and her mother had been wearing it when she died. After that it had sat in her mother's jewelry box, until her brother, Nathaniel, took it out one day to see if it was still in working order.

The angel was no bigger than Tessa's pinky finger, a tiny statuette made of brass, with folded bronze wings no larger than a cricket's. It had a delicate metal face with shut crescent eyelids, and hands crossed over a sword in front. A thin chain that looped beneath the wings allowed the angel to be worn around the neck like a locket.

Tessa knew the angel was made out of clockwork because if she lifted it to her ear she could hear the sound of its machinery, like the sound of a watch. Nate had exclaimed in surprise that it was still working after so many years, and he had looked in vain for a knob or a screw, or some other method by which the angel might be wound. But there had been nothing to find. With a shrug he'd given the angel to Tessa. From that moment she had never taken it off; even at night the angel lay against her chest as she slept, its constant *ticktock, ticktock* like the beating of a second heart.

She held it now, clutched between her fingers, as the *Main* nosed its way between other massive steamships to find a spot at the Southampton dock. Nate had insisted that she come to Southampton instead of Liverpool, where most transatlantic steamers arrived. He had claimed it was because Southampton was a much pleasanter place to arrive at, so Tessa couldn't help being a little disappointed by this, her first sight of England. It was drearily gray. Rain drummed down onto the spires of a distant church, while black smoke rose from the chimneys of ships and stained the already dull-colored sky. A crowd of people in dark clothes, holding umbrellas, stood on the docks. Tessa strained to see if her brother was among them, but the mist and spray from the ship were too thick for her to make out any individual in great detail.

Tessa shivered. The wind off the sea was chilly. All of Nate's letters had claimed that London was beautiful, the sun shining every day. Well, Tessa thought, hopefully the weather there was better than it was here, because she had no warm clothes with her, nothing more substantial than a woolen shawl that had belonged to Aunt Harriet, and a pair of thin gloves. She had sold most of her clothes to pay for her aunt's funeral, secure in the knowledge that her brother would buy her more when she arrived in London to live with him.

A shout went up. The *Main*, its shining black-painted hull gleaming wet with rain, had anchored, and tugs were plowing their way through the heaving gray water, ready to carry baggage and passengers to the shore. Passengers streamed off the ship, clearly desperate to feel land under their feet. So different from their departure from New York. The sky had been blue then, and a brass band had been playing. Though, with no one there to wish her good-bye, it had not been a merry occasion.

Hunching her shoulders, Tessa joined the disembarking crowd. Drops of rain stung her unprotected head and neck like pinpricks from icy little needles, and her hands, inside their insubstantial gloves, were clammy and wet with rain. Reaching the quay, she looked around eagerly, searching for a sight of Nate. It had been nearly two weeks since she'd spoken to a soul, having kept almost entirely to herself on board the *Main*. It would be wonderful to have her brother to talk to again.

He wasn't there. The wharves were heaped with stacks of luggage and all sorts of boxes and cargo, even mounds of fruit and vegetables wilting and dissolving in the rain. A steamer was departing for Le Havre nearby, and damp-looking sailors swarmed close by Tessa, shouting in French. She tried to move aside, only to be almost trampled by a throng of disembarking passengers hurrying for the shelter of the railway station.

But Nate was nowhere to be seen.

"You are Miss Gray?" The voice was guttural, heavily accented. A man had moved to stand in front of Tessa. He was tall, and was wearing a sweeping black coat and a tall hat, its brim collecting rainwater like a cistern. His eyes were peculiarly bulging, almost protuberant, like a frog's, his skin as rough-looking as scar tissue. Tessa had to fight the urge to cringe away from him. But he knew her name. Who here would know her name except someone who knew Nate, too?

"Yes?"

"Your brother sent me. Come with me."

"Where is he?" Tessa demanded, but the man was already walking away. His stride was uneven, as if he had a limp from an old injury. After a moment Tessa gathered up her skirts and hurried after him.

He wound through the crowd, moving ahead with purposeful speed. People jumped aside, muttering about his rudeness as he shouldered past, with Tessa nearly running to keep up. He turned abruptly around a pile of boxes, and came to a halt in front of a large, gleaming black coach. Gold letters had been painted across its side, but the rain and mist were too thick for Tessa to read them clearly.

The door of the carriage opened and a woman leaned out. She wore an enormous plumed hat that hid her face. "Miss Theresa Gray?"

CASSANDRA CLARE'S

#1 *New York Times* Bestselling Series

THE MORTAL INSTRUMENTS
THE INFERNAL DEVICES
THE DARK ARTIFICES

A thousand years ago, the Angel Raziel mixed his blood with the blood of men and created the race of the Nephilim. Human-angel hybrids, they walk among us, unseen but ever present, our invisible protectors.

They call themselves Shadowhunters.

CONTINUE THE ADVENTURES OF SIMON LEWIS,

one of the stars of Cassandra Clare's internationally bestselling Mortal Instruments series, in *Tales from the Shadowhunter Academy*. Packed with special appearances by characters from The Dark Artifices, The Mortal Instruments, and The Infernal Devices, *Tales from the Shadowhunter Academy* is a riveting short-story collection that follows the trials of Simon as he prepares to enter the next phase of his life: Shadowhunter.

PRINT AND EBOOK EDITIONS AVAILABLE

Learn more at shadowhunters.com and cassandraclare.com.

DISCOVER THE SHADOWHUNTER UNIVERSE:

The Infernal Devices | The Last Hours
The Mortal Instruments | The Dark Artifices
The Shadowhunter's Codex | The Bane Chronicles
Tales from the Shadowhunter Academy